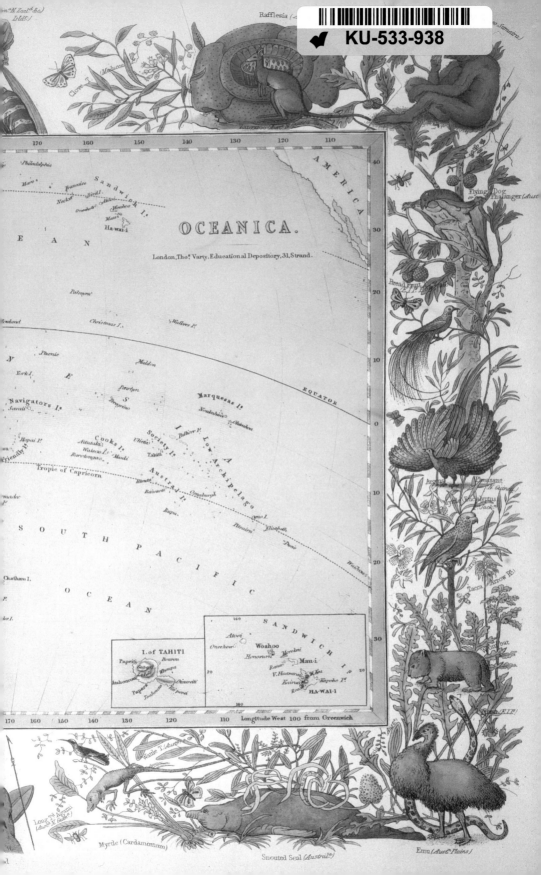

OCEANICA.

London, Thos. Varty, Educational Depository, 31, Strand.

Bettany's Book

Also by Thomas Keneally

Bettany's Book

THOMAS KENEALLY

SCEPTRE

First published in Great Britain in 2000 by Hodder & Stoughton
A division of Hodder Headline
A Sceptre book

10 9 8 7 6 5 4 3 2 1

A CIP catalogue record for this title is
available from the British Library

ISBN 0 340 61095 6

Printed and bound in Great Britain by
Clays Ltd, St Ives plc, Bungay, Suffolk

Hodder & Stoughton
A division of Hodder Headline
338 Euston Road
London NW1 3BH

To my ever committed and regularly infallible
friend and editor, Carole Welch

Foreword

Details of the pastoral life and wool-growing in nineteenth century Australia are taken from W.A. Brodribb's *Recollections of An Australian Squatter*, 1883, and Stephen H. Roberts's *The Squatting Age in Australia, 1835–1847*, 1935.

Many of the incidents of W.A. Brodribb's life occur also to Jonathan Bettany, but for the sake of Brodribb's memory it must be said that the intimate sins and failures attributed to Bettany in these pages are pure invention.

Similarly, I hasten to say that the incidents that take place at Sydney University and which involve academic turpitude are entirely fictional and are not based on any events I have ever heard of, nor are any of the characters based on Sydney University staff or students, past or present.

The quotations from Horace are taken from *The Odes of Horace* translated by James Michie, 1964, and *Horace*, Eduard Fraenkel, 1957. The English translations are my own work, though I did take my tone from the lyrical spirit of Michie's own free-flowing translations.

Any quotations from the Islamic scriptures are taken from *The Koran*, translated by N.J. Dawood, 1956.

I am grateful to Abbas Elzein of Sydney, himself a fine writer, for advice and the correction of any Arabic phrases which appear here.

For information on the work of NGOs and their field officers, I owe a debt to James Inglis, Jill Jamison, Graham Romanis, Sandra Heeney and Simon Williamson, who have all had a devoted interest in the Sudan. My daughter Jane gave similar help on matters to do with the Australian film industry. Needless to say, any errors or excesses appearing in the text are my own.

I would be wrong to conclude without thanking Louise Thurtell and Amanda O'Connell of Sydney and Carole Welch of London, the midwives of this long and complex text, and as ever, my wife Judith, who is under the persistent impression I am a writer.

Thomas Keneally, Sydney 2000

Part One

The simultaneous loss of her parents when she was nineteen had not seemed to throw any shadow across Dimp Bettany's bright eye. Even her more dutiful sister, Primrose, admitted how infrequently and with what a shock of strangeness she remembered the fact of the instant deaths of her parents. This end, which had come in a collision on one of the hundreds of kilometres of narrow stretches of the Pacific Highway, felt, when recollected, as if it meant less to her and Dimp than it decently should.

Perhaps that was because their parents had lived orderly lives and died in an exemplary way. Despite the head-on ferocity, there were very few visible injuries except for the fatal depressed fractures. Or it may have been because their mother had been ever distracted, fretful, remote; and their father, Gordon Bettany, as irresponsibly jovial as an uncle. Rather in the spirit of his life, he was said by the coroner to have died while sleeping in the passenger seat, and with an unregistered micro-second of massive concussion. Her life ending in that same micro-second, Angela Bettany, so the sisters were told and told each other, had suffered only a few seconds of apprehension, though that thought should have been pitiable enough to haunt them.

Dimp must think of them, Prim guessed, but it seemed an undue embarrassment to their tidy ghosts to ask her, and almost an affront to the joyous, rowdy woman Dimp had made of herself. Prim encountered them in dreams, but woke with more surprise than loss. While she was a student, Primrose would remind her dazzling sister in person or by phone each anniversary of the disaster, and there would be a pause in their talk, composed perhaps of two parts sadness and one part guilt.

'Come on,' Dimp said once, sniffing out her sister's uneasiness. 'You'd turned seventeen. Parents mean less to you when you're that age than at any other time of your life.'

But from the occasional references to parents, separated by hundreds of days in which Mr and Mrs Bettany barely got a mention, Prim came to feel that, if she and Dimp were to be good daughters of the dead, instead of offering the normal annual currency of wistfulness, nostalgia and the occasional disbelieving sense of vacancy, they owed a daily burden of grief, and that the failure to be a good daughter made her something of an exile, and thus prone to be rushed to orphan foolishness and to reckless journeys. She was the daughter who desired a conscientious and well-ordered life.

The sisters, Dimple and Primrose, had inherited their parents' bank account which was very nearly in overdraft. The family house in Turramurra, in which the sisters continued to live for four years under the supervision of neighbours who had thought well of their parents, had in the end to be sold. The sisters went to live in a grim little red-brick flat in Redfern. Dimp was by then twenty-three years old, just beginning her career. After settlement of their parents' debt the girls were left with a margin of little more than $25 000 each and, conscientiously, Prim chose to invest hers in a fund for her education and future.

In the early 1980s, Dimp Bettany, universally regarded as an unselfconsciously beautiful woman, of a darker and fuller handsomeness than her more abstractly appealing sister, found a job in the television documentary department of the Australian Broadcasting Corporation where she was soon liked by everyone. She was relieved to find that her name, as it appeared as assistant producer on credits, was interpreted by her colleagues as a shortening of Dymphna, instead of the reality – the achingly awful Dimple.

Dimp seemed to her more reserved sister Primrose – Prim by preference – to be above all a glowing, heedless orphan. Prim saw herself as an earnest undergraduate drudge with post-graduate ambitions, who required of herself a series of distinctions and credits in her sundry subjects – even an occasional high distinction. When she scored a high distinction in anthropology, she could picture her father saying, 'A high distinction at Sydney University! Imagine!'

Men distantly admired Primrose. Dimp was desired. Abundantly alive, a frequent laugher, carrying her orphan status lightly, Dimp seemed imperishably lit with inner light. The accepted wisdom in the ABC documentary department was that no one – farmer, couturier, politician, mountaineer – refused to be the subject of a documentary if Dimp Bettany was sent to ask them. No one – male or female – was immune from Dimp's famous good cheer, force of soul, looks and enthusiastic, sensual and childlike soul. It was the way, even when hungover, she

looked fresh-minted. And her sumptuous features shone with an unconscious spirituality, the spirituality of wanting to make a film. She was
avid for the nuances of character as revealed in the stories of strangers.

And she was of course an excellent greeter, counsellor to and assurer
of the subjects of documentaries – 'No, I don't think you need to change
your clothes ... Of course we have to make sure there's times for you
to have a rest ... No, I think the blue one's more your colour.' Even
though she dressed carelessly herself.

One of the documentary subjects Dimp worked on – who was to
change the course of her life – was an Italian by the name of Lorenzo
Cortini. A graduate of the military academy in Modena and an officer
in Mussolini's armies in Libya, Lorenzo had been a prisoner-of-war in
Australia during the Second World War. Meeting Dimp during an
informal press conference when he revisited Australia on the verge of old
age, this professional soldier had told her how appalled he had been
when his platoon, and the battalion they were part of, and the division
of which the battalion was part, showed very little resoluteness in
defending Mussolini's Libyan coastal fortress of Bardia from the Australians long before, in 1941. It was the Australian connection which
fascinated Dimp.

After being shipped to Australia as a prisoner-of-war, Cortini, Dimp
discovered, made three escape attempts. During each he found himself
generously protected by southern Italian sultana-growers in the Riverina,
along the Murray River. In meeting these immigrants, and depending on
them for refuge, he was thrown together with Italians far below him in
social stature, *Siciliani e Calabresi*, lower than the lowest non-swarthy
member of the platoon and crack regiment that had let him down at
Bardia, and less capable of speaking real Italian.

Some of those at whose firesides deep in the bush Lorenzo Cortini was
protected were laconic socialists. They called him Enzo and mocked in
raw dialect all the florid promises of a new Roman Empire which had
crumbled so easily before Australia's yokel soldiers at Bardia and
Benghazi. On the run, Lorenzo Cortini was reduced to wearing the rough
clothing of these people, eating their bowel-bruising cuisine, sleeping on
their bare floorboards, and bearing the papers and harsh name of a
deceased Calabrian peasant immigrant. The aristocrat from the military
academy hid beneath the lumpy beds of farmers in a dead man's suit,
the sweat and dust of anonymous labour clinging to its seams. In this
process Cortini became, as he told an engrossed Dimp, 'democratised'.

'On the last continent on earth, I discovered the size of the world.'

Going to Melbourne with his false alien papers, he lived in a boarding house in Coburg populated by metal workers and small-time salesmen, and fell in love with his landlady, a young, red-headed Australian widow named Maggie Slattery, a leftist within the ranks of the Australian Labor Party. Under her influence, Enzo volunteered to steal a union ballot box before the candidates his landlady favoured could be outvoted by a phalanx of right-wing Catholics. Waylaid on the way home, the ballot box in a basket on the front of his bicycle, the landlady's sweet company ahead of him, he was beaten up with the weapons of the antipodean working class – a cricket bat and two stumps.

To Dimp's delight, the tale of Lieutenant Lorenzo Cortini even possessed a relentless Inspector Javert figure, a fatherly federal policeman who hunted and ultimately recaptured him after his longer period at large.

The documentary Dimp helped make, and persuaded Enzo Cortini to participate in, related his return to Australia to visit the former high security prison in the country town of Hay, from which he had escaped. He had also come back to honour the Italian farmers of the Riverina who had hidden him, and to make a pilgrimage to Melbourne, where he had remained a year at large impersonating the deceased Calabrian. The crew Dimp worked with got excellent footage of both. With a palpating gesture of his right hand, Cortini called Melbourne 'the city of my heart'.

During Enzo Cortini's journeys over the route of his escape in the Australian bush, Dimp was his driver, adviser, companion, acting coach, manager, and confidante. Outside country motels in frosty Australian dawns, Lorenzo Cortini wore his overcoat over the shoulders, in a stylish Florentine manner, smoked a cigarette in that seemingly non-carcinogenic graceful way which characterised the heroes of *film noir*, and chattered away with his new Australian friend. What other intimacy or refuge Dimp gave Enzo on his Australian pilgrimage was a matter of speculation not only for the camera crew, but later, from the inconclusive account Dimp gave of it, for her more serious-minded sister, Prim.

Before Enzo returned to Italy, Dimp continued to spend time with him in Sydney, interviewing him in more depth and getting his experiences on tape. She had had since childhood a capacity to be consumed by stories, and this was now what she was inflamed by – the tale of the Fascist converted to a dream of fraternity by the great Australian rawness; the elegant Latin, under his fake, undistinguished name, selling little bottles of lotion house-to-house in wartime Melbourne to women wearied by loneliness. With his Italian cinema idol looks he was sometimes irresistibly drawn into the role of consoler of the Home Front.

Dimp had been persuaded by the family's solicitor to invest her portion of the proceeds from the Turramurra sale. But before Cortini's return to Italy (the documentary completed) Dimp withdrew the full amount to buy feature film rights to Cortini's life from the man himself ('I am, after all, Dimple *cara*, not a wealthy man!'), and to pay a screenwriter. She thought she had discovered an essentially Australian odyssey, and Cortini was its antipodean voyager. She found a Melbourne director, Frank Varduzzi, child of Italian immigrants himself, with one good feature film of the childhood-confessional variety behind him. Varduzzi became enthused too – after all, his grandparents and parents had been interned at the start of the Second World War, and he came from exactly that background of poor Italian immigrants at whose hands Cortini received his Australian education.

Lorenzo Cortini died in his sleep in Florence, but the film funding came through from sundry sources. The Australian Film Development Corporation invested what was then considered a generous fifty per cent, Film Victoria supplied twenty-five per cent, the Italian–Australian Federation was persuaded to contribute money, as were a string of private investors under the tax concession scheme named 10B(a). The film was shot for a modest $1 300 000 in the Victorian Riverina, Melbourne, and in a studio in Sydney, and made the careers of many people – Varduzzi; Colin Maberley, who played Cortini for $40 000 and within a year and a half was earning two million per flick; the cameraman Ossie Bendall; Sharon Bribie as the boarding house keeper. The film was entitled *Enzo Kangaroo*, was selected for showing in Directors' Week in Cannes, was snapped up too cheaply by an American distributor, and, according to the pattern by which distributors make the most money out of such films, made Dimp famous but returned little. But renowned, and much photographed, she had become a culture hero in a community which yearned for such figures.

Her film and perhaps a half dozen others rang in an enthusiastic era when accountants advised entrepreneurs to invest in films for their tax breaks. Lacking a project which called to her as fiercely as the Enzo story had, Dimp, who had acquired financial expertise at the cash-starved

ABC, had in fact done the budget for *Enzo Kangaroo*, was invited to speak for excellent fees at symposia for business investors. She also developed expertise in doing spreadsheet budgets for films, good and bad, generated by this investment. For despite the success of *Enzo Kangaroo*, she did not consider herself genuinely creative. Nor did she make it known that she received somewhat more predictable an income for doing these film-related tasks than she had as a producer. Her sister knew it, and other things, and was proud of her.

But years passed, and no tale arose to consume Dimp in the way Enzo's tale had.

At one of Dimp's breakfast tax seminars, a man wearing the name tag *Brendan D'Arcy*, the letters CEO, and the further elucidation: D'Arcy Coleman Mineral Venture, waited in line behind suited men and women, accountants with clients to advise, asking her for clarification of certain points. In the body of the room the tables were being stripped of their plates of half-eaten fruit and eggs. Other men and women were briskly rushing out the door to business, and only this fringe of questioners remained to protect the guest speaker from her habitual quandary, 'What in the hell shall I do with the rest of the day?'

Dimp had noticed D'Arcy during the seminar and, automatically answering questions, watched him join the line, wait, scrape his slightly unruly sandy hair, do some tie-straightening, and flinch at his watch every time he consulted it. She had heard of him in an indefinite way, but had never felt his urgent presence, and she rushed through her answers to the others to ensure he wouldn't leave. At last he stood in front of her, his large, beefily handsome face flushed and his sportsman's shoulders held crookedly.

'I'm Brendan D'Arcy,' he said like a complaint when his time came, watching the last accountant go and looking suspicious of the waiters. 'I liked your concise and humorous delivery.'

She thanked him. D'Arcy was big-boned, with generous features and eyes, which shone like an uncertain boy's.

'I want to ask you out,' he said, earnestly fixed on her face. 'I'm separated from my wife. You probably hear that from many men, but in my case you can check the files of the scurrilous *Sydney Morning Herald* last February and soon see whether I happen to be telling you the truth. The 'Stay in Touch' column. We made it, Robyn and I. No kids. Marriage annulment is under way, civil divorce to follow. No chance of reconciliation.'

Dimp tried to speak a normal sentence, like the ones she had been speaking until a moment ago, something about section 10B(a) of the federal *Film Finance Act*. 'Ah,' she said. 'I don't read the *Herald* ...'

'I have to tell you,' he continued with his leaden and yet fascinating sincerity, 'that you are a most exquisite and intelligent woman and that I would like to court you. I'm no seducer or casual fornicator. It's against my religion. If all this sounds mad as a cut snake, so be it. I was under necessity to say it. Would you accept my card?' At last he grinned. 'I would be very happy if it ever got to the stage where you knew that number by heart.'

D'Arcy was not to know that in taking the risk of such an unorthodox approach he was doing what was best calculated to attract Dimp. She was convinced by his entire demeanour and the redness of his face that this was not a normal speech for him, and the idea that this was an exceptional effort for him captivated her. Even though she was used to men making exceptional efforts, they had not done so on such a notable – or original – scale as D'Arcy. If he was working according to some *modus operandi*, she believed, he would surely not have used such a homely image as 'mad as a cut snake'. Prim would have rushed away, Dimp knew, appalled at his brawny and extravagant sincerity. Dimp saw a depth behind the gesture.

She felt a despicable colour creeping over her face, but such flushes of blood only made her look more startling. 'But you don't know anything about me.'

'I've heard you make a pretty good speech,' he said with a bluff but tentative smile. 'And we can't learn much more in here with these bloody waiters clattering away. Could I have your card, by any chance?'

'I don't have a card to give you. I don't carry them.'

'My God, a cardless person. I didn't know they still existed.'

'Well, I'm not really any sort of business woman. I have an ability to budget films and understand the sections of the *Tax Act* relating to film.'

'Ah,' he murmured. He spread out the sound, as if he savoured the originality of her lacking a card. He seemed to believe it supported his instincts about her. 'Do you know anything at all about me?'

Despite being a cursory student of financial pages, she had heard that company name, D'Arcy Coleman. It had begun as an old-fashioned gold-mining company – this man's grandfather or great-grandfather had

exploited reefs of gold in Queensland and Western Australia with a
Scotsman named Coleman, whose descendants, if they existed, must now
have little or no role in D'Arcy Coleman, since D'Arcy got all the press
attention.

Later she was to find out that he had turned his ancestral company
away from old-fashioned mining. He had been one of the first in
Australia to promote the concept of an Australian mineral futures
market, and had also created a venture capital division, operating from
offices in Sydney and Chicago, to raise finance for mining and drilling
operations from the Australian deserts to Siberia. The word 'Venture'
itself shone on his card, so it appeared to Dimp, with golden promise.
She wondered whether this man might extend his definition of venture
not only, as he had, into a blunt speech about desire, but into films,
perhaps her own.

The problem remained, however, that she did not have a film. When
driven along by Enzo's tale, she had believed that there were tales beyond
this one which she would not so much pick up but be picked up by.
She'd simply have to look around and a lovable, urgent story, howling
to be told, would present itself. It had not proved to be the truth. By
now she feared *Enzo* was a once-in-a-lifetime phenomenon, like *Citizen
Kane* for Orson Welles, all else seemingly smaller by contrast, the mere
filling of time while waiting for death. She had, for something to do,
taken an option on a book, a sort of Australian version of Chekhov,
about three tormented Edwardian sisters trapped in spinsterhood,
running a genteel hotel in the Blue Mountains. An engineer for the Zigzag
Railway asks to stay at the hotel. 'Ho-bloody-hum,' as Dimp told Prim.
The tale did not possess her. It was as easy to take a rest from, to post-
pone, as piano practice or an amateur painting class. It might make a
nice art-house film, but the audience would know how to connect the
dots from the first arrival of the engineer, about seven minutes into the
film. And when film functionaries at the Australian Film Institute or the
New South Wales Film Corporation found problems with it, Dimp found
herself strangely calm, and even consoled. For this film you did not go
begging door to door, insistent, making loud cajoling jokes. You casually
thought of who else should be contacted in a month's time. Film
Victoria? Okay, but I've got to do a few seminars first. And there was
time, friends told her. She was only twenty-six now. A child wonder.

On the morning D'Arcy turned up in front of her, Dimp had no creative risk on hand to match the scale of risk he seemed to be taking. A

CEO of venture, of futures, of glittering concepts, driven to reckless declarations, which waiters could perhaps overhear! She later wondered whether part of her early enchantment was a belief that she might catch a fervent idea from him.

Though he said he was no seducer, he was, within two weeks, Dimp's lover.

On meeting him, Prim liked D'Arcy but thought he was a more limited man than her sister seemed to believe. Prim was, however, so confused by men herself that she did not feel she had much authority to say anything. Occasionally, as she saw more of him, she would find herself waspishly answering some blunt assertion of his about politics or economics. Not that she knew much about either – she had just been accepted into the graduate anthropology program at the University of Sydney. 'Oh, anthropology!' he'd said, as if that were a complete key to her beliefs. She found irksome his male bent for taking the difficulties of his business too seriously, for speaking as if he had chosen a uniquely tough way of making a living or, more exactly, enhancing a fortune. He seemed to Prim to imply that the returns barely justified the outlay of effort, which was clearly a ridiculous idea. Had he never asked himself what it was like working by the year on one of the mining dredges operated by the companies whose money he found?

Love had made Dimp apolitical, and though vaguely agnostic, she found it almost endearing that Bren went to confession at St Canice's, Elizabeth Bay, once a month. She could imagine him wrestling sombrely with his conscience and confessing to improper desire for women and wealth, to neglect of his late father's sisters, termagants who lived in apartments at Potts Point. She was intrigued rather than appalled by the question of whether he felt bound to mention the times they made love, every incidence of sex, every departure from the theologically approved positions. Apparently his Jesuit confessor was already slated to perform their wedding ceremony. He'd always seemed to be modern, said Bren, considered the church annulment to be as good as granted, and had advised D'Arcy that the intent to marry cast a holiness, or at least a blamelessness, over sex with Dimp. 'They never talked like that in the old days,' said D'Arcy, whose charming father had apparently maintained some notorious affairs when affairs were really something: the risk of an eternity of flame and the social ignominy of being named co-respondent, all for two hours with a woman.

Some time after this conversation, D'Arcy's first marriage of five years

was indulgently annulled by Mother Church, a process Dimp was loath
to ask about, and his civil divorce was all but finalised, with Bren, to his
credit, never uttering a complaint about his first wife's financial and
property claims on him. But the priest had reinforced Bren's intention to
raise a difficult matter with Dimp, one he confessed he should perhaps
have mentioned earlier. All the medical evidence, he said, indicated he
was sterile. There was always a chance of intermittent or remissive
fertility. He and Robyn had considered adopting a child but felt that they
had never reached the plateau of mutual trust where it seemed the right
thing to do. He and Dimp could adopt, and a person never knew ...
Sometimes the very act of adopting made conception more likely. That
seemed to happen with supposedly sterile women, anyhow.

So intensely was Dimp captivated that she took hulking D'Arcy's
confession as a matter of lesser significance. 'We'll adopt children,' she
blithely told Prim. By now, apart from lecturing and doing the occasional
film budget, her job was still that of taking the three-sisters-and-
smouldering-engineer project around to the various state and federal
agencies which financed development, and talking with them by letter and
telephone. In fact her living continued to come from tax seminars. But
then the film investment rules were altered by the federal government, as
it seemed to Dimp, overnight. The tax advantages were taken away. Too
many bad films not recognisably Australian had been made purely for the
tax break, said the Minister for the Arts. As soon as the change was
mooted, Dimp was no longer a frequent seminar requirement.

About this time, while he and Dimp were inspecting a potential marital
house at Double Bay, Bren took Dimp aside by a sundeck railing over
the harbour. It was time for another of his unblinking, solemn talks.
'Now I like films as much as the next man, dear old Dimp,' he told her.
This habitual endearment – 'dear old Dimp' – made her pleasantly
imagine them as a doughty aging couple. 'But I know they're such risky
business. And there's so much else which will give you a return, including
forestry futures.' She loved him talking in this way, for having so many
investment options in his head, golden apples gravid on a brain stem. 'I
know from my experience with Robyn's family that money and advice
about money are something best offered to people you don't give a damn
about. The whole thing has so much ability to do harm. I think we ought
to take a pledge not to get involved as a couple on different sides of
contracts. I mean, by that, film contracts too.'

'Good idea,' she told him lightly. She had no film she was passionate enough to be suppliant about, so it was easy to see the reason of his statement.

'This is love speaking,' he assured her. 'You get that, don't you? This is love, not meanness.'

He explained that he had been reckless enough to give Robyn's family some useful intelligence about American silver futures. 'Don't go overboard with this,' he said he'd advised them. 'The price isn't a real value. It's a story about value.' They assured him they understood this. But Robyn's father, brother and brother-in-law all lost huge amounts, borrowed to the extreme limit of their investments in overvalued real estate in the eastern suburbs, and the infection reached D'Arcy and Robyn, or at least served as a trigger for the expression of profounder doubt.

And so the pact was made, and made all the more readily by Dimp because – in the increasing absence of tax-seminar orations and an obsessing film – she believed her true profession now to be D'Arcy's woman. But there were difficulties inherent in Dimp's role. Both sisters had inherited from someone – not their dapper father – a sartorial negligence. Their mother, they remembered, sometimes wore her lipstick inexactly, her slip would show beneath her dress, or a bra strap be exposed. Dimp therefore lacked the absorption with dress and decoration which might have made it possible for her to be, full-time, a rich man's consort. She wore clothing and used cosmetics carelessly. Her clothes, particularly as her marriage to Bren drew closer, were good quality, and carried the right labels – Chanel, Armani, bags and shoes by Prada, minimum requirements for the sort of people D'Arcy mixed with around Woollahra, Double Bay, Point Piper. But they hung indifferently on her, and achieved credibility only through the lustre of her brown hair, her green eyes, and broad cheeks. Uncharacteristic of the flagrant age she lived in, she hated large, carbuncular bracelets and rings. She favoured the small, the delicate, and D'Arcy seemed to like nothing better than to visit a jeweller with her, and have her explain to him the virtues of the discreet gem, the understated gold. There have been periods in history – the French revolutionary era, or amongst poets from the Elizabethan to the Romantic age – when an affected heedlessness of dress was the rage, and Dimp was so well-endowed a being, 'better rounded than her sister' as people had said throughout their adolescence, that even sloppiness looked like style on her. Only she and her sister knew that at a later age she would be seen as a charming but bedraggled old woman.

The Bettany girls had what was known as a protected childhood. They had been sent by their doomed parents to an all-girl grammar school on the sedate north shore of Sydney, and their party-going had been strictly supervised by their frenetically anxious mother and by a calm, intractable father who arrived to collect them at eleven wearing a cardigan, grey pants, slippers, his brilliantined auburn hair looking as carefully combed as it had when he left for work that morning. Their father represented a combination of elements the girls thought of as subtly combined to bring down on them the maximum of social torment, as he appeared handsomely squinting in his neat – though in the girls' eyes disreputable – clothes at the door, asking in a voice hardly to be heard above the party's clamour, 'Are Dimple and Primrose here?'

Their mother sent him, since no boy was ever trusted to take them home, yet Prim thought that if boys grew up to be like her father there must be some genial ones capable of it. Dimp, who from fifteen went to winter rugby matches at the boys' school, Knox Grammar, and was invited to a livelier range of parties than Prim, became an aficionado of the brief embrace, the open-mouthed kiss, and some more turbulent and unseemly mysteries still. Prim came along to parties in her sister's lively and generous wake, but after a while she got a reputation for being 'frigid'. The adolescent Dimp would advise Prim to cool it a bit, smile at the boys, relax. She was good-looking enough, bugger it! They all fancied her, for Christ's sake.

Dimp considered 'frigid' an insult, she didn't understand the subtle pride it gave her sister.

Dimp had got from somewhere a gift for earthiness, which had from childhood secretly amused Prim but alarmed her parents. She had the nature to study Australian coarseness. It had been reinforced by listening to some of the Knox boys, and even from studying patterns of speech in Australian soapies. To absorb an Australian rhythm, too, she had only to listen to snatches of talk from brickies working on their Bannockburn Street, Turramurra, neighbours' house. Though she was vigilant with what she said at school, she had an ambition to be known as a calling-a-spade-a-spade Australian, and her parents did not know where that came from.

Prim was in the meantime proud of her reputation as an ice-maiden, not least because at the Knox Grammar–Abbotsleigh School formal a particular type of boy would try to melt her down, and she liked to feel aloof from their hot breath, to feel the irrelevance of a kind of swelling in them, even more pervasive than the limited, boring rigidity in their groins. Seeming to be more innocent than she was, that was a great plan with these hulking, gasping boys. Showing them that she gave their dance floor erections no credit at all. That was better fun than acknowledging their heat, taking it with you out for some uncertain, unresolved fumble under an angophora by the rugby field. While Dimp was merciful and felt sorry for their urgent need, to Prim, icy virtue had joys that fingers-and-thumbs lust was incapable of supplying.

This conviction ensured that Prim went to university a virgin, where Dimp had preceded her as a male-loving daughter of experience. Boys who met Prim as an undergraduate felt a distant but readily defeated hope, while boys who met Dimp could not believe they had blundered on a sensual presence whose very company, the mere chance to buy her a schooner of beer at the Union, was an experience of bountiful promise.

Primrose was ultimately persuaded into two inconclusive and largely joyless couplings by a tall architecture student she met at the university Labor Club – led there by Dimp – where too much cask wine was always drunk. Dimp's turning up at the Labor Club, Prim found out, was considered such a political coup by a group of young Fabian socialists that she seemed to them a prize of the ideological wars. And though by now she defined herself as a thinking feminist, Primrose too was cherished by the Labor Club and found the sensation of being a prize less unwelcome than she was supposed to. From this glow, this delicious conceit, she found the courage for her intellectually stimulating but physically inept affair with the architecture student. While it lasted, she could for that time still be an icon, or – she wouldn't use the term aloud – a trophy, while safe within her known status as the architecture student's girlfriend.

At heart, Prim believed she neither had nor needed the capacity for love and its attendant exultations and horrors, its retching tears, yowling ecstasies and general unnecessary fuss. She understood from some of her younger lecturers that falling in love was a bourgeois construct, a metaphor for the sort of deep hormonal craze which was capable, if both partners played along, of leading to a mutually shared belief that their particular compulsion was worth a year's, or two or ten years' most testing and intimate investment.

She was thus taken by storm to find herself, in her first year as a post-graduate, bitten by the construct of falling in love with her graduate adviser, Professor Robert Auger. This occurred in an open-sided tent pitched at Turner Creek reservation in desert country two hundred and fifty kilometres south-west of Alice Springs, near a plug of conglomerate rock named Mount Bavaria or Gharrademu, a landmark which was the subject of a court hearing. Primrose and three other graduate students were seated on campstools in boiling air near the rear flaps of the tent that constituted the court. Since the other three were students well advanced on their dissertations, Prim had come here thinking of herself as Auger's best first-year MA, the only one invited to this land rights hearing in Central Australia.

Robert Auger, an American, had first come to this desert country in 1967 as a snub to the Vietnam draft and to study the Burranghyatti desert people. His being in Australia at the time was a matter of principle – he could have sought an exemption, but would not stoop to play that game. He 'got' the Burranghyatti at the right time, just as they were beginning to reconcile themselves to missions and reservations as a near full-time option.

While the mysteries of the Vietnam War possessed the attention of the bulk of his fellow citizens, American and Australian, Auger spent his research time in the presence of Tracker Tagami, a man then of about sixty years. Tagami was an elder of the tribe, in so far as the Burranghyatti possessed shared elders. For traditionally they travelled their sparsely watered country in small family groups – coalescing with relatives only at such major ceremonial sites and waterholes as the one at the base of Gharrademu, Mount Bavaria. Tagami, who had made Auger's repute, was deceased, but now his son, Noel Yangdandu, was the principal party to a land claim under the *Land Rights Act* for possession of the Mount Bavaria area. Professor Auger was the expert witness who could vouch for what Yangdandu's father had told him long before. If Mount Bavaria was a locus of primary meaning to Tracker, it was necessarily so for his son.

A Federal Court judge, appointed to hear the land claim under the *Land Rights Act*, sat in shorts and knee socks at a table deep in the tent's shade, listening avidly to the respected Professor Auger, advocacy anthropologist, now a man in his early forties, authoritative in a casually American sort of way. The middle-aged judge asked Auger to describe the number and frequency of the interviews he had held with Noel Yangdandu's father, Tracker Tagami, and whether there had been onlookers who disputed anything Tagami had said. Robert Auger – in country-music shirt, jeans, boots, and seeming more an anthropological ranger than a narrow scholar – referred smoothly to his notebooks, which had been the basis of sundry distinguished articles. According to Tracker's evidence, his hero ancestor, Baurigal, journeying in the void, had made stars descend, had hurled stones, turned beasts and two protean sisters, with one of whom he had copulated, into rocks. He had endowed a cave at Bavaria's base with his sustaining blood.

Tracker Tagami, Auger remembered, had been outraged by diamond drilling which had occurred west of Mount Bavaria in the mid 1960s. It had turned the earth inside out and chemicals had fouled two seasonal water holes in the rock plugs known as the Sisters. Later mining, said Auger, had destroyed tracts of land in which foods such as silky pear, flax onions, bush tomatoes, acacia seed and *ngurturl* trees with their succulent gum had been plentiful. This despoliation had been a powerful influence upon Noel Yangdandu to make the claim. 'Without Yangdandu's ceremonial knowledge and use of this country, the earth loses its significance, botanical, zoological or human,' Auger assured the judge, 'Though to us it might still seem peopled, to the Burranghyatti it will become a void, a fatal hole in the earth's fabric.'

Prim was enchanted by the vigorous subtlety of Auger's arguments, the way in which the judge set possible barriers to the success of the land claim, and the casual elegance with which Auger vaulted them.

Within the tent flap's shade, she could see the unmoving back of the claimant Noel. She knew him to be a handsome man, preternaturally thin and bow-legged from working as a stockman. From the students' campfire last night she and the other three aspirants had watched Auger and Noel drinking tea and laughing loudly but clannishly with other Burranghyatti men. The one male student had been invited over, and later went out with Noel and Auger in a four-wheel drive shooting feral cats, now a greater plague than miners in Noel's country.

And now, in the tented court, maleness rose and excluded her again. Some of the liturgical details of how Yangdandu and other men communally maintained and restored Baurigal's inheritance could not be uttered in front of women. Various aged and ageless women, square-bodied, thin-legged, with the broad stable features of desert Aboriginals, had already departed before the judge asked the three female students sitting in the last of the shade at the back of the tent if they would mind leaving.

Prim and the others gathered their studious notes and stepped out squinting from blue shade into brutal light. She saw the Burranghyatti women ahead of her, swaying to their own shade – the shade of brush dwellings fortified with sheets of plastic, wooden panels, corrugated iron and an occasional car door. Three such female householders who had not attended the court sat around a blanket in the shadow of a desert oak and began dealing cards, and in her giddiness Prim thought that they looked like world-makers as they passed magic tokens to each other, frowning, barely speaking. These women possessed the other half of their people's mysteries, the part that could be uttered only to women. Why couldn't she research the women's cosmos, on which the literature was thin?

Later, of course, she would blush for her vanity, for seeing a distressed and confused group as *her* potential material. Even then, in the early 1980s, Aboriginal peoples had begun demanding their totems be returned, the bones of their dead be restored to them from museums as far away as Scotland. It was an age in which a clamour arose about sacred and other native designs that had appeared, without acknowledgment of moral property, on tea towels and postcards. And anthropologists were the informers of the moral sense of the white majority. She felt her own moral sense, more than her vanity, blazing in the sun.

She and her fellows had been so careful not to intrude at Turner Creek that they had brought two tents with them – one was shared by the male student and the more senior of the women, who were lovers. Prim shared the second with the other unattached woman. The students had their own campfire, to which Auger began to bring some of the Burranghyatti people at night. They were mainly men who sat shyly on desert oak logs or on the red ground, and whose eyes confronted the flames rather than the faces of the eager researchers.

After such campfire meetings, Prim and the other students washed in an ablution block at the side of the clinic. On the second night in Turner Creek, Prim was returning damp-haired towards her tent, in a garden of soft darkness that burst into roses of fire here and there. Auger's clever face and lithe body appeared before her. His handsome mouth was creaked open in a smile which was very nearly silly.

'Hi, Primrose,' he said. 'Getting something out of this experience?'

Prim made the expected complimentary remarks.

'Yeah, but it's more complicated than they think. Mount Bavaria used to be the preserve of the Yurritji, but the Yurritji were wiped out by police and settlers while an overland telegraph was being pushed through in the 1880s. And so the Burranghyatti, who were related, reached out to absorb it. They began as kind of caretakers. They became the inheritors.'

'But isn't that a normal mechanism?' said Prim, brushing aside her wet hair from her brow.

'I don't want to confuse this guy, the judge,' said Auger. 'I'm taking things slow.'

He put a hand on her left shoulder. She wondered what it was doing there, professional mateship or something else. It seemed an honest enough, confiding gesture, yet it made her sweat. 'It's easy as pie to tell the full truth in the case of European property rights. We've got deeds, we've got fences. But ... the judge is aware, he's a bright guy.'

His left hand had now been lightly lifted to the other shoulder. He dragged her towards him and kissed the side of her face in an inexpert way that delighted her and reinforced his character as no more than a brilliant, uncertain boy. And now he began uttering the banalities of desire, breathing hard – again, in the tradition of the boy-men she had known. 'You're so damned beautiful and you're bright as a button,' he said, feeling beneath the khaki shirt for her breasts.

Since she would need to return to her companion in the tent and since she would be incapable of conducting the normal last-thing-at-night dialogue under canvas, she pulled away.

'I'm sorry,' he said, as she knew rebuffed men did. 'It won't happen again, Prim. I suppose it's the general intoxication of this case ...'

'Don't apologise,' she told him in a quick, strangulated voice.

She returned to her tent by torchlight, fearing that once she reached her sleeping bag, if she did not immediately switch out that small baton of light it might evince from her the whole unutterable story. Her tent-mate yawned and murmured, 'That sun draws everything out of you. But the air's brisk at night. Christ, I wish my boyfriend was here.'

Prim put on a sweater in the darkness, for the night air seeped through the pores of the tent. Even after what had happened, she had for Auger none of the normal revulsion she'd had for the men at the Labor Club. She had no sense that she had just taken part in a common and very nearly trite scene, in shared intellectual fervour between scholar and apprentice. But once she was in her sleeping bag, her pleasant fever was replaced by a distasteful question: Did he invite me to the Northern Territory just for this? Just to sound me out, to try it on? She was the only first year MA student he had asked. But if her looks had been more enviably normal, if people didn't talk like that all the time about Dimp and herself, if she were a pleasant hefty girl, if she were graced with those Scots and Irish freckles not uncommon in Australia, brought out to riot by the sun, she would certainly know where he stood in the essential matter of her intellectual promise. It was the panic of not knowing

either way which made her want to flee from this tent, from the cold
smell of sun-screen and insect repellent.

Prim fell profoundly asleep – the soothing sleep of the utterly
disgraced, the woman of no conceivable future. She had a dream of
attending a funeral and being forced to eat sponge cake by Auger's wife,
a political scientist. She woke in a divine daze, restored to happiness and
life after the sharpness of the dream. Something moved within her, the
serpent beneath the ribs, between the hips, in the bowl of her body. Real
life was not now centred in the nuances of the patrilineal descent amongst
Burranghyatti, but for the first time in her life in the nuances of her own
body.

Dressed, scrubbed, her brown hair pulled severely back and tied with
a green ribbon in a way which she knew to be both strict and playful,
she went off to breakfast with the others and then to the tent court. She
listened as evidence about the Yurritji massacre during the building of
the westward telegraph line was related by a newly flown-in historian
from the University of Adelaide, who had discovered a confessional diary
by an English surveyor. At the close of this evidence, Professor Auger
was invited back to comment on this sort of acquisition: the taking over
of the land and sites of slaughtered kinsmen. Handsome, righteous Auger
seemed a different man from the uncertain caressing lad of last night. He
was back in his realm of power, and reeled off similar recorded cases
from New South Wales in the 1840s to Western Australia in the 1920s.
It was tour-de-force stuff, and now and then his gaze moved down the
length of the tent and latched on to Prim's fixed eye.

That night Prim stayed on by the students' fire, which Auger had
managed to make the centre of his social evening conversations. Noel
Yangdandu and his tall cousins in their cowboy shirts and jeans talked
in jagged, laconic English about working on cattle stations from Oodna-
datta to the Roper River and west to Halls Creek. Their forebears had
seen their first horse only two or at most three generations ago, but these
fellows all looked like riders. The students asked about where this and
that man's country was. Men pointed into the night – north, south, east,
west, into the ancestor-graced darkness. One by one though, the
Burranghyatti men rose and vanished. The betrothed graduate students
sneaked off to their tent to crack a bottle of wine they had smuggled into
this officially dry reservation. Prim's tent-mate staggered off yawning.
Finally, only Prim and Auger were left before the dying fire.

They had nothing to say for a few minutes. He placed his hand on her wrist and said, 'Oh Prim.' She was delighted. She had reduced him from the polysyllabic cosmos he inhabited in the courtroom to just two syllables.

How does one woman betray another? By the superior authority of her desire. Its claims are greater than the mere retentiveness of wives. In a camp that seemed to her blind to their movements, Auger put his arm around Prim's shoulders and walked with her to his tent. Tearing at her clothes, laying his lips to her bared shoulder, he mentioned that there was a beautiful, star-struck place along Turner Creek that would be a better place for all this, but the evening cold was against it. 'I'll take you there one day,' he told her.

So occurred Prim's first experience of berserk, multiple, howling, wakeful, engrossed, transcendent sex. For the first time she knew that disabling sense of mutual congratulation which lovers bestow on each other once the summit is achieved. The only two mountain climbers in the world, ready to descend into a brief saddle of contentment before hauling each other skywards again!

She dragged herself back to her tent at 1 a.m., late enough to provoke talk, early enough to make talk not quite credible. In fact, in the drunken vanity of the hour she wanted her fellow graduate students to be at the one time ignorant and amazed.

On her return to Sydney, her addiction to Auger seemed more substantial than the known world, than the literal streams of traffic on Missenden and Parramatta Roads, whose purpose was purely to hem in Auger's scholarship at the University of Sydney. Auger had early told her that his marriage was loveless, and the mistake of his life. In loving Prim, he said, he was liberating his wife from lovelessness too. Again, this observation came to Prim as if it were extremely novel, rhetoric without pedigree, not just a stock cliché of affairs between eminent older men and worshipful disciples. His wife was an emotional manipulator, he told Prim. Her possessiveness had very nearly destroyed him, and his only solace had been his work. But now he went into his unhealthy contests with his wife arrayed and armoured in Prim's light. 'Let me tell you, Prim, there's nothing out in Gharrademu to compare with the perils in desert places of the heart, the waterless stretches.' His wife had delayed having children specifically because of their unhappiness, but he said he wanted children of Prim.

At the time, Prim and her sister were renting another place in Redfern, this time a dim nineteenth-century worker's cottage, into whose stairwell a light shaft had been cut to give the place a sunnier, more modern air. It was all too convenient that it should become the chief place of assignation for herself and Auger.

Hence Dimp got to meet Auger. Dimp, who was worldlier, who was not only beautiful but had robustness and an earthy common sense in matters of the heart, and had once or twice been where Prim now was, was at the moment there again with Brendan D'Arcy. And though Dimp frowned a great deal about Prim's affair while making coffee for herself, her sister, the visiting Professor Auger, she said little. But there was ultimately a fight in which Prim, who wanted the entire visible world to be engorged with her own passion, attacked Dimp for not liking Robert Auger.

'I just don't believe what he tells you about his marriage,' said Dimp. 'I've heard that sort of guff before.'

When the affair began, Prim had thought that it would be at most weeks before the Auger's avowedly failed marriage was abandoned. She was as yet innocent of the potency of a failed marriage over a triumphant affair. After four months, another journey to Central Australia together, a weekend of hiking in the Hunter Valley, a reconnaissance of an embattled Aboriginal settlement in Queensland, Dr/Mrs Auger had still not been told. His wife was unhappy in a vague sense, suspicious, Auger said, and would prove indifferent and scornful when she knew. He was waiting for the right moment to tell her that Primrose Bettany was willing to free her from her sour possessiveness. 'I have to wait until she's a little more stable,' he told Prim. She would be told once he was satisfied she had a grip on herself.

At first Prim followed an instinct that she must not be insistent. A further month passed and she became anxious. Another one, and she decided to take up the duty of stridency, and spent part of her time hating herself for asking the same question over and over, and the rest hating Auger and his wife. This was a time of angry, less languorous penetrations of her body. 'There you are, you bitch,' said Auger one day on her bed, conceding her his angry seed.

She had already been talking for some time to him about her dissertation: on the Burranghyatti women, not in terms of their traditional life but in their semi-reservationised state. Those women who were forced to leave the hearing tent during crucial male evidence – what of them? Had they possessed greater parity of ritual power and authority in their traditional desert life than male anthropologists had suspected? Or was it the crisis of coming in from the desert to the reservation which had diminished the male elders and given the women a new authority? Auger had referred Prim to the only other literature then available in this area. A dazzling article, he said, written in the seventies by a professor from the University of Minnesota, Dr Joyce Ackland. His praise for the material was spacious enough to make Prim faintly jealous, until Auger produced a conference program in which photographs of those who delivered the papers appeared, and Prim was despicably pleased to find Professor Ackland homely and nearing sixty.

Ackland, in any case, had written on the subject more from a traditional anthropological point of view. The thesis of her article was that the provision of stored and bore water via taps had altered the balance between men and water. It had taken urgency out of male rites designed to ensure the recurrence of water, the ceremonial maintaining of water sources in the desert being up until then substantially men's business. For it was the women who now turned on the reservation taps and fetched the water in jugs and pots from stand pipes. Or so Ackland's proposition went.

But Auger, though he admired Ackland's article, wondered whether the women's social powers had been increased not by tap water but by the way men succumbed to disorientation, bad diet, gaol and alcoholism. He showed Prim another article, by a West Australian academic – another elderly woman – who argued that, in their traditional life, women had had significant ritual input into maintaining water holes. Their new familiarity with taps, banal as such water might seem but ever a miraculous mother in the desert, was not a supplanting of the men but a continuation of female powers possessed before the reservation was put in place.

So Prim was to write a dissertation on both views and either reinforce one over the other, or reach a new synthesis of both. On a minute research grant, she spent two blistering months interviewing two middle-aged desert women, the Pidanu sisters, who had taken, at their christening by Lutheran missionaries in the 1960s, the names Betty and Dottie. She sat with them by the hour, playing gin rummy before, out of politeness, out of pure kindness, they took her, sometimes together, sometimes separately, to some local women's sites within hiking distance. At a cave beyond Mount Bavaria, the sisters each told her, sundry totemic beast-men, bird-men, lizard-children, disguising themselves as infants, persuaded a female ancestor, Kabiddi, to spill her milk for the convenience and succour of humankind.

Before she could attend any women's rites associated with this and other mysteries, Prim was privileged to find herself led off at dusk to a low escarpment near Turner Creek where, with white clay on her forehead and painful smoke from eucalyptus boughs in her eyes – the women smoking her ignorance out of her – she was admitted to the first, infant version of initiation. Great mysteries awaited her; she was certain of what would be a limitless, career-long association with these women, their aunts, daughters, nieces. She was a modern anthropologist, not looking at them through a long lens, but their intimate. For she was interested in all that awaited them – the solar-powered telephone, the satellite television – and not simply in the exotic aspects of where they had been in their previous, nomadic existence. And she would as a reward be one of those scholars who were named referentially, *reverentially*, in journals. 'Bettany's pioneering work with the Burranghyatti women in the Mount Bavaria region . . .' She would, of course, be argued with by later scholars on the scene, but her authority would supersede theirs. And in the tent courts, or the courts convened in some community hall in remoter Australia, she would serve the Burranghyatti people eloquently when they made their claims.

Returned to Sydney, Prim wrote a confident and combative dissertation – a critique both of Ackland and of the other scholar, Judith Verner – studded with footnotes from Strehlow to Tindale to Auger. Auger, who was a computer whiz, introduced her to the then fresh wonder of word processing and what it could do for a dissertation. 'I don't know how anything got written before the PC,' he told her.

Her writing ran parallel to her affair, which, though by now it made her as much miserable as ecstatic, she saw as her destiny. She entered a calm but firm phase of her discourse with Auger on the subject of what she called 'an honest confrontation' with his wife. The more Prim argued, and the more he delayed, the more a certain sort of confidence grew in her, something hollow, stale, yet somehow rampant and addictive. She became the demanding party in sex, he the frightened one who wanted to retreat to a few well-tried options. It was love in a kind of war. She was strangely delighted when Auger, gushing into her, yelled like an angry peon delivered of a load. 'Oh Christ,' he would say, 'that's it, that's it.' His voice seemed also to threaten that she might have earned other, fiercer degradations, and these would be delivered in time. It was amazing to her how long she was willing to live like this, in a kind of unresolved tranquillity.

Her dissertation done, she gave the computer disk and one of two copies she had printed from it to Auger's office. Then she applied to be admitted to the doctoral program at Sydney. Her fellow graduates, she was vaguely aware, nodded and said, 'Of course, of bloody course.' For they were applying to other places, to the University of Western Australia, to Northwestern or UCLA or Constanz or Tubingen. But they understood why she wanted to stay with Auger. After the event she would wonder at their casual good humour when more malice was justified.

Auger's office, near the university's renowned neo-Gothic quadrangle, was crowded with paintings of Central Australian dreamings from a range of desert cultures, carved birds from Arnhem Land decorated in the 'X-ray' style which celebrated the creatures' chief internal organs, and a spectacular bone casing with a shark painted on it. When she'd first visited it as an undergraduate, the office had impressed Prim as a sort of druid's cave, imbued with all that saved Australia, in her eyes, from its own torpor: the romance of the Aboriginal cosmology.

Now she was due to visit it because there was a perfunctory note from Auger in her mailbox, a note without the intimacy of an envelope. It asked her to visit his office any time from three onwards.

So she went. In this mood she was more ready to be robust, jolly, bossy with him than to be afraid at his unaccustomed mode of summons. When she went in there was a kind of shyness in Auger as he came around his desk, held her almost perfunctorily by the shoulders and kissed her cheek.

'I know what all this means,' she said, thinking he was about to tell her she had not been accepted into the doctoral program. He was about to tell her that there had been some fierce doctoral committee argument about her that he had lost.

He asked her to sit and they faced each other like strangers on opposite sides of the desk. 'Prim, listen. There's a problem with your dissertation,' he said at last. Her expectations fell another notch. Her Master's would be delayed.

He explained he had read her dissertation first and was concerned, 'for your sake as much as anyone's'. So he passed it on to Professor Rabin, because he wanted 'a more detached view'.

Prim would ever after remember precisely the way he looked out, levelly but with a small, painful, magisterial squint into the bright leafy trees across the lane, waving above rowdy students on their way to alfresco study in the Holme courtyard. She had a sudden sense that he was going to cast her off.

'So, you're going to send me for another spin around the block,' she said, and tried to laugh.

'Well, you see, I just wish I could.'

'Come on, Robert. Don't *wish* things. Tell me.'

He looked at her, his eyes not quite engaging, his face pale.

'Prim, it looks like you've put yourself outside my help.'

'What does that mean?'

'I find undigested lumps of Verner and Ackland in the middle of your dissertation. I mean, we all draw on each other in a way, but we're supposed to go through a process of making the scholarship our own and finding our own voice.'

Prim said, 'That's crazy. I referred to Ackland mainly to challenge some of her conclusions.'

Auger passed her dissertation. 'Why don't you look at page 25 from the paragraph beginning "On the basis of this evidence . . ." '

She took the marked pages. She still had residual faith that what she had written was in place, there in the text, amenable to calm explanation. But the passage was nothing that she had written, or remembered, or even particularly agreed with.

'I didn't write this,' she told him.

'Prim . . . that's the normal student denial.' So he had reduced her in a few seconds from friend, lover and colleague to temporising student.

She knew instantly what he had done. He had acted with a criminal determination no one would believe him capable of. For the sake of his grievous marriage, and to evade the frenzied lover asking, 'When? When?' he had altered her dissertation at source, on the disk. He had butchered it, robbed it of its connections, emasculated its argument and introduced undigested lumps of Verner and Ackland. Short of strangling her, he was sending her into thorough exile. He was extirpating her. And she knew even then that no one would believe he had gone to all this trouble.

His voice trembled as he read a series of page notations he had jotted down on a notepad. 'Turn to page 37, please. Then pages 42, 46 to 48, 53 to 55 . . .'

'You did this,' she said. He who was clever at word processors in an age when many scholars were still fighting a delaying war against them. He could – as the new phrase had it – 'desk-top publish' scholarly news-letters. So he had spent dark hours to alter matter through cut, paste, copy; to devise a new version of her dissertation. She flicked the pages and found the font correct but the contents largely strange. 'You did this, Robert.'

'Prim,' he said, looking out the window again, 'do you know how mad that sounds. I haven't betrayed you. You've betrayed me.' He seemed genuinely to believe it. 'It's like this – I don't think for a moment your direct purpose was to cheat. You don't need to. But I think you were actually testing me. Seeing if I would cover for you. Well, we may be great friends, Prim. But I can't cover for you on this.'

Everything was apparent to Prim now. 'You want to get rid of me – from the university. From all scholarly life. You don't want to be worried by me. You want your shitty marriage.'

'That's hysterical,' Auger said. Men could say that, hands spread concessively, chin lowered. It was one of their best tricks.

'My God, I didn't want to test you. I wanted to impress you. And I did. The real text. Weren't you impressed?'

'I can't be impressed with that,' he said, nodding to the text in her hands.

'I have another copy of what I wrote at home.'

'Of course you do,' he said. 'After all, weeks have passed since you put this one in.'

'Look, Robert, you *know* me. I've got too much intellectual vanity to play this sort of game.' Could someone else have done it, altered the text? A jealous woman student? 'Someone has tampered with this, and if it's not you, then I apologise.'

'I should think so,' said Auger. 'You do me very little credit, Prim.'

'How much credit do you do me?' she asked.

'Dr Rabin and I are required to report this to the dean.'

'This beggars belief,' said Prim. She stood up and walked about the office.

He knew he had routed her now. 'I can't avoid it. I have only to wait until another graduate student, or an academic working in this area seeks out your dissertation, and they'll notice it too, what Rabin and I have already noticed. It's a gross lift, Prim. I know I'm partly to blame for the fact you haven't been happy–'

'Don't you presume you can talk about my happiness,' she warned him. So he was happy to give that up, the consoling tone, and fall back on his habitual authority, that of a tenured academic eminent in his field.

'Well, I just know this whole time has been very stressful for you, Prim.

I know what you wanted out of our relationship. If I have added to your anguish in any way ...'

'*In any way?*'

'We can get you therapy,' he offered.

'Get therapy yourself,' she told him. She grew dizzy with an enormous just rage. She was determined against the odds to be believed by somebody.

'In any case,' said Auger, 'the dean is waiting to see you.'

'If I see the dean, I'll tell him everything.'

'So we've already got round to vengefulness, have we, Prim? I've already approached the dean, and confessed my association with you. There's forgiveness for lapses of sexual morality, Prim. But none for plagiarism.'

It was still incomprehensible: the last ten months described as a lapse! She could not find any handhold on such a fatuous word. 'Well,' she said, 'I very much want to see the dean.'

But the interview she had when she got to the dean's office was marked by the same kind of uncomprehending, brutal words Auger had uttered. One of them – again – was 'lapse', another was 'counselling'. 'But I can produce a copy of the dissertation in its true form,' said Prim. 'I'm sure you could,' said the dean. 'The point is the copy you did submit. And whatever it meant, whatever your motive ... attention-getting or otherwise ... it's still plagiarism.'

She must face reality, the dean told her, and admit the plagiarism. Otherwise the matter would have to be taken to the post-graduate committee and higher. After her excellent record, he was willing to accept that this had been an aberration created by stress. 'You may have,' he suggested tentatively, 'without deliberately knowing it, wanted to bring your unfortunate relationship with Professor Auger, the details of which he has confided to me, to a conclusion, and subconsciously thought the best way to do that was to offend him.' It was a sentence she laughed at madly at the time. A pompous, half-thought-out, Auger-suggested and amateurish stab at a psychological explanation.

When she told the dean that Auger had altered her dissertation, the dean politely called that paranoia. If it were the truth, anyhow, she could appeal. But with the greatest respect, the dean did not believe it.

The depiction of her as one who plagiarised for attention brought on disabling rage, then and later. It was so vast and appalling an accusation that she thought it capable of snuffing out her life with its hugeness. It proved to be an accusation that grew within her like a foreign, unchosen organism clamped around her vitals. Its malign nature made any further contest with these men, and with the man Auger, impossible to tolerate. Prim could neither confess to plagiarism nor throw herself on their mercy; neither take up their proffered counselling nor appeal to the vice-chancellor or the university senate. She could not bear to have the accusations, the comforting myth of attention-seeking, a plausible one in male eyes, raised again. She knew it would simply kill her.

She walked out of the university gates on Missenden Road and caught a cab home. There she found Brendan D'Arcy and Dimp drinking. She numbly drank some champagne with them and told them nothing.

'How is the thesis?' asked D'Arcy lightly, though he was so engrossed in his own happiness he did not wait for an answer. They insisted on taking her with them to a restaurant, where she conversed like a living being with a stake in things. It was only after she had been in the women's lavatory for half an hour that Dimp came looking for her.

'I'm giving up the university,' Primrose turned from the mirror to tell her sister.

'Now?'

'Yes.'

Dimp put a hand on her sister's shoulder. 'What is it?'

'All you have to know for now is I'm leaving.'

'That bloody Auger,' said Dimp. 'I'm so sorry.'

I will not weep at a name, Prim promised herself.

Dimp said, 'You must hate me for not doing more.'

'Why? You're innocent.'

'I should have intervened. I could read the omens, but I was too busy with Bren.'

'No, no.'

'Jesus, I should have warned you.'

'And I wouldn't have listened.'

'What will you do?'

'I'll go somewhere. You know what? I'd like to go to another country. What I mean is, another culture. Somewhere where I'm considered an aberration. Ugly if possible. No, maybe not ugly. That's self-pity. I'd like to go somewhere I'm considered neutral. A non-player.'

'Where could that be?' Dimp asked.

'I have some ideas,' said Prim. 'I have a degree, and some references from earlier in my career.'

'Come back to the table,' Dimp said softly, taking her arm.

'I can't.'

In fact, Prim barely emerged from the house in Redfern for the next three months. A strength in her forbade either suicide or full-blown mental illness, but in the end, for the sake of not being eaten alive nocturnally by the ridiculous remembered sentences of the dean and of Auger, she was forced to take a course of anti-depressants, hating herself the more, as if she were fulfilling out of a pill bottle the predictions of Auger, and comporting herself according to his lies.

Ultimately she went to Canberra, the national capital, a derisory choice of domicile for most Sydneysiders, and worked for an aid body, or NGO (non-government organisation), as such instrumentalities liked to call themselves. This one was named Austfam, was active in the South Pacific and Asia, and had a presence since the East African famines of the 1970s in Ethiopia, and a small office in the Sudan.

Dimp asked her repeatedly what she thought she was doing in Canberra, that artificial capital which imposed on its citizens sudden scarifying winter frosts and summer excesses of heat. But Prim had begun attending training courses run by the Australian Development Assistance Bureau and by the Australian Council of Overseas Aid. Most of her colleagues thought of Asian development as the primary Australian duty. Prim thought of the Sudan, where the Austfam office was run by an eccentric man named Crouch, and the post of assistant office administrator and field officer had just come on offer. Her decision to apply was motivated by altruism, but also by the fact that she lacked the facial markings, the orderly scarrings, the broad eyes and splendid pigmentation considered essential elements of beauty amongst many Sudanese.

She would not be desired there. And that was fine with her.

Prim went to the Austfam office in the city of Khartoum in 1984. In flight from the Auger business, she did not have the room to bring to the experience the enthusiasm of the tourist, or more cultural curiosity than she needed for her job. The broad-streeted city proper was held in place between the Blue and White Niles, which met each other – amidst beds of rich silt – in Central Khartoum's north-west corner. Near either of the rivers it was possible to imagine the city as fabled oasis, and the focus for the million square mile immensity of the republic. But south of that, on the rubbly, sandy earth of the New Extension, where head offices of many NGOs and other agencies were located, all the supposed aura and magnetism of the fabled rivers seemed remote to her. Prim's training, and the Austfam manuals she had read, had told her how to dress in East Africa – for example, long sleeves instead of short – and implied that for a woman there was a certain danger of committing errors of dress or behaviour if a person went wandering on her own. When she did go out with a woman acquaintance, over the White Nile to fabled Omdurman, a place everyone at parties in the New Extension told her she had to visit, she had for a while felt edgy and exposed. That feeling soon passed, but she was very happy in any case to stay close to the office–residence, located in a high-walled, two-storeyed, flat-roofed villa of plastered brick in the New Extension. Behind the house lay a little yard of dust, and a cinder-block garage which also served as quarters for a man named Erwit, Austfam Khartoum's earnest Eritrean driver.

Prim lived in a small, sweltering room behind the office, but took meals upstairs in Crouch's apartment. A peculiarly aged-looking man in his mid-thirties, Crouch stooped around the office, his brush of red hair all thrust forward spikily above features which appeared misanthropic. At first she mistook his air of melancholy for disenchantment with his job, and when she started attending Arabic classes with him each week at the monastery of the Vincentian Fathers in the New Extension, Prim found he had not achieved much competence in the language, and feared she too would not become fluent. She suspected that, despite all pretended breadth of intellect she was already, at twenty-four, too culturally set to enter and move with confidence in the new cosmos of Arabic.

Prim had worked at Khartoum's Austfam office no more than six months, chiefly looking after routine correspondence with the Sudanese Ministry of Health, with the Sudanese Commission of Refugees, with Austfam offices in Canberra and Sydney, when Crouch told her he was being considered for the job of heading the largest Austfam operation, in Cambodia. A few months later, it was confirmed.

Before he left, Crouch took Prim out for her first experience 'in the field'. They went to a water project at a village near the Nuba Hills, some four hundred miles south-west of the capital, where Austfam had helped fund a not particularly successful small dam. When they left the main road west, something like fervour entered Crouch's voice. Like Prim, he clearly found this country engaging, perhaps partly because it resembled remoter Australia. Even the gum Arabic bushes were acacias, and would not have seemed out of place in Australia's central deserts.

As they passed an informal plantation of these bushes, and saw little bowls placed at the base of the narrow trunks to catch the amber resin, he expatiated on that ancient industry – how gum Arabic resin had been until the age of synthetic chemicals the world's fixative. Pills, paints, lollies, said Crouch. 'Now the water basin's sunk to buggery, and people can't get the yield they want.'

Old men in dust-grey galabias took Crouch and Prim to a little dam, a quarter full of murky water, with lines of acacia trees laid out on the terraces above to hold the earth in place. Women were drawing up this water in plastic buckets with ropes attached. They would use it for watering stock, said Crouch. They were travelling quite a distance to take drinking water from an old British well – Crouch showed her on an ordnance map where it was. Prim would need to set up Austfam funding for a new well to be drilled.

As she and Crouch made their notes and assessments, these Sudanese, the long, narrow houses of mudbrick and adobe, the sacking and fabric at the unglassed windows, the fences of acacia, the goats nosing gravel in search of grass roots, all seemed as normal to her as the traffic of a country town in New South Wales. Unexpectedly, the dark, densely related male faces, beneath their skullcaps or with cloths tumbled turban-like on their heads, looked utterly natural, not marked by an exotic ethnicity. This, the usualness of the people she met, helped her forget she was an interloper. Some of these admirable-looking men were no doubt tyrannous fathers, tyrannous husbands. Their thin-faced wives were in the background, toting water is plastic cans, pounding millet, sitting by minute cooking fires in the lee of their houses, or looking out from beyond their shadowed lintels over raised shawls. For their sakes she must cease to be a ghost, an orphan. She must be of some effectiveness in the matter of water supply. That she might be in her way an unhappy woman did not count. That she was an orphan or even an imposter did not count either. They were willing to believe she and Crouch could release hidden water from the earth, and so she must believe she had that effectiveness too.

Of course, back in Khartoum, routine was still welcome, and so was the idea that she would soon, at least for a time, be working by herself. She had few doubts about her ability to keep the Austfam programs in the Sudan going.

Prim inherited from Crouch Austfam's share not only of drought-prone villages but of potential refugees from a recently renewed national war in the south of the country. There had always been a divide between the more Arab and Islamic North and the part-Christian, part-animist South. More Central African in appearance than their northern counterparts, the Southerners had always been uneasy partners in the Sudanese state. Southern officers and NCOs from the ranks of the Sudanese Army had rebelled against the government when it imposed Islamic law, the Sharia or Way, on the nation. A great part of the official Sudanese Army had recently descended upon the South to punish it for its rebellion and for its pretence of claiming sovereignty over the upper waters of the Blue and White Niles.

When the war began, regular troops, garlanded with flowers, marched and rolled in trucks and tanks along Sharia el Nil. The populace had called *Maah-ssalama*, God's blessing be with you, as young men went off to put paid to Southern insolence. But on their native ground of reed swamps, tall grass, clumps of bush and poorly marked roads, the Southerners – Dinka and Nuer cattle herders and others, the despised of the Republic, whom people in the North unself-consciously called *abids*, slaves – had not been easily subdued. It was apparent that a long conflict was in prospect. The Sudanese Army precariously held all the garrison towns, but in all their movements into open country the government troops were subject to attacks by the passionate Sudanese People's Liberation Army, the Southern rebels.

The people of the South were not only subject to being punished by government troops, but also by the Arab cattle-herding tribes, the Beggarah, who considered themselves part of the Islamic North and who had traditionally recruited slaves in the South. Now the Sudanese government had armed the Beggarah with semi-automatics, turning them into militias, empowering them to operate with impunity against their neighbours.

In Khartoum in the first weeks of the war Crouch had made a journey down into Bahr el Ghazal, one of the rebellious provinces, and wrote a report alerting Austfam in Sydney and Canberra that there would be a refugee problem. Southerners, whose villages had been suspected of harbouring the rebel troops, and whose livestock had been shot or taken by government soldiers, were vacating the zone of war, by train or on foot. They fled from the Sudanese Army and the Beggarah. They even fled their own, the Liberation Army, for crossfire took no account of one's ethnic identity. To begin with, over the space of a month or so, some 50 000 Southerners whose villages had been razed stampeded into the North, walking up the rail line to Darfur province, settling without livestock in wadis in the great dry grasslands. Officials from the Sudanese government, from the UN and a number of NGOs, colleagues of Prim and Crouch, rushed out from Khartoum with tents and medicine to intercept the refugees, and Crouch, in his last days in the Sudan, organised emergency shipments of tents, cots and blue plastic sheeting. Prim was delighted to have a hand in arranging these straightforward mercies. To her, after the subtle and defeated vanities of anthropology, they represented all the more a worthy and enriching exercise. The needs were so clear, and could be so directly met! She was redeeming herself through wells and shipments of Australian food aid.

Some ten months into what would prove to be her largely solitary posting, Prim got a radio telephone call from the Irish woman who ran the clinic at Adi Hamit, one of the refugee camps. She reported that the well Austfam had provided there had gone dry. A drilling crew was needed.

This was a chance for Prim to get more experience in the field, to travel to Adi Hamit with the drilling teams and make a report. Erwit, the Eritrean driver would accompany her. His technological expertise – he had serviced field telephones amongst the rebels in his country before coming out, half-dead with chronic bronchitis, to the Sudan in Crouch's truck – as well as his careful driving, reassured Prim. Prim also thought of the Dinka refugee midwife from Adi Hamit for whose education at the government School of Midwifery at the women's hospital in Omdurman Austfam had been paying. Prim had visited this midwife in the lean-to rooms where she lived behind the school, and then seen her recently receive her certificate. She must have been lonely in this city, surrounded by the other, the official Sudanese culture, and dressed not with Southern casual grace but in the North's sober swathes of white cloth and blue shawl – the price she paid for learning from Northerners how to deliver exiled Dinka babies. She studied at the School of Midwifery under a temporary Arab name – that was the rule – but her real name was Abuk Alier.

Prim visited her again and offered her a ride back to what could loosely be called 'home'. *Gidida*, a vehicle, said Prim. *Han-ruh Adi Hamit*, we go to Adi Hamit. When? *It-talat*, Tuesday. The newly graduated midwife smiled her seraphic Southern smile. According to Crouch's notes on her, she had seen a husband shot, and lost two children in some undisclosed way in the early months of the war. She was an uncharacteristically small-boned member of a race of lanky women, but identifiable as a wife, albeit a widow, by the patterns of ritual scars on her forehead, cheeks, temples. Abuk's surviving child lived with Abuk's mother in Adi Hamit.

The idea to travel with Erwit was altered when Prim received a call from the Englishman who had recently been appointed to run the European Community's development office in Khartoum. Prim had not yet met him at any of the NGO and agency parties she attended a few times a week, drinking tea, fruit juice and occasional illicit liquor with Danes, Brits, Germans, Americans. Crouch, spotting the loner in her, had emphasised the importance of these gatherings for maintaining contact with other people in the business, and she enjoyed the international character of these gatherings, at which some of the more adventurous were spaced-out by chewing the narcotic leaf, *khat*. There was automatic acceptance, but she could also achieve a sort of anonymity – just another youngish aid worker from a small NGO. Since he was even newer to the Sudan than she was, she had not yet met Stoner. His distractedness as he talked to her now smacked more of Liverpudlian rock group than Oxbridge languor.

'Oh, yeah. Look, I'm coming out with you, okay? To Adi Hamit, you know. If that's okay. I reckon it's time like. Time I went out there and saw the old Adi Hamit.'

'Well,' said Prim, 'I'll certainly have room.'

'No, I've got this big truck, love.' It came out as 'I go' this bi' trug, luv.' 'See, I share this compound where my office is with this Earthwater well-digging crowd. You can come out with me and ... you know, the diggers. You and I ... we've got a plane coming to fetch us back to Khartoum. Then my driver can bring the truck back in his own time.'

Prim told him she had to take back a midwife from the hospital in Omdurman.

'No problems, love. We got the room.'

The day before she was to leave, Prim discussed Stoner with an English friend, Helene Codderby, whom she had met at one of the NGO parties. Codderby was not an aid worker, but a journalist, and despite her seeming to know everything about the Sudan, she too had an air of isolation. Her father had been one of the last English bureaucrats to leave the Sudan, and she had come back as an adult. She was the sort of woman who must have looked aged in youth but had now achieved agelessness, and she seemed to hope that she would never go home to Britain.

Codderby took Prim's question about Stoner seriously, making the sort of dubious mouth which serves as a warning. 'He's a good fellow,' she said. 'Great fun. Marriage not solid.'

'What does "not solid" mean?' Prim asked.

Helene looked away. 'His wife hasn't joined him out here. But . . . yes, you'll be fine with him. You're capable of standing up for yourself. The only thing is, why's he going?'

'Why wouldn't he?'

'Well, has he heard some rumour about Darfur and wants to check it out? He's ambitious, and ambition makes people secretive.'

On a July morning, while Khartoum's air sat at a pleasant twenty-three degrees – it would climb towards forty degrees by mid-afternoon – Prim walked under clear skies towards the European Community's office at Street 33. She wore a cotton skirt to mid-knee and a khaki shirt buttoned to the wrist – civic propriety and the climate made such a combination advisable. She was burdened with a complicated pack which included a medical kit as well as her own belongings. Opposite the Farouk cemetery she turned into a yard where two drilling trucks and all their arcane equipment sat. Some Sudanese employees of Earthwater were slotted in amongst the esoteric gear. The large, check-shirted Canadian drill boss stood by the cabin of the leading vehicle and waved to Prim in a way that said, 'I'm just here for the work.' Earthwater was a Christian group whose desire was that every well should be sunk for God's love, but to meet the demand they had to hire roughnecks.

The man who turned out to be Stoner advanced on her from the shadow of a glossy four-wheel drive with the stars of the EC on its doors. He was tall, lazily awkward, crookedly handsome, with a Nordic pallor behind his tan. 'Oh yeah, Primrose, is it? Fergal. Got your gear? We got to collect your little woman, right?'

They were soon off, Prim in the rear seat. They drove out of the New Extension – Khartoum 2 as people called it – northwards, over the railway line through the city, across the Blue Nile Bridge then the northernmost White Nile Bridge into Omdurman. Omdurman was like a Latin Quarter, but had holiness as well – under a burnished dome was the Mahdi's tomb which infidels could not enter. Helene said of the great covered market called the *souk* that it wasn't up to scratch when compared with Cairo's. But when Prim had first gone there she had been fascinated enough, not so much by the jewellery but by the varieties of incense on display, and jars of *delkah*, an aromatic love oil. You could buy sure-fire love charms and amulets, and red silk threads which if worn on the right wrist of children protected them from the evil eye. Helene Codderby somehow bought her smuggled Scotch here.

The entire convoy stopped at Omdurman women's hospital, where Abuk the midwife seemed delighted to seat herself at Prim's side in Stoner's gleaming vehicle. A languid expert, the Sudanese driver, Rahmin, clicked with his tongue and assessed the crowded road, where in a melee of carts and dust, trucks and Mercedes, a white-uniformed cop stood on his pedestal at the crossroad, competently directing the flow. Stoner chatted intermittently with Rahmin in Arabic, but the man seemed keener to try out his English. He went into a rehearsed threnody for a lost Omdurman. 'No proper buildings,' he said. 'The better houses shrink. Everything once was green, now is dust.' Stoner studied his driver with a broad grin, and the man seemed flattered.

As if wanting a part in the discourse, the little midwife looked ahead at the wash of saffron light stretching away eternally above Omdurman's suburbs. '*Ya salaam hala-l-manzar!*' she said. 'Oh peace on this vista.'

The city was running out, and Rahmin swung temporarily off the ribbon of tar and compacted clay to overtake the drilling trucks. He did not wish to tolerate their dust. Acacias grew but grass was scarce either side of the road to el Obeid, and rain showed no sign of falling soon. Low dunes were exposed. Abuk slept neatly in her ornate midwife's uniform. Prim and Stoner discussed their careers to this point. Prim's tale was, as she told it, easily covered. Pulled out of her Master's. Joined Crouch. Here she was, waiting for his replacement. She gestured happily to the barren country beyond her window. She was pleased it held her safe.

'Me?' said Stoner. 'Okay, I was finishing up my Master's at York, and these bozos come round from the EC interviewing. They wanted to see me – you know, on my academic record purely. So I don't bother going to the interview, and like one of them calls me up and says, "We were expecting to see you." "Yeah," I said, "but you don't want guys like me." "Sure we do, if they speak Arabic." So I did my training course and then I was in the development office in Riyadh in Saudi, then a year in Lebanon, then here.'

'Lebanon,' said Prim.

'Yeah, my wife didn't like it. Cordelia. The old Cords. And now she wants to get the kids well started in primary school. Eight and seven. I'm home every three months anyhow.'

He was a good talker, but his contentment on this matter sounded brittle. As the acacias became shrubs and then stones, and they neared the city of el Obeid, passing the water tankers which travelled all the time between Khartoum and his waterless zone, Stoner lectured Prim effortlessly on rainfall, erratic and low around that thirsty, sprawling metropolis. Rolling down a street of neem trees amongst one-storey villas with their air of piety, quietude, decent reticence, he talked about the city's role as a formerly great marshalling point for caravans to reach critical mass before heading for Egypt or Arabia with gum arabic and slaves.

They kept on in afternoon torpor amongst table-topped hills and over rising earth – the Sudanese called this high, sloping plain the *Goz*. That night the party stayed at a small, barrack-like hotel. Rooms opened onto a U-shaped courtyard of dust, the mouth of the U being part-filled by an open-sided cookhouse where bread was baked and guests could sit and eat. Prim shared a room with the midwife who simply spread her shawl on one of the two beds and murmured contently, '*Il oda bita 'it-na* . . .' 'Our room,' she had said.

At that instant, Prim felt the loss of her sister like a positive rich presence. A succulent, phantom smile lit the near dark. Dimp's smile, at severest odds with her twee name. For the moment, Prim was amazed at the distance she had somehow and with a kind of hubris put between herself and Dimp. She was distracted by the burden of this awareness as she tried to read a novel by torchlight after the electricity went off at nine. Waiting for the surge of loneliness to pass, she heard the remote voices of men speaking English and Arabic, Stoner and the Canadian driller on one side of their room, the no fewer than five Sudanese members of the drilling team on the other.

Had these drillers been amongst those Sudanese who recently marched in Central Khartoum and the New Extension? She had heard the unmistakable tread and cries and drumbeats of a crowd passing the crossroads near her office–apartment. The first discontent at the government for embracing the war in the South, for wasting their international credits on it, for not winning it fast. The Sudanese pound and dinar were falling, and there had been at the same time a malign slump in the price of commodities the nation was best at producing. The white cotton-clad police and the khaki soldiers, who had suffered the same decline and hardship as the marchers, looked on tolerantly at the early marches. But after a few months, official good humour vanished. Prim saw the batons which had once lain indolently in the hands of witnessing police wielded with intent.

Off by eight, they crossed the Kordofan–Darfur border ahead of the drilling trucks. In an eternity of riven, yellow-grey tableland, the hard dirt road to Nyala could be discerned from the apparent blinding vacancy of the rest of the earth only by careful squinting. The Australian eye, as Prim regularly flattered herself, rejoiced in nuances, and was thus an eye fit for Africa: another reason – apart from shame and the desire for anonymous good works – she was suited to exile here.

It was mid-morning when they began to meet groups of villagers emerging from sidetracks onto the chief road. The speed of the truck and the cut of their white clothing gave the travellers either side of the road a false appearance of graceful and languid drift. At first it seemed that what they had encountered was an extended family on a line of travel, the too lean women carrying calabashes and bundles of belongings on their shawled heads or a child at breast or hip. Older men and women had staves and used the appearance of the drilling convoy as a reason to stop for breath. Some young men held out arms towards the trucks, but the children did not chase, instead with wide, sullen eyes watching Prim and Stoner and the others glide by. Stoner, looking over his shoulder, frowned at Prim. 'Generally you know it's the men who come to town,' he said, 'and they like to leave the women back home.'

Indeed, from what Prim had read, this line made sense if they were people migrating, farmers who had run short of food or cash and decided to become, at least for this season, city folk. Two hundred or so metres further along, a second and similar aberrant angular company was seen and then a third, and then the procession showed itself to be a long and continuous mass. A thousand and then three thousand people were easily passed in this manner. No obesity in them, no amplitude of flesh. They maintained a polite country reserve as they let the truck pass, expecting nothing from it. Prim felt now that she had seen only the rearguard of a host.

'Why don't we stop?' she asked, obligated, from banal pity if not from shock, to utter the question. All space, all food, all water, all analgesia Stoner's truck carried with it could not accommodate the miseries of this army in retreat.

Abuk the midwife had worn a particular frown as she looked out from under her shawl at these Northern people, by her calculation and theirs the favoured of the republic, impelled by failure of rains to seek Nyala, chief oasis and city of the south of Darfur. These people, Abuk seemed wide-eyed to observe, needed to undertake bitter marches too, could walk famishing, as she had once walked.

Stoner told Prim, for once every word connected to every other, meaning not diluted by pause, 'They want to arrive some place they can raise a little cash selling charcoal or fodder. And maybe they're hoping for a depot at Nyala. They're saying, *Inshallah*, if God wills it, there'll be food or work or both in the great city. Well, there's nothing there for them. That I can vouch for. Maybe there's some kind of little provincial government depot, but it won't handle this. Hey, pull up here, Rahmin!'

An extraordinary apparition, a truck top-heavy with people, some of them crowded even on to the cabin roof, was bearing into sight up a side track from the south. Stoner, dismounted, held up his hands preventively to advise Prim to stay where she was, but waved the drill trucks on. Prim wound up her window to keep the dust out, then wound it down again since Stoner, bandanna to mouth, wanted to talk to her.

'Okay, I'm going to talk to this geezer with the truck,' he told Prim, muttering into the dusty fabric of his neck cloth.

She smelled on the air the complicated and not unpleasant odour of the passing farmers, their children, their lean wives each with the ring of marriage in her right nostril. What woman would sell it even in the worst of times, even if it had a value? The marching families about her cried ragged and surreal greetings to Stoner. '*Ya Khawaga*!' they chorused with an unnecessary politeness. Greeting the foreigner, hoping his hands weren't as empty as they seemed. Stoner had produced a camera and was beginning to take pictures. Prim realised she had not included one of the office cameras in her pack.

Nearby, a boy of about fourteen in a grey-white *galabia* cried, '*Ma feesh aish*,' but was hissed at by a woman of his family. 'There is no food,' he had said.

'This looks like the real thing,' Stoner told her. 'There are fat-arsed people in Geneva and even in Khartoum who'd love to run up against this. Like Dimbleby discovering the Ethiopian famine in Wolo province. In Ethiopa, you know.'

'I think the hungry people in Wolo might have discovered it first,' said

Prim, finding that she had begun to tremble. And were these people starving? Well, who could tell. Food emergencies were not measured by inspecting people's skinniness. They were measured by the numbers who were desperate enough to take to the road, looking for work or a merciful cache.

'Yeah,' said Stoner, 'but you know what I mean. Your very first trip out here and you find *this*!'

That vacuous, ambitious idea rose almost by its own levity. Would they really say that in the case studies? The Darfur emergency discovered by Stoner and Bettany, Bettany and Stoner?

But the line of march of these people lay beyond the gaze of God's earthly instruments of mercy. If this was famine, it had been on no NGO's radar screen when they left Khartoum. Probably not on the radar screen of the government of the republic either, which was – according to rumour – regularly shielded from such knowledge by poor telephone systems and the reluctance of this or that regional official to radio through news of calamity.

The truck, top-heavy with passengers, rolled up. The engine cut for Stoner's raised hand, and there was no more than a murmur of conversation from the mass piled on its tray and on every surface. A tall, wrinkled man got down from the passenger's seat. He wore fuller cotton garments than the others, and sandals. He and Stoner greeted each other with waves of the hand and a handshake, and then a rapid conversation started during which the gentleman from the truck, a village sheik as Prim correctly guessed, addressed Stoner with the honorific *Sa'aada*, a title reserved for officialdom. Many of the foot travellers stopped and observed this discourse avidly, but did not push forward to climb on the contraption. At last the conversation, too fast for Prim's level of competence, ended, and the man nodded and returned to the truck where his driver was already starting the engine.

Stoner reported that he was sheik of a village twenty miles south. It was one of those villages belonging to a tribal group, in which land was held communally but not equally. 'Sounds better than it is in reality,' declared Stoner. The sheik was personally okay, according to Stoner. He grew tombac, chewing tobacco. He owned cattle and two trucks, he owned camels he hired out for ploughing. But he said the people who got by on millet and sesame were in a really bad state. No rains last year, late rains this. Last year he'd driven some men into Nyala, once the ground was ploughed, so they could get a job cutting fodder for the big cattle market there. But this year was worse – a lot of children had died. Allah took whomever He chose to take, the man had told Stoner. This spring God had taken children and goats. And now families, some of whom had improvidently eaten their seed crops, were making for Nyala, though those who still had millet seed had left someone behind to plant it.

All this – the deaths, the burials, the dying livestock, the hard successive days – had happened within the great shell of God's knowing, but to the universal ignorance of the world.

Stoner boarded the EC truck again. They overtook the sheik's groaning and swaying vehicle and Prim saw then a group of people heaping up a cairn of stone. Since a foot eloquently protruded from the structure, and children tottered up with more stones to mark the loss and protect the corpse from beasts, it looked obscenely stage-managed by some shot-happy cameraman. For the glimpsed scene was as immediate, yet as distanced from her by the frame of the truck window, as if she were watching a screen, perceiving a two-dimensional tragedy. Someone – Codderby or Crouch – had said great disasters rendered the victims more visible both in height and width, but took away their depth and their names. Only the victims of private and discreet murders had names.

The most astonishing thing in Prim's eyes was that Rahmin the driver took Stoner's truck away from the drift of the lines of marchers whom Stoner seemed so delighted to have found; and that no one protested, neither the marchers nor anyone in Stoner's vehicle. The Stoner–Bettany party and its preceding drilling trucks had specific objectives, a road plan, and diverged to Adi Hamit.

Stoner had the truck stopped at one stage, got out his field telephone pack and with the exemplary composure of the true bureaucrat radioed his office in Khartoum, for transmission to Brussels, the news that a previously unreported food emergency seemed to be in progress during the supposed rainy season in Darfur. With a quick eye for assessing such things, he told his office that because it would be even worse to the north, in the desolate ground near el Fasher, there may be at least 300 000 people imperilled. Seeming perhaps an overstatement to Prim's less trained eye, it would prove in time to be a fair estimate of the people who were now or would later be touched by whatever the term 'previously unreported food emergency' meant.

Prim felt somehow relieved to encounter the more normal levels of Suda-nese distress represented by Adi Hamit in its canyon between flat-topped hills. She had known they were close since the earth became bare, stripped for cooking fuel. They passed a Nissen-hutted, barb-wired food dump at the foot of an escarpment and penetrated blank afternoon light, and Abuk sat upright, smiling weightily and removing the cloth from her head. In this wide socket of the earth, open-sided tents and brush shelters with blue plastic roofs stretched away to a hazed infinity. Southern men and women, very different people from the people they had met on the road, walked out from beneath tent flaps and stood straight and thin, watching them pass with a wide-eyed lack of expectation. The men were middle-aged – there were not often young men in refugee camps. They were either dead, serving with the rebel SPLA, or trying to find work in cities. These were sundry tribes of Dinka. They had always been consid-ered noble, cicatriced on the face, and ornamented for special events with the blood of cattle. Prim had read of them at university, and seen the photographs Leni Riefenstahl, Hitler's cinematographer, took when – long after Hitler's fall – she came to the southern Sudan and to the cattle camps of the Dinka as to the cantonments of an African *herrenvolk*. The ivory rings which Riefenstahl had found so photogenic, the beaded vests which virgins had worn and from which their breasts protruded, and the sharp-edged bangles which men used for wrestling – none of it was visible in Adi Hamit. Leni should photograph them now, in their dust-impregnated T-shirts dimly marked with the logos of U2, the Chicago Bears, Celtic Football Club, Manchester United or the San Diego Chargers. Good people in Pittsburgh or Liverpool collected these shirts rendered obsolete for Western purposes by changes in marketing, spon-sorship, or design, and sent them to clothe the refugees. The lines of scarring on cheeks and foreheads remained though, and the forked scars worn in the flesh of the temples. These last, Prim knew from Leni's book, represented the hooves of cattle – in the case of the people of Adi Hamit, lost, confiscated or slaughtered cattle.

Even so early in her African career, Prim knew how such places as Adi Hamit ran – she had visited a number of them near the capital. The Sudanese government, having helped create this troublesome third citizenry of refugeeism, settled those fleeing from the South around half-viable wells hidden away from the towns, at a distance which allowed a dubious balance of care and of denial of responsibility. The Sudanese Commission of Refugees sent their army-fatigue wearing officers out to

administer the camps and the distribution of food within them. Some
NGO might supply a nurse, another might finance a well or a midwife.
UN tents arrived, but their number usually lagged behind the needs of
the emergency. And so sky-blue plastic tarpaulins provided the roofs for
stone and brush shelters, built more arduously here than amongst the
plenteous grasses and rushes of the Dinka refugees' native earth.

A stone building with a corrugated iron roof sported a Red Cross on
its door and in front the standard long bench provided for patients, and
a seat by the side window. Sudanese being inoculated traditionally came
up to windows beyond which sat doctors or nurses, and presented their
arms to the needle. Stoner's truck drew into the clinic building's thin
shade and Stoner, Prim and the midwife descended. Abuk stood smiling,
her splendid long head bare now, its temples marked by lines of ritual
scarring. Home, said her wide eyes, despite all she knew. Stoner said he
had to go off – to pay respects to the Commission of Refugees official
who lived at the food dump. Abuk was Austfam's responsibility, and
Prim walked with her, squinting, toward the doorway of the clinic. From
the screened-off rear of the structure, a little haggard woman in brown
shirt, pants and sandals appeared. 'Mother of God, it's darling Abuk,'
she cried. There were enthusiastic embracings, salutations in Dinka and
Arabic, translated into English by the white woman, seemingly for the
benefit of Prim.

'Yes, you will move into the tent right there by the clinic. Your mother,
your son too. And any fellow who wants to talk to you better talk to
me first.'

The clinic nurse turned to Prim and shook her hand vigorously.
'Thanks. Thanks a million. A few of the women are pretty close to term,
so she'll be very handy indeed. I'm Therese by the way. And you're Miss
Bettany from this Austfam crowd. Where's that miserable bugger
Crouch?'

Prim told the woman that Crouch had gone back to Australia and then
to Cambodia. She was expecting a replacement.

'Aren't we all?' asked Therese, hustling Prim and Abuk into the darkness of the clinic. The part-office, part-surgery was dim and had that
coolness of a place where at least the heat was restful. In one corner
stood her old-fashioned bulky radio transmitter. In the other white
cabinets with red crosses upon them.

'It's good to see those drilling trucks go past a little previous,' said the
nurse. 'You know the women have been walking twelve miles for water

over to Well 17 since the main well here gave up the ghost.'

Now women and children emerged from the laneways at the camp, ululating and crowding up to the clinc to greet Abuk. The midwife went to the door and the crowd drew her away, staring at her clothes, covering their mouths with long fingers.

'All right if you and Stoner sleep in the clinic here?' asked Therese.

'We're not an item,' protested Prim.

Therese said she didn't think they were. She invited Prim to 'settle in like a good child' while she went to make tea.

'Wait,' said Prim. 'We met something out there.'

'Oh yes?'

And Prim for the first time related the story of the journey, knowing by hearing herself tell the tale that she had somehow let a mist grow around the day's more massive events. 'Stoner can give you more details,' she promised Therese.

'Dear God,' said Therese. 'I'd heard things were bad out there.'

But she too seemed to be speaking of remote happenings, as if Adi Hamit was all the catastrophe she could afford to give her intimate attention. She asked a few questions – were the people in hundreds or thousands? – and then seemed gratefully to return to more immediate matters. 'That Abuk! Isn't she a darling? Awful history of course. But then everybody here has one. Did she tell you she was taken by the army? What happened is beyond imagining.' Therese gestured towards some vague conception of possible abuse which lay like an amputated but neutralised reality in the darkest corner of the clinic. 'Abuk was an *abid*. In the strictest meaning of the term. She was a slave, that little creature.'

'Surely not,' said Prim. The concept – Abuk a slave – struck her at once with an obscure but intense force. Its redolence was so strong. It was as if something live had not only nudged her mind but physically quickened within her, jolting her, making her stumble in search of equilibrium. She felt herself trembling, as she had on seeing the town-bound clans. But where they had numbed her, this enthralled her, producing in her a form of particular rage she had not felt this morning.

'It's a fact,' said the nurse. 'She was property of an officer. And let me say: With all that entails! See, her village was raided. She saw one of her children thrown on to the fire by soldiers, and another one hacked to death with a *banja* by militiamen. Death's very graphic down there in the South, by all accounts. The militia still ride round on horses, with big swords. And Kalashnikovs of course. They sold her to the officer, and when he was finished with her, he on-sold her to a farmer south of here. It isn't uncommon, you know.'

The tale of children hacked and ablaze hung in the air with its normal fearsome weight. Such stories were regularly heard, were the commonplace of discourse.

'But she's here now. How did she get away?' Prim heard her voice quaver.

'There's an Austrian woman – you know the one – what's-her-name? God almighty, I can't remember. Is it Trotsky? Something like that. Stoner probably knows her. Comes into the country with lots of money and just buys people back. In batches, sometimes. She's the only one who does it. They say she's a little nutty. The group she works for brings out this yearly report on her activities. But no one believes them because they're kind of Alleluia Jesus Protestant evangelicals. Anyhow, that was the woman bought her from the farmer, and then Abuk came here, where her mother and surviving child had turned up, and then she's selected to be a midwife. Great little woman. We should congratulate ourselves.'

Prim had heard at parties in Khartoum whispers of slavery and tales of anti-slavery antics by an Austrian woman. Veteran NGO people shook their heads and laughed over her occasional excursions to the Sudan. This was the first time Prim had heard the word 'slave' used of a face she knew, and the previously abstract term ran through her like a claim.

A Dinka woman in dyed cloth shirt and skirt brought in a plate of wheaten bread and tea. Smiling Abuk was with her, transformed, no longer wrapped up in layers of white, but wearing a shirt with a collar and floral-patterned skirt. She retained, as indicating her status, her sandals. They sat on stone benches and chairs around a little table.

What am I to do here? thought Prim. I am a refugee. I need the Sudan more than it needs me. But here is a woman to whom something worse than Auger has occurred.

The nurse spoke both in Arabic for Abuk's convenience, and English for Prim's 'So now, Abuk. Tell me again what's this clan of yours?'

'Ifo,' said Abuk. Then laboriously, in English, smiling at Prim, 'It is ... Ifo.'

'So when're you going to marry some thumping big feller from a related clan, eh?'

Abuk covered her mouth with her fingers and laughed. The Irish woman lowered her voice. 'You can get hellish fights here, even amongst middle-aged old duffers. You've got clans still quarrelling over their grandad's grazing rights, for dear God's sake. Meaningless, given their situation . . .'

Stoner, arriving, seemed grateful to turn to Prim. The Canadian from Earthwater was already meeting with the water committees, he said, tracking them down by asking at tent flaps. 'He's looking at these old British hydrogeological maps for the area too. Can you imagine? Those old Imperial guys, you know . . . beating the bloody Mahdi one day, out here the next day surveying for water. Got to give it to 'em. Rule bloody Britannia.'

He shook his head as if he had no stake in what they had done, was not quite himself a Briton.

Prim was conscious of Abuk, who sipped her tea absent-mindedly, like a woman who had never known want. Prim thought, *slave*. How astonishing, how old-fashioned, and yet how intimate a word.

After, still taken by the idea of Abuk's enslavement, she made her way through the last sting of the day's heat to a slightly elevated platform of soft red shale west of the camp. A crowd of women and children had gathered and were watching and chatting about the endeavours of Earthwater. Stakes had been driven into the ground and rope run from one to the other to create a security fence. The mud-pump and the drilling engine still sat on the trucks, and had not yet begun their work, but piping and drill parts, and what looked like lights and a small generator, had been neatly piled on blue plastic on the ground. All this energy exhilarated Prim. She could hear the seven or so men of the drilling team chortling with each other, apparently pleased with their progress.

As Prim ducked under the rope, the Canadian foreman strolled over to her to report. He'd drill from dark until his men got tired – about 2 a.m. He pointed out the way acacia bushes ran on the slope, and the line of certain termite mounds. Termites always built along the line of sub-surface aquifers.

The visit to the drilling site, the energy of the Canadian and the Sudanese drillers, restored her to clarity. It was not negligible to leave water behind, even if it was evident that aquifers of fossil water, once breached, could never be renewed. An emergency was an emergency and it was something to leave water here, in a cistern of steel, under a blue, anti-evaporative lid.

When she turned back to the clinic, advancing darkness made her party to, yet separated her from, all the night noises of the camp, from the

yelps of children and the smell of frying bread. You would think from
the eloquent voices that this was a happy town, in possession of itself.

Sleeping on a bench in the clinic, Prim woke once, to the flaying of
torchlight from the back of the building. Abuk was there, running to the
white cabinets then vanishing. Prim slipped on her boots and followed
the midwife out through the lean-to. She waited in a camp laneway,
looking into the lamplit interior of a tent, as after four hearty yells a
large-boned woman pushed out a blood-covered little exile.

Abid, thought Prim. Slave. Poor little bastard.

In the morning, Prim woke in her clothes without any memory of
having settled to sleep after attending that Dinka birth in the small hours.
Sitting upright, she could see, through a window without glass, a bare-
chested Stoner washing from a basin beneath a brush shelter. He looked
very businesslike for a man whose sentences were so crabwise and
tentative.

The light, already so sharp that some of the Dinka aged who had slept
in the open were hobbling to shade, reminded her of Central Australia,
of morning in the Burranghyatti reservation at Mount Bavaria. To dispel
that memory, she called to Stoner casually through the window.

'Could I use that after you?'

Stoner had an English sort of body, strong but without muscular
definition. She was unwelcomely reminded that by contrast Auger had
possessed a bough-swinging, tree-climbing stringiness, the inheritance of
his American boyhood. She watched Stoner pour out his used water and
fill the basin by dipper from the washing-water drum. Courteously, he
carried it indoors to her and set it at the bottom of her bench.

'Forgive the gallantry,' he murmured. As he went to where he had slept
and assembled his kit, she turned her back, took her shirt off, and washed
beneath her neck, under arms and breasts. Stoner, throughout her
ablutions, had the grace to go on packing. He turned when Prim had
hitched her voluminous brown pants on, had shed her dust-clogged
socks, and was functionally washing her feet.

'Listen, I gotta leave, okay?' he told her. 'In view of what we
saw ... I reckon you ought to come too.'

'I can't,' she said. 'The drilling ...'

'That Canadian bloke's reliable. He'll be back in the old corral in
Khartoum in a few days. But us? We owe it to everyone ... you know,

to test out the scale of what's happening. I suggest we go north through Nyala, check out conditions. Get a bigger picture.'

Therese had come in from her morning inspection. Last night's child was at mamma's breast, she said. All parties were in the pink. She sat down, an honest eavesdropper, as Stoner went on outlining his plans. 'Rahmin could drive us up to el Fasher and we can like fill in the provincial governor – I happen to know him. By the time we front him, we'll know more than we do now. And there'll be the two of us. Four eyes, okay?'

'That's a journey though!' Therese said, whistling. 'Trucks take days on that bloody awful road.'

'We'll do it in two.' He turned to Prim. 'I called the office. They'll send the plane to el Fasher for us Tuesday.'

'It isn't my job to go with you,' said Prim, and there was in her something like a fear of being dragged back to the mass of city-bound Darfur people.

'Jesus, toots!' Stoner argued. 'This is like the cataclysm, waiting for us, out there! Look, ever since Lebanon I got this repute as a wild bugger. There're people who'd rather ignore what I say. Plenty of 'em in government departments in Khartoum too. You don't carry any baggage that way.' He shook his head back and forth and held his long hands up in mock surrender. 'Okay, okay. It'll be very gratifying to stay here and, you know, see Dinkas laughing in a gush of water. But this is huge, and we'll only know how huge by reconnaissance.'

She could not deny the force of his argument, yet she had a sense of being conscripted. It struck her she wanted to stay to talk to Abuk – maybe through Therese's interpretation – about the midwife's enslavement. But forty minutes later, she made a final visit to the drillers as a prelude to going to Nyala and el Fasher with Stoner. At the drilling site the Sudanese team was already mixing cement to make a pad around what, it seemed, had been a successful strike. The Canadian was enthusiastic. They had hit an aquifer at a little less than 100 feet. The flow had been tested, he said, with an air compressor. Damn good readings. Acceptable pH and nitrate, good calcium and magnesium. His field microscope showed no faecal coliform, but if the camp expanded to higher ground to the west, the water would need regular re-testing. That would all be in the report, he said. He'd already reconnoitred a site for a second well, on the camp's southeast, above the clinic. They'd be finished everything in three days if the second well came in as easily as the first.

It was clear to Prim that, as Stoner had said, Earthwater and the Dinkas had no need of her presence that day.

Nyala was approached through a long canyon which gave way to a plateau. On the plateau too a scatter of people were moving, and Stoner consented to take on board a lean woman who lay by the side of the road with her husband and two children. Rahmin was not happy to admit these people to his white if dusty vehicle. The husband and children emitted a mousy smell of want and fever, yet they did not have an air of defeat, Prim thought. They travelled in hope, well or ill-founded.

Scattered groves of gum arabic and vacated fields of ploughed dust yielded in the end to the unofficial outskirts of Nyala. On the town's southern rim, by the great weathered timber enclosures of the cattle market, a huge shanty town of brush, stone, plastic, lath and old canvas spread. Because the world knew nothing of this settlement of shacks, because it was on no NGO's map and had been given as yet no international mercy, no yardage of fresh plastic or canvas, it seemed more disreputable than Adi Hamit. The old men of this emergency, squatting on the earth and squinting through cataract-dimmed eyes at this rare entity, a white vehicle with its tranquil blue badge, were unexcited. A few of the children of this new town felt well enough to chase the truck. Even at this extremity these people bore what Prim thought of as the onus of Islam: the pride in being numbered amongst the elect; the willingness to await the decisions of an intimate God.

Nyala's hospital was a two-storey building where, at the side door, Stoner showed admirable insistence to get the woman admitted, as the husband bowed to him and to Prim and even Rahmin, intoning, 'Shokran, Ya Doctour!'

'I'm not a doctor, sport,' said Stoner. To which the man responded with a resonant farewell. 'Assalamu Alaykum.' 'Depart in God's name.' Something like God's work certainly waited to be done, even by egotists like Stoner and herself.

Around the barely stocked stalls of the souk, the newly arrived women of the countryside, their faces covered against the sun, sat in what Prim read – perhaps wrongly, she realised – as postures of acceptance. They held sleeping or sick infants at breast or lap in gracious folds of dust-dulled cloth as children tottered around them, almost casually hunting for a sorghum grain or chickpea in the dust. Hardly anyone but an egg salesman was trading. Further up Sharia el Mellit, the stores which had shopfronts had shut themselves up tight to resist the rabble tide from out of town.

On the way north out of the city, they were in the presence of the great mountain which filled the sky to the west: Jabal Marra. Above the dirt road, raggedy tracks ascended the great, austere peak, its orange, brown, blue and grey slopes massive yet without snow, a barren mother, copious not with water but, high up, with sulphur springs. The el Fasher road ran over the lower slopes where in wadis trees grew on the strength of underground water. In such shade an occasional family took some rest, but the lines seemed thinner than yesterday's. 'Smaller ... you know ... smaller population,' said Stoner. As the EC truck progressed and Stoner made his calculations, Prim had a glimpse of an aged woman, perhaps as old as fifty, sitting under a tebeldi tree and surrounded by her clan, while a debate raged amongst the men as to the wisdom of some continuing to town, and the weak waiting. Whatever mercy Stoner and Prim were engaged in, it would likely be too late for this matriarch.

'What I can't understand,' Stoner announced, 'is that space is full of these damn satellites. Okay? You can read a numberplate in a street in Paris, or the brand of tissue a Bulgarian's using to blow his bloody nose. Yet the lines form up here in Darfur, and the satellites are blind as a bat to that! They're trained like, those satellite guys, to read rocket silos and camouflaged armour. But it's left to us, it's left to us travelling in a bloody thirty miles per hour truck if we're lucky to find *this* sort of thing and take a few pictures.'

That evening, on ground littered with stones, Prim, in light suddenly scant, began gathering rocks for a fireplace, soundly kicking each one before she lifted it, for fear of scorpions and camel spiders. Stoner, striding across the landscape in his huge boots, looking for kindling, sang 'Eleanor Rigby' in the authentic accent. Eastwards of the truck, Rahmin had spread a mat and completed the obeisance of his evening prayer. Eating quickly – tuna, flatbread, tea – they retired one by one to a rock platform up the slope where a rock cleft had been chosen to serve as the outdoor cloaca. Prim washed her arms and hands with the moisturised tissues Dimp sent her from Sydney. She settled herself on her bed-roll by the rear of the truck and watched the dark mass of Jabal Marra cut into the fields of stars.

Stoner, returned from the rock platform, intruded on her feelings of separateness and repose. Standing crookedly above her, he said, 'It'll be colder later.'

Prim yawned and said nothing, hoping it would dismiss him. But he got down on his haunches. He sounded languid. 'I mentioned I know the provincial governor. He's an army man, Colonel Unsa. Given what we've seen, Primrose, d'you think you'd like to have a word with him? If I can fix it, okay?'

'Me! I thought it was going to be *us*.'

'Well, see ... I'm supposed to work through the central government. Spilling the beans, you know, to a provincial governor first ... that'd be a violation of the protocols.'

Since he had deprived the night of all which had been sedative, she sat up. But who was she to complain?

Stoner said, 'I should warn you, you'll get nothing out of the bugger, not at first. He'll say you'll have to approach the Khartoum authorities. I'll do that anyhow. But when I do, it'll be like good for the sods to know that through you the responsible locals have been told. I mean, you might get something written out of him. Maybe something recommending the government to give you a bit of a hearing. A note from him ... that'd be fantastic.'

As much as ever she felt that the moral force of his demands was difficult to challenge. 'I have my NGO to think of,' she argued. 'It isn't that I don't want to help. But we have our way of doing business too.'

'My God, the man's not going to give Austfam any problems. His Excellency Colonel Unsa's chief demeanour will be a kind of haughty embarrassment. And by the way, I ought to tell you, he's a, you know, a sybarite. Keeps boys. Mustn't let your colonial puritanism show through, eh?'

He left without more argument and walked to his bed-roll. He still wore his boots. 'Do you always wear your footwear to bed?' she asked.

'Footwear,' he said, laughing at the nicety of the term. 'Okay, why do you behave as if you don't care how good-looking you are?' Prim felt a flush of anger at this banality. 'I'm not going to answer a question like that.'

He grinned crookedly and made a sceptical noise. 'Good night,' he said.

El Fasher was a traditional marshalling point for camel caravans, which would sound romantic, she realised, to those who'd never met a camel or a camel wrangler. In a sweltering mid-morning she saw the el Fasher minarets wavering in the haze. She and Stoner took rooms in the Berti, an old-fashioned hotel of what seemed to be crumbling mud brick adobe, and Stoner rang his contact, the governor's aide, and seemed with ease to arrange an interview for Prim. Stoner had done some calculations of uncertain value (at least in Prim's eyes) of the scale of what was, however measured, a disaster, and briefed Prim on her pitch to the governor.

Asked by Stoner and Prim if refugees had reached the city, the hotel owner said there were people living in hovels at a suburb named Mawashei, just by the huge camel trading market to the north. They were, he said, *nazihiin*, beggars, from some low-caste northern tribes like the Zaghawa who came to town each year to sell fodder and charcoal. Their women and children were with them, but only because Ramadan started in four weeks and in that time of charity the fasting city people were more likely to be kind to beggars. Don't you worry! the hotel manager said. That's what they're here for!

They drove to Mawashei, and its houses of sticks and pieces of fabric. Women and children were searching the afternoon dust outside a haulage garage for grains of sorghum, and – it seemed – for straw to eat as pottage. Stoner and Prim chatted with a turbaned, talkative man who lived there – of indefinite age, very thin, but of good morale. He told Stoner the provincial government had issued a ration of sorghum earlier in the month. It didn't have much more money though, he stated with a lack of bitterness. Did he come here every year? Stoner asked him. Oh yes, in the months when people waited for rain. If it rained he would go home to his village to the north-east and take his widowed mother, wife and children with him. But God willed no rain in the country last year, and rains were already late this year.

Women and children in the yards, and amongst the hobbled camels, looked as if they were combing the animals' fur, and the man admitted without any apparent shame that they were collecting camel fleas. Prim managed to ask him why in passable Arabic. He said, to eat of course.

At the *souk* Prim bought a long white dress for the interview, and a white shawl for her head and shoulders. She walked the few blocks to the palace, mentioned her appointment to the soldier at the gate in the wall, and was led within. From the courtyard the place had the look of a left-over barracks out of Kipling – a high wall, a working fountain, a garden and small parade ground, a U-shaped two-storeyed, plastered white building encasing the central space. The governor's office was on the upper level. A handsome army captain in fatigues met her at the bottom of the stairs, saluted, smiled as if signalling he was in conspiracy with her, and led her upstairs.

Colonel Unsa answered the knock, rising from a large desk by a wide-open French window. He was lean and good-looking, and he too wore military fatigues. He pointed Prim to a chair, which the captain adjusted for her before departing. Her only nervousness as she sat was to do with being an effective advocate for people who were more strangers to her than to him.

Sitting behind the great, ungracious desk, the governor gave off a mixed message of severity and whimsy. Stoner had warned Prim he was a cultivated sybarite, and he proved to be English-speaking, and with a posh accent – he'd been to the Royal Staff College some time back. They chatted about broad matters – he'd read a lot of Graham Greene, and loved and disapproved of his novels.

'Have you, for example, read *The Heart of the Matter*?' he asked lightly, like a man with a well-developed thesis. 'It represents high imperialism as far as I'm concerned. Africa existing merely as a nether-world to assure the damnation of whites who deserve it, cannot escape it, and – in their sins – desire it. I do hope young persons from the West have achieved a healthier view. After all, Africa is more than a highly coloured backdrop for flawed Europeans to anguish before.'

Prim felt edgy about defending Greene, since she had till this journey seen, and perhaps still did see, the Sudan as serving a purpose, a sanctuary in which she might be numbly safe. 'Don't you think though that if every Westerner knew as much about Africa as Greene, there'd be better lines of communications between the two worlds?'

The governor's eyes were alight. 'Ah, there you have it. The two worlds, you say. What happened to the third world on one hand, and on the other, one world of universal brotherhood?'

'Well ...' said Prim, feeling not so much bested but subjected to conjuring. She wondered if she had failed a test, but before she could go on, refreshments were brought in.

They were borne by the sort of people who lived in the camp at Adi Hamit, by two lovely Dinka boys dressed in immaculate *galabias*. Each was carrying a tray, one with tea cups and cinnamon sticks, and another a teapot and a plate of figs. Prim saw His Excellency's hand close round the lower arm of one of them, and wondered whether this was a caress, and if so, avuncular or indecent? Stoner had accused her of being a puritan, but it was more than the mere puritan in her that was appalled. Colonel Unsa saw it and explained that they were Dinka boys from the war zone. He was, he said, educating them. They would live in misery without him, he implied.

Prim tried to clear her brain of this new bug, the impulse to make an accusation, or an utterly stupid offer to buy the boys back. Out of respect for the chief debate, she decided, she must suppress that impulse and start talking about His Excellency's citizens, the people whom she had seen crowding into Nyala just to achieve visibility.

The colonel absorbed the news of what Prim and Stoner had witnessed around Nyala. He did not try to explain it away, he did not stoop to blaming the West and the spread of the desert, badmouthing the international commodity market and the International Monetary Fund, all the stuff more commonly heard around Khartoum.

'This sort of crisis,' he said, 'is hard to read. Did you take any film footage?'

'No. We have photographs still to be developed. But whatever my limitations, Fergal Stoner can read the signs.'

'Oh yes, I suppose he could,' said the governor, playfully evasive. 'After all, Mr Stoner represents Europe amongst us. But I'm sure you know that for many people in the countryside, coming to the city to work or beg while waiting for the harvest is a yearly event.'

This sounded dismissive enough to make Prim lean forward and draw together her knees in their immaculate fabric. 'Yes, but I'm told they don't move out in entire clans. Stoner and I saw whole clans. And there are entire clans at the camel markets too. And they tell us that you've made a special issue of sorghum.'

'Oh yes,' said His Excellency lightly.

'We wondered, if these are normal times, why is there a need of a special issue?'

'Well, of course, this is a year of special hardship. But even under special hardship, you know, people have their devices for getting through, and they have their pride.'

Since this was a thought Prim had had the day before in Mawashei, to hear it come from his lips was confusing. It was as if he could immediately see the advantage he had. Now he became dolorously sincere. 'An individual will sometimes starve rather than be fed by a person who takes away his pride. I've seen it happen. Even amongst the enemy in the South. And if poor people from north and west of el Fasher, from say the hills, or the banks of the el Ku, have pride which surpasses death, so does the nation. Before a nation holds out its hand to the world, it always considers the implications for its self-esteem. This should not surprise anyone. Look at the gulf between black and white health in the United States! No one in the US likes even well-meaning foreigners trying to influence policy on such matters.'

Prim had a sense of concerns being very pleasantly allayed; of the lessons of resignation being taught.

He said, 'I receive regular reports from village sheiks and policemen. What you have to say was not utterly unexpected. But I cannot myself authorise a survey of Darfur to determine the scale of distress. It's a huge area with poor roads, and I lack adequate staff. And I cannot myself invite any international relief effort. That is a decision reserved to the president himself, His Excellency President Jaafar el Nimeiri.'

Prim wanted to keep the right aloofness. Everyone said it was easy to be charmed by the Sudanese bureaucracy, by people like Unsa. It was easy, under the influence of the big sky, to go along with what had been said to her and Stoner earlier, something about God knowing and taking whomsoever he wanted. Since God is a being of deserts, of the great one-eyed sky met in deserts, it was seductively easy to take the God-like view; easy – even for a disbeliever – to shuffle the papers and sigh, and wait on God's will or something slower, a new direction from Khartoum. Prim was dressed in the pure white cotton that stood for Sudanese acceptance of the world as it is, and had to struggle against that tendency.

So she made a self-conscious attempt to summon conviction and zeal. 'I would like to ask you this. If I or someone else tries to get the permission of the president to conduct a more thorough survey, could we safely say that we have the approval of the governor of Darfur?' She felt the blood pounding in her throat. How could she make such a plea? A disconnected soul, ten months in the Sudan! 'And . . . would you consider putting that provisional approval in writing. For me to take to Khartoum?'

With a handsome smile he asked, 'That's Mr Stoner's idea, isn't it?' Then to her amazement he nodded and reached across his desk for a sheet of paper, writing in English a draft letter with an old-fashioned, chubby fountain pen. When he had finished, he read it to her.

> *Provincial Administrative Palace*
> *El Fasher*
> *Darfur Province*
> *Republic of Sudan*
> *22 April 1985*

To whom it may concern
The bearer of this letter brings to the provincial capital intelligence of a
supposed food emergency in the Nyala region. Her anecdotal evidence is
based on the observations not only of herself but of another experienced
aid officer, an officer of the European Economic Community, who calcu-
lated that the present emergency may affect as many as 300 000 people
or even more. The report is such as to warrant inquiry by Government,
and should His Excellency the President of the Republic authorise an
assessment and the initiation of an international relief operation, he may
depend upon the assistance of the Provincial Government.

He asked Prim whether that did it, and promised her it would be reliably
transmuted into Arabic. When she was effusive with her thanks, he held
up a hand, salmon-coloured on the palm. He called in a secretary, and
chatted with Prim until the letter was copied in Arabic in the outer office.
Between them, he and Prim polished off the pot of tea. And even grateful
for his generous letter, and not wanting to bite the hand that signed it,
she still wished to ask, Are you a slave-holder, you bastard?

She could not understand why the matter pressed on her. Even if she
were an abolitionist, she was not even sure slavery existed. Did she want
it to? Did its reality suit some fanatic need in her?

They celebrated her success at the palace with a meal of *gonnonia*,
sheep's stomach stewed with onions and tomatoes, eaten in the Berti's
dining room. Throughout she could not be utterly at ease. She watched
Stoner with an excessive, spooky fear that he might try to drag their
partnership further than it could be permitted to stretch. It was not so
much an offer of sex she feared. It was that she believed she would find
it beyond bearing if she saw in Stoner's face the same radiant, childlike
striving which had characterised Auger in seduction mode.

The next morning an Eyptian pilot from Nile Expeditions Charter turned up by cab and took them out to the edge of the town to a tarred airstrip, a radio beacon above its little white terminal building. As the pilot gathered up their movement permits with their passport-sized photographs attached, and went inside to have a chat about his flight plan, Stoner and Prim sat on chairs by the outer wall, watching as their Cessna was being filled, from a white, cylindrical reservoir of aviation fuel beside the runway, by a chain of young men in *galabias* and loose white turbans carrying watering cans with the roses taken off. These they handed up to a foreman who stood bare-headed, first on the starboard wing of the Cessna, then on the port. Prim was pleased to see that the Egyptian pilot, when the starboard tanks were full, checked them for water contamination with a gauge he carried.

Beside her on his plastic garden chair, Stoner said, 'You see that? They don't have enough foreign exchange to buy a fuel pump for el Fasher. Or they probably have a pump, but, you know, they can't afford the replacement parts.' He went on as if this were part of a seamless argument. 'What do you reckon if I took the liberty of inviting you to dinner at the Rimini?'

The Rimini Hotel in Khartoum was owned by Italians, a family which had been in the city for most of the century. In their dining room white-clad and turbaned Sudanese waiters, resembling to Prim's semi-informed eye classic Nubians from a film, served tall tumblers of iced lemonade, and plates of robust soup and Nile perch.

He looked at her frankly. 'Jesus, you're – you know – such a lovely bird.'

'Did you run out of courage to say that last night?'

'Hey, don't be a hard bitch.'

The idea of his nervousness made her brave.

'Listen, you'll get nowhere with the old lines! Besides, I couldn't go. I'm spending the night with Helene Codderby.'

'Are you?' he asked as if he knew it was a lie. He did not seem much disappointed. 'All right,' he conceded. 'But look, one thing I've got to tell you for, you know, free. Don't pursue this slave business.' She had mentioned to him not only the tale of Abuk Alier the midwife, but the two boys at the governor's palace. 'The whole thing's too arguable,' he said. 'Let's put the question in a, you know, a Western context. Take California say, where you'll find live-in maids, Mexican, working seven days for $50 a week and board and scared if they make demands they'll be reported to the immigration people. Say you wanted to make representations about that! Would it be the most fruitful thing to inform press and politicians that this is slavery? People would say, if this is slavery, why are so many men and women crossing the border every night to get in on it?'

Prim said nothing. She felt half-ashamed, like a person being chastised for a pornographic interest.

'If you so much as shout, "Slave!" no one out there in our world's going to listen. Whereas they'll listen to Darfur, see.'

Prim was willing to pretend that he had defused her callow moral imagination. The food crisis was certainly the immediate game. Besides, the pilot, beside whom she sat for the flight, mentioned some chance of a *haboob* – a sandstorm. For the first hour, however, they traversed the bell of unsullied blue above a sloping plain which ran illimitably down towards the shores of the White Nile. Higher than Jabal Marra, Prim savoured this map of desolation, with every nuance of earth, every wadi, exactly visible. The el Milk, a dry Mississippi, ran hundreds of miles north-south, and a robust play of light defined it, its banks as discernible as if they brimmed with living water.

But around ten o'clock, and within ten seconds, all the sharpness and clarity of earth vanished. A bottomless grey wall rose before them, an apparently static explosion of earth into air. Its top was close and level with the nose of the aircraft. Prim felt very little turbulence. The great globe of dust seemed too concerned with its own inner physics to give the charter plane a shaking. She avoided asking the pilot whether this moiling ball, huge as a moon, could affect the engines. She knew it could penetrate a scarf and fill a mouth. In Khartoum she had sat with all doors and windows shut against the sibilant pinging of the raging grit, and seen the particles intrude beneath an unplugged rim of door.

'Time we tried it,' the pilot cried merrily. He eased the controls imperceptibly forward, and the world vanished. A greyness thicker than cloud pressed up against each window. No margin of air existed between it and the windscreen. The interior of the plane became instantly fierce. For a while Prim played with a ventilator beside her, jiggling and twisting, as if coolness could be persuaded to enter. At ground level in Darfur, the famished moved with game dignity to non-existent succour. In the South forces armed with AK-47s moved against each other with Old Testament fervour. Why should she still believe herself the immortal centre of things?

'Tell me if you see the ground,' the pilot cried.

At a little over 2000 feet, give or take the margin of error the pilot was willing to ignore, Prim and Stoner simultaneously saw a road and densely packed houses of mud brick. 'There, there,' they both cried. But then the sight was swallowed again, and the pilot took the plane up. Prim felt a strong annoyance. She had discovered the ground for him, and he had lost it on her. Somewhere below, shut in, were the secure comfort of her books, her bed in the corner, her prints of Fred Williams's Australian landscapes affixed to the wall with little gobbets of dry putty.

But the second descent and attempt to find Khartoum was successful. At 1800 feet they saw again streets of dust and shuttered houses, exquisite in the fog of sand. With restored professional certitude, the pilot banked the plane in air which was now blue-grey, the air of a London winter dusk, though it was still mid-morning in Khartoum. Far out, away to their right, Prim saw Khartoum airport, end-on, all its lights glittering, and wind seemed to blow their aircraft into line with this illumined avenue. The touchdown was accomplished with an almost flamboyant delicacy, and they taxied off to the charter company hangar, the hut which served as company office. A number of charter pilots – Egyptians, Frenchmen who had flown aircraft for the Chaddian forces, handsome Somalis – emerged in company uniforms and epaulettes and began shaking the hand of the Egyptian and clapping him on the shoulder, a fraternal exhibition which seemed to confirm that there had been some peril. The terminal itself lay shut tight. No big jet, with its tendency to ingest birds and debris, could do what the Egyptian's plane had done.

Landed now in the miasma of this storm, they found the air intolerably dense, scalding and yet still. They took a taxi to Stoner's office at the EC compound which was empty except for the doorman, who reclined on cement in the corridor. He opened up the office where, beneath creaky fans, Stoner and Prim wrote and faxed further reports of the Darfur emergency to their respective headquarters, asking them to be ready to act, and to use their good offices to alert governments and exploit diplomatic channels.

But Stoner had not quite finished asking Prim for favours. He got the doorman to make them tea and as he and Prim sat in air dense as cotton wool, muttered, 'I know this other bloke.'

'What other bloke?' Prim asked.

'Well, he's a Sudanese doctor. Got a practice in Khartoum. Does some gynaecology. Now most Sudanese guys will, you know, divorce their

wives if they see a male doctor, so his practice is limited to the liberal
bourgeoisie ... bit of a shrinking class in the good old Sudan. But this
doctor's well-connected to the president's office. His cousin's an
economic aide to the president. His name's Doctor Sherif Taha.
Maybe ... you know ... you could go and see him.'

'Another damn hoop to jump through?' she asked.

'Well, it's like the problem with Colonel Unsa. EC people aren't
supposed to go breaking down doors.'

'And so I've got to go and see this doctor, and ask him to introduce
me to his cousin. And what do I have to do for you after that? What
other odd jobs?'

'Okay, it isn't like my fault there's a bloody disaster down there,' said
Stoner with some justice. 'I promise to do my part – I'll send out a story
on the BBC by way of that stick the Codderby woman. The Sudanese
won't like it, but it'll help mount pressure.'

It was vanity to think he might be trying to cement her to him by
setting her tasks. And yet, even in the face of the Darfur catastrophe, she
feared that.

'All right,' she said. 'But after this, I'll go back to taking orders from
Austfam, not from you. That doctor again?'

'Sherif Taha,' said Stoner.

'Okay. I'll see him,' said Primrose. Having been delivered safely from
the huge ball of sand, she felt she must go the full distance.

'Good girl,' sighed Stoner.

Back at the offices of Austfam, she found a letter which Erwit the
Eritrean driver had put aside for her, a letter which was clearly from
Dimp.

Woolarang
Double Bay
21 April 1985

Dearest Prim,
*Sent yesterday to Khartoum the things you ordered. Imagine them not
being able to afford importing tampons any more! Come home for sweet
Christ's sake! I don't know why you've chosen to stay in that place,
particularly since they've left you in the lurch and not appointed any
replacement for that Crouch fellow. Is that industrial justice? I ask.
You're running the whole place and getting a mere assistant field officer's
pay. Tax-free, I can hear you say. So what, if you can't buy tampons!*

*Now look, that bastard Dr Robert bloody Auger has buggered off –
got a chair at some cow university in America. He's absolutely forgotten
round here. Lechers are okay, you know what they want. But lying and
forging, that's too much for me. Enough said. I know you'll be shitty at
me for mentioning A–u–g–e–r. But I'm bloody shipping you tampons,
so be nice.*

*The matter of Bren: I can't believe how long this crowd at the Holy
Roman Rota – that's the marriage court of the Vatican – are taking to
come up with the annulment. The archdiocese here has already recommended it, so apparently it's as good as in the bag. But the Rota are
taking longer than the first marriage lasted, and the longer they take the
more conscious I become of Bren's first wife, Robyn, of whom I have
no clear picture but whose reality this bloody delay seems to reinforce.*

*In the meantime, don't come back if you're still deluded enough to
think anyone gives a damn about the* affaire *Auger. It's not that they do
know. It's the expectation that they might know – that's what you're
scared of. But you could surely make a life somewhere they sell aspirin
over the counter.*

*I even have proof that sensible people are giving up on the Sudan.
There was a fellow from Foreign Affairs at a dinner we went to the other
night, and he told me, while every other boring bastard in the room was
talking bauxite and molybdenum, that the government's own agency is
edging out of Africa anyhow. Asia's closer, more definitely our business
and, he says, somewhat less volatile and more responsive in every sense
to the development dollar. If you want to see results for your aid dollar,
Asia's the go! Sudan – he just laughed. The crazy invalid. The sick man.
And as you have pointed out, the sick poor bloody woman too. So the
most intractable case of all is of course the place you – with your infallible nose for these things – have chosen as your domicile.*

*So consider your region, eh sis? If you have to work in places with
cerebral malaria, choose somewhere where your dear native Southern
land has diplomatic and commercial stakes.*

*Hey, if that annulment ever comes through, will you come to the
wedding? It'll be nice. Bren has a Jesuit lined up to do it. None of those
nuptial masses. Just a little ceremony. Vows, and a prayer for the bride.
Who is, to be believed or otherwise, until you come home, your admiring
and very concerned poor old sod of a sister.*

Dimp

As Prim read the pleasant, plain letter from her sister, a mild fever shook her shoulders. Perhaps as a result of too many shocks on the road, she developed something like the flu overnight, as if her body wanted to accommodate her with a reason to call Dr Sherif Taha and make an appointment in halting Arabic. His listing in the English language directory for Khartoum had the subtext: 'Sudan Institute of Epidemiology', and in smaller print still he admitted to being involved in general and obstetrical practice, to have qualified at Guy's hospital in London and to have a Master of Science degree in tropical fevers from Louisiana State University. Two empires had given him the nod, thought Prim.

The doctor himself answered the phone, recognised her foreignness, and said resonantly, in an Anglo-American accent, 'I speak English.' When she explained her business he sounded suspicious. She could go, after all, to one of the UN or NGO doctors. But he told her in the end that he could see her late that morning.

Doctor Taha's surgery was in a good address, on Sharia el Baladaya, a few blocks from a renowned mosque, the el Kabir, and in some senses well-located for foreign custom, not far from the US Embassy. Next door to Blue Nile Petroleum Exports, Sherif Taha's plate, advertising the institute and enumerating his degrees, stood on a high adobe wall by an unlocked but barely ajar metal gate, through which Prim stepped into an enclosed garden where shrubs, small palms and acacias grew and cast a crowded shade. This court had the old-fashioned air of having been carefully planted in the era when Khartoum had been a city which prided itself on its oasis-hood, before the Sahara had seized so much of the surrounding landscape. It was designed to delight and soothe the eye of travellers who came to it through wastes of alkaline sand, claypans, fields of stone.

Seated on benches amongst the shrubs were five Sudanese women, one of them in a black veil and mask. They all grew silent, and the four whose faces were not already covered drew their shawls over their mouths and noses and looked at Prim with the region's limpid fixity. The thing about the mask, she had already discovered, was that it enabled the women who wore it to be bolder in their gaze towards outsiders. Finding a bench in a deeper corner of the garden, Prim knew that with part of their souls they regarded her glacially: an unclean woman, an infidel not so much theologically but in sexual custom. But there was curiosity too, perhaps an eagerness to sisterhood, and in the contempt, if it existed, there also lay something like envy.

A woman patient emerged from the door, swathed in white, adjusting her shawl over her mouth, carrying her gynaecological secrets calmly. Obviously, some better-off Khartoum women brought their problems to Doctor Sherif. Prim had heard plenty about complications arising from the practice of genital circumcision of female children, common to both Coptic Christianity and to Islam, pre-dating both religions.

It was then, in the wake of the departing patient, that Prim first saw Sherif Taha. He wore a crisp white shirt, a cricket-club-style tie, and fawn pants over long legs and black shoes. A stethoscope hung around his neck. He was quite luminously dark, or so Prim chose to describe him to herself. Maybe the west of Sudan had had some input into who he was.

Dr Taha's long face fascinated her. He was ageless yet his hair had begun to recede neatly from the front corners of his brow. His lips were long but not prominent. He was very tall, very thin and altogether an exquisite fellow.

Prim had before now noticed a striking quality of many Sudanese faces – an extraordinary repose of features. She saw it on the street in 1985 as in the historic photographs of supporters of the Mahdi, many of them prisoners of the British and Egyptians, displayed in the Khalifa's house in Omdurman. And here it was in the features of a physician who had studied and lived in London and Louisiana.

It was not yet her turn. 'Mrs Ab-Dahali?' he called, with an almost tender boredom in his voice. A woman rose from a bench, and Dr Sherif stood back and let her pass, his eyes sweeping once remotely across the other presences in his courtyard, finding Prim's face and nodding briefly at this novelty: a European client.

Prim no longer felt residual irritation at Stoner for sending her here, and her throat ached all the more. She was content to wait, and at last the doctor showed the shawled Mrs Ab-Dahali to his door, watching her go with an eloquent bunching of his lips and a brief wiping of one half of his brow. He called, 'Miss Primrose Bettany?' with a somewhat formal intonation, and amongst the two remaining patients in the garden there was a rustle either of disapproval or curiosity, or both.

In his shady office, he gestured her towards a chair and sat down himself. 'Primrose Bettany,' he said, as if it were 'Westminster Cathedral' or 'Sydney Opera House'. 'Australian, you told me?'

She admitted it.

'That's one for the books!'

'I work for an NGO here. Austfam.'

'The Sudan of the southern hemisphere, Australia,' he remarked with a languid smile. 'Another desert country.'

'In some ways, yes,' she conceded.

'And why have you come to see me?' He spoke now with a tired directness. Prim was delighted to be able to mention her throat. Dr Taha stood with a light, approached her chair, and shone a beam down it, demanding of her the normal 'Agh' sound.

'I would like to take a swab of that,' he said when done. 'It could be staph. When I have it identified, I shall give you a prescription for antibiotics. I'm sure you'll be able to get them at the UN clinic.'

He frowned at her a moment. If with Austfam, why hadn't she gone to the UN clinic anyhow? But then, courteously suppressing doubt, he opened a chrome rectangle, and took from it a long stick with sterile cotton wool wadded at one end. 'You may feel a slight choking sensation, Miss Bettany. I think it will help to hold your nose while I take the swab.'

She was conscious of his hand on her jaw, his knuckle against her lower lip. 'Just a little patience now. Almost done.'

Withdrawing the swab, he crossed the room and dropped it into a glass test tube into which he put a stopper. Swallowing, Prim asked, 'You do your own tests?'

'Yes, here in the Sudan we must be, as they say in America, "multi-skilled".'

He washed his hands and returned to her, murmuring in a way both confiding and uninsistent, 'Does that cover your problems then, Miss Bettany?'

She thought what a trustworthy man he was. It was there in the fact that there were husbands who were willing to permit their wives to consult him on gynaecological matters. Yet this Dr Taha was permitted to treat women behind a closed door! The trust some Sudanese men and women had in him seemed a reason Prim herself should trust him.

'I have a sore throat,' she said, 'as you see. But I also fear that I'm here as part of a conspiracy. A stratagem would be a better word. I've come at the suggestion of the EC development officer here, a fellow named Fergal Stoner. He spoke as if you'd met him.'

'I have. A public health seminar at the Hilton.' And he smiled, as if he found funny the idea of Stoner and himself at a public health seminar in a republic which could barely afford hospital beds. 'But a conspiracy,' he said, rolling his eyes. 'This is a great relief from the ennui of surgery hours!'

Prim told him at a brisk pace about astounding Darfur, the lines encountered and the road to Nyala, and the written undertaking of the Governor of Darfur, which she took from an envelope and showed him. She assured him that she and Stoner would be able to support the letter and their oral account with photographs which at least had impressionistic force. She admitted too that Stoner had said he, Sherif, had a cousin . . .

'Doctor Babikir Hamadain,' Dr Taha supplied.

'Yes, an economic adviser, Stoner tells me. To President Nimeiri.'

'That's right,' the doctor agreed, faintly astonished, engaging her with his frank, broad eyes. 'He's quite an intelligence gatherer, that man from Yorkshire. As for Darfur, I'm not surprised. If I had the resources, I might even be there myself. What could an epidemiologist or a public health freak do, I see you ask?'

She intended to but he forestalled her by answering himself.

'Vain and bloated with method as he may be, the epidemiologist at least maps the aetiology of diseases which strike and end the lives of the famished. You must know this already. I'm likely to be the chap who asks ravaged women which of their children succumbed, and of what. This is, perhaps understandably, a low priority with the Sudan Ministry of Health. Like all bureaucrats they don't want to be embarrassed by the figures. They want *good* figures. I want whatever comes up. This sort of study is of little use to the present victims, but one hopes it might if properly considered help future ones.'

'I think you would find this crisis an engrossing one,' said Prim. 'If that's the word.'

'I have no line of research funding. Now news of every failure of food supply, and of every attendant epidemic, comes to me from strangers like you.' Am I a stranger? asked Prim of herself. 'For example, from professors from Columbia or the University of Leicester or Tubingen. Foreign aid workers like yourself . . .' He shook his head and drew his eyes back to her. 'Forgive me, Miss Bettany. I should have said "interested outsiders".'

'No, you might have been right the first time,' Prim admitted. 'The governor gave me a talking to. On the arrogance of intruders. On the impatience of the West too.'

'That's common,' Sherif rumbled, 'dear lordy, it's common. We like to tell people: accept the principle of *Inshallah*! We are not impatient because clearly God is not! It's the great Sudanese excuse.' He made a casual, salaam-like, palm-exposing gesture of his right hand. '*I* do not mind the arrogance of intruders. I simply mind that I have no resources. My institute exists on paper. Some would call it a folly to keep that sign by my gate. If I signed on with UNESCO say, I might be able to be their pet epidemiologist, but I would probably be sent to Laos or somewhere similar.'

'And you aren't tempted?' asked Prim, pleased he wasn't.

'Well, I'm something of a patriot. My grandfather was a member of the White Flag League. Trans-racial, trans-sectarian. He was young, he was dashing, he believed in Woodrow Wilson's principles. Self-determination for the Sudanese. He would weep if he saw what has befallen us. We're self-determined, right enough. We've determined ourselves into catastrophe. You must think I am such a complainer.'

'No, not at all,' said Prim, who was enjoying his forthrightness.

His eyes fell on her again, casual and piercing. 'Forgive me for saying this, but we should conclude our business soon. I have old-fashioned fellow citizens who watch these premises with a sour eye and need little encouragement to draw the worst of conclusions. This letter you have from Darfur ... that sort of thing isn't always easy to extract. You realise, I suppose, it might have a subtle purpose.'

'I'm sorry, I don't understand.'

'Provincial governors are habitually discontented with Khartoum. You may have given him, your Colonel Unsa, the chance to register that discontent.'

She felt abashed that Dr Sherif Taha looked at her and saw a bumbling naivety.

'Well, all I care about,' she said, 'is the extreme situation in Darfur. I don't mind if I've been used.'

'So on to Doctor Hamadain?' asked Sherif, smiling.

'I can't see any reason why not,' Prim told him.

'The chief reason is me. I'm disapproved of by some of my relatives and friends. They think me something of a Westerner in disguise. In fact I feel fundamentally Sudanese, in a way which evades the accepted definition of the moment.' Laughing softly, and turning his face briefly to the wall, he seemed to find the normal prejudice of his fellows more endearing than dangerous. 'But having warned you of that ... and on the grounds that you have been such an exemplary patient ... I'm willing to speak with my cousin and arrange for an appointment. You, however, should be the one to hand the letter over. What would be dismissed as impolite if it came through the normal lines of communication, such as they are, would be more understandable coming through you, Miss Bettany.'

'Because they'd think I'm crass? Is that it?'

'I'm sorry,' he said, shaking his head and still retaining the smile. 'I heard you speak and I thought straight away, that's the frank voice of the New World. Which you possess, Miss Bettany, in good measure, and which I shall do my utmost to preserve by curing your throat. Now, the president is a very stubborn man. However, rumour has it my cousin possesses some residual influence over him. I wonder what will happen when this president falls and my cousin goes into exile? He who is so Sudanese! And yet, he'll probably teach economics at George Mason University or the Polytechnique in Lyons!' The prospect seemed to amuse Sherif and a small, nearly silent stutter of laughter broke from him. His placid, enormous eyes crossed Prim's face. 'I hope that you, Miss Bettany, will still be here with us then to point out our needs and failings in your gracious manner.'

He picked up his telephone and made a call. His two dominant mannerisms so far had been an engaging frown and a nonchalant, almost silent laugh. But now he adopted a straight, sober face, the face of one confronting a camera, and pointed to the phone in a way to indicate to Prim that the illustrious Doctor Hamadain was on the line. Prim sat forward while an extended though calm argument in Arabic raged between the cousins.

At last Dr Sherif Taha put the phone down.

'I have your address, do I not? I shall collect you at seven o'clock this evening.'

Prim, delighted, rose when he did, shook his hand hurriedly, and left at once. Beyond the gate, she heard him call another patient and close the front door of his surgery. Walking to the Austfam truck with emphatic steps, she talked almost aloud to herself on an empty pavement.

'No chance,' she said. 'Forget it. *No bloody chance . . .*'

Dr Sherif Taha arrived outside the Austfam office–residence at the promised hour. Prim had been looking out for him from the window of her small sitting room above the office. She had dressed for her visit to the presidential aide in the style she had adopted for the visit in el Fasher to Colonel Unsa, although this dress was her normal floral one, which fell below the knee. She wore no make-up, and her hair was brushed back but uncovered. She did not move from her window until Sherif came in through the unlocked gate and knocked on the office door downstairs. Running her hands over her skirt, she descended into the darkened office to meet him. As she neared the front door, she rubbed her cheeks, for she suspected she might have developed a fatuous paleness. When she unlocked it she was pleased to rediscover him in all his long bones and tallness. She felt as surprised as if she had not been expecting him. She saw his smile.

'Ah, wise Miss Bettany,' he said, assessing her. 'I was intending to advise you to dress conservatively, but you are such an old hand that you did.'

He strode ahead of her out through the gate and to his car, opening a rear passenger door for her.

'Miss Bettany,' he said, 'some of these gentlemen bureaucrats are old-fashioned. It might be easier for us if you sit in the back for our grand entry.'

She slid into the back, adopting the pose appropriate to a chauffeured woman. The antique green Mercedes was full of that potent leathery and chemical smell which the sun of equatorial countries calls forth from upholstery. There were no fussy seat belts to worry with. The Sudanese took the view that war, malaria, malnutrition or dysentery were more likely to end a life than vehicular collision.

Sitting in front of her by the big, knobbly steering wheel, Sherif Taha seemed familiar to Prim, as if this were not a first journey with him but one in a series.

He drove at a ceremonial pace, and ceremoniousness seemed the mark of his character. He was steering north, out of the New Extension and along dusty Sharia el Muk Nimir towards the railway.

The triangle of land between the south side of the Blue Nile and the east bank of the White had been the official centre of Khartoum since the Egyptians had taken over Sudan in the 1820s. Their adobe buildings were long gone, however, and the broad, riverbank streets like Sharia el Nil reminded Prim of Australian country towns, often laid out by nineteenth-century British army engineers in avenues wide as a football ground. The British had also left in Khartoum their stone and brick two-or-three-storey, wide-verandahed administrative buildings. After independence, the new government had continued to find them suitable, and a large compound of these buildings, halfway between the Grand Hotel and the University of Khartoum, housed the Ministry of the Interior and the Ministry of Police.

Here Sherif drove up to a gate and, leaning out of his car window, with casual grace talked a khaki-clad guard into admitting them. At the top of a set of steps flanked by a dusty garden, a junior bureaucrat in a western suit was waiting for them and ushered them along white corridors, and after knocking, took them into a three-windowed office. This contained a tall, tranquil man in an immaculate white thobe-like gown who stood waiting by a desk. He seemed slighter than Sherif, but they shared a family resemblance and possessed the same air of composure.

Dr Hamadain lowered to the desktop some papers he had been reading and came forward. The two cousins gave each other salaams and embraced. But Hamadain did not shake Prim's hand when introduced, keeping a remoter and more professional air. As they sat, hot tea was brought in a large enamel teapot which would have done honour to some dreary office in Whitehall. The old tea man was already pouring white sugar into Prim's glass, and she held up her hand to restrain him when perhaps three spoonfuls had landed in it. This was considered a restrained use of sugar by any Sudanese, and the old man frowned at the odd ways of foreigners.

As soon as the cousin was behind his desk, and had taken a sip of tea, Sherif began.

Miss Bettany, he explained, while recently visiting a refugee camp for Southerners, had beheld in the general populace signs of distress. 'I think she is a reliable person, and on that basis, I bring her in contact with you.'

Prim was left to tell her own story, which she did with a dry mouth. She brought out photographs collected that afternoon from Stoner, and Dr Hamadain consulted them. She had a sense that they fortified somewhat her own equivocal, Western voice. 'As you see, there are women and children on the road with their menfolk. By all accounts that is exceptional.' She explained how she and her colleagues had decided to investigate northwards towards el Fasher, a region which though less populous had traditionally had a struggle to produce its grain needs. She was careful to use phrases like, 'so I've been told', after each of her assertions about the nature of the emergency. After all, she was still in her first year in the Sudan.

When she had finished, the president's aide inhaled, taking his time. 'We have heard some reports of the failure of rains and a harvest crisis in Darfur. But not on the scale you report. You mention colleagues. Were you travelling with other people?'

'I was travelling with Fergal Stoner, the EC man.'

A half smile came over Dr Hamadain's lips. 'Did he ask you to come here?'

'No,' said Prim, and hoped the lie was not too transparent. 'But I know he has already informed his headquarters about what he saw.'

'I suppose,' said Hamadain, 'you and Mr Stoner would like to see a reconnaissance in force, approved by the government of the Republic, followed by appropriate emergency action?'

'And not only Stoner and myself, doctor.' Subject to the approval of the central government, she said, His Excellency the Governor of the province was willing to see an emergency effort. And so she handed over her letter.

As Sherif's cousin read the letter, Prim looked to Sherif for some Western-style relief, a wink or a nod. She saw his reposed features, and his eyes fixed on some middle point in the triangle created by himself, Prim, and his cousin.

Sherif's cousin asked, 'May I take a photocopy?' and stood, as if he intended to do the photocopying himself. He did not leave at once, however, conversing in Arabic with Sherif, at a speed at which she could not comprehend. Their manner neither included nor excluded her. Their air of remoteness was, she decided, both off-putting and delicious.

'Excuse me then,' said the cousin at length, and left the office by a different door from the one they had entered.

'How do you think we are going?' she could not avoid asking Sherif.

Sherif produced his temperate smile. 'Excellent in terms of this problem,' he said.

'What does that mean?'

'My cousin believes that the president will not be able to resist the threat that such a letter presents. It is a straw in the wind, after all. In writing that letter and sending it through you, Colonel Unsa is signalling his willingness to be replaced rather than continue to tolerate this regime. Unsa, you see, retained a Mandarin exterior and pretended reluctance. But you might have been a godsend to him.'

Prim felt, yet again, a novice. 'So I *have* been used as a messenger.'

'Well, there *is* politics in it. On the other hand, the governor and you are at one in not wanting the people in the province to suffer.'

'And where does your cousin fit then?' Prim asked in a whisper, hoping that this office, unlike all such offices in movies, was not bugged or observed or listened in to in some way.

Sherif did not seem fearful, yet answered in the faintest of voices. 'My cousin is barely upset to receive you, Miss Bettany. Like all aides to chief executives, he wishes to make the president more responsive. Just on rainfall figures alone, the president should be aware that something like what you have seen is occurring. And the fact that my cousin has risked confronting a failing president could serve him well in the future.' He laughed without any ill will, seeing her bemusement. 'These guys confuse me too, Miss Bettany. Perhaps that is why I'm in disfavour. My last application to travel internally, in my own country, was refused.'

Dr Hamadain returned now, gave her formal thanks, handed back her letter, and did not sit. 'It is charming to have met you,' he said. 'I know that you are not English but in a sense post-colonial like us. I believe your experience has been a more constructive one, and though your nation is characterised by huge tracts of desert like ours, you do not have the lines of the starving, no matter how severe the drought. Thank you for coming to see me.'

The cousins embraced and Sherif led Prim out into the night. When the car was clear of the front gate, Sherif stopped, opened her door and invited her to join him in the front seat. As they drove off again, he was taken by a spate of laughter. 'Well you've solved *that* one,' he told her.

'And you think solving this one will make the others harder?'

'No. You might get a minor repute for being intrusive. By the way, would you consider asking me to tea at your office?'

'Certainly,' said Prim at once. His request had been uttered so gently, without any apparent design.

'I have a bottle of Scotch under the passenger seat. A flogging offence, of course. I quite like its tang in tea.' He laughed.

'Oh,' asked Prim, delighted, 'you mean this evening?'

'Unless the confrontation with my cousin exhausted you.'

'No, I found it stimulating.'

Above the office Prim's three rooms consisted of a small kitchen, an L-shaped living room facing the street, and beyond it a bedroom. She was still delighted to have such a place to herself. It was here, upstairs, that tea and whisky should be drunk, rather than in the office downstairs.

She led Sherif up the stairs, stamping her feet too energetically, as if to show that she was used to holding utterly business-like conferences in her living quarters. 'So what will it be? Tea English-style? Tea Sudanese-style? Or whisky to start?'

'Tea English-style,' said Sherif in his utterly silken voice behind her. 'Then, perhaps, whisky.'

She showed him into the living room. 'There's a pile of the *Guardian Weekly*,' she told him. 'Excuse me.' She went into the kitchen to make the tea. There were just two matching cup and saucer sets amongst the chaotic collection of low-grade china Crouch had left her. She stayed restless in the kitchen until the water boiled and was poured, until the tea drew. Then she carried it to him on a tray, along with some Scottish shortbreads her friend Helene Codderby had given her. As an afterthought, she forced some ice cubes out of the little ice tray in the refrigerator, put them in a bowl, and put one clean glass, then two, near the tea cups.

'Australian then,' said Sherif as she brought the tray into the living room. 'My English friends tell me that Australians are outspoken to a fault. But it does not seem correct in your case, this characterisation, Miss Bettany.'

'Well, I'm not characteristic, I suppose. My sister, Dimp, is a gloriously outspoken woman and chastises me for being reserved. You see, we consider outspokenness a national strength. She wants me to fit the national mould.'

'Look,' he said then, 'I did invite myself to tea for a specific purpose. There are benefits I believe I may be able to bring you, and vice versa. That camp to which you supply personnel, the one out in Darfur – Adi Hamit, is it? And camps like el Sherif west of town here. These camps already abound but will abound more. Are you equipped to do a comprehensive public health survey of them?'

'No, I'm being kept busy here. Paperwork. But I'm not equipped even if I had the time. Crouch, my predecessor, told me that a team from the Melbourne office was due to visit me, and all the camps we're involved in. They would survey them all. But I've heard nothing.'

Sherif lifted both hands. 'Your cold sounds better.'

'I think that facing Dr Hamadain frightened the bugs.'

'But back to the surveys. I would very much like to be able to make a useful map of refugee populations – the grief, the skills, the resources people have lost and bring with them, their level of hygiene – the whole story! So not only can you discover how best to assist, but they can discover what to call on in each other. I'm in a position where I need the patronage of some NGO under which to work. It's sad. When I finished in America, I had my chance to apply for all the big jobs – University of Leicester, University of California at San Francisco.' He adopted the voice of a rapper. 'They's got all the gear, but ah'm here!'

Prim heard herself laugh. She was both relieved and depressed that Sherif had had such a practical motive for coming indoors with her.

Putting down his tea cup, he spoke of how he could save Austfam and other NGOs money – they would be able to identify what people most needed, and which people most needed it. Baseline data, he said. To find skills and strengths within the community. To identify IMR and crude birth rate, and improve the chances of children at birth and up to five years.

Prim's mind scrambled. IMR. Infant Mortality Rate, she remembered. Sherif was still talking with a sort of dolorous intensity. 'I can set up questionnaires and train a team right here. Now, for example, for survey purposes, you've got an Eritrean engineer in the backyard who can speak Tigrean and Arabic.'

'How do you know that?'

'He used to be a wardsman at the hospital in North Khartoum. Your friend Crouch brought him out of Eritrea and got him a hospital job before taking him back as his driver. But he could be a skilled member of a survey team. Whatever training he doesn't have, I can give him. We can do it all, out of this office. Design a 40-minute questionnaire we can put to people – the mothers of refugee families say. And the wonderful thing we could do, Miss Bettany – unlike the Ministry of Health – is that we could share the results with the people we survey, so that they too can make their arrangements. Oh, I know, they're semi-literate, the despised of the earth. But they have a great eye for any chance of leverage. It would cost Austfam a few thousand dollars a survey. I can send your people my CV and references and past surveys I've conducted, and I would, of course, offer my services voluntarily.'

The concept of working with Sherif elated Prim. 'But surely,' she asked, 'there are far more esteemed organisations than ours?'

He shook his head but did not answer. 'Let's have some whisky. Will you have some?' She nodded. It was illegal under Sharia, but a less-than-observant child of the Prophet was urging it upon her. She experienced unbidden daydreams about joint work, of glory accrued in Sydney and Canberra.

She allocated ice to the glasses and he poured for both of them – in each case a middling quantity. The drinks stood untouched as he returned to the topic.

'Look,' he said, 'there'll probably be no end of epidemiologists and public health experts turning up in the Sudan. What a juicy study it makes, after all! Columbia, University of Pennsylvania, Oxford, so on. But I want my little, half-dead institute, which I started on a Ministry of Health contract and a little inherited money from a venerated uncle, to have a place in the record. A Sudanese voice, you see. There will one day be a generation of young Sudanese so strong that they can manage their own future within the world, and I do not want them to say, "Our miseries were counted by the British, by the Americans, by the Italians and the Germans. But where were our own?" I am humiliated by the present situation, which is not of your making, but derives from the dependence, the equivocation of the Ministry of Health. I would, if you would permit it in your reports, like the Sudanese Institute of Epidemiology to be counted amongst the counters. And I know it will do some good here. The Ministry of Health is surely not interested in the hidden skills within an illiterate refugee community. But I am interested in that because, if the phrase is not too melodramatic, salvation comes from within. Cheers.' He lifted his whisky, and after sipping, kept it close to his face, savouring its bite, and lazily stirring the ice within it with long fingers.

'I can train you and Erwit in the evenings on how a survey should be conducted, and the questions asked. You'll be part of what could be called a Monitoring Committee. So would I. I can also draw in skilled personnel from other locations – from amongst the staff of two Khartoum hospitals, should we need them. And we could use women who are already there, in the camps. In this quack's humble opinion, local women are good brains for the job of surveys. The *women* see the young die.'

Prim put her whisky glass down. There had been a great deal happening. The routine of the last few months was to her like a lost garden. Potent intention, not only her own, but Stoner's and Sherif's, now ran below the surface of her skin. She had the indecency, even in the light of what she had beheld in Darfur, to be elated by possibilities. She did not dare down her drink. Unlike Dimp, who wanted booze to be part of every moment of exaltation, she was scared her powers of discrimination would be flooded.

She drank some of her tepid tea. 'Well, I would have to submit these ideas to Austfam. But I can't see obvious reason why we could not work together.'

'Well, that's splendid,' said Sherif. He sat forward, as if about to leave. 'No doubt, you wish to call your accomplice, Mr Stoner.'

'Oh yes,' she said. Her conference with Hamadain had become remote during all this talk of health surveys. 'He wouldn't be there, of course. I'll let him know first thing tomorrow.'

Sherif quickly drained his drink, pulled from his pocket a tiny atomiser, and sprayed his open mouth so that, on the street, he would seem law-abiding.

'May I leave the bottle here as a deposit against future debriefings?'

'Of course.'

He rose, pleading some operations he had to attend to in the morning at Omdurman women's hospital. When she questioned him he mentioned ovarian cysts – a peculiar specialty for someone interested in public health and epidemiology.

'Middle-class women?' asked Prim.

'Oh yes. But also I repair fistulas which are looked upon as a curse by Sudanese society. That is good and satisfying work, since a simple proce-dure gives women back their womanhood. I enjoyed our meeting, Miss Bettany. I hope we will meet again soon.'

Prim knew walking with him to the car, to extend their contact, would not be allowed under the protocols of Sudanese street culture. She saw him to the door, locked up, took a few steps towards the base of the stairs, but leaned back against the filing cabinet full of reports of food dumps established, wells dug, midwives trained, livestock distributed – the largesse of Austfam.

'Sherif Taha,' she murmured. 'Oh Jesus.' She was desperately tempted to believe that whatever Auger had stolen from her had been brought back to her door by Sherif's angular goodwill.

Next morning Stoner was predictably pleased to hear from her – 'You know, delighted!' Two mornings later she heard from him. 'It's on! Congratulations. Not only do we two bozos locate a famine, we chivvy permission to study its extent and initiate the relief effort! You'll come with us, in the recce phase?'

Prim found in the days following her excursion with Sherif and his visit to her residence that she began to take more notice of Helene Codderby's prognostications on the BBC African News and of the *Sudan Post*, the English language newspaper, as if the country was suddenly more

intimately connected to her. And the destiny of President Nimeiri seemed
also to engross her in a new way. Nimeiri, who had advanced modern
agriculture and brought the peasants in to work as labourers in the cotton
plantations, now faced a collapse in commodity prices. To pay his excessive foreign debt and the expense of war, he was earning less and less.
Students and other critics went to prison for being vociferous. The president had gathered in the support of the Muslim Brotherhood and the
National Islamic Front (the NIF) and various church leaders in the provinces. But even the radicals of the NIF were disgruntled with him. They
wanted a more thorough-going and efficient Islamic republic than he
could provide. The president had not yet, and was unlikely to confess
publicly to the Darfur problem. There was enough bad news for him in
the capital, without his drawing on the disaster in Darfur.

In the meantime, Dr Taha's curriculum vitae was brought to the office
by a hospital messenger. There were references and supporting papers,
one of them published in the *United States Journal of Public Health* and
entitled 'The Aetiological Fraction in the Case of the Water Supply of
Shendi, Sudan, 1982–3.' To it, Sherif had attached a note. 'This study
grew from a contract the Ministry of Health financed. Though I believed
that under the terms of the arrangement I was free to publish, the
ministry took a dim view.'

Prim sent these documents to Canberra with an accompanying letter
which indicated the distinct services and the prestige she believed a man
of his qualifications could offer Austfam. She had not yet had any feed-
back from Canberra and did not know whether she was considered
heroine or villain for her report from Darfur. If the former, they would
answer her wishes and authorise her to work with Sherif.

As she waited, she remembered and weighed the content of his
sentences – plain words, but informed by rhythm, by a musical emphasis
which made them more significant than they might seem. She held in her
head an image of his hands, functionality again masking something more
significant. Fistulae, he had said. An act of mercy worked within rubber
gloves on a series of birth-induced ruptures connecting bladder to uterus,
or in some ill-starred cases bowel to uterus. Womanhood thereby
restored to women traditionally thought unclean and accursed.

Even though Canberra had not spoken, Sherif rang and said he'd like
to take her through the questions he believed should be asked in any
community health survey. She agreed that he should come to the office–
residence the next day about five in the afternoon. Since that was an

hour when he could, with more propriety than last time, be invited
upstairs into the living room, in early afternoon heat she was overtaken
by what she considered nesting instincts. She tidied the small kitchen, the
L-shaped living room facing the street, and then the bedroom. She did
not expect him to visit there, and in fact she was devoted to the idea he
should neither be there or be imagined to be there. But she didn't want
any imperfection from within to penetrate what he would see. Nurse-
like, she unnecessarily straightened the thin raucous quilt of red, green,
yellow, blue, bought for her bed in the Omdurman *souk*. It was like the
bed of a nun or a patient, iron, knobby, covered in chipped blue paint.

There was not much to do. All she had to do to the living room was
close and fold a rice-paper *Guardian Weekly*, which crackled like rubbed
lizard-skin in the dry air, and remove a coffee cup. She dreaded the
arrival of the promised senior colleague from Austfam, which would
mean turning this space into a bedroom, hers.

In Canberra it was the next calendar day and morning faxes from
Austfam headquarters were arriving as Sherif pressed the bell at the gate
and announced himself. She met him at the open office door. He was in
shirt sleeves and carried a raffia bag, not by the handles but scrunched
at its neck. He frowned, hearing the fax machine. 'But you have incoming
mail.'

'Oh,' said Prim, 'I don't need to look at that till tomorrow. Most of
it's projects in Asia, anyhow.'

'Ah,' said Sherif. 'They used to say, trade follows the flag. Now it's
aid that follows the flag.'

The raffia bag proved to contain gin. Dr Taha seemed to have a
mission to provide her with a cocktail cabinet, in a republic which
forbade such things. 'Not that I encourage you, Miss Bettany, to be
lawless.'

In her living room, over tea, and later at an Eritrean restaurant on the
Blue Nile where they ate dinner with Erwit, Sherif – who already knew
what questions should be posed and data should be sought in random
sample surveys of what he called 'displaced communities' – asked for
suggestions from Prim.

Agreed on the significance of Infant Mortality Rate and its relationship
to the Crude Birth Rate, they made notes on the corners of the paper
tablecloth left free by the large metal dishes of *injera* bread, by the bowls
of lamb and chickpea paste, as they decided what other baseline data
should be gathered.

'Those people most in need within the camp? Those who have no animals?' asked Prim.

'Sure,' said Sherif and tilted his head.

'Listen, you know what questions to ask. You don't need me to dream them up.'

'You are, after all, the boss. I'm the volunteer.'

So the discussion continued. Who had skills which might generate income? Mat-making? Curio-making? Tailoring, embroidery? Refugees could take these goods for sale to *souks* in villages. Not to be forgotten: those with earning power as shamans. The women who wrote love amulets. Yes, charcoal-burning, as she had seen at Mawashei. Teaching. Could likely women be financed to become teachers? So the hardest up were those without animals *and* without any source of income or any skills to trade. But say there was some income, couldn't it be used to create a co-operative store? Couldn't it be used to buy a motor-driven mill so that women who were able to grow or buy a little grain didn't become weakened by the hours-long daily task of grinding it so it could be cooked?

Further questions. Total number of persons in households, ages and sex of family members, tribe, place of origin, former occupations – pastoralist, farmer, both? Reasons for coming to somewhere like Adi Hamit? Slaughter, burning, confiscation of cattle? Terror, hunger, both?

Sherif kept returning not only to the benefits of such inquiries, but to their moral force. 'I published the Shendi article, which concerned water-borne parasites, from professional vanity, to which I am perhaps too susceptible. But also – if this is not too grand a term – to bear witness.'

The dishes were taken away by a waiter. Erwit had gone off to talk with the restaurant owner, a man from Asmara who, like Erwit, had been a rebel soldier in Eritrea's war against Ethiopia, another of the sad, vast wars of the region. Prim and Sherif began tearing off the notes they had made on the butcher's paper table-cover. Sherif would need them to devise a questionnaire for the planned surveys.

'You realise,' said Prim, 'that within a week or two I could be involved in the relief effort in Darfur.'

He said of course. That was a chief priority.

'And there's one other thing,' she told him.

'Oh?' he said, and frowned.

This is work he wants to do with me, Prim thought.

'Nothing directly to do with this. Let's put in a question about slavery.

We don't have to publish it. But let's test if the phenomenon is widespread.'

'Slavery,' said Sherif flatly.

'Yes. Another issue that arose from my journey out to Darfur. Mind you, Stoner says the term is very loosely used.'

'Maybe you should find someone who is in a condition of slavery, and ask them what they think of the term?'

'I intend to,' said Prim. 'I believe I've already met one who has been. But how would I find another such person? Well, through these surveys.'

He did not seem as hostile to the proposition of slavery's possible existence as Stoner had been. 'You should speak to my friend, Mrs Khalda el Shol. Everyone calls her Mrs el Rahzi, since she's married to the famous Professor el Rahzi. He's professor of politics at the University of Khartoum. I have been frequently invited to their house and I am sure they would be delighted to see you. Khalda was one of our first feminists. Our Germaine Greer.' He laughed. 'She's made some inquiries in this matter, and she knows slavery activists. Would you like to visit her?'

'I'd love to meet your friend.'

'There's also a German or Austrian woman named Baroness von Trotke. Then there's a woman bush pilot, Connie Everdale, from Loki-chokio in Kenya. She used to fly whisky to Khartoum and *khat*, the narcotic, to Somalia, but she saw the light of revelation in middle life. Those two visit Khartoum sometimes, and Mrs el Rahzi greets them and confers with them. A very good woman, Mrs el Rahzi. Sometimes she takes one of the slaves – if that's what the people the baroness rescued really are – as a servant.'

'It sounds very much like abolitionists in the nineteenth century,' said Prim.

'Except that slavery *is* illegal in the Sudan,' Sherif told her – a warning against exaggeration.

The reconnaissance party to investigate Darfur gathered in Khartoum the same day Peter Whitloaf, the chief executive of Austfam, wrote enthusiastically about involving Dr Taha, initially for two health surveys. Any chance of doing a community somewhere in the South? asked Peter. A sort of pre-refugee study? Whitloaf said that her report to Austfam from Darfur had been admirable, careful – she had not been betrayed into hyperbole. He asked her if she thought she could carry the office for a while longer on her own. 'You certainly seem to have made extraordinary contacts there. Theoretically, of course, you should get yearly leave and I know you have a sister back here, in Sydney. It's just that Cambodia and the Pakistan monsoon between them seem to be absorbing all our spare personnel.'

He said that he would write a request to the Minister for Health asking that Dr Sherif Taha be granted permission to work under contract for Austfam and given all facilities, including travel permits, to make his work possible.

Prim showed the letter to Sherif, whose vast eyes coruscated. Prim rejoiced that they now had a licence for unlimited future meetings and travels.

The party was made up of Saudi representatives of the Red Crescent, three European Community officers, Americans from US Aid, Norwegians and British from Save the Children, and three bureaucrats from the Sudanese Ministry of Health. The party was to be divided into three teams, with Prim and Stoner in separate teams. Darfur was divided into three sectors, the smallest in the more densely populated south of Darfur, and two others named Central North and North-East. Each team was allotted towns or villages to visit. If to cover the ground one team needed help from another, they could call them in by radio.

Prim travelled with Erwit in her own vehicle in convoy with the personnel of the North-East team. They found the villages of north-east Darfur more depopulated – there had been a scatter of rain a few weeks past, and then a determined dry spell. In some cases, women and old men, left behind to tend and protect the house while the rest of the family made off to find work or food in the big towns, told them the millet crop had already been baked to death in the earth.

The leader of the North-East team, a Dutchman named Martin, told Prim after their visit to el Fasher and Mawashei, which had if anything swelled as a camp in the few weeks since Stoner and she had been there, that his estimate was that this crisis would kill 200 000 people.

Prim was sceptical. 'As many as that?' she asked.

'Of course. Why would you argue with such a figure?'

'These people are clever, that's all. Adaptive. They're so determined. They're not very willing to lie down.'

She had seen thin women, encouraged by a light scatter of rain to return from the city to plant millet, beating at termite nests to expose the grains that ants had stolen in better years. Would 200 000 of them and their children perish? She remembered the day she and Stoner first encountered the columns and observed a death, a limb protruding from a grave of stones. Could that happen 200 000 times?

As the first relief convoy for Darfur gathered on 21 May, the government of President Nimeiri, subjected to even fiercer wounds than those inflicted by the letter of the provincial governor of Darfur, was overthrown by the army. It seemed a remarkably easy transition – the chief parties to the relief operations in Darfur did not need to let themselves be distracted. Large resources of international emergency food had been gathered in warehouses in North Khartoum, Omdurman, and at the edge of the New Extension, and the new regime seemed happy to see the Darfur crisis attended to.

The effort was by consent of all participants named Project West. Stoner and his staff, with the officials of the Office of African Emergency, were principally responsible for the creation of an office in Khartoum named the Office for the Co-ordination of Humanitarian Affairs. They controlled a fleet of nearly four hundred trucks, and the movement of food.

Prim and Erwit were at a truck marshalling point on the western edge of Omdurman when the radio announced that the Military Council had appointed an interim civilian prime minister, who was soon pleased to cite the Darfur crisis as an indication of Dr Nimeiri's maladministration.

The co-ordination office had assigned to Austfam an emergency feeding station in the town of Abu Grada, situated on a wadi below nubbly hills in north-east Darfur, reached by convoluted and obscure tracks in the clay. The town was a settlement of stone, mud and brush habitations occupied by people of the Fur tribe.

When the first relief truck arrived it was mobbed by people of all ages, and as Prim and Erwit joined the person in immediate charge of the proposed feeding station, a young Indian man named Pradesh from Save the Children, the cries of hungry women and youths were so intense that bags of sorghum needed to be opened on the truck itself, and people's pannikins filled directly. Prim handed high-protein biscuits and powdered milk over the sideboards of the truck into reaching hands, some of which held pots. She saw that victimhood – although she still had doubts that these people would wish to be described as victims – did not improve human habits.

As this first, frenzied, panicky issue was in progress, an old man, who turned out to be the uncle of the town's sheik, appeared on a wooden crutch and chastised his fellow citizens for forgetting their pride, for being raucous, for pushing the weak out of the way. His intervention permitted a conference between Prim, Pradesh and the sheik himself to take place in the shade of a brush shelter outside a mud-walled cluster of huts which belonged to the sheik's clan. The old uncle sat by reminiscing on how the wadis, in his youth, had been full of trees, and the rainfall reliable. El Fasher, where half the town had gone in desperation to find work, had been a green city.

Under the sheik's patronage, lists of townspeople were drawn up. Tents and tarpaulins were erected in a thicket of acacias, and supplies unloaded there. An instant feeding station was thus created. It worked by a simple equation – 5 tonnes of high-protein biscuit, and 10 US tons of sorghum were sufficient for two weeks short ration to the 2457 people whose names were on the rolls. In the next seven weeks, 157 US tons of sorghum, 43 US tons of powdered milk, and 85 tonnes of high-protein biscuit were distributed in Austfam's name. By then the Darfur famine had been written about in *The Times*, the *New York Times*, and the *Washington Post*, and *The Times* had declared, like the Dutchman, that 200 000 lives were about to be lost. As famished as the citizens of the town, and their brethren now returning to Abu Grada from the cities, as regularly as babies perished of gastroenteritis or measles and were carried away by fathers to a cemetery area in a ravine and buried in the earth beneath heaped stones, Prim found it hard to believe so many would become victims. Such was the fame of the Darfur emergency that a Canadian NGO took over Abu Grada after some weeks.

In this time Prim discovered some of the subtleties of such emergencies. Food saved, but could also corrupt. She and Pradesh needed to complain to the sheik about families who managed to pass themselves off as greater in number than they were, or who tried to hoard and sell on to town merchants. The sheik himself was a problem: he was something of a town bank, and had loans out everywhere. He had declared no moratorium in this hard time for his borrowers, though he was genially open to adjusting repayment.

Prim, as thoroughly absorbed in the tasks of storage, distribution and record-keeping as she had ever hoped to be, was still possessed at most conscious moments by the thought of Sherif, or by the redolence of his character.

When the Canadian NGO took over Abu Grada, and Prim was back in Khartoum, feeling enlarged by the zealousness of what she had been engaged in, and suspicious of how that might cause her to act towards Sherif. Soon he visited with a draft proposal and questionnaire to send to Canberra. He also said that his Friday afternoons were free, and when he asked had she seen the *souk* in Omdurman, she found herself saying, 'Just a flying visit.'

Thus she travelled as if for the first time in the aromatic avenues of spice dealers, amongst women who displayed coffee beans, ground nuts and fruit on woven panniers, past the stalls of the makers of filigreed jewellery and the sellers of amulets. Sherif said the small size of the produce market showed how scant Sudanese product was, and showed how poorly infrastructure – roads, railways – operated. But Prim shook her head. She did not want, amongst the fortune-teller stalls, to be distracted by politics.

The hornet's nest dome of the tomb of the Mahdi hung over their Omdurman excursion. The Mahdi's supporters had overrun the Anglo-Egyptian forces in the Sudan, and he had not lived to see General Kitchener take the country back for the British in 1898. Yet his ghost was so potent that Kitchener had destroyed the mausoleum. Rebuilt in modern times, entry to it was forbidden to infidels, but the house of the Khalifa, the Mahdi's successor, was available to all-comers. Prim realised she had scarcely looked at it when Helene Codderby had brought her touring. She was suddenly engrossed by relics of the Mahdi's war and Kitchener's invasion, on which Sherif was calmly discursive. After God gave him his victories, said Sherif, the Mahdi lived and died in 'heroic depravity'.

Prim wished to believe that her lack of interest the time Helene took her there to see mementos of past Sudanese travail, and the patchwork uniforms of the Mahdi's devout soldiers, had been due to her having been in the country such a short time, of having no sense of its diversity. Besides, Sherif knew so much more even than Helene – he knew in religious terms what the diamond-shaped patches of cloth on each uniform stood for. She could see him as a calm, convinced warrior, driving out the occupying unbeliever.

Prim had a long-standing arrangement with Helene to visit the whirling dervishes in Omdurman, who danced to achieve union with God. She had found regular reasons for putting it off. When, a few days later, Sherif suggested it, she agreed to go with him. He drove her across the

White Nile bridge, left the car by the soccer stadium, and walked through a suburb of shanties before arriving in a square in front of a mosque named after a famous mystic, Hamad el Niil. This was late May, when temperatures were at an apogee, yet Prim had a sense, moving in long-sleeved blouse and knee-length skirt, of pushing aerobically through the heated air, her thin hands brown as an Egyptian's.

By the gate of the mosque a flautist was surrounded by drummers, and in front of them was the sheik of the mosque wearing black and kneeling on a carpet of red. Red, Sherif told her, was the colour of unity with God. The flute was joined by drums, by whose thudding the dervishes appeared in fez-like hats and black cloaks from the direction of the nearby graveyard. They approached the sheik, kissed his hand and began to whirl, while the orchestra played and sang of the divine union which the dancers strove to achieve through giddiness.

The dancers shed their black overgarments and danced in patchwork tunics, just like the garments of the soldiers of the Mahdi. The name 'whirling dervish' had been applied to all the Mahdi's troops but, said Sherif, it was only a minority of Sudanese who pursued Sufism, the mystic side of Islam. The Mahdi himself had danced towards God in a giddiness of eroticism.

Why did Sherif insist on taking her to such places? Why share a meeting in a palm-shaded tea-house at the city's dusty Botanic Gardens, during which he talked drowsily, in a tannin-sated voice, about the spread of desert since his grandparents' days, about his father who had been elderly when he was born, and a mother who died young of meningitis. As he spoke, the contours of his sentences felt so familiar to her that she forgot for minutes at a time that she was not Sudanese.

Since the successful graduation of Abuk Alier, Austfam was supporting two more women at the School of Midwifery attached to the women's hospital in Omdurman. Partly from duty, partly out of interest, Prim visited them, and they walked her through the wards. In one room she saw an exquisite young Sudanese woman, dark-skinned but with well-defined Arab features, lying on a bed, dressed in long white skirt and embroidered shirt. Her eyes were skilfully accentuated with kohl, and the tips of her fingers were darkened with henna, as were the ankles and soles of her feet. Prim and the midwives-in-training possessed enough Arabic between them to speak with her, and during the conversation her eyes kept straying to the door. She was waiting for her husband. She was to go home that day with her new child, who was sleeping, and for its father's arrival she was beautified. A severe-looking nurse, dressed in layers of white, joined the group, and proved jovial. They all shared the young mother's exaltation at having given birth to a healthy Sudanese boy, and now she was prettified and – neither the nurse nor the wife were embarrassed to say it – sewn up again. The labia had been sutured together – *infibulated* was the medical term – allowing only enough space for sex. Thus the vagina was restored to a tightness considered beneficial to any marriage. The midwives unabashedly discussed the practice – all the women of the region seemed to talk freely about it, but only in all-female company. Infibulation provided the eternally, the artificially unstretched vagina, demanded by men – even of the educated urban middle class to which this woman's husband belonged – and promoted by mothers who had been through it all themselves. The severe-looking nurse turned to Prim and said in English, 'It pleases her husband, who gives her gifts.'

Thus Sherif could not be interested in her, Prim believed; even if she tried she could not make herself lovely with kohl and henna. She was the sort of obsessed Western woman who had lost the gift for loveliness, though beauty might still perversely cling for a time. And she could certainly not countenance infibulation: her culture disposed her to see it as a regional lunacy, just as the lack of infibulation made the West seem lunatical to many Africans. Yet her imagination was fired by the joy and wifely alacrity of the young woman waiting, a restored bride, for the bridegroom. Well, it was just another case of women being suckers, and she had been an adequate sucker. But she could never provide such a display, such a waiting, such a sacrifice of flesh, even for Sherif.

Unhenna-ed and uncut, Prim had good reason to be armed against the fatal soppiness of womanhood. Yet in a recurrent daydream which arose without any conscious welcome from her, she saw herself grafted to Sherif. This was not in any frankly erotic way – she could avoid thinking about his chest, the mystery of his penis, the more frankly legible contour of his arse. She imagined herself instead as a little bio-packet of material, lodged under his skin, a kind of slow-release, beneficial substance which became assumed into him, growing, breathing, declining and willingly dying with him. This, she was aware, was desire attempting a conceit, imagination trying to lead her to the bed but dancing behind an image more medical than sexual. She felt obligated to see through all these tricks.

Secure in seeing through herself, in her contempt for fantasy, she invited him to the office to arrange dates for the proposed Adi Hamit survey. It could not occur before September, she would need to tell him. She would be involved in Darfur, or in the office, working with the relief effort, until then.

He came to the office and brought his normal surreptitious bottle of booze, this time vodka. The dates for the Adi Hamit survey finalised, they moved upstairs for a drink. 'I am pleased to have such a pleasant boss,' he told her. When he got up to go, she reached from her seat and took his wrist. 'Stay a bit longer,' she said. Outraged with herself, she could hear her own pulse.

She realised then that she would need to lead him to her bed simply because it provided the only arena for the energies now running in the room. On the way in he said nothing: no noble exhortations to think again, no confession he had been waiting to be led in by her for a week or a month. Earnestly she unbuttoned his shirt and saw that dense, African body below. It had a young man's lustrous hair on it. So he was still young beneath the middle-aged demeanour.

He took over, undressing her with a set of scarcely audible sighs, and was so swollen, she observed, that he had scant time to say the expected and demanded things. But he said she was very beautiful. 'I haven't got any kohl or henna,' she told him. 'No *delkah*.'

'What's all this chatter,' he asked her. After cupping and praising her breasts, by entering he drove from her body all the skilled arguments about versions of womanhood, ornamentation and device. She grabbed his hips. She held him roughly. She demanded he reach a certain limit only she knew well. He must be dragged, and incited to do superbly. She saw her knees lock him to the task. Imagine, she thought. Imagine.

In Prim's first five years in the Sudan, Dimp had pleaded with her frequently to repent of her wilful choice of life in Khartoum and take a post somewhere more accessible. At the very least, she said, Prim should come home for a visit. Dimp made plans to visit Khartoum herself in 1986, not least to inspect the lover to whom Prim made occasional and typically guarded references in her letters. But then Bren's annulment came through, and her marriage was planned.

Dimp had an unquestioning sense that she should be married to Bren. She was the sort of woman to whom the initial risks a man took were of great and binding significance. His first ardent approach to her at the film-tax seminar was a gesture of appropriate and compelling scale. She had not doubted since that hour that she was bound to him by it.

On top of that, the trouble he had taken seeking an annulment, to cancel at its root one marriage so that she was his first wife, was a rite of extreme ardour to her. In her view of the world, it was an unnecessary process, but she was impressed by how much it meant to him, of how it added weight to his purpose.

At the time of the wedding, Prim sent her warmest wishes but pleaded that an emergency in the Southern, tropical part of the country, where Austfam maintained a feeding station, made it impossible for her to come back. It was apparent Prim was engaged in pressing humanitarian efforts, but pleased to be.

Prim took some leave the following year but found reason not to fly further than London. She was still grotesquely scared of coming home. Bren did not want his wife to go and fetch her, either. It might be counter-productive, he suggested with his lumbering canniness. Well, maybe they could call in briefly, detouring from the Gulf, on a trip to Europe.

For whatever reason – though Dimp had no doubt of her love for her sister, or her sister's for her – no visit, either way, occurred.

Some time after her marriage to D'Arcy, in a Southern Hemisphere summer, when she and her husband were happily established on the edge of the massive harbour in their house named Woolarang at Double Bay, Dimp faxed her sister. She had just heard on Radio National that the elected government of the Sudan which had come into being a little time after Nimeiri's fall, had been deposed by a group of army officers. So, Dimp understood, Prim had by 1989 lived under three Sudanese governments – the supposedly Marxist government of President Nimeiri, the civilian government just toppled, and now a military council. This seemed another reason for her to come home. Military rule surely would make Prim's spartan life even less comfortable.

The second subject of the fax was a Sydney barrister named Frank Benedetto. Dimp was sure Prim had met him at a party, before she left Australia. 'He acted for Bren's company once. A pleasant, bear-like sort of fellow, you know. Recently made a Queen's Counsel – I wonder what his Italian mum and dad think of that! Well, he got a Master's degree in pastoral history before he did law! That is, a degree in sheep!'

This man Benedetto told Dimp that he liked to visit all the old houses of the squattocracy in New South Wales and Victoria, and whenever there was an auction involving one of those old places, he would turn up to bid. 'Second-generation Australian,' wrote Dimp to her sister, 'but he's more interested in that stuff than the rest of us!' Recently he had attended the sell-up of a sheep station named Eudowrie in the Riverina, the estate of a deceased, remote Bettany cousin, an old man – someone they had not met, unless perhaps, when they were infants, their father had taken them to visit the place. Dimp had a hazy memory of visiting some broad, wide-open pastures, of herself and Prim chasing lambs, and an old man telling them to stop because it wasn't good for the lambs' hearts.

Benedetto's reason for turning up at this sheep station auction was that he believed a nineteenth-century manuscript entitled *Sheep Breeding and the Pastoral Life in New South Wales*, a work published in 1882 by a Bettany ancestor, Jonathan Bettany, was likely to be part of the estate. 'You remember the book,' Dimp told her sister. 'Father sometimes showed it to guests. It had that bloody big fold-out map of pastoral leases in the back which made about as much sense as an anatomical drawing. It had riveting chapter headings like "How to Choose a Balanced Flock", or "The Tobacco Water Cure for Scab in Sheep", or "Thoughts anent the New Land Bill now before Parliament". He wrote of a diphtheria epidemic which hit the Monaro, but even made that boring. But he's a hero to this Benedetto.'

At the auction, Frank Benedetto bought the station papers, the stock books and so on, and the prize, the manuscript of *Sheep Breeding*, for a mere $8000, and passed them on to the Mitchell Library for nothing – an act of largesse such as particularly the son of Calabrian immigrant peasants might relish. But Dimp reported to Prim:

There were some other and more private documents of our esteemed ancestor nearly-Sir-Jonathan, Member of the Legislative Assembly for New South Wales – 'Missed a knighthood by a whisker,' as Dad used to say – which came with the papers. Benedetto knew from Bren and from Enzo Kangaroo that I was a fully paid-up Bettany, and he thought I should have what he called these 'more private' papers. He sent the stuff by courier. So I have the documents, and can tell from a quick read that Benedetto has behaved with great delicacy.

The main item Benedetto's given me is a sort of confessional journal from Jonathan Bettany – it's headed Bettany's Book *and reads almost as*

*if it were written with publication in mind, a far more literary publication
than* Sheep Breeding. *This may be a rare intimately personal account of
Australian pastoral life, and that makes it all the more interesting that
Benedetto gave it up out of some sort of sensibility! If it's to be
published ... well, he thinks that ought to be up to me. Then there's a
series of letters written in her convict condition by his wife, our ancestor,
of the revealing kind all of us maybe write in hours of stress but which
we might hope to get rid of before we die. I intend to exercise some rare
discipline and leave them until I've transcribed a large slab of the
memoir, which I'll send to you in bits.*

*But – and this is fascinating – these papers show that Mrs Bettany,
our ancestor Sarah, was not only a convict, but Jewish as well. Don't
you wish our poor parents were around for that piece of news? To hear
that! The wife of nearly-Sir Jonathan Bettany, great man of sheep! Isn't
it stimulating? I wonder if that modicum of Hebraic blood explains my
filmic tendencies, and your career as a pilgrim.*

Amongst the documents, said Dimp, was a picture of nearly-Sir Jonathan
and nearly-Lady Bettany, as they were in the flesh and as they might
have been aggrandised if his pastoral Free Trade party had remained in
government in Macquarie Street a little longer.

*He is sitting, she is standing, according to what you'd loosely call the
habit of the time. He is older, a little paunchier than the ideal pioneer
should be, but not too much so. A very handsome, square-faced, clear-
eyed fellow with eyes a bit startled by life or the photographer's flash.
Wearing a very well-cut suit, but the way a man who is muscular does,
as if he's just waiting to throw it off, put on dungarees and jump into
the saddle again. He certainly loved bloody sheep!*

But Dimp was not content to mention the photograph, and promise to
send it on to Khartoum. It had clearly precipitated in her, a woman
nearly without clan, a tide of clannish analysis.

*As for her, Sarah, the wife, she is luscious. A-1. Splendid. Dominant. A
long head, piercing dark eyes full of intelligence. A superb figure despite
the five kids she bore him. So, muted along the way by a few Scots
brunettes, she's clearly the wellspring of our problems, Prim, of – I might*

as well bloody say it, since every other bastard does – our beauty. Came to us through father, those fine lines he had in his sixties and even in his casket, even in death. Those darker features were not quite Anglo-Scots, were they? They were what attracted and scared the hell out of Mum. What's in this picture, a kind of alien lushness from Poland or Russia – or even from somewhere like Persia, something Sephardic Jewish – that's what attracted her to Dad, but then she was panicked by it in us. Poor old thing, she tried to tamp it down for our own good with our pretty, crocheted, bloody silly names – Dimple for me, Primrose for you.

For the time being Dimp promised to attach a good photocopy of the photograph.

So I am sending you in batches what I have transcribed of the old boy's journal, and the old girl's letters, in a belief that it's important to know what the founding virtues of your ancestors were. But, more important, to know what were the founding crimes.

Such a statement, Prim thought when she read it in Khartoum, was pure Dimp. She inspected the photocopy of the photograph. The splendid upright woman did have a face a bit like Dimp's. But there was in Bettany's eye, she was sure, some of her own discontent. More than she would ever tell her sister, Prim fancied she saw in him a desire like her own: to find new landscapes in which to remake himself.

MY CHILDHOOD AND JOURNEY TO NEW SOUTH WALES
My father used tell my brother Simon and myself in the vaguest terms that when he was young he was very like the poet Horace. He had been raised on Quintus Horatius Flaccus (BC 65–8), *Odes, Books I–IV*, and Horace was the classic poet he loved above all, and attempted to teach the colonial-hearty Batchelor boys and ourselves at Hydebrae, west of Ross, Van Diemen's Land, now Tasmania.

Father's constant references to Horace may have been in part his way of letting us know that in his youth, like the poet, he had committed some crime, or let me use my kindly mother's phrase, some 'mistake of politics'. It was clear to me even then that his crime had been more a matter of enthusiasm, since, unlike *real* convicts and felons, he was

respected by the better people in Hobart and Ross. They accepted that
whatever he had done – something ill-advised and republican – had been
a matter of a good heart, exuberance and earnest intent. It was a sin
from which everyone, including himself, had long recovered. Mother,
Simon, myself, were after all its beneficiaries. It had brought us from a
small house in Manchester, in a sunless street with a cloaca in the midst
of it and typhus on every corner, to temperate and robust Hobart.
O, happy crime – *peccatum felix*. Or so it seemed to us.

The small disadvantage of our situation was that everyone knew father
was a former ticket-of-leave man as all in Rome knew that Horace's
father was a freed slave. But it was taken for granted that only the
meanest of people mentioned it aloud. So few of these were there, and
so well was father greeted by the progressive settlers such as the Batchelors, that he was as empty of any grievance as were Horace's sunnier
verses.

> *Vino et lucernis Medus acinates*
> *immane quantum discrepat: impium*
> *lenite clamorem, sodales,*
> *Et cubito remanete presso.*
>
> By wine and the light of lamps
> Drawn Median daggers are inappropriate,
> So soften the row, mates,
> And keep your elbows tucked in place.

As I got older, I gathered a little more intelligence of father's mistake,
and of my English antecedents.

'According to Suetonius,' father told the Batchelor boys and my
brother Simon and me one day, 'Horace's father was a *salsamentarius*,
a seller of salted fish. Similarly, my father was a fishmonger from Widnes.
And like Horace's father he possessed a noble mind.'

In the trap on the way home from the little Anglican church in Ross
one Sunday, Mother said dreamily – she often gave her most important
news in a state of false torpor – 'I like Anglicans greatly. They're less
likely to lose their common sense than Wesleyans. Your father's father
was a Wesleyan, and interpreted the words of the Gospels in a fanatic
way.'

I wondered what this fanatic way might have been, for I intended to avoid it. In a book from the case of books Mother had packed for us to bring to join Father, I found an old history of Greece, and inside its cover, in an arduously achieved hand, misted by the increasing greyness of the paper, the words, 'The Society of Spencean Philanthropists.' Then, in the back of another of Father's old books I found a verse:

Hark how the Trumpet's Sound
Proclaims the Land around
The Jubilee;
Tells all the poor oppressed
No more shall they be cess'd
Nor landlords more molest,
Their Property.

I waited several weeks before I asked my mother, one howling Tasmanian winter's evening by the fire, 'Ma, could you tell me what is the Society of Spencean Philanthropists?'

My mother looked up from needlework with a severe fright in her eyes.

'Where did you hear of them, Jonathan?'

'Someone mentioned them. It might have been that parson, the Reverend Munroe, at Mr Batchelor's.'

'What did he say about them?'

'He said something about having known them ... Not here! In England.'

'How would he know of them? Was he trying to blacken your father?'

I had got deep in, since it was her acutest fear that someone would discuss my father's crime. 'No, no. Was Father one of these Philanthropists?'

'Your grandfather was one of that cracked fraternity,' she said in a lowered voice, without lifting her eyes, as if the shame were hers. 'He influenced your father, but he no longer does.'

'Well, he's dead, isn't he, Ma?' I remarked.

'Yes, he is dead, nor does he have any influence.'

At that age I was simple-minded enough to think that the two things – dead, no influence – were the same.

After I had reassured my mother, she in turn told me that Spence had been a Londoner who put fanatic weight on those parts of the Gospels which had to do with property. The rights of the poor, the verses in

which Christ called on his followers to sell all they had to give to the
poor, the difficulties for rich men entering heaven, and so on – all that
Spence and his Spenceans interpreted by the letter, and so expressed
contempt for the rights of property. 'Wesleyan, of course,' said my
mother. 'That is why your father and I have now embraced the Anglican
faith, since you never hear such folly from them.'

I would not have said Father had 'embraced' the Anglican faith. The
verb was too strong for his good-humoured attendance at Sunday service.
He had begun attending before we all arrived, while he was still an
assigned convict tutor to the Batchelors, permitted by some arrangement
of Mr Batchelor with the Convict Department to wear a suit.

As part of their belief that Christ wanted property equally distributed,
Mother explained, the Philanthropists wanted the monarchy removed,
and the king of England banished or punished in some French Jacobin
manner. I found this all hard to believe – not that men would propose
it, but that *this* was the nature of my genial father's dereliction.

For by now we were possessors of a pleasant 2000 acre farm, Tiverton,
adjoining the Batchelor estate, and Father, having achieved not only his
ticket-of-leave but being in receipt too of a conditional pardon, had hired
a young free settler to run the farm while he himself conducted four days
a week a respected law practice in Hobart. The habit of ownership had
grown on him. But my grandfather, the fishmonger, had been one of the
chief distributors of Spence's tracts and seditious newspapers – the *Giant
Killer*, or *Anti-Landlord*, for instance – in the North. He was typical,
said Mother, of the self-educated tradesmen, the law clerks, the Wesleyan
preachers of a particular stripe who belonged to that society, and into
which my father had been born.

Naturally, while Mother was willing to talk, I pressed the issue and
found that Father had tried to swear into the Philanthropists the son of
a prominent Tib Street cloth merchant. It was not to be wondered at that
after the Philanthropists had already rioted in London, at Spa Fields –
about which until that moment I had heard nothing – the authorities
should treat my gentle father as if he was of the same colour as the
extremists. But he was not – he would never have been a credible
comrade of the cockade-wearing men who tried to take the Tower and
the Bank of London, their malice, incompetence and drunkenness all
rivalling each other.

The less than fair reality was that Father had been one of the few
Philanthropists transported. That had been due to the excessive fervour

in sentencing by the Manchester magistrates. 'Your father was always,' said Mother, 'too easily influenced by the sight of misery amongst people whose names he did not even know.' That was why his transportation was such a blessing, for whatever could be said of Van Diemen's Land, no one starved, and indeed the lower classes, particularly as represented in the felon and ticket-of-leave ranks, distracted anyone from too much compassion by their frankness, their vulgarity, their poor morals and their dram-drinking.

Now I really saw why Horace was my father's favourite. Take this example: Horace's former-slave father, involved in the fish trade, had sent his son to Athens to study philosophy. Similarly, my grandfather the fishmonger had indentured his son as a law clerk to an 'eminent solicitor' (my mother's term of course). While Horace studied, the assassins of the Emperor Julius Caesar, Brutus and Cassius, arrived in Athens and turned the heads of all the students. While my father studied, he was influenced by his own father towards the Spencean Philanthropists. Having been appointed a military tribune by Brutus, Horace saw him as his fellow philosopher, and volunteered to serve in his republican forces on the battlefield of Philippi, just as Father had agreed to recruit and perhaps fight for the radical Philanthropists. Horace found himself no soldier, just as Father had found himself no revolutionary.

After the republicans were defeated, just as surely as the Spencean Philanthropists were, Horace's property in Apulia had been confiscated for his crime, and yet he came to Rome and through cleverness and charm became a friend of Maecenas, the noble-hearted chief adviser of the young Emperor Augustus. And so ultimately and for a time he was appointed secretary to the Emperor himself!

Father was not secretary to an Emperor, nor had he come to Rome but, in the manner of empires, was sent to a remote island exile. However, he had had a Maecenas, and that Maecenas was Mr William Batchelor, soon to dominate the Van Diemen's Land Legislative Council. Horace's brief flirtation with republicanism was estimated by Maecenas to be an instance more of philosophic exuberance than of any genuine ill will against the institutions of society. So too was Father's by kindly Mr Batchelor.

About the time my closest friend Charlie Batchelor and I reached manhood, news of great pastoral reaches available on the mainland, in New South Wales, arrived in Van Diemen's Land and left us excited. My younger brother, Simon, was similarly stimulated. Our fathers would, after Sunday dinner at Hydebrae, take the maps out. Of all the immensity of New South Wales, only an area as big as Ireland was detailed on these maps. A stretch of coastline somewhat less than three hundred miles, and country inland, about one hundred and fifty miles, as far as the Lachlan river. The Lachlan was the Styx of the mainland, so it seemed – all was oblivion and nullity beyond. Within the line lay the area where government operated, enforced affairs, provided land title, and named things. The limits, beyond which government's writ ceased to run, and things were not named, were called 'the Limits of Location'. The Governor of New South Wales hoped that settlers would constrain themselves to the area within the Limits, and even implied that those who went beyond lacked legitimacy. But even as boys, through reading Hobart newspapers, we knew that many mainland settlers from reputable families had gone beyond the line – that it was not considered dishonourable to do so, and that all of us would try it if we could, expanding the repute of our fathers' names to an extent not possible in the pleasant but narrow valleys of Van Diemen's Land.

Charlie travelled from Hobart to Sydney with me on the sloop *Emu* in a late Australian summer whose air of hope and novelty I shall never forget. Charlie was twenty-four, and a compact, dark-complexioned young man – he attributed his looks to a Cornish grandmother, and owed his hard-headedness and wariness to the Batchelor way of doing things. I was twenty-three, tall and somewhat sandy in appearance, with blue eyes my mother called 'Danish'. Though the son of an elevated convict, I uneasily considered myself Charlie's equal, and there was never anything in Charlie's demeanour to say the contrary.

Visitors from England arriving in that port of Sydney declare its harbour vast and admirable, but for my money it did not match in splendour the long, green approaches to Hobart. Similarly much had been made of the deportment of the 'canaries', the convict labourers in yellow cloth, and of the profligacy and high colour of former London prostitutes, drunk at ten in the morning, lounging at the gates of their little cottages and crying out in eminently resistible lewdness to the passersby. The thing was that Charlie and I were used to felons – Hobart was full of them. There was no novelty for us here, nor had we a reason to visit any of the grandees, the merchants or wool-brokers, of Macquarie Street or Point Piper. We would possess the city ultimately, in our way, we did not doubt. But for now we wished to possess the interior.

I knew that Charlie travelled with some genuine capital in his money belt, as well as having opened an account in the Bank of Australia, the bank favoured by free landholders. I knew too that he had instructions from his father to go to country within the western limits, country on whose qualities Mr Batchelor had been corresponding with some settler of his acquaintance from New South Wales. Charlie was not only to buy a farm of his own on the family's behalf, but was also to purchase some well-balanced flocks of Spanish Merino sheep, by all accounts far preferred in New South Wales than the Romneys and Leicesters of Van Diemen's Land, and put them out to graze to homesteaders within the Limits of Location, according to the arrangement named 'thirds', an arrangement said to be as ancient as the Old Testament. By it, a settler would take an investor's flocks, run them at pasture, pay the annual expenses of convicts to shepherd them and watch them into hurdles by night, bear the expense of shearing and carting the wool to market, and all other incidental expenses from year to year. In return for which he would receive one-third of the wool, and one-third of the annual increase, the lambs to be divided at weaning time each year, that is, about the same time of year as Charlie and I first arrived in Sydney.

My task, however, as suited a man whose resources were far more limited, was to establish in partnership with Charlie some place open for settlement beyond the Limits of Location – that is, to find pastoral land, available free, which had never been grazed since the hand of God set time thundering. The land beyond! Charlie and I would stock it with sheep and cattle, some of them mine, and we would share the costs of equipment for establishing ourselves there, and again I would keep stock books and run his livestock on the normal system of thirds.

So, first, I must search for remoter country. I had, as I have already indicated, limited resources. I possessed a letter of credit for £400 with the Savings Bank of New South Wales, one of whose directors had been transported with my father years past, the Savings Bank being considered the preserve of mad democrats and pardoned convicts and much inferior to the Bank of Australia. This £400 was made up of my wages from my father's farm, Tiverton, and a patrimony of £250 my father had generously settled on me when I turned twenty-three. My first chief item of expenditure was the purchase for £12 of one of those hardy New South Wales stock horses named walers, after New South Wales. These horses were Arab in part, Welsh and Indian in others. The horse in question was a three-year-old, and I was happy to find it had already been named Hobbes, since Father was an admirer of Hobbes's *Leviathan*. 'Hobbes is one of the makers of the world we have,' he told me levelly when I was eighteen. 'He devised the social contract, which benefits us here better than it did back there. Thus he is a prophet of the new world.'

For my journey I had also acquired a saddle, a bridle, a pair of saddle-bags to contain razor, shirts, stockings, spare moleskins, a sealskin cape, a blanket and a kangaroo skin, and the second pistol I had bought to go with the one my father had given me. And, perhaps above all, my copy of Horace, a shield in the barbarous but wonderful outer regions. With the benefit of this equipment, I was a young man precisely where he wanted to be, going precisely where I wanted to go, fitted out with all the wonders of my society, with the affections of distant parents, and the backing of the Batchelors.

Since Charlie had some more business than me in Sydney, he agreed to meet me in Goulburn in a month's time, and I started off, making first for the inland county of Argyle, named in sentiment and perhaps for reassurance after the county in Scotland. My track led me through the little produce market and garrison town of Liverpool, where I had never seen soldiers look paler under their sunburn, nor more stricken with boredom. Past it I was in billowing green-brown country, which resembled very much a massive hide stretched out and spiked to the earth's inner frame with the sometimes white, sometimes fire-blackened shafts of eucalypt trees running limitless to the west. This earth had a very different feel from the dense woods of Van Diemen's Land: more open, that is, more dominated by the sun, and more perilous.

I had sewn £80 into my saddle lining, in case of the bushrangers and outlaws of whom the *London Illustrated News* wrote with such relish. Anyone was welcome, if they asked, to the thirteen shillings and eight pence I carried in my fob. I felt in no way constrained or frightened however. I felt in that most wonderful of Australian eras that I had the run of the unsullied earth.

So Hobbes and I proceeded past Campbelltown and the pastures of Camden, very fine country for animals but grabbed early, even before my father committed his Horatian crime! This was land thick with convict shepherds. Yorkshiremen, children of Erin, Scots from the High-lands, the latter, as my father said, nearly more understandable when they spoke Erse than when they spoke English. And they, in tune with my father's hopeful attitude towards transportation, seemed to be living a life better than they expected. Deliverance through sentence: they had anticipated Hades and been given Arcady. They would wave a eucalyptus staff at the traveller and cry 'Gidday to you Surrh'.

Eighty miles on my way, the little town of Berrima sat, like Ross, on its alluvial ground. But beyond Bong Bong, the country became very lonely, a phenomenon I nonetheless welcomed. Poor soil here, old and unredeemed. Scrawny bush covered it. I got to the summit of the Towrang Hill and looked down into much lovelier ground, with two small rivers running through it, Mulwaree Ponds and the Wollondilli. They met a little below the township of Goulburn. The town itself, spread outwards from Mulwaree Ponds like an encampment, had a population of nearly 3500 souls, one of whom – a Mr Finlay – I had an introduction to.

I arrived at dusk – by way of a red clay driveway – at an excellent brick and sandstone house, a relative rarity in this part of New South Wales. Through trees from his front verandah, the roof of Finlay's brewery could be seen, designed to supply the thirsty county of Argyle.

Finlay was a man of severe features, and his wife in her dark beauty reminded me of handsome Mrs Batchelor. That evening at dinner, I became something of a favourite of his perhaps fourteen-year-old, lustrous daughter, Phoebe. She was of a different order of beauty to that of her mother – it was as if they had decided between them to cover the allotted glories available to womankind, and Phoebe, fair and with green eyes, was in other respects her splendid mater's child. When after dinner, however, she attempted to follow her father and myself onto the verandah, Mr Finlay had only to murmur, 'Please!' to make her disappear, flitting with her golden hair indoors. '*They* don't understand,' he told me, and by *they*, he seemed to mean colonial children. There was a rigidity in his neat frame, his exact shoulders. I read it as representing success. But I was nonetheless pleased to hear him say at the end of our pipe-smoking, 'You must speak to me about investing in livestock with you if you find suitable ground, John.' Thirds, again. The glorious, ancient and now antipodean arrangement which made the world possible for the son of a Spencean Philanthropist.

Phoebe, on leaving the verandah in semi-obedience, had worn a curious little unabashed smile, whose glow remained after the lamps indoors were turned down. *O matre pulchra filia pulchrior*, I reflected of the Finlay women, borrowing the line from Horace. 'O beautiful mother to a yet more beautiful daughter.'

I was delighted visiting Hobbes over the next day to see how quickly my pony took on condition grazing in Mr Finlay's paddock. When on the second morning I saddled him, I was watched from the yard fence by lovely Mrs Finlay, who carried a parasol and was shaded as well by a huge hat, and by Phoebe, echoes of each other, one of the olive cast, one of the light peach. Mrs Finlay said, 'I can see that you are excited at the prospects of the wilderness.'

I admitted that I was.

She said that I must consider myself free to stay with them again whenever I tired of isolation and was passing Goulburn. She said it with some wistfulness, not like a woman who could afford to return to Europe whenever she chose.

The beautiful child, Phoebe, proclaimed, 'I wish I were going to the country out there. Goulburn is marked by nothing but torpor.'

'No it's not,' said her mother. 'It's just your new word.' She murmured to me, 'The young may sometimes fall in love with a word.'

'I would not want to marry,' Phoebe insisted, 'a man who was content with Goulburn's torpor.'

Her mother extended a finger, and spoke with a melancholy fondness. 'Your father will send you to Europe to be tidied up if you fling around abstract nouns as if they were stones.' But then the three of us began laughing like guilty schoolchildren, as if in Mr Finlay's shadow. 'I would be delighted one day to have a daughter like you,' I told Phoebe, but she glowered at me, as if I had cast her in an inferior role in a play.

South of the Finlay estate I entered the area of pasture and native coachwood named the Limestone Plains, where there were few public houses or boarding houses. At the core of each day, about noon, I unsaddled Hobbes and ate a slab of damper with mutton supplied by my host of the previous night and read newspapers from my saddlebag. In the dusk I would look for a glimmer of light or a thread of smoke. I was close to the invisible line, the southern edge of the Limits of Location. Here rich men lived in slab huts, and the owner would call a convict servant to unsaddle a traveller's horse, and turn it out into a grassy paddock. Lying on my kangaroo skin rug, surrounded by other travellers or convict servants and stockmen similarly encouched, I slept deeply by the doused fire. This was hospitality, this was comfort, on the edge of the defined, the outer regions of the limits. Better comfort, I was certain, and a surer hand than you could have anywhere else on earth.

When I left one settler, he would give me instructions on how to reach the next, and I divided the bush of Australia, sure of my time, sure of success, into sweet little daily lumps of twenty or thirty miles in extent,

about the range of my pony *per diem*, and about the extent of sheep and
cattle runs in that part. I soon knew, though I was not precisely sure
when it happened, that I had passed beyond the limits.

I stayed about then with a gentleman at a place named Baldalgo, in a
long, crude slab hut of a kind I would be happy to occupy. He was an
Oxford man, and had a dresser full of classic texts. His father was Arch-
deacon of Wells. He lived joyously in conditions hardly better than those
in which an English herder lived, with smoky sheep's-fat lamps throwing
shadows over his dirt floor, and his only medical remedies being bottles
of spirits and a box of antacid powder. For his casual good humour
alone, his contentment, good fortune and cultivation, I would willingly
have traded places with him.

Further south, the Oxford man had told me, on the edge of the earth,
there was an occupier named Treloar, who lived in Sydney but kept cattle
and sheep in that area under the care of an overseer and convict shepherds. Beyond him lay no occupier at all.

I remarked that there seemed to be few natives in this area.

'You will see them,' he promised me, 'coming and going and being a
pest to your livestock. Sensible chaps, however, they stay in this area
only for the summer, so we will soon be free of them and all their trouble
for some months. The women you know, pox my shepherds.'

I was uncomfortable with this one sour note, since it intruded upon
my Arcadian expectations. 'I thought the pox was a European disease,'
I said, 'and that we are guilty of passing it to them.'

'Oh, in the first instance, yes. But they get it worse than any European
woman would and give it back to the shepherds in a rich, full-blown
form.'

The high plain I rode out on next morning was broad, sometimes with
large glacial stones standing on the earth, and to the west a long range
of mountains, higher than anything in the British Isles. If you crossed
them, the Oxford man had told me, you came ultimately to Port Phillip.
They were streaked even in this late summer with fingers of remaining
snow.

Now gentlemen's fires grew very rare. I came upon the occasional
shepherd's hut of bark and slab timber, and dossed down with English
thieves or Irish rick-burners, or machine-breakers from Nottingham and
Yorkshire. But often I preferred my own company, or more accurately
the company of the country. One late summer night I lay in a scatter of
trees and saw fire moving in an incandescent line along the wooded

ridges. I felt that the Oxford man's dresser of great and benign works were nothing against the scale of the night, which was graced and silvered not only by fire but by a near-full moon.

At some hour I was gently slapped awake by a rise in the breeze. From where I lay I could see every silver underside of every leaf, shimmering greyly above my head. And all around me, marking every limit of my body, my hands swung wide, was the companionable odour of an ancient earth, a great body of unique musk. This worshipful, strange aroma, undisturbed by any human scent but my own, was the product of protean soil laid down before Adam, of the residue of God's first experiments with trees.

I stood up on a potent impulse and removed all my clothes – the clothes of an English or Scottish or Irish farmer, lacking only leggings. I felt the air across my chest like the hand of a father. I was the Englishman over-come with enthusiasm for a barbarous place. I believe that people at Home would have said: this is merely the heathenism which too ripe an alien adventure will raise in the young mind. I was not inhibited by any such reflection. I walked a little way, barefooted, and then lay down in nakedness on loamy earth and began to scoop it up and inhale it. The earth groaned, so I thought, like the beloved, caressed. I rose and walked towards the fluid line of fire – it did not so much advance as roll over the earth sideways like a great viper, leaving what it touched blackened. Past standing stones and up amongst grey-leafed trees I approached it, but not – I hurry to say – with any impulse to self-immolation. Just the same I felt no pain in my feet, and though once falling on my knees, very hard, felt no discomfort. Evoking no surprise in me, the night moaned in its manner, and moaned again. Above me the fire maintained its slow, remote progress – it lacked malice towards me. I tripped on a sandstone ledge, and now felt my skin broken and the great joy drain from me. 'What is this?' I was forced to ask myself. I wanted to get back to Hobbes and dress.

A native child of perhaps four years came tottering along the uneven rise I stood upon. He was as naked as I, and grinning as if it were a contest. His hand was out to claim mine.

'What is it?' I asked.

The native boy who had seized my hand led me some thirty or forty yards, and I bent over now, ashamed, as in a Biblical tale, of my nakedness.

Down the far slope of the hill sat a native woman in a fragment of dress that covered one breast. Foam marked her mouth, and her lips were a little parted. She had *rigor* and was some hours dead. She bore no visible wound and it seemed that something caustic, the fruits of industry in a land far from industry, had been fed to her. The boy seemed to demonstrate her to me, to reach his hands out to show me her seeming easiness, her contentment with her angle of repose. Yet she already had the sick scent of death.

'Is this your Mama?' I asked him. Grinning still, he began to weep, keening and trying with his small hands to heap up leaves and stones around her legs. I put my own hand very firmly on his shoulder to aid him in his distress, and he looked up once, and went so far as to widen the smile, so pronounced for its contrast of anthracite skin and ivory teeth.

I could do nothing but recite aloud, bare as Adam, a *Paternoster* and Psalms 52 and 54 as the little boy continued to scoop and mourn. I must have made, beneath that moon, a ridiculous and helpless sight, but now I had a resolve to get the child away. 'Come, come, come,' I told him. 'I'll fix Mama.' I lifted him and he protested only very softly, and I hobbled with him in my arms back down to my camp and campfire so distinct by starlight now. On this descent the earth hurt my feet savagely, in a way which had not been the case on my ecstatic ascent, and I was very pleased to near my boots and my jacket.

I sat the child by the fire which rubied his smiling face. He pointed into its heart and made a grinning yet grief-stricken comment of approval. I had some shears with me from Goulburn – they were a pair which Mr Finlay had forced upon me. So I picked up my ample blanket and cut a two-foot strip from one end of it. I wrapped this around him and searched for a section of twine I knew was somewhere in my bags, and found it and used it to help fix the blanket at his neck.

He said suddenly, 'Jolly good.' And as if he wanted me to know his gratitude he turned his face full to me and beamed further. I could see he had very fine canine teeth.

At some stage of this business of warming and clothing and pinning up the blanket on the child, I began to bandy the name Felix about. It was not quite a kindly name – his smile had nothing to do with hilarity. Yet it occurred to me, I think, without ill feeling in a country where giving a nickname to another human is considered a form of welcome. 'Hold still there, Felix,' I said. 'Warm those cold little hands, Felix.'

'Smiley' would have done as well, except that it seemed to mock what

was too mad a smiling purpose in the child. 'Felix', involving as it did
the little Latin I had, was a civilised gesture on a barbarous night, and
it had an edge of protest to it as well, as I recalled Horace's words. '*Quo
me, Bacche*,' I wanted to protest, '*rapis tui plenum?*' (Bacchus, what are
you doing with me, as I fill with your godhead? Into what forests and
caverns are you forcing me . . .) For Bacchus had been the night's appropriate god. I had been drunk, after all, without even drinking, and I had
been led as by a god into unfamiliar experiences.

The boy, whimpering and the grimace relaxing a little, sank into a
sleep. Would he wake, this child, who, I now saw clearly, was mulatto,
half-white, half-black? Might it not be merciful if he did not?

Now, clothed but lacking a shovel, I climbed the hill again, and heaped
boulders and stones over the young woman, inspecting her not too
closely, working with some tenderness for Felix's sake. This method of
semi-interment, I had heard many times, was the preferred burial rite
of the natives.

When we woke at dawn, so remotely located and out of the range of
kindly breakfasts, I shared with the child Felix some of the dried beef
I carried, which he ate with a frank appetite and with a quantity of water
from my sealskin bag. Then he staggered away a distance, parted his
blanket coat and urinated very functionally. Throughout this process
his facial rictus remained. When he returned I reached out and took his
cheeks in my hands and tried to ease the grimace with my thumbs,
pressing down on the creases that divided the chaps from the area of
flesh beneath the nose. But he would not let go of his awful grin. I let
him have his way, and when we set off, put him over the saddle in front
of me. He would utter an occasional sentence when he saw some bird
or passed an isolated boulder, and his arms would work beneath his
makeshift cape.

As we climbed to a high plain about mid-morning, I found what were
beyond dispute wagon tracks and a swathe through the grassland such
as is made by even a small herd of cattle. These marks I began contentedly to follow, but took as usual my noon rest. That was my father's
advice: do not let circumstances flood out routine. The child, having been
fed, slept almost instantly in a patch of sun amongst the tall but scattered
trees we found ourselves in. I myself dropped, pipe in teeth, into a medi-
tative drowse.

I woke to find perhaps thirty native men of sundry ages scattered about
our grove – the men, with spears in their hands, considering me calmly.

In the trees above some cloaked old gins, as we call native women, could be seen. The manner of the men was not such as to make me even think of my two loaded pistols in my saddlebag. I felt pleased that they had come for their child! Though someone with more missionary spirit might have wanted to retain him, to introduce him to the benefits of being *us*, I went at once and shook him awake. I took him by the hand – he was pliable to being led – and brought him to two or three older men who were close. Because they wore kangaroo skin capes around their shoulders, they might have recognised my good intent in Felix's blanket cape.

Nudging the boy towards them I caught the whiff of their barbarity, or whatever you would like to call their strangeness – half-rancid, half-woodsmoke. The boy walked past these gentlemen, and with a yelp a young woman broke from behind a tree and scooped him up against her breasts. But two of the older women emerged from thickets of stone and eucalyptus trees with digging sticks in their hands and began lashing at the young woman's lower legs, so that she put Felix down and danced, jumped and howled to get away. I did not know what any of this meant, yet it looked more like an enactment than discipline.

I gazed at one of the old men and touched my face. 'Why does he grin?' I asked, myself then grinning with clenched teeth. The men stared at me, judges in Israel, an austere panel. The most apparently senior one displayed for a second the same sort of extreme grin. I could not tell whether this was courtesy, explanation, satire or dismissal. But he turned his back and moved away at an easy, long-thighed, if bow-legged, gait. The others followed, older women beating the howling gin, or *lubra*, as younger women were sometimes called, away from Felix, who covered one eye with a hand but seemed to observe the entire departure through his other orb. He muttered, but was not moved yet to tears. It seemed mere seconds before he and I were on our own, in vacated country with each other.

The tracks I had earlier seen led me and my young companion into a narrowly contained valley, a rocky escarpment showing to the west. About four o'clock, as the light was getting flinty and the air cold, I saw two little slab cabins and a stockyard with three horses. Smoke came up promisingly from one cabin, but from somewhere amongst the blackbutt trees two miles off on the ridge above came a parallel tuft of smoke – the native people who had rejected Felix, or an illegal still from which some lawless passholder or absconder made his living. After tethering Hobbes, I let a drowsy Felix down. He tottered off but I restrained him with a hand.

A bark door had already creaked open. 'Heard you on your way,' an appeasing and somehow untrustworthy voice said. It came from some-where in the north of England, though it did not owe its archness to any region.

'Turn my horse out in the yard?' I asked in the normal, rough New South Wales way, not wanting to be thought above myself. Grammati-cally all I needed was the gruff vernacular appropriate to the slab hut before which I stood.

Felix had descended from Hobbes in a way which made it plain he wanted to be taken in my arms. When I lifted him, he seemed to fall at once asleep.

'A fine little fellow,' said the voice whose owner now stood in the shade of his bark verandah.

As I advanced with Felix I saw a tall, stooping man with a long face and features kippered by sun. He seemed to be ageless, though he might have been forty years. I carried the child past him indoors, and was at once aware of a number of presences in the room – other journeyers and stockmen.

'Set the child there,' said the man, following me and pointing to an oily sheepskin in the corner.

While I put Felix down on it, the tall man watched me through squinting, unscannable eyes.

By the fire two men in boots, dungarees and red shirts sat, smoking pipes, on bits of log. Their wine-dark eyes, set amidst leathery skin and huge amounts of hair, moved languidly over me. They had pannikins of liquor in their hands. I saw one of them reach out with his foot and nudge the boot of the other, to make sure he had properly weighed my entry. They were, I guessed, former prisoners of the queen. The same could be said for the man who had invited me in and who stood by the table, amiable in a worn shirt and moleskins tied below the knees.

'So yeh're welcome to the yard, mister,' he told me. 'Let me fill these boys' pannikins. Make this home yeh own and when yeh're ready join us by the fire.'

He went up to the hairy men seated on logs. Their crude possum skin coats lay by them on the floor. He refilled their mugs with a clear and thus potent liquor from a stone jug, then set it down on his slab timber table, returned to me, winked, and nodded towards the door, despite his earlier invitation to warm myself, asking for a conference.

Outside, the hutkeeper's breath flumed in the steely afternoon. 'Even at this time of year, sir, it can be cold evenings.' We walked across to Hobbes. 'Oh Jesus,' he said, but disapprovingly. 'Nice bloody little pony, sir. And bloody nice tack.'

I looked at him askance.

'Those visitors of mine indoors. Nameless fellows. Aren't such bad fellows as all that. But flogged men, yeh see. Therefore spoiled men. Runaways from work gangs. No ticket-of-leave like myself. Nothing to lose. Which makes nice pony and nice tack a problem. Unless, of course, they like yeh. They have their code, yeh know.'

'I'd heard,' I said, beginning to unsaddle Hobbes, whose back smoked in the failing light. I asked his name.

'I'm Goldspink, sir, the overseer. This is Mr Treloar's run, Bulwa Mountain, ye're on. But my stockman and wagon-driver are off at an outstation, so I am solitary here to welcome yeh.'

I told Goldspink my own name.

'Has a Biblical ring, thinks I,' he told me. 'Well then my dear Mr Bettany, I'd say don't put yer tack in the outhouse. Sleep on yer saddle, if I were yeh. Use saddle bags as a bed bolster and adopt no airs. Drink little and seem to drink much. That's the rule in this part of the known and unknown world, sir. No trouble with me, sir. Did I say I have my ticket-of-leave?' And he pulled from his pocket a creased and grimy certificate, unfolded it and showed me his name and the absolving signature of Governor Bourke. And though he was playing at old world servility, he was also making sure I knew I'd get none here.

We turned Hobbes into the home yard, and Goldspink closed the gate. 'I wonder where yeh found the little black man?'

'I encountered him last night,' I told him, as if it did not matter.

I carried the bridle, saddle and bags on my shoulder back into the slab hut. The men by the fire, Goldspink had implied and I had guessed, had permanently escaped from government service and were living wild in the bush off kangaroo and stolen livestock. In carrying indoors to them my bank notes and cash sewn in my saddle, I may have more or less carried my death warrant. But I was calm. Indeed, I was stimulated, as if I had come here for this encounter, this test.

In the corner the sheepskin was now over Felix's head. I could not assess the conditon of his face. One of the men by the fire gestured lazily with a hand to acknowledge my entry. They talked deeply and in lowered voices to each other in the Irish tongue – in Van Diemen's Land as in New South Wales a common method of Gaelic convicts for closing the shutters on strangers. I placed my saddle and bridle and bags in the hut corner, making of them a rampart around the child. Goldspink poured me a tin mug full of grog, and I sat at the table in the middle of the hut, not wanting to claim a place too close to the fire, and momentarily stung my lips with it.

'Very good,' I told Goldspink.

As the Irish runaways by the fire continued to exclude me from their company, I told Goldspink about Felix and my afternoon meeting with the natives. I wanted to narrate the story enthusiastically, as an exceptional narrative. But the way Goldspink nodded his head was meant to tell me that this was a tale he was used to. He looked at the absconders too, suggesting with his hands I keep what I said unheard by them. 'These lads live to the west,' he told me. 'Savage bastards. Take black women as *dibbunuk*. When they're done or tired, they poison the poor gins.'

I didn't have to ask what *dibbunuk* meant. So, was I proposing to share a hut with the killers of native women?

'I saw the little boy smiling,' said Goldspink. 'I'd smile round those lads, sir.'

'But if it's true, what you're suggesting, I must go. I must report the death.'

'On a night like this, sir? Yer intentions to speak to authorities would be pretty bloody clear. Wouldn't they, sir?'

'Let them be clear!' I said.

'But do ye have the latest pistols, sir, to ward such fellows off? And the infant ... How could yeh go off in the night and take the infant?'

And the nearest magistrate was in Goulburn, a huge march away. Nonetheless my father had been careful never to permit his family to exclude the savages from the list of humankind – he retained that from his Spencean Philanthropist days. The death would need reporting, and if the men by the fire were accounted guilty, so should it be.

So began a peculiar night. Leaving the absconders by the fire with their pipes, I helped Goldspink cook some damper and offered him a little of my tea to pay for the night's accommodation and the liquor I had pretended to savour. At Goldspink's call, the Irish escapees joined us at table. I sat with the sleepy child in my arms, placing morsels of mutton in his mouth. He kept his face averted from what might have been his mother's murderers, yet with the demeanour of a normally shy infant.

Through their asking from each other for salt or a slab of damper, I discovered their preferred names were Tadgh and Captain, Tadgh no more older than I behind the thickets of hair and what weather had done to his face. Captain, a wishful name, had grey in his russet beard and sometimes Tadgh called him Captain Rowan, and sometimes Tadgh's name, Brody, emerged. In their company, which proved not uncongenial, it was most weirdly easy to forget by the second what Goldspink had accused them of.

'Whatever part of God's Britain d'you come from?' Captain Rowan asked me from the blue.

I looked at him levelly. 'I am Manchester-born,' I told him.

'I see now,' said Rowan, chewing mutton. 'Find that babby?'

'Found him in the bush.'

'You're the lucky one.'

He looked to Tadgh to laugh with him, but the young man's features remained innocently dark, though his eyes never left me.

The meal over, the two runaways were up without apology to attend to nature.

'Very well then,' said Goldspink, while the absconders were out of the hut. 'Those lads like yeh well enough for now. It won't be so easy when yeh come back with livestock. Capital is blessing and curse for a fellow, I can say, being utterly flat myself. Now it would be twenty-five miles from my ample residence here to the hut of Mr Treloar's last shepherds. But I could show a young fellow of capital, if that's what yeh are, a little something beyond, to the south-west. Grassy uplands there. High meadow would be another name for it. Not all of the quality of the country closer in ... the best has a way of going first, as is clear and plain.'

I agreed that was obvious truth and stood up, disguising my hope that Goldspink might be of aid to me, and put down the sleeping native child in our nest of rugs in the corner. Goldspink followed me. 'If I showed yeh something to yer liking, I surmise I could expect a small capital reward?'

I chose not to be too forthcoming. 'My resources are naturally enough deposited with the bank. But I would pledge an appropriate gratuity.'

'A poor fellow dreams of herds,' Goldspink murmured without bitterness.

The runaway Irishmen strode back indoors and settled themselves by the fire. This closeness to the hearth was their unspoken reward for being dangerous and hard to predict, for leading an uncertain life.

'When could this visit to the right land be arranged?' I asked Gold-spink, probably too eagerly.

'Why tomorrow,' he said. 'While yeh're a guest of the country.'

Settled against my saddle, for some reason I was very much at ease. Outside a huge wind scraped against the ridge. Astoundingly, in view of the company I was resting in, with the child of the murdered woman by my side, I contentedly put my hand into a saddlebag, hugging it to me, and took out the Horatian *Odes*. Through fighting at Philippi with the republican assassins of Caesar, Horace destroyed his own father, Horatius Senior, an up-jumped slave whose land in Venusia was confiscated as penalty for his son's folly. On the other hand my father, without once wielding a knife, had by Jacobin fervour saved his children from landless Manchester, and brought his son to such a fine fire as this, amongst the lost and the absconded, and on the edge of huge pastures to be delivered to me directly from God's hand with Goldspink as possible midwife.

I looked occasionally to the fire, where Captain Rowan had wrapped up his russet body in skins and was sleeping. But then the younger man, Tadgh was there above me, fully dressed though on bare feet.

'The babby, mister,' he remarked.

'Yes?' I said. He was scratching the stitching of my saddle with a toe. I resisted punching his ankle.

'You ought leave him alone.'

'I found him by his dead mother.'

Was this the ambush? Would I have room at least to stand up to defend myself? I had eased onto my elbow and then half sat up.

'I know, I know the tale,' said the rogue with utter indifference.

'His people won't take him.'

'I know that one too,' said Tadgh. 'It's the taint, you see.'

'I think it all disgraceful.'

Tadgh laughed privately. 'Oh Jesus now, it certainly is that. But if kind you should shoot him, before some shepherd of Treloar takes unkind hold of him.'

I felt rash. 'No one will take hold, kind or unkind. I intend to present him to the authorities.'

'Ah then. Those authorities. They're the boys all right.' He yawned. 'Poor little feller, he is. See this now?' He turned, dropped his coat off his shoulders and pulled up his shirt. Sure enough, his back had the tracks of the flail criss-crossing it, and the dead blue and white of scar. 'Read this testament, sir. It's an old language, this one. Older than the Barns of Joseph.'

'Barns of Joseph?'

He went on displaying the scars. 'Those pyramids built by slaves, sir, in Pharaoh's Land. If you read this right you see it's my title deed to the mountains beyond. I hope a man like yourself could respect such a document.'

'It is not a licence for doing whatever you want.'

Facing me from his bed of laths and leather opposite, Goldspink, frowning, clearly hoped I would not spoil his night or my prospects by making any improbable protest.

'Well, sir,' Brody said in a murmur which sounded very like exhaustion, 'I think it might be a licence to be let breathe, you understand.' And he pulled his coat on again and went without looking at me and lay near his friend.

I was not further disturbed at any point of the night.

When I woke the next dawn I found the hut empty of humans and invaded by grey light from the half-opened door. The absconders were vanished. But so were Felix and Goldspink. I jumped from my blankets and ran barefoot out into the frost-rimed shadow of Goldspink's bark portico. From here, the overseer could be dimly seen beyond a screen of saplings, stooping at the stream below the hut. He seemed to be watching over his shoulder and yelled, 'The boy, Mr Bettany!' the instant he saw me. I ran to join him, and found him hauling naked Felix from the stream. 'I found him floating in the stream when I came for ablutions,' said Goldspink. 'He must've wandered out earlier and the boys pushed him under.' I admit I wondered if the truth was that he'd been drowning him himself when I woke, and had now converted murder to a rescue. But my suspicion was lulled when he put the limp boy up against a tree trunk and said with unfeigned moral bemusement, 'The interesting thing – they would have done it as a mercy.'

I took Felix in my arms and squeezed him until he coughed and his eyes flickered, and turning him over, shook his body until he retched water. Behind me, Goldspink said, 'The Captain and Tadgh are gone from the scene. I need to say though, sir, as an honest Christian, I've seen that boy and his mother. They lived near one of my stockmen for a time. The boy may know my face, I think.'

Felix, redeemed a second time in a few days, coughed and gagged in my arms.

'So it might have been your stockman who used her and tired of her?'

'Please, sir, please!' said Goldspink with such earnest outrage that I felt bound to believe him. 'I would not put my Mr Treloar in such a bad position as to draw the border police down on Bulwa Mountain. That above all is what the man hates. Intrusion from the government, sir. Magistrates he hates; surveyors he abominates; clerks from the Colonial Secretary or the Convict Department raise his special ire, sir. As for inquiries about natives ... well, I think ye've got the drift. What I say to yeh, sir, is this. After I've pointed out the likely country to yeh, take the little chap away to Goulburn and put him with a missionary.'

'Nice of you to spend my money for me,' I commented, still holding the reviving Felix upside down.

He held out a preventive hand. 'Sir, I wouldn't presume to say. But the tiny fellow should be put anywhere safe!'

Felix's eyes opened and my own eyes all at once clouded with tears. I smiled at him with something like parental relief, then rushed him back to the hut and swathed him in the rough but comforting texture of a possum rug. He did not howl – he made a low, monotonous humming. The more he revived the more his crazed grin was restored. Casting about, I found Felix's little blanket-cum-cape in a corner. Whether he wandered forth to his accident, or was rudely snatched by Tadgh and the Captain, he had gone out naked to his death.

Behind me Goldspink was industriously feeding the fire with the dry wood of the region which conveniently fell from trees and provided kindling without the necessity of an axe. Such were the mercies of this marred paradise, which like Eden had suffered its founding murder, and in which, depending on one's angle of view, a child had been half-redeemed or half-murdered.

'Course,' Goldspink said, 'there's likelihood of other gentlemen coming through here asking after country. I would like to put ye in place before that should happen. I shall show ye wondrous country, sir.' How I liked that phrase 'wondrous country'.

I offered Goldspink £30 if he agreed to act as my guide. I wished to see the promised region as soon as I might, so that I could cut blazes on trees and know, however briefly, the land for which I would need to buy stock. So we packed quickly, then Goldspink and I, with a restored but restive Felix travelling perforce on my saddle, rode out past Treloar's last, squalid shepherd's hut. There Goldspink dismounted to talk to the hut-keeper, and I was thinking of descending too, to put some tea into Felix, but the poor, near-mute, grimacing child let out a whimper of protest.

'You will see nice country, Felix,' I promised him above the wind.

Goldspink reappeared from the hut, and we crossed a little creek in rising country and rode through a pass between wooded ridges, during which it seemed the child was torpid or asleep. We were now south of Treloar's last sheep and, on Goldspink's advice, I marked a number of trees with a hatchet he had brought with him, and saw to my joy that all trees and boulders were free of human scars. The light was sharp as we came into a great, open natural parkland, scattered with trees and strewn about with great smooth stones which looked deliberately placed, like the work of some tribe who believed in a plurality of gods. On the mountain ahead, to the south-west, great storm clouds lay like a promise, and a river, its track marked by native oaks, its surface high, threw back the shifting sun's cold light.

'This country,' said Goldspink, 'our native stockman tells me is named Nugan Ganway.'

'What's it mean?' I was happy for it to mean anything at all.

'Dratted if I know, sir. Maybe the little lad can tell yeh. The natives have these names ... I'd say it meant: plenty gibbers, big bloody stones, or something similar. Yeh see there that hollow hill above the river? That's a good place to put a hut, I'd say.'

He indicated the dome of a low, boulder-strewn hill. So the site of my future homestead was pointed out by the ambiguous Goldspink, though that did not mean I had grounds to reject the idea. I had already extracted the £30 in bank notes and had it in my jacket. I paid it over now, to release him. For I wanted to be rid of him. If he rode hard, and into the early evening, he could make his southernmost shepherds' hut.

'Look to the little chap there now!' he cried as his horse trotted off and left Felix and me to our own sweet devices. I rode up into the saddle-backed hill Goldspink had pointed out and made my camp there, secure from winds. Making fire and brewing tea, I let the poor bemused child rest, fed him occasional sips from my mug, and lumps of mutton from my saddlebag. I was Horace in Venusia, in benign hills, by kindly streams.

'Jolly good,' said the poor child.

As much as I already felt for him and was growing to like him I had not come to New South Wales to become guardian of a black child. Returning north and seeing a thread of smoke from a wooded ridge to my west, a sign of natives, I was overtaken by the sense that, given the misadventures which had been imposed upon him, he was surely better with his own, who were just then cooking wallaby or kangaroo above us. They could not, seeing him from a height, alone in the plain, abandoned by myself, finally reject him. I could not deny him a final chance for reunion with his kind.

When he was drowsy after our midday meal I sat him in his little blanket surcout under a tree and made gestures of such friendly but firm emphasis that he knew he was to stay there. His mouth contorted but no tears came, and I mounted Hobbes and rode away, but kept the child always in sight. I must have ridden two miles on to a saddle amidst hills from which in a sparkling day I could see him seated still in place, reduced by distance to a scintilla, a little jot on the hour's huge manuscript. I would have liked to have had a glass to train on him, and I swore I'd bring one back to Nugan Ganway with me. I waited and he did not move. I hoped he slept. His fidelity to remaining a speck was terrible for me to see, and though I waited some time there was no sign of anyone emerging to claim him, and the smoke from the ridge had vanished. It had been a simple-minded concept of mine anyhow, and I realised it grew from a disordered and wrong-headed feeling that in this country I was perpetually watched by the sable brethren. Now, in that immense natural Australian sphere which lay before me, the remote child took on the look of the sort of ragged fragment of life only a brute could abandon.

I turned Hobbes about and rode back down to him. As I went I felt a strange delight that the little fellow was not lost to me. I was reclaiming him with a new seriousness of intent now. As I neared he stood up. I had only permissively to pat Hobbes's crop, and the small, grinning, humourless, homunculus, the child of unimagined gods, was with a fluid action lodged in front of me again in the saddle, and tucked into my body.

At noon some days later, we reached at last that excellent and happy household of Mr Finlay of Goulburn, where I waited for Charlie Batchelor to arrive back from the west, having left a message for him as arranged at Mandelson's Hotel. I would happily have recruited Felix into this instructive company. But he was rather younger than Finlay's son, and I did not know what the father would have thought of joining the English child with the native child. I left the boy therefore with the Finlays' Irish cook. She seemed pleased to have him, and promised to look after him over the next few nights, though she asked me, 'Whatever is it wrong with the little feller's face there, sir?'

Going to the house, I waited for handsome Mrs Finlay to rise from her afternoon rest and for Mr Finlay to return from a visit to one of his outlying stations. I contemplated setting out to report the death of a native woman to the police magistrate. But it would be better to wait for Mr Finlay to introduce me, as the magistrate would treat my story seriously if I came recommended.

Aimless for now, I stumbled into the library looking for something to read, and saw the daughter and the little son of the household being tutored. As I went to withdraw, the fair-haired daughter, Phoebe, left her seat and rushed to me, taking me by the wrist.

'*Monsieur Juneau*,' she said to the tutor, who stood watching her tiredly. '*Nous avons un visiteur. Monsieur Juneau, permettez moi de vous presenter Monsieur Bettany. Monsieur Bettany, Monsieur Juneau.*' Juneau, who wore a butternut, rough-woven suit and no neckcloth must have been one of the Canadian prisoners, the rebels of Quebec, whom many householders sought to employ to teach their colonial children the rudiments of French. '*Monsieur Bettany est un Vandemonien*,' the beautiful but forthright girl told her harried convict teacher. My father had begun, like him, as a teacher of free children. 'Not a citizen of Van Diemen's Land,' I corrected her, lest she lead me ill-equipped into a morass of French. 'I am a citizen of New South Wales now. What's that? *Nouveaux Galles de Sud?*' Indeed, the hope of my land lay more warmly and certainly in me than the last time I had seen her.

Soon Mr Finlay intended to send these children away from him – he had spoken of Harrow for his son and for his daughter a Swiss finishing school. I wondered if they would do better there than they would with sad-eyed Juneau, who had the face of a cultivated man.

On his return, I found that Mr Finlay had kindly invited people to dinner to meet me, and was pleased to hear that one of them would be Mr Gonfleur, the police magistrate, and his wife. Gonfleur, as it turned out, was an older man with a kind of opaque humour in his face and, from the way he talked, half an eye on planned return and retirement to

Norfolk. Mrs Gonfleur too pined for the fens. They wanted quit of the country I had only just found! I looked for an opportunity to alert Mr Gonfleur to the murder of Felix's mother but was interrupted by the arrival of Charlie Batchelor. He was better dressed than I, who wore the same trousers I had worn on my ride, with one of Mr Finlay's borrowed coats and my spare boots. In his compact, olive handsomeness, his colonial wiriness, Charlie was a robust sight.

We sat almost at once to dinner, drinking claret from Finlay's own vineyard. The men at table questioned me about the land I had located, and Charlie listened keenly to what I said on that. But they, as complimentary as they were of my efforts, moved quickly to Charlie and his search for a property to the west. It was ever thus in New South Wales that whomsoever you met, you could always work up a conversation about land and livestock. As Charlie answered, he engaged my eye and smiled at me. 'Jonathan,' he told me, 'I have not yet found the property I wanted but I have used my capital to purchase three thousand ewes. I've put them out with two settlers, north in the Bathurst area, and at Menai, for three years. I have of course enough in reserve to stock your place, Jonathan. It's the best thing to do while prices are high and while I look further west. My Menai gentleman, MacLean—'

'Captain Maclean of Menai?' asked Mr Finlay, in his voice the measure of approbation for which Charlie was looking.

'Yes, and Barton of the Bathurst region. And of course I have my joint effort at this . . .'

I could not believe he had forgotten the name of the land I had found. That it did not have for him the nature of an essential password.

'These fellows you've left your stock with, they are trustworthy men?' I asked, as much to annoy him or bring him back to himself as anything else. 'After all, Charlie, we know nothing of this colony.'

Mr Finlay and his friends were laughing. 'Do you think these men are absconders or ticket-of-leave men, Mr Bettany? No one would dare say they did not keep exact stock books. Well-kept stock books are the basis of most New South Wales friendships and of New South Wales honour. There's little enough honour anywhere else, the dear God knows.'

Everyone at table was willing to chuckle at my doubts about Charlie's stock holders, Captain McLean and Mr Barton, who had honour other sections of the populace lacked. Mr and Mrs Gonfleur, Mr and Mrs Finlay, and Charlie all shared in this communion of honour, and it seemed to me their laughter was the laugh of free people against convict people, *and* against their offspring, if I chose to have sensitive feelings, which I had taken a vow to prevent myself ever indulging in. For my mother had always been careful to instruct me that my father, though rash, had a nobility of impulse which transcended the banalities of trading which characterises free settlers. He was thus higher, not lower, than many an aimless free settler who stumbled upon colonial wealth, and as a result of that happy accident imitatively adopted the rituals of an honour which was not innate. *Captain* Maclean? Was *captain* such a dazzling rank? It was, I thought, losing my head a second, a characteristic New South Wales one – the bush was scattered with captains, but rarely with colonels and never with generals.

'And a man might always inspect their books,' said Charlie now, adopting his mode of being the hard-headed Australian. 'Just in case their English honour overlooks a few strays.'

But this was all right. All chuckled. A gentleman could make jokes about a colonial gentleman's shavings and dodges! But then I calmed myself. This joke of Charlie's, I thought, was the sort of daring witticism he had acquired from my father, his tutor, from my father's version of that great surviving spirit, Horace, which could flame first under one dispensation – republican – then under another – imperial, and be a man under both. Charlie's observation suddenly made me at home at this table of men who pretended they were something more elevated than in fact was the case. What would Mr Gonfleur be, returned to England? A man who had held an obscure job in an obscure colony, and – very likely – never stopped boring people about it. And Charlie subtly knew this, and the reason he knew it was my father's urbanity as a tutor.

'And are you all spent out?' I asked Charlie as a joke.

'It depends what you have for us, Jonathan. Tell me. This place of yours . . .'

I did not answer at once, and the table looked at me. I began. 'Some one hundred and sixty miles south of this spot, beyond the land occupied by Mr Treloar, lies a huge, high natural pound of at least two hundred square miles in extent. It is good open pasture scattered with boulders and seems to me particularly suited for sheep. It is bounded by some creeks of the Murrumbidgee River on the north, and its natural limit is set only by snowclad mountains which separate it, or so I presume, from the Port Phillip regions beyond.'

'And how high is this pasturage?' asked Charlie, his eyes alight.

'A little more than two thousand feet, I am told.' It was a guess but proved a surprisingly accurate one. 'The lank kangaroo grasses in profusion. Native herbs and sedges. I would assess it to be excellent sheep country though capable of frost, even sometimes in summer.' I remembered the wetness of Goldspink's home yard the morning Felix was hauled from the stream. 'As for cattle, well, cattle are hardy, as they say.'

Mrs Finlay suddenly spoke from her ignored place at the table's end. 'This country has made a profound impression upon you, Mr Bettany.'

'Oh,' I said, 'I feel that though I have just seen it, I have blazed its trees and feel it is the country of my heart.'

'Bravo,' she said. 'Not too many other men can make such a happy assertion.'

'Yes indeed,' said Mr Finlay. 'You have made a mighty ride.'

'And seen things,' I announced, as if preparing Mr Gonfleur, 'not usually encountered.'

At last the two women dutifully withdrew, and we who had stood for their departure stretched luxuriously and yawned. Loosening his neckcloth, Mr Finlay fetched port from the sideboard and we gathered to one end of the table.

'Mrs Finlay tells me you brought a little sable chap in on your pony,' remarked Mr Finlay, pouring.

'I have been waiting all night to talk to Mr Gonfleur of this,' I admitted with relief. I related how I had found the boy's mother, and promised Mr Gonfleur that with the help of Goldspink I could lead him to the absconders to whom the responsibility for her death could credibly be affixed. Mr Gonfleur held up both hands crossed at the wrist, a gesture designed as if to halt charging horses.

'My young friend. I must say I believe we are years from the first successful prosecution for the murder of a native woman, regrettably common as that phenomenon might be. We are indeed years from placing a magistrate in the area in which your alleged murder occurred. This is not Van Diemen's Land, neat as a nut and nicely contained. First you, the groundbreaker, sir! And then some years or decades after you, we hope, the institutions and the reach of law.'

'So I am to let them go free, in the same reach of country as I inhabit?'

'I admire your refined conscience, Mr Bettany. I too consider the killing of a native to be murder. But how to sheet it home to fellows? And could it not equally have been one of Treloar's shepherds?'

I told him they had tried to drown Felix before they departed Treloar's.

'Well,' he said, and I could gauge his frustration as an official of the system of justice, 'I am sad to tell you they are far down the list of matters to be attended to. There are enough such murders *within* my district. I have had two ticket-of-leave women strangled by some evil chap in the past month. I shall deny this was ever said. But if you are aware of the genuine guilt of these fellows, perhaps when you are established you could arm your men and take your own recourse.'

There was a low, sputtering laugh from Mr Finlay. But I found I was reluctant to let the serpent of the spoiled blood of the Captain and Tadgh into my new-found garden.

'But if nothing can be done for the mother, what is one to do with the child?' I asked.

'You might take him to clergymen, who locate such cases.'

'I am not sure ...'

'Well, if you've developed an affection for the little savage, we have a most reforming schoolmaster here in Goulburn might take him. Advertises in the *Vindicator*.'

'Hugely pious,' Mr Finlay remarked, suddenly a little drunk. 'Name of Loosely. He takes the children of thieves and promises them peerages, or at least a seat in the Commons.'

'I think such a pedagogic policy is splendid, Johnny,' Charlie suggested to me with a wink. 'Send your little Negrito chap there!'

Later I would think that it is often in our lightest moments and with casual remarks that we summon up real eventualities. Sore-headed in the morning, I was pleased to find a copy of the rather Whiggish, emancipist *Vindicator* in the breakfast room, and looked for notice of Mr Loosely's school. I read:

Modern Evangelical School,
Mr Matthew Loosely (MA, Oxon.), former Secretary, Anti-Slavery Society, Bristol; Corresponding Secretary, Prison Reform Society, London, is pleased to announce the commencement of a Grammar School designed for both colonial and English-born students, conducted according to the principles of the Common Book of Prayer and deploying a curriculum which includes, as well as the study of the Classics, due attention to History, Natural Science, Deportment and Social Behaviour. Mr Loosely is pleased to stand

by the principle that the children of both Bond and Free settlers are equally welcome, for how else is the principle of Liberal Brotherhood and Social Cohesion to be imbued in a colony which will not Forever be based on the Labour of Assigned Slaves? Prospectuses available from the school, 27 Grafton Street, and from the offices of the Goulburn *Vindicator*.

It was precisely the sort of school Mr Finlay would go to great expense not to send his son to. I fetched young, compliant Felix from the cook. He certainly seemed to possess a great capacity to study and adapt to habits one might have thought were strange to him. For he sat up drinking tea from a cup like a little Englishman. Still wearing his blanket cape as well as a small pair of knee pants the cook had in decency found for him, he grimaced studiously as I led him away from her kindly presence. The cook clasped my hand, as convict cooks were not unknown in their Gaelic familiarity to do, and said with tears flowing, 'Sir, if I might say to you be kindly. I had three wee creatures myself I must leave behind when I was shipped.'

A groom saddled Hobbes, and we mounted and were away. I found the Grafton Street address and left Felix standing beneath a tree outside the small colonial cottage. After knocking at the part-open front door, and getting no answer but the drone of a male voice from within, I entered to discover Mr Matthew Loosely instructing an assortment of some seven colonial children. Some bare-footed, they sat in the second of two upright pews, and attached to the back of the seat in front of them was a flap of wood which could be raised to make a desk of sorts. Mr Loosely's children indeed appeared to be the children of pardoned convicts who lived in town, where some of them ran profitable businesses, including – as Mr Gonfleur had complained at one point last night – illicit stills in Goulburn's skirtings of bush.

The instructor, a little brownish-complexioned man no older than thirty, was pointing to a map of the Roman Empire which hung from an easel, and introducing his charges to the mysteries of Rome's First Servile War, taking a very sympathetic view of the slave general Eunus. 'These slave men and women of Sicily were not distinguished from their masters in any way. So the resentment which immortal souls naturally harbour towards bondage sought merely a spark to ignite it. The spark was provided, children, by a tyrannous master named Damophilus, a landowner of Enna.' He pointed to the map of Sicily as a red-headed cornstalk child reverently yawned. I could see that Mr Loosely blazed with a sort of banked energy, and I noticed in his pupils both a lack of timidity and a liveliness I could not help but approve of. He noticed me observing him from the door, and called, 'Mrs Loosely. Please.' Mrs Loosely, tall, pale and full in the body, entered from a door, and he handed her the pointing stick as indication she was in temporary command.

'Sir, follow me,' he said and led me out into the patch of garden in front of his house to converse.

'Mr Loosely,' I began, 'I listened fascinated while eavesdropping at your door.'

'Thank you, sir. We must remember that the history of the servile rebellions of Rome was written to glorify those who suppressed them. The offspring of former assigned convicts may need that critical knowledge to negotiate their way in this society, and see history written aright.'

I pointed out the waiting Felix.

Mr Loosely peered. 'Is he black, or is he a mulatto?'

'I do not absolutely know the answer to that question. But I think half-caste.'

'Oh,' he said in a particular way so that I realised he presumed the child was mine. 'And his name?'

'His name is ... his name is Felix. I found him by his dead mother beyond the limits nearly two hundred miles from here. He is a promising little fellow who seems to be about four years of age, and I would be happy to pay for him to attend your academy should you find room for him amongst your boarders. I assume you have boarders?'

'The two with shoes are boarders,' he told me flatly. 'In that regard, what the child is wearing now would not be satisfactory.'

'I would fit him out fully,' I told Mr Loosely, 'or leave a sum with you out of which it could be done. And since I intend to live remotely, I could leave with you an amount which would see him set up for at least a year with you. Mr Finlay could vouch for me.'

'The extreme Exclusivist!' murmured Mr Loosely, with a rumour of a smile. 'But I shall accept your good character if you will accept my MA.'

'Is there any doubt about that?' I asked with a half smile, though I had wondered.

'I give you my word of honour that I am utterly equipped to turn the children of convicts into scholars and that even though men in far-off places, especially New South Wales, regularly and falsely claim home distinctions, such as college degrees from Oxford and her lesser sister Cambridge, my qualifications are utterly as stated. I would not blame you for doubting though.'

'I envy you your capacity to look down on Cambridge,' I told him. 'I am afraid my Vandemonian father could not in the end afford to send me there.' Not that I grieved in any way for that. Cambridge would have distracted me from my discovery of mainland Australia, restricting me perhaps to some Hobart law office. 'But the question which has occurred to me,' I continued, pressing close upon what I knew would raise passion in him, 'is whether there might be any member of the sable brethren who is capable of achieving a baccalaureate. You have in this child, whom I will present to you, and of whose welfare I shall, despite my remote station, never be negligent, perhaps the chance for such a thing. You have the proof to all of Australia that there exists no inherent flaw in the native race. I have seen this child, and he has travelled with me, and I have observed him to have as much intellectual capacity as any convict child. His silences and reticence seem related more to the horrors he has seen than to any inherent intellectual inferiority.'

Loosely was certainly tickled by the glorious vanity of it. He laughed. 'No more intellectual inferiority, I take it, than any Exclusive's son or daughter.'

This is what my father, young and inflamed, must have been like, wanting to turn society on its head and shake it till the money fell from its pockets and rang around the ears of the despised.

In the spirit and exuberance of our joint experiment, I handed over a £5 bank note to him, but he insisted that two pounds would do for the moment, and from that he would fit Felix out. I was delighted, being now a party to a grand social experiment. It was an experiment I would not care to discuss with Mr Finlay or Charlie, who might think it over-imaginative and a fatuous thing. But I felt that every shilling I handed Loosely celebrated my father, and his quiet belief in the civilised impulse.

I took Felix by the hand, muttering reassurances to him, and brought him over. Mr Loosely asked me what was wrong with his face and I told him it was a rictus. 'I believe I can cure that,' said Mr Loosely lightly, in a way which I was somehow confident did not imply cruelty. I patted Felix on the head and shook his limp hand, and we left him sitting with his awful compliance, more affecting than the wailing of ten other children, on a bench in the hallway as Mr Loosely saw me out to Hobbes.

'I am the grandson of a West Indian slave,' he told me suddenly. 'Otherwise I am a European. But I cherish that despised blood that runs in me, as despised blood ran in the tribe of Judah. I shall cherish the little fellow.'

'Good,' I said. And then, as a riposte, suddenly in competition with him for humble origins: 'Nor am I the heedless gentleman you consider me to be. My father was a convict.'

'It is possible to state any fact baldly,' he said, 'but impossible to get to the truth behind it.'

In the Horatian scepticism of that statement, we shook hands and I rode off to Mr Finlay's, the Exclusive's, to make my final arrangements with Charlie before going to purchase a herd and flocks.

I was pleased that evening when Mr Finlay, ignorant of my democratic seditions with Mr Loosely, asked me into his office with its bound stock books reaching back until 1821, the history of a considerable empire which had never yet known a servile war, and asked me if I believed the investment I would have from Charlie would fully stock my station.

'No,' I said. 'It is a vast country and we are mere beginners.'

'Then,' he said, 'in the interests of encouraging the young, I am willing to have drawn up an order for £2000 to be spent on a flock of sheep on the normal arrangements, and in consideration of the normal one-third return. Mind you, Mr Bettany, I say a flock. I do not want it spent on shepherds, structures, wagons, implements, supplies. It remains very properly the concern of yourself and Mr Batchelor to provide these things.'

Of course, I told him. The normal, delightful arrangement. What was best was that I presumed that since I last saw him he had made inquiries of Mr Batchelor into my family and he, the high priest of Exclusives, had overlooked whatever taint attached to the noble impulses behind my father's crime. I was flushed with gratitude, and assured him I would not alienate a single penny of his to the meanest item of tack or to an ounce of hard soap.

'One thing,' he said. 'I have never known a district of New South Wales where the Leicester failed to do well. They have excellent hardihood and will handle your harsh upland well.' I had not thought of my country as 'harsh upland', but was willing to forgive his blunt assessment. 'I mention that,' he continued, 'simply because wool-breeding in New South Wales is very different from that of Van Diemen's Land, and a world removed from the short staple British business, which is in any case being supplanted by our wool. I will, of course, expect a strict accounting.'

Enthusiastically, I told him he would have it. I felt guilty at the snide things Mr Loosely had said of him, and I thought that he had now shown the truest nobility. I wanted to envisage that one day in the age of my prime I should behave as amply to some young pilgrim.

I rode at once through the town of Goulburn to Mandelson's Hotel, to break to Charlie Batchelor the delightful news of Mr Finlay's offer to invest with us. Charlie was in his room writing letters to Van Diemen's Land and, without a second's thought, I blurted out the details of Finlay's kind gesture.

To my amazement, Charlie's face became suffused with blood, and he stood up and walked about the room saying, 'Damn, damn. My God, Jonathan, I had thought of warning you! But I surmised the fact that you ... well that your father had a penal record ... would stop him from interfering with us.'

I was as hurt as I ever was when people tried to reduce me to a mere outfall of my father's penal past. 'Is that what this is?' I asked. 'Interference?'

'That is exactly what this is, and damn him to hell! Why do you think I stayed here instead of at the Finlay's? To avoid exactly such an offer! He can see in you what I have always seen. Industry and probity and vigour. And he knows that this land is worth exploiting, but is fully absorbed in the service of that he already owns. So we shall do the work for him at a fraction of what it would cost him to do himself. What breed does he want you to buy?'

'Leicester,' I told him. 'After all they have been so outrageously successful as mutton, and they grow a long wool.'

'And one which is less prized than the Merino. As for mutton, how will you sell mutton from this Nugan Ganway? The only clients for fat mutton are yourself and the natives! Oh perhaps he would like to see the flocks mixed up and the mean quality of our wool lowered. And if it doesn't happen, what does he lose? He can ask for his Leicesters back at any time and sell them in Goulburn. Thus, typically, he puts in a fragment of money, he determines what the enterprise shall be, and makes us do the work.'

Though I argued that Charlie was misjudging Mr Finlay, I could see that I had not had as unqualified a success as I had first thought.

'Oh it's typical of you and your type,' Charlie suddenly raged. 'Either too perverse or too innocent! There is a flaw in the passions, that's the problem, the founding disorder ...'

But he would not say any more. For a second I wanted to do him damage and he could see it. And though he was a slighter man than me, he was agile, so that I believed later it was fear of hurting me further, rather than my rage, which caused him to stop. He certainly wore a regretful face.

'Forgive me, Jonathan. I've overdone things.' He shook his head. 'A flaw in the passions ... That is a description not of you but of your petulant friend.'

How could I hold a grievance against a fellow who apologised so handsomely?

'The dreadful thing,' he continued, 'is that one cannot oppose him. His influence is too strong.'

I said simply, 'I am going to the saleyards east of Parramatta to buy stock. I shall ensure your section of the flock and mine are Merino. I hope you will trust me to do a reasonable job.'

'Of course, of course,' he said, shaking his head, and making apologetic gestures with his hands, so we were friends again, though edgy. The air, as much as it sang with promise, was taut.

I mentioned an acquaintance of my father, a surgeon in Parramatta. I would depend on him to select me the correct overseer. 'Mr Gonfleur has said I can fetch shepherds and hut-keepers from the Parramatta depot.'

'My dear fellow, I trust you absolutely,' said Charlie.

'Then what, may I ask, are the details of your movements?'

'Yass, and then I shall be back here within ten days. I intend to spend the early part of your setting up with you. Unlike Mr Finlay, I want to see this country which so excites you.'

And he smiled, and suddenly was crossing back towards me to shake my hand.

WHEN SHE RECEIVED THE FIRST SECTION of *Bettany's Book*, Prim read it with a strange unease. Though she avoided returning to Australia, the idea of Dimp, happy and secure there, acted as a stabilising pole to what she thought of as her own rootless, intense life. But, knowing her sister better than anyone alive, and given that she had never fully liked D'Arcy, she feared that Dimp's happiness was somehow fragile and that her sister's equilibrium, by some careless touch, could be destroyed. Some aspects of Dimp's present enthusiasm spoke subtly to these misgivings.

AUSTFAM Headquarters
29th Ave East
New Extension
Khartoum
16 May 1989

Dearest Dimp,
A great pleasure to get back from an excursion of mine – to Nairobi in fact – and hear from you about Benedetto and these documents. I'm now re-reading that first section of Bettany's more secret book. As for the Jewish great-granny, I agree with you: that is a novelty, and if I were younger I might find myself using it to alter my image of myself – even as an ego boost, to justify myself. You know the sort of thing: I carry persecuted blood, no wonder I was out of place in Sydney!

Now I don't intend to use it like that. What good would it do me? What light would it cast? I can see you though, telling everyone about it – reiterating it. Especially to Bren. I wouldn't be surprised if you started dividing the weekend between Mass with the Jesuits and the Bondi synagogue.

I admit what you sent me does read better than Sheep Breeding and the Pastoral Life in New South Wales, *or whatever it's called. But there's something I feel have to warn you about. I know it's boring, and I sound like a maiden aunt, but I must say it to you that you have a tendency to look for signs in the heavens, or signs anywhere. You mention 'founding crimes', and it's a little thing, but it just sounds as if you might be getting yourself ready for something extreme. You use the phrase as if they're crimes you might be bound to reproduce. You're not.*

Every person on earth has sixteen great-grandparents, including the one from which they get their name. We didn't get what you insist on calling our beauty from this one woman, but from seven others as well. And similarly we didn't get our souls from this one man and woman, even if we share their name – we got it from seven other men and seven other women as well. I know I already sound pompous, all this cautioning, especially since you're the older sister, and it's just a journal. But I don't want you poring over it as if it's some map of your own life. I feel it's my younger sister's duty to say this: ancestor worship is one of the chief religions of the Sudan, but it is unnecessary to practise it in Double Bay.

Well, again I'm embarrassed to talk like this, but I can smell your worst ideas coming before you have them.

But I'll give you I was engrossed at the first bundle of transcribed material. Here in good old Sudan, where the national grid is starting to go down regularly, or the hydro-electric station at the Rosieres Dam cuts out because of attacks from agents of the SPLA, I made sure to have a torch by my bed so that I could read it at a gulp.

I don't intend to be influenced or haunted by it by day. There's too much light here for that. And life is too busy. The Southern urchins we've all got used to meeting in the streets of Central Khartoum – Shamassa, they're called, sunshine kids – have just been moved out of town to a stretch of wasteland beyond Omdurman, and Austfam are supplying two wells there, because there's nothing otherwise. There's a strong rumour that these kids are used as a blood bank for government soldiers wounded in the South. In any case, you can see that the sun and politics take away strength from us all here. Not what great-grandfather did!

In affection and well-placed suspicion,
Prim

PRIM WAS CORRECT IN SURMISING THAT from the first passage, Jonathan Bettany's book engendered enthusiasm in Dimp. For her it was the authentic voice of Australian pastoral fervour, the joy, and in Bettany's terms, the wonder, of taking and stocking pristine land. A new awareness of Australian history, by the time Benedetto handed the Bettany document to Dimp, was recasting the first graziers as heedless occupiers of tribal earth and dispossessors of the most ancient hunter–gatherer societies on earth. This new way of looking at Australian history, combined with the blandness of the way the whole business had been taught her as a schoolgirl on Sydney's north shore, at first made Benedetto's interest in old pastoralists seem very quaint.

But in her ancestor's informal memoir she encountered the voice of a young man enchanted and enriched by the new world he entered and believed himself to be remaking. His was the wonderment of Adam before the Fall, and his innocence was a crucial part of the Australian record. The potent European dream of limitless livestock on limitless pasture apparently realised in enormous New South Wales! Bettany's discovery of Nugan Ganway engaged Dimp's filmmaker's passion in a way nothing else had since *Enzo Kangaroo*.

Along with Bettany's journal, there were the letters of the literate Jewish convict woman, the Female Factory woman. These letters too Dimp began zealously to transcribe for her sister. For not only did she intend to use this material for her own purposes, she was not sure that Prim would deal with Bettany's difficult handwriting, and knew she might use the narrowness of Sarah's as an excuse not to read. In an attempt to find something more on this woman, Sarah Bernard, Dimp went to the New South Wales State Archives in Globe Street, a small alley down near the Quay, where she had sometimes saved Bren a few thousand dollars by researching the history of this or that mining lease.

She knew from the letters that Sarah Bernard had travelled to Australia on the ship *Whisper*. Dimp found from the microfiched muster for the ship that it had made an ocean transit of 130 days from Sheerness. *Whisper*'s Surgeon Superintendent, a man named Bugle, had written beside Sarah Bernard's name a number of details: her place of trial, Manchester; her crime, 'Stealing Clothing', and her ship number, which was 97. She was marked as possessing 'Reading and Writing', and being 'Married'. In the column headed 'General Description', he gave a summary of the appearance of this twenty-two-year-old on the eve of her first stepping ashore on the continent of Australia. She was: '5 ft 8 and 1/4 inches tall, dark complexioned, exceeding fair, eyes brown, no facial mark. Jagged scar between shoulder and upper left breast. Scar back of second finger left hand and back of right ankle.'

Dimp went through the list of all the women on board the *Whisper* – it came to nearly two hundred – and was somehow excited to discover that amongst all the red-faced, 'plain' and even 'disagreeable' females, there was an occasional 'fair', but no other 'exceeding fair'. And since Bernard was also described as 'dark complexioned', 'exceeding fair' clearly did not mean blonde, but rather extremely beautiful, at least in Bugle's eyes.

Excited by this touch of humanity in the system, even if it meant only a flicker of desire on the part of the surgeon, Dimp was enchanted to find that she could retrieve a forgotten convict woman's looks at twenty-two from beyond that huge barrier of time. You couldn't do that with free immigrants, she knew, since unlike Sarah Bernard, they had the freedom not to be defined.

Dimp looked up the report of Surgeon Superintendent Bugle – it was on microfilm copied from the Public Record Office in London. On all the long journey, Sarah Bernard had not consulted him. Women went or were taken to him with hysteria, pneumonia, catarrh, bloody dysentery and, occasionally, syphilis. Two of them died of scurvy and gastroenteritis, one perished of pneumonia, one of 'a cerebral fever', two of bloody dysentery. Surgeon Bugle, whose strong suit did not seem to have been gynaecological, mentioned no specifically female illnesses and wrote about his women as if they were male prisoners in petticoats. He complained that those who died on board had been too long held in English prisons beforehand. He did not want to be accused of any negligence himself.

The only Public Record Office document relating to the captain of *Whisper* was a letter from that gentleman dated March 3, 1837, and addressed to George Pulteney, Clerk of the Transport Board.

My Dear Pulteney,

I know you don't have the supreme power you deserve with the Transport Board, but next time those gentlemen are all sitting around a table deciding how the business of taking women to Australia should be managed, and what the appropriate demeanour of all parties ought to be, perhaps you could point out the inadvisability of appointing Surgeon Superintendents who wish to run ships on evangelical and improving lines. I've had a most vexing journey, not in terms of the ship herself, though she's a shallow-drafted little thing and swings about a lot.

But I am hugely vexed throughout by Surgeon Bugle's management of the ship, and his unwillingness to listen to me, who have, someone should point out to him, made two previous such journeys. On Nevis and Jerusalem, good old Slattery the Surgeon Superintendent approached me before we left Sheerness and told me that he had always found it very suitable for the women to form associations with the sailors and unmarried garrison. The young women were thereby helped and protected, and their influence for good order on the prison deck was increased tenfold.

But Bugle comes aboard, declaring himself a Corresponding Member of the London Bible Society, for dear Jesus's sake! He demands that I punish sailors who form associations with women on the prison deck! He'd rather chain the women than let them associate with my sailors, or the soldiers of the 40th. All very well, but this mode of proceeding creates its own toll in my opinion. On Slattery's and my first voyage – on

Nevis – only two deaths. On our second, only two. Bugle, trying to regulate even the passage of lewd sentiments between the crew and the women, limited exercise hours and put a strict limit to the number of mess orderlies on deck at the one time. And of course, outlawed dancing to musical instruments, a procedure which under Slattery kept the girls in good spirits and alleviated the lethargy of scurvy.

And so, six deaths when two would have done. Six deaths which more deck time and more air, and even the company of men, might have reduced. In the tropics, let me assure you, he did not want any of the women brought up to sleep on deck, to relieve the temperature below! Better to have the girls in one hundred and five degrees below than the chance of a sailor distracted in the top-gallants by a sleeping thigh.

You'll see the damn fool's log, and it will read sweetly and plausibly, I know. But I urge that the idiot should never be allowed to board a transport again. I don't know what he thought he was preventing, after all. For the women, so rigidly impeded on deck, about the galley and elsewhere, sought unnatural solace from each other.

This reference to 'unnatural solace' was probably jaundiced, Dimp decided the tone of the letter was that of a choleric old bugger! It was clear though, from reading the letters of Sarah Bernard, that women enduring profound misery had been driven into fierce sisterly loyalties. It was there in the potent friendship between Sarah Bernard and a convict named Alice Aldread, twenty-three years, described by Bugle as 'fair' who had been judged guilty of murder and her sentence altered to transportation for life.

Dimp found this fierce friendship compelling, and Bernard's letters indicated that she was an ardent but not a flippant woman, the opposite of the bawdy Cockney trollops of convict mythology. Already Dimp wanted to use their rawness and eloquence to fuel the texture of the Bettany story. She foresaw herself handing them to an actress – 'This is background reading for your character.' On a set somewhere in the bush, in a clearing beneath hard ridges, with curlews calling. She foresaw herself writing to Prim about them too. 'This also is a third world woman, because the past is the third world.'

⇒

Letter No 1, SARAH BERNARD

Alice
My God that I should find myself lacking your company and surrounded
by these people here! Cramps in my belly and behind a wall nine feet
high. They have put us for protection in a place which is called a shelter
but has features of a gaol or a madhouse and is known as the Female
Factory. It has taken two days coming up the river from Sydney to be
locked up here on the charge of being defenceless. The chief of the consta-
bles on the boat which brought me here is a fellow named Long who
told me: It's to save you from the world, which is a worse world here
than anywhere else.

Coming here Long knew the camp spots though – the little beaches
and the rivulets that come down the face of the rocks. He had a large
fire made and we who were women from both a Sheerness and a Dublin
ship slept to the left – the constables to the right – on soft ground in
gentle air at the start of what here is named winter. I slept well under
the government of Long with barely a sway of the earth beneath a head
grown accustomed to the sea and its movements. But ever missing Alice
your friendly caress.

The Female Factory of Parramatta. A name which may be taken either
way. The place where women are crafted. The place where women craft
themselves awaiting liberty. I believed myself safer in Long's boat than
in this loud bedlam of Irish women – they hoot at a person in their
tongue and call out all the time to Jesus and Mary when they speak
English. Constable Long did not permit rum in his long boat. But there
are some who have it here, brought in by some garrison soldier of the
40th Regiment or some constable.

Of this place I can tell you – Alice Aldread – that your supposed
madness – which is solely grief – would go unnoticed in a general babble.
And I do not remember the face of my husband McWhirter the soldier,
nor the face of Mr Duncannon my esteemed former employer nor the
face of Surgeon Bugle. I remember Alice Aldread whole – every margin
of skin and every little blemish of purple under the pale. You who have
murdered a husband and must be separated out by Bugle into your own
class of one to eat different rations – cornmeal instead of wheat – no
tea – no comfort of tea – in some hut for lunatics! You who would guard
me here so easily under the weight and authority of your murder! Having
your prettiness and bright eye and your youth which saved you from the

more awful but quicker punishment. The short jump as against the long sea.

If here you would be separate from the mass of us for having given Prussian Blue to your awful old husband. You would be a special category 3 and in your own cell. But I know I could get to see you here. For we women of highest category are permitted much movement and live in large downstairs rooms with broken windows. The Irish women who are the majority here drop off half the word and call them the Tories. We are crowded in the east Tory and I have talked of noise already. But you would not believe the noise. You would make it all less loud – less howling – less laughter and acid glaring. You have done Alice Aldread what these little chemise thieves and bacon stealers have not done! They are peasants who will make up some fable about me I can tell. And you could stop them – these loud women young and aged who walk in the aisle between the beds like women born and grown and come to womanhood here. The air they have is that they have inherited hell and are sure of their title to it.

A watchful little red-complexioned woman and prisoner who has a girl child of nearly two still at breast has the cot on one side of mine. This in the corner of an islet of cots jammed up solid by the wall across from broken window panes. Mrs Pallmire our Matron has us arrange and spread them either side of the Tory for the visit of Surgeon Strope on Thursday each second week. Surgeon Strope is on the look out in God's crow's nest. But not the same high crow's nest Surgeon Bugle was in. Surgeon Strope does not exhort us to cast our souls upon the Saviour as bread upon water. He thinks the worst of us straight off and says to us: Do not be mistaken that congress between women makes those who practise it mad.

That is his story. I think congress with men is an equal especial cause of lunatics and all the women know this but say nothing. He does not bother noticing the broken windows. They have been broken in some rage by this or that woman. They will be broken again thinks he.

So on one side of me a large woman with a reddish weathered face and on the other side this reddish little one with the child. They look at each other – the little reddish one wanting the larger one's protection and the larger one in envy of the watchful nature and the good cheer of the little one. For the little one with the child is not unkind nor kind. Holding her child she is looking for a sign – I think – which will be given neither by hand nor tongue but will be seen at once by all. A sign that it is at last the right thing for her to speak to me at length. I swear she is looking in my direction with a kindly ghost of a smile but when I return the gaze she is all at once looking at the ceiling. She smokes very daintily a little clay pipe which she holds like a flute between her tiny brown fingers. The memory of some summer's evening when she was in the open smoking and watchful – the memory of smoking between dances – it's still there in her fingers.

The larger woman speaks to me in a spirit of instruction – thus:

Aren't you an unlucky little woman to be here?

She says little though I'm as tall as she.

The way she speaks says more that they are unlucky to have me than I am to have them. She says:

There are no more women sent to New South Wales now. They send all the English whores they need these days to Hobart.

This is not meant as a joke. She and her little red friend then start talking about me in their language with much movement of their eyes. It is a language in which no Bible or book or scholarship has ever been written and it defeats me. And they swing back into the mother tongue now and then without thinking.

Will she keep us awake with the colic again? the big red woman asks of the gazing infant of the little one. There is a musical lilt there – in her talking to the child – which I find pleasing. The big red one notices that.

You're looking at a woman who has been here some six or seven years, she tells me.

I turn my eyes to the little mother with pipe and infant and half a smile but she of course looks away on the instant:

The big creature says: Not my friend. I mean myself. Returned to the Factory when my master gave me rum at Christmas. He is at large but here I am held safe from the evil influence of a kind of fellow I wouldn't mind running into again some day. As soon as I can manage it.

She is not telling me all this for some idle purpose. She is telling me that I might know she is a serious woman with her own notable history. She says: You are looking at a woman bidden to the needlework class of Her Ladyship the Mrs Governor. Did you ever know that of Her Ladyship? That she gave out needlework classes to such as me?

As expected I say No. The big woman nods as if she knows that much about me – that my ignorance can't be helped.

The big red one says: Then before your dear woman Mrs Governor went off to die she had thirty of us better reputed over into the parlour to learn the needlework. I was one. I have been at this place longer than Mrs Governor's been a ghost. You might see her coming up to the window to look for girls for the sewing.

I wait for laughter or a big red-eyed wink. But none comes nor does the little woman titter. So perhaps they believe it and have seen the spirit there at the broken windows. But again it all goes to prove the standing of the big red one.

She says: I been here as long as that. Eternal rest give unto her. I still do the sewing. On the other hand, you'll be one of them laundry.

Indeed I have already been placed to work in the laundry.

But I tell her I have needlework.

The big one says: But not Mrs Governors needlework. That means you are one of them laundry.

So she goes on instructing me on how she stands at the peak of the Factory and I somewhere far down its slope. In this Hades of women and against the face of the big one red as a tyrant I hanker for your softer face and surer speech. How I wish I could face her off with you, for needlework cannot stand up against murder – against lovely fair unblemished killing of husbands.

On Saturday Parramatta's dirty linen comes here in baskets on the back of a wagon. Shirts – shifts – chemises – all worn close to the bodies and soiled by the bodies of the lambs who live beyond the walls. Linen from the bed of the visiting surgeon and from the solitary bedroom of His Excellency – he thinks it is improving and a good example to have us do his laundry. Shirts from his bowed neck. Heaps of linen from others too. Linen grey not from bad laundering but from sweat and journeys. Table linen which has been wiped across lips and here gravy darker than blood and there some sauce of berries purpler than a king.

On the floor below the Tory – in a cellar reached by steps from the outside of the building – we boil the colony linen in copper tubs. The women around me are all turned pink and the linen a dead lolling sopping white. Under our caps our hair hangs limp across our view and we flat-iron for days upon days. Perhaps a day and a half of boiling and four days at the flat-iron – that is my labour Alice. Women who have been longest in the Factory or have influence are set to fold and pack the hampers.

Yesterday evening the big red one comes and sits on my cot uninvited. I was flushed and ugly from ironing:

If in your buckled shoes – says she – if in your buckled shoes, I wouldn't comb my hair again little chicken. Let it hang is what we say. Rub starch into your cheeks or dirt. It is best. Mrs Matron Pallmire has an eye on you.

Why should I let my hair hang? I ask her but she does not tell me. I am full of fear and need your counsel my Alice. It is useless but I cry anyhow: Can you not come?

One of the great lumps of constables comes to the laundry now and tells me I have a guest in the garden. I ask who it is and he says just one of those Sydney constables. It seems that to him they are an inferior kind of constable altogether.

I go and find the yard wide and empty at this hour. It was once gardened by an earlier Matron but is now unloved. By a plain wooden table where women sometimes gather sits Constable Long in blue jacket and canvas boots. I am happy to see him for he helps my hopes by treating me carefully – this very leathered man. The sun of this place has worked on a complexion which had once been faint and fair. There are a few scars of salt sores on his lips. For when not bringing women upriver in open boats he has laboured in the great harbour at Sydney Cove.

He says I look flushed and I agree I pretty well am flushed. He has an easy smile. He tells me he has a letter from my friend. I ask him, Friend? Since I did not know I had mentioned your name Alice.

He tells me: But yes the murderess. She is they reckon insolent and thus they have put her in the asylum for now. My own patrol took her up the river to the madhouse, and I told the warden that she was calm in the boat. And she was exactly calm. It is loss of hope I believe.

But I knew they had put her amongst the lunatics, I told him. It happened as we parted at the Dock Yard. They called it hysterics and all the knowing women about the place said she's for Tarban Creek.

Long nods and says he was there again lately and looked in at her hut and let her write a note for me. He says: She is apart from the murder a better class of woman.

I ask him how he remembered who I was.

He says: Oh I remember you. You said to me as we loaded you – you said you were a very dangerous woman. You see you thought I might do you harm and wanted to frighten me.

I say: I do not remember saying dangerous. It was a foolish thing to say.

He says: In my own way I am dangerous myself. Though innocent too if judged by the court of heaven.

He hands me your letter then. The letter of my Alice. It is written on medical orderly book paper. You tell me in it you do not know why you so acted up – a sort of rage – you looked at the strange place and felt that rage. You do me the honour to say I was the last certain thing you had and were being taken off you. You say: Have no doubt you are much thought of by this girl. Not everyone wants to know a Prussick Acid poisoner reprieved from hanging but you never held back from being my dear friend.

I look up aching from your good letter. Constable Long tries not to look keenly at me but is looking so.

I ask him: When she comes here will they let me see her? I ask him though I know he has no power.

He tells me: The rule says no – they want to save you from the influence of bad women.

So I argue: Her husband rushed to poison her too. He took arsenic for his health. He was a being of poison. He was embalmed in his own poison. And – and on top – he fed her on nothing and upbraided her like a child and flaunted his ratty old will at her to show how he would forget her in death.

Long says in conviction: It is always like that in murder. The world just does not know how it is.

It seems he had once thought of murder. He looks away.

If I murdered someone – I tell him – they'd surely hang me. I look capable of it – though I've never had occasion. But they could not hang a sweet thing like Alice.

That's right he said and with a slight smile. They could not hang her.

And what about you then? I ask him growing bold. Your soul? How does it stand with what you did?

Oh I sit pretty quiet on what I did. Threatening notice against some hound of a landlord. Hammered it to a door. Life sentence. And now I'm seven years in and have a ticket to seek employment.

I tell him: How I desire a ticket of leave. But tell me! Threatening notice does not sound like a life sentence.

Oh it might be in Ireland. If you put the notice on the door post and broke the door in.

Whose door then?

The Marquis of Sligo! But not in that county. At his door in Westport Mayo.

His air of freedom shines for a second in his eyes. I want that thing –

to catch it as a person catches a disease. To be scratched on the arm with it and a sore to grow. A scar to form over this part of me named the Female Factory.

He tells me: You are a decent woman. I intend to press on any master of mine your merits as a housekeeper. For I am sure you possess them. I will if adequate be overseer at a homestead. But you could be its mistress of management.

He did not dare look at me and was half-ashamed of drawing up his simple plans so boldly in the Factory yard. But it was no place for them. They hung above the weeds like redeemed Christ and his saints in glass hanging above our heads at Saint Anne in Manchester. There I first began at the urging of my father my inspections of religions and I think that he and I both wanted Christ to see me as a true English girl and not a girl of the shul and synagogue. Yet though I loved the Church – people whispered but they did not sniffle and rage at God as if he was a customer in some little shop – though I loved St Anne I saw the eye of Christ had an absent look. I was not in his schemes. He was concerned with bigger fish. And the plans of Long had the sniff of plans meant for bigger fish too. A sprat such as me would not be dragged up in that net of glory!

Says I: I wish to breathe any air but this. I wish Alice to breathe too.

Oh may that day come for you Alice and for your true friend

Sarah

Letter No 2, SARAH BERNARD

Marked by her: A LETTER NOT TO BE SENT

My dearest Alice

I write to you but also do not write to you. For this is not a letter I wish you to read, but I cannot prevent writing it or thinking of you as the being I would best like to receive this catalogue of miseries. As his last act before he goes to the west and over the mountains – lucky fellow – to what must be better country Long the convict constable has said he will see you get a scribble from me. But not this scribble.

The little red mother Carty gives me more time of day than previous. She tells me something of the time when the Visiting Justice had the Pallmires thrown out of this post and pious people named Mr and Mrs

Chapman from London put in their place. But the Irish women – the big red woman and the little one and all the rest – did not like the pious people since they tried to wean them of their superstitions such as Rosary beads and all that magic. Those women – including my little mother who sleeps at my side and whose baby girl I sometimes comfort at night – would rather have their superstitions than fair and just treatments. Or else they simply do not believe anyone can give them fair treatment and prefer the devil they know. Many of these women find it easy to be loud and to profane and utter divine names raucously. Even now I hear them yell Thundering Jaysus, Jaysus Mary and All the Saints. They put the Chapmans to flight with such roaring of the name of the Christian Messiah. And whether or not they had a beloved sister amongst their fellows they played nonetheless at prison caresses and flash speech just to scare the Chapmans off. The pious two told the Governor that the women of the Tories were depraved beyond uttering and unredeemed. The Governor sent them away to find work in a better place if such exists here or anywhere else. And Mr and Mrs Matron Pallmire – being at the least used to the Factory – were put back in the post. When I observed her upon coming here Mrs Pallmire looked as if she had been here forever since Pharaoh's days. She carries the air as she enters – a plump and pretty woman though nearly fifty years – that she knows every twitch of this place.

These Irish girls take me by surprise by being content with Mr and Mrs Matron's old tricks – the boiling down of the beef into a soup so we cannot measure what we have eaten. Tricks of short-weighting with the baked loaves. The reddish women tell me Mr and Mrs Matron supply some beef and baked rolls to hotels and a dining house in the town of Parramatta. Perhaps the Governor dining out in his solitude as a widower eats our bread at his table. But the Pallmires remain so forward and confident about their crimes – it is as if they were free of inquiry.

Why do I not now want you to come here and yet at the same time wish it? I do not want it since you are too lovely. Though I am pained to think that similar things might occur in your asylum on the river. Wrongs might be done there without any hope of complaint or redemption – for how easy it is to discount the wrongs of the mad.

There has been a recent night when after dinner and the locking of the Tory Mrs Matron let herself in again with a key. She peers about amused and her plump features look roundish and kind. She sits on the end of the bed of the large brick-red woman who has always guyed me and *begins chatting with the girls about. Her voice is low – as if she doesn't want infants woken. Some of the women rise and go looking for panni-kins for Mrs Pallmire brings forth from under her petticoats a stone flagon of rum. She begins pouring the rum for this and that woman – the little mother too – and all the time she is saying I hope you are well ladies. And they joke back boldly. As well as you let us be Mrs Matron. Mrs Pallmire murmurs: Don't be saying that girls for you'll have me and my big man in strife. She pours a very heavy pannikin and offers it to me. A quarter as much might have been to my taste and good health. But so timid does the convict state leave all but the best that I meekly resolve to take that much and then to offer the other half to the Irish girl or to an ill old woman – Annie Hamilton at the end of the Tory. For you know I am not a drinker. I remember a Passover at my father's uncle's little hovel in Manchester when they had Jewish wine at the table. I was a little girl and before me this glass of wine which I drank not as the uncle told me but as one might cherry water. Now I also had to hide this small piece of the unleavened bread – the Afikoman I think it was called – the youngest at the board is meant to take and hide it. And my great uncle was crying out: Who has the Afikoman? Who has the Afikoman? He had a penny in his hand to pay me for it – such is the Israelite custom. So I walked towards him hiding the bread in my hand and before getting to him I vomited from the wine. Oh she is no Gentile they laughing told my father. She cannot drink wine!*

Hence now I am willing to give away this killing dosage of rum to the Irish who are good at it. I rise to do it and Mrs Matron cries out to me to hold hard and where do I think I am going? I tell her to Annie Hamilton to give her a sip or two. Mrs Matron says: That woman is a malingerer! That woman Hamilton would be happy to give me and my big man an evil repute.

But I know Annie has no malice – her mess prefect who is a London woman gives her less than a ration. Annie has limped to the nurse and the nurse told her: If you go into the hospital you will have solely liquid rations. This Annie – Yorkshire and a very simple woman – did not want liquid rations being hungry enough on full. So Annie stays wasting in the Tory.

Mrs Matron Pallmire orders me to drink the lot up and I stare at the dark syrup surface of that Indian rum and stare and stare. I think if I swallow this then I have no watchfulness left. Some of the Irish girls start laughing. Worst of all some turn their heads as if for pity. It seems all at once that they are not for all their talk bosom souls to Mrs Matron but that they know that they are without power and shrink from her.

Giddy and choking I drink the burning mug at her urging and am pleased to be done with it. I feel it like a hand in my vital organs and a hand across my sight but at least it is done. But she tells me: Have some more, and she pours it full again for me though not for any of the other women who are about. There you are – she says – you have no jollity. We will get you back to the jollity you had in your patch at home with your husband the soldier. So she knows my husband McWhirter was a soldier. So she has studied me when earlier I thought she had not noticed me. Excellent Jamaica says the big red woman Connolly who wishes she could be in the same relation to the full pannikin as I am. They have all finished drinking in quick order. It is true these Gentiles I see have a great facility with liquors.

Then the women go back to their business – the talking and packing of pipes with tobacco and the coddling of babies. The little mother Carty is crazed with rummy affection and kisses her baby with great flourishes not two yards from where I sit though she might as well be in another room. Mrs Pallmire considers me as I choke the stuff down and get silly. It is nothing like your suffering dear Alice but her gleaming eye which is now to my view tiny and fierce as a parrot's is awful. I know it has no love for me and I am afraid.

She says to me: You are a learned little troll aren't you and dark as a gipsy. Are you an Assyrian or some such or are you a Jewess? So this McWhirter of yours? Uncircumcised? That must have been in the nature of a novelty for a Jewess.

I must stop this account for the moment – I write it in the corner of our misgrown Factory garden with women looking at me sideways for writing fluent. It is as if my quick writing backs up all the ill they might have heard of me.

I have taken six days of misery to write this far on the paper Sean Long gave me and soon I shall need to start using the pages I tear from between the covers of tracts left by the Reverend Arnett. Just now Mrs Matron can be heard from the Tory again but without a bottle. She is ordering women to set out the cots at proper distances for the Visiting Surgeon. Good order she cries. And proper space. And cleanliness.

At this point Sarah Bernard clearly ceased writing for a time, but soon resumed.

I continue my awful news – Alice – addressed to you but kept a secret to myself. For if you think of the Factory as a harbour to be reached and if you knew it was not you might in your hut and mad dormitory at Tarban lose all hope.

As related I was under the urging and pouring and pouring and urging of Mrs Matron Pallmire to drink pannikins of tar black spirit. Soon I suffer that prickling kind and unsureness which I most hate in the bottle and which best ensures I am no toper. The other women have left the awful merrymaking and swung away to other conversations and here we are a drinking party of two – private in a crowded loud place.

She tells me: I must have someone to set the table. Her table – I had never seen it – is in a stone apartment of two floors away from the Tory but reached by covered walks. The floor below is their offices and a dry store. Some women have been there to the Pallmires to work and sew and do not seem to like it on reflection. The Irish point them out and nod with that old knowingness they all at least pretend to! These women who have worked in the Pallmire apartment are treated with respect and distance but it seems they have been returned here to enjoy less of a future than ordinary girls of the Tories. Hence there's a quandary knotted between the eyes of such women. Where to now?

I wonder now if when Mrs Pallmire urges me to swallow more and then more tarry spirit I obey her from a weak and lost souls desire to cloak oneself in unknowing? I cannot say. Imprisonment clogs up all the usual exercises of the spirit. So when I believe I have reached the limit where I cannot safely stand she stands up with her bottle still in hand and in a way signalling that I am to follow her which I do and go out a door she unlocks for me with perhaps every woman in the crowded Tory knowing she is leading me out but no woman turning her eyes to us. She pushes me out the door in the Tory and into open air which turns me giddier still. Then one more door is unlocked and up the steps and over the bridge to her home above the store. In the dining room with three windows I begin to set the table and she tells me to lay places for three. She tells me as I stumble and drop things that I am well-trained and it is good to see. Some Irish and the Scots she says have not seen so much as a spoon before. When the table is ready in the best Tib Street Manchester form – and she does not have bad china but very good – we sit down at it and she pours more rum for herself and me but does not touch hers. I can scarce remember the entry of Steward Pallmire her husband. He has his strong shoulders and wide throat. And this short but very burly fellow comes up the stairs yelling: Dove who have we got from the Tories?

He smiles at us both as he sits down at the table where rum and water have already been set. I am taken to the kitchen where a pot of split pea soup sits on the fire. I am to serve it even to my own place at table. Such a disordered world is that of the Pallmires and the Factory that a meal I would dream of as a meal in a thousand can only be taken in a fuddled state and in a mad scene where I am server and guest of these two very strange souls. If I am to pour and serve soup then why must I be tipsy? I bend to lift the soup pot. The heat of my fear meets its heat. In serving I make many slopping errors which do not cause them anger but laughter. They have eight hundred women to wash their tablecloth and scrub their board. There were Kings of Poland who did not live like them.

I have no memory of the serving of beef and potatoes. I awoke in near naked disarray in the half light – in a great blazing pain of head and limb and yet colder than a corpse. This is in the corner of a room. A bed sits like a bark high above me and I struggle up and find Mr Pallmire neat as an old Greek under opossum skin rugs. I can hear from another room Mrs Matron Pallmire snoring in sleep and I know that they have a madness in place of a scale which I have no experience of. Not only all my joints are so hard put upon by the bare boards but I have a sore memory as well. I remember his strength on top of me but it was not the strength of a hero – it could have been pushed away I believe. I did not push him away. I thought: Oh be quiet and let him be done. I am dumb earth that lets itself be taken and trespassed on. I think: Oh this madness of the Pallmires piled on top of their power without limit – this is too much to fight against. I remember he called me a dry Puritan. Now of course I want the hour back to fight in. Yet it contained all that was of bad order and all I least wanted to look at.

I pick myself up as the bile surges up my burnt throat onto my tongue. I say something within my narrow power to Mr Pallmire's sleeping form. I cry: Next time do not make me drink fire! But the Steward Pallmire has the appalling hide not to notice but to sleep on. So I gather myself. I do not wish to return to the Tory but I do not wish to stay here. At least in the Tory I could read the outline of what I've been through in the way other women will look at me in jealousy and spite. But then they could not know that I have yielded in awe of what was happening and that to yield in awe is the most awful laziness of spirit. I stand a time in the Pallmire's kitchen. Will I wait here – good servant forever –

for Mrs Pallmire? But then I start to move and a big night constable I meet on the bridgeway moves to open a door and let me back into the Tory where women are stirring for the day. I tell you before the God both of Jews and Christians that I would have pitched frenzied head first off that bridge to lumpy paving beneath it but for one thought which is the thought of you Alice in your deeper peril. And once inside I am helped by the kind presence of the little freckled mother Carty. For I find my cot with its two slices of blanket and there is the little mother sitting up on her cot in the dawn holding her baby and without the big red creature to overshadow her – Connolly is perhaps at the jakes at the end of the Tory. Carty stares at me with just one speck of sister mercy in her weary eye. She says: That Mrs Matron likes to pick the ones who will not give Mr Matron the pox. What a thumping great blackguard that fellow is! She is reaching out a little red hand but then sneezes and her baby daughter cries. And to her that is as large a matter as a woman – myself – who has been used evilly and consents as a coward to evil usage in this world of the Pallmire Factory.

But I now too feel I have the knot on the forehead and a pale look. In one I am ice and I am fire. I near despair of the ambition to get you to this place since I have until now thought it the lesser Sheol – the gentler Hell. But now though yearning I do not want to see you here for this is the madhouse worse than Tarban Creek.

But the thought comes: If next time I determine not to be rendered so drunk then I can be gritty and watchful. Or at the least your faithful
Sarah

Dimp kept working energetically through the record of Bettany's early Nugan Ganway career, which she determined Prim would receive and respond to. With this history calling to her, Prim was surely less likely to remain in Sudan. For Prim's choice of life there was, Dimp believed, what nineteenth-century people called a 'notion', a conceit of which she could be cured by a wholesome genealogical interest. Dimp had a poor understanding of how profoundly placed her sister was in Africa. As much as Prim tried to convince her, Dimp seemed never to believe that the Sudan was more than a random, self-punishing fancy of her sister.

WE STOCK NUGAN GANWAY

I made excellent time to the orderly little town of Liverpool by harrying Hobbes along so fast that I needed to leave him in Narellan to graze in the care of a ticket-of-leave man, and hire a mare to get me the rest of the way. I took the road north then for the saleyards. I would happily have camped by them, wishing to temper my body for its years of joyous hardship, but a letter from my father, which I had collected in Goulburn, mentioned that his old friend, a surgeon named Dr Peter Strope, presently stationed at Parramatta, had been a little aggrieved that I had not visited him on my way inland. Strope had helped my father on his ship and, upon arrival, extricated him quickly from the convict depot, sending him to join the household of the Batchelors. Clearly he should not have to tolerate this offence.

So instead of a quick transit to the saleyards, I called into the Strope household, a little stone cottage which lay nearly in the shadow of the men's gaol in Parramatta. Dr Strope's stone house came to him as part of his post as Visiting Surgeon to the Parramatta orphanages and to the Female Factory. Small in the body and narrow in the shoulders, with a pinched little face, he struck me as a very plain saviour.

Looked at in himself Strope was the kind of man not uncommon in the penal colonies. His eyes had grown hooded, his mouth a thin gash. It was as if he knew one or two things more than were comfortable. A man of middling talent, a farmer by disposition, he had a few hundred acres a little to the west.

'Mrs Strope does not like it here,' he confessed to me early in the evening. 'In a town half free and half bond, who can really be called free?'

But chiefly – over the lamb, that antipodean staple – he was interested in what my plans were. 'This is not a time to delay. In fact even in the outer regions some of the best country is already taken.' He forced the corners of his mouth back into a grimace of approval. 'These Limits of Location, these Nineteen Counties beyond which no man is meant by government to tread ... your generation has too much spirit *not* to violate them. But the further you go, the more you will need a splendid overseer.'

I thought of Goldspink, Mr Treloar's canny but un-admirable overseer. I wanted someone better. I wanted a fellow pilgrim.

'Yes,' I confessed, 'I mean to speak to the magistrate here about that.'

'But I know the fellow you want. It's a former convict constable named

Long who goes to the magistrate every morning to inquire whether he has been applied for. In a place of abysmal servants, he would make an excellent one. We will see him in the morning, if you like.'.

I said I would like it very much, and the topic turned to his work. It weighed on him, he said, the demands government made of him. 'Once a week I need to ride to Blacktown to inspect the sable brethren there.' Tuesday it is the Catholic orphanage, the next day the State orphanage. On Thursdays I am permitted to receive polite patients, and on Fridays I visit the Female Factory. Whenever I make an inspection of the general arrangements of that place, I seem to cause amusement amongst the Irish women who make extensive commentaries on my behaviour in what I can only call their ungainly language. I am often sorry that I ever left Van Diemen's Land where, despite everything, I think society has achieved a higher average urbanity than in New South Wales.'

I uttered the customary condolences, but reflected that I would be far from corruption and *urbanity* in my deep wing of the bush.

Strope lowered his voice, to a level at which I had to lean forward. 'The problem as in all these systems is that the women are not the greatest criminals, as repulsive as many of them might be. The Factory Steward and his wife the Matron are amongst the two most abominable people I know, and in New South Wales this is a description indeed. The Matron and her husband, you see, know the system and run the Factory in a manner which presents an undisturbed surface to the public eye. It is the habit of higher officials than myself to overlook the sins of Matron and Steward, and so I must overlook them too. Thus the Steward has begun to be emboldened. He now takes convict women to the inns in town, and drinks with them. I shudder to speculate what happens thereafter, what his pleasure might be. I know that should I report him he would have an explanation which would suit the Colonial Secretary, who prefers not to think about the Factory. And so, what am I to do?'

I was appalled that this was what had happened to a kindly man who considered himself virtuous – that New South Wales had reduced him to this moral inertia. I was pleased that my only contact with the official side of New South Wales would be to employ shepherds and stockmen.

Rested the next morning, I felt more kindly towards the doctor as he rode with me to a large brick inn named the George, and led me to a stable at the back, where in a series of stalls a number of apparently newly released felons were lolling amongst straw. Strope called for Long, and he came forward, tall, lean-faced, wearing a blue coat, canvas pants and big boots which he probably retained, as a favour of government, from his career as a constable. His manner was restrained and wary yet correct.

Strope said, 'This is Mr Bettany. He is starting a new pastoral run in the interior, and is looking for an overseer. As a start, stock must be purchased.'

Long fixed me with a melancholy but, I thought, generous eye. 'Ah well, stock!' he intoned in a rhythmic, Celtic voice which gratefully did not have any tone of blather. 'There I think Mr Bettany could do all right altogether. We've barely had a proper rain the past eight months around Parramatta, and the cattle are slipping a little in condition. If you could get yourself some thin darlings, Mr Bettany, and rest them on good pasture on your way inland . . .'

'It is Merino and Leicester sheep above all though, Long,' I told him. 'I shall let the cattle have the run of the hills. But fine wool, that is the game. Do you think you might be up to the task of overseer?'

'Well, I suppose I have had management of men as constable.'

Strope said, 'Long had management of the boats which brought the women to the Factory and behaved well in keeping them orderly. Indeed, how can he be replaced?'

'But do you have any experience in livestock?'

'I have worked in fine wool, Your Honour. With Leicesters, in another place.' He meant, I think, the place he'd been transported from. 'They're a fine mix of talents, those boys! But everyone tells me the Saxon Merino, though shorter in staple, has a great amount of crimp and is the sheep for the further country.'

I smiled to think that the convict shared the same high opinion on the virtues of the Leicester as exclusive Mr Finlay.

'I suggest, Mr Bettany,' said the doctor, 'that you take Long with you to the stockyards, and thus assess his strengths.'

Dr Strope indeed had his official calls to make, and so I rented Long a horse. If he proved his mettle I would soon need to buy him one.

As we rode past the end of Church Street, we saw the great structure of the Female Factory beyond the river.

'There it is,' I told Long. 'The house of unruly women.'

Long murmured, 'Oh, it is not as bottomless a hell as they say, Mr Bettany.'

'Oh no? Why do you say so?'

'I was constable bringing the women upriver to here. You would find women of lesser crimes and honest backgrounds there lately.'

We rode a little further, looking at the high walls of the place, perhaps ten feet, I think. Though of course I said nothing of Surgeon Strope's confidences of the night before, Long seemed willing to address the very views Strope had uttered. 'You see, they are loud girls in there, but loud is not the same thing as vile. If ever you got as far as needing a house-keeper, I know at least one good woman who inhabits that place.'

'Well, we are years from that, I'd say.'

'Yes. And the woman herself is likewise years from being one.'

Arriving at the saleyards and tethering the horses, Long moved with me in the dust very companionably, amongst yards of shorthorn cattle. A stock agent came forth from a hut with his dusty cravat and descended upon us, full of advice we didn't need, as we climbed from yard to yard choosing our bulls, our steers and heifers, and watched the stockmen run them down races to holding pens. There were no choices I made that Long took issue with, no choice he suggested which was not worth making. The agent stood by bawling out his professional incantation, hammering the palm of his left hand with his right fist. 'All calves under six months given in with the lot.' And Long murmured quite properly, 'I should bloody well expect it.'

We had worked with great and impeccable urgency, the best way to do things. Long and I next inspected some Saxon Merinos at pasture beyond the yards. Into pens made of split saplings, with much hallooing and waving of arms, we drove rams; two, four and six-tooth ewes; and wethers and weaners of both sexes. Then we looked at some Leicesters for Mr Finlay's share. I was once more impressed by Long's competence, so much so that, leaving him to finish the task, I rode into town to draw Mr Finlay's and Charlie Batchelor's money from the bank. And so the purchase of livestock was completed in hours! We left our selected live-stock overnight, and went back to town where we finalised the purchase of a wagon, bullocks, three dogs and a string of six horses. In Goulburn we would still need to buy supplies, tar, shears, soap, woolsacks. But the pace at which two men, co-operating together, being of one mind, could put together flocks, mobs and necessaries excited me.

At the inn from whose stables he had emerged, Long would introduce me later in the day to a ticket-of-leave man named Clancy. 'He is not, mind you,' Long warned me beforehand, 'a perfect fellow, but I can gouge work from him. He is a sailor, and so not without some order to his mind.'

Clancy proved a stocky, dark man, an American. I found by questioning that he claimed to be a half-Cherokee Indian, and the other half Irish. He had been tried in Liverpool, the original Liverpool on the Mersey, for assault. He was experienced at driving bullocks and carts. I took both him and Long to the magistrate, signed two papers, and suddenly they were mine in earnest.

It was a common enough tale of New South Wales, that a settler might travel west with two ticket-of-leave men, who could give him his quietus, take all, and go bushranging. Yet I had every confidence that this was not the plan with Long and Clancy. After less than a day in Long's company, I would have entrusted him with my life. He seemed a universe removed from the unreliable Goldspink, and I discovered why in the stableyard at the George Inn that dusk, when I had a discussion with him concerning terms of employment. An overseer was entitled to £20 a year. But Long told me, 'Sir, I have no use for such a sum in the deep countryside. If you pay me £10 per annum, and give me 10 per centum of the increase on the cattle when I receive my conditional pardon ... perhaps that would satisfy Your Honour.'

I told him that the arrangement was very welcome to me. Since the entire enterprise must be financed, in terms of all the necessities of sheep-raising and cattle-farming, by myself and Charlie, I knew that ten per cent of increase on the cattle – the cattle being entirely a secondary matter to me – was a more welcome formula than £10 expended now. I saw too that it gave Long a motivation for industry, and in a modest sense, my partner, with an interest in what was to my benefit.

'Consider that the arrangement,' I told him.

But to move my livestock inland, I would need more fellows than Long and Clancy.

Such was the demand for labour in New South Wales that all the men who had been with Long at the stables of the George were now vanished, employed by farmers. Long suggested that we visit the police magistrate, because he knew there were still men who had been waiting at the Parramatta depot for the bench of magistrates to release the money they had earned as prisoners.

So we went back to the police magistrate at his office, which was located on the same patch of saffron clay as the depot. He knew or, at least, suspected that though any men I took with me were to be marked down as working in the Goulburn region, I was actually taking them to work a previously ungrazed country far beyond the limits. He led Long and myself to a barracks on the west of the clay square. Here, in a long room, a number of male convicts selected for assignment or else holders of tickets for the first time were sitting on their berths, most of them dressed in dungarees and red flannel shirts, or in some cases in sheepskin jackets as protection from the brisk morning. Only a few wore the canary yellow fabric of their servitude. Their faces were full of a dull inexpectancy and even passivity, and I was pleased Long was with me to read these leathered features, and penetrate their take-me-or-bloody-leave-me air.

'These fellows are the ones who have "Nothing Recorded" on their sheets,' the police magistrate told us, indicating a group of men in a corner marked with a large A. 'That is, they are members of the "well-behaved" category. I try not to pass on bad fruit to people who need reliable labour, particularly since you say you will be at a great distance and there will be no authorities to help you.'

At the magistrate's order a ragged line of men was formed. One was a freckled, wizened gentleman who held a dusty copy of *The Edinburgh Review* in his hand. I asked him his name and he told me, 'Shegog, mister,' and squinted at me. I wondered what to make of this fellow who carried his own entertainment with him.

The magistrate consulted a roll of paper. 'Stole tobacco to the value of 30 shillings.'

'He might do, sir,' said Long.

A big, watchful man next attracted my attention. His name was O'Dallow, it seemed, and I think that even then I imagined that his crime might have been a technical or a protest one. The magistrate informed me that he had hamstrung a cow. 'So you have experience of livestock,' I remarked.

'I do,' said O'Dallow, 'working for Mr Clench of Myall Brush.'

'And hamstringing a cow in Ireland.'

'That was ... That *houghing*, as we call it, was a matter between a tithe proctor and myself, sir.' He did not pretend to too much virtue. He did not plead his case. Long spoke to him in Irish and then turned to enlighten me.

'He says it was his own cow, sir. He houghed it to stop the proctor taking it off. All I can say is I've seen that sort of thing, Mr Bettany.'

O'Dallow seemed unwilling to be described as having committed a justifiable crime. 'But tell me, sir,' he said. 'Would a man have a waler to ride in your employment?'

'I have five or six store horses,' I told him. 'Those who ride well can ride them. The others will travel by foot or wagon.'

'I adore to work cattle, sir,' he darkly told me, more like a lament than an expression of taste.

I felt in me the inappropriate impulses of improvement, to let the space of Nugan Ganway amend this man. This was something I had from my father, and I understood its peril. I wanted to be more like Mr Finlay and Charlie Batchelor, who were not burdened by delusions about the redemption of man.

In startlingly quick time, with help from Long and the magistrate, I chose another eight men, making selections on the flimsiest grounds. This was the nature of employment in New South Wales. The value of my choices could only be proven by living with the service of these fellows over time.

The sight of Long droving my cattle away from the saleyards gave me a pang. They looked so lowly I was pleased that Charlie Batchelor was not there to see what my stewardship had produced. Clancy called from his wagon, 'They'll look a heap better, Mr Bettany, after a week's grazing on those limestone plains.'

I looked at my men, most in the new red flannel shirts, striped pants and boots which I had bought them at an outfitters in Parramatta, but distinguished by their coats of all marsupial and livestock background, from the kangaroo to the Merino. They had their lag reticence, their determination not to appear too earnest, too clever, too orderly, too respectful or too alacritous. They were of the whole cloth of the convict system. Would they stand by me?

Assisted by the three sheepdogs we had acquired, I followed our sheep on Hobbes, putting the Leicesters behind in the especial care of sullen but intelligent O'Dallow and one other man. These sheepdogs were splendid, glossy creatures named Boxer, Brutus and Bet, and it was hoped that Bet the bitch would provide litters of future dogs for Nugan Ganway.

As we passed through the town of Liverpool, I saw from my position in the rear, and with a recurrence of self-doubt, that ticket-of-leave men waiting outside the courthouse in yellow smocks and dungarees jokily took their hats off to mark our passage, finding in our herd of cattle a metaphor for a funeral. My men, who included the quasi-scholarly

Shegog travelling on foot with a bag of journals, cried dark curses back. I was pleased to note the proprietorial affront with which Shegog cried, 'To hell with the lot of you. We're driving the beasts casual and easy, and we'll be lords of flocks when you bastards are still begging for a dram.'

And while I kept fearing to see some old heifer the stock agent had managed to slip into our numbers fall over dead, the cattle kept on with that bovine tenacity which is part of the endearing quality of the short-horn beast.

Our conversations on that first droving journey were delightful. When Long spelled me at the rear of the flock, I rode by the wagon and asked Clancy about New York, which I had read of in the *Illustrated London News* as the coming place of the New World.

'Oh,' he told me, 'it is the devil's own port. A narrow and stinking place, Mr Bettany, and into the toe of the city is packed the worst of humankind. No tide fails to wash up a murdered corpse or the bodies of strangled babes.'

'But that is what critics say of Sydney,' I protested.

'True enough. But in Sydney a fellow could blame the System.' He hammered his chest. 'Fellows like myself are counted to be fallen and have no pretence of manners. But where does a fellow look to find the blame for what New York is? They are a fast crew, let me tell you!'

I did not disclose either to Long or Clancy the news that my own father had been a member of a secret and illegal society in his youth, but perhaps the information was already there, tacit in the manner in which we conversed on that first journey. My demeanour, whether activated by some sort of vanity or not, consisted of this: behold, I do not dismiss any man!

As we came to the little town of Picton, a curricle coach pulled away from the hotel and I saw two ladies inside. I had promised the men ale in Picton, so we turned the herd off onto the common, heavily grazed as it was. Ordering the ale from the owner in the taproom, I mentioned that by the look of the carriage which just passed down the road, he had had guests of quality.

'You know that old Scotch bastard in Goulburn?' asked the publican – a typical New South Wales man, perhaps a former time-server, and very free with his language. You would not have found in Ross or any other town of Van Diemen's Land a hotelier who referred to former guests or their connections so. 'Finlay,' he said, and before I could stand to a full height and defend Mr Finlay, he was rattling on. 'That was Mrs Finlay and a lady companion in the surrey there. Goes to Sydney every chance she gets. As you bloody would eh? Married to such a miserable old crank.'

'Mr Finlay has been generous to me,' I warned the man. 'And Mrs Finlay has many preparations to make in Sydney. Her daughter is to study in Europe.'

He tossed his head and concentrated on the settling froth in the pots of ale. 'If you sit on the verandah,' he said, 'I'll deliver them to you. No harm was meant. All serene, my boy.'

I had intended the ale to be some kind of secular communion, to bring together the intentions of Long, the men and myself, to give my pastoral sergeants a sense of our corps. For the same reason I amazed the publican by ordering the men a table in the dining room. We would eat splendid the first afternoon of our joint careers! But letting Clancy near the public house was the first great error of the long drove to the great upper plain of Maneroo and Nugan Ganway. While Long and I and, in their own knot, the other men, were content to drink ale on the verandah, and later feast on lamb chops in the dining room, Clancy certainly had ale but also kept, by secret arrangement with the owner, a rum bottle in a back room, which he apparently visited frequently on a series of plausible excuses, including calls of nature. From the window at which Long and I ate our meat and potatoes we could see the quite extensive sight of my cattle and sheep grazing the broad common, and that, not the flitting presence of Clancy, absorbed my attention. Long himself kept his eye on our 2500 head, and on Boxer, Brutus and Bet, who lay in the dust contentedly and with a watchfulness of their own, rising authoritatively whenever any sheep violated the concept of the desirable compactness of the flock which these wonderful dogs carried in their heads.

Clancy had finished one clandestine bottle at the guzzle and had broached the second before Long and I read the signs, and that was mere seconds before he fell useless to the floor. Our other men ironically clapped and cheered this collapse. The publican entered the dining room and said jovially, 'I thought it would be too much for him. It is overproof-to-blazes he has been swallowing.'

It was no use arguing with this amoral creature, but what should we do with sodden Clancy? Long got up from his chair, lifted the raving and bubbling Clancy over his shoulder, and went outside with him. He was promptly back, saying he had dumped Clancy in the wagon and, seated again, he cleaned dust or the redolence of Clancy off his fingers by wiping them on the tail of the tablecloth.

'Perhaps we should find another driver,' I murmured to him.

'It is my fault,' said the Irishman. 'Since didn't I recommend the rascal? I would not tell you what should be done, sir. But how likely is it we could find anyone to your liking? I shall give the blackguard the most thorough warnings when he is upright once more.'

'And warnings will suffice?' I asked.

Long smiled and lowered his lean face. 'It suffices when they are proper meted. In the meantime it's the sad truth there are no perfect men here, Mr Bettany. All the perfect men are in Parliament.'

Long soon left the table again, and when I had settled the bill and brought the rest of the men out of the inn, we were arrested by a scream from the wagon. Long had the barely resuscitated Clancy naked at the tail of the cart and was beating him earnestly with a knout of rope. Clancy was not tethered but somehow knew that to move away would entail worse punishment. This was what Long meant by warnings and, remembering the magistrate's advice that in the high plain Long and I would be the sole authority, I chose not to intervene for the moment. But presently, when he brought the knout crashing across Clancy's jaw line, I moved up and ordered him to cease. He gave the grey and tottering Clancy his clothing back, and then stepped away, looked at me, blinking rage out of his eyes, and said, 'We shall not be shamed or delayed further, Mr Bettany.'

I was pleased Long possessed such volatility, but flattered myself I didn't. Perhaps it was in such excess of feeling that crime arose. If so, where was my father's share? I had not seen it. It was hidden now beneath the restrained features of a Tasmanian sheep farmer and solicitor.

That night we slept amongst tall trees and a light frost settled as I profoundly rested.

I AM PROPOSED TO, AND START BUILDING A HOMESTEAD

When I reached Goulburn and reported to Mr Finlay, as I expected he told me to bring the flocks into pasture of his, and he sat astride a black mare beside me as we watched our sheep into his fields. As Long, my men and the dogs drove them in he murmured, 'Passable, passable,' which from his canny tongue meant something like, 'Excellent! Excellent!'

Since Mrs Finlay was in Sydney, Mr Finlay's daughter of fourteen or fifteen years, Phoebe, a young lady with whom both Hobbes and I had become favourites during our recent visit, was *ex officio* chatelaine of the house. Phoebe, as I have already mentioned, had a grand prospect. Her father intended to send her to Europe for instruction and finishing, and so she would return to New South Wales a young woman of accomplishment. There was a particular school in Geneva to which a number of young titled British women were sent. Mr Finlay told me at table how many letters he had needed to write to the English and French nuns of Geneva, who had educated the noblewomen of Europe over the past century and a half. He had needed to enlist the help of the Colonial Secretary in Whitehall, with whom he'd been to school in Edinburgh.

But despite his evident weakness for British titles, Mr Finlay seemed a devout Australian and could not see his daughter, once she had been adequately exposed to the cultural glories of the world, embracing any other future than that of a New South Wales woman. Neither, it seemed, could Phoebe, as I discovered in the most remarkable and perilous way.

I woke on my last night at the Finlays to find Phoebe standing in my room in her nightclothes but at a great distance from my bed and by the window, where moonlight did something to soften her childlike – although not utterly childlike – form. She was present in the manner of someone who has entered a hall to make a speech and was just clearing her voice to begin.

I sat up, feeling naked in my nightshirt.

'Mr Bettany,' she announced. 'I regret to wake you. But I think you might care to know that at the end of my European polishing I should like to join you on your tableland. I could be your helpmeet. Because I leave for Europe in six weeks, I must seek a guarantee from you. Are you willing to delay marrying for four years? Until I return to New South Wales?'

I knew she would not appreciate laughter from me. I said that I was flattered, and then realised that I was indeed, and I felt a sort of midnight urgency to give her my strongest undertaking. But wisely I resisted it. I explained it was a large decision for a man, and I would need to consider it.

'God will guide you,' she told me airily, but also with such vigour and confident prescience that I feared she could not be sent away with some adult prevarication as the only fruit from her dialogue with me.

'I hope He will,' I managed to say.

Fortunately this pious hope seemed to satisfy her, for she began to leave, her white feet crossing the boards to the door. But before vanishing she laid down a condition, which coming from the lips of one so young, surprised me. 'I would, of course, expect you to remain utterly chaste in the interim.'

Once she was gone it was possible to look on all that had passed as, in a sense, play acting, and I could not understand why I remained half-awake for the rest of the night and woke at dawn feeling not ecstatic but pleasantly exhilarated. I was the least impetuous of young men – I was determined that no one would accuse me of rashness, as my father had been accused.

When I left that morning, being seen away from the portico by Mr Finlay, Phoebe strolled beside me, in a way which might indicate harmless infatuation to her parent. I had my speech prepared to explain to her that she would meet young men, though it was unlikely that where I intended to spend the next four years I would meet young women.

'What do you say to my concept?' she asked me and I saw her green eyes raised to me, and her wonderful heart-shaped face.

'I can't make any serious pledge even if I wanted to,' I said. 'Let's decide nothing till you sail home again. For I wish to leave you room for affections which may develop in you. If that happened, if you felt a warmth for another person in the interim, then I would not believe I would have the right to feel betrayed at all.'

I was saying, perhaps too ambiguously, that she would grow out of it. But, looking up at me, she adopted a determined, level gaze.

'You know me very poorly,' she said, shaking her head and turning back to the house. That was the last I was to see of Phoebe Finlay until after she had been 'polished', and learned to sketch and stitch petit-point and carry on a full conversation in French.

By mid-morning, inhaling the sweet dust my flocks and herds kicked up, I was convinced that the total discourse between Phoebe and myself had been so much vapour. It astonished me that she had the condidence to come to my room, but I imagined that might represent a forthright colonial innocence, and I was a little uncertain whether that innocence and determination were admirable or not. But since I had behaved properly, and the school in Geneva would teach her less recklessness, I was more than prepared to let the question go unanswered. With any luck I would have passed forever out of her head by the time she crossed the equator. Some young ship's officer might very well receive from her a chaste but determined visit of the kind I had experienced. I hoped he would behave well towards her.

It would be hard to overstate the conditions of raw and squalid bush democracy under which Charlie Batchelor, my convict overseer Long, my stockmen and shepherds lived in our new, casually named country. We shared our two large tents informally, and no man ate better beef and bread than another, since the conditions did not favour preference. Charlie and I believed we were reforming the earth, and blazed with confidence that in this new and immaculate world we would be made new, immaculate men.

The flavour of those splendid days can be had from a letter I wrote to my parents, and innocently made a copy of for the day when as a successful older man I might wish to include it, edited perhaps, in memoirs for the instruction of future pastoralists.

The place we have chosen as our campsite – our centre – in Nugan Ganway is a generous and gentle hollow atop a blunted ridge. Granite stones large as a Van Diemen's Land residence are spread about this ridge in clusters and save us from the south-westerlies which in this region are always present, sometimes as a murmur, sometimes in full-throated fury.

Each morning, the two squads of shepherds leave here and take their respective flocks off to pasture in different directions, and at night drive them back closer to the camp. Here they enclose each large flock in a separate fold, within hurdles we have made out of brushwood. A nightwatchman guards the sheep from the native dogs which are seen in this area and which are said to be able to smell the blood in the sheep's veins. Ultimately these two flocks, with their rams, two, four and six teeth ewes, wethers and weaners of both sexes will be placed with their shepherds miles from each other and from our central habitations, to reduce the risk of boxing, or undue commingling.

Our shorthorn cattle graze wide, left for now to their own plenteous, unfenced and natural devices. This is the opposite of well-ordered Van Diemen's Land, but the size of the country allows different methods. The herd finds for the moment the natural fords in the river below our encampment and stands ankle deep to drink from the same water which sustains us.

After our dinner of mutton and tea, which one of our shepherds has taught us to sweeten with a gum from a particular species of tree, we crowd into our tents. Charlie and I are not always under the same canvas. All men equally smell of campfire and innocent sweat. I thank God for allowing us to be many Adams in this place of barbarous name but grand quietude.

But it becomes evident from the effluvia of some of the men that the huts will need to be built before the weather turns warmer.

Lightning has been our companion. You would laugh to see me, Father, wrapped in a possum skin under the thunderous canvas reading Horace by the light of a tallow lamp made from a jam tin, and by the tempest's flaring, intermittent gusts of white light.

'Iam satis terris nives atque diraes
grandinis misit Pater . . .'

Remember that? I make translations designed to satisfy that eminent Tasmanian tutor Mr Bettany with as much accuracy of cadence and meaning as I can muster. 'I am content now with this ordeal, the snow and hail storms which the Father has sent, and the thunder bolts thrown red-handedly at the sacred summits, and the terror awoken in the city . . .' Or the terror awoken in the bush of Australia, one might say.

You would tell us, Father, you would tell Simon and myself that the great poet's father did not altogether escape the taunt which adheres to persons even of remote servile origin. Your monitions rang like a generous warning that the ill-advised and malicious might seek to harm us. But I feel that any risk of such an unjust reflection upon us, deriving often from men less worthy by far than yourself and than the great Horace, has been outrun here in deepest New South Wales, and simply has no place in this vast plain and under our fraternal canvas. For this is conundrum country, which seems to make all of us equally servants, all of us equally masters. My shepherds and my hutmen may not yet be conscious of this reality, yet they walk on the earth, and talk amongst themselves, as if the truth had somehow penetrated them.

Yet in this Eden lay elements hard to command and many serpents. We needed to build two residences, a shearing shed and a stockyard, as well as two further-out huts for our shepherds. And so we sent a party off in the wagon under Long, with axes, wedges and adzes, to cut logs. They returned chastened. They had been able to cut much bark for the roofs but the most likely looking trees on the ridges above had blunted the blades and proven knotted.

We needed to consult with someone local, probably Treloar's overseer Goldspink, about suitable local wood for splitting, but we were busy so contented ourselves to stay under canvas for the time being.

Two days later, as Charlie and I rode out to one of the flocks, we saw two horsemen descend a far-off ridge, bulky creatures in their shaggy possum or kangaroo skin coats who seemed too top-heavy for their delicate Hobbes-like ponies.

'Are these the absconders?' I asked aloud.

'The absconders?' Charlie asked me in return.

We paused and Charlie eased forward in his saddle, and began filling his pipe. We gazed across the plain towards the western mountains. As the two horsemen came on, they proved not to be alone in the landscape. A mile beyond them, by a tree-marked creek, was the almost alien sight of one of our flocks grazing docilely in the care of a shepherd. Only a black, darting dog, Boxer, introduced frenzy to the scene. Charlie did not seem afflicted by any frantic or subtle thought but by a clear vision of how the wild miles of pasture before him represented substance: how grass might be transmuted, by the vehicle of sheep, to fibre and thus to wealth. More conscious of the approaching riders, I explained what I had until now told Charlie only cursorily, and not adequately to engage his interest; of my meeting with the absconders Rowan and Brody, of their attempted drowning of the Aboriginal child, and of my adhering to the advice of the Goulburn magistrate Mr Gonfleur and placing Felix in Mr Loosely's school, a detail which made Charlie chuckle and shake his head.

'I suspect it would suit this Goldspink's mischievous character,' I told Charlie, 'to fetch the very same men down on me now.'

'And when they get here, would you have me help you hang them?' asked Charlie, amused still, unshocked by anything I told him. He looked at me indulgently, as if he had been in New South Wales twenty years and understood all its grammar perfectly. It was the same gaze he had directed into the middle air, above the plain. 'I would let it go, my good chap,' he said. 'New South Wales is so vast and so incapable of being policed that I'm advised one sends some crumbs in the direction of absconders lest they come down from their hills at night and snatch the whole loaf.'

'No,' I told him. 'If it is the same men, I shall have it out with them.'

'Well, they will certainly be happy to have a frank discussion,' he said, openly laughing. How had he so easefully given up being a Tasmanian man of ideals to become a cynical New South Welshman?

'We should not ride out like hosts to meet them,' I told him. 'We should wait for them in camp.'

Fortunately Long was there by the tents, returned from visiting a flock in the other, eastern, direction and drinking his tea from the pint pot at the campfire. The speed with which our men had committed themselves to their work, undemanding and possibly stupefying as it might be, was to a large extent due not to my wisdom but to his authority. I told him that I thought absconders were approaching, and asked him to stand with us to greet them.

The men who approached us on their ponies, crackling their way across the not yet fully evaporated frost, were identifiably the two I had met at Goldspink's hut, and as if they had foreknowledge of our diffi-culties in hut-building, they carried axes, heads encased in scarred leather, at their horses necks. When they reined to a halt they showed no embarrassment and did not dismount at once, but considered Charlie and Long and myself for a while. The red-bearded one, Rowan, self-styled the Captain, said to me, 'We have met before this, sir.'

'By Christ, get down!' called Charlie in a huge voice.

'By Christ then we will, mate,' said the second, younger one, Tadgh. And they did, at their own speed.

When they stood before us, their hands innocently occupied with holding the reins of their horses, I said quietly, 'I did not want to see you again, unless it was before a magistrate. Whatever befell a native woman whose body I saw, I know for certain you sought to drown that child I had with me.'

'As one might drown a kitten,' said Rowan. 'To save you the trouble of it.'

'Then you anticipated my desires with a murder!'

'We did not think it murder. It was a mercy, to stop him starving.'

'Good heavens, then you would anticipate *God*'s desire with a murder!'

'I don't know what God's desire is. To a fellow positioned such as I am, it can sometimes seem twisted.'

Long stepped up to him, the supposed Captain, and pushed his shoulder. Though Rowan took Long by the wrist, I was pleased to see that Long would not be held. He began chastising the two absconders in the Irish tongue. Their tones began in anger and then ran to a quiet intensity. Long seemed very much on top of them – he evinced their respect or their fear or both. Now they waited by mutely as Long turned to Charlie and me to explain their arrival.

They had seen our campfires and approved, it seemed, our choice of site for a homestead. They were used to building from the timber of the area, and they thought they might come down to offer their temporary labour.

I was bewildered by this idea, but Charlie was soon well-advanced in negotiating a price for the home, a further hut, the habitations of the shepherds, and for other split logs sufficient for the erecting of a serviceable shearing shed. Somehow these men, who had chosen to treat Felix as an unwanted animal, and who were incapable of being rendered contrite about it, knew well enough we were from Van Diemen's Land and began by proposing a contract fee of £45. Charlie argued them down to £20 and asked them to be kind enough to wait there and – if they chose – have some tea. 'I shall need to confer with my partner, Mr Bettany.'

Thus, meekly, the absconders went and sat on a log, facing Long and two of the hut-keepers, continuing with seeming jolliness their reminiscences sometimes in the English but also in the Irish tongue.

A little way off I opened a parallel discourse with Charlie.

'It is dishonour to employ these men,' I argued. 'We must send them away.'

'And thereafter be forever watchful of them?'

'If that is the price.'

'Their actions are not without reason, Jonathan. It is you solely who believes this impossible child has a future of any description.'

'I don't believe you could talk in such a way.'

'Dear God, I don't have to justify myself. I say I would not drown the child, but can see why they might! In the meantime, are we to go hut-less?'

He stepped away, to the place where the vigorous discourse between Long and the absconders was drawing to a close in flurries of dark, sputtering language. I frowned, thoroughly disappointed in myself at the prospect of admitting such men into my equation but wondering what else was to be done.

'Then enough!' Charlie cried. Long and the absconders stood up. 'It is not yet for us to pursue or curtail you gentlemen,' Charlie told the absconders. 'But we know of your acts, we know! It is not in our interest to send for police and to find out your habitation. If we suffered depredations – let me tell you! – it would quickly come to be within our interests indeed. For the moment you are fellow inhabitants of this country and we do not wish to see you unless we call for it, do you understand? While you are here companionably, we are willing to be companionable. An intrusion upon our flocks would create rigour in us, and motivate us to combine with Treloar's fellows and seek you out.'

'Do you want huts built then?'

Charlie said of course we did.

'So the rest is rigmarole,' said Rowan, 'but we understand you.'

Thus the contract was quickly concluded.

Charlie came back to me, 'Jonathan, cheer up. If we chose to capture them and did not achieve it at a gulp, their vengeance would be awful. This is unknown land to us, but not, I think, to them.'

'But there are still principles, Charlie. Even at such a distance.'

'Oh yes. Their principle is that they want £10 before they begin work.' Charlie laughed. 'It seems they have sometimes been duped by gentlemen in the bush.'

We retired to our tent and organised the appropriate bank notes. Out by the fire again, I watched Charlie hand a note to each of them, and they folded it, their eyes on me, into obscure pockets in their inner jackets. The comfort was that in accepting these notes they were folding into their jackets a potential doom. They could only be spent in towns like Braidwood or Goulburn, and spending them brought peril that a passing detachment of border police might recapture them.

The two lightly nodded to Charlie and me and walked up the rise behind our homestead tent. They were looking as it happened for redbutt and beefwood, which split well. Soon the sound of their axes indicated they had found some.

Later, I took Long aside. 'What do you and these men talk about?'

'We talk of experience, Mr Bettany. The usual things transported people speak of.'

'And what was their crime?'

'Same as O'Dallow's. They cut the hocks of cattle,' he told me levelly. 'Then they had a hard ship coming to New South Wales and a tyrannous master on the Hunter River.' His eyes were full on mine, and deep enough to suggest that with similar hardships he might have become something like them.

Just then, the two absconders came across the rise, hauling a log on their shoulders, and I was distracted into a sudden joy. It was now apparent in a new way that here on my hill amongst inhuman granite marbles a European habitation would for the first time be raised, and if by questionable hands, then by the sole hands to be had.

In nights that crackled with cold we had our first lambing. Charlie and Clancy worked with the shepherds and hut-keepers of the eastern flocks, Long and myself with the Leicesters and Merinos of the western. Generally, the ewes gave birth with a biblical simplicity – except in some cases when in frosty midnight, Long and I must wrench the lambs into the world with our hands. The men deftly plied their knives, castrating the males of the flock and sealing the wounds with a dab of tar. There was tenderness from these harsh fellows when they brought a quick end to the occasional sickly ewe, or carried lambs into the warmth of the hut fire.

At the end of a mere few days, our flocks had doubled! Mr Finlay's share of the increase were marked with a simple tar stroke – I felt he might delight to be identified as number 1 – mine were marked with a cross, and Charlie's with a C. Reflecting that this Arcadian place seemed anxious to reward us for our early gestures of faith and enthusiasm, I took a note of all the lambs of each flock in my stock book.

Then Charlie mounted up on his barrel-chested mare and was bent on going. On the way through Goulburn, he would employ more felon shepherds, and advance them ten shillings to make their way to me. He rode off, very happy, and by the end of the winter four more men bearing convict travel passports arrived, having walked and taken rides on wagons for part of the way from Goulburn. They seemed in high, wary fettle, and were very welcome, since they allowed me to separate out sections of the stock into their care. O'Dallow, whom Long had retained as his lieutenant, knew two of them, and there were reunions in the Gaelic tongue which were close to enthusiastic on O'Dallow's part.

In all our pastoral energy and hut-building and lambing, we had not yet encountered the local savages. But at dawn one morning Clancy came into our hut, the one shared for the moment by Long and myself, and told us there was a party of natives on the hill to the south-west, the one from which the absconders had taken their redbutt and beefwood timber amongst whose split uprights we now lived. As I gathered myself for this encounter I asked Clancy what he read of them.

'Jesus, Mr Bettany,' he said. 'They walk down here like the relatives coming to Christmas breakfast.'

At this moment one set of our shepherds and their two separate flocks were located still at the homestead area, where the pasture remained good. The hut-keeper of this party, the scholarly convict Shegog, at night slept in a little portable box, a coffin-like structure with handles protruding at either end and a door in the side, all designed to permit him to rest between the flocks for which at the onset of darkness he became nightwatchman. His job was to forestall the depredations of the mad, fierce, skilful native dogs, which lived, like the absconders, in the ridges and descended to rip out fifty throats in a few minutes, reducing with lightning savagery the cries of their victims to a sigh and stupefying the rest of the flock. So Shegog was for his colleagues cook and housekeeper by day, flock-tender and light sleeper in his little hutch by night, an existence which I would not have chosen for myself, and which appealed largely to eccentric men.

Shegog came up to me now and addressed me in that strange way, one eye on the sky, one off to the side. 'These creatures here,' he told me, 'might be related to the ones I knew and learnt to converse with in the County of Murray. Would you choose me to talk to them now?'

I was dubious of Shegog's linguistics but authorised him anyhow. What could be the harm?

I could now see a little way up the hill to the south-west a scene I was familiar with from my experiences with Felix. The leading screen of native men, dressed in their possum cloaks for a season which still retained a trace of cold, and bearing lances as casually as walking sticks, were descending into the socket of earth where our homestead buildings stood. They were talking amongst each other, but only sometimes now and then did their conversation take on a heightened quality, an urgency. I could smell the sharp, particular redolence of these warriors and elders, and see again, higher up the hill behind them, children flitting, and women of all ages swathed in skin coats above thin, bare legs. I could hear too the more distant, sharp, speculative chatter of the women. Were these the same group who had rejected Felix? I had no way of telling.

'Do the heathens expect to spear our livestock?' Long, jealous of his promised increase, asked at his side.

Shegog reassured him, 'They would not have brought mother and all the kiddies if they did.'

Closer now to the men, Shegog took up an extraordinary posture. He spread his arms wide, so that he looked like a thin-legged bird, and approached them with an exaggerated, high-stepping gait. It seemed he knew what he was doing, for there were immediate explosions of laughter from the old men who stood at the centre of the line, as from the women, old and young, further up the hill. Abruptly he abandoned the peculiar stance and took up something more normal, though I think the man was eccentric and nothing was quite normal with him. Long and several of the other men were laughing nearly as much as the natives.

Shegog began greeting them, a few words at a time, and the old men nodded at last and began to speak back, again, one or two words at a time, like say a Spaniard talking to an Italian, testing the shared features of this or that word.

'He's a thorough wizard, that little fellow, isn't he?' asked Long in a murmur.

The hut-keeper made an inclusive gesture, indicating the hill we stood on, the entire plateau, all its solitary stones, all its rugged forest, all its broad pasture. The discourse went on, the sentences got longer. Then Shegog turned back to us. 'The old men keep saying 'bogong-bogong'. Thus, many bogong moths.' He lifted one hand, and adopted a pedagogic pose. 'They produce the plural by repetition of the word.'

'These are those great thumping moths,' said Long, 'which plague us.'

Indeed, since the weather had turned a little warmer, huge muscular moths had begun invading the huts, crazy for treacle and the flame of our mutton-fat lamps. When one such moth in its frenzy had collided with my forehead, it had felt like a punch from a small child. At the tail end of the tribal crowd facing us I saw women idly peeling moths off the outer layers of the congregations which had settled on a tree trunk and feeding them to the children, who munched them with apparent relish, while not for a second taking their eyes off their elders' encounter with the strangers.

'So they are the Moth people,' I said.

'In previous employment,' Shegog the hut-keeper told me, 'I dined off the moths myself, for variety. But don't concern yourself, sir. At the close of summer, when the cold weather returns, both moths and sable brethren shall disappear. One good frost and these visitors will be on their way to lower ground, down beyond Treloar's Bulwa Mountain station. Then the new moths and our seasonal visitors will reappear when spring is well advanced. I saw it on my former station!'

Things the great Macaulay and Carlyle, splendid figures of the literary world, contributors to the journals Shegog cherished, had not dreamed of, their furthest disciple had seen!

Behind us, just a stroll backwards, a pint pot of tea hung over our outdoor fire and permanently brewed. I walked back, the native males pressing forward all the more to watch me, poured some tea into a pannikin, mixed in sugar, and had Long take it to the line of elders. I did not choose to do this myself. I felt reluctant to establish some sort of trade between peers; that is, I, the occupier and owner-at-heart of this country, was unwilling to greet those gnarled old men as some sort of native equivalent to myself. As they were occupying themselves with the tea, I had Clancy pour some pounds of wheaten flour and pass them in a bag to the elders. We handed over as well a few twists of tobacco. It was clear that, as I surmised, they knew from their winters in neighbouring country about the uses of tobacco, for they held it up and mimed chewing it. We laughed, and a thin old man of authority cried, 'Baccy, baccy!' which caused a bright smile from all his fellows.

Communication having succeeded to this point, the serious-minded Long took over negotiations from Shegog and pointed to the nearby flocks. 'Woolly fellows,' he cried. 'You don't bloody spear 'em, you understand?' He made lancing movements and then raised an imaginary rifle to his shoulder and pointed it at our visitors. 'You understand that?'

This threat caused so much jollity amongst the visitors that under his lean and weathered features Long reddened, as if caught out in his most secret desires – to enjoy this country without interference. The black men went on chatting as if we were not there, and the women further up the hill were occupied in their own business, part of which was to keep their children from us and distract them. Only two or three older women who sat on the ground resting and whose dragging dugs showed beneath their cloaks of kangaroo, seemed to watch us at all intently. As if at a signal none of us were aware of, the men casually turned away from us and strolled up the hill, collecting as they went the sundry other elements of their group, and disappearing in the verticals of forest very quickly.

They seemed to have concluded that we were harmless, which did not please Long, with his hunger for eventual herds.

It is October and my first shearing! Consider this: shepherds, hut-keepers, Clancy, O'Dallow all standing in a line in the stream – some of them are waist-deep, in waters not always kindly or dependable. And with Boxer, Brutus, Bet and myself harrying them, the sheep race across, going from soap-filled hand to soap-filled hand. Tar and other substances, including

New South Wales's infamous Bathurst burrs, adhere to the wool despite the best work of my men. That is not our business. Let the buyer clean the wool after he has bought it and given us our reward!

Soon all the sheep stand, drying in the sun, in the stockyards by the shearing shed, which we have erected from the timbers cut for us by the absconders. O'Dallow and Long show the men how to sharpen their shears on holystone – we do not have the luxury of a honing wheel.

Immediately after the wool-washing in the river, for which I rewarded each man with two glasses of rum to keep any chill out, we sat at a great outdoor fire, dining as ever on mutton and damper. I let their chatter wash over me, their teasing peculiarities of which I had no knowledge, and I felt that glorious sense that life was both very simple and gloriously complicated. Above us, threads of smoke marked out the places where the moth-eaters were. But they were a mere chorus to our preparations for taking the fleece.

The next morning, when I came out of the little two-room homestead hut, I saw the least welcome inhabitants of the region, the absconders in their eternal layers of skins, approaching. One of their horses, a grey, moved lazily, but the other was of daintier dimensions and, by comparison, danced across the frost-seared pasture.

'We saw the washing going on,' the Captain told me (though I am determined never to call him by such a ridiculous name). 'Do you wish for two sets of hands?'

'I have adequate hands.'

Rowan said, 'Well maybe. If youse want to be still shearing at Christmas!'

I wondered what Christmas was to him, and what kind of Yules he had spent.

'We are at your call,' he continued. 'A pound a day for the two of us and four glasses of rum. It's the normal thing.'

I called Long and we stood aside for a moment. They waited without anxiety, surveying countryside they might have thought of as their own.

'They want a pound a day for two of them,' I told him. 'It's similar to their log-splitting. But where would they spend it?'

Long nodded, for he knew. 'Oh sir, they creep to shebeens and into certain western towns. If they prove incompetent, which I much doubt they will, for they are country lads, then, sir, you can send them away. God knows we need every hand.'

Long's advice in this as in everything else would never betray me, yet

I did wonder if he saw himself in those lost men, saw a mirror of his own want, his crime and his anger in them. I expect that he believed one thing divided him from Captain Rowan. He had a promise of five per cent of our cattle. And he had not had the lash.

'As long as they work,' I said, yielding to sin and lawlessness in the gathering of the fleece, as I had earlier in the building of huts. I was getting used to such arrangements.

I did not want for models of how I should behave during the shearing of the flock. I had seen Mr Batchelor and my father march up and down the boards between the pens where men cut the wool with, if one was lucky, gliding motions of the shears. Many times I had heard my father calling amused instructions and, seeing the shears bite flesh here and there, cry with a whimsy which might have sounded worse to the men than tyranny, 'Jimmy, are you shearing or do you want to extract the gall bladder by way of surgery!' My father had been a great generator of good humour on the boards at Ross, as I tried to be here, though seeking to be sometimes masterly like Mr Batchelor. The absconders were the fastest workers, though they moved the shears with broad gestures and sometimes cut the sheep, barely pausing for Shegog to apply tar to the cut. Whatever I said by way of good humour to other men, I did not extend it to Rowan and Tadgh.

Long and I took the fleeces on a bench, then O'Dallow, Clancy, Long and I laid them in, one above another, head to tail, tail to head, head to tail, in a wool press of cut planks and logs, using all our weight to push down on the log which acted as lever and lowering the great boulder bound to it by rope onto the rectangular press. This earth which had known nothing but fire and stillness thus produced its first wool.

When all the sheep were shorn and turned out of the yards, I stood again by a fire with shepherds and hut-keepers and overseer, drinking tea and rum, and felt the weight and friction of my European nature against this lovely place, and praised its divinities.

My Merinos yielded an average of five pounds of fleece each at Nugan Ganway's first shearing, as did Charlie's sheep, which were looked after by the party to the east of the homestead. Mr Finlay's Leicesters gave more – over six pounds per sheep – but even in its greasy form, lying on the dirt floor of the shearing shed, I could see how superior the Merino wool stood with its greater crimp and density.

Over 1700 pounds of wool was thus pressed and stored in wool packs, which were in turn manhandled and levered onto the wagon. It made a tall, beetling mass, tethered with rope, but looked insecure and fragile as human prosperity. The bullocks, which had had an easeful winter, would draw the fleece to market. I had decided I would travel with Clancy and conduct the negotiations myself, confidently leaving Long to manage the men. I had promised him that during the summer we would muster in our cattle, and assess his promised percentage of the natural increase on them. I could tell from his smouldering delight at my calculations that he had a peasant hunger to own livestock, and that, on the hoof, it would ever be perfectly acceptable to him. With such visions in his head, he would be a more exacting master than I needed to be.

As for flocks, there now seemed no reason why Nugan Ganway should not provide pasture for some 20 000 sheep. I relished these figures.

THE SARAH DOCUMENTS WOULD RESOUND with Prim. She would see that she too was in a sort of Female Factory, confined – more broadly and benignly than Sarah Bernard – by consent and affection, but mostly by fear of leaving the Sudan and going home. By the time she came to read the Bernard letters and the Bettany transcripts she was conscious of having chosen, two years past, her Sudanese exile over all else and of having slighted her sister. In late 1987 she had received a faxed wedding invitation from Dimp. At the time, Prim had recently returned from Adi Hamit, where with Sherif, Erwit and two Khartoum nurses, and the help of the resident clinic sister Therese and the midwife Abuk, she has used Sherif's questionnaire to ask Dinka women about the health of their families. From the answers, Sherif had calculated the Crude Death Rate and Infant Mortality Rate and other indices of need, and Prim had sent a copy of the final analysis of the survey to Dimp, expecting her to be reassured and somehow reconciled by it.

Instead, the reply was full of Dimp's own compelling business, though she thanked Prim for the report from Adi Hamit. 'What a place! My little sister right there! Sometimes I wish I was with you, my clever, brave, unselfish sis, making a filmed record perhaps.' But she passed quickly to the real news.

Well, I can't be. The annulment is at last through, and Bren is free in conscience to marry me, which is set to occur next February. I can't express the happiness of this. To be his wife seems an extraordinary kind

of reward – at the end of such a wait, too. Come and share my happiness.
You're overdue for leave. Couldn't you come ... please? Why not bring
this Sherif fellow you're so keen on? You're so scant with details on the
poor bugger! You just don't satisfy the obvious questionings of your
prurient sister. Let me see the bloke in person, and draw my own conclu-
sions. Just think, he'd shake Sydney up! Why don't you just settle here?
Come home. You can swamp any memory of the Auger business by
having a handsome African lover and being the most beautiful couple in
Sydney.

We're talking about the last weekend of February, Saturday the 24th.
We'll be married by a Jesuit at St Canice's, but without some of the florid
touches of big church weddings. I'm ringing round restaurants to find
which ones are available for that weekend. If you and Sherif came – that
would be the star act!

As for Bren, he's as enthusiastic as a great loutish dog, and he's going
round sniffing out houses. There's one at Double Bay, right on the
harbour, above a little beach – Seven Shillings Beach. This house which,
if he buys it will turn out to be the fanciest abode this poor blowsy body
has known, is a sort of opulent Californian adobe expansion of what
was once a plain old Federation two-storey. It has three enormous
sundecks above the water! Does that enrage you adequately?

So can you come back for the wedding, if not forever?

Please make the arrangements if you can. We are, after all, sole close
relatives to each other. Come home and be appalled by the way we live.

All my love,
Dimple D'Arcy-to-be

Prim knew her sister had every right to expect her to be at the wedding.
Without her, Dimp would be able to muster to the nuptials only an aging
uncle and aunt-in-law. Contrary to all reason though, Prim felt stampeded by the thought of Sydney. Could she go back there as a chummy,
affectionate sister?

Out of shame she made a plane booking, but the thought of February
still filled her with persistent terror. As it turned out, a severe malaria
would come to her aid. Three months before the wedding, in December
1987, she felt an excruciating joint pain, an unprecedented headache,
and her temperature mounted to 104 degrees. She was admitted on Sherif's advice to the UN clinic in Khartoum and for five days suffered the
most severe cerebral derangement in which the entire cosmos, from God

to her dead parents to Auger to the Pidanu sisters, pressed in on her for urgent discourse. Hence a micro-organism rescued her from the need to travel home for her sister's wedding. When her temperature fell to normal levels she was extremely weak and bedridden for a further two weeks, during which it was not difficult to manoeuvre a number of doctors, including Sherif, into doubting the wisdom of her flying to Australia soon. In fact, by the wedding's date she was robust again, and disquieted with being in her office in Khartoum. But the day passed, and Dimp was off on a honeymoon in Thailand to which any hankering she might have had earlier for blood relatives wasn't relevant.

And Prim was busy. It was a time when the Sudanese military had withdrawn from direct civil government and permitted a new prime minister to be elected. It proved to be Sadiq el Mahdi, an urbane-looking man who wore a business suit rather than military or traditional garb. But that did not bring any change as regards the war in the South. It was still being fought, and refugees abounded, fallout from unrecorded village tragedies.

It was an easy time to forget her failing of Dimp. Fergal Stoner, not content to fall back on his renown as proclaimer of the Darfur famine, had devised a scheme by which food could be equitably distributed, by permission of the combatant parties, in both the North and South. He presented the gleaming logistics of his plan to EC headquarters in Brussels and to the new government of Sudan, which was resistant, seeing itself forced, by typically self-serving Western appeals to conscience, into talks with those it perceived as Southern terrorists.

For a while it had looked as if Stoner's plan was stymied. Helene Codderby told Prim there was a chance Stoner would be sacked for overreaching. 'Darfur was famous, of course, but there's a sense he talked the numbers up. And now the government suspects he's had secret meetings here, in restaurants and rooms around the city, with rebel agents, you know, the SPLA.'

Some system of relief was clearly needed. Only a scatter of aircraft had been permitted to take aid south, and had been shot at by Southern rebels not involved in the preliminary negotiations. The Red Crescent had distributed some relief food by Nile barge, but its ministrations had been limited to a few towns. In the end economics helped Stoner. An expensive government end-it-all campaign in the South has been blunted in the marshes and along the bush tracks which were the South's roads. With the nation's debt still rising, the prime minister came under pressure from the United States and the World Bank to settle the costly war. And if the South could be supplied with food, people would stay at home, and the government would not be burdened with masses of refugees.

Stoner called Prim in her office. 'Had you heard about my scheme for the South being, you know, picked up?'

'Congratulations. What's it called? The Stoner Plan?'

'Ha bloody ha! It's called Operation Safety. A hopeful title, right?'

Prim worked on logistics at Stoner's office in the New Extension, not far from her own office. Amongst other tasks she had to liaise with a UN official named Anwar, stationed in the Republic of Chad, over funding for a fleet of six Ilyushin transport planes he intended to bring to Khartoum. At last Prim assembled the funding for the charter from Australian, Canadian and Scandinavian NGOs operating in the Sudan, and a delighted Anwar told her it would be a mere few days before his Ilyushins, the UN logo freshly stencilled in lavender on their flanks, would land in Khartoum. They would be filled with rice, UN high protein biscuit, wheat and sorghum, and go south.

She went with Stoner to Khartoum airport to greet Anwar's armada as it touched down. It was piloted, in the spirit of the event, by men from everywhere: Kenya, Egypt, Belgium, New Zealand. Anwar himself was accompanied by his Bolivian lover Julio. They had found their haven in Chad, just as Prim had found hers in the Sudan.

So as Anwar, Julio, Stoner crammed themselves along with her onto little seats, their knees tight up against the strapped cargo, it was not only possible to forget the larger questions, but also her failure of her sister. They were on their way to Aweil, after all, a dangerous market town and garrison to the west of the Nuba Hills.

Prim was with Stoner when he held respectful talks with the Sudanese brigade commander in the fortified military headquarters in the town. The commandant gave his permission for the opening of a feeding centre at a site south of the town. In this clearing, in a landscape of tall grass, palms, and equatorially lush trees, Stoner and Prim helped to pitch UNESCO bell-tents for Anwar and Julio to live in as they set up this first station and established a network of depots in the Bahr el Ghazal province. Trucks rented from contractors in Aweil, with 'laissez-passer' on both sides, would move the food.

At a small table in the depot clearing, Prim and Stoner ate dinner of wheaten bread and kebabs with Anwar and Julio on the second night. During the meal, tall men in military fatigues turned up to share the food. They proved to be rebel officers, long-limbed, lean-handed, ritual scarring on their cheeks, dining within sight of the garrison lights of Aweil. The night air, laden with heat and ambiguity, swelled the throat.

Flown back to Khartoum, Prim spent unexciting but utterly engrossing weeks resupplying Anwar and Julio, whose depot was merely the first gesture of a broader plan to feed, restock and reseed a thousand villages depleted by war. She intended to fly back to Aweil, and had Austfam's permission to take Dr Sherif Taha with her. His health survey at Adi Hamit had been so useful. Now he would conduct an investigation into the health and morale of the refugees on the edge of this southern town. On the strength of Austfam's approval of him, he had the grudging permission too of the Sudanese Ministry of Health. His proposed study was considered, for good or ill, ground-breaking, at least in its potential.

All this activity, all this application to the needs of Southerners, distracted Prim from the truth: that she had abandoned her sister to marriage, and her solitary monomania over ancestors.

Letter No 3, SARAH BERNARD

Marked by her: NOT FOR SENDING

Dearest Alice
I have begun to think of strong means to make up for my weakness. Yes I would face hanging for murder if I needed to. There are knives sharp and blunt at table. I envisage myself taking them to hand. I see in my mind blood and potato falling from the mouth of Steward Pallmire and I hear the howls of Mrs Matron while I say: You thought I lacked any power but I was able to do this. It would be a lesson to all. I am ready to try it and only sometimes think what will befall my Alice on her own and inside that place where you are – and this where I am.

Well vice has been forestalled in its path and so has revenge. Because up from the river come one hundred and twenty further women from a new Dublin ship Eurydice. *I note amongst the freckled ones a number of fair beings and wonder in my shame can some of them stand as victims in my stead.*

And I find that Mrs Pallmire seeks me out in all the rush of settling these women in and wishes to drink tea with me. I cannot explain how

*she wants that. But in some way I have suddenly become her familiar.
She tells me: You are a true lady. It is strangeness itself yet who can say
that drinking tea in her kitchen is not an improvement over what last
happened. In the Tory in my new and sudden standing as servant and
confiding friend to Mrs Pallmire I am safe from mockery. But I see Mrs
Pallmire pause by a young woman fresh from Eurydice who grows silent
and raises her eyes to the exalted Mrs Matron and there is in them a
cow-like fear. I know this was the same exact gaze the poor girl raised
to the magistrate at trial. It is a gaze pleading for punishment though
she does not know that.*

*That same Mrs Pallmire takes from me the burden of destroying Mr
Steward Pallmire. She is suddenly pleased to count herself my protector.
I am meant to work in her house. But chiefly I sit and listen to her talk.
She tells me that she met Pallmire when they were seventeen years – he
working as an errand boy and porter in training at the county orphanage
in Guildford and she as a servant. He was always very wry – so she says.
She gleams when she says it. This is a very strange affection between
them. She says he always had funny little songs. Then she asks me about
my husband.*

*I say: I was married to Corporal McWhirter. He was tall and had pale
skin but he was moderate in drink. He did not have funny little songs.
He went to Jamaica with his regiment. When in Manchester City prison
I had a letter from his brother who was a soldier in another regiment.
Fever had killed him. It kills men in greater numbers in the West Indies
than any cannon. But though I was really widowed M for married
somehow went beside my widowed name when I was put onto the ship.*

*I commence bawling at that or rather tears leak out. I want to say he
was a good man which was as much as I can remember to say for him.
But I will not say it in front of her since it has no meaning for her. She
thought Steward Pallmire a good man and a trump and likely rogue.
Nothing to be said to her that means anything! In any case and whatever
their condition – married or widowed or in exile – women cannot speak.
Or they can speak but are not heard. Their words do not cause the
smallest change in the course of this world which belongs to men.*

*And Mrs Pallmire asks: You did a silly thing when he was sent away
to Jamaica?*

*I confessed to her that that is what some said. They said of me: Foolish
girl without the love and guidance of her husband! The magistrate
tempered my sentence to fourteen years on that account but could not*

overlook the offence. As for innocence it is a word a person does not utter here without creating gales of laughter. The other women believe you my dear Alice when you tell how you were incited to poison your husband and what a Cyclops he was. They are reverent when you talk of your old husband. Doting son of an aged mother who exhorted him on her deathbed – as you have told me my dear – to mind his health by taking small dosages of arsenic and mercury salts – all of which he had to hand being a dyer.

They listened in silence when you tell them you took from his dyeing shop the substances of his trade. Red alizarin from the madder root. Mixed with alkaline salts it was potent but merely made him queasy. Yellow picric acid and Prussian blue were what you were driven to. It is an ornate crime and it stands telling again and again and is so unlike the dreary daily crimes of the rest of us. For them we cannot cry: Innocence!

And as I sit drinking tea with Matron Pallmire I am but one year done with my sentence and have six years to run before I get the half freedom of my ticket. I believe that as soon as I have done the correct services by you my Alice and given you rescue I must surely lie down under the weight of that time and perish by my own will.

We spend an hour together – this is Mrs Pallmire and me – when the tin box of tea on the sideboard has only a few leaves in it. Go across the hallway – says Mrs Matron – and into the side bedroom. Take the tin with you and fill it from there. I walk as she has instructed and open a door and find myself in a room where it is hard to move for hampers of piled soap on one side and cases of tea of which one has its lid prised. From it in that hushed cave of treasures I refill the tin not using a measure but holding up handfuls of dark china leaf. See how it falls into the caddy. I have lived by measures – an ounce here and one and a half ounces there – since I was first imprisoned. The room beggars my belief and it is for this room – for the permission to conduct this room and other rooms and fill them with plenty – that Mr Steward Pallmire is permitted by his wife to have his compensation from the girls in the Factory. This room contains what Mrs Pallmire finds precious and its piled-up preciousness with her can be felt in here.

I had discovered them in their hoarding – these two Pallmire people who give the women in the Tories four ounces of soap to last them for two weeks for body and clothing. These people who eke to each of us a few ounces of tea and there are women here who would sell their souls for tea or tay as the little red brick woman Carty calls it. Her sweetest

*comfort. All the riches of soap and tea are in this room and God knows
what in other rooms!*

*Yes – so I tell the Pallmires silently – you have been careless with me
and I shall make a record. I am not a stupid woman. I have the cleverness
to write a letter. And when next I am sent to a room like this one I shall
make a count.*

*Knowing this I feel well at once. I feel too that small amounts are the
failing of the convict women. We were innocent enough to take small
quantities – crimes in ounces and mere pinches – not in pounds and
pounds stored up.*

*I say to myself then: I have you two! I have Mrs Julius Caesar Matron
and Mr Julius Caesar God-Almighty Steward Pallmire. I am altogether
very pleased without thinking how rash it is to think this way inside the
Factory. I think that our rescue Alice is in knowing what I know.*

I put my name to this now and one day she shall read.

Sarah

⁀

I TAKE OUR WOOL TO SALE

Clancy and I with our towering load, and with the axles holding up
splendidly, slept at night beneath our wagon. We avoided Goldspink's
homestead, and the man's odious company, and so traversed the limestone plains, sheltering only one night in an overseer's bush hut before
our approach to Goulburn. I set Clancy to camp near the racecourse but
rode up on Hobbes to Finlay's house. I was quite elated at the idea of a
proper bed and glass windows and good china, as well as breathing
within brick and exactly timbered walls after months of living in the
midst of bark and beefwood.

The convict woman who was housekeeper met me at the door and
asked me in at once, but I was disappointed to find that the house
possessed a cold air, as if it were being only half lived in. Of course, with
the lively Phoebe gone there was bound to be a sense of vacancy.

The housekeeper had told me that Mrs Finlay was away visiting relatives in Yass, but that Mr Finlay, who was out at the moment, had
particularly said he wished to see me when I came through. Did I need
anything?

Since my only baths in the past months had been in the Murrumbidgee
River, I asked her could a bath be poured. A zinc tub was quickly filled

for me, and I sat amongst the steam in miraculous luxury, contemplating my coming wealth and mulling over the maker's name imprinted in the flange of the bath: Tatlow and Sons, Manchester. That man, I thought, that Tatlow and not only his sons but also his daughters would one day wear cloth woven from the pastures of Nugan Ganway. Since I had made wool out of the world of Nugan Ganway, I felt an interest in all that was made on earth. Bettany was, like Tatlow and Sons, a creator.

I shaved off a large part of the beard I had grown, and then shaved again in case handsome Mrs Finlay returned home. Then, emergent from the bathroom, I was given the choice between a bedroom to rest in and a library to read in, and chose the library. The *Sydney Herald* had an essay on the grief convict servants caused their masters.

It was nearly six o'clock that evening when the housekeeper knocked on the library door and told me Mr Finlay was waiting for me in the front parlour. It was said in a hushed way, as if Mr Finlay were not used to being delayed. I found him behind his big front window, looking out at the sweet blue of an Australian dusk. He held in his hand, which was extended as if he had just finished reading, several sheets of writing paper.

'Good evening, Mr Finlay,' I said after a polite cough. 'It is a great pleasure to see you, not least because I wanted to discuss what you would consider a minimum price for your Leicester wool.'

'Not now,' he said, not looking at me but holding out the papers. 'For the moment would you read aloud from the third paragraph on page 1 to the end of the second paragraph on page 2 of this letter from my daughter?'

Confused by his lack of welcome, I needed to ask him could he nominate the passages again. He repeated them in insistent tones, like a man teaching the wilful or the idiotic. I took the pages and fumbled with them. At the head of the first, in an earnest hand, rich in copperplate flourish, was written 'The Convent of the Soeurs de Sacre Coeur, Genève, June 27th, 1838'. The letter was nearly four months old.

How curious, I thought, that the English gentry, who so mistrusted Papists, would so willingly commit their daughters to be trained by nuns. But French nuns ... they were considered elegant and safe. My eyes glanced over a mention of a forthcoming expedition by coach the young ladies of the Sacre Coeur would make to Frutigen.

But the third paragraph on page one began, 'Though it is possible to regret the raw nature of new country, I must tell you that no life other than that of New South Wales will satisfy me. Before I left Lansdown

Park, I proposed an arrangement to Mr Bettany by which he would in the end marry me and take me into new country. The sight of European men, who have not known and cannot know the size or the nature of our continent, confirms me in the wisdom of this compact. Since a dutiful daughter reports such decisions, I must report that I intend upon my return to fulfil our agreement and to marry Mr Bettany. This means I must live if necessary in a bark hut as his spouse, and this I thought it right to inform you in good time. I look forward to an existence as Mr Bettany's spouse, and it is something of which all my fellow students not only approve but at which they express envy.

'If then you should meet Mr Bettany in the interim, I would ask you to exercise the duty of a wise parent and treat him with all the courtesy of a future spouse of your daughter and of father to your grandchildren.'

I looked up in confusion. I could not believe a promise exacted from me by a child, a half-joking pledge, could turn on me like this.

'Perhaps you could explain,' suggested Mr Finlay, 'what Mrs Finlay and I are to make of our daughter's statement.'

'A promise was half-given, it's true. It was given as in a play . . .' Even to myself I sounded flustered, like a man lashing about. It had been a joke, or nearly a joke. But I could not quite say that, just the same. I could not have her parents say, 'Mr Bettany thinks your letter a joke.' So far from New South Wales by the waters of Geneva, an accusation of silliness might be very wounding to the girl.

'Please,' I said, 'it was a fantastic idea your daughter proposed almost as a whimsy.' I realised that this was a very poor substitute for calling her foolish. 'Naturally I thought a European education would remove her from that sort of intention. Visiting your relatives in Scotland, I assumed she would meet some suitable young Englishman . . .'

It was time to be silent. I could see Mr Finlay's dark eyes running through various phases of furious disbelief. 'I would have thought that as a courtesy,' he said, 'I, who have welcomed you to my house and extended to you pasture not otherwise available, could have been confided in.'

'Certainly,' I said. 'Had I thought the idea a genuine one, I would have done so.' But I confessed to myself that I had in a way, and however briefly, enjoyed the secrecy of our contract.

Becoming more and more severe within his compact, manly body, Mr Finlay said, 'I cannot help but wonder under what circumstances this supposed betrothal was arranged?'

How could I say, she came to my room! 'Let me tell you, those circumstances . . . they were utterly innocent.'

'A Vandemonian and the son of a convict speaks to me of utter innocence?'

The jibe brought on the normal panic in me, a panic of rage but also of the inescapability of my description. It seemed to me once more so obvious and so universal that whoever looked at me saw above all a felon's child. No matter how much of their fleece I had brought them, no matter the stock books I kept, or how I comported myself, the intervening description of who I was cast its yellow, questionable light on all I did.

'Did you mention the concept?' asked – or more accurately – demanded Mr Finlay. 'Which she then took up with her normal girlish enthusiasm?'

How could I let myself be accused of planting such an idea in a child's mind? For to Mr Finlay it was, no doubt, the sort of thing the offspring of convicts did all the time.

'No,' I insisted. 'It was a fanciful suggestion of your daughter, as I've said. I would like to take as much blame as is appropriate, but my mind was very much set, and happily so, on the enterprise of finding my own station beyond the limits.'

'And so you closed the matter off then?' asked acute Mr Finlay. 'You told her that it was unseemly and ridiculous and impossible?'

'Ah,' was all I could say, looking to at least two of the corners of the room for aid which they could not offer. 'You will sometimes promise a young person something for the sake of pleasantness. And because you know that all undertakings will evaporate under the pressure of time.'

Mr Finlay now did something very confusing in the midst of this intense quarrel. He sat down. 'I mention the fact of your father being an emancipated felon. I did not know that till, on his last journey here, Charles Batchelor let it slip.'

I did not like to see my father dismissed in those few words. 'My father is a transportee, that can't be denied. Surely I didn't tell you otherwise?'

'No, but the letter from Mr Batchelor concerning you was so enthusiastic, and it did not mention it.'

'The Batchelors were always very kind to our family and treated us as members of theirs.'

'But surely I expressed my views on emancipists when you were at dinner here.'

I felt myself possessed by my unruly blood.

'Are you trying to say, Mr Finlay, that apart from any objectionable aspects of my role in your daughter's daydream, my problems stem from my paternity?'

'You would not want me to dissemble on that matter, I take it?'

Charlie had been right. Mr Finlay was a gross interferer and a gleaner of power. I apologised for my neglect of him and his wife, thanked him for his past kindnesses, and then said, 'But I think I must go now, since you entered into our business arrangement under a false impression that I was the child of free settlers. That I have kept correct stock and wool books, and I have some quite splendid wool out on the wagon, much of the longer staple wool being yours – that is clearly nothing to your mind. When I have found the opportunity to sell it, I shall recompense you.'

'Very well,' said Mr Finlay. 'I expect ten pence a pound from my share of the wool. I would be very pleased to forget that sum if you write to my daughter and tell her that any sort of connection between the two of you is ridiculous. That you live in a bark hut surrounded by natives and by the lowest of the felonry.'

'And am a felon myself, no doubt,' I said.

He ignored my irony, and I knew that in some ways his offer was reasonable. But the thought that he was enjoying, was congratulating himself on having me skewered on the immutable iron of my father's transportation brought out a fierce reluctance in me. Also, I had a sharp vision of Phoebe's face against the white of her gown as she made her preposterous speech in moonlight. There was something in her that could not be traded for ten pence per pound of Leicester wool.

'I would be very pleased to oblige such a generous offer,' I told him, 'but I can't. You see, we owe your daughter's letter the courtesy, in my book, of not letting her know the two of us have discussed it in terms of wool prices.'

Now Mr Finlay looked away as if to an unseen witness. 'Dear God,' he murmured, 'I think there is still some sort of ambition in the man.'

'Oh,' I said, 'there is certainly ambition, but it is not directed at your daughter.'

'Very well,' he said. 'I shall expect an accounting. You'll deal with my agent, Mr Tute of the Bank of Australia. You may deliver my Leicesters to me before Christmas. You may keep your one-third of the increase, but I would like to see an appropriate and at least plausible record. Please do not delay in rendering me that record or in returning my sheep. Since you occupy land beyond the limits, your tenure is insecure, and I have friends at the newly formed Land Commission who could make it extremely insecure indeed.'

I told him he could have his Leicesters back well before Christmas. I decided I would send them up in the care of the sullen O'Dallow, who could be depended upon not to show excessive respect. Then, profoundly offended, I left the Finlay house, its chance of a splendid dinner and tea of a delicate tint in a china cup.

My flock had been diminished, and must somehow be restored – obviously from the money earned by the sale of wool. I would therefore not have many reserves of cash to deposit in the Bank of Australia or the Savings Bank at Goulburn. I was above all tormented by the revived image of the young Phoebe, and thus spent a doubly tormented night resting beneath the wagon with Clancy, and ended in rousing him early so that I could get away from the hated reach of Mr Finlay.

Hope kept me lively on the way over the divide and down the terraces of the foothills, where at every stop I was vigilant to keep Clancy out of the pubs we passed. If he got drunk I did not have the wagon-driving skills to keep up the pace, and certainly lacked the breadth of profane language to make the bullocks take me seriously. In warm, humid days and country flat and pleasant we drew near the area called the Black Huts.

Ahead of us, in this nondescript little village of aged slab-timber huts which gave the place a look of pervasive greyness, natives could be seen walking in the streets in shirts and with blankets over their shoulders. An occasional white settler rode the main street past a small stone bank and a large brick hotel. The place had no look of being a golden town.

Yet energy suffused the landscape as a slim man in a plum-coloured swallow-tailed coat, nankeen pants and neat tan leather riding boots came thundering out of the town on a very fine roan mare. Drawing level with us, he hauled his mount to a stop, jumped down and ran up to me, his eyes frankly on our load of fleece.

'Sir,' he said breathlessly, in a Yorkshire accent from which in the north country way he dropped all definite articles. 'Sir, name is Barley and I am a Sydney wool merchant. I started out early along road on offchance of encountering such a load as yours. May I ask where you come from, sir?'

But he did not wait for an answer, walking instead to the bales of wool on the wagon and having a look at the name on them: a rough stencil cut by Long had provided the woolsacks with the inked words 'NUGAN GANWAY' together with the letters 'CBJB'.

'My dear Lord,' said Barley, 'I've been meeting wagons three years now and each year names multiply as if it were infinite out there. Tell me, is Nugan Ganway located just this side of infinity?'

I said that it was far south of Goulburn and he started to laugh like someone wishing to share a joke, fraternally. 'I'm sure I might have a pleasant proposition for you, Mr Nugan Ganway. But it must await my inspection. With your permission ... ' He took from his pocket a knife and at the same time a courteous needle and heavy thread. He hauled himself by the ropes on the load onto the great structure of bales, and with only the rims of his tan boots keeping purchase on the edge of the wagon he set about cutting some sacks open to sample the wool. The needle and thread were for Clancy to re-sew whichever sacks he opened.

He slit only three of the wool packs, two on one side of the wagon, then one on the other, thrusting in his hand and surveying the handfuls of fibre he extracted. He seemed engrossed but made no comment on them until he jumped down and waited with me, chattering away, while Clancy mended the packs.

'Now, sir,' he said. 'When your man is done with that, could I prevail upon him to remove some outer packs? Not you, sir, not you of course, but some squatters are careful to put all fine fleece on outside of load. It is utterly customary for a chap in my position to look within load, and I know you would not consider that in any way a personal affront.'

I was taken by the fact that he had as much energy for the wool as I. I looked at his eager face and glittering eyes – he was slightly shorter than me, with a big-nosed, terrier look which, taken with his general energy of manner made him easy to like. I said I would not be offended by his request, but that some of the bales were of Leicester wool from the same station. Clancy removed some of the bales and Barley climbed again aboard the wagon to test the Leicester and other inner sacks of wool. He plied his knife, pulled out a handful and considered it. Jumping down a last time, I was pleased to see he played none of the normal games one would expect of a wool broker. There were no frowns, no sighs supposedly induced by poor quality in what he had just inspected.

'This strikes me as wool grown at altitude, sir,' he observed.

I admitted that much of my property was at 1500 feet and some of it, the hills in which my herd of cattle was located, higher.

'Well I must say this is excellent, sir, excellent crimp and scale. You have done very well in my opinion, my dear Lord, yes. Nine pence a pound won't do for this, at least for your Merino! I shall have to offer you 10 pence ha'penny to stop you from being intercepted by other merchants.

'You see, sir, that little town yon will by noon today be full of Sydney wool merchants, but none as jovial as Barley, I promise, and few as willing to be generous. If you would trust a good fellow and honour me with your business, sir, I can weigh your wool this afternoon – there are facilities for it, a large scales, in town. Money would be handed to you over dinner tonight at the Wool Pack Inn in Liverpool, a few miles beyond.'

I quelled the intoxication I felt. This previously unknown sprite had emerged from the landscape to be the first to praise the Nugan Ganway fleece.

'I must,' I told him, 'in consideration of my partners, consult other dealers and their clerks.' He managed a frank grimace of disappointment.

Dusting his hands, he took a pair of fawn gloves from his pocket and put them on.

'In that case, sir, I must bid you good morning. But if you should see me at Liverpool and Parramatta crossroads, where agents less energetic and more brazen than young and fortunate Barley are at this hour barely rousing from their beds and complaining at being in bush, then I shall greet you as a friend whatever happens, and we may feel need to discuss things further.' He nodded, briskly remounted, and rode away, a natural in the saddle. I was sad to see him go. I wanted to come to terms with him if possible.

Clancy and I rolled through the Black Huts, and in a few miles neared the famous inn called the Wool Pack, at the place where the road from Parramatta joined the Liverpool road on the edge of that small village. In a great space before the inn we saw an armada of bullock trucks groaning with wool, and scattered amongst them the sleek town phaetons of Sydney wool merchants. The verandah of the Wool Pack seethed with men in more or less the same town uniform Barley had worn, and men too like Clancy and myself, dust in their coats and broad brimmed hats, trousers which had known river, mud, and the blood of sheep.

The clerk at the Wool Pack told me that all the rooms were three times full, so I rode across the junction towards Liverpool to the Dangling Man where I found a room in which to put my shirt and bed roll. On the crowded verandah of the place many other pastoral gentlemen were sitting, smoking pipes and drinking ale. I saw one settler who had not bothered to shave rush up to another and cry, 'Eight pence a pound, Mr Tucker. How does that make you feel?' And the two of them were laughing, a year in the bush redeemed at 8 pence per pound.

It seemed these gentlemen had not met Mr Barley.

My accommodation settled, and with the firm intention of later rewarding Clancy with a bottle of rum, a prospect I did not distract him with at this stage, I went back to the wagon and waited for visits from some of the gentleman wool merchants. Few of them were as pleasant or enthusiastic as Barley. They gave instead a sour appearance of weariness. Most of them had clerks whom they made climb up and bring down handfuls of wool – no clambering for them. Nor did they have the courtesy of needle and thread, so that Clancy and I were required to reseal the packs by our own devices. Some of them offered as little as 9 pence, others 10. One of them offended me by offering 7 pence ha'penny.

'Where is your station?' he asked. He had already been drinking, and there was a map of pink veins on his cheeks.

'South of the County of Argyle, on the plateau, up against the southern ranges.'

'Well, sir, why don't you call a spade a spade? That's the Maneroo country, as I fully expected from the quality of the wool. That is not prime wool country, sir. That is passable wool country.'

And so they came, inspecting the handfuls of wool as if they were the entrails of chickens, looking for omens of coming great houses, of better phaetons, of rarer bay mounts, of imported crystal, of exporting their sons to Oxford and their daughters to finishing schools. By 11 o'clock I had been offered 11 pence ha'penny by a sour old man in a frock coat. At his offer, I remembered hearing, at the age of twelve, an old Tasmanian ticket-of-leave man, a West Country fellow, in conversation with my father, saying, 'There be great wealth in ha'pennies.'

At noon I went back to the Dangling Man for some ale and bread, and I saw the same two men I had noticed earlier, one rushing up to the other and exclaiming, 'Nine pence a pound, Clarence. What do you think of that?' By the door, as this sentence was uttered, I was grateful to see Barley sitting in a big cane chair, looking hot yet composed.

He smiled at me, and looked the most humane man in all this wild scene. 'Actors employed by certain wool brokers, Mr Bettany,' he called to me. 'In the hope of talking the sellers down. This is the great Australian drama. Ah, but did great fortune, as distinct from a pound here and there, ever derive from low stratagems?'

'Perhaps more than we would like to think,' I told him.

'I do not presume you have come to see me on business, Mr Bettany, but it is requisite that brokers buy the pints. Could I pay for a pint or dram of your pleasure?'

I accepted and we entered the interior of the hotel, moving across a sawdusted floor in a dark press of excited men. Barley greeted a number of settlers by name. This one from Yass, another from the Liverpool Plains, whose respect he obviously had earned in dealings earlier that morning or in previous years. He was exactly the sort of good fellow who would be a clever clerk in England, but the maker of a fortune in New South Wales. As I knew and hoped, colonies exist to exalt the humble. And here at least no one resented a northern English accent if it came with the right price. He returned his attention to me as the pints he had ordered were delivered to the counter by a florid, no doubt ticket-of-leave, barmaid. Barley held his glass upright.

'Mr Bettany,' he urged me. 'I ask you to imagine Garroway's famed coffee house in Change Alley, Cornhill, London. Renowned, my friend, renowned. Dim lit. Dimmer than this. For it's late in English winter. London merchants sit around before their coffee ready to bid on Australian fleece. They have already bought what they want of Irish and Saxon wool, but they know that it is no longer height of quality, and they await this robust fleece from ends of earth. Auctioneer mounts his stand and promises them something of the best.'

'Have you been there?' I asked.

'With my master from Salford, when I was young,' he nodded. 'I was raised in wool trade. And I can see a future – not perhaps coming European winter but succeeding one – when Nugan Ganway wool has repute it deserves. A reputation as a staple. And so on this day sixteen months hence, a bale with your markings is placed on table and opened. Auctioneer says, "It is Nugan Ganway wool, such as we first saw last year." Dealers, hard men, believe me, Mr Bettany, hard men, wealthy men, canny, now lean forward in respect. A mark is made on candle on auctioneer's bench. Bids must be made before candle burns down as low as that mark. Nugan Ganway, shipped by Robert Barley, Sydney, New South Wales. Hard and avaricious fellows lean forward, Bettany. That is a moment! And so year by year that wool goes to Garroway's, and candle is marked, and bids are uttered in a husky tremble, and are no sooner uttered than topped, sir, topped. When I bid for your wool, Mr Bettany, I bid for a lifetime of wool, year after year until we are old men. Old men blessed by fortune.' And then he raised his pint and drank with me. 'So,' he concluded, 'I would be honoured to match your best bid.'

So there, at the close of his Yorkshire eloquence, I sold him my first wool shipment. We were so compatible as we talked that he asked me to join his family for a Sydney Christmas. He said that was the squatters' time, when men came from remote stations and stayed with prosperous relatives and friends and waited through the warmth of January for the Squatters' Ball. There they met their future wives. He could see no reason I should not leave Nugan Ganway with my overseer and spend two happy summer months with him, with Christmas dinner at his house at Darling Point – chicken, turkey, pork pies, puddings, sherry, wine and ales, and then a cooling of the person in the waters of Port Jackson, 'weather-eyeing it', to use Barley's phrase, for sharks. He repeated the verdict of an American whaling captain on the beauty of Sydney women, namely that even the lowest in society, the ticket-of-leave man's daughter, fed on colonial doughboys, was unparalleled. "Boston or New Bedford could not hold a candle, sir."

As I drank, I tested this daydream against the reality of my life. I found that the rawness of the conditions at Nugan Ganway, my own rawness over Mr Finlay's attitude, and the revival in my mind of Phoebe, who by her rash letter had somehow managed to create her own space there, all made me unwilling to waste time walking into a room full of Sydney women. And I also found, deep into my fourth pint, that I wanted no misunderstanding between Barley and myself.

'You realise my father was a Van Diemen's Land convict?' I suddenly asked Barley. I did not do my usual trick of saying what a minor, almost admirable crime he had committed.

'By God,' said Barley, 'At least one-fourth of all fine wool settlers, I would say, have been in chains in their day ... '

'Yes, but don't say people fail to remark on it. You have just remarked yourself, Mr Barley. If, say, I were charming, which I very much doubt, wouldn't they say, "Charming for a convict's son", and if I did not behave well, would they not say, "Well, what could you expect?"'

'Oh my friend, I am not in a position to say such things. Who was my father? He was a servant came in Governor Darling's party. Like a felon he had his hidden virtue and like a felon needed to crush his cleverness down into a hidden place within. There be high Tories of Sydney who speak in way you mention, as if they ride high above the mass, which is unlikely – many are former officers of low station, and some have convict mothers too! I tell you so you see me correctly – I am a Whig. Though people in wool generally tend towards Tory-dom, a result of their long acquaintance with sheep! But I am a Whig of my own kind. Most want transport system ended. I want it kept going because it redeems convict shepherds and it serves all wool, sir, all fine Merino fleece.' He broke into laughter. 'If you be convict's son, Bettany, you are a sign that clever lads can't be kept down.'

The wool clip weighed, Clancy drove it into Sydney, to Barley's warehouse. With the gentleman himself, I rode into Sydney too for a brief visit and met his wife at their white-limed sandstone house. She was a Northumbrian, thickly accented, but seemed as merry a soul as Barley himself. As for the projected Squatters' Ball, the Tory wool merchants of Sydney would need to wait another year before I was established enough to allow them to run the risk of meeting me.

We went sailing on a skiff of Barley's in the harbour, thumping along over waves kicked up by a sou-easter. As we pulled the skiff ashore, Barley straightened and said to me, 'Would you accept some money of mine, on the normal thirds basis, into the operation at Nugan Ganway? It is simply that I know a competent man when I see him. There is, sir, an outrageous incompetence amongst some pastoral gents.'

Intoxicated as I was by the sun and that resonant thump of water in my head, I said I was delighted to consider it. After dinner I told him I would write to my friend, Charlie Batchelor, and if it was satisfactory to him, then we would welcome Mr Barley as a partner.

He seemed too to pick up on my thoughts. I reflected that I would have the joy of banking my wool money, and within a quarter of an hour, as if in answer to my thoughts, he said, 'My advice, by which I mean advice from other reliable men, is to bank in part with Bank of Australia and in part with Savings Bank. Savings Bank, freed convict as it may be, has great underpinning resources from a Mr Samuel Terry, a tobacco thief in England, who made a fortune in this town as a merchant. Bank of Australia is certainly bank of supposed respectable men, but is, I hear, based on property prices and not as immune to vagaries of markets.'

I thought of Mr Finlay, who had occasionally carolled the Bank of Australia as the only worthwhile institution. Now, due to a word from Barley, I would divide my funds, putting half with one, half with the other. I concluded there was a considerable beneficial amount to be learned from Mr Barley, who could not afford definite articles but could afford generosity.

One of my duties returning through Goulburn was to call in on young Felix at Mr Loosely's Universal Academy. I found that esteemed peda-gogue in splendid spirits, and he sent out to the yard for Felix to be fetched into the parlour. For some reason, while I waited I felt uneasy. Had I done the right thing by this small pilgrim? But as he entered in breeches, shirt and boots without socks, I noticed that in the months since I had seen him, he had become a boy. Under a kindly regime, his facial constriction had nearly disappeared. He had not quite reached a hand-shaking age and so I was reduced to the patriarchal business of head-patting.

Mr Loosely turned to me and in a lowered voice murmured, 'He has extraordinary facility, sir.' He took down a book from the shelves – *A Child's Life of Isaac Newton*. It had large and majestic print. He handed it to the boy. 'Read, would you, Felix?'

Felix read in a melodious and well-paced voice. 'The infant Isaac Newton did not utter a word until the age of two, and his grandparents wondered aloud if the child would grow up mute. But his mother always reassured them with the words, "Isaac is not slow to speak. It is simply that he has not chosen what to say. When he does speak, the world will not easily be returned to the way it previously existed." '

I was of course gratified. I laid aside some pocket money for the boy and prepared to leave with that feeling of comfort a man has when his semi-accidental arrangements yield sublime results.

'You must return, sir,' said Mr Loosely at his gate. 'This boy bears watching.'

Part Two

The day of Dimp Bettany's wedding was clear, hot, humid, beneath a massive, sharp-edged Sydney sky. Out of a casual respect for the fact that Bren had been to the altar previously, and from a natural reticence about fashion, Dimp dressed like a second wife, in a cream sheath. On her head she wore a simple construction of flowers. After photographs and felicitations outside the church, she and Bren were flown down harbour to the wedding feast at a beachside restaurant in a helicopter belonging to a mining corporation associated with Bren.

Dimp's side of the party was outnumbered by Bren's aunts, uncles and cousins, let alone by his friends. She lacked an attendant sister, but then Bren lacked both his parents too. His father was ten years dead; his mother – who had borne Bren in her mid thirties – had recently died of a stroke.

Most of Dimp's old crew from *Enzo Kangaroo* came, even the lonely-looking star Colin Maberley, who had played Enzo and arrived from location-shooting in New Zealand. For the wives of lawyers, miners and venture capitalists on Bren's side, Maberley's magical and wistful presence outweighed that of any other personage, perhaps even that of the bride and groom.

Dimp had always suspected Prim would not come, and understood why. Her absence left a margin of dark but inert vacancy on an otherwise sharp, exultant day. 'The poor girl's had malaria,' Dimp explained when asked about her sister. The naming of a tropical disease seemed to satisfy the curious and validate Dimp as a splendid waif and dazzling orphan, worthy of the respect of all witnesses to the wedding.

Prim's absence counted in, Dimp's experience of her wedding day was seamless. It was to her that simplest of images. It expanded like a flower to the sun, petal by petal, joyful quarter-hour by joyful quarter-hour. She had no doubts. In her view, the essential nature of the separate histories she and Bren had lived was that they would coincide on this crystalline

Sydney day, in a city so designed for marriage that most photographs of weddings were outdoor ones.

One of the quieter presences on Bren's side of the wedding party was Frank Benedetto, the lawyer who had given Dimp the gift of the Bettany papers and the stray letters of Sarah Bernard. To an observer he resembled any other wedding guest, though he was not as raucous as Bren's boyhood friends, who took the fact they had known Bren since adolescence as their mandate to get fraternally drunk, to sing songs which meant little to anyone but them. Benedetto was not a party to the jokes of Bren's boyhood. He had attended a Marist Brothers school in the far west of Sydney. His childhood had been spent some crucial miles from Bren's, and under less promising auguries.

ULTIMATELY SHERIF'S VISIT TO THE SOUTH with his team, including Erwit, would produce 'A Random Sample Survey of Families with Young Children in Aweil, Bahr el Ghazal Province, Republic of Sudan'. It would be published, to the great excitement and considerable kudos of Austfam in Canberra, in the British journal *Public Health Abstracts*.

It first stated that between July and August 1988, Dr Sherif Taha's survey team, including Ms Primrose Bettany, Acting Administrator, Austfam, Khartoum, had discovered that Aweil's population had increased by some 25 000 people now living east of the town, on the edge of the extensive cattle market, and also on the road southwards from the town, in shelters of mud and brush and with only the most rudimentary water supply and sanitation. The new arrivals were displaced Dinkas, whose villages had been overrun by the parties to the conflict in the South, and whose livestock had been confiscated by either the Sudanese army or the forces of the SPLA.

The Dinkas had come to town chiefly to escape the battle zone of the open countryside, and the Sudanese garrison considered them potential sympathisers with and members, albeit extremely depleted and malnourished ones, of the SPLA, the rebel army.

Prim, Sherif, Erwit and the five Khartoum nurses who made up the team, walked from one brush hovel to another asking families if they would answer questions. Given that she was a stranger and so was Erwit, and given the uncertainty of the refugees' situation, Prim was surprised at how willing they were to tell their stories, to answer Sherif's questionnaire about dispossession, child mortality, and livestock ownership previous and present.

The article in *Public Health Abstracts* concentrated on infant health. It spoke of such indicators of child health as Height for Weight, and MUAC (mid-upper arm circumference), and of Z, the wastage factor.

Most of the children less than five years old, 62 per cent, said the article, had a wastage score of $Z-2$. This meant severe hunger, and the number was all the more alarming to Prim since, as Sherif pointed out to her, these children were the survivors of a crisis which had already killed many of their brothers and sisters.

The death rate of children below five years was 25.88 per 10 000 children per day or 724.64 per four-week month. The children were buried in improvised graveyards, small stone enclosures, near the town. The very high infant mortality rate was explained in part by a measles epidemic which was in progress when the Austfam team arrived in Aweil, before health teams had been able to initiate their vaccination programs. There was evidence, wrote the survey team, that the efficacy of measles vaccinations could be vitiated by the high temperatures of the region and the lack of refrigeration for vaccine storage.

In sweltering Aweil, the survey team had stayed at and worked from the beige and blue Boz Hotel in the centre of town, near the two-storey barracks, in a main street with a *souk* from which Sudanese policemen armed with long canes excluded the refugee children. Prim had two jobs: supporting the efforts of Anwar and Julio, and participating in the survey.

As the survey would be published, whether for pity's sake or for the sake of truth-telling, fear of joint authorship made Prim, in the thundery, super-heated August of Aweil, uneasy with Sherif. In irrational hours it seemed to her a genuine risk that Auger or an Auger colleague would write to *Public Health Abstracts* and detail the impropriety of her ever being credited with any authorship. With the constant dismal news emerging from Sherif's measurements of children and questionnaire for mothers, and the general equatorial sweatiness of the place, Prim was pleased towards the end of the month to have to return with Sherif and the team to the less dense air of Khartoum and facilitate a further food drop for Anwar and Julio.

There, working in her still office, she heard on the BBC African news one afternoon the exact, clear voice of Helene Codderby reporting that hostilities had broken out again in the Aweil region. Sudanese Army regulars, it was claimed, were pushing the SPLA south towards Malek. There was no mention of Anwar and Julio, but the next day Stoner called Prim and told her in his most melancholy, hesitant way that they were in his office. They had come close to dying in crossfire as the rebels and the army fought for their depot. The rebels, said a shaken Anwar, thought the depot was being used to give credit to the army, and the army thought it had been used to succour rebels. Its existence had become a *casus belli*, and while the program they had instituted at Aweil still operated, the army had insisted that they, thank you very much, would run it from now on. In what spirit it might be run, whether it would be used to feed government troops, Anwar and Julio would not know, for they were out of the place. They were under suspicion of sustaining rebel peoples.

'I'm going to protest to the government *and* the SPLA,' said an outraged Prim. 'There's Australian rice and wheat down there. Austfam paid for some of the aircraft charter!'

'Good thing,' said Stoner in the same dismal tone. 'But, I mean, Operation Safety's not going to end. It's just that Julio and Anwar are out.'

Prim was still outraged. She was particularly angered that Stoner seemed so resigned. 'This is a scandal. And what aid worker is safe, if they fight over food dumps?'

'Yeah, well,' he said. 'Look, the food itself ... let's not be too overdramatic. It's only agricultural excess, isn't it? It's not as if it's costing the poor of Australia anything. There's a tougher issue. Our Ilyushins were seized this morning by the military.'

'*Seized?*'

'Yeah, the charter's been taken over by the army. They have the authority under the Emergency Laws, see. The planes'll be used to supply the new big push.'

'You mean, with the UN's logo on the side?'

'Oh, yeah, holy moley,' said Stoner. 'I hadn't thought of that.'

Prim said, 'I bet they want to keep the UN markings for protective colouring. The rebels don't fire on UN planes. But when they see them disgorging men and cannons – that'll change their minds.'

'Wait a tick. Let me talk to the boys.'

Within five minutes he was back on the phone. Prim was already searching through the office cupboard and had found a used can of white paint left from Crouch's time, and a selection of hardened brushes. She was in a state of vengeful grief: Operation Safety was such a sane plan, it had seemed at first to create a new reality. But obviously, it would be permitted to operate only within the bounds of the military convenience of the parties to the war.

There was a profounder weariness in Stoner's voice now. From his storeroom he had blue housepaint, three litres, and brushes. He and the boys would go out to the airport . . .

'Collect me on the way,' she insisted and, waiting, set to thinning Crouch's ancient white paint.

From the front seat of Stoner's truck, Julio and Anwar greeted Prim wanly. The last time they had seen her they had been remaking the earth. Now they were merely engaged in a gesture, and might not be permitted to accomplish even that.

Everyone still had the appropriate passes: of their sundry organisations and of Operation Safety. With these, and a lot of persuasion in Arabic from Anwar and Stoner, they were admitted through successive screens of reluctant NCOs onto the apron of the airfield. '*Amreeka?*' Stoner was always asked. 'British,' he would say, pretending to less Arabic than he had. '*Shnatuk. El tayarah. Ilyushin.*' His bags were still on the Ilyushins, he claimed. Incredibly, they were permitted to drive around the edge of the airport to where about thirty assorted military aircraft waited on the far side.

The Sudanese Army, it had seemed to Prim until recently, always dressed in what she thought of as a quaintly British manner, their berets, shirts, trousers and gaiters had a Second World War cut to them, as if still supplied by warehouses the British had left behind thirty years past. But the troops guarding the airport perimeter, and at ease in the door-ways of hangars, were dressed in snappy, fresh-looking camouflage gear which bespoke a new level of military purpose. A company of young Sudanese soldiers in camouflage were loading their packs through the rear door of one of the transports on whose flank the UN insignia still shone. The charter company pilots, African and European, stood by in the wing's shade, watching. Anwar got out and went to the officer directing the troops and was suddenly loud and eloquent, pointing to the plane, raging, holding up his fingers. '*Sittah*! Six. With a threatening politeness the officer ordered him to clear off; '*Imshi*'. Stoner, watching from his truck, was inflamed. '*Imshi* yourself, you bastard!' he cried through the window.

Prim and Julio were already at the rear of the truck. While Julio levered cans of blue paint open with a screwdriver, Prim stirred the opened cans

with a stick. They were all enraged and willing to be shot for their right
to erase the debased symbols.

The officer called to Anwar, who was coming back to the truck to
take up his brush. 'The plane's ready to depart,' he yelled. '*Essabaah*'.
This morning. Anwar turned back to the man, holding forth the UN pass
hung around his neck, and pointed at the task they were engaged in, the
work which had to be done. One of the charter pilots, a Frenchman,
came out of the shade. 'I told them to remove the UN signs,' he said. 'I
told them. It makes this trip easy for them, but the future hard for us.
The rebels will start shooting at everything. I told him. But be neat, guys,
be neat!'

So Prim and the others were not impeded, and as the officer and his
company boarded a plane, took up the streaky white and fresh blue paint
cans.

The team of four spent an hour effacing the pretence of compassion
and human courtesy from the sides of the remaining three cargo planes
as young Sudanese men in camouflage kit with the sweetest of mute faces
approached the cargo doors, loading cases of artillery shells aboard, gifts
for Anwar's former regions, Aweil and Malek.

Slavery remained an issue for Prim through all her Austfam duties; it
would return to her in dreams and in small-hour wakings. She had questioned a number of Dinka refugees in the town of Aweil who claimed
one or more of their children had been taken away by government troops
or militias, and for whose freedom the family had needed to pay over
the last of their cattle. And Sherif introduced her to the middle-aged
Sudanese woman, Khalda el Rahzi, he had described as being concerned
with the matter of hostage-taking in the South and with – the word Sherif
hesitated to use – slavery.

Sherif had taken Prim to the el Rahzis' for dinner one Sunday night.
They drove there, as Sherif said, 'Louisiana-style', together in the front
seat of his old Mercedes and were admitted to the el Rahzis' high-walled
stone villa, on the southern edge of the university, by a tall young man
dressed in shirt, pants and sandals. He wore glasses and had the look of
a student.

'Hello,' he said, in English. 'I'm Safi. My parents have me on the door
this evening. I hope I look adequately august.' He laughed, a big half-
made man, all bones. He led them into a broad hallway from which the

house seemed to spread out without constraint, and he dashed ahead to
a sideboard on which stood a tray of iced fruit drinks which he offered
to them.

Glass in hand, they were led into a living room where Western style
chairs stood against the wall but a long, low lacquered table occupied
the centre of the room. Khalda el Rahzi, shorter than her son, bare-
headed here at home and dressed in a long blue gown, greeted them. She
wore the nostril ring of marriage, Prim saw, along with her repute for
feminism. Her firm neck was decorated with a circlet of ancient coins.
She suggested in English they put down their drinks a second, as a
Southern-looking woman, a servant, approached them with a copper
ewer of water and a bowl, a white towel folded over her wrist. Prim was
delighted by such rites of hospitality. She relished in particular the way
Sherif turned his hands and his wrists under the thread of water the
servant poured. It was a sinuous and balletic exercise, more an inheritance than a mere practice of hygiene. Then, with rinsed hands, they were
led by Mrs el Rahzi towards her husband and amongst the guests.

The professor, a tall, slightly heavy man with grizzled hair, pleasant
features and an urbane air wore a light suit rather like Sherif's. 'Now, if
you would like some gin or whisky, Miss Bettany,' he murmured, 'it
would not be looked upon amiss.' Prim said the juice was fine, and so
introductions began.

Sherif appeared to know everyone there. A man as tall and perhaps
younger than Sherif, dressed in a long thobe-like garment and a loose
vest, turned out to be a lawyer named el Dhouma. He had a great deal
of whimsy in his eyes, and murmured to Sherif, but for Prim's sake, 'We
went to school together in Almarada, isn't that so, Dr Sherif?'

'That is precisely correct,' said Sherif, making great ceremony of the
handshake, his shoulder leaning in towards el Dhouma's. 'Dr el Dhouma
was the absolute star of the law school at the University of Khartoum.
As to the name of the star of the school of medicine, I leave you to guess.'

The company laughed, and a suited young man standing near Safi said,
'It depends which era you're dealing with.'

'You are as usual right, Dr Siddiq,' said Sherif. 'Your era was a much
more illustrious one than mine.'

At Professor el Rahzi's invitation the guests began disposing themselves
on cushions around the low table. Mrs el Rahzi disappeared to look at
the final preparations for dinner, and Prim observed the Sudanese cour-
tesies as she had learned of them through reading manuals prepared for

her kind by various NGOs. In her long floral dress, she knelt with knees together, reaching behind her to stretch the dress hem over the soles of her low-heeled shoes. All around her the men, emitting sighs, settled cross-legged, a posture considered unacceptable for women.

Just then the doorbell rang again, and the guest whom Safi admitted this time was was Helene Codderby.

Professor el Rahzi said, 'You must think us barbarians, Miss Codderby, that we sat to table before you arrived.'

'I certainly don't,' said Helene, having her hands rinsed. 'I rang your wife earlier to apologise in advance that I'd be a latecomer. I've been at a press conference at the Finance Ministry and I'm ravenous.'

Prim saw Doctor Siddiq and el Dhouma smile at each other, a shared joke. Helene Codderby smiled at Prim and took a cushion next to her, while Sherif reclined on Prim's right. Helene only had time to whisper, 'My God, that dear old Sherif of yours. He *is* an absolute hunk, isn't he?' Khalda led into the room two young women in white who each carried trays of bowls of the opening course, lentil soup. Setting to, Helene and the men did not leave their bowls on the table, but held them in their left hand as they spooned away at a hectic pace.

Prim had felt her heart expand under Helene's simple, womanly compliment.

The soup consumed, and Mrs el Rahzi moving to the kitchen to attend to the next course, a silence grew which was filled with a sudden, half-nervous comment from the el Rahzis's son, Safi. He turned to el Dhouma. 'After all my father says of you, I was surprised to hear you were the lawyer who represents the National Islamic Front.'

Prim sensed a slight uneasiness amongst the older members of the company at what would be considered a confrontational remark. People like the el Rahzis looked askance at the National Islamic Front, though for subtler reasons than the Western press, with its caricatures of turbaned fundamentalist zealots. They understood, if they did not agree thoroughly with, the Front's desire to fight the West's baleful politics and culture by bringing about a more stringently regulated Islamic state than presently existed even under Sharia.

Before el Dhouma could reply, Safi went on, 'My father tells me you were a declared socialist as a student.'

'Please,' rumbled the professor, 'make a fool of yourself on your own bat, dear Safi, but don't drag me in.'

'No,' said el Dhouma, nodding with weary good humour, as if this were for him a much-heard question, 'I think you wouldn't be surprised, my young friend, to find that I am still a socialist, but so are many of the NIF. Their agenda is not simply religious. You would consider many of them very civilised chaps, and excellent patriots.'

There was the polite hint of a snort from the boy.

El Dhouma continued patiently. 'Many of the leadership are progressives. But they are not shallow humanists as say, the Democrats in the United States pretend to be. They are progressives within a tradition – an Islamic tradition. With due regard for our esteemed women guests, the NIF see the rootless, anti-Arab opportunism which lies behind the facade of Western democracy.'

'And these are the sorts of propositions used to justify the Sharia and the war?' Safi asked.

Professor el Rahzi began laughing. 'Enough of the Socratic method, young man!'

'You mustn't think I mind the subject at all,' el Dhouma insisted. 'I find my clients an interesting bunch not least for the way they combine theology and political theory. Some are from the mystical tradition, and others from the hard-headed political side of things. And as for science – which in America or Britain is seen to be at loggerheads with religion – well, I had a fascinating chat the other day with a man from the science sub-committee of the Front. An older man, a graduate in science from the University of Khartoum. I shan't name him . . .'

'Do,' cried young Dr Siddiq. 'If he's fascinating and has a crazy theory, it's probably an uncle of mine!'

El Dhouma let the laughter die. 'No, I shan't name him. But consider, he asked me, the Resurrection of the Dead as predicted in the Koran . . . "Man thinks that We shall not assemble his bones. Yes truly! Yes, We are able to restore his very fingers!" Well, my friend on the science sub-committee begins from the justifiable theological premise that the Resurrection of the Dead is inevitable and certain to occur. He also argues that it offends piety to believe that there is a single scientific error in the Koran. So how shall we rise from the dead? For the answer he goes to the Big Bang theory. That too must lie latent in Revelation. The idea of the universe being in expansion is raised by one of the Suras, he says.'

It seemed to Prim that the Sudanese in the room were capable of mental recitation of the Sura in question. El Dhouma went on.

'It's a matter of pride to this man that the Koran countenanced the concept of an enlarging cosmos. Compare that with the Vatican, which fought a rearguard action against the idea of a sun-centred galaxy, though it was forced to accept reality in the end. In any case, my friend the scientist–theologian argues a correlation between the Big Bang and Einstein's Theory of Relativity on the one hand, and on the other the Sura which reads, "We shall roll up the heavens as a recorder rolls up a written scroll." The idea is that the universe expands, but at its limit of explosion it will inevitably begin contracting. And when that happens, time – which is the measurement of the continuum of expansion – will be reversed and rolled up like a scroll. Or like a rewound tape in a tape-recorder. In that reversal of time, we shall rise from the dead, this old man argues – all under the pull of the running down of time. We shall be old before we are young. We shall be aged before we are born. The future will be our past. All our evil deeds will occur and then feed themselves back painfully to their initial intent. We will feel the anguish of our evil long before we have done it, while all our good deeds will joyously emerge and be connected by a golden thread to their founding impulses. In the reversal of time, says this old man, there will be heaven in our decency and hell in our malice. And we shall carry all our sins and all our virtue back with us into the womb. This will continue until the last man and woman have replayed their lives backwards and disappeared into the water from which God first brought them. And so the entire universe will rush backwards to its final, founding explosion in the hand of God.'

There was silence in the room, a reverence for the august nature of this idea, even if it did come from the National Islamic Front. El Dhouma turned to Safi. 'You see, my clients are not unimaginative people.'

'But,' said Safi, with a smile, falling back on his inherited charm, 'they wouldn't be willing to eat dinner with two such charming infidels as Miss Primrose and Miss Helene?'

Everyone chuckled again, and Prim savoured the old-fashioned nature of the English spoken by these men. Soon Mrs el Rahzi was back again with her two women. They carried platters of *kisra* flatbread, bowls of white rice, tomatoes stuffed with minced beef, bowls of fool beans and *shata* sauce, and lamb stew. As all was laid before him, el Dhouma toasted the feast with a glass of grapefruit juice, invoking 'the plenty of our country, the continued exile of that weak man Nimeiri . . .'

'May he enjoy Paris,' sang Siddiq, since that was the city of Nimeiri's exile. But el Dhouma was not quite finished. He still had his glass in the air.

'. . . and the well-meaning compassion and fellow feeling of our foreign friends.'

'Well-meaning,' said Sherif, winking at Prim. She did not think it such a bad word.

Eating heartily, the Sudanese men, Mrs el Rahzi and Helene Codderby sopped up the lamb stew with their *kisra* bread. But after a time, noticing that Prim still used her cutlery, Sherif lifted up some stew on a fork and ate it companionably with her. Prim listened as the men talked. Dr Siddiq had just been appointed to a post in the Ministry of Health. 'I'll be living somewhere out there on the banks of the Atbara.'

It was when the crème caramels were brought in, and Mrs el Rahzi picked up her spoon and the dessert and admired the sheen of its surface, that Prim took the chance to lean across the narrow space occupied by Helene and say, in a lowered voice, 'I believe you're involved in the question of slavery. However that might be defined.'

Mrs el Rahzi went on working delicately with her spoon at the crème caramel, and did not lift her eyes from the task. 'It's true the term is a sliding one. It is sometimes not as clear-cut as in *Uncle Tom's Cabin*. Yet it is almost traditional, and it's endemic.' She smiled, finished her dessert. 'Helene, why don't you bring your friend, Miss Bettany, out to the kitchen to watch how Sudanese coffee is made?'

Sherif raised an eyebrow and struggled upright. Apart from that, the men barely noticed when the women rose, excused themselves as a phalanx, and left. So, in good company, Prim entered the large kitchen in which there was an enduring redolence of spices. In a patch of light beyond the back door, the two young women who had borne the trays in and out had squatted, white linen shawls over their heads, and were frying coffee beans over a small charcoal heater. They would sometimes reach into the pan with bare fingers and flip this or that imperfect bean out, dropping it on the ground.

Mrs el Rahzi went to her cupboard, extracted a bottle of J & B whisky, poured a glass and handed it neat to Helene. 'Prim knows I've got hollow legs when it comes to this stuff,' said Helene. Khalda el Rahzi gestured with the bottle to Prim, who decided to wait for the coffee. They sat on three stools in a close circle.

'What sparked your interest?' asked Mrs el Rahzi.

Prim recounted her contact with the Dinka midwife. She mentioned too the servant boys in the governor's headquarters in el Fasher.

'Yes,' said Mrs el Rahzi. 'The victims know they've been traded into bondage. You see, down in the South the Arab tribes such as the Beggarah have been capturing hostages, and trading in them, for centuries. One is reminded of kidnapping amongst some Southern Italians – a way of life. Certainly it is possible for Westerners, uninformed about Sudanese history, to come here and be over-excited by what they see and hear.' Mrs el Rahzi spread her hands. 'But if slavery is the buying and selling of people, if you look at it in that strictest sense, then you'd have to say, yes, there is slavery in the Sudan.'

'I once used that term on the BBC,' said Helene Codderby, happy with her whisky, 'but the government went crazy.'

'If you can prove a case,' murmured Mrs el Rahzi, 'the police will often act on it. However, that happens only occasionally.'

Helene had two-thirds finished her tumbler, and had the look of a woman who might ask for a refill. 'Most NGOs don't want to buy into the question – it's too explosive, and it's hard enough pursuing famine relief. And anyhow, the war is what drives it, and makes it easy. So Stoner virtually makes a stab at ending the war by making the parties agree to relief in the South! That's his way. A failed one, but an honest try.'

Who could escape being possessed by these women's calm acknowledgments of the buying and selling of human flesh? Prim couldn't, she knew.

'This fine woman here ...' said Helene, indicating Mrs el Rahzi, '... this woman here has herself redeemed a number.'

'I've contributed a little when certain people were pointed out to me as worthy cases,' said Khalda el Rahzi. 'As the so-called owners of these people would say, the cash I gave over was compensation for the training, educational cost and general investment which had been put into them.' Mrs el Rahzi yawned – the labour of her dinner party! 'I have a servant who was bought out and whom you might wish to interview at your convenience. And the next time the Baroness von Trotke is in Khartoum, or her friend Connie Everdale, we shall organise a meeting.'

The women at the fire tray outside the door were now decanting the coffee sludge from the intensely brewed *jebena* coffee. Mrs el Rahzi, Prim and Helene, whisky downed, followed the coffee and the tray of small cups back into the dining room. El Dhouma watched Prim with his benign irony.

Revivified by the coffee, Prim and Sherif said their goodbyes and made their way out to Sherif's green Mercedes. Sherif asked, in his ornate, slightly creaky way, 'Why do you smile, my Miss Bettany?' She smiled to know that they possessed the confidence, the euphoria of people who would in coming hours be mutually exhilarated, rewarded, sated.

'I think it is appropriate in matters of seduction,' said Sherif, putting both hands on the steering wheel, 'that if a man has genuine tender feelings for a woman, he be willing to take her to his place, rather than just routinely to bear his desire to her address, where she has to face the scrutiny and comments of neighbours.'

Prim reached out and caressed his elbow. 'Okay,' she said. 'Just get us on the road, sport.'

And yet after a hectic hour with Sherif, her mind reverted to the astonishing and redolent fact of slavery, as uttered by her new friend Khalda and her old one Helene.

Though in her association with Sherif, Prim tried occasionally but inconclusively to employ the traditional aromatic ointments of Sudanese lovemaking, dousing her breasts and thighs with *delkah*, it did not seem to attract added ardour from Sherif.

'It is not necessary, that goo,' Sherif reassured her. She felt fortunate to have been found by him, for he was not concerned by her ineptitude at the craft of seduction.

He seemed to find the inevitable sexual confessions of earlier life easier than she did. She glossed over Auger as a generic married man. Sherif talked with boyish relish of his American experience. Prim felt she was getting to know more than she wished to know about the medical student he had been engaged to – a great-grandchild of the slaves, he said, a strong-minded but naïve young woman from a family of Shreveport middle-class Baptists. It seemed from his anecdotes that he thought her nature too demanding and strident. But the worst thing, he said, was that he found the community of 'respectable blacks' from which she came, and to which she aspired, stupefying and perilous to the soul. Memory was both muted and urgent in them, said Sherif. It showed itself in the way visitors to the house, friends of the parents, talked endlessly about his manners, how good they were. He concluded that with one side of their souls they rejoiced in their enslaved history specifically because, to use his terms, 'it had house-trained them'. An African who could manage to be as urbane as they believed themselves to be struck them as a novelty. The girl's mother one day said to guests, as an explanation of

Sherif's courtliness, 'Oh, but he's been three years at Louisiana State.'

But his fiancée wisely saw right through him, he admitted. 'Right to the selfish core. She knew she would not get from me an easy life. That I would have opinions to the point of discomfort.'

Prim, by the time Dimp started sending her the Bettany journal and letters had for some two years or more been willing to marry Sherif. He was her cherished companion who had redeemed her from the shame of the Auger business, opened the Sudan to her, and enabled her and Austfam to tell the truth about refugees. Yet she and Sherif were mutually embarrassed when the unspoken tension of the question occasionally brought it to the surface.

He said once, 'There will be a time when I can marry you, but it is not yet. Is it selfish to say that marriage is for both of us too difficult?' Somehow, she was willing to believe that he wanted his nation to be settled and stable first. Like many others, he suspected that improvement was at hand. There was too much pressure from too many good men and women in the Sudan. The prime minister, Sadiq el Mahdi, would surely for the sake of fiscal health and idealism ultimately evoke a pluralist Sudan! Not that Sherif and other Sudanese lacked pride in their Islamic history, in their descent from the seers, devotees, generals who had come out of the provinces to fight the British and Egyptians, their desire for Khartoum backed by the will of God.

So, he implied, he was waiting for an end to Sharia, an end to the war, and thus, it seemed, a fair and balanced environment for marriage. Prim was curiously content to wait also, since in a way she too felt the air aching towards a settlement, a beneficial resolution.

In the meantime, she cherished him more than she could convey to him or anyone else. Her lyricism was internal, not visible. The love poetry she wrote she kept to herself. She would hand it over perhaps when the Sudan and she and Sherif achieved between them some happy plateau.

Good morning, my good Nile,
I heard your living current in the night,
and sought your deeper wells, the Arabic and the Nilotic.
I have been calm in your dark pools.
I have heard the underflow however.
Better than you I hear
the drums, whirling and incantations
of your nubile mothers, and see

the quiet dusk submission to the east of your scholar forebears.
And all your heresies move lively
in cold clear depths, like muscled perch, the river's king and queen.
You who are heretic to the Sudan
in failing to read God's will in Crude Death Rate.
And to the West a heretic for seeing that the world is not to be
*   perfected ...*
And yet you know a world turned upside down is
still the world.
Beneath the rowdy moons of your tranquillity
and by the cunning war machines of your own peace,
I sit in shade and bless the river.

Prim received the Bettany and Bernard documents, as arranged and tran-scribed by Dimp, at regular intervals – usually about ten pages of transcript at a time. Each time a parcel arrived, Prim felt a combination of annoyance and fascination, as if her sister were using them as some sort of ancestral magic to make her come home. She always delayed reading them, as if her own enthusiasms and sins were likely to be exposed. She pretended they possessed for her only curiosity value, yet as firmly as she tried to make little of them, Dimp in Sydney tried to make much.

This is as big as Enzo Kangaroo, *but it's got my own blood in it! I'm surreptitiously making notes for a screenplay. I don't know if it's ancestor worship and I don't care. I THINK IT'S THE NEW GRAND PROJECT. The more I read the more I know that, and the less confident I grow as well! What about these Moth people, eh? Can't you just see it? All the ambiguities, black and white. But you read it and you can barely raise a fax that comments on it. Well ... I'll be quiet for now.*

To be aghast at the past, to be stimulated by it in Dimp's particular way, was a luxury of plush cities like Sydney, Prim thought. In the Sudan, the preposterous past served only as prelude to an even more astounding present, more Gothic – or should it be more baroque – than anything a previous age could yield up.

Prim thus feared that in her fever over their ancestors, Dimp was drum-ming up something from the depths of her sensibility. Something dangerous and engorged would bob to the surface and be a peril to shipping. Her fear seemed validated when a letter arrived which spoke of some sort of revelation Dimp had experienced at Sydney airport. It was not a revelation in a religious sense, but rather one of those instantaneous changes of direction or of viewing the world which were at the same time both Dimp's greatest strength and vice.

According to Dimp's letter, she suffered this most dangerous reversal of sight on a day she'd been on her way to Melbourne to see old friends in the Victorian Film Office – the ones who had given her the development financing on *Enzo Kangaroo*.

I know whatever development cash they give me won't be enough for the writer I have in mind, but it'll be a start. And I also know, so you needn't say it, there are bigger tales in the cosmos! But film's not built to redeem anything. The story is all. The story has to levitate its producer, get her off her arse. And it's an established fact that the earth's despised themselves would rather watch ET *than watch a social realist version of their plight. Honest!*

Dimp's flight was delayed three and a half hours by an aircraft refuellers' strike, and the lounge at the Qantas Club filled up as catering staff tried to fuel those huge aircraft. Dimp sat with her little cup of coffee and the *Australian* amongst men in suits all fuming into cellular phones with loud, groaning self-absorption. As she waited, she saw a woman with auburn hair and wearing a fawn suit stepping amongst the full-throated malcontents. This woman looked stylish in a habitual sort of way, as if she dressed well every day. Dimp had always wanted to be that kind of woman! This one also looked like a genuine woman of business, carrying a briefcase and a cup of coffee deftly in the one hand as if she were used to having something else, a laptop maybe, or a file, in the other. There was something familiar about her – it began to tease Dimp all the more because the woman seemed to be making directly for her. In the end she stood above Dimp and asked tentatively, 'Dimple Bettany?' Dimp mounted the defence of her marriage. 'Dimp D'Arcy,' she said. The woman said, 'Well, I'm Robyn D'Arcy. How are you?'

So this was Bren's first wife! Little wonder that with her hair shortened since the days of her failed marriage her features were at the same time remembered and forgotten. She was good-looking, thought Dimp, with a Slavic kind of face.

In bewilderment, Dimp asked Robyn D'Arcy to take a seat. Slotting herself into the chair, she had the air of a woman who lived in a succession of chairs for many busy convenings, daily. Bren had depicted this woman as an occasional virago, but she did not look like it that morning: she looked like a servant of reason and order. A copyright lawyer. Bottle designs, patterns on tea-towels, computer software.

And she had introduced herself as D'Arcy. She still retained Bren's name. Was that a flag of convenience, a form of vengeance, or a running sore?

Dimp looked at the pissed-off men in suits all around. They would probably like to be diverted by two women screaming at each other, in battle over a name. But in fact Robyn wanted to discuss destinations. Where was Dimp going? Melbourne. Robyn was going to Melbourne too.

She asked how Brendan was in the way a person asks about the health of an uncle. Dimp stumbled out an answer. For the moment she half-hoped Robyn might call her a slut in front of the entire company and tell her to leave the lounge. Dimp would have limped out more happily than she now sat playing tea parties with this intimately known stranger.

'He'll live to be a hundred,' said Robyn. 'You can't kill them, you know. The D'Arcys. As much as they deserve it.'

'His parents are both dead though.'

'Oh yes,' said Robyn. 'I give you that. But at a great age, especially the old man. They were made of teak. Their longevity means you're going to be stuck with Bren deep into the next century.' The idea amused her, but gently, without an edge. 'Does he have you going to Mass?'

'Occasionally. The Jesuits.'

'He got me going back to Mass, and discussing theology. And now I can't stop. That's not very fair is it? All I'm left with from my marriage is a sort of dogged faith.'

Dimp, wanting to switch subjects, asked, 'Do you have a new ...'

Robyn understood. She said 'Oh, yes,' and mentioned the name of a Supreme Court judge. He must have sighted her during a case, liked her fair hair, healthy face, brisk manner. 'His wife died. We hope to be married next year. Quietly. It's a bit intimidating, press-wise, to remarry, when you're Bren's cast-off. And hard for my friend too, given his position. It tends to be the subject of ... of what you would call ironic report.'

Even now, no bitterness. She should be offering classes in the Zen of divorce.

And that made it even more certain that Dimp would say, 'You know, in case you wondered: I didn't meet Bren until after, you know, that bloody annulment business began.'

No bloody aplomb at all, thought Dimp. The first wife smiled, damn her, and said she knew. 'I know you're no scarlet woman, if there is such a thing anymore. I just hope, though, the judge will cure me of this Mass thing. Because they're missionaries, you know, the D'Arcy's. They visit the natives and rearrange the insides of their heads.' She said it more like an anthropologist than a wronged person, and Dimp began laughing with her. What a likeable woman, bugger it! Robyn continued, 'My parents were Serbian, but though they were agnostics, Bren saw me as Orthodox and so, ripe for conversion.'

Robyn's situation reminded Dimp of Bren's grandfather who, while serving as an infantry captain in the Middle East during the Second World War, met and wooed the daughter of a Lebanese surgeon from Alexandria. Dimp knew the story and had seen the pictures. A hulking, immortal-looking young man and a Mediterranean beauty with darkness and bemusement in her eyes, grinning their way down an avenue of Desert Rat officers making a nuptial arch of raised swords outside some domed church in Cairo.

Robyn agreed, 'I got the impression that they've always done this – married out, made a raid, and brought back with them not only a young body but a young soul as well. I bet he had you promise to raise any kids as Catholics.' Dimp had made that promise. 'Except there'll be no kids, will there?' Robyn observed. 'Bren's great shame. He fires blanks, as they say.' It was the first thing she'd said which could have been seen as bitter.

'We intend to adopt,' said Dimp.

'So did we. Another contribution to the Kingdom of Heaven.'

Dimp rushed to Bren's defence: to give him his due, he'd made his sterility clear. Robyn – and Bren – had found out a year or so before he left her. That is, in the third year of their marriage. And now she really began to talk.

When Bren moved out, he'd sought the annulment through the Archdiocese of Sydney. That meant both he and Robyn had to submit to some marriage counselling, and then be interviewed by a panel of priests, a psychiatrist and even a physician. The physician's task was to question Robyn as a means to showing that the marriage had been consummated – penetration, ejaculation. Bren wasn't claiming it hadn't happened, nor was she. But it had to be cleared out of the way. If the marriage hadn't been consummated, they were entitled to a more or less on the spot annulment – known as 'the Petrine privilege'. When the doctor examined her, Robyn had told him, 'It doesn't prove anything, you know. I had lovers before Bren.'

'Pardon me for asking,' asked Dimp. 'But why did you submit to all this?'

Robyn looked at her, a little dolefully but without resentment. 'Pride,' she said. 'In a weird way I went along with the process as a way of sending it up. I really thought they'd break down and apologise, and not only the priests and doctors, but Bren too. You see, he'd really convinced himself that when he married me, he'd been unfit to understand the marriage contract, the true weight of the vows. And so, he was arguing, the marriage was invalid. He said it was his own fault, that he'd brought inadequate consent to the contract. But *I* hadn't brought inadequate consent. And I wasn't going to pretend there was something lacking with the contract *I'd* entered. For Christ's sake, I did bloody contracts at law school. I dug my heels in at one stage. If we were to be divorced, it had to be simply a civil divorce based on incompatibility! Not some fiction that we'd been unfit to enter the marriage. I wanted him to divorce me civilly and remarry someone else civilly if that was what he wanted, and have the guts to flirt with damnation!'

In the end, she said, she saw it was hopeless, and submitted herself, out of a kind of weariness, a resentful kindness, to further questioning by the Catholic psychiatrist. He asked her about lesbianism (because if she had lesbian tendencies, that would have been something Bren hadn't known, and lack of full knowledge could bring the contract unstuck). A priest, a canon lawyer, questioned her about her maturity at the time of the marriage. Had she entered it with due discretion? She asked them who in God's name would marry if they did it 'with due discretion'? Who would marry, she asked the priests, if they had an adequate map of the other party's DNA, just for a start?

But this reaction was taken by these very serious men, anxious to enable Bren and Robyn, if possible, to get out of marriage without losing their souls, as a sign that indeed she might have been deficient in the elements which make up a contract. As for Bren, he earnestly satisfied them on that score. And so the Archdiocese referred the documents to the Canon Law courts – the Rota – in Rome and, after an inordinate time, the annulment decree was issued and sent to Sydney.

Quite some time had passed by the time Robyn got to this point of the narrative, and the airline had opened the bar to deal with the complaints of the crowd of business travellers. Robyn and Dimp went to get some wine. Dimp felt she needed it. She had noticed a change in Robyn, from dispassion to a calm but profound anger. The Church, not willing to permit divorce for breakdown or for cruelty, was willing to go probing back to the day when Robyn had appeared in white at Riverview College chapel and given her smiling, awed, liquid consent. They had dug back to that day and found her 'I dos' not up to snuff. That, rather than the split-up as such, was what was corroding Robyn, and as it took longer and longer to refuel the planes, both wives, like old schoolfriends, went back to the bar until, when the Melbourne flight was at last called three-and-a-half hours too late, Robyn and Prim boarded it in tipsy, edgy sisterhood. Robyn had a weight off her mind. She had transferred it to Dimp.

'From that point there was a curse on my journey,' Dimp would confess to Prim in her letter.

Honest! I didn't do much good with Film Victoria, and I was delayed long enough to have to stay overnight, and in my hotel room sat upright from a dream and began bawling like an orphan. Until I heard Robyn's story I'd thought of the annulment as a touching amount of trouble for Bren to go to. But now I began to ask: If Bren's marriage to Robyn was lacking in this due discretion stuff, what of his marriage to me? Were my vows any better than hers? And as for Bren, if he couldn't make a valid contract at twenty-seven, why could he make one at thirty-three? If Robyn was invalid, why wasn't I invalid too? And how do I know I'm not?

So I've been miserable as hell. You remember the time you found a famine out of the blue. I feel like I've found a blight out of the blue. The annulment once was a fringe charm of our whole approach to marriage. Now it seems like a mess of legalism at its centre. Give me a good talking to, eh?

Prim had a suspicion that her sister's enthusiasm for Bettany's memoir, for Bettany's continual self-examination and seriousness, had somehow set her up to make too much of the first wife's story of annulment. And the idea that Dimp might, with a Bettany-like solemnity, look for some single disabling element in her life and so would make too much of the annulment, caused in Prim a mixture of severity and panic. In Prim's map of the universe it was Dimp's job to make sensible, whimsical progress, singing as she went. Prim was tempted to send an urgent chastising fax, but then thought Bren might see it.

'*You're turning me into a conspirator,*' Prim complained by letter, taking up the disciplinary tone she didn't seem capable of avoiding.

And as you always tell me, you don't have to invite me to be censorious, so here's some censoriousness for you! Listen, you're a woman of too many damned omens. You meet Brendan's ex-wife at the airport, and so you don't do well at Film Victoria! As if the one were contained in the other. And . . . if you and Robyn D'Arcy don't even believe in the annulment process, how could either of you be invalidated by it? Does Robyn still want to be married to Bren? No. And if she did at the time, she shouldn't have gone through with the process out of perversity or pride or whatever it was.

I'm going to get tough with you, and ask this: Are you sure you weren't daydreaming about being unmarried before you met Robyn? You depict your doubt as if it were a pain that came in the middle of the night. But I don't believe it. If it's a pain, it might have been one you were waiting to recognise, half-hoping it would strike. For the rest, you're his wife, true and solid. I don't think you ought to go looking in former wives for signs that you're not! You're not the most obvious wife for him, but that's what excited him and you.

Why don't you adopt that child you've been talking about? Why not do that as quickly as it can be arranged? There are plenty of them around here, desperate Southern Sudanese kids. All handsome to behold. Of course it's not as easy as just taking one. You have a disadvantage with the Sudanese government of being outside Islam. And one of the chief marks of not being of Islamic background is amply demonstrated by your letter: you dramatise your life in an unwarranted way. Free of all risk of war and hunger and epidemic, you make risks up. That's what you've done with Robyn's rigmarole about annulment.

This is a harsh letter, but I'm busy. I thought there were refugees when I first came here! But it was nothing compared to the present! There is for example a nearly instant refugee centre in the Red Sea Hills for Nubas and others. The new camp is hundreds of miles away from the Nubas' homeland. The government drives people there, to leave a free zone for army operations on the edge of the South. And we're putting the midwives and the water into this instant town of twenty, thirty thousand.

Each of whom has real, not notional problems! See! So just live on with what you have. I try to.

She signed the letter in fear. If robust Dimp couldn't find her way past a great doubt, how could Prim?

⌒

PRIM FELT MORE COMFORTABLE WITH THE letters of the convict Sarah Bernard than with the journal of Jonathan Bettany. Not only did she consider they resonated with an anguish not unlike the anguish of a slave, but Dimp did not seem to take from them any undue cues for her own life. Bettany's journal was full of such moral honesty that it seemed to be laying down a basis of explanation for some later, exorbitant crime. There was a sense of a drift towards an abyss, and it made Prim anxious. Sarah Bernard, however, could be looked at without flinching, as a sister already in the abyss, and falling.

⌒

Letter No 4, SARAH BERNARD

Marked by her: A LETTER FOR NOT SENDING

My Alice
This sort of thing happens: a woman comes up thin but broad-shouldered and gives me a sharp little jab at the bottom of the stomach. As I gag I think how brave she is to take that risk – I could report her to the Pallmires and get her put in a cell. And she goes further and says: Don't esteem yeself, duck. I cannot acquire breath fast enough to tell her she need not worry – that I have no grounds for esteem.

But why should they not be angry – these girls so often hungry? Since Mr Matron cum Steward dishes them out the bony segments of beef and bone that cannot be eaten. For the richer cuts they know one should visit the butcher shops of sundry friends of Mr Pallmire. And they think me party to that scheme. They think me sated. Whereas my heart shrinks and my mouth seems full only of acid.

I think certain plans of vengeance and I harbour the idea that the distractions of the new Irish women from Eurydice had saved me from all humiliations. Now I tell you that is not the truth. I am armoured against great humiliations but not against unexpected and lesser ones.

Thus Mrs Matron appears again in the Tory and a silence falls. Handling the keys at her belt she says to me: Sarah my girl. Get the Sunday petticoat out of your clothing bag. Since it is afternoon I murmur I will not go again.

But Mrs Pallmire is not enraged. She touches my wrist. I can understand you are a tender one. She says it like a sister. I know you are a woman of qualities and thus I have made you my day servant. You must trust me and get the Sunday petticoat.

I do this now – the clothing bag is under my cot. She tells me: Also get the shoes with buckles. Out in the garden Mr Pallmire stands in a serge jacket. I see why some would like him from that smile on his meaty face. They would think him an honest beast. There is a woman from another Tory there in her Sunday petticoat. A slighter woman than myself and brown haired under her cap. She is young but attired precisely as me.

Mr Matron tells me: This is Elizabeth. Elizabeth you are looking at Sarah Bernard. Now we are going to have a fine time in the George Inn.

And so we all get in a cart and set off out of the gate and through the streets within sight of the house of the Governor on its slope. And we go into the door of the George Inn where a large and red faced woman is on the doorstep bawling: Bring my Johnny! Bring my Johnny! And so into the better taproom as frequented – says Mr Pallmire in his jolly way – by the quality and no ticket of leave.

At the top of the George is a room for dining but Mr and Mrs Pallmire are here for drinking and for display – to have us petticoated two there to show their power. To show official men and women with what ease of control the Pallmires govern the Factory. I come to believe we are here for little better purpose than that Mr Pallmire might be jibed and joshed and ribbed to his soul's content by other men when he goes outside to relieve himself. So we are joined by two butchers and a cooper and they drink merrily and wink.

Oh she is not a good talker – so says Pallmire of me when I will not converse well with the cooper. He says: A pretty countenance but a sour spirit. And I am standing there as the cooper questions whether this could be so when I see entering the front door of the George the Visiting Surgeon of the Factory Doctor Strope. He leads his wife who wears a bonnet. As he passes the door to the taproom his eyes light directly on mine and I believe at once he sees all and chooses to ignore all. I see that in knowing of the hoarding of the Pallmires I know nothing which Doctor Strope does not know and does not join with the broad world in not wishing to know. And so he passes on to dinner with his lady.

If I am to punish the Pallmires I must go higher – to people who really do not know the character of the Pallmires and so might be surprised and shocked.

Who these heavenly creatures might however be is unknown as yet to your abased friend

Sarah

IN POSSESSION

On my return to Nugan Ganway, at my first inspection of Shegog's shepherd's hut, I found a woman of the Moth people in residence, wearing a skirt of flour sacking and making with some skill a damper on a bed of coals in the open air. The Moth people were still in the region and had rented Shegog one of their women for tobacco and tea. Some such association must have produced the genius Felix.

As we rode up the native woman stood up watchfully, bending only occasionally to flip one-handedly the damper on the glowing coals. The eyes of this handsome anthracite woman were utterly vacant of scheming. For her sake I did not choose to yell commands into the smelly shambles of Shegog's hut, but called out his name and invited him to appear.

I brought to the encounter with Shegog, who now presented himself, scratching, a body of settler wisdom which said that though there must be inevitable congress between shepherds and natives, to allow one's drovers to keep a native woman indoors was likely to create small wars both amongst the felons, and between us and the natives. The Moth people, out of resentment or what they saw as a familial relationship with Shegog, might also feel themselves entitled to kill cattle or sheep. Nor did I want to find, littering the pastures of Nugan Ganway, the poisoned bodies of native women of whom shepherds had tired.

I took Shegog aside, intending to talk straight. The woman was continuing with her damper-making.

'Is that woman *your* bushwife, Shegog, or is she a common convenience to you and the others?'

'I am repelled by such an idea as "common convenience",' he told me.

'I think you might call her my bushwife if you wished to use an over-arching term. She is a splendid and unspoilt woman if – like all her sisters – a little rank. She is my Diana of the Australian wood.'

'Under any system of mythology,' I told him, 'she represents great trouble for us. You are to send her away.'

He considered me and a tear broke out in one of his ill-assorted eyes.

'Sir,' he said, 'this is not a lightly assumed affection.'

'I'm sure you are a good man, Shegog. But you must send her away. Come with me and do it.'

Shegog looked dolefully down his nose and said, 'Go, my darling. Go!'

It seemed to be settled. But a week later, I found yet another native woman in residence, asleep in the hut. Again a confrontation – I had Long forcibly drag Shegog out into the open by the shoulder, bony and thin as it was, and sit him on a log by the door. Was this his station or mine? I asked him. He was kind enough to concede that he believed it was mine. I felt that I must show my own authority now, not depend on Long. On the trodden earth outside his door, I flattened him with a blow which stung my hand. As the woman woke and began wailing, I was privately disturbed to see that my attack had pushed Shegog's teeth into his lip and caused his mouth to bleed. He stood testing the injury philo-sophically, like a man who had suffered a thousand such blows and was only interested in placing it in its order in a table of remembered assaults.

'If she is here when I next come,' I told him, 'I shall send you back to the magistrate with an evil report.'

'It is not the same woman, you know. She simply looks the same to you, Mr Bettany. The natives plague us to take their women.'

'And they want rations?'

'Some of our flour ration,' he conceded. 'It is our ration, and we reason that if we feed them they hold off spearing the sheep.'

I said, 'My Heaven, he should be a defending lawyer.'

The woman crept out of the door with a kangaroo cloak about her shoulders and a length of burlap about her thighs. She stood by a tree looking anxious, and emitting a low continuous wail which I knew would increase in volume if we punished Shegog as he deserved. As in Van Diemen's Land, the natives seemed a soft-hearted race.

I turned to Long. 'How does Shegog meet so many natives? We have hardly seen any.'

But the hutkeeper had not yet finished educating us. 'Let me tell you, Mr Bettany, they were back the day after I sent the other lubra off. You see, it's apparent they do not think we can be of any harm to their women. They think of us as phantoms, they think us chimeras. They have strict rules of congress amongst themselves, for they see themselves to be the sole true humans. But their estimation of us is that we don't count. Thus fornication – if you'll pardon the blunt abstract noun, Mr Bettany – fornication with a white man is not a violation to them, no more than a thought. Not even a thought. It is a dream. And for having the dream, she receives, Mr Bettany, some tea and flour.'

He shrugged and I looked at this too real and too alarmed native woman and wondered if all the phantoms of Shegog's hut had shared her.

'Oh you are a deep scoundrel,' said Long. 'You will keep your tea and flour and stop them spearing sheep both.'

'I would love to accommodate that hopeful proposition, Mr Irishman,' Shegog advised him. 'But it might take cannons.'

Adopting peaceable gestures, I approached the woman. She was still and looked at me levelly.

'Come,' I told her. 'Come with me.' I led her by the wrist, as she made a slight, querulous *Oooh* sound in a silken voice and I beheld with a shock that she was beautiful. I felt the coarse delicacy of her lower arm. I was amazed and not a little confused to hear this woman's utterance as all the more familiar for being so strange. I could not forgive, but I suddenly understood, Shegog's interest in her.

I put her in the care of Long. She was quite content, it seemed, to stand while he took the rope he carried at his pommel and tied it firmly but not too severely around her waist. He attached the free end to his saddle. We would lead her home. We walked through the bright day, willing to lead our horses and be reflective. Attached to us by one strand of thin rope, the woman appeared not so much a captive but a companion, making no complaint but powerfully suffusing our thoughts. The woman-less nature of our lives had been made achingly clear. We had until that second thought it admirable. Now there was a chance we thought it regrettable. Yet though in the wilderness now christened Nugan Ganway I had known the stings of the flesh without which there is no virtue, I had no intention of taking a bushwife. What honour was there in it? Seduction with flour and tea leaves? Seduction by trade, of a woman who thought you no more than a provider of tobacco?

But I knew too that both Long and I were frightened that whoever spoke next might, unless very careful, reveal too severe a need.

I nonetheless took the risk. 'Do you suppose Shegog and his shepherds used the poor woman communally?'

In his careful way, as if I were asking him to solve calculus, Long answered. 'All I know, Mr Bettany, is that even if Shegog turned this girl away from the hut, his shepherds might outvote him. You see, some parsons and surgeons start encouraging the men to vote on sundry matters on the ships, as a means of improving their minds. And the fellows get the habit.'

And thus Athenian democracy is employed, I thought, to retain and abuse a native woman!

'Well,' I told him, delighted to overtop my inner unease with a show of appropriate authority, 'I shall let them know they are all outvoted by me.'

I could very nearly hear pulleys and mechanisms of mind and soul grind in Long. 'It seems, Mr Bettany, that if there happened to be a white woman here it would serve more than a single purpose.' It was 'pair-puss' as Long said it in his hard Irish accent. 'It would lift the minds of fellows and put the manners on them. For I do know a reliable woman at the Female Factory. Learned, virtuous and with reserve, as they say.' 'Rissairve'. I had never noticed nor been so reduced to petulance before by the way this good servant spoke his English. Nor was the distance, the chariness of 'as they say' welcome to me. I wanted to bark, 'As *who* says?'

But I swallowed my spite. 'I believe it may still be a little early. Although you claim for her some rare enough New South Wales qualities.'

'It is of no concern,' said Long. But I felt a moment's inane smugness that he had in his way expressed a liking for this unknown, virtuous convict woman.

We could now see the smoke of two native fires on the ridge above us. Not wanting to aggrieve any sensitive native elders by treating their sister like a trussed, dragged slave, we made a casual approach to the area in which the Moth people were spending their Australian spring. The archaic trees and the great jumbles of huge stones large as houses we met as we ascended had the air about them not of a season but of centuries, and the woman who had caused such discontent in Long and myself began singing low but with a piercing, nasal intonation. When Long slipped the rope from her wrist she seemed content to wait with us. It was true. We were her phantasms. She might wake from us when she chose – at least she thought so.

'And though they might think we're nothing,' said Long as if answering my thought, 'yet they take the pox quick enough. There's pox now amongst Docker's shepherds. They have given it to some women. I warn our people.'

Sometimes he gave me important news in this tangential way. As ever his information seemed broader and superior to mine. I turned to the woman who stood as if waiting to be dismissed. She said something and laughed frankly. Long and I were thus at least amusing chimeras.

Now she turned away and began calling to unseen friends on the hill above. The air filled with shrieks, her own and those of other women. She was still near us though, as if everything on earth – staying, returning – was of equal value to her.

I thought of Horace and some of his apposite, remarkable lines.

'*Mater saeva Cupidinum . . .*'

'The savage goddess of
amours, allied with wild freedom, returns me to
desires which I thought were dead.'

In trying to rid ourselves of the young woman we shooed her ahead of us and so ourselves rose up the slope. I noticed that many of the harsher-barked trees around were covered with fat grey moths, often – it seemed – to a depth of three or four. These were the bogongs which had again, like last summer, begun invading our huts, and sat in layered torpor on many a yardpost. Above me, some native children, perhaps six-years-old to ten years, studiously ate from a tree, easefully plucking the moths away and devouring them like nougat. Seeing us, these children ran off to another source further up the slope, where they resumed eating with a glazed and sated contentment. Beyond them stood a group of older men, one so old that even in this warm air he was wrapped heavily in what seemed two kangaroo-skin cloaks. There were perhaps twenty men in his party. Some sat on the ground to watch us, others remained standing, but all their air was that of gentlemen in a country of plenty.

I led the woman up to the men and, using mime, gentle pushing and other gestures of rejection, I indicated that we did not want any more such generosity. Even as I worked at this, I was overtaken by a sense that I was involved in a futile lesson. It was not helped by the fact that some of the men exposed their robust crooked teeth and laughed at me. Meanwhile the woman skirted the men and vanished at the same casual pace at which we had brought her here.

To demonstrate to them that I was no chimera and would not vanish from this country, I went to one of the many moth-encased tree trunks, peeled one plump, torpid insect off the surface of the mass, and without even plucking its wings, determinedly ate it whole. This act of small bravery proved far more pleasant than I expected. The moth tasted like a sweet nut, and I swallowed it without any hardship, and would have willingly taken another.

The elders hooted fraternally this time as if I had offered them a compliment. But had I proved my substantial nature so much as shown myself a clever manikin?

An adventure to bring in December! We needed to go into the mountains to muster our cattle which, left to range, wandered off into the range to the east, the one Goldspink and Treloar called the Tinderies. I will not rehearse here the joys and perils of such an experience. But we were rather short of men who could ride well. O'Dallow was a ferocious bush hussar. Sean Long too rode with a Celtic vigour. One of the newer men, named Presscart, though born to be a weaver rather than to the saddle, had somehow acquired the gift of riding in New South Wales. He was a personable fellow, a fresh-faced Englishman who had been tried in Shropshire for his part in helping to destroy a mill full of mechanical looms, which he had thought would take away the living of himself and his parents.

Of all of us, only Long and O'Dallow were competent at using a stock-whip, producing that sound that threatened to split the day apart and which compelled cattle.

I was nervous, I confess, taking my short-handed felon cavalry into broken, rocky and wooded country, full of peculiar hazards – the nest holes of the large slothful wombat, for example. But Long said to me that this was the country for which the light, sure-footed New South Wales stock horses, the walers such as Hobbes, were bred. Brothers in that confidence, we rose up the mountain slopes and encountered scattered members of the herd, which broke away through the striking verticals of the ghost gums. Separating into two parties, Long's and mine, each of which ended miles from the other, we ascended harder than the cattle, and outflanked and drove them towards a central gully which would serve to funnel them down to the plain.

I saw my overseer amidst the dust and raucous animal protests as his party and mine drew close. Long was zealous in heading off with whistles and howls and plying of his whip the young bulls which tried to break out of our thin cordon. The dog with his party – Brutus – keeping always close to him, worked in an ecstasy.

There is a crazed exhilaration in rushing cattle down a wooded mountain with brush-covered dips and mounds and hazards. At the bottom of the hill and in more open country they slowed, became less frenzied, more compliantly herdish and somewhat more compliant too in entering the stockyards. Here we separated out the steers and some of the calves for sale in Goulburn. Similarly heifers, and what we pretentiously called the mad bushians – a term reserved for a young bull born in the hills which had not yet seen a human, unless it were perhaps a glimpse of one of the Moth people. None of my cattle had yet suffered the brand – white paint daubed on the herd I bought earlier that year had served to mark them. The mature calves had not even that. But now I had a brand with a modified B above a bar. This would go onto the hides of all except the few cattle which carried Treloar's brand, the modified T, and they would need to be returned to him for honour's sake.

On a breezeless, hot afternoon, we were still at the branding when a near-empty wagon appeared through the dust our activities had thrown up. It proved to be a tall Liverpudlian from Goulburn, one Finnerty, who had heard from Treloar that I had taken up the Nugan Ganway country. He addressed me in his jagged accent and said he would undertake each quarter to freight goods and mail to us and from us, as he had for some two years been freighting goods and mail to Goldspink at Treloar's run. This first call of his was speculative, although he had brought some rum and canned plum duff in case I wanted to greet the coming Christmas in some style.

And amongst what Finnerty carried as mail contractor was a letter from my two-years-younger brother, Simon, which I reproduce in part. At the time I would consider it plain and read it blithely enough, but on revisiting it years later, I saw that it reliably contained all the omens of the ultimate grief of our family.

'I am happy to tell you,' wrote Simon, 'that I recently made an exploration of the Port Phillip and Melbourne area and find that all the best land has had the eyes studiously picked out of it by fellows who were there before me – which means not an aeon but a mere two or so years before me.'

In this empire, a man has to be quick and born in the right second to seize a start. In a twinkling that thing we call the wilderness or 'the bush', the hoary nothingness, becomes some former army officer's or prison guard's rural estate!

I intend to settle in the eastern section, as it is called – along a river they call the Broken. Now, consider the chart, what there is of it! The Broken is a location which will put me on the road between yourself and Port Phillip. If one day you should choose to drop over your alps and visit me – a mere ride of two hundred or so miles over snow-blocked passes and thick forest and amidst the local natives who are said to be very martial – then you shall be very welcome. One day indeed you might bring sheep to me for fattening and for droving to the Melbourne village, where mutton has a huge price! Thus we might combine commerce with brotherhood.

Simon went on to say that Mother seemed now to be unwell in a general but

... by no means dangerous way. I think it is that her children are leaving, and perhaps with them the basis for so much social activity in Ross and with the Batchelors out at Hydebrae. But Father is in strapping form, attending four days a week his law office in Hobart, and spending the other three days at the farm at Tiverton, conferring with the overseer Frume, drinking a little with him ...

Frume, I remembered, was a convict Luddite, a wrecker of machines, like my fellow, Presscart. In England, clearly, it had not been such an uncommon crime.

He rejoices for all our sakes in the London price of wool, as I hope does his son in New South Wales.

Now, most importantly, do you remember Elizabeth Purves, of the Purves family of Sorell? She has done me that greatest of honours ... When I am established on my run, I shall return to Van Diemen's Land for the wedding, which I well understand you may be unable to attend in view of your remoteness. My Elizabeth insists she wishes to occupy my Broken River station as my Companion on this Earth.

Finnerty had also brought a letter for Long. It was all the way from Ireland – the postmark said 'Sligo' – but when I handed it to Long, he

seemed to be defeated by this reminder of lost places and secreted it
straight off with a grimed hand into the pocket of his brown trousers.

On Nugan Ganway's first Christmas morning Long and I rode out to
the huts with some rum and canned plum duff. The men expressed their
thanks plainly and so very touchingly. I was pleased to find no black
gins around the place, though God knows that men like Shegog might
have temporarily sent them away. The native fires could be seen on the
hills, as banal today as on other days. Long and I rode back to the
homestead half-tipsy, observed by a line of placid natives on the ridge
above.

We drank some rum with Clancy and O'Dallow in their hut, a few
yards from my own, and then one of the men carried a rough Christmas
dinner to the homestead, where Long and I dined in masterly isolation,
talking of nothing but our recent muster and the increase figures. Long
was entitled to have deposited in the savings bank in his name his small
portion from our first sale of steers and calves. We were dining on
nothing but mutton and some beef as usual, enhanced however by the
appetite morning rum had given us and spiked up by the pot of mustard
I had also bought from Finnerty. As I ate and we conversed, I noticed
that the letter Long had received weeks earlier now lay beside his plate.
At last I pointed to the letter. 'News from home?'

'Yes, yes.'

'No bad news in your letter, I hope.'

There was silence. I could hear Clancy and O'Dallow and a few other
men singing in the second hut.

'It is written in a dense style,' he told me. 'In a script I have to do
battle with.'

'The work of a notary or a scribe, I suppose.'

'My papers say Reading and Writing, and I can get the better of some
print. But not fully read this.'

'I don't wish to intrude, Sean. But I would be pleased to supply that
service.' I knew as soon as I spoke that this was not a good offer to make
on Christmas Day. In his world few wrote letters idly.

He thought, ate some more mutton, sipped his rum. Then Clancy
brought us two bowls in which lay segments of the modern miracle of
English canned pudding, and when that was reduced to fragments, Long
abruptly passed the letter to me.

I unfolded it and found it was indeed a densely written letter. I hoped the poor fellow had not been trying to make sense of it for days.

'Dear Son,' I read aloud, 'With this come my devout prayers for your endless well-being. I am reconciled to the woeful truth I shall never see you in this world again but think daily on the hope of that better location where we shall be face to face without the veil of distance.'

I heard Long grunt, as if to cast doubt on the idea of better places.

'There is no day passes that I fail to think of you and what your life must be. I see your dear wife and children, young Sean Pat being now nine years of age and yourself reborn. To behold him is at the one time a joy and a sharp sorrow. He is sturdy and has your quiet manner, so I am left to hope he does not harbour dark plans and eat his soul alive as did you. Your dear wife's family is a well of kindnesses to me – I thank God they are so numerous, for they have supported her and me in your absence.'

Long packed a pipe as he told me casually, 'Yes, I was married, Mr Bettany.'

'I knew that,' I said. 'But somehow it means more now . . .'

'I signed that paper men can sign. To petition that she be sent here to join me. But nothing's been heard. There's plenty of English wives brought out. But in Ireland you have Dublin Castle, and it never finds the means.'

'Your son though?'

'I have two of them. One older than Sean Pat. They'll join me perhaps when they're grown and I'm prosperous.' Yet he did not suggest his wife might come. 'Would you ever mind reading on now, Mr Bettany?'

I did, and was soon sorry. 'We have just had here the saddest news which I hate to break to you of your dear brother Martin's death with the army in the Indies. It was fever, and old Mr Mulcahy who served in the Indies as a boy came to the wake to your dear brother's memory and said that fever is awful in the Indies or in Jamaica . . .'

I broke off and said, 'My dear fellow, this is all dreadful news.'

Long looked at his hand and murmured, 'God rest him then.'

I could not read on in this phase of bereavement. The silence grew. I said, 'Your brother was a soldier then?'

'Ah, he was with me in the little act we arranged for the Marquis of Sligo.' They had, it seemed, while wearing some thin disguise, broken into the marquis's house to utter threats over rent. This was the old marquis, he told me. I had indeed read in a copy of the *Times* at Barley's place that the father had been succeeded by a somewhat more open-handed, Whiggish son. 'There's five whole battalions of the 60th Regiment and they fill them up from the gaols. They counted me a little old for that purpose, but they took Martin, and he knew it for a fever ticket.'

He drank some rum and coughed a great deal. I was at that point overcome by a partially tipsy passion to challenge his stoicism. I reached across and poured more rum into his pannikin. He took it up and tipped it onto the earth floor, the first Australian libation I had seen. I was not offended but filled my own mug and did likewise, pouring it out.

'For the spirit,' he murmured. 'May the souls of the faithful departed ... Dear Jesus, if I'd taken better thought, we might both be by the turf fire for this feast with everyone around us. I understand perfectly now there is no overturning of what is called the law. I did not know then that it could move me so far through space. That it could move me so far and be waiting here to receive me too. So here we are.'

'Here we are,' I agreed, percipient with liquor. 'Life is all accidents.'

Long was in the meanwhile shaking his head. 'The mortal being scarce has time on this earth for regret or complaint. Do you mind, Mr Bettany?' He nodded to the letter again. He did not want my tipsy reflections.

I read on. 'The air in the Indies is so bad, we hear. But who would have thought it could strike down a soul like Martin's? He is at the right hand of the Virgin now, which must be our solace.'

At that Long nodded. 'It must be,' he said, though not sounding as if he meant it in quite the way the letter did.

I concluded reading at a good pace. 'Your wife and children – as do I – long to have a word from you. We hear of you that you have been made a constable in New South Wales! Such a thing! The Drynan family have heard this from Thomas Drynan of Barryshaun who works at shepherding for a New South Wales magistrate.

'So in hope of a note and in shared sorrow but with sure and certain expectation of the Resurrection, I am Your one own Mother.'

I let the missive settle in the room, and its sadness wash over me, the *lacrimae rerum*, on a day when I was doing so well, and existed exactly where I hoped to be. After another sip of the liquor, which was good Indian stuff, not some Parramatta rotgut, I said, 'Should you need to write ... or any assistance ... my note paper and pens are here for your use. I could also ...'

'You could also write it for me in copperlate and add a Latin tag.' He sounded just an ounce shy of hostility. I could see that the same excellent liquor was making him a little more direct as well.

'If you wish, I could,' I said.

'The text that must operate here, Mr Bettany is this: Let the dead bury their dead!'

'This is a little harsh on a wife. And a mother.'

'Oh the harshness is not mine. One should ask Dublin Castle about that. And I have seen men waste by writing notes, and receiving notes, and pretending that these others, the left behind, are – for real purpose – the living. And being disheartened when the breathing presence can in no way be conjured. Not for me, sir. That's not for me as I am now.'

'Even so,' I argued. 'A word. You should write a word surely. Something to be shown to your children. A scrap of writing with your name on it.'

He thought a while, then said, 'It might be a sop to them, and a sop to me. Those who have crossed that line we have all crossed, we do not write a piddling letter, Mr Bettany. It would be a scar on their sight. What man, once gone, would try to scar his children?' He suddenly raised a hand and pointed upwards and to the vague north-west, in the direction of impossibly distant Europe. 'I regard them,' he said. 'I regard them, and so do not open the wound.'

I was slow, trying to frame an answer to this.

Long spoke again. 'After seven years of no contact, a man is able to present himself to a minister of religion and swear that he has not written letters for seven years, and neither his wife. That they are, that is, dead to each other ... I will not lie about such a thing. I will not say I have neither written nor received if I have written and received. I am trying to be a sensible man.'

'It is not for me to tempt you,' I told him.

'My brother,' he said. 'Could you and I, Mr Bettany, drink a health to his good rest?'

And so we did.

Shegog has been speared! One of his shepherds appeared at my door in the middle of a hot night and screamed the news. 'We told you we need bloody carbines!' he howled. Leaving Long to organise Clancy and O'Dallow into a homestead guard, I rode out on Hobbes, carrying the shepherd behind me on my saddle.

The second shepherd had carried Shegog from the place he took his wound by the door and into the hut. Now that same shepherd was with some timidity waiting for us, carrying a hardwood cudgel which looked like something a native had once made and given him as a present. I saw in the mutton-fat lamplight that Shegog looked pitiable, laid on one of the rough cots and seeming almost luminously white-grey, with a froth of blood on his lips, and a broken spear stuck in deep below his heart. The shepherd with the cudgel explained the severity of the wound. 'Them sables use a fluked bone to gash a fellow open!' he whispered in my ear. I could feel the hot breath of his terror against my neck.

Shegog complained in a thin voice, 'Oh it won't come out, Mr Bettany. Save me if you can.'

'Don't speak,' I said as consolingly as I could.

'I feel well enough you know, Mr Bettany, more of coldness than ache.'

He coughed some more blood, and again I said, 'Don't speak, dear fellow.'

But he was a speaker, a rare Australian orator. As if, having lived a more self-examined life than some felons, it was his duty now to die a self-examined death. 'I am a Presbyterian, sir. Despite my fallen state . . .' A paroxysm came but could not stop him. We all wished he would be quiet and die. '. . . God is not pleased to see his Christian children impaled. Go out now, Mr Bettany. Go out and fire your carbine in the dark, so they know there's a vengeance coming.'

I wondered whether the sound of my carbine would dissuade the natives from further attack, or merely make pursuing them all the more difficult. I could not refuse a man though whose darkest blood was bubbling at his lip. Outside, in the bright, silken deep night I discharged the weapon, and the noise went bumping round the boulders and recoiled from hills. Only the sheep in the fold Shegog had been guarding responded by scurrying. The cudgel-owning shepherd had followed me out. He said, 'They were angry because poor old Shegog had poxed their women. He's an awful ladies' man for an ugly fellow. He thought he was jake and clean when we first come here, but the pox has come back in full flower for poor old Goggy.'

We went inside and recited in ragged unison the Lord's Prayer, and I uttered two psalms from memory. Shegog looked more studious than in pain, and expired with a whimper around first light, the shaft still inextricable in him, as the natives intended it should be. I felt acutely that his was the first blood spilt on Nugan Ganway, and diseased as it might

have been, there was no question it altered the complexion of the landscape. I felt an irrational reluctance to bury him at once, as if the fact of
his murder would be thereby erased. So I wrapped him in wet burlap for
a day.

I had during that time returned to my hut–homestead and opened the
lock on a chest which contained some seven carbines and ball cartridges.
Like many other cases of recourse to arms, this one had less than meri-
torious origins, but the men must not only behave – they must also have
means to defend themselves and their flocks. So the firearm entered
Nugan Ganway's history, and I felt dispirited that it had. Not everyone
would use such a potent implement with wisdom.

The memory of a stratagem first attempted in Van Diemen's Land
cheered me up, and I fetched some pages and ink and began to draw
cautionary pictures.

In the first image, arduously but definitely depicted in ink, I showed two
black men projecting a spear into a white man's chest, and then a response:
two white men firing long-barrel carbines and felling a black man.

The second set of images was of two white men shooting down a native
and then, with black and white for witness, of the two culprits hung
from a tree for murder.

Next, a sketch of native men spearing a sheep, and being pursued by
white men for it. Last, a group of black men spearing a kangaroo, and
being offered the hand of fraternity by a settler who bore some resemblance to me.

The secret was to find an elder and give him these unambiguous pictographs. Another Van Diemen's Land device that might be useful was to
choose an appropriate elder, to observe the one the natives most
respected, and proclaim him king, giving him an appropriate chain of
office, making him responsible for the behaviour of his people.

I gave one carbine each to my most trusted men, saying, 'We are not
at war with these people. We seek to enforce the peace, that is all. No
wild shots!'

Clancy and O'Dallow said nothing. Their eyes took on a distance and
so I warned them again, and showed them my pictographs. 'Persuasion,'
I said. 'Persuasion.'

I guessed that after Shegog's death the Moth people would have wisely
taken to the wooded heights. I rode off that afternoon south-west with
a carbine at my saddle, one at O'Dallow's, and Shegog's two shepherds,
unarmed (we had simply left that outpost's sheep in their folds). A second

party led by Long and equipped with a copy of my treaty-in-pictures, went more northerly, towards Treloar's run. We looked in our progress for the usual threads of smoke which would betray the location of these people. I saw none, and my party had to wait until the next morning before we encountered anyone at all, a lean old woman wrapped in a kangaroo skin rug. She talked to us quite companionably as we passed. One of Shegog's shepherds called to her, 'Yes, rave on, you old bitch.' Perhaps she had been left there to die, as was rumoured to be the economic custom of all natives.

Finding nothing else, we came to tall hills which flanked the pass marking the southern end of my land licence. We normally called this, if we called it anything, the Gap. From here one could see the line of snowy alps stretched diagonally across our front. Shegog's murderers had not taken this route.

Returning, we found Long still gone, but the men left behind at my station had by now built a coffin of rough slabs and put Shegog within, and we buried him with the point of the lance still within him. Convict scholar, lecher, and in part, maker of his own murder.

It was late afternoon before Long's party arrived back at Nugan Ganway main station. Long carried a small boy, smaller than Felix when I had first met him, folded within his arms as he held the reins. He dismounted, drew down the child and walked across the yard to report to me. The child was not passive as Felix had been. It yowled and writhed, and Long did not look very pleased with himself. I asked him inside, and he seemed bewildered about where to place the infant and sat with the squirming child in his arms.

'Where does he come from?' I asked, expecting to hear an unhappy account.

'Sir,' Long explained, 'so along we go and encounter a party of men, women and children, with me trying to talk to an old man. But the young men began to make warlike sounds – you know what they're like! I saw the women and children running off. I tried to show your pictures to the old man but the young fellows made spear-throwing gestures and screamed something – Wallah! Wallah! – something like that. Whatever it was, they were not telling us to enter their habitation and make ourselves welcome.' He turned to the little wrestling bundle in his arms and made soothing noises. 'Do settle, small heathen!' he said, and the child did a little and he returned to the tale. 'Young Presscart was sure they were about to send me off on the same path as Shegog and impale me. He was hugging his firearm and of course it went off. This child's mother, a little beyond us and higher up the rise was killed, and his relatives, thinking him dead too, left the place in an utter rush, the young men turning back to tell me this was not a finished business.'

I put my head in my hands. 'Oh dear God!' I said. So there had now been, within little more than a day, parallel murders on Nugan Ganway.

'Why did you not leave the child there?' I asked.

'We meant to, but he howled worse when left, and so, thought I, I should take him and return him later to his people.'

I told Long to take out the child for the moment and bring in Presscart, loom-breaker, horseman, and now killer of natives. I questioned the young man and told him I had put considerable trust in him by placing a carbine in his care.

'Maybe I wasn't ripe for such trust,' he replied. 'I have rarely had a firearm in my hands and it went off without my meaning it.'

There was no doubting how close to tears he was, how horrified by the blood he had let. I would have liked to call it murder, but could not.

Long came back with the child. It did not weep any more, and Long went on quite tenderly soothing him with tea. This, it struck me, was a full-blood infant. What a noble experiment, I thought for a while, to take such a child to Mr Loosely. If Felix could read the life of Isaac Newton, would a full-blood child read it better? But this, I realised, was a Satanic impulse. We must return him, as much as progressive Mr Loosely would welcome him.

And as we watched the child, calm now, totter about my house, opening boxes, inquiring into things, with a genial content, Long was still worried I, at whatever inconvenience of time, might inflexibly hand the young man Presscart over to a magistrate for punishment. Presscart was a good fellow, he insisted, who got teased for crying for his own lost babies, and would not knowingly harm other infants, even sable ones.

'After all,' I reminded Long, 'I have drawn pictures of a white man punished for killing a black one. It is part of the contract.'

'But we haven't managed to get the natives to take to the contract yet, sir.'

I had a sense I think even then that my convenient hesitation on this matter might return to savage us all.

I nicknamed the native child Long had brought home Hector, for though he had not been killed by Achilles in the form of Presscart's carbine, his mother had been. When in time the Moth people presented themselves to Long and myself during our ride in search of them, there seemed to be no rancour – in fact I wondered if they had seasons of peace, unknown to us, like the sixteen days of peace which had always accompanied the old games at Olympia. We returned the child by putting him down from my horse once within sight of his people, and, unlike what had happened when I had tried the same plan with Felix, the native women came down, dilly bags hanging from their wrists and elbows, and picked him up with whoops of delight. Hector had shown himself an affectionate and jolly child who had none of the wariness of Felix, and I think Long may have been a little sad to see him reclaimed.

Over the coming years Hector would prove to be a frequent visitor to Nugan Ganway. He always approached without fear, and Presscart and Long would teach him riding and roping a steer and other tricks not native to his people.

But in the year of his mother's murder, I still needed to conclude a peace with the Moth people. On a day when Long and I encountered a staring band of men, with Long watchful in his saddle, I dismounted and offered a thin-legged old man at the head of this party some of my tea from my saddlebag. Then I made a fire and Long and I sat with this fellow and his brethren drinking it. It was possible to believe Shegog had not died, and nor had Hector's mother. I began with the matter of names and by the normal clumsy gestures convinced the old man to call me Bepp'ny. With probably equal inaccuracy, I discovered his name to be Durra or Dhurra. I took out my pictographs and pointed out the contracts in each frame. I was pleased young warriors and even some women crowded up to inspect them too. I could hear their warm gasps and smell the bodies, chief olfactory component of which seemed to be stale animal fats they rubbed on their skin. I could not have proved the exculpatory, extenuating aspects of Presscart's crime with my basic pictures. But I believed I had expiated the native woman's blood by taking care of and returning the child, rather than indulging in the improving vanity of sending him to Loosely.

Durra was delighted with my pictographs and thrust them into the air, waving them, as his people hooted all around him. I put the pictographs in a leather pouch he could wear about his neck – his copy, the Moth people's copy, of the compact between us.

'What a genial people,' I exclaimed as we rode away.

I had Clancy fashion a little breastplate of metal which could be

suspended on a chain from the neck. On one of our future meetings I
awarded it to Durra. I knew from a notice in a *Goulburn Herald* Finnerty
brought me that a more formal chain of chieftainship could be ordered
from a jeweller and engraver in Goulburn. I ordered one with 'Durra,
King of the Nugan Ganway Natives' etched in the breastplate. The
following year I drank tea with him again and presented him with the
chain. He seemed to comprehend the contract inherent in this act, and I
thought again what an understanding set of men and women these people
could be. But always dreaming of the day when I could send Felix to
come to them like an apparition, and make all clear.

Those first three years of my possession of Nugan Ganway happened,
as I and the world would soon discover, to be the finest three years ever
for putting livestock in such country. The great levellers of weather and
prices and the rest, which would eventually and for a time make a very
poor town indeed of Sydney, later hung over us, and would in the end
make dust of many. But we were not aware of such dull restrictions in
my first three years in New South Wales, and in that time some provident
tendency in me equipped me to make use of this age of plenty, for I lived
carefully and restocked – as it turned out – wisely.

Here are some figures from my stockbook for the time just before
lambing as my fourth year of occupation of Nugan Ganway began.

'The sheep stand thus, after deducting losses amongst the beasts at the
rate of 5 per cent, and the sale of 1800 old ewes, and adding in the
80 per cent increase of the flocks:

Breeding ewes, 3 years old 4720
Ditto, 2 years old 5540
Three-year-old wethers 3803
Ditto, two-year-old 4758
Ewe lambs, 11 months old 6400
Wether lambs, ditto 5857
Rams 200
Total ...... 31 278'

My profits for the previous year (half of which went, of course, to
Messers Barley and Batchelor), read:

'To the sale of 150 700 lbs of wool, at mean price of 10 pence
ha'penny in the grease £6630

To the sale of 3700 three-year-old wethers, at 10 shillings each ......
£1850

Total ...... £8480'

I had as always, being a fellow enchanted by figures, to resist their fascination, lest their imitation of solidity induce me to make silly choices.

Despite Barley's charming yearly invitations, I did not go to Sydney to lord it, to rent or buy a good house, and present myself at the front doors of tailors' establishments. I had returned all wool profits into buying new livestock and supplying an increasing number of shepherds from the convict depots of Sydney and Goulburn, as advertised in the *Government Gazette* which Finnerty now brought to me by wagon.

For I needed in my third year to employ, besides Long, Clancy, Presscart and O'Dallow, some two dozen shepherds and hutkeepers. Yet I was proud no one could accuse me of prodigality. As I set off with the wool that third October, with the two Nugan Ganway wagons I now owned and some five others rented from Goulburn and groaning with fleece, I was very proud of those wary instincts inherited from my mother, who simply could not understand rashness. I soon found I was no perfect member of that earth-wide Communion of Saints of whom I was a distantly placed member.

For there is a confession which must be made here in this personal journal, in the hope that such frankness might constitute a decent act of repentance. I had always known I must keep myself separate from the native women if I were to set a mark for my men to imitate, yet I fancied that it did not constitute much of a hardship. My energies were bent to my flocks, and my main discourse with the Moth people, whose tribal name I discovered from inquiry in Sydney was Ngarigo, had been aimed not at sociability for its own sake but at impressing on them the concept that Saxon Merino sheep were not *animal nullius*, game to be slaughtered like the kangaroo or the possum. Yet I had noticed that many of their younger women were in extraordinary ways handsome, their handsomeness enhanced by their air of extreme ancientness, not of their persons but of their manners. I was always given pause, by their innocence – and also by thoughts as to which of these daughters of Eve carried in them Shegog's appalling disease, and to which others it had spread. That infection, if acquired, could unfit me for the eventual fullness of decent manhood utterly.

Now I found that, as my father had once said, commenting – to my mother's disapproval – on a parishioner of the Anglican Church in Ross, moral pride is itself a good preparation for crime.

At our meeting that third October at the town of Black Huts, Barley had ordered some splendid French brandy. My load of wool, already sold to Barley, was securely fastened on my wagons in the dusk outside the Dangling Man Hotel. A sense of the wholeness of the world had entered my head through the good price Barley had offered – 10 pence ha'penny a pound – and the angelic, limitless hope that figure held out.

Barley, being both my co-seller and my buyer, given that he had a share in the wool, was in lively spirits and in his company one felt uniquely blessed, that Athens and Rome were as nothing beside the Black Huts, and though Mycaenas and Horace may have been friends, their friendship was not quite at the peak as the friendship between Bettany and Barley.

'Even, my friend Bettany,' Barley said, 'within confines of frail flesh, a chap could not help but stand on his hind legs on such a night in such a market, and howl at moon for glory!'

I remember too Barley's paleness by lamplight. 'If wife were here,' he told me sincerely, 'she would have wisely counselled me to more modest intake.' Suddenly he was gone, and I was alone, wrapped in the golden blanket of my own senses and comfortable in what felt like hero-hood. A bare-headed young woman, one of a set of girls who made themselves accommodating to both the men who sold the wool and those who purchased it, approached me now. Her auburn hair was somewhat tousled and she had knowing eyes. She sat and asked could she take a dram of the brandy, and since two-thirds of our third bottle of the evening lay undrunk, I permitted her. 'I'll pour for myself,' she told me, 'since ye seem a little distray.' I found this greatly amusing, and she put out her hand and said. 'Ye're a poor child unused to bein' squiffy. Ain't it so?'

She asked me then, straight out, did I like trolls named Cecily, since Cecily was her name. I remember assuring her that I particularly admired that name. I launched into encomiums in its honour. Then, inevitably, she asked me what I considered time spent with a Cecily might cost. Did I think it might be worth 10 shillings? Man of business even in my cups, I beat her down to a mere crown.

The next morning I was of course in hell, but towards afternoon I began to feel that I might at some remote time live and breathe and have moral being. I met Barley at one stage in the corridor, where his freckles showed up on preternatural pallor. 'I leave for Sydney this afternoon, dear Bettany. Will you not come this year and lave yourself in harbour?'

I assured him that I would visit him one year, but I felt unworthy of his hearth, of any urbane hearth.

'I needed my dear wife to act as rudder in my folly.' His pronunciation – 'rooder' – and his woeful face restored me momentarily to laughter, but it did not last. For distraction that forenoon I sat in the parlour, and waited to gather myself for my own departure by doing a little book work in my journal on the glittering price received per pound, and the more I wrote and made those lifeless figures, the more I was convinced that what I clearly needed was a wife and helpmeet. Land and a flock were no longer adequate.

I returned to Nugan Ganway, and tried to lose myself in work at that slacker, summer time of year. All that season I expected some pernicious display to break out in my flesh as punishment for my sportive, drunken night with the woman at the Black Huts. No sign of the disease presented itself though. Accursed Cecily, whom I had for some minutes or hours mistaken for a creature of splendour, was a woman to be praised in that regard.

And on some days Miss Phoebe Finlay in adult form, a being of inexact, fair features, returned to my mind as my possible and fated spouse. At others, riding out to check on my out-stations, I would find myself dismissing this child-bride from my head and making a stern pledge to attend the Squatters' Ball the next January.

As if to reproach me and mock my need, a compelling missive reached me, by way of Finnerty's wagon.

Genève,
May 24 of Anno Domini 1838
Dear Mr Bettany,
I am normally prevented by reasons of propriety from writing to anyone other than my family. I write to you in horror at the concept of you which my father seems to promote in his letters to me, and I hope that you do not suffer from these slanders where you are. Since I know them to be false, they therefore make me truer. I look forward on my return to New South Wales to taking my own direction and to making independent choices. If our compact stands, I am still prepared to be your wife, for I retain a true affection. I shall see you in your distant station, and enjoy the prospect.

Yours sincerely,
Phoebe Finlay
PS: Do not answer this, as I will not be allowed to receive it.

I thought, this is not like the letter her father read to me. This had a levelly determined tone, and a certain restraint: 'true affection' was invoked, a relatively modest emotion. I considered writing to her anyhow and asking her on the basis of her obvious maturity of attitude to refrain from such letters. But then I thought, would she use any letter of mine as a stick to enrage her dangerous father?

I was secure that between Phoebe and me lay oceans and continents of other men, English clergymen, soldiers, scholars, ships' officers, merchants, gentlemen farmers. I was content to see how her 'true affection' would last these contacts. And yet with one side of my mind I relished her letter, and hoped that she would appear one day, an ivory woman amongst my leathered men.

There was at this season a considerable time to daydream. Long and I were engaged in the practice – though Long's thoughts seemed too sombre ever to be called by that sunny title 'daydream' – one dusk in our homestead at the heart of wild pastures, not yet stricken with the first frost, when he put his mug of tea down, stood up and told me a party of horsemen, out of our sight from here, were bearing down on the Murrumbidgee stream which lay below our hill, and approaching our homestead. He had a remarkable set of senses and yet I doubted what he said. A party? Parties had no reason to come to Nugan Ganway.

I considered drawing out my carbine and ball cartridges which lay under my lath bed. Long waved a lean hand in the blue light. 'It could be the county hunt,' he said, and his mouth cracked open in silent laughter. Yet we both felt a reclusive annoyance at being intruded upon. We walked without arms out of the boulder-clad basin in which our house stood, and by the stockyard Clancy, O'Dallow and Presscart had also gathered, frowning. We beheld, coming down the opposing slope to the river, a group of six mounted men, one of whom resembled a figure stumbled into Nugan Ganway from a European opera. He was mounted on a beautiful grey, almost silver in that light, and wore a shining pillbox hat, a brilliant green jacket of a military cut, blue trousers, and gleaming boots suited to a Napoleonic cavalry charge. My fellows, in red flannel shirts and breeches, gazed on him with disbelief. This leader of the mounted party flew gallantly across the Murrumbidgee, throwing splashes up into the brilliant dusk light. The other riders, though trying to keep up to him, were more reluctant to make the show of it which he had. As they came up the slope to the higher ground, we saw that the chief figure was accompanied by four convict constables in blue jackets and canvas pants, and a black trooper in a blue coat, his bare feet poking comfortably out of his stirrups.

They drew up and tethered their horses to the stockyard rails, in which Hobbes and Long's horse, Dingo, reacted to their arrival with as much bad grace and suspicion as did Long and I. The Napoleonic man had swung from his saddle with much vigour. Now, his boot leather squeaking and slapping, he marched with equal flourish towards our party.

'Sir, sir,' he cried out to me earnestly as he advanced. 'Are you aware of the new *Land Occupation Act*?' Long and I smiled at each other. *What a conversationalist!* Long's glance pronounced.

'May I present myself, Captain Richard Peske, with a final "e". I am newly appointed Land Commissioner for this district under the Act.'

I felt uneasy at once, but Long and I fraternally maintained our indolent bush postures. 'I was not sure we had the honour to possess a Land Commissioner,' I said.

He strained for augustness behind his lightly freckled cheeks. 'Indeed you didn't, sir. I am the first one appointed to this south-west region below Braidwood. Superlative country, count myself very fortunate, I do. Now, sir, I do possess your name, but I confess it is in my journal in the saddlebag and it has slipped my mind. It is painful for me to tell you, sir, that your occupation of this country is illicit, and that you must abandon this area. It may be that your flocks are forfeit – I shall have to consult the Chief Superintendent on that matter.'

Surrounded by my huge acreage I did not at once feel panic. I told him he could not expect me to take him seriously.

'That is a common response,' he admitted. 'But I think that if you consult the new Act, you will find that I possess authorities only slightly less – in these matters – than a Roman emperor.'

'You can be sure I'll consult the Act. I also have powerful partners.'

'Well . . .' he whacked his fine moleskin trousers with the pair of leather gloves he had taken off while speaking, 'partners don't signify in this business. If you ride south from here in the direction of the Port Phillip Pass, you will come to a sharp little pass named by that Polish gentleman Lhotsky as Dainer's Gap. Do you happen ever to have been there?'

I had visited it looking for the Moth people after Shegog's murder. 'I have been that far once or twice,' I said.

'Well, we have been up there and are coming from there now. We find, as Mr Treloar told us, there is a native cairn on one side and two trees blazed by him six months before you ever visited this place.'

'Ah, that's where Mr Treloar has been. For I have never sighted
him. However, from what I've heard he was pleased to have me to settle
this area, since he himself could obviously not afford to stock this tableland.'

'He has not said that to me,' said Captain Peske, cool in a blithe sort
of way. 'He has appealed to me to give him a licence over this area, and
I have no reason, on the grounds of the marks he has made to the south,
to deny it. He is rather chagrined, I have to say, at the small number of
cattle you returned to him after your muster.'

'I was scrupulous, for God's sake. I can show you my books.'

How I protested! I had stocked this land, kept peace with the natives,
kept my servants in good order.

'Did anyone tell you to invest in this land?' asked Peske. 'I don't mean
Treloar's questionable overseer. I mean anyone with any authority?'

'I told you. Treloar. Not that he has any ultimate authority. The chief
authority was the custom of the land beyond the limits. The divine
vacancy of the place was the authorisation, and I stocked that vacancy.'

Peske looked at me from under knotted brows, as if he were up to my
tricks. 'Sir, sir, sir. These matters have already been settled in most areas
of the country, and only your distance from the seat of administration
has allowed you such a good run. Now I can't answer for what Mr
Treloar might have said to you, but in any case, Mr Treloar is of an
altered mind. And he has previously marked and blazed this particular
quarter of the earth.'

Long was staring steadily and with a murderous frown at the Land
Commissioner. All I could do was go on arguing, somewhere between a
bellow and a bleat. 'One native cairn and two marked trees. You'll try
to expel me for one cairn and two damned trees? When I have taken a
vacuum and given it substance?'

'Ah, now you're falling back on a principle more abstract than that
provided for by the *Land Occupation Act*,' he told me. 'This land, though
unoccupied, has always belonged to the Crown. You took it without
permission . . .'

'But if that's true, it's true of Treloar too. Yet Treloar has your
blessing, and I am the one who is to be cast out!'

Peske's constables were growing bored and looking away at the blue
mountains of evening. Did this ridiculous freckled gallant ride round
routinely telling people they had lost their pasture and that their flocks
were forfeit?

'You might as well ride away,' I assured him. 'It will take greater force than you have at your disposal to push me off.'

'Now you are talking like some Irish or Scots revolutionary. Wouldn't you be ashamed to be taken away in chains to Braidwood?'

'I *would* be shamed. I would also be howling angry.'

'Your anger would not signify anything,' said Captain Peske, again slapping the ham of his tight-trousered leg. 'I am more than accustomed to anger. It is a product of my calling.'

'I shall challenge you in the Lords.'

'In London? That would be very expensive.'

He looked so owl-wise that I began to laugh. This must be a joke put together by Charlie Batchelor. Maybe Charlie was visiting me, and had sent these fellows in costume ahead. And now he was concealed behind some tree, laughing!

'We have in case all night to argue,' I told the operatic captain in his uniform devised by no known army. The overarching law, like the curlews in the high trees, where the last light remained only for a moment, would need to sleep. 'You and your men require shelter and refreshment. You can have that, but not my land.'

Peske sounded both sympathetic and doubtful. 'You would not, I trust, slaughter us in our blankets as the Campbells did the MacDonalds?'

I looked levelly at him. 'Come inside.'

'Well,' Peske said, 'though I'm aware of being a nuisance to you, Mr Bettany, I find the concept of a rum-tea delightful, should you have rum. But I am reluctant in the grievous circumstances to impose.'

Long made up a drum of tea and cooked damper, and entertained the constables outside while the black trooper started his own campfire in the lee of some boulders beyond the stockyards. It was Long's way of ensuring I could have time alone with the ridiculous Peske, who sat with me at my sheet-bark table drinking tea laced with rum as politely as if he had not just told me to leave Nugan Ganway. He annoyed me further by feeling the freedom to inspect my small bookcase, which these days had come to accommodate such works as Wainwright's *Sheep Breeding*, a bound volume of the *Illustrated London News* I had bought in Liverpool after selling my sheep, Macaulay's *Essays*, the King James version of the Bible, Curry's *The Punic Wars*, a work on Euclidean geometry, as well as the founding volume of my bush library, *The Odes of Horace*. He pulled this last out and began to leaf through it. He looked at the inscription inside the cover, and my father's name.

'Robert Bettany,' he said. 'But I knew a Mr Robert Bettany. My old tutor in Van Diemen's Land. Excellent old chap, emancipated felon of some kind. Quite a burning zeal for dear old Horace.'

'Your old tutor?'

'Well, not so much mine. He taught boys called the Batchelors, and I went to stay with their family while my mother was ill.'

He was a fellow for thunderous declarations. Having with utter certainty declared himself a Roman emperor, he now revealed himself as my father's pupil.

'That emancipated felon, as you call him, with the passion for Horace ... that is my father. I remember you. Your mother ...'

'Yes, she died a year later in Hobart Town. Charitable creatures, the Batchelors. But your father ...? *Your* father? Really?'

I was not as worried any more, for I remembered the wide-eyed, tear-reddened child this usurper had been when I too was a small boy. His father had been the Crown Solicitor of Van Diemen's Land, and, in the absence of a mother, it seemed young Peske had cleaved fast to the forces of authority, had somehow acquired the (you could be sure) colonial title of 'Captain' – his passion for military clothing indicated the amateur campaigner! – and become a Land Commissioner to serve the *Land Occupation Act* in New South Wales.

'So my father taught you Horace.' I now made my own declaration. 'And your old friend Charlie Batchelor is my partner here on Nugan Ganway.'

'But you are surely not little Bettany whom I knew?' Peske asked. (He may of course have been thinking of my brother, Simon, but I would for the sake of my land claim be any little Bettany he chose.)

'You are surely not the little Peske whom I knew?' I countered.

He whistled and shook his head. Then he said, as if to honour my father, '... *dum loquimur, fugit invida aetas; carpe diem, quam minimum credula postero*' 'While we speak, jealous time runs its way. Since you can have little faith in the morrow, seize the day!'

He put the book reverently away and came and sat opposite me, meekly refilling his mug of tea and daring to spice it with rum.

'And Charlie Batchelor himself is your partner?'

'Absolutely. These are in large part his sheep you would confiscate! I wish you well with it, not least when the news gets back to Hobart.'

He considered this bleakly for a while. 'Oh my God this puts me in a pickle. Bettany, my God it does!' He shook his head. 'You have done pretty well here, you know.'

'Not according to you.'

He actually groaned. 'It's not really Treloar who wants you gone. He was conscripted by others, and I in turn was conscripted. Not as if I were someone's lackey. I came here willingly on the report of an eminent gentleman.'

'Finlay,' I suggested.

'Yes. It is on the demand of Mr Finlay of the county of Argyle that I am instructed to move against you in Treloar's name. How is your father, by the way? I didn't ask.'

'My father's well and practising law in Hobart. But Finlay wants me ejected?'

'My dear friend, you have no idea what a scoundrel he makes you seem. I came out here determined to evict that scoundrel, that ... well, I dare not use the words he used. What I find is no apparent scoundrel at all but a civilised chap who happens to be old Bettany's son.'

I swallowed a sick anger which had risen in me. 'What is it Finlay tells you, and no doubt others, about me?'

'Oh you sound a squalid man indeed in his mouth, dear young Bettany. That's why I rode up here ready to give you the full force of all legal devices open to me. According to Finlay you are the leering son of a felon who tried to suppress the information of who you were, and who has poured your efforts into the seduction of his daughter as a means of acquiring some of his wealth. Because of your designs, he claims, he went to the trouble of sending his daughter to an academy in Switzerland!'

I hurled my mug of tea, still hot, past Peske's ear. It landed in the fire, where I was content to leave it sizzle and blacken as a proxy for Mr Finlay. I roared, 'Let me say that where he has not chosen to confuse cause and effect, he is a liar, and I shall challenge anyone who stands for the concept that he is in any way an honest man.'

Peske laughed silently, laughter which had more fear than hilarity in it.

'Come, young Bettany. This is not some duelling place like Italy or Ireland.'

'If it's not,' I told him, 'it's a bloody pity.'

'Well,' said Peske, by now well-fortified, 'I will admit that calm regard for truth is often borne away when there is some chance of gain. If you ask me why Finlay would want your livestock confiscated, I can tell you that confiscated sheep go for knock-down prices, not at usual market rates. I don't know, and I will deny I said it if you say I did, but perhaps the desire to pick up your Merinos cheaply further warped the picture Mr Finlay purports to have of you.'

'I won't beg, Mr Peske —'

'Captain. Mr Bettany. Captain, if you don't mind.'

'I won't beg, Captain. But in a case of clear tyranny, whose servant you set out to be and seem now to have repented of, what can you do for me?'

Peske thought for a time. 'It is very true that during the short existence of Land Commissioners, my colleagues in the business have given us a repute for following an independent line and never giving anyone quite what they want. I suggest to you, Mr Bettany, that in the next few days you make some blazes on trees some forty miles south of here. I will use them as the basis of awarding this station to you. I will suggest to Mr Treloar that he is entitled by his blaze to stock the high land between Dainer's Gap and the summit. I know he does not want to, his desire for that country being purely to accommodate Mr Finlay, but he will feel he is receiving some joy. You will have to pay license fees to cover Nugan Ganway, £10 for every twenty square miles – yes, you must, since that is the law, and no one's malice. I shall leave your flocks untouched and adjudge you the legal leaseholder. I will hope that if ever I take up settling, no friend of Mr Finlay's becomes my Land Commissioner.'

At dawn the next day Long was surprised and not a little pleased to discover that we were not leaving Nugan Ganway. My licenses had cost me £30, for which Peske accepted a cheque on the Savings Bank and gave a receipt.

I now had paper for this land, and official title.

AFTER PRIM'S FIRST VISIT TO Khalda el Rahzi's house, she began to interview young men and women known to the eminent Mrs el Rahzi who claimed to have been subjected to slavery. Sometimes accommodatingly Mrs el Rahzi acted as translator, or at least as verifier of what Prim herself could make out, but on other occasions Prim used a sceptic like Dr Sherif Taha.

Prim sent copies of the transcripts of interview to Peter Whitloaf, the Director of Austfam; to the United Nations High Commissioner for Refugees; to the International Committee of the Red Cross in Geneva; and to the sundry national entities of Save the Children.

In the meantime, she could not fight off the likelihood of a visit to
Australia. The place exercised its own subtle gravity, but Dimp represented a more direct pull, and invited Prim to attend a third anniversary
party in Sydney.

*Do come and see my dear D'Arcy, the annul-er, in his earnest impersona-
tion of being my husband. Okay, I speak fondly, of course. But in spite
of the good talking to you gave me, in the night, when a person is at her
maddest, I do wake and I think he didn't love Robyn enough and he
doesn't love me enough to risk the fires of hell. In the darkness, this can
for twenty minutes or so seem a big issue. It begs the whole question of
whether I'm worth risking damnation for, a proposition I very much
doubt! But the idea of the suitor being willing to go to Hades for us
must be deep in our brains, because the story is in all cultures, isn't it,
including Orpheus going to hell to rescue Eurydice? And now the question is, would D'Arcy go to Hades to fetch me back without first getting
his return ticket stamped by the Vatican?*

*But we're going to celebrate the loving ambiguities which bind us, me
and Bren, next February, last weekend of the month, with an anniversary
party. And it would be wonderful for our morale if you could come so
that we could both feast our eyes on our only living close relative.*

Dimp also announced she'd nearly finished a screenplay on Jonathan
Bettany – his love of sheep and other things – wonderful stuff, she said.

*Like many of the guilt-stricken, he's not very effective. Except in some
ways. I mean he distributes carbines to his shepherds and stockmen as
if they're picks or shovels, and we know those Monaro tribes – that he
called the Moth people – were decimated, cowed and driven off. He gives
us the signal by talking about them as a problem – and his men deal
with the problem out of his sight and at a distance from his own trigger
finger. He might instruct them one way, but they pick up the message
his own morality won't let him utter, and they do the job. And yet he
hates massacres and pursues those who commit them – have you read
that bit yet?*

*If you can come this February, we'll buy you a first-class ticket! Bring
Sherif too. No argument. D'Arcy can afford it. He'll claim it off his tax
if he has a single conversation with you about Sudanese mines and
resources.*

Though Prim did not rush to read the Bettany transcripts when they arrived, she was engrossed, despite herself, although she felt guiltily that any interest she showed might somehow act as a subliminal message to Dimp to take it all too seriously.

One day Sherif saw pages of the transcripts heaped on Prim's coffee table.

'What are these?' he asked.

'I told you. These are the pages of ancestor worship my sister sends me.'

'The oldest religion,' said Sherif. 'At least, the only one people never lapse from. How much land did your old ancestor hold?'

'By the end of his life, about 2500 square miles.'

Sherif whistled. 'What a pity he is not around now to fund our little surveys.'

Prim held up the pages of Dimp's letter. 'My sister wants me to visit her for her wedding anniversary. Next February. I don't know what to do.'

'Go!' said Sherif. He knew of her reluctance to go home and worried about her annual failure to return. So now, again, he said, 'This time, go!'

Prim put both hands to her forehead and rocked her head gently. 'I don't want to, of course, but I don't know how to tell her.'

'No wonder we have such affection for each other,' said Sherif. 'I am an internally displaced person, and you're a refugee. Do you think it proper, my dear, to use Sudan as a bolthole?'

'But it's more than that.'

'It can be more than that only after you have been home and reduced Australia to size.'

Prim felt panic coursing up her arms, against the flow of her blood.

'Would you come?' she asked.

'No, not this time. I can be a fit companion next time. And I look forward to it.'

'You're serious?'

'Never more,' said Sherif.

So, with a sort of heady nausea, Prim understood that she must go home, and must somehow return intact from the experience.

BETTANY AND MARRIAGE

I had been for a time suffused by the excitement of a visit I'd made on my way home from the previous wool sale, the one during which my lapse from grace occurred at the Black Huts. On the way back home to Nugan Ganway, my very unease made it appropriate that I should visit Felix at Mr Loosely's academy in Goulburn.

It was mid-afternoon on a sunny spring day when I reached Grafton Street and stood with the eminent Mr Loosely on his back verandah watching his wife reading to a set of enchanted young scholars. They sat beneath the shade of a native beech on ground which sloped away pleasantly to the Mulwaree Ponds. Mrs Loosely happened to be reading from that evangelical classic, *The Pilgrim's Progress*. She read musically and well, in the voice of a woman who enjoyed fighting the good fight.

For the first time in two years I saw Felix, a robust lad of about eight years now. Though of mixed blood – and it may have been, as Goldspink had once suggested, Rowan's or Brody's absconders blood in his veins – he possessed the most handsome features of the Ngarigo. The awful grin for which I had given the boy his name had been eased by the passage of years, kindly instruction, and wonderment at the tale Mrs Loosely read. The rictus of old eased further as he lent ear to John Bunyan's great book, listening along with other little pilgrims who were mainly the children of more or less prosperous liberated convicts.

Mr Loosely called to Felix, who proceeded out of the circle and accepted my extended hand.

I said, 'How are you, young man?'

He answered precisely. 'I am very well, sir, thank you for asking.'

Thin Mrs Loosely, book in hand, smiled and Mr Loosely said, 'Felix, this is your benefactor, Mr Bettany.'

'I remember,' said Felix, bunching his mouth a little as in his infancy.

'We must talk privately,' Mr Loosely murmured to me. 'We may wish to speak to you later, Felix,' he told the boy, who nodded and rejoined the group of young New South Welshmen.

Loosely took me to his small parlour, and we sat by his little deal table, which served as a desk. His bookshelves, however, around the wall, were enviably full.

'As you know, Mr Bettany, this school is based on the fraternity of humankind. I stood up for the freed convict, but I am now shocked to find that the former convict, in some cases, comes to me and complains that I have taken in a native. Apparently his children are too refined to learn their letters, their numbers, their divinity, their manners in the presence of a native child!'

I wondered at first was he asking me to pay a further fee still than the one I had already paid him, and I made some hints in that direction, but he did not take them up. His disappointment was not financial but political in nature; or perhaps I should say, philosophical.

'What sort of race are we,' asked Mr Loosely, 'when one group accepts liberation purely as the platform from which to oppress others? This is a great mystery to me, since it means that even in the midst of their oppression, their sojournings by the river of Babylon, their containment, their floggings, their misuse, they somehow admire the flogger, the oppressor, the misuser.'

He seemed so distressed that he stood for a while shaking his head. 'You must consider,' I suggested, 'the great Horace, who was never free of the slur that he was the child of a slave. It suffuses his poetry and his self-estimation, but it is fuel to his genius.'

'No, no, you are right,' he said. 'Such heartburn as I have just expressed is a small price for what I have to tell you. I rejoice to inform you now that, far from being a threat to civilised impulses, the child you brought to me is a dazzling intellect. It is as if all the yearning for light which has lain pent up in these people for centuries, even for millennia has been released in him, has driven him to read and write and cipher. He is, let me tell you, a gem at mathematics. In the past year he has learned to figure long division in his head, without recourse to paper, and he demonstrates a hunger for learning rare amongst British children.'

These claims made me nervous, even though I had been struck by the child's urbanity in the yard and had heard him read very competently some years earlier. 'You're sure, Mr Loosely, that you are not disposed by your progressive nature to help this child along? To see things which may not be there?'

Loosely did not seem at all offended by my *caveat*. 'We shall call the child in, and you may perhaps make inquiry of him.'

He went to the door and called to his wife to fetch Felix. As the boy knocked and entered, his eyes seemed to me liquid and quick.

Mr Loosely said, 'Young man, since this is your patron who brought you out of the bush and keeps you here at his own cost, I expect you would be happy to display your skills to him.'

Felix turned to me and said, in an accent halfway between that of the children of the convicts and Loosely's regional idiom, 'I would be very happy to do so, sir.'

Loosely said, 'I wonder, Felix, would you be so kind as to tell your patron how many times 13 goes into 128?'

Felix adopted momentarily a warp in his face equivalent to what I had first encountered, but it eased within a few seconds. 'Nine with a remainder of 11,' said Felix.

'And now,' asked Mr Loosely, 'multiply 436 by, say, 321.'

Felix closed his eyes. Seconds passed. Loosely smiled.

Felix slowly but confidently uttered his results '139 956.'

Mr Loosely thanked Felix, murmured to me, 'In his head, sir, in his head,' and then picked up from his desk a book of *Macaulay's Essays*, a work I possessed myself at Nugan Ganway.

'Would you please read that for your dear benefactor, Mr Bettany?'

Taking the book, far more sophisticated than the child's life of Newton he had read from for me years past, young Felix closed his eyes so that only a slit of vision must have remained. He considered the book so long that Mr Loosely turned to me as if to reassure me that this was the boy's normal demeanour towards the essays of famous Britons. Perhaps ten seconds passed before Felix began to read: 'There is great force about this speech. Cicero had not attained that perfect mastery of the whole art of rhetoric which he possessed at a later period. But on the other hand there is a freedom, a boldness, a zeal for popular rights, a scorn of the vicious and insolent gang whom he afterwards called the *boni*, which makes these early speeches more pleasing than the latter.'

Looking at me, Mr Loosely reached out and took Macaulay away from Felix.

'Thank you very much. Mr Bettany, in case you think I have falsely rehearsed this scene, would you care to put to Felix some problems of your own? Avoid for now pounds, shillings and pence equations, since I have not yet acquainted him with the banalities of finance.'

I was delighted to be part of such a joyful experiment, but told Mr Loosely that there was no need for me to check the powers of Felix. Indeed, I told him, the normal process was that the schoolmaster tried to convince the parent that the child lacked qualities which time would often very well prove the child possessed in better portions than his original denouncer.

I shook the boy's hand again but with added warmth, and Mr Loosely dismissed him.

The child left and we sat again. Mr Loosely fidgeted with the loose cover of the Macaulay.

'I do not know whether what I have daily witnessed and you and I have temporarily seen here has had time to reveal its full possibilities to you, Mr Bettany. I am a school teacher, you are a young man of great promise, a settler. Now the talents of Felix clearly derive not from the debased European half of his soul but from that wandering daughter of Eve, his mother, the native. I ask you this: what if the desire for learning, thwarted by centuries of nomadism in such hearts as Felix's, lies out beyond us, in the bush, amongst all the children of the natives? What if our children have somehow been sated over centuries with European scholarship, and turn dully to the light? What if, on your land holding, on all the stations within and without the limits of settlement, all the children of the natives – without even knowing it at the thinking level of their minds – wait to take to the skills of enlightenment with the same fury with which young Felix has taken them up?'

It was one of those ideas which would go through even the dullest man like an electric shock.

'It is of course possible,' I told him. 'The ignorant consider these people as less than human, but I have no doubt about their humanity.'

'From what I have heard of the behaviour of convict shepherds and overseers, it is likely that there will be other murdered mothers and other Felixes. I would like to see men such as yourself devote a fragment of their wool clip to the education of these children. All in the hope that thereby learning will be renewed, nature revived, and society reconciled from top to bottom.'

'These are honourable objectives,' I told him.

'Send to me another Felix – I have already written to other settlers with the same request. Write to the governor of New South Wales, Sir George Gipps, who is a progressive man, and ask him to finance my school, so that the economic burden – which a good man such as yourself is willing to assume, but which other more fallible men might not welcome – can be taken by the state. I would take one native child for two pounds a year, and two for three pounds. There is of course no profit to me in this.'

'But,' I said, 'there is an orphaned child of the natives – I have called him Hector – who is always at my homestead. He has a ready aptitude too.'

'I do not doubt it. Orphaned? Full-blooded perhaps.'

'Yes.'

'Could you bring him to me without creating problems with the sables?'

I promised that Hector would be brought to him.

Early the following month, when the child was present at the stockyard trying to persuade Long and O'Dallow to let him ride horses, I approached Durra and told him I would be taking the boy off, and when he understood he told some of Hector's aunts who exhibited a short and passionate burst of grief. But Hector himself seemed willing to ride anywhere a horse would take him. I gave to Presscart, who had by accident killed Hector's mother, the job of taking Hector to Mr Loosely. I also wrote to Governor Gipps as Loosely had requested, and recommended His Excellency to extend his patronage to him. Thus I was already in an excited frame of mind when the most startling events overtook me.

So busy had we been at Nugan Ganway that Long's lost brothers, the Irish absconders, were presences whose exact shape I had forgotten. They reimposed their existence on me, however, one dusk in late summer by riding up to the homestead. We had all heard them coming and were outside to meet them, and the one named Martin Rowan, or the Captain, who had once held Felix's head in a stream, took from his jacket a sheet of paper he said he had been given at Treloar's.

He and the younger one, Tadgh Brody, dismounted and stood about explaining themselves in Irish to Long and O'Dallow, in whose company they were willing to adjust their mouths to gashes of brotherly amusement. On coarse, journal paper, the note merely said:

Dear Mr Bettany,
I do not have the honour of your acquaintance but must tell you that your betrothed Phoebe Finlay is with me at Treloar's in the care of Mr Goldspink. I have escorted Miss Finlay from Goulburn. She is quite ill from a storm we passed through. Could you kindly visit her at your first chance and restore her spirits.

Sister Catherine (from the community of the
Sisters of Charity in Goulburn, New South Wales)

My betrothed, Phoebe Finlay? I interrupted the amusements of the two absconders and took them aside.

'What is this about?'

'There's a holy woman and a young one there,' Rowan told me.

'Poor young woman's got the collywobbles,' said Brody.

Did these two share a hut with them, the miraculously nearby Phoebe and her friend?

I should have been afraid, to honour the tradition of the habitual bachelor, but I was excited. It was as if Phoebe had been summoned by my secret need of what Barley called a 'rudder'. But she was ill, and I was instantly anxious. In my memory she had that delicacy which might easily be borne away by a fever.

Though dark was approaching, I packed my saddlebags. As I gathered myself within the house, the men drank tea by a fire in the open. Before leaving, I took Long aside. He was to see the absconders went that night. Nugan Ganway was to be no scene of extended Celtic reunion. I rode out on the now seven-year-old Hobbes and behind me, from the direction of our large, shaggy-barked woolshed, there seemed to rise hoots of convict amusement. I found that my hands were trembling on the reins, but I ascribed it to a feverishness I had that month.

It was a night and a day to Treloar's boundary, and the first thing I saw on the ridge above Goldspink's homestead, apart from some cattle and horses in the yard, was the strange sight of a nun sitting in brown habit in the shade of the verandah reading to a bare-breasted black woman wearing a sacking skirt. Goldspink, in the manner of the late Shegog, had clearly taken a housekeeper – a very young one too.

I rode hurriedly down, past the very handsome four-wheeler in which Phoebe had obviously been travelling. The young native woman was alarmed at my approach and ran inside to hide. The nun stood her ground as I dismounted and approached her. She seemed a handsome woman with a slight reddish coloration beneath her cheeks.

'You wrote to me,' I said. 'I'm Bettany.'

'Sister Catherine of the Cork congregation of the Sisters of Charity,' she told me.

The nun looked no older than I was, and it was just as well she wore such a complicated and archaic garb, to cause Goldspink's stockmen to think twice about offering her any insult. She was empowered by this same archaic dress, it seemed, to look me straight in the eye.

'Your betrothed has a pneumonic fever,' she said. 'She came straight from her ship over the mountains, came to us and cast herself on our care.'

'Cast herself on your care?'

'On our community. It seemed she was after being with the French nuns in Geneva, you see. So she sought us out without returning to her home.' She held her hand up: enough questions. 'Now I'm sure she will be the better for your visit, Mr Bettany.' She led me at once into the hut. It was grey and cramped within, this interior I remembered from my first meeting with Felix. The native housekeeper kept a wary station by the fireplace, and Goldspink was not in sight. But at the other end of the hut, in an alcove screened by blankets and netting, lay Phoebe. The bark window flap behind her head was propped wide to admit air, and the lovely, sleeping, clearly much-matured Phoebe seemed by her rasping to be in need of that element. The nun had her dressed even at this distance in the bush, in the proper regalia of the ill: white linen, with a white linen bonnet around her head.

Though she was sick, she was – I was pleased to see – not anywhere near sick unto death. Her eyes had a blueness beneath them. Snow on a sad afternoon, I thought. I looked at her body beneath the sheet and saw she had become a taller woman in Geneva, by four or five inches. I took a nearly parental, anxious joy in that. Thinking her sleeping, I felt stunned when she reached out her hand and took mine. After my years in Nugan Ganway, her skin felt exquisitely delicate. Bark, leather, the fouled and burred and mud-matted coats of sheep were what I was accustomed to. This flesh was a manifestation from another universe. It partook of the utterly new, but what caused me to fall in love in the most unabstract way was the *habitual* way she reached for my hand, the habitual and playful way she tugged it, as if she'd reproved me for my reluctance to grab her fingers in the same way a hundred times in the past. Of course, I saw! That's what Barley had meant by a rudder.

'So you are now the great man of sheep and cattle,' she said. The irony she spoke with was habitual too. It was in a way a *married* irony. I liked that, and seriously intended to taste more of it.

'I am a man still struggling to be that. Where are your parents?'

'A woman shall leave her family ...' she said, paraphrasing the Scripture.

'No,' I said. 'The text says, "A *man* shall leave his family and cleave ..."' The hotness of the verb prevented me from finishing. I thought of Cecily for a second before banishing her forever.

'Well, what's good for the goose,' she said.

'Does your father know you're here?'

'Not here precisely,' she said. I was aware that the nun was still present, and frankly enjoying her chaperone role and the secrets it brought her. 'He told me all the slanders. It was my duty not to hear them. And I set off. But it is not as if I have abandoned the proprieties. I travelled with a nun, *á la mode Européenne*.'

'You travelled too hard, my young friend,' murmured Sister Catherine behind me. 'You nearly had me with the pneumonic too.'

'It is a total wonder that you came,' Phoebe told me. 'Yet I knew you would.'

But she was so young still, and I thought of Horace.

'*Nondum subacta ferre iugum valet cervice, nondum munia comparis . . .*' 'She is not yet of such a strength as to bear the iron yoke of marriage, or the lustful weight of a rearing bull . . .'

Phoebe's eyes translucently closed. She murmured on the edge of awareness, 'I shall rest well now you have arrived.'

The nun gave a jerk of her head which told me to leave. One could well imagine her as a strong-minded farmwife. She seemed accustomed to being obeyed. So now we went outside again, past the screen and onto the verandah. Here we replenished our pannikins of tea. We had offered one to the so-called housekeeper, but she had shaken her head, gone outside and run away to the nearest tree and sat behind it, to get away from my gaze.

'She thinks you have the evil eye,' said Sister Catherine, much amused. 'Just like at home. There's nothing new amongst the poor fallen children of Eve.' She looked levelly at me. 'I would hope for Phoebe's sake you have not taken a native woman into your house, Mr Bettany, as seems to be the habit of this country, men being such heedless souls.'

'You can be assured,' I said. But I was disarmed by her depiction of us.

'You can imagine that after such a journey and so much conflict, with the pneumonic added in on top, that the girl has no need to confront that sort of thing.'

Her insistence stung me a little. 'Neither she nor you will find anything in that regard. If it's your business.'

'My business or not, I'm pleased to hear it. But I'm sad to say it makes you an uncommon man in the bush. It strikes me that if we had more sisters, we should at once create a refuge in the bush for these dark women most misused and least rewarded. But there's only four of us in Goulburn, and we must see to our own convict women.'

'You know the country?'

'I know the lie of it and I have been escorting women to the outer stations before today. But on top, the good child offered us such a fee, and fees are very welcome with Mother Ignatius. Ever are we short of that quantity, and the bishop gives us nothing but a certain ration of his disapproval.'

'Why disapproval?' I asked

'Ah,' she said, waving her hand, 'he is an English Benedictine, ever threatening to excommunicate us. He considers us disobedient women. The Canon Law, he says, and even the rules of our Order, require that we travel always in pairs, and we say, if there were eight of us, and the country small in extent, we would be happy to have a sister with us for prayer, correction and companionship. But the Canon Law was not written for us as we are in this country! We say we would obey it to the absolute letter if there had ever been a time like this before, or a place like this. Here the rules must yield to faith. We must go out ourselves, in solitary armour against all perils, and in the company solely of angels.'

I was still not utterly at ease with this turbulent nun who seemed to find both the world and the wilderness so legible. 'Couldn't it be said though that you encouraged her to defy her father?'

Sister Catherine stood up, whistled loudly as a farm girl to the housekeeper behind the tree and started waving her back towards us. The woman came only halfway back, and stood in the shade.

'No,' said the nun, sitting down to her pannikin of tea again, shrugging at her half-success with the native woman. 'It could only be said that a young woman was determined to come south on her own resources, and even at the cost of her reputation, for she intended to visit you at your station. And so I accompanied her to give her the protection of my habit.'

'She would have been safe in my company,' I told the nun with some sullenness.

'I'm sure,' said the woman in return. 'But would the world know that?'

I mulled over my tea. The native housekeeper returned to Sister Catherine by stealth, and the nun picked up the book of instruction from a bench on the verandah, a sort of primer she had brought with her in case she encountered ignorance which could be conquered. So the lesson began again.

I sat quietly and in increasing content. Sometimes I would yield to go to the window flap and look in at the resting Phoebe, and linger there confidently above her fever. It was the breadth of what Phoebe had done which startled and compelled me. I have since seen that people are bound together by the power, the madness of what one or sometimes both of them have done for the sake of union. There was of course an inadequacy on my side, no breadth of gesture. I would not have had the strength to advise Phoebe to do what she had done, but now she *had* done it, I was a captive of her act, her grandeur. Her arrival here was in its scale like a vast transaction in acres given, livestock offered. It was enough to bind me and provide me with the founding landmark of our love. I did not so much fall in love as find myself claimed by it. Many young men looked to nature for symbols of their love, but to me the effects of nature seemed predictable and work-a-day when put beside what Phoebe had done at great cost to her bodily fabric, which was now recovering from the strain in Goldspink's hut.

Later, I went in unimpeded by the nun and replaced a tepidly damp rag which sat on her brow with another one well-drenched in the bucket of cool creek water in the corner of the room. Goldspink had still not returned to sully the air in which these services were performed.

He came in later in the day with two of his stockmen who were nearly indistinguishable from the absconders. When he saw me he cursed them out of the house and made speeches about having the gentry indoors – myself, Phoebe – and what a welcome variation it provided, and what a charming feminine presence Sister Catherine was. 'A woman,' said Goldspink out of her hearing, 'if a neutered one.' He wiped his brow. 'One wonders what she makes of a fellow.'

Phoebe was anxious to leave Goldspink's uneasy shack, and within two days her pneumonic fever had passed. It was clear that she still meant to visit Nugan Ganway under Catherine's guardianship, and so we started off, the nun driving the good four-wheeler in which she had brought Phoebe southwards, Phoebe in the back, on the cushions, wrapped in a blanket and smiling. Since I rode at her side, we could converse. I tried to speak to her about her father's anger, building even now, surely.

'He spoke of suing you for alienation of affections,' she told me, her face unclouded. 'My mother will not let him. My father says one thing and means another. There is a Biblical name for that. I am afraid it is "whited sepulchre". I am not an ungracious daughter, am I? You probably think me one. But returning to New South Wales I felt at once that I must be saved from his house.'

'But why? It's a fine house. You would surrender it for the prospect of slab timber and bark?'

'I do not find I can inhabit that house. I can't say why, so you need not press me.'

To listen to her speak was to feel a moral giddiness and a fear at her ardour. Sometimes I wondered was she edging me towards some reckless act. But I was enchanted by the very sensation.

So we made our arrangements. After she had seen Nugan Ganway, and our raw pastures, she would go with the nun to visit her young friends Mr and Mrs Parslow who had a little sheep farm, far to the north, near the village of Braidwood. There she would make the church arrangements for our wedding, and inform me by letter, and I would make my way there.

The two women, Sister Catherine and Phoebe, spent a week at Nugan Ganway, sharing my hut while Long and I crowded in with Clancy and O'Dallow. The nun felt a natural sisterhood towards Long, for one could feel in him, beneath his bush aptitudes, the mighty engine of his soul, grieving and puzzling away, running like a huge river to the sea. She liked to tease his seriousness, unleashing in herself a kind of rustic flirtatiousness.

Phoebe was delighted by everything other women might find off-putting at Nugan Ganway. To her the smell of mutton-fat lamps seemed incense. When I think of her conversation that week I remember not words but a solidity of mutual purpose. I slept badly in my lath cot in O'Dallow's hut. Separated from me by virginal starlight lay the true help-meet, a woman to whom the necessary physical coarseness of Nugan Ganway in no way bespoke barbarism, but promise.

I was startled one evening, by the shearing shed in our circle of buildings, to observe Sister Catherine seated on a chair in the shade talking to the two absconders, who crossleggedly occupied a log. My impulse was to tell them to go – for it seemed that they knew more of what was afoot at Nugan Ganway than Nugan Ganway ever knew of them. It was also difficult to read their demeanour towards Sister Catherine. They looked up from beneath eyebrows which seemed at dusk to be hooded against a reality they would not be barbarous enough to speak of to the nun. But they also watched me pass, and speculated whether this was the day I would decide to move against them. All parties had known from the start that such a day would come. All parties were relieved that it was not yet. Consoled after a manner, they soon rode away into the long blue evening of my higher pastures.

Every evening after Phoebe retired, Sister Catherine sat on a hard stool on my verandah and read from a black book with a gilt cross on its cover. 'I saw the wild men here,' I told her.

'They wanted me to write to their mothers in Kerry,' said Sister Catherine. 'I tested the poor fellows. Surely, I said, they would soon have their tickets-of-leave and be able to go to Sydney and themselves write. But they said no, they were dead men under this system, their names were in the *Government Gazette*, and one day troopers would come for them.'

'Perhaps you should also found a mission to the absconders,' I told her. 'They are greater savages than anyone else in this region.'

'Ah,' the nun sighed, 'there are so early in the history of the place so many sadnesses.'

'I must ask you again, sister, to reflect on my betrothed girl's towering certainty; that this is the life for her, and no other will do! She has fought off a strong and wealthy parent to seize this pastoral poverty. I am not sure that when I am older I would wish such a place on a daughter of mine.'

I gestured for emphasis towards the darkness, full of the burr of late summer insects crying out for their lives.

'What Phoebe proposes is Christ's gift to you,' the nun told me. 'Receive it in joy.'

So I had confirmed to me from a vestal mouth what I already suspected: that through the scale of her acts Phoebe had earned a lifetime of my love.

I sent Phoebe and Sister Catherine to the Parslows in Braidwood in the care of Long. Long returned at last with a letter.

Mullambee via Braidwood
March 12 of Anno Domini 1839
My most darling Mr Bettany,
Do not be angry with Long, who is a decent fellow torn in two when Sister Catherine announced – just a little way beyond Treloar's – that she must return to Goulburn, was needed by her sisters, would love to see me wed – though of course she would not be permitted to attend the ceremony – but feared such thoughts were all vanity, with so much waiting in Goulburn to be done. She was so insistent and so certain of

*the Lord's protection for herself, and of leaving me to Long's guidance!
And Long knew he must stay with me. I moved from the nuns' four-
wheeler to Long's wagon and wept as we waved the good Catherine off.
None of this is Long's fault. She could not be dissuaded.*

*I am surprised to find that though I am of more than adequate age,
the minister here in Braidwood, a fellow named Chenniger, delayed
making a decision as to whether to marry us without my father's written
consent. He cites church law, but since I am eighteen I think it is pure
old fear, and am very surprised that a man whose stock in trade – so to
speak – is eternal truth and the love of Christ should be so scared by
acreage and livestock in the quantity in which my father possesses them.*

*I went and found then with the help of my friend Cynthia Parslow a
Wesleyan clergyman named Hollyhead who is a friend of Mr Loosely of
Goulburn. He certified my age and said he was willing to perform the
ceremony. I had a certain idea that you would prefer, as a man of
promise, to be wed in the Anglican church, even though Hollyhead is a
far more devout man than the Reverend Mr Chenniger, and is not a
spare-time farmer like that gentleman but spends most of his week in the
saddle, visiting settlers and convict shepherds and trying to protect the
natives from such as Goldspink. If I cannot persuade Mr Chenniger,
would you object to being wed by Mr Hollyhead, since I feel he is closer
to the principles on which our marriage will, I trust, be founded? I would
be very happy if you would permit this small departure from what you
would probably find normal.*

*I would be very much obliged, if in the company of your best suit you
arrived in Braidwood by December 10th. I am very happy staying at the
Parslows' here. They have a simple style of life and rejoice, as I trust we
will, in their Australian existence.*

Yours eternally,
Phoebe Finlay

This question of churches distracted me from concern for the headstrong
nun and the unchosen responsibility thus placed on Long. If I had ever
thought of marriage, I had imagined myself wed in the reasonable solemnity of the Church of England. My father sometimes complained, even
in Van Diemen's Land, that the sleek Church of England, unlike the
fervent Methodists of his youth, rejoiced in the world as it was, and
participated in its most immediate rewards. Yet that is why my mother
and I preferred it.

I ordered from Kurntz Jewellers of Pitt Street, Sydney, a ring of diamonds, emeralds and sapphires to be delivered to me care of the Royal Hotel, Braidwood.

One of the most startling mercies of great civic and religious mysteries such as marriage is that they convince those who undergo the rite that for the moment they lie at the centre of nature and of God's plan. The Anglican Mr Chenniger eventually consented to officiate at the marriage, a fact at which my mother, with her dislike of Methodists for what they had done to my father, later expressed herself by letter to be very gratified. But the Reverend Chenniger proved very dour about too much colour or excessive ritual in his church. He clearly thought the act itself, the 'Till death do we part', had sufficient grace and hope about it that the flowers, the silverware, the bunting and incense which Phoebe wanted (having got a taste for such things in Geneva) would contribute no more.

Before the wedding, at my rooms at the Royal Hotel, I was delighted to find that Charlie Batchelor had ridden all the way from Yass for this event, and had brought with him Miss Dines, the Australian-born young woman whose hand he had sought, and her Scottish mother. Mr Barley was also present with apologies that his rudder had not accompanied him from Sydney. And then on the verandah, in a dove-grey swan-tailed coat of somewhat better cut than the suit I had purchased two days before from a limited range in Mr Sutler's, the Braidwood tailor, was my friend the Land Commissioner Peske. All these friends had been notified and summoned by energetic Phoebe.

'I thought I might as well come,' Peske told me, 'and make a complete enemy out of Mr Finlay. Surely though those Finlays are coming to this?'

I told him I believed not, that there had been no answer to the letter I had been careful to send them.

'Awfully difficult, my friend,' he told me, 'without the mama and pa, even though Finlay is such a thorough old brute.'

He laughed in a way I did not entirely enjoy. Fortunately we were joined by Barley and by Charlie Batchelor, and the three of them sat with me on the hotel verandah, smoking cheroots. Their job, they said, was to keep me calm. It had been a summer of low rain and that was a topic of talk, since rain was in all senses the fountainhead.

Peske said, 'About your girl's papa, I believe he has had a hard time.'

I had not heard anything of this myself.

'Has the same problem I have,' said Barley. 'Got involved in wool speculation in Sydney, thinking he could be amply recompensed from

London. But London merchants have ganged up on us – had to happen! – and he bought at high price, sold at 7 pence ha'penny.'

I had heard, of course, something of the decline in London prices. The *Sydney Herald* in the parlour of the Royal made frequent comment on it. 'You are not in trouble yourself, I hope,' I told Barley.

'I have a good banker,' murmured Barley, unembittered by the shifts of markets. 'But I have a great plan. I had let contracts for the building near Semi-Circular Quay of two large storage warehouses. I shall, if you like, hoard wool, and release it to London auction houses when it suits me and at my price.'

Charlie applauded this. And even in the blur of fear, the watchfulness for omens, the strange weakness induced by desire of the beloved, all of which I suspected was the standard condition of bridegrooms, it was a delight to see Barley's eyes glitter. 'I hope I am what you'd call a New South Wales patriot,' he murmured to me. A little exuberant from brandy, he cast his hands up and said through lips clamped on a cheroot, 'But we should try to call tune, not have tune called for us.'

At the marriage, these men occupied my side of the church, small as a Van Diemen's Land chapel but, in a world of slab timber, built of red brick to convey its permanence. And on lovely, be-satined Phoebe's side of the congregation were her friends Cynthia and Robert Parslow and their friends, who included the police magistrate. The absence of her parents seemed to mean little to Phoebe, but Peske's barb was still in me and I wondered if her parent-less condition at the altar would be one of those shadows bound to grow with time and distance.

Afterwards in the dining room of the Royal Hotel, in the exultation of my new condition of marriage, in front of a feast I knew I could well afford and seated by my miraculously determined wife in her dress of white satin, I felt delighted to throw my arm round Peske. He was the only one to straddle in friendship all parties to this particular act of matrimony, since he happened to be a friend of the Parslows too. I felt uppermost a dazed delight that Phoebe and I now possessed the extraordinary authority of sitting together to eternity without asking anyone's authority or pardon.

It was ten o'clock at night, but there was still pudding to be served, when Peske and I wandered, cigars a'mouth, into the hallway to find an outhouse, or what is more pleasant to men in our condition, the edge of an expansive paddock where, shoulder to shoulder and reflecting tipsily on the splendour of the night, we could ease ourselves. We did not get that far, however. In the corridor, at the table where the maid normally sat arranging accommodations for guests, a woman stood forlornly. Peske performed his version of a gallant British officer, in so far as he had learned it in the militia in Van Diemen's Land, and cried, 'Madame, could we find you a seat?'

The woman raised her face. It was Mrs Finlay, in a handsome brown riding dress, its hem smeared with wet clay from the harsh road she had travelled, and holding an oilskin coat in one hand. I rushed to her, full of concern to make her welcome. Behind me Peske said, 'Oh, I see. Forgive me. A fellow should now vanish.'

Mrs Finlay's head quivered involuntarily. 'I had meant to be here to speak to you before your marriage. But I wasted too much time and was too influenced by my husband. Then, when I did decide to come, a wheel came off the trap as we crossed over the Gourock Range, and now of course it is eternally too late, Mr Bettany.' I felt no great threat from her words, and as she shook her head, she seemed weary and philosophic rather than absorbed by either active anger or dread.

'Come in,' I pleaded, gesturing towards the door through which we could hear the noise of our guests laughing and a Braidwood ticket-of-leave man playing the fiddle. 'There is still plenty of food.'

I was thinking that a brandy would do this stranger, who happened by sacramental mystery to be my mother-in-law, even more good than food.

'No,' she said. 'I didn't come here for this ill-advised festival, Mr Bettany. This . . .' she gestured towards the door I had pointed out earlier, 'is the product of both foolishness and unworldliness on the part of many, including you, Mr Bettany. My husband, too, made his contribution.' It was the second time she had said something disapproving of Mr Finlay, and I found that astonishing in a woman who had been tight-lipped on her husband in the past. 'I can tell you I am here in defiance of him, and this is the first time in twenty years that I can say that. This is the character of your proceedings. In making your heedless marriage, you may well have destroyed my own.'

I made the best defence I could. 'Isn't all marriage heedless by nature? Can it ever decently be like the ordering of provisions?'

Naturally she showed a weary contempt for these trite arguments. 'There is a parlour in there,' she said, pointing to a small room off the corridor. 'I'll wait for you there.'

'But let me bring you something to eat and drink.'

She told me she would order her own refreshments. 'Don't tell Phoebe I am here,' she said. 'I am not equipped to face her yet.'

'Your own daughter, Mrs Finlay.'

'Yes, but she has scorn for me as yet.'

Leaving her, and abandoning Peske to his solitary relief in the outer dark of the stableyard, I returned to the banquet room, where I kissed a dew of sweat on my wife's forehead and smiled and made much of her. While she was talking to three young married women at one end of the table, I slipped away to meet her mother.

Mrs Finlay was seated waiting for me, her face still abnormally pale in the lamplight, and her clothes unchanged, but opened at the neck. She had a teacup by her. A sweet odour emanated from it, and there may have been some rum in there too.

'Your daughter would be so pleased to see you here, Mrs Finlay,' I began.

'I fear I might see her soon enough in any case, Mr Bettany. You are the beneficiary, I hate to tell you, of a persistent novel-reading by my daughter. In a novel, a marriage is not a marriage and love is not love unless it is preceded by prohibitions from fathers, and the threat of disinheritance. Even the mother of the tale, though sometimes depicted as understanding, is meant to be a disappointed crone in whom no blood flows, and a witch on the matter of her daughter's desires. In such books, marriage is always of this nature, a dangerous compact worth dying for in the teeth of an angry world and angrier parents.'

I could not help but feel a little pulse of anger. 'It seems to me your husband may have read some of those books too. He was very ready to see me as the man of bad family who wants to corner a fortune.'

She shook her head and turned her face away into the dark. 'It is his politics, not novels, which produced such beliefs. Also, may I say, a certain wisdom?'

'But not in my case,' I told her tightly, well settled in my anger now that it had begun to flow. 'He tried to have me pitched off my country. And my country is the limits of what I desire.'

'Your country and my daughter,' she murmured. 'The point is that novels are all she knows about marriage. She knows nothing of other matters, of what a man is likely to demand of a wife.'

My anger died and I began blushing. Yet I remembered Phoebe at the end of the table speaking to the other wives. Surely, amongst themselves, some knowledge was passed.

Mrs Finlay continued. 'You see, she believes she has done everything fiction states to be material to a marriage. She has defied her parents, been adequately disinherited, and undertaken bold strategies to make her intentions known to the beloved! She has filled the role of the heroine. This to her is marriage fully defined. She is, after all, barely more than eighteen. I fear she will be routed by, appalled by that what men and women would consider normal. She will flee home to us, which will not be the best thing for her.'

I shook my head. There was something oppressive here, the concept that a young woman could use me – as Mrs Finlay was saying – as a mere device to mock her parents, or to follow the right sort of literary precedent. 'I don't wish . . .' I began.

But Mrs Finlay interrupted me wearily. 'Ah, I think you will find you would be unique if you did not wish, and if you lacked the normal unruly nature of your kind – by which I mean, mankind. I can see you frowning.'

'Well, of course I am,' I admitted. 'That doesn't mean . . .' Again it was impossible to finish. I found it something of a wonder that a girl, my girl, who had grown up in the County of Argyle in New South Wales, a distant and turbulent province with a repute for ungovernable passions of the flesh, both natural and perverse, could yet retain an angelic northern European innocence! It was wonderful and somehow desolating at the same time.

I saw Mrs Finlay assessing me. She was a lovely woman reduced by a kind of wistful fear. 'If I appear now I shall destroy my daughter's fiction. But you may tell her that I love her and will see her at a future time. In the meantime I am willing to depend on you for kindness. So let me go to a room, and I shall have vanished by the time you and she appear in the morning. You should go back to the banquet now.'

I assured her I would not harm Phoebe in any way.

She smiled generously. 'Marriage itself is often the harm. But thank you.' She reached a hand and took hold of my sleeve. 'You are not a bad young fellow. I wish you no ill.'

I returned to the feast in a somewhat less hilarious state than I had left it.

Phoebe and I were at last shown to the nuptial room by our friends, and, as Peske said, 'left to our delights'. When the door closed and our retinue could be heard withdrawing to their own rooms or returning to the dining room, Phoebe turned with lustrous eyes and kissed me at length. This, I thought on her mother's authority, was – however delightful – from books. It was the point at which novels ended.

'We should prepare,' she told me.

'Yes, you must be ready for a long rest, after such a day.'

'Such a day?' she asked, raising perfect eyebrows, as if I had amused her by quaintness. 'Jonathan, do you wish to wash now, and undress?'

'No. You prepare, my darling. I shall sit and read a while.'

'Very well. But I shall need help in lifting off my wedding dress.'

Phoebe stepped out of her satin wedding slippers and I took the weight of the hoop of the dress as Phoebe raised it off her body. She, in bodice and drawers, and I in my wedding suit lowered it to the ground, where it stood by its own stiffness.

'Phoebe,' I said. 'How you must have suffered in that.'

'I suffered but I gloried,' she told me.

A screen with embroidered swans had been erected and a servant had placed soap, a water basin and towels in its lee. Phoebe went behind this screen, and I sat, still fully dressed, and read a *Goulburn Herald* report I had already read once yesterday on the civic amenities and industries of Brussels, in the new kingdom of Belgium. The very remoteness of the subject matter was a delightful comfort to me in my exhausted and ov instructed condition, as behind the screen Phoebe washed and sang to herself in French. The young flexibility of her voice touched me, so that I was moved to a frank but hopeless desire.

I remained seated, and Phoebe emerged from the screen in milk-white feet and a long white muslin gown, very simple, very charming. Still singing absently to herself, she knelt a second by the near side of the bed, said in silence what seemed like perfunctory and routine prayers, and got beneath the sheets. I dropped my paper, crookedly pulled my chair across to her, took her hand and kissed it. 'It has been a very hard long day for you, dearest Phoebe,' I said.

She lifted my hand and kissed it, in deliberate mimicry. 'And for you.'

'You should sleep now.' I closed my own eyes and yawned a little as if she were a child in need of a demonstration. But Phoebe pulled my head down suddenly and to my delight and confusion gave me a long, thorough, knowing kiss. I was bewildered, since the mother had told me such a kiss was not within the child's giving. 'Eros and Morpheus,' she said. 'Love and sleep. Do they go hand-in-hand? Not according to what I've heard, Jonathan.'

There was another kiss, to which I responded thoroughly, and soon sleep was abandoned. It transpired, as I discovered in later wondering and delighted conversations with my wife, that not only had Phoebe read inno- cent 'romances of sighs' favoured by the English, but had acquired as well a full map of what might be called love in the flesh from certain white- covered French novels which the girls of the Geneva *academie* passed amongst themselves. On top of that, many of the French and Spanish maidens who attended the *academie* were willing to speak matter-of-factly of the joys of marriage awaiting them, of which they had had a full and frank account from older sisters, cousins and even from younger aunts, and had also speculated on the question of taking young lovers should they be required to marry older men. Lastly, it seemed young men of the town would on spring nights climb the walls of the *academie* after the lights had gone out and call to the young women in their rooms, sometimes with a particular piquancy of suggestion which was itself an introduction to the mysteries of Eros. Some of the bravest girls managed midnight meet- ings with young men in a summerhouse in the gardens, and though these ended with honour intact and virginity retained, the adventurous girls who returned from these assignations related to their sisters every detail of the boys' most ardent and concrete wishes.

I wondered whether Mr and Mrs Finlay would be pleased or disap- pointed to find that their daughter had not entered marriage as blindly as they believed.

☙

Letter No 5, SARAH BERNARD

My Dearest Friend
I confess to you I have written letters I did not want you to see and have kept to myself – so terrible might this place be thought to be even by you who are amongst the mad! But the lunaticks may not have the wit to be as evil in purpose as is this place. It grieves me you must come one day here for the next stage of your supposed reforming. Though I know you may prove safer in the narrow cell of your category than in the public raucous wards. I have become a friend of the Matron and to tell you this is more a confession of shame than a boast. But it means I am secure from certain things and I have been careful to use my place here to give a little more sugar and tobacco twist to the Irish women around me in

the Tory who stand by me when some of their kind would seek to tear me to pieces. Let me tell you this: Steward and Matron Pallmire behave like very emperors and empresses and their quarters are both quarters and storehouse for all they have amassed. They know how things are done and profit by that.

But never mind. I write to tell you I have found a small amount of power over them both. On some nights I sleep in the Matron's house and sometimes on a litter in a room full of sugar from the West Indies where poor Corporal McWhirter perished. And on such a night Mr Steward Pallmire came to the door and opened it. He was shuddering from rum as you might believe. I said: Go Away! And he looked as shocked as any old tyrant. As shocked if I might say as that old tyrant of yours when the venom cut his breath! I said: Go away sir! Mrs Pallmire will not permit it. He called me a name but just for something to say. And I was surprised I now felt no threat though I had felt much threat earlier. So he turned away and belched and went off like a curbed child. For he knows his wife and I have begun to talk at length. It seems as if she needed a friend. That is the strange thing. They might be kings and queens but lack airs. And they simply do what they do.

I thought then I have some power and must practise at it to bring Alice here. And once here to make her safe! I was all at once redeemed you see.

This letter you might think is all boast. But I am blithe to have a little of my might back – that is all. That is why I write. I will use what is now my influence with Mrs Pallmire. Do not hope over much but hope some! And know that not only a boast do I include on this page but at the same time my true heart.

Your friend in life and death
Sar

A reply from Alice Aldread lay amongst Sarah Bernard's letters.

Lovingest Sar
I send this to you by a constable for a high price. I am in such trouble here the surgeon disliking me. You must get me to the Factory for it can not be worse and must be better. My life and soul depends on it for I am so misused here. One thing is I shall see your kindly face.

Yours ever
Alice A

PRIM WOKE IN STILL, COOL AIR which seemed – no other concept fitted – laundered. This was strange enough by the standards of Khartoum to cause her an instant of frenzy in which she knew nothing – not her name, her starting-out point, nor this destination. But then the stampede of her brain gave her back the faculty to name her place. She was in a bedroom in her sister's house, the house of Mr and Mrs Brendan D'Arcy. The curtains were drawn, but she knew the window looked south over blue reaches of water to Shark Island and a distant Opera House and Harbour Bridge. She rose and verified this with some fear. For this was the landscape of her shame. But she was pleased to see too that the afternoon sun, reddening subtly down-harbour, carried barely a flavour of reproach. Thought of in Khartoum, the Auger affair seemed perhaps a pervasive tale of Sydney. Had Mrs Auger entertained people with the tale of the berserk student who had been so naively besotted with her husband the professor that she had stolen the words and opinions of an international scholar to impress him? 'Ah yes, the plagiarist!' She had felt the reflex of terror when, on boarding a Qantas flight in Rome, having flown from Khartoum to Rome on the ethnically neutral Austrian airlines, she had heard the Australian intonation of the pilot, that long, dry accent merciless as the Mount Bavaria landscape, and just as full of ambiguity.

But now that she woke beside that great pool of blue harbour, she could see by the nature of the light that these fears had been vain. She knew she could deal with this situation, not with total confidence but with valour. And the place, as seen from her window, had an air of vast, splendid, loutish indifference. Sydney, as ever, was sailing on its heedless way towards dusk, hauling intact its plentiful and traditional cargo of sins, rackets, venalities, forgeries, accommodations and systems of favours. It was also true – how had she forgotten it? – that it was always this year's fish, this week's, that were frying in Sydney. Dazzled by harbour light, the city had a short memory. Social commentators, historians, said that. So Sherif could have been here, sleeping the profound sleep of a tourist who had flown from Khartoum to Rome to Sydney. Sherif could have woken here with bewilderment in his eyes, and she could have been, in her own city, the expert, the casual local. 'Darling, you're in Sydney! Look ... Do you see those ferries!'

In three nights time, the anniversary would occur. Before then Prim

was to meet her boss Peter Whitloaf in Sydney, and then, the day after
the celebration, make a speech in Canberra to the United Nations Association and supporters of UNESCO and sundry NGOs. On Tuesday she
would leave Australia and be back in the Sudan in nine or ten days.

Dimp's unpretending delight at seeing her – sudden energetic hugs,
shrilling expletives – had been both wonderful and scary, a cheque
presented against a bank of sisterhood and love which was supposed to
be located in her, in Prim. She feared she looked good only on paper,
and was a ghost company. The ghost of the Nile. As always it was Dimp
who seemed so substantial, so present.

Prim wandered out, on the third of four floors, into a house full of
stillness. She delighted in the works on the walls – Dimp had acquired
these paintings for D'Arcy, and amongst them were the now fashionable
native artists, the desert ochres of people not utterly unrelated to the
Burranghyatti – the renowned Clifford Possum Tjapaltjarri for one. On
the walls of the hugest room, the harbour was echoed by two nineteenth-
century paintings of that great reach of water by Conrad Martens, and
by the light-drenched works of Australian impressionists like Roland
Wakelin and Grace Cossington Smith, their late 1920s, early 1930s
preoccupation with the great arch of the Harbour Bridge rising incom-
plete into the sky. On a far wall hung a Brett Whiteley nude-by-the-
harbour, and a flamboyant John Olsen celebrative of this particular
place, the bowl of deep blue by the shores of which her sister and Bren
lived, and the emblematic gold of sky above. There was further Australian vividness scattered through the rooms: Ned Kelly; the explorers
Burke and Wills whom Central Australia consumed; the Australian
digger and the mad bride of the bush, a woman dashing in her phan-
tasmal veil through the vertical of the ghost gums. Prim half-amusedly
recognised her former Sydney existence in this harpy–victim. She, Primrose herself, with her phantom, sullied veil, run mad in Sudan?

Distantly, from the blue water beyond the windows, the voice of a
commentator on a tour ferry could be heard, and the vivid paintings of
this huge sitting room continued to echo the nature of things beyond the
glass doors onto the sundeck.

Dimp and her husband arrived home at the same time, at dusk, loudly
entering. Bren said, 'Jesus, a man could do a glass of wine.' And then he
lowered his voice, 'Do you think your little sister's up?'

Prim remained quiet like a child hiding, as Dimp, business-suited but
with her jacket undone, went to check Prim's bedroom, came frowning

towards the front of the house and discovered her. 'Here she is! She's up!' And there was no doubting the delight, even the relief, which entered Dimp's face, as if she knew explicitly how indefinite Prim felt, how skittish and likely to bolt. She subjected her flighty sister to an intense scrutiny and murmured presciently, 'Bet you're sad you didn't bring your bloke! Fucking's the best cure for jet lag.'

'He'd be fascinated by the paintings. He's the sort of man who would want to know everything. He'd be asking me about Burke and Wills and what they meant.'

Brendan, in shirtsleeves – a tailored Italian shirt – came through carrying bottle and glasses on a tray, and with easy command led the women to face the low sun on his massive, tiled sundeck. Out here, Dimp put her hand on her sister's shoulder as they all sat at a white table.

'You've got to miss this, where you are now,' said Dimp with the standard Sydneysider pride. It was their great and simple vanity, this unmerited harbour which had fallen into their hands and which had imposed a particular style on their lives.

'Of course I miss it,' Prim said at last, but it came out as the sullen enthusiasm of a teenager.

Dimp inclined her head to murmur, 'I reckon I know why you wouldn't bring your Sudanese fella.'

'The truth is,' Prim lied, 'he's very busy.'

Prim could see, behind her sister's face pressed up close to her own, her own features submerged.

'Oh yeah, yeah. Too busy eh? The truth is, you were scared he'd become the tame fuzzy-wuzzy at the party, and be patronised.'

With a tug, Dimp undid the string at the neck of her blouse. It reminded Prim how the small Dimple Bettany had always wrestled within her clothes, and would unconsciously unbutton herself at the wrists, the school tie already hanging loose from her collar. All the teachers asking her why she was not more like her little sister Primrose, and Dimp so incapable of imagining or desiring regularity in her dress that she did not even take her sister aside later for vengeful slaps.

Prim said, 'Sherif has to scramble to put together a living. And he's too proud to let me buy him a ticket.'

'Yeah. But just the same ... I'd love to see the guy,' said Dimp, then turned to her husband, who was still struggling with the wine cork, and asked, 'How do you think my little sister looks?'

'Right up to the family standard for pulchritude,' said Brendan, pouring glassfuls, passing them to Prim and Dimp and then himself hungrily drinking. 'Christ, much needed. You must be zonked, Prim.'

'I'm fine. It's just a bit unreal, being back.'

She was delighted that all peevishness seemed to have gone from her voice. The hateful tone from the inept past, from Auger-obsession. She did not want to be the mad, sullen bride.

Dimp smiled lusciously. 'If you're a little culture-shocked now, it'll get worse with the party. Rich bastards who don't deserve to exchange the time of day with a true labourer in the vineyard like yourself.'

'Rich bastards,' nodded Bren, still concentrating on his wine. 'In other words, undeserving friends of mine. But you know I've come to a theory – no, not a theory – a *conclusion* on wealth.'

'Save us that,' said Dimp.

'No. I'll run it by your sister and see what she thinks. I mean, I know a lot of the rich, she knows a lot of the poor. Between us we have the basis of an opinion.' He turned to Prim. 'My theory's this. Wealth is generally interpreted in economic and political terms, and so it's a great cause of social unrest. But wouldn't people on both sides of the economic divide be a bloody sight happier if they knew that wealth or affluence or whatever you want to call it is a biological outcome as much as it is the fall-out of an economic system? It's like having red hair, say, as much as it is about the classic Marxist view of capital.'

Dimp said, 'Holy bloody hell. Wealth's genetic as long as your father leaves you a bloody goldmining company!' She winked at her sister. 'This is Bren the thinker at work.'

'Well, I won't bother responding to the goldmining gibe,' said Bren with good humour, 'except to tell your sister that gold was in the pits when I began my public life, that's why I went into the venture business. My father didn't leave me a Chicago office. But say gold was flourishing when I started, and say my father did have a Chicago office to service Canadian and US mining companies. Aren't such assets themselves genetic markers? As much as an ability to be good at rugby or to be able to paint well?'

'The answer,' said Dimp, 'is no.'

'But,' Bren continued, 'I'm not arguing this in a way which counts wealth as a superior gift or something. The simple truth is that most of the wealthy people I know are that way because they can't bear not being that way. Everyone vaguely wants wealth, but not everyone needs it to be able to breathe. Others have some little genetic spur that makes them, above every-thing else, want to race pigeons, or paint, or study classical Greek.'

'Genetic spurs eh?' said Dimp. She seemed to be enjoying herself, Prim was happy to see. All her talk about the annulment seemed distant from this sundeck, and its wine and disorganised chatter. 'That's funny talk for a bloke who sees God's will in all things. So God chooses the wealthy by giving them these little DNA sprigs.'

'Yeah, but biology is part of the divine plan too, the rules of the game he created and plays by.'

But then Prim saw a shift behind her sister's eyes. Even if Dimp's tone remained jovial, the conversation was no longer mere game-playing. 'Pity he didn't make a game where we're not all ripping each other's throats out all the time. And if biology drove you to me, why did God need you to get an annulment from the Holy See?'

'Oh come on,' said Bren, looking at his wine. 'Low blow!'

Prim saw from the peculiar narrowing of Dimp's mouth she was familiar with from childhood, and from the rounding of D'Arcy's shoulders, that the harsh edge of an unappeasable discord had been casually reached. It was frightening to see that the annulment question did seem to lie at the bottom of all argument.

But Dimp was ashamed that she had let the beast out into the daylight, and turned quickly to her sister.

'From tomorrow, there'll be a bit of noise in the house. The housekeeper will be back and people delivering stuff, and one of Bren's secretaries supervising everything.'

'It doesn't matter,' said Prim, wanting herself to fill the air with busy sound. 'I have to have coffee with people from the Sydney office of Austfam tomorrow.'

Bren abandoned the question of wealth, biology and God's will. 'By the way – tell me if you're too tired to discuss this – but you wouldn't know a place called Adiel, would you?'

'No, I'm sorry.' And she tried to sound it.

'How about Melut?'

'Melut's down south, on the White Nile.'

'That's the one.'

Prim smiled. 'You know more about the Sudan already than most outsiders.'

He shrugged. 'It's what we do. D'Arcy Coleman Venture, I mean. My Chicago office found the capital for a Canadian company, Alberta Petroleum, to go into a joint venture with the Sudanese government extracting oil from a well at Adiel. After extraction, they pump it to the river and ship it north by barge. I've got to tell you, it was a decent sum we raised. The deal was made in good faith with the government, which assured us it had sovereignty and control over the area.'

'Sovereignty shifts around a bit down there.'

'That's what we found out.'

'But are you still involved in the well? Isn't it the problem of this Canadian company now?'

'I'm not directly involved. I have to keep tabs. I have to be ready to restructure the financial deal in case of problems. And there have been problems. A month ago a group of rebels turned up at the well and told the Alberta personnel that the site would be attacked if they did not immediately withdraw.'

'I really had no idea,' said Prim.

'The next thing is,' Bren went on, 'I see a memo telling me that the Sudanese government has moved a battalion of infantry with armoured support to secure the well area.'

'The government can't afford to lose sites of that nature,' Prim told him like a professional briefer. 'If they want to pay their foreign debt and go on fighting the war.'

'And doing something about their bloody awful deficit,' said Bren.

'How did the battalion manage?'

'Pretty ordinary. They were routed one night, some of the Sudanese personnel and one Canadian driller shot, and outbuildings burnt. But the rebels didn't attack the well itself, because they say it and the oil in it belongs to them ... what are they called? The Southern People's something or other.'

'Liberation Army, SPLA. Although it has factions. It could be the SPLMA, the Liberation Movement Army! There are tribal and political differences in the South.'

There was a sudden, more muscular mood change from Bren. 'There always bloody are! I wish the bastards would just let my friends extract the oil, that's all.'

Dimp laughed, jolly again. 'Look at my capitalist! Isn't he a lad?' She winked at Prim.

When you lived in four levels of grandeur on Sydney Harbour, Prim understood, it *would* seem reasonable that the politics of distant places should readjust themselves to your desire.

'Do you stand to lose much then?' she asked, exaggerating the compassion in her voice.

'If it goes totally bad I stand to lose commissions,' he said jovially, but smiling to put her at ease about her sister's future. 'Of course it's not really my money to start with, and it's all underwritten and insured to buggery. But apart from the commissions, it means the people my staff approach to raise future capital will not be as open to us as before. Look, I'm not asking for sympathy, but if you put the world together, all in all, with Aborigines in Australia, Blackfoot Indians in Canada, the SPL – whatever it is – in the Sudan, the sort of deals I put together become harder and harder to conclude, and less frequent. And I've got a sumptuous woman to maintain.'

'Don't give the bastard any sympathy,' Dimp told Prim.

Yet he had a sort of hulking charm which made it easy for Prim to simulate concern. He was a pleasant fellow, brisk, meaning well. But she had never fully seen what it was that had attracted Dimp, who displayed a faint, indulgent tiredness as she listened to him.

Prim was delighted to have got through the conversation well – to have saved it in fact, to have re-channelled it. She had feared, coming home, that she might manifest herself as one of those censorious aid workers. 'Business is down? Tough luck! You ought to see how people live in the Sudan!' She knew that some people had always mistaken her shyness for censure anyhow, and was therefore pleased that with a hard case like Bren she had been able to seem a contributor of interesting fact.

The offices of Austfam were not in any of the high-rent buildings around Sydney Cove but in that seedy stretch west of the point where George Street becomes Parramatta Road. In the spirit of their surroundings and their trade, the employees of Austfam dressed more for down-at-heel comfort – old batik dresses, open neck shirts – than for corporate success. There was very little slickness at Austfam.

Peter Whitloaf, the head of the NGO, who commuted between Sydney and Canberra, was an exemplary beanpole. In his cardigan, he looked like a Trappist monk in mufti. But Prim knew enough by now, from meeting such folk as Stoner, that here at the bosom of aid and development bodies could be found, as well as an undeniable altruism, at least as intense a voracity to prove, to survive, to succeed, as anywhere else in the human scheme. And a hunger for funds, which other NGOs competed for as well, and for credit, credit being something she had unintentionally acquired for Austfam in the case of the Darfur emergency and through Sherif's health surveys.

Peter was both a decent fellow and an operator. Formerly a federal minister's press secretary, he was at Austfam by choice. After Prim had been greeted, pecked on the cheek, and answered the inquiries of the outer office staff – 'Yes, I am thinner. It's the malaria from a few years back' – she was welcomed by Peter Whitloaf like an uncle encountering a favourite if over-exuberant niece.

'Prim,' he said. 'Ah, still a girl, still a girl.'

In his office they talked about what he called 'Austfam's footprint' in the Sudan. Peter said how delighted the board of Austfam was at the community health studies Prim had organised. They had not only served as a useful guide for those deploying aid in the field, he said, they had also raised the profile of Austfam in 'the literature'.

'This Sherif is a godsend,' he continued without apparent irony. 'Which brings me to the question of the new Khartoum administrator we've been promising to send you.'

Of course, she saw at once. They must intend to end her solitary residence at Austfam, Khartoum. So she felt more than pleased when Whitloaf hurried to say, 'I'm afraid I have to tell you I don't think we can find a second person yet. But there's a consultant Austfam employs. He'd like to visit before the end of the year and make an assessment of our operations. That would take a month or two. I wondered if you felt you could hold out another year on your own?'

'Oh yes,' said Prim. 'I can manage.'

'Well, that's the bad news. The good news is we would like to make you officially our senior office administrator there. You'd get five or six thousand more in salary. But there's a minor problem about it. This promotion would make you totally responsible for Austfam's good name, and totally and exclusively dedicate you to Austfam's work, in the Sudan.'

'Of course,' she said.

Whitloaf looked at the ceiling. 'These letters of yours to the United Nations, the International Committee of the Red Cross and so on, which you've been kind enough to copy for us. The ones about . . . about slavery of a kind. Southern people in unjust forms of bondage – that comes as no surprise, I suppose . . . But this interest of yours is a bit worrying to us.' He looked at her direct. 'Some of the board think it an internal administrative matter for the Sudanese government, and that buying into it is extraneous to our mandate in the area.'

PART TWO

Prim felt the blood move to her face. 'I don't agree with them. It's part of the refugee problem, and there's no doubt the refugee problem's within our mandate.' She wondered if her anger was inordinate.

'Look, Prim, when we go into a Third World country we all pick up the politics and our opinions are swayed one way and another. And sometimes it's true that despite being neutral we find ourselves becoming proactive. We might decide a certain rebel group is better and juster at distributing equity than the government. So we send a little more aid their way than the government might like, and we get threats from various ministries as a result. But over-involvement in this slave business has the risk of getting us into real trouble with Khartoum. Here's a government which says, again and again and angrily, that there's no systemic slavery in the South or North and that if there are residual cases the culprits will be prosecuted. And yet in the same city there is a woman representing an aid group who says, here is instance after instance of slavery.'

'Are we to be totally driven in our actions by the claims of governments?' asked Prim.

'Of course not. But beside the true, visible problems, this one is ... you know, it's controversial. Unproven, if you like. And that word – "slavery" – has such a melodramatic weight. And Sunday, in Canberra ... you must remember that your audience are generally middle-aged and older people who've been committed to the support of bodies like ours since their youth. We don't want to distract any of them from the main game. Whereas the slave-liberators – I have heard of them, including the *von* woman – are attending to a minute part of the tapestry of African misery. But they demand centre-stage for it. It's part of their absolutist, Bible-bashing view of the world.'

'For Christ's sake,' said Prim and stood up.

'I didn't want to make you angry,' said Peter Whitloaf. 'I actually thought I was offering you a promotion and a fraternal caution.'

'And I don't get the one if I don't take the other?'

'I didn't say that.'

'Look, Peter, the subjects, the people I interview. *They* think they were part of a system of literal slavery.'

'Only after the *von* woman had told them that by paying money for them.'

'No, their knowledge is deeper than that. Bloody hell, Peter, read my case histories!'

'Well, they're certainly illustrative of a problem. But is it slavery in the *Uncle Tom's Cabin* sense?'

She found herself laughing, richly, like Dimp. 'I've had this argument so many times. With Sherif even. Maybe this is a *man* thing, after all. Women – von Trotke, my friend Mrs el Rahzi, even the BBC correspondent Helene Codderby – they all think slavery exists. The chaps, however, won't believe it on any terms.'

'Thanks a million,' said Whitloaf, regarding the ceiling again.

'We're told by her critics that if von Trotke goes round buying adolescents back, she is driving the price up and encouraging more captures. But that doesn't prove that there isn't a slave market. It proves there *is* a market, subject to supply and demand, like toothbrushes and bottles of gin. But if I want to be my own boss in Khartoum I can't say that? That there's a market?'

'I'd prefer you didn't if you're speaking for us. On Sunday, these people want to hear about our development and aid programs.'

'I actually intended to tell them about development and aid.'

'And the health surveys?'

'Yes.'

'Good.'

'Ah, but I have a mind to change my speech now.'

'Don't.'

They sat in a silence which seemed to make Peter uneasy, but he kept his long neck stiff, willing her to do the right thing.

In the street after leaving the office, Prim was all at once suddenly overcome by the absence of Sherif. She felt something like a digestive leadenness, a pain in the joints, but it all carried his name. Perhaps what she felt now was exhaustion at having kept a strong hand over her edginess, her capacity to whine and threaten, the capacity which had soured Auger. She had managed herself well, she was conscious, both when discussing the inconsiderateness of the southern Sudanese rebels with Bren, and this morning while arguing robustly, rather as Dimp would argue, the semantics of bondage with Peter. Her depression descended further as she neared the bus stop.

But as she paid her fare, seated amongst middle-aged men retired too early by the mechanism of corporate downsizing and emitting a faint, defeated musk of late-summer sweat, and watching young mothers come to town with their children to buy bigger school shoes or larger shirts, she reached towards Dimp for an antidote to melancholy, and envisaged the paintings she had cleverly bought, and felt a new surge of affection. She would give Dimp the best of presents, something infinitely superior to the set of Bach cantatas she had already bought her. She would enjoy the party in its own right. She would at last reduce the distance between herself and the event. She would be sociable in a new way, and thus enjoy the night as Dimp would enjoy it. That was a redeeming pledge.

Hence, next morning, when Dimp had an appointment for hair, face, nails and leg-waxing at Evelyn's beauty parlour in Double Bay, and wanted Prim to go with her, she went along happily, though she had always been wary of beautification. From the windscreen of the car the vigorous light of a Saturday morning in Sydney looked supremely familiar. Yet everyone seemed so healthy. People in their forties looked agelessly young. She had forgotten too, in flat Khartoum, how hilly her home city was. Dimp drove sagely, squinting in concentration at New South Head Road and its cinemas and coffee shops.

In her side-street salon, their hairdresser-in-chief was Evelyn herself, supervising the team of women who went to work on the two sisters. Tall and thin and calling everyone, 'Darls', Evelyn greeted Dimp with a simple heartiness.

'Oh, the adorable Dimp D'Arcy,' she shrilled.

She led them to the waxing room, and within the peach-coloured walls they hung their clothes, changed into short terry-towelling gowns and lay together on parallel tables to have their legs waxed. Evelyn, telling them she would see them later, left them to the waxer's mercies.

'What are you both wearing?' asked the waxer, after their initial small talk. 'You know, at the party?'

Prim had until this moment thought that regretfully the only thing she had that was party-suitable was the white embroidered gown she had bought in el Fasher years before, a stand-by that she still wore on visits to the el Rahzis. Now, as the waxer began to pull off the strips of cloth, stinging her by peeling out the hair of her lower legs, she realised that it would perfectly fit the event. What it lost in texture would be gained by its novelty. As the hair came off her lower legs, Prim felt the long neglected glands of her vanity begin to secrete. She felt as if she were about to be initiated into a delightful tribe, where simple things said – 'You've had this done regularly?' – carried a complicated subtext to do with the sisterhood of desirability.

Afterwards, the waxer soothed their stinging legs by rubbing them with balm, and so sent them forth to Evelyn.

'Your hair's lovely, darls, but so brittle,' Evelyn told Prim as she languidly inspected it after it was sleek and shampooed.

'That's the Sudan,' said Dimp, from her chair. 'My sister lives in the Sudan.'

'In the Sudan,' said Prim, like a woman who daily thought of her hair, 'it doesn't matter how hard you try.'

'That's the Sahara, isn't it?' asked Evelyn, massaging her scalp, a sensation Prim was enjoying more than she would have thought.

'Close enough to it,' said Prim.

Dimp winked at her, at one in her strategy.

'Does you husband's job take you there?'

'No,' Prim said blithely, her soul evened out by shampoo. 'I'm not married.'

'Oh but you will be, darls,' Evelyn assured her. 'A honey like you.'

While their hair was blow-dried and styled – yet another experience Prim found delightful, soothing, therapeutic, and a relief from intractable questions – their nails were attended to. This is the Western equivalent, Prim thought, of the henna, the tattoos, the *delkah*. Next, their faces were made up – or 'made over', to quote Evelyn – at dressing tables by enthusiastic young women.

So, glowing, Dimp and Prim left Evelyn's, walking with the slight stiffness of their enhanced perfection, and sat at an outside table in front of a Hungarian coffee shop and patisserie.

'That's what I love about Double Bay,' Dimp said. 'It's Budapest transported. Not a misplaced England. You can hear the bloody Danube pulsing away.'

And indeed from a sound system within the patisserie, a violin and an accordion played a languorous, worldly Magyar tune. Prim tried to imagine herself and Sherif in this place at the end of the world, taking excellent coffee, done in the style the Hungarians had learned from the Tartars. Men and women looked at them. Two radiant sisters, sharing the one pastry.

Dimp leaned forward again. 'That Auger thing still has its hooks in you, doesn't it?'

'Less and less,' said Prim. 'I believe I can look you in the eye and say less since I came home.'

'You should have come home sooner.'

'Well . . . a person doesn't know that. Coming home taught me there's no danger in coming home. Not yet, anyhow.'

'That's good. You've been delivered of your demon. Good for you, sis.' By her emphasis, Dimp implied she was still possessed of her own devils.

'Come on,' said Prim warily. 'That annulment thing. You're not serious, are you?'

'God, yes. For some bloody reason I still am.'

'And yet you knew about it. You knew about it even when I was making an idiot of myself with Auger.'

Dimp stared at her for the undistracted half-second the competitive, honking traffic streaming into Double Bay permitted. 'It isn't just that if one marriage can be annulled another can be with the same ease. It's also the other thing: Bren has told both of us, his first wife, and me, he loved us. But he didn't love us enough to cover his miserable Irish –Lebanese arse.'

'But that's ridiculous,' Prim argued. 'Love is always conditional.'

'Yes. But there's one side of my soul says otherwise. I'd like him for his own sake to take a risk. I don't mean "venture capital", which is a flash phrase for minting money. What I want is for him to risk everything. Sometimes I can't help myself thinking it's my mission to bring him to it. Look, verbally, he's willing to make unconditional commitments. But then I find he's got a stainless steel guarantee from a canon lawyer. Christ, what sort of love is that?'

'The sort you live with. And have a party to honour.'

'Yeah, yeah,' said Dimp as more coffee arrived. She scooped some cinnamon-laden cream off the top. 'You're right, of course. But being right doesn't quite swing it.'

Prim was all at once the older sister, the wise counsellor. 'You'll feel better after the party.'

'I'd like to come to Canberra with you tomorrow,' said Dimp.

'Won't you be tired?'

'Tired *and* emotional. But I want to hear one of your outrageous speeches.'

'Outrageous?'

'Yes, you remember. You always gave the weirdest speeches at school. I mean, the weirdest and the most interesting. Remember that time you were thrown out of the debating team for saying Australia was a Third World country?'

'I can't remember that,' said Prim.

Dimp began laughing with a raucousness which did not quite suit her present peerlessness. Her legs were alabaster smooth though, and that was a start.

The social confidence built in Prim at Evelyn's salon disappeared with the first guest to enter Dimp's house. Not that there was any awesome authority, any clear intimidating opulence amongst the guests. The men tended to dress down, lean and serious, with trimmed hair, and collar-less white shirts under baggy linen jackets, they looked rather like Prim's (and perhaps their own) idea of French film directors rather than the merchant bankers, venture capitalists, brokers, lawyers who were Bren's preferred company. Even when Dimp's friends from film, the director of *Enzo Kangaroo*, Frank Varduzzi, and his wife, Septima, arrived, Prim felt just as lost, almost to the point of impoliteness. The promise of that morning, the promise of drawing normal, sociable breath, evaporated.

For a while, Dimp brought everyone up to meet her, as part of the house tour, and that made things better – 'My sister came all the way from Khartoum! Just to be at our anniversary!' But soon the guests arrived in such numbers that this nicety became impossible. She noticed Bren enjoying himself with a group of balding men. Occasional bursts of male laughter punctuated what seemed to be Bren's enjoyably glum economic prophecies. A handsome red-headed woman, ample in an emerald dress, came bouncing up to Prim where she stood leaning on the stone balustrade above the harbour. She had the expectant smile of someone who was about to be recognised.

'Skinny Bettany,' she said, reviving a nickname even Prim herself had forgotten. 'Primrose. You remember me? I was in Dimp's class at Abbots-leigh. Sue Crosier. You *must* remember me. I was the one who was jealous because your sister had that great nickname. Tits!'

Prim did remember, discerned the child's face behind the woman's. In the years before the Bettany parents died in their car smash, she had been one of Dimp's gang of part-sullen, part-hilarious, adolescent cadres. The memory was welcome, Prim was pleased to find, and she felt her social impulses at last unleashed. Conversation could now make its own heed-less, instinctive way, in Sydney as in Khartoum.

'I wish I'd done what you did,' said this former child named Sue. 'I've often thought about it. Little Skinny Bettany. Doing it hard in some shithole, eh? What shithole is it?'

'The Sudan. And you're pulling my leg.'

'No! I've never spent time anywhere interesting. Potty-training is as close to squalor as I've ever got. And I've got two kids now. Do you remember a fellow called Jason Eckhardt? Played rugby for the Walla- bies, which is a huge deal with men we meet. Secret of his success. Well, I married him, and the kids both tore their way out of me like bloody flankers breaking away from the scrum.'

'I haven't had the guts yet to have children,' said Prim.

'Because the world's supposed to be so bad? I suppose it is where you live.'

'No. I just wouldn't ... have the courage. And by the way, that's probably why I'm in Khartoum. I lack the guts to live normally here. And I couldn't join a convent. So ...'

'Boy, you *are* hard on yourself. You always were a serious one, even though every fourteen-year-old boy had the hots for you.'

'You know,' Prim said, 'I think of those times and I realise that despite the boredom, perhaps as few as fifty million people in the entirety of history have ever lived as well as we did then. As securely.'

'Oh, this is the chastisement is it, young Skinny?'

'No. But no one lives as securely as that in the Sudan. No one.' Prim felt the wine, anxiously imbibed, now speaking with welcome authority. 'It's just good to see that despite all our good fortune, we had what everyone has. Divine discontent.'

'Well, I've certainly got it. Look around you. The people within fifty metres of us are the people with whom I will spend, unless Jason does the dirty on them in business, every Saturday night from now until I'm on a walking frame. Every single Saturday night. Unless I'm watching my son, who's four and shows every sign of playing rugby for Australia. That would be quite a nice break, actually.'

'You have an unlimited future,' Prim asserted, giving a stranger advice with great assurance. 'One day you could even do the same work I'm doing if that was what you wanted. I mean, when the children grow up.'

'Oh, Jason would be very bloody happy about that!'

Had Sherif come, Prim realised, all these conversations would have been different. People would have become earnest. Earnestness was what Africans were for.

She was aware now of a large young man with a half-whimsical smile, wearing a fairly beaten-up fawn jacket, waiting for a chance to insert himself into the conversation.

'It's the gorgeous Frank Benedetto,' said Sue Crosier, hugging his large fawn arm close to her, still with ambitions to be the flagrant schoolgirl. 'When are you going to ditch that solicitor friend of yours and let me clear out with you?'

'What are you doing about ten o'clock on Tuesday morning?' he proposed, and kissed her cheek lightly. 'No, you deserve better than me.'

'Not at all. It's not what we deserve but what we fancy. I'll be available as soon as I've dropped the kids at kindergarten.'

Primrose admired these easy flirtations. Benedetto and Dimp's old school friend had such an exact sense of where dalliance ended and seriousness and hurt set in. They had learnt it somehow, had in youth clearly plucked down some lesson that was in the air, above their heads.

Benedetto nodded towards Prim. 'You're so obviously Dimple's sister. I'm the fellow who sent Dimp those papers of your ancestors. I hope they didn't contain too many shocks.'

'It was very sensitive of you, Mr Benedetto, to care.'

'Well, I'd be a historian if it paid the rent better. But all I wanted was the old boy's manuscript: *Sheep Breeding and the Pastoral Life*.'

'You didn't read the private journal and the letters?'

'Well, I began reading and saw that both became kind of confessional. So I thought they were your business, and Dimp's. I couldn't just hand them over to the public library without Dimp seeing them first.'

'They've excited her,' said Prim.

Benedetto smiled. 'Well, she's a woman of gracious enthusiasm.'

'Oh dear!' said Sue. She was vamping it up, choosing to take Benedetto's confession melodramatically as a sign that he had affection for Dimp, and not for her.

'I really am concerned only,' Benedetto said, 'with the question of how these Englishmen, Scots and Irish made their fortunes. I'm a dry-as-dust historian, I'm afraid, and a very poor Italian indeed, because their love life means very little to me. It's the romance of the fleece, the Australian pastorale, I'm into.'

'But I think you should have felt free to have a read of the stuff. After all, Dimp intends to broadcast it all to the world in a film.'

'Yes. Native born Australians have a facility to broadcast the faults of their ancestors in a way which would be considered improper, best kept in the family, in Calabria. But then that's all Calabrians have, their pride.

If we had harbour views,' he gestured out across the water, 'perhaps we could be heedless blabbermouths too.'

This was needlessly philosophic for Sue, who excused herself.

'So,' said Frank. 'Do you really read the Bettany material your sister sends you, in your house in Khartoum?'

'She asks me the same thing, pretty continually,' Prim told him. 'But the answer – anyhow – is yes. But I ... well, I don't want to get into conversation with her about it. It seems she's a little over-stimulated by it. These things reverberate for her.'

Benedetto said, 'She's a storyteller, you see. She hasn't stopped being one, just because of all this ...' He gestured towards the interior of the house and then up-harbour.

A sun-tanned couple came up – they had been out sailing all day and had a maritime glow – and engaged Benedetto in talk of a court case. Benedetto had a pleasant way of making obscure legal points to the man, who was clearly a lawyer himself, and then restating them in succinct English for the sake of Prim and the man's wife. The case was a challenge by a group of East Arnhem Land elders – people who lived some 1500 kilometres north of the mysteries of Mount Bavaria – against a proposed bauxite mine. The elders were seeking to present their case directly to the International Court of Justice in The Hague, and Benedetto was their counsel. Their grounds would be a point of international law as old as Grotius, said Benedetto. The wife asked a little coldly why they would not be happy with the bauxite royalties they would receive. Well, said Benedetto, their sense of the world, their security in who they were, depended on securing an area of coastline between Cape Arnhem and Port Bradshaw against further bauxite mining.

'It's very complex, isn't it?' asked the wife, though it sounded more like warning than comment.

'And don't you think,' said the husband, 'this appealing to outside tribunals could set an irksome if not dangerous precedent? On the one hand, legal progressives like you, Frank, couldn't wait to cut out Australian appeals to the Privy Council of Great Britain. But here you are encouraging an appeal to another outside court, this International Court of Justice.'

Benedetto raised his big hands gently to the right elbow of the husband, the left of the wife, including them and, by glance, Prim, in a fraternity of the enlightened. 'Well, this isn't an appeal. But I accept your point. You and I know that conservative Australia hates anyone to go to outside arbiters. It's a post-colonial insecurity. We have input into The Hague though. It's *our* court as well as the world's. And we'd like it to stick to judging the real baddies – people in Eastern Europe, Asia, South America – not nice girls and boys like us. But ... it's available, and as you know, clients want to use the courts that are available.'

This calm exposition fascinated Prim, but the couple made some unconvinced remarks and drifted off to talk with others about their day's sailing.

'What does Bren think of all this?' Prim asked Benedetto. 'I mean, you're trying to stop mining, no less!'

'He hates me and he loves me.' Benedetto seemed to relish Bren's ambiguity. 'I've represented miners often enough. And he knows enough to understand secure title is in everyone's best interest. As much as miners jump up and down, they've got nothing to complain of here. In other countries, their mines get blown up by the locals!' Benedetto gave way to the affectionate laugh of a man who possesses many friends and understands his enemies, and Prim's splendid sister, dressed with her normal dazzling inadvertence in a long silk gown painted with pink and scarlet tropical flowers, appeared at her side.

'Are you two going to consider talking to other people tonight?' Dimp asked, but her grin had an uncertain and annoyed quality, something Prim remembered from childhood, nothing as raw or inane as suppressed jealousy, but an annoyed ingredient of it. It was the first indication Prim had that her sister was capable of finding Benedetto interesting as more than a supplier of obscure family documents.

Morning came too early for Prim. Surely Dimp would stay in bed and miss Canberra. But no, she was already up, lipstick applied with more energy than accuracy, dressed for business in a suit, to catch the cab and take her sister to Canberra. Dimp slept in the window seat for the short hop from Sydney to Canberra, the early sun lighting her face and, Prim thought, illuminating a definite drag of discontent in the skin. In the bright brown landscape of the lower Monaro – Jonathan Bettany might have sighted these pastures on his way to places such as Yass – only Canberra looked fogbound from 20 000 feet, and so they descended to Australia's only misty town of that morning.

After the long night – they had enjoyed a last, sweetly meaningless glass of wine with Bren at 2 a.m. on the balcony – it might have been a pleasant thing for both sisters to wrap themselves in the woolly comfort of fog, but the sun was already burning off the vapours and there was no risk that the miasmas would make inroads on the sessions of the annual conference of the United Nations Association.

There was a homeliness about a parliament which was constructed within the contours of a hill, as Canberra's was. Delivered to the gloom of the underground Parliament House car park, Prim and Dimp ascended to a confused pearliness of light.

Inside, Dimp told her as they entered the building's reception hall, those marble columns were meant to reproduce the verticals of grey gums, the dun eucalypts of the Australian bush. But there was something in Australian flora, in the Australia of Jonathan Bettany, which resisted marble. Prim had not much sense as she passed amongst these stone saplings that she was coming to the heart of a home forest.

The meeting was held in the Senate hearing room, and at its rear stood a table with tea bags and Nescafe, the same table which could have been found in a thousand remote shires of Australia. The Australians had the same faith as the Sudanese – that tea was a solution. They had somewhat greater reasons to hope so.

A pleasant middle-aged woman who had until recently been a senator showed dazed Prim the rostrum and the microphone. The room filled with awesome rapidity, and decent faces were raised towards her.

'We might start,' said the former senator.

Prim saw her sister settle two rows from the back of the hall. A rare bird amongst the wise ones, amongst these men and women whose passion for international affairs, and not their relationship to the speaker, dictated the order of their day. She saw Peter Whitloaf, looking wan, settle himself not far from Dimp.

The former senator introduced Prim and she stood.

'I'm Primrose Bettany, Acting Administrator, Austfam, Khartoum.'

She was surprised to see her name float away safely above the heads of the listeners. She began to speak of the meat and potatoes of emergency and development aid, as she had with Whitloaf. Adi Hamit was a good stand-by for this, as were a dozen other camps. Midwives, health workers, Operation Safety. The supply of seed and livestock to Abu Grada, the town in Darfur allotted to Austfam after the 1985 emergency. Sherif's work. Why it was that in December there was the largest incidence of respiratory disease in Adi Hamit. Mortality rates, the nutritional status of children under five, and of women. A disquisition on the war and its impact upon Sudanese society and its well-being. A cautious examination of the failure of government policies. And many safe sentences were uttered beginning with, 'Austfam participated in …'; 'Austfam initiated …'; 'Austfam met the expense of training …' Whitloaf's face was raised in something like hope.

'It would be appropriate,' said Prim, 'to end with some personal observations.' Peter Whitloaf crossed his hands on his knee and stared at his knuckles. Prim saw too the radiant, proud, engrossed face of Dimp. Obviously Dimp had no idea that her sister had given a very ordinary report to this point – to her it was all new material, it was as if it had been conjured and was thus as clever as film, fiction, or any of the forms beloved of Dimp.

'One impression is that the concept of famine is very poorly understood by us. As fruitful as it might be in gathering money for emergency aid, the term makes no allowance for the fact that seasonal malnutrition is common every year in the Sudan and elsewhere. Plots are planted at the beginning of the rainy season. Men, and their entire families, sometimes leave their village to find work at that stage, but in confident hope of returning for harvest. They are often seasonally hungry in May, June, July – most millet, other than fiercely guarded seed millet, has been eaten by this time. The husbands might go and sell fodder or charcoal for cash or food. But if the rain does not come, and the crop fails, then malnutrition claims the entire year, as it did in the Darfur emergency. Nonetheless, we are scarcely entitled to look at people suffering these events as utterly hapless, as purely and simply victims.

'Yet if we think of much aid advertising, particularly emergency aid advertising, images of haplessness and victimhood come to mind. We can each of us here envisage the skeletal women and children who are favoured in some posters; women and children who are in fact probably long dead by the time their images are presented to the eyes of the West. Such images are of people so removed from us by hunger, so inhuman in their skeletal condition, that though we pity them, they have become a different kind of being, they are pure ineffectuality, and the one recourse open to them is death.'

Whitloaf raised his head suddenly here, but seemed to have resolved to bear her exuberance bravely.

'One thing I learned working for Austfam is simply this: when we see these figures, we should salute them as the figures of heroes rather than flinchingly behold them as the figures of sub-humans from another economic planet which we shall never visit. For if such a figure was a Sudanese woman, a shrunken baby at her breast, she has seen seedlings die and fields crack beneath the sun. She has seen drought lower the water level in the well in her village. She has walked fifteen miles a day to fetch the family water from some water source not yet dried up. She has hauled that meagre ration back to her family. She has asked: Do I wash, do I cook? What do I drink and what does the family goat drink? And as the dry continues she fights the easy options – she tries not to feed her children the family's millet seed, the seed of the next harvest. I knew a woman who mixed her seed millet with sand and buried it in the earth to prevent her hungry children eating it. But then the drought takes the family livestock. She has tried to drive them to market perhaps, but there has not been water or pasture along the way. And in the towns the price of the millet she wishes to buy has increased ten-fold. For a time of emergency is as ever a splendid time for speculators to buy livestock cheaply and sell grain expensively.'

At this stage, Prim detected that a few people in the room began frowning as if she was leading them on an unexpected and puzzling journey. But she was embarked now. There was only one way down from this intimately harboured argument of hers.

'So now, the skeletal mother we see on the poster, has tried with some craft to bridge the gap. She has collected edible or inedible grasses on hillsides, and boiled them with a handful of millet. She has fed her family and kept them alive on the seed of the thorn grass, the fruit of the *zisiphus* bush, the occasional collection of watermelon seeds, or of groundnut meal residue. She has set bear traps. She has broken open termite mounds and sought with her hands for the grains of millet that ants have stolen and stored in their chambers. She has dug up rats' nests looking even for the husks of grain. She has combed camels for edible insects. And then, she has found that all this is not enough.

'But her huge, vacant eyes, which are now used on a poster as a blandishment to make us generous, are not the product of too much passivity. They may be the product of too much activity. When the last grain has been eaten, the last grass has blown away, she lifts her children and begins to walk. It is difficult to carry a child across a loveless landscape, bearing on your shoulder a gourd of water and a satchel with some traces of groundnut meal in it. By the time she reaches the feeding station, sits in some shanty town near a cattle or camel market, she may have plans to make a living as a charcoal burner, but now the essential properties of a living being have been leached out of her by gastroenteritis or malaria, by an unlucky fever or loss of the minerals of her body. Or she has recently given birth, perhaps on her path to the feeding station, and now her one new child hangs like a hank of flesh upon a breast which lacks milk.

'She is a woman who, though without resources, had plans for her continued existence for herself and her children, but now her flesh has been reduced, and she is in the condition in which we behold her on the famine poster. But this is not a woman whose image we should easily exploit, nor should we flinch from her or feel distant from her. For she has exercised the limits of all her human skill, her capacity for adaptation, her gift for expediency and her loving familial choices. She is the Madonna of this century. We should all acknowledge with profound humility her exultant human valour ...'

It struck Prim now, as an orator awaking from a trance, that her audience were still perhaps in it. Dimp watched her with a huge approving frown. But there was no way back to wells dug, inoculations given, nutrition levels assessed. She had daydreamed of defying Whitloaf and uttering the heterodox word: slavery. But she could not see how she could make a segue in that direction. Her Madonna stood centre stage. The slave would have to wait until she had exited the stage.

'You have been very patient,' she said.

There was generous but somehow ambiguous applause. She knew she had not delivered the normal aid-worker speech. She was asked if she would answer a few questions. Only one of them was in the vaguest sense to do with the latter part of her speech. A woman began her question with the statement, 'Yes, Miss Bettany. I find those images of scarecrow women very hard to look at too.' This woman was no fool, yet she had permitted Prim's eccentric argument to penetrate only the first layer of skin.

Dimp and Prim stayed for one speech after lunch and then left for the airport. The day was bright by now and they looked out from Canberra's terminal windows at the ancient quietude of dun hills.

Dimp said, 'Next time you should go down and see the sheep station of nearly-Sir-Jonathan. It's still there.'

'You've visited it?'

'Yes. It all happened in concrete time and place, after all. The people who own Nugan Ganway now claim their homestead is built on top of the original, in a dip in the hills, just like nearly-Sir-Jonathan says.'

Dimp seemed wan, and Prim reached for her sister's hand and stroked the wrist. It was a broader and less angular wrist than her own.

'I'd like to do that with you,' she said. 'Yes.'

Dimp smiled palely. 'Two and a half hour's drive from here. More or less.'

'You shouldn't have come, after that big party.'

'No, no,' Dimp insisted. 'I wanted to. My smart sister. You know the woman who mixed the seed millet with dirt? That got to me . . . Our old Jewish great-granny. She strikes me as that sort of woman. Unstoppable. Though just as likely to be a poster girl for some damn misery or other. But not, of course, by her own choice.'

To remind her sister that what was said in the speech concerned modern women in Darfur and elsewhere would have seemed particularly priggish just then. Instead Prim imagined the two of them in some distant safe year. Two aged women who had worked it all out – or whatever in their lives could not be resolved had passed. It seemed to Prim a desirable plateau of simple comforts.

'All right,' she said to her proud sister who needed comfort, 'we'll have a bloody big gin and tonic on the plane.'

⌐

Letter No. 6, SARAH BERNARD

Dearest Alice

Your appeal causes me distress but I am taking action. I speak to Mrs Matron as we are drinking tea and conversing together. And it seems to me all threads of power meet at her. I ask: Could you get a Category 1 woman from the Asylum if she is not mad to start with? She asks what the woman did.

I tell her how I met you first in Manchester county prison where your solicitor let you wither and wait in a public cell – though he could have dipped into your husband's money to pay for something better. As I tell her I remember when I came to that dark prison ward how you shone like a star with your every kindness. Remember that woman with the two children? Receiver of stolen goods? Both her tots had bad bowels and the whole ward full of a reek of thin shit! You wept softly. I thought this woman should not be here. Not this angel! You were above that place.

I tell Mrs Matron: The woman I speak of was married to a dyer many years older – a tyrannous man of very crooked desires and in the way of taking poisons for the sake of his health.

Mrs Matron looks under her rounded eyebrows. So this is your ducky is it? You want your ducky friend here?

It seemed that despite her might she is jealous to keep the tea and time she and I spend together.

But she is talking of helping. She says: I could claim that because of the death of mad old Martha I have a spare billet in Category 3 – the one category a poisoning woman could be in. But that would be in a cell of seven feet by five in the far wing. But, better for your friend than the narrow cell named a coffin she might have had in the execution yard had the judge not been moved to pity! Then Mrs Matron goes on: I would like to be kindly but cannot have it otherwise than Category 3. The Visiting Justice would create a frenzy if I put her in with you!

But when the Visiting Justice is not visiting she does what she likes – this Matron Pallmire. But for the start I shall see my Alice in the cell of mad Martha – this is the cell of an old woman returned many times to the Factory by her masters for being tipsy. This is however but a start for you. But a start my friend Alice.

Mrs Matron sounds wearied when she says: I have never had a felon woman I could so easily chatter with and if you are to remain that to me I imagine I must keep you happy.

So I hope you will soon be delivered from the madhouse by the inter-cession of your true friend

Sarah

And Sarah Bernard did manage to have her friend moved to the Female Factory, since her next letter, numbered No 7 by Dimp, spoke of ecstatic reunion.

Letter No 7, SARAH BERNARD

Loving Alice,
It proved so easy to persuade them that I should be admitted to your cell. Mrs Matron calls the turnkey and says simply to take me to the prison wing of Category 3. Because I am now paid to supervise the laundry I can give a lummox like him sixpence – to keep everybody sweet. A nothing price to feel your hand on my wrist dearest Alice.

And now you are here at last like a simple miscreant! I urge you to behave cunningly and well for I have plans for deliverance whether it be yours or mine. Next step is Category 1 – for I am such a friend of Mrs Matron that I can protect you in such a place as the Factory. How I wish you were a simple mean thief like your best and unworthy friend is. I could see a faster rescue for both of us. But be brave lovely Alice and keep in your heart that gravest and most crafty patience which is in you if you do not give way to useless railing. Mr and Mrs Matron have very dark souls and will howl in hell. Yet they might be used as our aid.

But what a great pity that Mrs Matron dances in towards the end of my visit and looks down her plump nose saying: This is your friend then. Nice to have a friend like this who is pretty. It is wonderful to see in her this jealousy. Yet how can she be jealous of a wretch? There is enough of her soul left that she can see how secret rooms hoarded with sugar and flour are not a sufficiency to the soul. As is your sisterhood to me!

She paid you that praise – do you remember? She praised the two of us. She tells you: You do not look like Category 3 but then you are a friend of Sarah so of course you would not have the look of a witless thief.

Her praise is as they say mixed blessings. But fear not since I ask myself the one question all the time. It is this – How to use up Mrs Matron before she uses us up.

You were thinner. That grieves me but I can bulk out your rations now you are beneath the same roof as

Your loving Sarah.

MARRIED LIFE AT NUGAN GANWAY

There was little enough nuptial holiday for Phoebe. She was impatient with the concept in any case, and determined to join our male cantonment in the bush. All the suggestions her friends made concerning the employment of convict servants she dismissed. The greatest and most miraculous index of what a spirit she had was that though trained in a Swiss academy for young women and prepared thus for the life of a European country estate managed with the help of servants, she took with a joyous zeal to the life of the bush hut. While waiting with her friends the Parslows for our marriage to take place, she had been studying books on colonial domestic management. She had the good grace to

relish our life, its awkwardness and wrong-headedness, its want of refinements. By now we had advanced from cooking the food for the
homestead on communal outdoor fires to cooking in a separate bark
outbuilding, and Phoebe joyously insisted on taking over those duties
too, with occasional advice from O'Dallow, whom she liked for his Celtic
morbidness and amusingly negative view of the world.

She cooked, for an example, a vast supply of plum duff, and O'Dallow,
sniffing it, said, 'Well they might turn up, those absconders, with this
sweetness in the air, Mrs Bettany, and then you'll have the blackguards
by the nose.'

It seemed all sin, squalor and ill will were lifted from us for a joyous
nuptial season. But neither nature nor the malice of men, which is itself
part of nature, let much stand as still as I would like it to be. Riding in
to our homestead from a visit to a southern hut one day, I found two
well-saddled horses in the stockyard with the insignia of the queen on
their blue saddlecloths and a blue-coated constable sitting on a log
conversing with the wagon-driver Clancy. Inside, a hulking police magistrate, in a navy-blue uniform with silver crown at its collar, was drinking
tea in the parlour with Phoebe, who raised a stricken face to me.

'Look who we have,' she told me. 'Police Magistrate Purler has come
all the way from Goulburn.'

She announced it politely but as if to say: Grief has too quickly entered
our lives.

I thought myself, after many years, the inflexibility of law has arrived
at Nugan Ganway – as distinct from the mere fictions of law with which
Peske had played. Yet Purler himself did not much resemble grief, being
florid, youngish, bear-like. He wore a black beard and his pistols rested
for safety's sake on a side table, dangerous beasts asleep for the
moment.

Phoebe jumped up. 'I'll get you a cup,' she announced, making for the
sideboard. But something impalpable stopped her in her tracks, as if the
task were beyond her. Had the great and glorious barbarity of Nugan
Ganway reached and overwhelmed her in that second?

'Oh my dear,' I said with both a smile and conviction, 'isn't this
precisely why we need a maid and housekeeper?'

Nonetheless I was a little mystified and concerned as I got up, took
her by the elbow and helped her back to the table, and then fetched the
cup and saucer myself. It was Spode china I had ordered from Sydney as
a sign of our increasing capacity for refinement. I should announce here

too that candles and whale-oil lamps now lit the interior of my household. Decent furniture – a bed, a table, a desk, a bookcase – had been
brought in over time by Finnerty's wagons, and an extra slab timber
bedroom appended to the one room which Long and I had previously
occupied. I had set Clancy to work lining this nuptial room with pages
from the London illustrated papers, so that the eye might equally be
caught by the visage of Lord Melbourne or 'A Vista of the Highlands'
or 'A View of Vauxhall Gardens'. Thus we now had bedroom as well as
a parlour-cum-dining room.

So I left Phoebe in her chair, in her sweet redolence and temporary
silence, and turned towards the not unpleasant, honest and horsy combination of odours from Purler's uniform.

'How can it be?' asked Phoebe suddenly, and I could see now that she
was very forlorn. 'My friend Catherine is gone.'

'The nun?' I asked, though I knew precisely whom she meant.

'I have been under insistent pressure from her superior to make
inquiry,' said Purler, 'into the whereabouts of that nun who was sent
south here with your wife. She has not returned to Goulburn. It was
presumed by some that she stayed in the bush or fled to Sydney for . . .'
Purler seemed embarrassed, '. . . for propriety's sake.'

'What do you mean, propriety?'

'Well, when the chief nun began to complain, I fear the Goulburn
authorities may have thought, "The woman has fled, has found a man."
But the chief nun went on haranguing, and so inquiries were made in
Goulburn, Yass, Parramatta, Sydney. But the woman couldn't be found
there. And so I was asked to search the country where she was last seen,
and Mrs Bettany has told me the circumstances of her parting with the
woman.'

I reached and took Phoebe's pale hand. She murmured to me, 'It was
my insistence that she come here.'

For Phoebe's sake I defended Catherine. 'She was sure of herself and
her life,' I told the magistrate. 'She is not suddenly an absconder from
what she believes so thoroughly.'

'You mention absconders. I've heard from Treloar there are two
absconders, are there not, domiciled somewhere in the mountains
beyond?'

'That's right,' I said. 'Rowan and Brody. It is the first time I have had
any word or question concerning them from anyone in an official
position.'

'Were you expecting some word?'

'Some years ago I suspected them of perhaps using and then poisoning a native woman. And of having tried to drown her child.'

'Is this true?' asked Phoebe, her green eyes widening. This was an awful shock to her image of our Australian Arcady. Until now, she probably believed she had encountered the extremes of vice chiefly in her Geneva classmates, in the young men who climbed the wall, and perhaps in unreliable Goldspink. She might think poorly of her father, but his wealth had kept her safe from the realities of the penal colony.

'But some of your fellows here, to whom I spoke, tell me these men come down to your place to shear.'

'That's right,' I admitted bravely. How could that be understood by a man who lived within limits of the sanctioned world, at Goulburn? 'I reported the death of the native woman to your predecessor Magistrate Gonfleur at Goulburn some years ago. He laughed at me, or more accurately at the possibility of doing anything.' I was becoming angry, and that was a sign that at some level of my mind I had always considered my relations with the outlaws to be improper. Nonetheless, I kept attacking. 'After all, in the case of Rowan and Brody, the law has been very late in making an appearance. And I can say of them this. In some ways they are less sly, and almost – one could say – more honest than men such as Goldspink.'

'Well, Treloar likes him not for his character but because he has done a good pastoral job,' said Purler. 'Mr Treloar has many interests, and is more concerned, I'd say, in a chap's capacity to keep shepherds and stockmen in order than in his moral fibre. And it seems that, like you, Goldspink welcomed the absconders, Rowan and Brody.'

I felt a surge of irritation at being associated with Goldspink, as if I were an equally chancy source of information.

'These associations – I'll say it again – they began before the government of Great Britain or of New South Wales recognised the existence of Nugan Ganway or Treloar's Bulwa Mountain. They are not chosen arrangements. They have been forced upon us by the peculiar nature of what we are doing, without the benefit of advice from magistrates.'

Magistrate Purler drew his chin in and sat back. 'I can assure you I am not unacquainted with the circumstances under which this country was occupied, Mr Bettany.'

I looked at this man, probably an English gentleman farmer's son with a grammar school education, who now exercised in a most distant wing of New South Wales the blunt and not particularly refined power to sentence recalcitrant convicts to fifty lashes, to return women to the Female Factory, and, if he could find them, to return absconders to a fierce retribution. I had to admit, though, there was a worldly under-standing in the way with which he had dealt with my momentary vexation.

'Catherine. That's the question. Where is she?' said Phoebe, dragging Purler and myself back to the real issue. Then Phoebe uttered a sentiment which could equally be applied to herself as to the nun. 'Her faith was so simple that one can't bear to think of her coming to harm.'

The police magistrate looked at me, and I could now see that he knew more than he was saying.

'Goldspink,' he murmured, 'who buys illegal moonshine from the absconders, and perhaps the occasional other person's cattle, said that he saw them recently, that they arrived in a four-wheeler. I asked him, where would they get a four-wheeler? He told me that he never inquired too closely into anything concerning them, he made points not dissimilar to your own, but did so with more heat and less grace than you have shown, Mr Bettany. He says he saw them go off then, one of them driving the four-wheeler, the other riding beside him and leading a horse. So they vanished. He had feared they had got the vehicle from you, but knew the dangers of questioning them too closely on that.'

I told the magistrate that I had not owned a four-wheeler until a little time before the wedding. Magistrate Purler gave out a huge sigh over his tea cup. 'A four-wheeler might not be very serviceable where they were going, in the wild mountains. Perhaps they had a buyer in mind. Perhaps they merely meant to take it out of our sight.'

'Please,' said Phoebe, standing, her hands trembling, 'I shall make more tea.'

We both said no need, but could see that she wanted to be busy. She went out to our primitive bark kitchen.

'Spode china,' Purler murmured to me, smiling without malice. 'And yet the young lady insists on doing all her own work.'

'She is involved in her bush idyll, Mr Purler, God bless her. It takes a little time to find out that there are serpents in the garden.'

'Oh, that there are. I chose not to tell you this while your wife was here. One of my native trackers of the border police has already indeed found the nun's body high up in the direction of Mount Bimberi beyond Mount Bulwa. She was many weeks deceased, her clothing was scattered, and according to Doctor Alladair of Cooma Creek her neck had been broken. Either she had been taken there and killed or killed elsewhere and thrown there!'

I groaned and called to dear God, all the useless utterances of a bereavement. That this good woman could come all this way voluntarily on a convict transport and die horribly on a distant, unearthly mountain.

'What did you do with the remains?' I asked, knowing as if by instinct how important such a consideration would have been for Catherine.

'Perforce we had to bury them where they lay,' Purler told me. 'We lacked lead-lined coffins and such. I believe that this woman's sisters in Goulburn are quite desolate and will later translate it to Goulburn, since they think the nun a martyr of the new country.'

So now I began to calculate the culprits. Could it have been the Moth people who had attacked and desecrated handsome Catherine? That was not likely, I thought. It might have been one or other of Goldspink's shepherds, and Goldspink himself had the credibly sly fury in him to do it. But he said he had seen the absconders with a four-wheeler. Their possible guilt must be tested as a first option.

'We must watch Goldspink,' I told Purler, 'but above all we must find Rowan and Brody.'

I realised that this was the long-delayed business pending for Nugan Ganway. Though the Captain and Tadgh had often enough discovered me, I knew that the day would come when I must discover them. I wanted very much to weigh in their presence the question as to whether they had ravaged and killed the dedicated Catherine.

'You will assist with your men?' Purler asked.

'I will assist. Two of them speak the same tongue as the absconders.'

We agreed that with three of my men – Long, Clancy, Presscart – I would meet him and his border police at Treloar's at noon in three days time. That much was easy to organise. The hard thing came after Purler, refusing my hospitality for the night and wanting to rejoin his border police detachment, rode away and left me to go to our bark and slab kitchen and tell Phoebe that her friend and fellow pilgrim had been found murdered and misused. Phoebe had been cooking lamb by the recipe out of a book named *Food Selection and Preparation*, and now she kept absentmindedly basting while looking at me with mute horror. I stressed murder, rather than rape. I told her I must join the search for the killers. But O'Dallow would stand watch at Nugan Ganway. She had nothing to fear. With summer ended, the Moth people were gone.

'I am not afraid of the Moth people anyhow,' she told me through tears. I felt her desolation: the great adventure of her marriage, the story designed to one day enchant grandchildren, had turned on her like a cunning device. The decent impulses of adventure which had united two such different women as herself and Catherine and were driven by her brave blood and imagination had helped produce this obscene and dreadful result.

She insisted on cooking the lamb superbly, as lamb had never before been cooked on Nugan Ganway, but then ate none of it. I ended in taking it to the men, who fell on it with eager appetite. I found Phoebe waiting for me on the verandah when I returned, gave her some brandy, helped her to our bed and kept strong hold of her hand as she closed her eyes on a world she had thought, till this afternoon, to be the landscape of assured happiness.

Three days later I arrived with Long and Presscart at Goldspink's homestead to find a detachment of border police and a black tracker – a native man of diminutive size recruited from some other region, dressed in blue coat and breeches but utterly barefoot – all under the overall command of Purler. But also on the verandah sat my friend Peske, in his green Land Commissioner's jacket.

'Awful business, old man,' he called with an absolutely contented smile. 'I trust it hasn't distressed your dear little girl too much.' His coat was hung about with two bandoliers and a cartridge belt, and he looked fit to munition the entire expedition.

Everybody was of sober demeanour and Purler seemed to have taken on a higher seriousness than he had displayed at Nugan Ganway, and certainly a more intense air of command. Goldspink was bustling about, boiling water for tea, but booted and ready to ride himself. He suggested to Purler that this was an hour and an expedition where a little spirits might have been forgivable or even to be advised. But Purler, enormous in his uniform and sheepskin coat, ignored him.

'We have two trackers,' Peske told me, his persistent good humour and blitheness making me doubt his good sense. 'Friend Purler's first chap is already out along the trail of these rogues a little. These Waradgery trackers are utter wizards. They can sort out trace from trace, and from right here in the yard the fellow picked precisely the tracks Goldspink reported – a four-wheeler, two horses, one led, one ridden.'

He settled back, utterly happy with every aspect of the colony and its gradual reaching out for absconders and like anachronisms.

Indoors, we supplemented the mutton in our saddlebags with some of
Goldspink's fresh damper, and by the time I got out into the yard, a tall
tracker was there, returned from his reconnaissance, a great frown on
his long flat forehead as he talked to Purler.

'I find 'em, Mr Purler,' I heard him say. 'Goan off toward them fellers
there.' And the 'fellers' he pointed to were the tangle of mountains almost
directly west – quite credibly so, since it was a stretch of country named
the Kiandra, whose ownership was uncertain, whose precipitous gorges
we avoided, and towards which even Long's attitude, if he suspected
cattle had wandered somewhere in that locality, was very nearly one of
resignation.

'They couldn't get a four-wheeler up there,' I heard Peske say.

At last we set off behind Purler's trackers, who rode barefooted in
their police pants and engaged in a sort of shy collaboration at the head
of our party. I rode Hobbes, who still served me and was now a mature
beast of eight years, and had learned a kind of endurance and patience,
I believed, not common in the horses of Van Diemen's Land. On gradually rising ground, first open, then wooded, the trackers would pause
now and then to drop to the ground and discuss matters in the brisk,
elliptical language which sounded like that of the Moth people but which
was very likely different.

According to the trackers the two absconders had somehow got the
four-wheeler up here, bouncing its ironbound wheels over rocks. At dusk
the trackers led us to the edge of the ridge we were then on and pointed
out to us the wreckage of the four-wheeler at the bottom of the drop.
Purler and one of the trackers climbed down to it. 'No horse down here,'
Purler called to us, though we could see that already. So they had taken
the horse out of its traces and pushed the dray over the edge, giving up
the crazy struggle with the terrain. After further conference at the top of
the ridge, the police trackers told us that after the vehicle had been
pushed into the abyss, the three horses had continued along the ridge,
two horsemen leading the carriage horse.

Things were looking very poor for Rowan and Brody, and we moved
with greater wariness. We were running out of light when we came upon
a primitive pot still. It sat on a dry stone mount above a quenched fire.
This must have been the fire from which the absconders had supplied
themselves and my outlying shepherds with moonshine, hauling up stolen
sacks of grain for distillation. So we were now close to them, perhaps as
close as two or three miles. A grey, wispy dusk was falling, and already

there was a sense of an early seasonal frost. So, uneasy, we were forced to camp.

There were three languages in that camp – the trackers discoursed in some brand of Waradgery, and Long strolled over to a second fire and spoke his Gaelic earnestly to some of the Irish constables of the border police. He once provoked hard laughter with something he said, but he was not himself, for the crime weighed on him.

Though we needed them high, we kept the fires low, having circled them with substantial stones which we dragged up one by one to hem in the modest flames lest they be seen by the absconders. Peske prattled on in a fraternal murmur, speaking of his fiancée's family, who were settlers at Gundaroo. He was very proud of his future wife. She was colonial-born, he said, and less affected than some others. It was a sentiment which, given his own affectations, caused Purler and myself to smile.

I was prompted to muse what Horace would have made of our miserable, drizzly, sparely warmed camp. He would of course have a sentiment for it. 'Contracto melius parve cupidine vestigalia porrigam ... By narrowing my desires I shall increase my real revenues.' But, having thrown away his shield and renounced militancy in his youth, he would not have much liked this wineless, songless place.

The dawn came up grey, and with a snarling wind. We revived a portion of ashes for tea and ate cold damper and slab mutton. We left our horses, hobbled, behind. Our party edged forward silently behind the trackers, who would now and then noiselessly turn to make hushing motions with their hands. At last the shorter black tracker came back and told Purler that the absconders' hut was due ahead.

The hut we sighted in a frosty clearing up through the trees above us was, in a colony of mean dwellings, the most miserable habitation I had ever seen. Clay caulking had fallen out of the cracks between slabs, and wind and rain seemed welcome to enter. The rickety bark roof looked ripe to be blown away. Convict shepherds were lords by comparison. Though around every homestead lies an accumulation of bleached bones and partial skeletons of sheep and cattle, the ramshackle little refuge of Rowan and Brody was surrounded by absolute ramparts and hedges of white, the remains of livestock shot and eaten to sustain their years beyond the law. Amongst the bones, the three horses of the household grazed.

The first human movement we saw was of a shivering native woman dressed merely in a man's shirt who emerged and hurled in our direction the night waste of the absconders. She went inside and then the Captain, Rowan, strolled out smoking a pipe in his shirt sleeves, a hardy creature, one had to give him that. Purler had just then sent some of his troopers around the clearing, to the back of the hut. The border police had a repute for clumsiness and I feared that Rowan, smoking and exchanging some words with the three horses in his yard, might look up at once, aghast, hearing the infallible noise of encirclement. But he went on chatting to himself, a man who seemed so normal that it was hard mentally to assign to him the savagery of which he was apparently guilty. Yet one of his three horses looked to me to be very close to the one I remembered from Sister Catherine's four-wheeler.

'We will talk to him now,' murmured Purler to me.

Goldspink, on my left, heard this. 'Sir,' he suggested, 'shoot the bastard.'

'It isn't appropriate,' said Purler dismissively.

'Do we need to wait for Brody to present himself?' I asked.

'I take your point,' said Purler. 'Better to.'

But at that second Brody himself appeared anyhow, in breeches and flannel shirt, sniffed the cold, high air, raised his quite boyish features to the leaden sky and exchanged an observation with his companion. Rising now behind a shaggy-barked gum tree and stepping around it, Purler cried without any excessive tones of drama, 'Peter Rowan and James Brody. From the evidence as it exists I am required to question you about the murder of a woman. I think you know which woman. Don't look that way – my men are there also.' Brody seemed to be about to take flight. 'Order your friend Brody to be still, Rowan. Persuade him of it, like a good fellow!'

But Brody did not cease backing, and Rowan himself, though he had not stopped smoking and had laid what seemed a very unsurprised eye upon us, turned and ran with his young companion into the hut. Long, the coolest of men, the one most appalled by this crime, most ashamed of it, stood and shot off his carbine, and the bullet struck Rowan in the hip. If he lives, thought I crazily, he will have that to show with the scars on his back. Rowan was however not the sort of man to be stopped by any wound short of a fatal one, and Brody and he crashed through their door and into their hut, which was at once pushed shut. Within seconds, while we – in a very unmilitary manner – were still standing there in view on the clearing's edge, a torrent of fire poured through the window flaps of the hut. One would have thought the absconders were firing pistols and carbines two-handed, or that the native woman was reloading for them, or that they possessed a depot of armaments. I could feel the velocity of musket and pistol balls all around me, but had a novice's immunity to them.

There was a pause then, in which we all walked back to the shelter of the trees, quite calmly. Peske, who proved to be the only casualty, held up a shattered, bloody hand. 'Well, it's not my writing hand,' he managed.

Once we had tree trunks between us and the absconders, in a sensible voice Purler called upon them to come out. They fired again – we could hear bullets thrashing foliage and embedding in wood, yet once again we were charmed and none of us were struck. We poured in a fire of our own, and I observed that one of Purler's constables was binding up Peske's hand, Peske himself unsuccessfully attempting to move his fingers, and not seeming very upset when he could not.

Purler asked that they let the native woman out of the hut, since her howling was pitiful. This, after a time, happened – the door opened and the woman came running towards us, keening, galloping through our thin ranks. We let her go thinking she could be retrieved and fed and consoled if necessary. But we would never see her again. Events in the clearing would delay us too long.

Purler called on us all to blaze away now. With my new carbine I shot the bark door to shreds, thinking that such a demonstration would surely persuade them to emerge. They abandoned the hut rightly enough, with an athletic suddenness, raging out the door, Rowan not slowed at all by his wound. It was, as we all decided later, a form of suicide but one which put the onus of despatching them fairly and squarely upon us. At the time, I think it fair to say, they frightened us, these primitive men stranger than savages, so far beyond our interpretation, moral or social, howling down on us in their shirt sleeves, a carbine in one hand and pistol in the other. I know that my ball was one of those which entered Rowan, and those who discharged carbines to my right tore Brody's body to pieces.

Approaching the fallen absconders in sudden silence, we saw that Rowan had his face to the sky, and although his shirt was utterly soaked with blood from his chest, he was capable of calling robustly again and again, something which sounded to me like 'Olung! Olung!' An energetic Goldspink was the first to reach him, and put his carbine to Rowan's head, ready to dispatch him finally. Long, however, pushed him aside, crying, 'Keep your distance, you pagan bastard!'

The fact was that Rowan had been calling for Long in Irish.

His lips frothing redly, Rowan had his last conversation of all with Long in the Gaelic tongue, and, occasionally looking sideways at the rest of us, Long sombrely listened and answered, tears falling down his cheeks.

'Aye,' Goldspink told me, 'those bastards stick together in their gibberage.'

Long stood up as if to talk to us, and Rowan howled, 'Into your hands I commit my spirit.' His wounds were appalling, and without another word Long turned the barrel of Rowan's own undischarged carbine to the man's head and fired. The trackers keened, and one of the border policemen was as ill as I wished to be.

'Why, sir, in God's name and on whose authority did you do that?' Purler roared at Long.

'He would not have lived to be moved.'

'I'll have you flogged.'

'It will add to the gore of the day,' said Long.

Purler stood, audibly snorting. 'And did he make a confession?'

'He did not, sir,' said Long, 'but asked for pardon.'

'Pardon?' asked Peske, his lips drawn back now with the increasing pain of his wound.

I noticed Long go across the clearing and speak to Clancy, who had hung his head against a tree like one drained of strength. 'No false tears, Yankee,' he said. 'It's the way of this awful world, that's all.'

The first winter of our marriage was one of poor rain. Little snow fell on the distant hills, and hardly any on our pastures. Some two thousand of the Merinos died famished and were devoured by crows, and the increase at lambing was the poorest to that time. Yet we got the wool in that year, and Phoebe insisted upon cooking for the men, a task so endless that I began to suspect that she might need two servants, not one. Phoebe rode beside me in a convoy as Clancy and seven others, some hired from the new hamlet of Cooma Creek, dragged our wool to Mr Barley. My wife was a wonderful horsewoman, able to gallop side-saddle, one dress-clad knee hooked up over the pommel in a manner perhaps considered not totally acceptable in Europe, or even closer in Sydney, but of adequate modesty to any fair observer and warranted here by the uneven nature of the countryside.

Phoebe had gradually softened a little her uncompromising attitude towards living her life in the bush to the full limit of its harshness. I was surprised but pleased when she let me pay £80 to buy a better carriage than we had driven in until now, a well-sprung phaeton and a team of horses from a gentleman recently arrived in Cooma Creek, a young Scot called Dr Alladair, who needed the price of the vehicle to establish his medical practice there. So a physician had arrived as close as thirty miles from the Nugan Ganway homestead. I resolved to keep a watch on his behaviour and repute, for if Phoebe was to bear children and consent to give birth at Cooma Creek, to which I could be easily summoned, he might act as her physician.

Phoebe travelled with me in our new four-wheeler, with Hobbes and her favourite mare Glory trotting empty-saddled behind. There were to be encountered, despite the brown-greyness of the plain, some wonders of an enlarging world. North of Bredbo, on the borders of the County of Argyle, a young Jew, a relative of Mandelson, had built a stone inn. His dark-eyed wife made a great deal of Phoebe, for Phoebe constituted a promise that no wild borders which she inhabited could be taken as utterly barbarous. While Phoebe and I occupied one of the rooms, Clancy and the wagoneers slept beneath the loads of fleece.

A little way along the track the next morning we met a curiously laden wagon coming south and accompanied by Mr Treloar on horseback.

'Mr Bettany,' he cried, admiring my four-wheeler, 'you travel in elegance.'

I had met my neighbour only once before, in Sydney at the Squatters' Ball. Encountering his square and rather jaundiced face there – he was a man of perhaps fifty years – I had never forgotten that he was once willing to be a cohort with Mr Finlay in my ejection from Nugan Ganway. Naturally I treated him politely rather than as a friend, and I looked about for casual topics of conversation, of which the most obvious was the enormous steel pot atop his wagon.

'Oh,' he said, 'that is a boiler. Didn't you know that closer in those of us who are left in the wool trade have taken recourse to boiling the sheep for tallow. Boiled up the sheep are worth something in the London market. I admire your bravery in taking wool to Sydney.'

'I have not been told otherwise by my agent,' I said. 'He must consider a market still exists.'

'Some bailiffs were selling sheep they had seized for tuppence a head,' Treloar told me. 'Until they calculated they were worth 6 shillings boiled to tallow. And at such a time as this the governor chooses to appoint

Protectors of Aborigines, to prevent us dealing with those who spear our devalued stock! It is the Whig sensibility run mad!'

'Is that why you have moved your overseer?' For Long had darkly told me, soon after the deaths of the absconders, that he had gone to visit Goldspink on some business or other and Goldspink was gone, across the alps, to a new station of Treloar's.

'Yes, he works well and frightens the savages, but that is not permitted any more! So I have moved him over the alps where he can at least competently work without hindrances such as Protectors, or Weepers, or Creepers, or whatever His Excellency might call them.'

After a few more complaints about the efforts of government and markets to cramp his income, he excused himself and caught up with his wagon and boiler.

In Goulburn we took rooms at Mandelson's Hotel, where Phoebe was to my surprise persuaded to wait for me while I rushed the wagons to Barley. We had no intention of approaching the Finlay house but, at my urging, Phoebe let her mother know that we had rooms at Mandelson's Hotel. Mrs Finlay, her eyes still seeming bruised as if from within, had the grace to come. She entered from the stable wearing a veil and avoiding servants. 'No one will ever succeed in making me slink in that manner,' Phoebe later declared. Seeing her married daughter in the parlour of our rooms, she began to weep, and Phoebe joined her in tears.

'When I think it might have been both of you,' said Mrs Finlay, referring to Catherine's murder, which had been canvassed in all the papers, and about which a booklet, *The Fatal End of Rowan and Brody*, had been published in Sydney.

'But the men are dead now,' Phoebe reassured her mother.

I wondered if Mrs Finlay could read in her daughter's demeanour that Phoebe had proved herself to be more than an unworldly, novel-skewed maiden. But her concerns seemed, at this meeting, elsewhere. I had heard tales of Mr Finlay's shrinkage as a grandee, all due to heavy borrowings and the fall in wool price. But I could not believe that Mr Finlay was in any serious danger – if there was shrinkage, he was well-placed to bear it. The sadness in my mother-in-law's eyes surely arose from some other source than business.

When I found some excuse to leave them for a while, Mrs Finlay told Phoebe that when our wedding banns had been read in the church in Braidwood and noted in the *Goulburn Herald*, Mr Finlay had consulted lawyers about stopping the marriage, but Phoebe was, by a mere few months, old enough to dispense with parental permission. He had of course angrily adjusted his will. But, said Mrs Finlay, life was now teaching him that he was not a god, and he hoped, and she hoped, for a reconciliation.

Phoebe, more like her father than she knew, said to me, 'He will need to be appeasing indeed to win back my duty.'

I had time before setting out again to take Phoebe to Mr Loosely's to see Felix, now some nine years old. Felix was brought into the parlour and seemed both robust and sober, bowing in a genteel manner towards Phoebe. I was filled with sufficient admiration and affection that I was tempted to take him back to Nugan Ganway there and then, and he increased the desire by reading at Mr Loosely's request from an essay of Praed's and some Latin verse from Ovid. But it would be criminal of me to foreshorten an education which was proceeding so well.

Nonetheless, Mr Loosely did not seem as exhilarated by the skill of Felix as he was depressed by what he called in my presence 'the pervasive oafishness of the colonial children'. We greeted the child Hector, too, who was happily and aimlessly digging up mud in the black soil of the academy yard. I asked Loosely, 'Does Hector not possess the genius of his cousin Felix?' The master made a strange gesture as if plucking an invisible apple from the air.

'He is of course of the full blood native strain, and perhaps the light within him has further to travel to reach the surface.' As if he meant to illustrate this point in mime, Loosely raised both hands close to his face and vibrated them. 'But the light will emerge from beneath the nomadic overlay, I am sure.'

I was saddened to see that it was not only in Mr Loosely that a species of desperate wistfulness resided, but – as we rode back to Mandelson's for our dinner – in Phoebe as well. We ate in the hotel dining room, and her polite near-silence lasted through soup. After I had asked her five times whether she was well, she said that if she told me what was plaguing her peace I would hate her. I insisted that hatred was out of the question; so was displeasure. She said then in a small voice, 'It has been known for men alone in remote regions to make bushwives out of the native women ...'

That was it: she had wondered whether I had had such a wife and whether Felix was somehow my son! I was able to laugh, and reassure her, but with some guilt burning on my palate, deriving from my association with the woman Cecily.

'Consult the calendar,' I said jovially, to show I did not feel offended. 'I have been in New South Wales seven years. Felix is nine or perhaps ten years old.'

She became confused with shame and incoherent with apology. 'I didn't mean to ... Any insane fancy will arise and stick in me as if it were a real thing ... Any insane fancy ... How can you begin to overlook ...?' And so she unnecessarily went on.

I closed my hand on hers. It was a joy to bring her simple soothing.

Leaving Phoebe in the Mandelsons' care, and in the teeth of all the decline recorded by both the *Heralds*, Goulburn and Sydney, I drove my wool to Sydney. The country was browned by drought, far worse than Nugan Ganway. Boiling-down works mounted on ovens of brick or stone were burning sullenly in every town and, it seemed, littered every dusty pasture. The livestock of New South Wales was being rendered by slow fire: hoof, fleece, bone, hide. The air possessed a leaden taint, and vistas were hidden by malodorous smoke. What would a settler think, travelling this road for the first time, a stench of failure pervading the air?

Yet an undefeated Mr Barley was reliably waiting for me in his glossy blue phaeton, but in a less crazed and competitive atmosphere, at the Black Huts. He could, because he was able to store for better days, offer me 4 pence per pound. Why were others not availing themselves of his generosity? I asked ironically.

'My friend Bettany,' he murmured. 'One more bad year and I will be finished for storage room and up to my rafters. My rudder and spouse says to me, "How can'st thou be sure wool will ever come back, and for that matter, rain will ever come back?" And I say, "Mrs Barley, my dear, there will always be need of worsted." And I hope to dear Lord I'm right.'

'Amen,' I supplied. 'I have been lucky.'

'You have been wise, friend Bettany. You have not spent wild money on overpriced acreage. You have set aside, and banks owe you and not otherwise. You've done it exemplary. All shall be creamy with you, I'm sure.'

We dined at the Dangling Man, less than a feverish place now, barely discernible as the scene of my earlier folly. We were the only ones that evening in the dining room, and had it not been for the raucousness of the wagoners in the taproom the place would have utterly lacked liveliness. I had the supreme excuse of Phoebe not to linger there more than a night, but turned back with my own two wagons the next morning, allowing my chartered ones to bear the wool clip on to Barley's warehouses.

I drove the four-wheeler hard for Goulburn and was delighted to enter

Mandelson's and find Phoebe, plumper and looking healthy on Mrs Mandelson's cuisine and playing the piano like one of the family. She had had another visit from her mother, but was delighted to board the phaeton again and roll home.

Some acts of hostility from the Moth people occurred that summer. One morning a hutkeeper arrived with the news that during the night there had been some sort of hecatomb of animals. O'Dallow and I rode out and found at an open plain we had named Ten Mile, an aggrieved convict shepherd standing watch over a wattle-fenced fold in which some hundreds of sheep lay massed in death from spear wounds and clubbing. There appeared to be no purpose of sustenance – a few tails had been cut off as a delicacy, it seemed, but only as an afterthought.

On journeys to my sundry outposts I took a few of my men on a swing into the ranges, in the hope of meeting Durra. By this time he had been the recipient of an especially engraved chain ordered from Goulburn, with his name on it, a chain which he had accepted with laughter but also with solemnity – a symbol of the pictographic pact I had shown him and which he gave every evidence of understanding.

Phoebe often rode with me on these journeys. One day when we were riding north-west, to the shepherding station we called Presscart's, some younger native men approached gesturing with spears and clubs, and screaming something akin to 'Mallah! Mallah!' at us.

Long cried, 'Speared sheep, you blackguards! Not good! Not good at all!'

But I did wonder whether Shegog's disease was running in their women, fouling their families, and it was for that they had made a wanton slaughter of sheep.

Phoebe, splendidly brave, soothed her horse, and seemed to bring curiosity rather than dread to her first sighting of the natives.

No other molestations occurred that summer.

It was a delight to wake one morning in March and hear a thunder of rain and detect, through the threads of water pouring on the floor, the weak points in our bark roof. In my joy I stood directly under one such shower-bath, still wearing my nightdress, while Phoebe laughed like a bell, and then, the merriment still in her voice, told me that she believed herself with child. Thus, she went on solemnly, as if I might be disappointed, she could not ride out with me for the time being.

My delight was tempered by the fact she proposed to give birth at Nugan Ganway without any help except the assistance of nature. I had other plans – perhaps she could be with her friends the Parslows near Braidwood, or she could take a lodging at Cooma Creek where the young Scots physician, Alladair, had opened his surgery. I returned to the subject of female servants for Phoebe.

I asked Long one day, 'You know a reliable convict woman, haven't I heard you say?'

'She is a solid girl,' he said, 'and no trouble-maker. Since they found the Matron and Steward of the Factory to be dishonest she's been at work at a magistrate's house but says she would prefer a remoter post.'

I asked him did he have the woman's address, and it appeared he had received a letter from her. He had not brought it to me to be read. Perhaps he found tedious the counsels which had attended my earlier reading of his letter from his family, and had gone to one of the literate stockmen like Presscart. Her post with a magistrate westwards of Sydney was a temporary one, and she would soon be advertised in the *Government Gazette*, said Long, and may even have been already applied for. After all, she could read and write fluently.

I questioned him about her character, since he did not seem to make mistakes in these matters. Could she be trusted to take up a firearm if that became necessary for the protection of my wife? He was sure the woman would be a true companion to Mrs Bettany.

I thought it best to write directly to the Parramatta magistrate for whom this woman, Sarah Bernard, was presently in service. But first I must persuade Phoebe.

I broached the subject over tea one afternoon, as the air was full of curlew and currawong cries which seemed no more than the voice of a wistful earth on the edge of our particular high pasture winter. She must have a companion, I insisted. Surely she did not wish to go on cooking and maintaining our hut throughout the hardships of motherhood.

'I would be happy to,' she told me.

'But I don't wish you to become a drudge.'

'Do you think I look a drudge? Is that the news you attempt to break to me by talking about housekeepers?'

But she was not serious.

'You are a rose,' I told her. 'You are a rose and you are aware you are. That is not the matter of argument.'

'What is this woman's name?'

'Her name is Sarah Bernard. She is known to Long from his days as a constable.'

I knew she trusted Long.

'So Long thinks her nice and wants her here. It is not my place in life to accommodate Eros for Long's sake.'

'Is that how lowly you think of Long? Long and Eros have nothing to do with the question.'

So blithely do we make pronouncements which later recoil and grind our flesh.

Phoebe said, 'Well, I am reconciled to try her for three months. If I do not like her, I shall return her to the depot without prejudice and without any debate.'

And it was, I knew, futile to enter into debate – she brought to everything the same mental rigour she had brought to achieving our marriage. For example, I often thought of vain and obdurate Mr Finlay with flinches of regret, but not – it seemed – Phoebe, who had the courage to lead a ruthless life. I was delighted to have wed such a woman warrior.

SARAH BERNARD HAD BEEN QUICKLY DISENCHANTED by her friend's presence in the Factory, and Alice Adread seemed to spark a series of rapid changes there.

Letter No 8, SARAH BERNARD

Friend Alice

I write because such is my shock. I cannot tell you the horror of seeing you appear at the Pallmire table when you were meant to be safe from them in your cell. It is my fault that Matron Pallmire saw you and set out to sully things. So now you live in two places: the house of the Matron and Steward on one side and on the other your little Category 3 cell. I ever wished to release you from the cells by my means not theirs.

It does not seem right of you to drink rum at their breakfast table. Oh my friend you seemed to drink it in delight and were winking and smiling at him. I know women in our position lack a choice. But should the choice be winking and smiling at the beast? Oh I confess that I am not in such a pure condition as to make any hard judgements on the matter. And perhaps your seeming jollity was despair with a grin.

I can give no counsel but to say: Do not sink to smile and chortle with them. My mind races on your behalf. You must understand that if you

*are discovered by Surgeon or Magistrate to be out of your cell you will
be blamed and the Pallmires will explain it away and keep their power.
They have all the world under a spell.*

I notice how you cough when the rum hits your throat. Are you sickening? How I hope not!

For I am still your friend named

Sarah

Alice Aldread was quick and heated with a reply.

Sarah

*Well they have me back in my cell now since Visiting Surgeon is coming
and Mr Pallmire absent! And you are right to say you cannot judge my
laughing and seeming jolly. You may keep a long face and think there is
nothing worse than the company of Mr and Mrs. So you want a long
face from me too. But to me the worse thing is the cell we Class 3 women
have to sit in with knees to chin. You know well I was never a girl to
be shut in. Confined. I would have gone mad on old* Whisper *but for
you with me.*

*But that Class 3 cell where I now spend two nights and should spend
seven is worse to me than Mr Pallmire. So there is no sense in you writing
a letter saying Mr Pallmire is worse when I know to be shut in is worse.
In this world all is use! And I would rather be used in a clean house
than in a dirty little cell of seven feet length.*

*I am not a girl for crying out Alas and Woe is me. So do not take time
to be shocked or to be a judge!*

*You say in every letter: friend – good friend – best friend. And I tell
you that all these thoughts of defeating this man Pallmire and this woman
are a mad thing. You will not do it. For it cannot be done. You must
wait and be reconciled. You cannot rescue yourself. You cannot rescue
me. And better not to try.*

And my cough. I have been coughing since Whisper *so nothing new.
It is improved not harmed by kitchen warmth and rum. For I like rum.
It is a poison I admire. What is to be said then? What is to be done?
The asylum was one room in hell and this another and we move about
them. That is the story. The story of Sarah and her dear friend*

Alice

And so a reply from Sarah.

Letter No 9, SARAH BERNARD

Friend Alice
You say to me I cannot bring about a rescue! And I tell you I shall not
cease to try. As to you playing up so to Mr and Mrs I can only agree
that women are mysterious creatures and cannot be easily read or judged
by any other soul. I mean with a greater fervour than ever to liberate
you and I have started to take measure of all that Mr and Mrs Pallmire
hold in their house. Do you know that in a side room intended for chil-
dren some two hundred pounds of soap is stored in wax paper? Where
children should sing dumb soap sits.

Lady Gipps the wife of the Governor has asked for some well-behaved
women to be sent to her – the list to be made up by Mrs Matron. The
good Lady Gipps wishes these women to visit Government House for
needlework lessons. Says Mrs Matron: It is lovely! Wait until you see it!
So from the way she talks it seems my name is to go on the list. Is this
the opening of the cell door for us unhappy girls? Being your true friend
who does not judge but now signs herself

Sarah

It seemed that Sarah Bernard was daily moved to prove to Alice that
useful efforts might be made against the Pallmires' interests.

Letter No 10, SARAH BERNARD

My dearest Alice
I have learned sewing on the verandah and in the parlours of Govern-
ment House. This is a habitation of grace and light as Mrs Matron has
said. The wife of the Governor walks from one to another of us. She is
very lean and very pale and I think not so well. Her scent is of a coldness
and a holiness. When my old papa the Jew decided I must be shown the
good order of the Christian faith and how it was all white linen and
calmness and no ranting Hassids he took me to St Anne Tib Street. There
was a cold and calm came down in the second after the candles were
snuffed. To my ear and nose Lady Gipps has this same calm and holy
coldness. It is only when we leave her house and start off back to the
Factory that the heat rises up off the clay pan and flies crawl without a
by your leave into our eyes – as if we were already dead. Only then do
we feel the state of bondage reach out and take us in again.

This Lady Gipps is the woman to hope in though – when they are finished it is to her I must hand over my lists of what Mr and Mrs Matron retain in their house. Then I would hope we – you and I Alice – will have a proper reward and dignity. But how can a person be sure that they and not you are punished? That is the pause on all I do.

And one other thing is true. I understand your laughter yet every time I hear it I am sapped of will and find reason for delay where I should find reason for daring. But I shall look for the opening to be brave and be clever for the sake of my dear friend despite all.

You might destroy me with this letter but I trust you not to. As for your most loving friend it is still

Sarah

A firm answer came from Alice.

Sar

For now we must be content I think with what we see of each other in Tory and at the house of Mrs Matron! You should not write letters since it is dangerous to us both. I know not where you keep safe your letters and lists and other guff you write. You tell me you make out copies of all you write to me. It is as if you wish to show God what you have written, or at least some gentleman somewhere. Well that is you! That is your nature Sar – that you write and copy and I do not quarrel with it!

Let us just exchange a word when we can rather than the letters. I am sick of eating paper since there is no hiding place for me whether in the Class 3 cell or in the house. And what is the use? You say Sar that you want to do this and dream of doing that but all you have done till now is enjoy the smell of Mrs Governor. Until there is something done there is nothing to write.

I am still your friend.

Alice

Driven by such scorn, Sarah Bernard took her extreme risk.

Letter No 11, SARAH BERNARD

Marked by her hand: THIS MUST BE DESTROYED
Dearest Alice
I am still – as you see from this – in ownership of some of the blue government paper which Mrs Pallmire hoards. But despite my supply I had recently heeded your call not to write about helpless intentions of mine which never come to ought. Well things have come to more than ought now for I have done what I proposed to do. It was when I saw he had given you a blue kerchief for round your neck. It was a mark of such a special favour and when Mrs Matron saw it I could see in her eyes that she was lost – she looked like a girl who is snubbed by a boy.

And now we shall see what our friendship is because if you were to show this letter to Mr Pallmire or pass on the news of my purpose then I would know your constant friendship has been altered for the worse by Mr Pallmire. But you are not to be angry to hear me say I am willing to be sunk in a hole in the earth or drowned or strangled or sent to the Hunter River or Norfolk Island or whatever Mr Pallmire might do to protect his place in the earth.

I have heard too the sewing classes at Government House are coming to an end because of Mrs Governor being poor in health. Mrs Matron says the good woman is bound to return to England soon for she has the notion and desire to breathe her last at the house of her parents. This makes me understand my dear friend that I must act soon.

I have made a copy for you of what I write to Mrs Governor. And I mean to put in her hands all the accounting I have made of things stored in the rooms of the Pallmires. And again I wish to know if you are my friend since I mean to tell you where I hide the record of all hoarded stock. It is under tea chests in one of the rooms. Since there is no bottom to the avarice of this couple and the childless yearning of Mrs Pallmire for loot and bounty I have hid my record under stores she does not need yet will never dispose of. I tell you for I wish to know whether you are still my Alice or the Alice of Mr Pallmire.

Here is what I mean to hand to Mrs Governor at the next and last needlework class:

Madam the wife of the Governor
Parramatta
New South Wales
Dear Lady Gipps
I trust you to see to it that – in saying what no one else will say – I am protected and awarded the favour of my Ticket of Leave which is due in a little time in any case.

I join to this letter the lists I have made of all the goods the Steward and Matron Pallmire have kept in their house for their own joy and use and profit without the knowledge of the Governor and against the interests of the poor women in their charge. I have put on each page the date on which this measure of goods was held in their house and counted by me. As for the butchery a day of inspection would show that the better cuts do not go from there to the women of the cells and Tories but to the sundry butchers of the town. I know from your dear presence that you would not be pleased to hear of this misuse of goods and of prisoners. I know that though your gaze is mild it is also strait.

As well as this Mr Matron misuses a Category 3 woman whom he keeps increasingly in his house. This is in no way the fault of the poor girl – it is Mr Pallmire who orders it of a girl who has no power.

I trust all my future and my very breath into your hands. And I trust above all into your hands that poor Category 3 girl whose name is Alice Aldread. She is found guilty of manslaughter. But she has created no trouble in the colony and may be at peril from the women at the Factory who think that she has had some special treatment through no fault of hers from the Pallmires. That she has had but it has been of little joy to her. She must be put somewhere else and – if you will provide for it in your grace – her ticket of leave advanced.

When women have no way to turn they look to a sister. If you will forgive me I dare see you as my kind sister and look in utter hope to you.

Your petitioner
Sarah Bernard

RETURNED BY WAY OF ROME TO THE Sudan and a subtly smiling Sherif, Prim heard from Erwit that Fergal Stoner had been calling.

'Oh,' she said, 'he wants to make some use or other of Austfam, to help him on his way to glory in Brussels.' But an amused affection for the man ensured she called him anyhow, before anyone else.

'My wife's coming out to see me,' Stoner told her.

'You must be happy about that.'

'Yes. I hope to persuade her to move here permanently – you know, show her the foreign school, and what nice friends I have. Come to a cocktail party at my place, okay?'

He nominated a date, and Prim agreed to attend. 'But are you actually serving cocktails? I mean, liquor?'

'Yeah, well there'll be a room off the courtyard stocked with gin and vodka. For infidels like you. They both go pretty well with fruit juice.'

The house the EC had given Stoner was in Almoradah, a fashionable suburb with imposing houses worthy of a wealthy district in Saudi Arabia. Prim looked forward to going. She found that her brief time spent with Dimp had somehow encouraged her to be more conventionally curious about such matters as the sort of woman rash enough to marry Stoner.

In the end Prim did not arrive at Stoner's with Sherif – the morning of the party she received a panicked telephone call from a tremulous Helene Codderby. 'Could you take me along with you, Primrose?' asked Helene, sounding strangely unsure for a woman who knew her way so well in the Sudan. 'Please. Please! It's just something I feel I can't face on my own. All those strangers.'

Prim was surprised at that word, strangers. To Helene few people in Khartoum were strangers.

So Prim and Helene entered by a double gate, through a little garden and to the door where a tall Southern Sudanese man pointed them into the shining, tiled interior of the house. They traversed the corridor to a broad shady courtyard, where young men in jackets, galabias, and white turbans came and went with bread and chickpea paste, delicious little cubes of lamb and dried tomatoes, and fruit juice. An unaltered Stoner came lolloping up, tall, bony, brown, but – Prim thought – a little boyishly flushed.

'Prim, dear old Codders!' he shouted. 'Let me introduce you to Claudia straight away.' For some reason his lips brushed Prim's cheek.

Claudia turned to them, green-eyed, lanky like her husband, handsome, large-jawed, and very northern European in complexion. The high sky seemed a violation of her pale skin as she moved from light to shade to meet them. She did not look timid, which was the idea Prim had somehow got from Stoner. So it was not fear of equatorial regions which had kept her in Britain.

'Hello,' she said in that English manner, putting emphasis on the double 'l' and stretching out the 'o'. Stoner described the two of them – Prim and Codders – what they did in Khartoum. 'See,' he told his wife, 'I've got loads of company here. And so would you.'

His wife did not resent this didacticism. 'It's not the company,' said Claudia Stoner smiling broadly at her guests. There was no trace of Yorkshire in her voice. 'It's that I don't like the heat. But I suppose the marriage vows transcend temperature. When the children are old enough for boarding school . . .'

Stoner dropped his voice and pointed to a door in the far corner of the courtyard. 'There's vodka in there should you need it. In the upper cupboards. Infidel gallons of the rubbish.'

New arrivals were already queuing behind them to meet Claudia Stoner, and so Helene and Prim stood aside. They found themselves no more than a yard from Dr Hamadain, in a cotton suit, and Safi el Rahzi, the student, in shirt sleeves. Hamadain had recently been courted back home by the government from a professorship at George Mason College in Washington. Safi was in full eloquence on some subject, and did not want to pause, but Sherif's urbane cousin held a hand up to halt the conversation and greeted them both by name. Helene Codderby – atypically – had nothing to say, and it was Prim who was left to congratulate Hamadain on his return and new post with the government.

'Yes,' said Helene, oddly distracted, 'Ministry of the Interior, isn't it?'

'I am special adviser to the minister, yes. Troubled times, I'm afraid.' His face shone with a sense of survival and of engagement.

Safi said, a little loudly, 'We were discussing guerilla training. I don't mean the guerillas in the South. There was a rumour printed in the *Washington Post* that our government is training guerillas for activity against the Israelis.'

'And I was telling my young friend here,' said Dr Hamadain, 'that if it is so, the Ministry of the Interior does not know about it.'

'Perhaps someone has omitted to tell the minister,' said young Safi with a smile. 'The *Washington Post* said these operatives included not only Palestinians and Libyans, but Pakistanis as well. Mind you, though I mistrust anarchist-style protest and random bombings, I am no lover of the Israelis. They took my grandfather prisoner in the Seven Days' War. But . . . guerillas?'

'Your grandfather was an Egyptian then?' asked Prim.

'No, he was one of our soldiers who volunteered. My mother's father. A professional soldier and an enlightened man.'

The conversation ended there for the moment, for Sherif turned up, strolling in bare-headed, a half smile on his face, waiting to be introduced to Stoner's wife. Prim went through that much commented-upon transformation: the entry of the lover alters the air, gives two-thirds of its humanity to the party. Prim was wearing the same gold-collared, loose white native dress she had worn to Dimp's party and wore to almost every party in the Sudan. It sat on her body easily. She had a light shawl around her shoulders – something she had learned not from the Sudanese but from her mother. 'To de-accentuate the bosom, dear.' Sherif must have found it a fetching combination, for he whispered in her ear, 'How are you, my little white ruffian?'

An hour passed with Professor el Rahzi telling tales of his days at the London School of Economics and at Oxford. He was particularly hopeful, he told Sherif and Prim when the rest of the party drifted away, that the government was about to be forced to resolve the conflict in the South. The World Bank, which had been lenient with repayment reductions earlier, was putting pressure on now, had refused to ratify a new deal on its debt, designed to ease interest repayments until the war was won. To maintain a war in a world of falling commodity prices was, everyone had agreed, grotesque. But there must be secure Sudanese sovereignty over the South – that was the trouble – and that would take long peace talks. However, peace talks would attract international goodwill and investment, said the professor.

Sherif asked Prim in a lowered voice, 'Are you taking Helene home?'

Prim nodded. 'If I can find her.'

'I think you'll find her in the booze room,' said Sherif with a smile. 'I shall see you later, my soul hopes ...'

'Your soul can rest assured,' said Prim.

There was a fleeting contact of hands, and she went to the room in the corner, knocked lightly on the door and tentatively opened it. She heard a gasp and thought she had surprised lovers, but in fact it was Helene Codderby weeping, a tumbler of what looked like water, but proved to be raw vodka, placed beside her on the table at which she sat.

'Helene! My God, what's the matter?'

Helene gamely composed herself. 'I'm in love, bugger it!'

Prim came to the table, leant on it, and made the normal gestures –

hand on shoulder, rubbing of the upper arm. 'But what's wrong with that?'

'Do you know what I find just a little offensive?' said Helene. 'I'm in love with the bastard. But when he wants someone to act as a warning to his wife, he uses not me but you. You're the one he kissed in front of her. He doesn't say, "Here's the charming Codderby, who is your rival." What he says is, "Here is the delicious Prim Bettany, so you'd better watch out!"' Her face contorted with tears again. 'I don't blame you in any way. It's not your fault any more than it's mine that I'm a plain old hank of a woman.' And she went on shuddering with grief.

Prim couldn't stop herself asking, 'Are you really telling me, Helene, that . . .?'

'Of course. Better part of eighteen months. I was beginning to think it would grow into something until now. He's a very driven man that way.' More tears. 'He likes his bloody home comforts, but he always has a plan for any stray woman.'

'Jesus Christ,' murmured Prim, fetching a glass and the vodka from the upper cupboard, and pouring herself some.

'The point is,' said Helene, 'that he wanted his wife to think it might be you, not me. I've got to admit you've got a special kind of danger written all over you. It's the charm of not knowing how good-looking, and so how dangerous, you really bloody well are. It's just as well you've got Sherif to look after you.'

They drank a while in silence. 'It has been the best and worst time of my life,' said Helene. 'But dear Lord, I'm suffering the sufferings of the sinner now. I'm drinking a bitter bloody cup. Bottoms up!'

They finished their drink.

'I know it's selfish of me,' Helene said. 'But do you think we could sneak out, if you don't mind? I don't want to see the bastard, and I don't want to see his bloody English rose of a spouse.'

They left the room and walked along the shadowed verandah and out by the corridor towards the street. Prim thought that perhaps it was not even safe being considered plain by both Westerners and Sudanese. It hadn't saved Helene who, like any betrayed sister, sputtered with grief all the way to the truck.

A few days after the welcoming party for Stoner's wife, Prim received a call from Stoner, and felt disposed to treat it with suspicion. 'Claudia and I,' said Stoner, 'wondered if you and your lovely doctor would like to join us at the Rimini tonight for dinner? I think Claudia's a little, you know, envious of you.'

So now he wanted to play married and betrothed couples! But she would not let him get away with it.

'I don't know that I want to,' said Prim. 'There's no problem with Claudia. But Helene Codderby is pretty unhappy.'

'Oh Jesus,' murmured Stoner.

'Don't worry. I won't blab on you, you treacherous bastard.'

Stoner had lowered his voice. 'Look, I never made any undertakings to Codders, okay? She knew the score. And what's a bloke to do now that the missus has moved in?'

This was the truth – Helene had never implied he had made promises. He was not Auger. He was a lesser barbarian. On the one hand loyalty to Helene ought to prevent Prim going to dinner with the Stoners – Helene would be horrified to hear of it if she did. But on the other, she and Stoner had painted over UN insignia on the sides of transports and discovered a supposed famine.

'I don't think we ought to come at the moment,' she said.

'But Jesus, Prim, a man's not a monk!'

'No. You're not a monk anyhow. You're a total bastard.'

In a louder voice than he had been using, he said cheerily, 'Guilty, Your Honour.'

'Yet everyone forgives you. I know I'll forgive you, but not just yet. Thanks for the invitation. And love to Claudia.'

In fact she spent the early part of the evening at Helene Codderby's little apartment in the city centre, over whose rooftop the minaret of a mosque passed a dramatic shadow in late afternoon, and where they sat drinking tea.

The subject of Stoner and the turpitude of men was soon exhausted. Quite naturally, politics came up next. 'What were Safi el Rahzi and Doctor Hamadain talking about?' asked Prim. 'Pro-Palestinian guerilla squads training in the Sudan. Did you know anything about this?' She had a few hours before been specifically reminded of the conversation at Stoner's by hearing on the radio of yet another clash between Israelis and Palestinians in Hebron. Two Palestinians were dead. Paying the price, as Prim thought of it, for two thousand years of European anti-Semitism.

'Yes,' said Helene, dismally sipping her tea and grimacing. 'It's all the truth. There's a camp out to the west, between here and Shendi. That's where they're billeted and trained until they're needed. Islamic freedom fighters. Young fellows. High morale.'

'This is really an astonishing country, Helene.'

'Hamadain's right. There may be ministers in the government who don't know. The prime minister may not even know. That's how it goes here.'

'That's how it goes anywhere, if you can believe the spy movies.'

'If you can believe the spy movies. Do you think men suffer like this?'

'I think women have been asking that very question for some time.'

'But it doesn't happen to a girl like you.'

'What bloody rubbish,' said Prim with an almost angry urgency. 'Of course it's happened to me.' And with those words, Prim felt an electric jolt in her womb, something like, she imagined, a child turning over, but not in happiness. 'It was a professor–student thing. It's the reason I'm here. I'll tell you that much, but no more. End of story.'

Helene looked at her from under lowered eyebrows. 'You know, I'm utterly delighted to hear that. Aren't I a bitch?'

'Yes,' said Prim. 'Of course you are.'

And in the shadow of the minaret, the finger of God, they both laughed and drained their tea.

At two o'clock in the morning, Prim was woken at Sherif's house by a banging at the door and presumed, for some reason to do with a recent but unremembered dream, it was the police. Bolting upright, she saw by the now switched on bedside light that Sherif was already wide awake.

Sherif shook his head and went off frowning to answer the door. Professor el Rahzi had once admiringly said, 'He's rubbed a lot of noses at the Ministry of Health,' but surely that was not grounds for arrest. Adultery was, under the Sharia. But fornication?

She followed Sherif, stylish in his thin cotton bathrobe, going to meet destiny with grace, downstairs and through his office. He opened the door without inquiring, without inching it open and squinting forth, but with the authority of a man who would not accept he had anything to hide. Helene Codderby nearly toppled into the room. For a second or two, Prim wondered with a little impatience whether they were going to be subjected to howling, small-hours, he-done-me-wrong lamentations.

'What is it, Helene?' she called from the stairs.

'The fighters, the bastards, the terrorists, whatever they are. They've come into town and blown up the Rimini. Two grenades in the dining room. Fergal and Claudia are both dead. Fergal's hard to identify, but Claudia's face is intact. The bastards killed a Saudi Arabian, an Egyptian engineer, two waiters and Fergal and Claudia. Jesus! Can you believe that? Jesus!'

'Oh God,' said Prim, coming forward and hugging her. 'Oh Helene. The EC people called you?'

'The police called me. The police knew I knew Fergal. What do you think of that? A state where everybody knows everything, and nothing gets bloody done. I identified the bodies. The poor bloody shredded bodies.' She was babbling with grief now. 'They didn't know what hit them. She would have died with his bullshit in her ear. He would have died full of the usual plans. Oh Fergal! Fergal. You sod!'

Prim was aware not only of shock, the guilt and horror of the reality that she might have occupied the same deadly table, but of loss as well, loss of the villainous ally, the predictable friend, the manipulator without whom nothing happened, without whom there was no lover for Helene, no bread for the stricken, no succour and, of course, no father for his children.

Prim, while still embracing Helene, saw that Sherif had turned ash-grey. 'That the Stoners should have to pay . . .' he murmured.

Prim sat up the rest of the night with Helene, as she poured out her utterance of love, bewilderment, resentment, not least against the victim. They worked through tea and got onto whisky, and then Helene announced that Prim and Sherif must accompany her during the morning to an address in Central Khartoum, where Fergal and Claudia Stoner would be placed in lead-lined coffins for shipment on the next night's flight from Nairobi to London.

'So soon?' asked Prim.

'Oh Jesus,' said Helene, 'They are dead. Don't doubt me. They are dead.'

And yet when they went to what proved to be the police mortuary, and saw Fergal and Claudia hauled in plastic sacks, tied at both ends, into their respective lead coffins, Prim still thought, 'They are leaving too soon.' It was as if they were relieving their killers of the reproachful weight of their presence. Helene could not be comforted and was nearly mad with grief.

The throwing of the two grenades into the dining room of the Rimini, had left the upper floor of the building blackened, since one of the grenades which had killed the Stoners had also started a fire from a burst gas cylinder. Afterwards, when Prim drove through Central Khartoum, the black and shattered upper floor always drew her eye. It was as if the Rimini's Italian proprietors meant to leave their upstairs floor in ruins as a reproach, with shutters hanging, blasted, by one hinge. Displaced Southern urchins and the children of the urban poor still begged at the front door and visitors still defiantly came, as if in protest at the randomness of terror.

Diplomatic pressure from the British and Egyptian governments caused Sadiq el Mahdi, the prime minister, to expel half a dozen men, three Libyans, two Pakistanis, an Egyptian – who may have been involved in clandestine operations in the Sudan. It altered nothing. There were places on the Lebanese border where these men were greeted as heroes, said Helene Codderby. They had shown that the West could not with impunity support the shooting down of Palestinians in Hebron.

An urbane but very formal Spaniard replaced Stoner. A more careful, more diplomatic, less intrusive presence, he seemed to Prim to keep Stoner's programs, particularly the one in the South, merely ticking along. The air of expectation, of coming redemption, which had somehow always attached to Stoner, had vanished.

One night Prim woke alone in a panic and crisis of her own – Sherif was off at the hospital on some emergency. What am I doing? Stoner dies. The war goes on, and so the slave reports go on too, and nothing alters. The health surveys are made, and the refugee camps proliferate. Australian flour is intermittently flown south, but who does it feed? Wells are dug but run dry. I am here now because of Sherif, she realised. And this, though a superlative reason, did not seem an adequate justification for taking up space on the Nile, for inhaling this particular good, dry air. She knew that one day she would have to go home, and that this was as inevitable as death, but closer.

Letter No 12, SARAH BERNARD

Marked by her: BE SURE TO DESTROY THIS
Dearest Alice
The first thing I know there is trouble Mr Pallmire enters the kitchen when I am drinking some tea. Mr Pallmire says: Bernard come with me! I wonder am I to be beaten but he takes me into one of the little store-rooms near the butchery – it has a drain in the centre and there is a pile of hard soap on the floor – a little mountain of it – and he gives me a mallet and says: Break it up Bernard. Break it up and when you have done you are to get in the constables to wash it down the drain. I see that it is fluster and fear and not rage which is at work in the man now. He leaves me as if I were his most trustworthy servant and I break away with the mallet though the soap is very hard and as I hammer away I rejoice within me.

I take my time but nobody comes and interrupts me. But when I emerge to drink tea at one o'clock what would I see but a magistrate I had never seen before and unfamiliar constables at the walk bridge and hammering at the door of the Pallmires. And other strange constables are on guard before the butchery and the storeroom door. When Mr and Mrs Pallmire are led away, the women of the factory come up out of the laundry and whistle and hoot and shriek to leave the poor ears of the Pallmires ringing. And amongst the loudest are my old friends – the little brick red woman Carty and the hefty brick red woman Connolly.

Then I see you in the kitchen window with the blue kerchief and try to go to talk to you. But the new magistrate – a young man – asks me come with him. I gather my canvas bag and go with him to a carriage and later find myself amongst his servants in a well-ordered farmhouse beyond Parramatta. Here I am given very little duties indeed – except the housekeeper gives me ironing which is a memory of the Factory. He had me into his parlour to quiz me and I have told him about you Alice. He has promised that you will be sheltered and given consideration. He said that he would remove you from the Factory to a trusted position in Parramatta Gaol on probation, And in view of the damage done to you if you were good for two years he would have you in process for a ticket. All I can tell you is his household is very sober and there is an air of truth here. He is a disciple of John Wesley though he gave me a lecture on why the Wesleyans had been foolish to depart the Church of England.

As for me I can tell you the Visiting Surgeon and this good magistrate are determined that I should be rewarded for my devotion to truth which is – I hope you will believe me – also a devotion to you. I have been allowed to write to Long at his station. He is a man I trust above all others. Wherever I go I shall mention your name as a good servant. I can if all parties are agreeable be assigned to that station which I believe I would like since it is according to Long far from the malice of most men.

I do not doubt you Alice. You were true and kept the secret which could have been sold with profit and at my deepest cost to the Pallmires. You are indeed a decent woman as I always knew.

Your firm friend
Sarah

Letter No 13, SARAH BERNARD

Brave Alice
You should receive this since I have asked Constable Henley at the Factory to deliver my letters to you in the hospital at Parramatta Gaol for five shillings to be sent in September by bank order from Goulburn. Should I get an indication this is not done then Henley can go sing. I was so sad to find your coughing has worsened but I will get you to a better and tonic clime – you will be better I know in this drier country inland.

We are a little army of women – nine of us – with tickets of leave and passports to travel inland and have been put here for the night in the cell of the convict depot at Liverpool. Not for doing wrong but for the same reason the Female Factory was put in place – to protect us from the men and the men from us. The greatest surprise is that I share this journey with my former Tory friends the little red woman Carty and her protector Connolly. The girl child of Carty is with us – she lies asleep on the cell floor. All the while her mother and the large red woman and some of the others stand at the window swapping pleasant words with constables and convicts – many speak their language but I hear others say: You come out here dearie and I shall properly stamp your ticket better than a magistrate. They laugh like women who have learned nothing from their ordeal. But now I see through that and I think they have learned something. They have a plan and are both looking for a husband. Whoever weds the big red one will be subject to her fierce rule but even here we see so few women that someone would eagerly wed her.

The little freckled one who has a good heart keeps wondering aloud

*how I am given a ticket of leave a year early but explains it thus: It must
be because you are given to learning!*

*All the activity of human souls in these places along the road! There
are black men in top coats and no pants or wearing a possum skin rug.
There are unhappy soldiers of the 50th Regiment who wake up for me
the ghost of my dear husband Corporal McWhirter. It seems a military
life is barely superior to the life of a felon though I must say I am
damned – yes damned – if mine shall not be superior to that of any dolt
of a soldier.*

*My employer is to be a Mr Bettany of a district named Maneroo and
a station named Nugan Ganway. He has been persuaded by my friend
Sean Long that I am what he needs – namely a housekeeper and
educated. I hope you will agree – friend Alice – that I am something of
that nature. When I was called by the Parramatta magistrate to hear of
my assignment – they said it: an educated woman. I know it is vanity to
like to hear such things but I like it Alice.*

*With women from the Factory I was marched by a constable to Church
Street Parramatta and given into the care of the Scottish driver of a
furniture wagon. This fellow was warned of cancellation of his ticket if
he set hand on us and failed to have us report to police magistrates along
the way. It is handsome furniture on the wagon for a man named Batchelor who is at a station named Inchecor beyond the distant town of
Yass – the wagon driver Tolhurst keeps marvelling someone can afford
such niceties in hard times. People in this outer world of the colony speak
of hard times till one is sick. We could my dear friend tell them of real
hard times. But would they be interested?*

*The land is not mountainous at all but Tolhurst tells us the mountains
are ahead. You will all be pushing and heaving says he. Even the bairn.*

*But I know it from breathing the air. At the heart of the country of
slavery we shall have our freedom my darling friend. With friendship and
company – the chief ingredients of a good life. More from my destination.*

Yours Ever

Sarah

IN THE APRIL OF STONER'S DEATH, the windows at Prim's flat needed to
be closed against sharp little grains of sand pinging by the million against
the glass, eating the paint on the metal window frames. Under a low grey

dome, cars moved by noon with headlights on. No planes penetrated the murk because Air Sudan pilots, who connected the Republic to Arabia, the Gulf, Ethiopia, to the world's current, were on strike. The rumour was that the government lacked the money to pay them. Thus a double isolation held the capital in place. In the city, captive to grit, prices of food had risen beyond all reason and the Sudanese *dinar* and pound were worth maybe half of what they had been six weeks before when Prim had returned to Khartoum from Australia. The war in the South was in its permanently unresolved condition, the government still able with any certainty to call itself a government only in the garrisoned towns such as Aweil.

Prim was suffering from some recurrent gastroenteritic virus she had caught, she believed, on one of the two planes she took to get back home. Sherif knelt beside her, placing damp cloths on her forehead, caressing her neck with a washer as the squalls of grit attacked and receded.

Recovering in this turning season, Prim found even Sherif could be edgy. It was, she understood, the edginess of guilt – his country had failed to take care of Fergal and Claudia Stoner.

'You'll write about Africa, won't you?' Sherif asked, in a murmur with some acid to it. 'Murderous Africa. You worry it out, you shake your head.'

'No. Not like you think.'

'Good,' he said after a time. 'Africa can be interpreted only from the inside.'

'If you don't know I know that,' she protested, 'we've reached a pretty pass.'

One morning, which happened to be wind-less and clear, Prim answered a call from Mrs el Rahzi, who said, 'There is a particular Austrian woman you have expressed an interest in meeting.'

An Austrian woman. It must be the Baroness von Trotke who had brought children out of slavery. 'I see,' said Prim.

'Well, she has flown up by charter aircraft from Kenya with her Canadian friend, and we are about to have tea. Could you join us, do you think?'

'Immediately,' Prim said. She called for Erwit, who loped inside in his ever-clean white shirt, grey pants and sandals to mind the office and phone in her absence. Prim drove with some haste along the Sharia el Muk Nimir, over the heat-emitting railway line towards the city proper. North-east past St. James's Circuit and the Sudan Club to the elegant houses behind the University of Khartoum. She parked and rang at the el Rahzis' gate. Through gaps amidst the buildings of the university she could see trucks rolling along the embankment of the Blue Nile like promises of normality. It was suddenly hard to believe that, as Helene Codderby claimed, somewhere officers were arguing with each other about what to do with this government, this war, this political entity of the Sudan.

Mrs el Rahzi herself – smiling, prompt, beauteous – opened up to let Prim in. 'Come through to the garden,' she said. 'It's a good day at last for sitting outdoors.' Through the cool, wide corridor they reached the garden, with the sudden kindness of well-cropped brown grass somewhat faded and swamped with sandy fall-out from the skies. Here, flowering acacias and three palms grew. 'The lungs of the residence!' Mrs el Rahzi often commented.

In shade provided by an awning, two white women, seated at the table before half-drunk milk teas and a plate of honey cake, stood up to greet Prim. One was lean, with pale skin, her brown hair in a tight bun and her style graceful and languid; the other a small, husky woman with cropped blonde hair and an honest grin. The tall one, of course, the one with the Hapsburg languor, was von Trotke. 'Connie Everdale,' said the shorter woman, shaking hands and confirming Prim's assumptions. 'I'm madam's pilot.'

'She is Jehu the charioteer,' said the baroness, laughing musically, in faintly accented English. 'Her chariots are afire. She can land a Beechcraft or a Cessna on a schilling.'

'Please let us all sit again,' said Mrs el Rahzi. The party obeyed her as she poured tea for Prim.

'I hear,' said the baroness in her high, amused voice, which reminded Prim in a way of Sherif's modulation, 'that you are one of those rare NGO people who believe in the literal existence of Sudanese slavery.'

'Yes, though I have the indulgence of Austfam to pursue the matter purely as an individual,' said Prim. 'My superiors are uneasy.'

'Oh yes,' said the baroness, and Connie Everdale nodded and reached for more honey cake. 'I can predict what their arguments are since I am so well-acquainted with them from other sources. The West had, at one stage, industrial slavery in the metaphorical sense. Conscripting under-age boys into armies or rebel fronts is endemic in Africa. What of a family fostering a Southern child into a household and requiring it to go to a Koranic school and change its name? European settler families used to do that sort of thing, taking in this or that African boy as a kind of house-slave, giving him a Christian name, and so on.'

Prim smiled. 'They're some of the objections I've heard, yes.'

'Well, honey, let me ask something,' said blonde Connie Everdale. 'If they are not slaves, why do we have to pay to get them back?'

'Oh that is easily answered,' said the baroness, still playing the role of sceptic. 'Why, we are obviously naïve to spray money about, and so we encourage the practice of child seizure!'

'And so, you see, hon, if slavery exists,' Connie Everdale concluded, 'we're the slavers, buying and selling. Honest to God, that's what we get told.'

Mrs el Rahzi rose with the tea pot and went around replenishing cups.

'So are you based in Kenya now?' Prim wanted to know of the baroness.

'Not exactly. I flew from Rome to Nairobi, and my friend here, the good Constance, collected me in one of her aircraft and took me up to Lokichokio where she lives.' Lokichokio was a town in northern Kenya, close to the Sudanese border. Prim knew that much of the food and medicine of the continuing but shrunken Operation Safety was flown into the southern Sudan from there on aircraft chartered by Save the Children, the Red Cross, and others. 'Connie has a veritable armada of aircraft.' Baroness von Trotke's eyes glittered. 'Six or seven Cessnas, four Beech-craft, two old DC6s, three Ilyushins, and two Sharps. You know the Sharps? Like a butterbox in structure, yet it flies.'

'Good passenger payload,' murmured Connie dreamily. 'And low maintenance. That's what we came up here in.'

'Yes, I've spent a few days in Lokichokio, and now Connie has flown me up to Khartoum to see friends, amongst whom Khalda is top of the list.'

Connie and the baroness beamed at Khalda and Prim.

The idea of Connie's bush squadron intrigued Prim. She asked the pilot who her clients were, to charter all these aircraft.

'A lot of NGOs,' said Connie airily. 'Some government ministries. Before ... that's before I accepted Jesus as my saviour, let me tell you straight out that I made my money out of flying *khat* into Somalia and around Sudan. I'd willingly fly cargoes of *khat* now if that's what it took, if that's what gave me the funds to buy out cargoes of misused kids from the South. But the baroness here is a little strict about hallucinogens and narcotics.'

'The principle of double effect,' the baroness, raising her chin, stated. 'You can't use a bad means to achieve a good end.'

Connie said, 'I used to take *khat* myself. I was a mad kid when I first came to Kenya in the late fifties.'

'And now they still think you're mad,' said the baroness with her tinkling laugh. 'So at least you are consistent.'

'That's what my mama said to me, spouse of dear Doctor Everdale of Stratford, Ontario. "You seem bent on difference, my girl." '

'I think you're very brave,' Prim murmured, and turned to the baroness. 'When you ... go to work ... what's the process exactly?'

The baroness nodded, delighted to have a potential disciple. 'I have a network of Sudanese friends in the South – some of them are Coptic priests, some Sudanese officers, some rebels. When they visit this or that house, they're shocked to find this or that young person in a state of slavery. They report to me and over time I build up a map of where the young are being held, go down there, hire a truck and drive from place to place buying them back and returning them to their families.'

'But this time we're doing it different,' Connie told Prim. 'We're flying into the South together. The details are under wraps for now.'

The baroness pressed on. 'We were wondering if your time and situation here would permit you to join us as an observer on our forthcoming excursion. We are going from here in two days, weather allowing. And don't worry about any danger. We know the terrain.'

The idea of travelling with the baroness and Connie, of verifying the truth of enslavement, filled Prim with a certain fear and exhilaration. Of course, Peter Whitloaf would be appalled.

Prim asked the least important question first. 'How much time would that occupy?'

'Maybe a week,' said the baroness, 'by the time you had a good look around Lokichokio and went on to Nairobi to catch a commercial jet back to Khartoum.'

'I could get you down to Nairobi,' offered Connie, 'and with your NGO passport and my reputation, you shouldn't have too many troubles.'

Prim took thought again. 'My NGO won't want me to go. You mention Lokichokio and Nairobi. But first you land in the South? To load up?'

Connie Everdale put her finger to her lips, in a 'walls have ears' sort of gesture. 'I wouldn't worry about it, hon. I've touched down in the

328328

328

328

328

328

328

328

328

328

328

3283328

328

328

328

328

328

328

328

328

328

328

328

328

328

328

328

328

328

328

328

328

328

328

South hundreds of times, and no one knows I've even been there. But like the baroness says, it's up to you.'

'I want to go,' said Prim. One day she might be able to give a testimony of what she saw – the transaction, the liberation. She would need to tell a lie or a half truth to Peter Whitloaf, but it seemed a small price.

'We're meeting an agent this time,' Connie explained. 'He'll bring the kids to us. He's a man in the Arab militia. You know, the Beggarah. You've heard of those guys?'

The baroness trilled a correction. 'Actually the fellow we're dealing with is a Rizeighat, one of the sub-groups. Have you heard of them?'

The Sudan abounded with ethnic sub-groups, but Prim had heard of the Rizeighat. They provided a fierce pro-government militia and figured in many of the narratives of slaves.

The baroness said, 'Last of all, we are taking a highly reputable Khartoum man with us to act as our negotiator.'

'What sort of person would volunteer for that?'

The baroness smiled faintly. 'For now, if you will forgive me, it remains a small secret.'

Tempted and appalled, Prim turned to Mrs el Rahzi. 'Could I have more tea, please?'

The professor's wife smiled and said, 'You are between two hard cases with this pair.'

Prim gathered herself to send a half-true totally deceiving fax to Canberra.

FROM: *Austfam, Khartoum/Prim Bettany*
TO: *Peter Whitloaf, CEO, Austfam, Canberra*
DATE: *May 6 1989*
1 page message

Dear Peter,
I have a chance to fly down to Lokichokio by charter plane at no expense to myself or Austfam to have a look at southern Sudanese reception centres in northern Kenya. I shall then return to Khartoum from Nairobi at my own expense. I hope that in this reasonable cause you will forgive an absence of a week from the Khartoum office.

Prim

As easily as Prim could deceive Peter Whitloaf for a good end, she could not undertake the flight without telling Sherif.

He listened quietly when she told him she intended seeking leave from Austfam to fly to Lokichokio to look at some of the refugee arrangements down there. She was flying with a woman named Connie Everdale. At Connie's name, he raised a hand. 'And I know, I know. Those women are in Khartoum!'

'What women?'

'Those slavery nuts. I bet you've talked to them. You are actually going to be foolish enough to fly with that Austrian woman and land in the South?'

'Look, I must. Connie's done it so often. She says it's routine.'

'Maybe. One day it will turn non-routine. Besides that, you will remove Sudanese nationals to a foreign country?'

'Sudanese slaves,' she said.

He shook his head in long, slow sweeps. 'I don't want you to do it. It's a foolish thing to do. What's to become of me if anything should happen to you? I would find life impossible.'

'You've been yourself to the South with me.'

'That was authorised. This is piracy.'

She pretended to think about this for a while. In reality the imperative to accompany the baroness and Connie was lodged solidly under her ribs.

'I have to go. Forgive me.'

'I'm not sure I shall. You represent an NGO. And what you plan, apart from the danger of being shot down, is illegal.'

'Like drinking gin,' Prim suggested.

'Well, you'll go without any blessing from me. I think it's an indulgence, and a dangerous one. Reconsider. Please.'

But even for Sherif Prim would not reconsider.

On the night before the flight she and Sherif sat glumly, drinking tea together, Sherif in a rare sulky mood. Faxed approval from Peter Whitloaf allowing her to visit northern Kenya, a region of plentiful refugee camps, had come through.

Connie Everdale had advised Prim that the first day might be long. No *haboobs* were predicted, but the Air Sudan strike was still in progress on the designated morning. Prim arrived at Khartoum airport, eastwards from the New Extension, at 5 a.m., and found the main terminal closed and guarded by soldiers. She was permitted to stroll to the hangar for charter services. Here she found the baroness and Connie, dressed in full blouses, skirts and heavy boots, in the shade of a hangar before which a box-like but sizeable aircraft, the much-discussed Sharps, stood in its dull silver metal, its fuselage marked with sober blue and white lettering: Northern Kenya Charter Services. The women were drinking tea reflectively from mugs, and offered Prim a cup.

'It ain't pretty,' said Connie, seeing Prim frown at the sight of this apparently ungainly aircraft, 'but it's got the range.'

Through that hour's pure light, undistorted yet by a high sun, a sad-looking customs official in khaki shirt and trousers strolled up from an office a hundred yards away and asked to see their passports.

He was still weighing the passports in his hand when Professor el Rahzi emerged from a taxi in front of the charter services hangar. Today he was dressed not in his normal traditional mode, but for the bush, in khaki pants and shirt, just like the immigration man. When he saw the official the professor added his own passport to the pile the man was holding.

'Off to Lokichokio, professor?'

'And returning from Nairobi,' said the professor helpfully.

'Very well, come with me.' And the immigration official, taking all the passports, led Rahzi off to an office.

'Typical,' said Connie, wagging her close-cropped blonde head. 'Had to wait for a guy to turn up before he could do business.'

'What is Professor el Rahzi doing here?' asked Prim.

Connie lowered her voice. 'He's our respectable Sudanese gentleman in good standing. These Arab militia guys don't always like doing business with an old tart from Stratford, Ontario.'

'Or an old tart from Vienna, when it come to that,' said the baroness in her fluting voice.

The professor emerged from the immigration hut, crossed the patch of sunlight, and came to the women. He waved the batch of passports. 'We are permitted to go to Kenya with the blessing of the government of the Sudan,' he announced with a broad smile.

With the casual fatalism African people, black and white, feel towards aircraft, the party boarded through the fuselage door. The baroness, Connie, and the professor sat stooped in the cargo space where some blankets, plastic bottles of water, and packages marked 'High-Protein Biscuit' were casually stacked. Here they studied a map Connie had produced from a briefcase. It showed in its contours the White Nile swamps, and hilly country. Towns were marked to the level of individual structures – the settlements of Mbili and Kawajena, on the road to Wau, middled between reed swamp and plateau.

The professor's large finger was indicating a line beyond a water-course which ran towards the Bo River. 'Here,' he said, 'on an east-west axis. Marked by two red oil drums on one side, and two on the other.'

Connie Everdale had an old-fashioned pair of protractors in her hands, and began plotting a course from the raw landing place the professor had indicated to her home airfield. 'Forty-nine degrees 15 minutes 23 seconds south to Lokichokio. Keep Juba well to starboard, there's artillery there. Then Mount Kinyeti to starboard too. I can pick up the Kakuma track from the Sudan–Kenya border with eyes shut.' She punched the map with her finger. 'Two and a bit hours tops.'

It was a comfort to hear Connie speak of the line of flight they would take after their ill-advised southern landing. Connie took the chart forward with her to the cockpit.

'You like to sit with me, Primrose?' she called over her shoulder.

The baroness and the professor disposed themselves in passenger seats, as Prim came forward to take her place beside Connie. Connie handed her earphones and indicated she should wear them. After some clipped communications with the tower, still apparently staffed in this season of *haboobs*, strike and civil doubt, the fragile-feeling, boxy aircraft trembled at Connie's throttle thrusts and dragged itself, a little crookedly it seemed to Prim, down the runway dazzled by early light. They bumped along a few feet, it seemed, above the flat rooftops of Khartoum, banked across the opaque Blue Nile, crossed the White Nile, and levelled out above the burnished dome of the Khalifa's palace. Prim strained in her seat to see how the baroness was faring, and saw her with closed eyes and clasped hands. Baroness von Trotke had such a worldly presence it was easy for Prim to forget she was an evangelical Christian and might pray at points of departure. The professor, Prim saw, was reading the international weekly edition of the *Guardian*. Now they swung over the dam twenty miles south of the city and across the irrigated fields of the Gezira, the broad triangle of fertile soil produced by the drawing together of both Niles. Patterned cotton fields stretched away into haze. A glory of government planning, so it was once thought. The client farmers and labourers were these days discontented about the world price – to them, another item in the exploitation of the Islamic world by the West.

As the plane reached higher in a sky utterly lacking in vapour, Connie aligned the nose above the dam, twenty miles south of Khartoum, with the general drift of the White Nile.

It was at once apparent to Prim how broadly and with what languid grace the river tried to distribute its kindnesses, mothering the hard surfaces of the angry republic, embracing quadrants, spaciously expanding into reed swamps, cunningly defeating exploration. It was a mother who, working twenty-four hours a day, could still not soothe her rabid child.

'*Bahr el Abiad*,' murmured Connie through the earphones. 'White Nile.'

Prim had noticed similar awed intonations of the names of the river by other Europeans. Seeing it, they were forced to name it softly. So profoundly did this river run in everyone's cortex, the first great river of our infant storybooks, the one earliest drawn, told stories of, made the basis of essays and projects and drawings in all our childhood classrooms.

But then the river was lost behind them. Visual relief to the great grey-yellow-tan orb below was provided by the Kordofan plateau ahead, whose wadis they soon crossed. The plateau, traversed, fell away to lowlands again. One high brown plug of mountain – *Jabal el Liri*, said Connie – rose through a base of haze to the east. From such a height the landscape seemed apolitical and formless, possessing only the property of vastness. Above all it seemed to lack strategic meaning, and lacked, too, either an angry or suffering populace. It was as if no eye existed amongst the papyrus swamps, the grasslands and the folded hills.

Connie asked through the earphones, 'You got a guy, hon?'

'I wouldn't put it like that,' said Prim. It sounded a starched, defensive reply even to herself.

'Well, let's say a good friend then?' said Connie, getting her number, and squinting out amused at the prodigious sky above them, in which, far beyond the dazzle, lay a hint of the universe's intense dark. Why couldn't she yield, like Dimp, and accept the normal, banal words – *boyfriend, fella, bloke, guy, squeeze, lover*? What exclusivity did she claim for her desires? For he was a guy, he was a lover! She had sat joyously on his prick, howled to absorb him, urged him to pay his substance away. Wanting to hold all his resources forever and, above all others, in her blood's dark bank. Wasn't that what anyone did? Wasn't that what it meant to have 'a guy'?

'You could call him a guy,' Prim conceded. 'He's a doctor in Khartoum.'

'Sudanese?' asked Connie.

'Yes.'

'Hey ... none of my business, but watch it, hon.'

'Very Westernised,' Prim said, as if Sherif needed defending. 'Studied in England and America.'

'Oh yeah. Some of 'em like white women. They like forthrightness and light-coloured hair. But only when it's going their way.'

'You?' Prim asked, changing the angle of the discourse. 'Are you married?'

'I was married four years – '58 to '62. No kids. I was a bad wife and mad at the time. Honest. I get the sweats in the dead of night just thinking what I was like. My folks wanted me in a sanatorium. It was the flying thing, combined with the fact I was such a miserable bitch. None of the purpose of all that misery I lived through was clear to me until round about seven years back.'

'When you had your ... conversion?'

'When I said yes to Jesus. I felt all the foulness, but above all the madness lifted off me. A good thing too, because I felt heavy-burdened and was beginning to wonder should I just fly a plane into a mountain. The way I see it, you take on a sufficient weight of the world's pleasures, woes and sins, and then they reach critical mass and kill you. My sins in the commission were light as a feather, but they weighed tons in retrospect.'

'What happened, if you don't mind telling me?'

'No, not at all. I'd already done one run for the baroness. Thought she was pretty much an eccentric, which she surely is. Anyhow, there's this mission near my airstrip. It's American, run for the past thirty years by a couple named the Wagons. If they needed a plane, they chartered me. The Mission of Jesus True Saviour – they'll take the kids we pick up into their dormitories there. Anyhow, I was flying this old guy Caleb Wagon and his wife down to Nairobi for some medical treatment he needed, and old Caleb was sitting beside me, in this single engine Cessna, and we're chatting through the earphones like you and me. And I asked him what he used to do – and of all things he was in youth a sales rep going round six southern states of the US selling syrups to factories and restaurants, and so on. And it was such a big business that his boss and he used to take their favourite clients to Las Vegas and – to quote Caleb – "supply them with ladies". He woke up one morning with a mouth like a cesspit and went to a window and looked out, and there was this grey haze over everything in Vegas. None of the normal stuff, no clear, eye-scorching, wake-up-and-go-for-a-swim weather. I suppose something like one of our *haboobs*. And he says that without the Strip and the palm trees to distract him, there was a vacancy inside his head. And a voice inside him went, "This can't go on." And when he told me this in my plane on the way to Nairobi, it was as if the same voice went off in my head. Even though I was flying along at 10 000 feet, I felt I was in a pit I'd dug myself, or like I was trapped between two stone walls, with only a sliver of sky showing. And then I felt something with wings come down on me and lift me out of the pit and over the mountains, till I was at last level with myself, with the altitude of the Cessna. My soul, which after all was flying the body and in danger of forgetting it was, was at last on a level course. Like that, I was reunited to myself. But I knew I hadn't done it myself, lifted myself up on wings, reconciled my body and soul. Not to put too fine a point on it, Jesus had lifted me.'

'How did you know that?'

'I just knew while it was happening. It was the Holy Spirit of Christ. And I thought, I mustn't ever let myself get separated again. By the way, see that reed swamp and meander down there? That's the Jor, flows into the *Bahr el Ghazal*, flows into the Nile. In other words, we're in the South, hon.'

Prim was aware now of an increased degree of watchfulness in Connie Everdale. The army had placed occasional anti-aircraft batteries throughout the South to frighten off aircraft whose flights had not been authorised by Khartoum. Though they were widely scattered, and though Connie rode on the wings of the Holy Spirit, a given aircraft might be unlucky. Randomness was the special terror of the agnostic, Prim knew, and randomness weighed somewhat on her.

The earth had now changed to look more Central African. Apart from forests of reed and water hyacinth, there were date palms and thickets of trees. This was a land over which sovereignty was always uncertain. Ahead lay green hills, off-shoots of a plateau which swept up from Zaire and Chad. The professor appeared behind Connie and shouted in her ear, referring to his map and occasionally looking at his watch. At last he and Connie nodded a number of times and he went back to his seat. Connie threw a partially unfolded map in Prim's lap. It was much marked in ballpoint pen and dog-eared.

'See that long north-south running watercourse? Yell if you spot it.'

On the map, the informal airstrip was marked in ballpoint. Amongst tall, leafy trees, Prim saw the glint of water in reeds. 'There,' she cried –

and then almost instantly a dirt and grassland runway came into sight. Its only attendant structure was a brush-covered shelter, a *rakubah*, set along the perimeter like a parody of a terminal. Prim relaxed. The air, other than the normal turbulence, seemed vacant of malice. They landed and rolled along the earth with a surprising smoothness. From her place beside Connie, Prim saw, packed in by the edge of the trees and into the shade of the shelter, young men in khaki fatigues sitting shoulder to shoulder, Kalashnikovs on their laps. What their presence meant Prim chose not to inquire of Connie.

Connie dragged back the throttle and cut the engines with a flourish, and a thunderous silence rushed down on Prim.

'Ah the blessed silence afterwards!' Connie said, but satirically.

She left the cockpit area first and in passing the professor said, 'Okay prof, come and meet your old pal.' She yanked the door in the side open. 'Out, out,' Connie urged the baroness and Prim. 'Without the engines running, these things turn into ovens.'

Stepping down to the airstrip behind the baroness and the professor, Prim felt the weight of a different proposition: an equatorial sun in a region of tropic rainfall. Ahead of her the professor put out his arms in greeting. Towards him from the *rakubah* loped a tall man with the beginning of grey in his wiry hair. Obviously a Southerner, no visible admixture of Arab in his blood, this fellow wore army fatigues whose pants did not cover his ankles, had sandals on his feet, but was hatless. On his belt he carried a military-style holster and pistol. He performed a ritual embrace, laying his head profoundly against both the professor's shoulders.

'*Wa alaikum'ssalam*,' said el Rahzi. 'And let us pray for peace.' The professor turned back to the baroness, Connie and Prim. 'May I present John Along, a former student of mine at Khartoum University.'

Lanky John Along shook the women's hands. Prim felt both the reluctant hardness and yet the elegance of his hand.

'John is a Dinka, and was a Sudanese army staff officer when I met him. I do not judge his involvement in all this.' El Rahzi gestured at the equatorial sky. 'Indeed,' he continued, 'we could not have made such a happy landing without Colonel Along.'

'Welcome, welcome,' said Along. 'The Rizeighat colonel himself is close. Please, wait in the shade.'

He gestured to the *rakubah*, in whose shade many of his soldiers were massed. Prim chose to remember an incident which had not come to mind

earlier. Two years past some Rizeighat militia units had filled a train at
the rail head at Wau with Dinkas they had driven out of their homes
and, whether or not at some gesture of resistance from a Southerner,
fired into the cattle trucks and set them alight. Helene Codderby had
reported to the BBC for the African News that some sources, including
survivors, put the death toll at 1500.

As the four from the plane approached the brush shelter, Along's
troops, who seemed young and unsullen, stood up graciously and vacated
the shade. Along suggested the visitors take refreshment, and a young
soldier brought anodised cups of black, sugared tea to them on a chipped
tray painted with red and white flowers. The professor took a sip.

By now Connie Everdale and the baroness were seated, or more accurately, Connie was reclining and seemed to have a mind to take a nap.
'See,' she said to Prim, 'this is a coalition across the divide. To save kids.'

Prim looked at John Along's boy soldiers of the southern Sudanese
People's Liberation Army, sitting in mottled shade on the edge of the
bush. Their faces, too, seemed to her to be the faces of redeemable
children.

Despite talk of 'near' and 'soon', the morning lengthened and insects
shrieked. Some of the boy soldiers wrapped their pale brown cloaks
around their eyes and slept. The humidity was fierce, and silenced all.
Connie, the baroness, Prim and the professor drenched handkerchiefs and
neck cloths with water, and the professor gallantly filled everyone's tea
glass with water again and again. By a little after noon it seemed the air
had grown too molten to be sustained upon the tongue. Yet Prim saw
many boy soldiers still slept.

'Ai-ai-ai,' said the baroness, considering them. 'What must it be like
to fight and to bleed in this air!'

About mid-afternoon John Along murmured something to the
professor. Prim noticed Along's soldiers beginning to rise and move
about.

'The Rizeighat fellow has made contact with my patrols,' Along
announced for general consumption.

Connie, circles of sweat under her armpits, stood and brushed down
her skirt. 'Alleluia,' she said. 'Best thing is, we won't have to doss here
overnight.'

Out of the bush to the west of the airstrip emerged two vehicles, a
four-wheel drive preceding, a two-tonner behind. They rolled down
towards the brush shelter, and on drawing to a stop, the lead truck

disgorged a half-dozen armed men. These Rizeighat militia were slightly but not definitively lighter-skinned than Along's boys, but not dressed so differently, though they wore informally wound *ghutras*, piled turban-wise, on their heads. As the professor walked forward to meet him, the man who led them, casually carrying his semi-automatic across the back of his shoulders, had on his youngish face a look of intense resignation. The officer's aides – or armed youths – strolled up in a less than regimented column, while behind them an uncertain number of other and obviously younger boys were being unloaded from the two-tonner by a handful of militiamen. These were the subject of the contract the baroness hoped to make.

Two lines each of about a dozen stringy boy children formed up. Some of them were garbed in dusty thobe-like garments, of the kind worn by children to Koranic schools. Others were in grimy T-shirts, the logos of football teams quenched in the fabric by dust, and khaki shorts massive by the standards of their legs. Contrary to other supposed 'victims' Prim had met, these seemed blank-eyed, obedient and inexpectant.

Now the Rizeighat militia leader let his gun down to the ground with one hand and made a profound obeisance to the professor. Next he nodded with joined hands towards the baroness, Connie and Prim. *'Assalamu Alaykum!'* he said, devout in greeting.

'Better help me with the water,' Connie Everdale told Prim. She led her off through the grass to the Sharps, and they mounted the steps. They were clearly to be the handmaidens of the process. It was over-warm within, but Connie worked fast, taking up one multi-litre pack of water and handing Prim another, with a pack of plastic cups beside.

Outside, a negotiation was in progress between the baroness, the professor, the Rizeighat officer and John Along. Prim passed, pouring water into plastic cups, down one line of children, who exuded sweat, fear and the smell of dust and dung. The boys did not reach for the cups of water until they were proffered. They had spent their times in some hard school.

Prim became aware of whispering, and was relieved to find two boys trading satiric grins, finding her as laughable an authority as boys their age – ten to thirteen – were meant to find all such figures. Yet they all told her *shokran*, thanks, as they had no doubt been instructed by their masters, whoever these might have been.

Coming level with a light-skinned Rizeighat militia guard, Prim studied his face a second and offered him a cup of water. Before accepting, the man, who could not have been more than twenty-two, joined his hands, and bowed his head. He too had been to a hard school.

Glancing back to the *rakubah*, Prim caught a glimpse of the baroness pulling green rolls of American dollars out of her satchel.

It seemed the business part of the affair was done, and the baroness crossed to the ragged line of children and began to stroll amongst them, lifting a chin here, prying a mouth open, inspecting eyes, in some ways the very model of an assessor of slaves. She asked them in Arabic to please sit down. They did so and their Arab guards towered above them.

The baroness addressed Prim, 'I'm sorry we cannot go yet. To seal the arrangement we must drink tea with both the Arab and Colonel Along. Leave the water canister here for the boys.' Prim followed her to the brush shelter. 'Don't,' the baroness murmured, 'be influenced against our friend, the Rizeighat colonel, el Zubair. He is not the only one who benefits from my satchel of notes. Companies of the SPLA are not so well-provided. Along must scrounge ammunition, bandages, drugs. He will be taking a quotient to his war purse.'

'This is an astonishing arrangement,' said Prim.

'Come,' said the baroness. 'It will be a rare experience for el Zubair. Drinking tea with women.'

And the baroness strode off in her Hapsburg manner to the *rakubah* brush shelter to which some of Along's soldiers were already delivering once more a great tin pot of tea, and anodised cups, and a plate of wheaten bread.

The party sat a long time with Colonel el Zubair, a man in his mid-forties, Prim guessed, and a lively conversationalist. There was leisurely tea drinking and discussion of the war to which they were all in their way party. The colonels, El Zubair and Along, seemed to think it a not totally crazy concept that they should take refreshment together and make slighty remarks about the regular army and the government in Khartoum.

Given that it seemed a Martha and Mary relationship between the baroness and Connie, Connie became restless to be either flying again or housekeeping. Since the former was impossible, she touched Prim's shoulder and asked her to come to the plane with her and break out some high-protein biscuits for the kids who, she told Prim, had probably travelled all day without food. Connie and Prim were still passing out the thick, grainy slabs to both Rizeighat guards and boys when the high-level tea party beneath the brush shelter came to a close.

It was a curious cargo now. Twenty-five boys fitted into sundry seats, without the restraint of seat belts, which dangled disorderedly around the seats. Compared to the perils these children had encountered, the threat of air turbulence seemed minor. Though some sat, others – those by windows – stood bolt upright, their shoulders trembling to every vibration. They had entered the furiously heated aircraft with awful obedience, though they had by then begun to talk sparsely, watchfully, to each other, and seemed composed once altitude and the engines drew cool air into the cabin. There was still by Western standards, and by the standards of the cheeky *shamassa* children of Central Khartoum's streets, an abnormal lack of conversation, as if these arts had been quenched in them. Amongst them Prim and the baroness moved like flight stewards with more high-protein biscuit and water. In her high, musical voice, the baroness told the boys, '*Dohret el mye-yah*', enunciating exactly and pointing to the toilet aft. Their work done, Prim and the baroness sat at last in the back row of seats.

'I understand now,' said Prim, 'that I barely know how you operate. You were expecting some twenty boys, Connie said. Twenty-five turned up.'

'Exactly,' said the baroness. She laughed briefly. 'Strained the exchequer. Our friend the militia officer el Zubair excelled himself. Of course, a man of authority, a Rizeighat sheik of a considerable village. Perhaps as many as two or three of these kids were in his own possession. Then at an invitation to sell, sent him across the lines by Along – if indeed there are lines – el Zubair has gone around amongst his neighbours in the Arab quarters of the towns and on the farms collecting Dinka boys, promising people a good price. So then he contacts Along with a progress report, they organise a meeting place, an airstrip. Next, Along faxes the professor and lets Connie know the approximate number – but it's often more, let me tell you.'

'They're all boys.' said Prim. 'Why no girls?'

'El Zubair said it would be boys this time, and we can't argue. His decision may, charitably considered, have been based on the reality that boys are most at risk of bloodshed – due to conscription by some commander less urbane than Colonel Along.'

For a while Prim contemplated in uneasy admiration the deft process of deliverance the baroness had devised. Such a brave endeavour! She felt churlish to question it, but she did.

'Forgive me for raising this, but have you ever suspected this man, el Zubair, or others like him, might be tempted to abduct more and more boys, purely for the potential cash reward? I know you told me your critics make this claim.'

The baroness nodded, raising her eyes, her chin pointed towards the juddering roof of the plane. 'For one thing, if it were so, why does el Zubair stop at twenty-five? Believe me, my dear girl, there are adequate numbers already serving in slavery to supply el Zubair's side of the market a thousand, two thousand times over.'

'But then, I can't help thinking,' Prim persisted, wishing that for the moment she could let the question rest, but as unable to do so, as desirous of teasing out the issue as when in Adi Hamit she first heard the word 'slave', 'if there is such a massive trade – and I believe like you there is – isn't a flight like this a mere gesture?'

'Dear girl,' said the baroness, with the most oblique trace of annoyance, 'you speak as if we were indulging ourselves, liberating some, ignoring the rest. You must think of the evidence gathered from these boys, names, histories. These will be sent to the UN Human Rights Commission, the UNHCR, the State Department, the British Foreign Office, and on and on, until the reality cannot be any longer denied. These children, processed and then returned to their families, are worth more than their individual weight, as precious as that might be.'

Prim looked out across the sea of children's heads, some quiescent, bobbing to look out windows. Conversations had started, larger boys talked over raised chins to smaller, and Prim could not help hope that something normal, some schoolboy cuffing, pushing, scragging might break out as a sign that these ageless children had been restored, at a cost, to their boyhoods.

Letter No 14, SARAH BERNARD

Friend Alice
We are in the town of Goulburn – we came down to it from the last ridge aboard the furniture wagon of the Scot Tolhurst. We walk to the

centre of the town past road gangs who yell at us in the usual way. In
the barracks we find first a constable and then a solid young police
magistrate in his navy blue coat who was just sitting to his luncheon. So
we stand together in the yard and we all think how the Factory is behind
and the magistrate is in front of us – he has come out to see us with a
gravy catching square of good linen in his hand. So the system is here
too. This fellow is the system in Goulburn and though he cannot be more
than thirty two years he has that same air of being in command since
ancient times.

He has us now follow him to his table and we stand by it – the little
woman Carty holding her daughter tight to stop her wandering about
the room and maybe upsetting a cruet and ruining her mother's record
as a fresh minted citizen of New South Wales. The big magistrate starts
eating bits of mutton – he is delicate in manner and does not stuff his
mouth – and at the same time asks: Do you have any complaints about
your treatment during your journey? Did the wagoner chap treat you
well?

Big brick red Connolly says: Yer Honner he had been warned off.

As he should be says the police magistrate. He then says to Carty
without dropping his fork and nodding at the bundle held by her: That
is a baby boy?

Carty says: It is my little Molly sir. She was famous in the Factory for
saying it is my little Molly – the way someone might say: Here comes
the Prince of Wales!

Well then the police magistrate says with some potato in his mouth
now. Very well you have the option to mind her and raise her far from
dens of thieves and whores. You can give her value.

The little red brick mother says all the while glowing: That is what I
mean to.

He rings a bell and a constable enters. The magistrate says: Take these
women to the nuns. To us he says: The nuns are better at keeping girls
safe at large in Goulburn.

My Papist companions look at each other and halfway smile and
halfway frown. They were as frightened as I at the idea of trading constables for nuns.

The constable leads us out into the afternoon warmth and says not to
one but all of us: You're a pretty parcel. What lucky old buggers getting
you for a piece of joy?! Any of you interested in matrimony with a single
constable?

Though he is sallow and nearly all his teeth gone yet he had firm wrists. He was not like solid Long but he was dressed neat.

The constable leads us with his shoulders all drooping with pretended loss through streets and to the gate of a little flat cottage like other flat cottages but with a cross affixed to the top of its gabled gate. Here right within the gate lies a garden of cabbages and potatoes.

Says the convict constable: Should you think you've met the full force of the Convict Department System you aint met Sister Ignatius yet. Iggy is behind the veil a true killer and a scourge of her fallen sisters.

His hammering on the door gets answered by a small woman wearing a high starched apron. She could have been a sister of our little mother Carty for she has that same look – the look of the convict ship and the Female Factory. Will you get the Head Missus? the ugly constable asks her. Soon a wiry little wisp of a woman dressed in nunnish brown garb arrives and the constable hands her our papers. This woman is about the age of Mrs Matron. She looks the papers over. She is full of business. She says: Ah Miss Bernard you have a little time to wait with us for the Nugan Ganway people will not soon be here. You Mrs Carty – we shall take you and your infant by wagon tomorrow to your place of employment – not ten miles from here. And you Miss Connolly we may well take you later today. But first let us drink tea like the very nearly free women we all now happen to be.

Rigorous as any warden she jerks her head and we follow her down a corridor.

I am chilled to find one door barred like a prison and behind it are cots and a scrawny badly used woman sitting in there yelling. Damn the scrodding Pope and damn you and damn Jesus who put me here! The nun tells us it is the cell for those unsatisfactories returned from assignment as servants for crimes committed against their masters. The young police magistrate Mr Purler – says the nun – trusts us better than he does his own convict constables to keep them guard. Mind you my ladies that woman in there is not a woman returned for being misused by her employer but for misusing. She thinks she can hurt me but I cannot be hurt easily. My four sisters and I have made the same journey you have. We have been cast on the water and reborn of it.

The big red woman Connolly asks her: You were not transported surely.

We were transported of our own will. I travelled on Almorah on the convict deck from Cork to look to the interests of my countrywomen.

All my sisters – all the four of them – did the same. And one of them murdered here by ungodly men.

Murdered you say? the little woman Carty asks. A nun murdered? A nun murdered? Murthered is how she says it.

Says the nun: We tested God perhaps too much by sending her unprotected into the wilderness. It was all a chosen task for this woman and we could not argue with it nor could we scorn. It was by our own choice that we tempted God by taking to the wide waters of the earth and tending the rope burned hands of the sailors and eating the same diet as prisoners and going down into the mad furnace of the convict deck off Africa.

We listened hard to her. The barrier we put up on hearing advice from most free women was that when they told us what to do they did not know. This woman with the name of a man – this Ignatius – she knows.

She sits us down at a big table and the woman in the high apron pours us china cups of tea on a table that smells of beeswax. Get them some currant cake too says Sister Ignatius who has joined us at the table. A slab of currant cake and a knife are placed in front of us. Help yourself and pass on – so Ignatius advises. Go on. You are ticket of leave women now and must get used to the normal doing of things.

It is excellent cake too and full of a kind of promise. It is sweet. Ignatius puts before us food and drink like good news. And this is a darling cake – the little red woman Carty said – feeding it to her child. We grind it in our mouths. It tastes of our new small but growing power and hope.

The tea and the cake are now drunk and Ignatius stands and says: Well we will all go and deliver Miss Connolly here to her employment at the chandlery. It is peculiar to hear the big red woman called Miss Connolly.

We all put on our bonnets again and set out with Ignatius leading us through the garden of cabbages and potatoes and through the sound of afternoon wood chopping. Carty carries her little freckled girl who is placid. We step aside meekly into a garden to let sheep be driven through a crossroads and we pass the Commercial Hotel. On its verandah men who would normally shout to us merely whisper to each other because – I am sure – of Ignatius. As we walk she is instructing the big red one Connolly – though her counsels are designed in a way for all three of us.

She says: If you have any torment at the hands of Mr or Mrs Schottfeld who own the chandlery you are not to abscond for that is the way to certain retribution. You are to come to me. But – mark you – no silly complaints. I speak of cruel blows or forcing liquor upon you or worse

*things. It would be the very sin of pride she says to claim before the Lord
I have the police magistrate in my pocket. But it is largely the truth. I
do have that vain young man there.*

*The idea makes us all break into shared laughter. She seems to approve
of that. We have not laughed such sincere laughter yet on our journey
and now she supplies that lack out of her own invention.*

*The door of the chandlery with Schottfeld written above it is closed
and we all peer through the glass and see that within there is some
disorder. Barrels are overturned and rope snakes uncoiled everywhere
over counters and heaps of coir doormats and jute sacking can be seen.*

*Dearest Mother! says Ignatius tightly and begins knocking on the glass.
Now she tries the handle of the front door and it gives and the door
opens.*

*We travel in a file behind Ignatius down the disordered corridors of
the chandlery amidst the stands of picks and shovels and the savage
blades of ploughs and axes. We can hear from beyond a half open door
at the back of the chandlery the noise of crying and then considerable
curses. Leave a bloody man at a time like this! cries – indeed – a man.
And more: Travel all the way and nurse his cholera on board and then
die on the edge of happiness. On the edge of bloody wealth. What sort
of a woman is this? – so the voice asks. What sort?*

*This is from the storeroom and since Ignatius has emboldened us we
step through with her into it. Everywhere are pieces of iron and beams
of timber and a man of about forty five years by my guess sits on a stool
in the middle of the floor. He seems even sitting to be drunkenly
unsteady. From the rafter above him hang nooses in ropes of this gauge
and that so that he has left himself provided with many choices for
ending his existence. The man at the stool at last sees Ignatius and raises
to her a face of ghastly torment.*

She has left me – he says – my light and only recourse.

Mrs Schottfeld? asks Ignatius.

*A fever two nights ago and then an onset of flux and at midnight last
night a seizure. She is in her coffin at the Carberry undertakers. Where
I seek at once to join her.*

*The many nooses he has made for himself show he is not fully decided
on this but devoutly wants it.*

*Ignatius seems to think him undecided too. For, says Ignatius: Living
blood cries out for life. The close comes quickly enough in this veil of
tears without being rushed along with sundry thicknesses of rope.*

The close cannot be quick enough – so says the man who is Mr Schottfeld.

But I have brought your new servant. You must meet Rose Connolly.

Rose Connolly the large red woman. Half friend and half mocker she bows to Mr Schottfeld who considers her.

He holds his head backwards for better viewing. There is nothing that that great lummox can do for me he says. Servants are for the living.

All the more therefore are they for you Mr Schottfeld. Naturally Rose cannot now stay on the premises with you but I shall leave her here each day under the care and supervision of one of my sisters. Ignatius then turned to Connolly. You must begin to prepare a meal for Mr Schottfeld. Look in the pantry in the cookhouse – there will be something for you to get ready.

The large red one looks stricken at this idea and taken with panic but moves off like a woman using limbs she has suspected to be damaged and has not tested again until now. At the same time Ignatius picks up the two thirds empty bottle of brandy by the chair and carries it to the window where she opens the stiff pane and pours the last of the spirits away into the open air. The little red mother licks her lips at such needless waste but says nothing.

The nun is commanding with Mr Schottfeld. You must for now take to your bed for a man must not make such an awful decision as this without rest.

And he goes and does it – this tear streaked unpretty man who was willing at least to think of dying for loss.

To my amazement Connolly obeys Ignatius as the man had and finds some smoked ham in the pantry. Under the direction of Ignatius too the little red mother and I mount ladders and untie the nooses and put the store in order. Then home we go amazed to tea which we eat at the big polished table with two other servants awaiting wagons to their masters and with Ignatius and two of her sisters.

I say at table: They call this a convent do they mother?

It is what I call a convent dear Miss Bernard. It is not what one of those English Benedictine priests in Sydney would call a convent.

I could join Ignatius willingly and at the expense of believing anything and might have done so except that I would need I suppose to take back my pledges to my sweet Alice.

Whose friend hereby for now signs her name

Sarah

I RECEIVE A FIERCE LETTER

I told Phoebe that as well as writing for a housekeeper I would write to her parents with the good news of our impending parenthood. I was always left uneasy by her indifference to her mother and father. I did not doubt her love, but she seemed to think she had centuries and not simply fragile years to make peace, to find a place for them in the tale she was living.

'Write to my mother,' she told me knowingly. 'She will be edified and even a little surprised. But don't write to my father. He is not ready for a letter yet.'

I had by now had definite news of Mr Finlay's present problem: he had needed to sell some land at Yass and the brewery in Goulburn, and in a falling market. The air of respect with which these transactions were reported in the *Sydney Herald* and even in the very different and more rankly populist *Goulburn Herald* indicated that these were temporary stratagems undertaken to buttress an inherently robust fortune. Towards other men desperately selling assets they were not as kind.

The autumn rain made me more hopeful for the lambing, yet it was about lambing-time that I got a fierce answer from Finlay concerning Phoebe's pregnancy.

Dear Sir,

I am appalled to find that you should have imposed a child upon my daughter, no doubt with the intent of claiming my property through it. I take it this infant is designed to produce appeasement, since what brute could oppose the claims of blood and grandchildren! I love my lost daughter and await her return, but in the meantime am left to assure you that no shift, no device you can think of, no felon cunning available to you can make you or your succession welcome to me.

I do ask you to desist from imposing any further contact upon me.

Happily, Mrs Finlay had somehow got control of the envelope and enclosed an imperious but more welcome note of her own.

Please give all my love to my daughter and use her well. When she knows where she will lay in, if it be with the Parslows of Braidwood, I would use every endeavour to visit her there.

I showed Phoebe her mother's note as if it had been the brisk extent of the letter. The father's letter I destroyed, not forgetting to make a copy for my journal however, as if that were some sort of vengeance, or a little trap which would one day spring on him. I knew once and for all not to go near the Finlay house, for whatever my demeanour might be, I would be greeted with the standard insult.

MY NEW HOUSEKEEPER

The price of wethers had crept up a little thanks to the autumn rain, and so I took some to Goulburn with Long and my drovers. Phoebe, who was beginning to thicken with child, came with me, saying this was the last excursion she would be able to make for some time. We scudded along royally in our phaeton, in front of the dust of the herd. The men pitched a tent for us each night, and laid out our swags, buttressed by the upholstered green cushions from the phaeton.

I had raised with Phoebe the invitation of the new minister at Cooma Creek, Reverend Mr Paltinglass and his wife, that she should have her lying-in at the little brick vicarage in Cooma, to be delivered there with the help of a midwife and the young Scots doctor Alladair. But when again I suggested that she write and tell her parents that she would have her child in Cooma, she became very short with me, and it was only after we were settled in our tent with a lamp hanging from its central pole that she told me, 'You might tell my mother if you wish. As for Father, he is still playing at his game of having begotten an ungrateful child.'

I kissed her but it did occur to me that she too was still engaged in a game of vengeance. If Phoebe had a fault, I concluded as we conversed, it was an innate intolerance of her parents. She was dismissive of her brother, George, too. He had gone to Harrow and was now about to enter Oxford. Perhaps as a reaction to his father's sturdy sense of the material world there was a presumption that he might become a minister of the Church of England.

Other than getting a not-so-bad price at the saleyards of 9 shillings per beast, and sending a man to deliver a note to Mrs Finlay, I had two duties to attend to before Phoebe and I left Goulburn. I had been disturbed by Mr Loosely's air of wistfulness the last time I visited his Academy in Grafton Street, and wished to see how Felix and Hector

were. As I approached the gate of Mr Loosely's admirable experimental
school I saw disturbing signs of decay. The academy's front gardens,
where the pupils were put to work learning botany and primitive agriculture, looked – with the hard summer long over – unwatered. Stakes
designed to hold up vines had collapsed, and amongst the withered stalks
sat a half-caste child of about six years of age, attempting to extract a
little bell from inside a ball made of raffia. He wore only a faded blue
shirt and the poor child seemed to be myopic, barely able to see the glint
of the blue bell within the strands of wicker.

I rapped on the door, and a desolate-eyed convict maid opened it.
Behind her I could hear a hubbub of children which sounded disordered,
not at all like the unleashed voice of native Australian scholarship which
had been Mr Loosely's objective.

'Is Mr Loosely well?' I asked the convict woman.

'Not on your oath, sir,' she told me. 'Not so lively at all.'

She put me in the parlour, where I sat facing the wall where Loosely's
map of China was crookedly hung. Little, wispy Mrs Loosely hurried
in at last. She wore a grey apron on which some stains, perhaps of
modelling clay, showed. She made no attempt to explain the turmoil
of children I could hear from the yard. 'Mr Bettany,' she said. 'Did
you read that the Governor of New South Wales has withdrawn his
grace from us?'

I admitted I had not.

'So we are without support. Our black children are to go to Blacktown,
our white to the Devil. This is Mr Loosely's reward.' Her face quivered.
'How easily he could have founded another sad colonial grammar school
for the children of the moneyed class . . . Or he could have been a master
at the best British school, if his angels had not driven him here. And the
stipend he sought in place of the affluence which could have been his
has now been cut off.'

'I had no idea. What reason did His Excellency give?'

'There have been malicious rumours concerning beatings, and our
enemies have not omitted to throw in slanders about the drinking of hard
liquor.'

'By Mr Loosely?'

'That in despair he gave some to scholars too. To children.'

I shook my head. No wonder the wife seemed so beset, so worn to a
wire. As I wondered what to say and do, the door was pushed open and
Mr Loosely was there, wax-pale, unshaven, wearing only his nightshirt

and showing gingery straggles of whiskers. Having thrown the door wide, he entered normally, like a schoolmaster in august possession of all his appropriate weeds and wits, and closed it quietly. Then he came across to the table, sat down opposite me and gathered himself as if to be frank.

'Mr Bettany,' he said, 'that second child you sent me is a failure. He has not proven to be a primal well of yearning waiting to be undammed. This child, unsullied with the blood of the European Cain, this child from that supposedly limitless mine of the intellect's longing, is a cretin, an utter idiot. I expected the fullness of raw intelligence. I got a fool. I became a fool myself for having held out such a vision to the Viceroy. On his last visit His Excellency was acutely disappointed to behold the place and to quiz the children.'

'You are not well, my friend,' I said.

Poor mad-eyed Loosely shook his head. 'I don't know what is happening to me. I have interminable flux.'

As he sat trembling in his nightshirt and complaining more to God than to me, his wife reached for his wrist and turned her pale eyes to me. Loosely gathered himself. 'The power of the child Hector's ignorance is what oppressed me. I had set tasks in ciphering and copying. He failed once, and again, but – sir – I was patient, waiting for that mighty serpent of knowledge to arise. But whatever I asked, at each turn I might as well have been asking him to translate the Rosetta Stone. I brought him brandy and said, 'Drink that, you oaf. Your mind is incapable of being rendered less prehensile than it already is.'

'You forced brandy on Hector?' I was beginning to see why His Excellency might have been shocked. 'That child is my ward.'

An acute and childlike alarm rose in the faces both of Mr and Mrs Loosely. Mrs Loosely raised both hands. 'It was unwise. But Mr Loosely had not slept. He was so disappointed, you see.'

'But how can that excuse such an act?' I asked.

Mr Loosely fibrillated his hands madly in front of his face. 'How indeed, sir? How indeed? But doctor has given me opium for the pain of that bare ignorance ...' He gestured towards the noise of his residual pupils from the yard. 'Their ignorance is a spike in my flesh.'

He lowered his head on the table then and Mrs Loosely explained, 'He thinks they have made him sick because they can't do long multiplication. He has encountered but one gem, your boy Felix. Apart from that, it is barrenness ...' She gestured towards the air.

'My dear sir,' I told Loosely, 'you must see a really good physician.'

I was stricken for him, and for Hector. He had suggested this vain experiment but I had gone along with it, delivering poor Hector to him like an amateur botanist bringing some rare vine. I took a £5 note from my pocket and passed it with minimum gesture to Mrs Loosely.

'You must both look after yourselves,' I said.

'What will become of us?' she asked.

'I will write to His Excellency and urge a government pension,' I told her.

But she seemed to think that was not likely to work. 'I have, praise God, a well-to-do family in Abingdon on the Thames, and will need to apply to them for great help.' She took the £5 note nonetheless.

Poor Mr Loosely rose and put the back of his hand to his forehead. 'Oh the old grief creeps on me,' he said, and walked out.

Mrs Loosely went running into the corridor behind him. 'Winnie, Winnie, put Mr Loosely into his bed.'

Naturally, on her return, I asked her if I could see Felix and Hector. She took me to the back door, from which we could see the yard where perhaps twenty ill-clad children were making the noise of two hundred.

'I shall stop here. I am the matron indoors, but Felix is the only one they will obey outdoors. He is the monitor for the open air.'

I saw them both at once, Felix standing and holding apart a white urchin from a black one, Hector. Hector was bare-bottomed, and they both wore threads and had no jackets despite the advancing New South Wales winter.

Mrs Loosely said, 'We have cut down on clothing since Mr Loosely's dosages became so expensive.'

It struck me then that of course he was deranged. Because some fool of a doctor had told Loosely to consume laudanum, his judgement had vanished. Hence the pin-point eyes, the bloody flux, the craziness of forcing brandy upon poor Hector. Even the idea to force grammar and geometry on Hector may have been opium-driven. Yet I had been persuaded to go along with it.

I went down into the yard, and Felix saw me and gave up with a grateful sigh all efforts to mediate between Hector and the other child. He was now a handsome boy of nearly ten years, and stepped towards me and said, 'Mr Bettany, could you take me away from here? I have learned enough.'

'I think I will take you away,' I told him. 'I had no concept . . .'

A number of the yard urchins, the children of convicts, drew close to listen.

'I will work very hard as your stockman.'

'Mr Loosely says you are too clever to be a stockman.'

'No,' he said, smiling. 'I am a stockman here.' And he looked around the churned, unruly yard.

'But don't you have loyalty to Mr Loosely?' I asked him. 'Now he is ill?'

He did not answer.

Hector now took my hand. There was wariness in his eyes. What was to be done with him?

'Can you ride?' I asked Felix. I had a clear image of the two of us, riding with vast flocks beneath snowy escarpments.

'Yes,' he told me, and indicated an old nag beyond the yard fence, grazing in a paddock.

'I think I could put you on a better horse than that one,' I told him. 'And the tongue you spoke as a child ... you remember that? How to talk to the Moth people ...?'

'*Utique, domne!*' he told me in classroom Latin. Yes Master. A child pitiably trying to show he had studied dutifully.

I went therefore and made it finally plain to Mrs Loosely that I was taking both boys. I told them to go to the resident children's dormitory and collect what they owned. They came back still without shoes or jackets. Felix carried a Latin Primer named *Liber Primus et Secundus*, and Hector a top, which he held close to his lips, as if to say, 'No books for me.'

Behind me Mrs Loosely cried with a fluting voice, 'We intended to buy more winter clothes before too long, Mr Bettany. But tradesmen are not very understanding in this town.' By that she obviously meant that they wanted to be paid.

'Why did your husband and yourself not inform me?' I asked.

But then I had not visited the academy regularly enough. I had let Loosely fly to pieces without any intrusion from me.

That was the last I saw of these people destroyed by the sort of excessive hopes which abound in the air of young colonies. I did hear that after Mr Loosely had had some treatment or other in Sydney, they went home and disappeared into the mass of Britons.

Hector and Felix were deposited with Long and Clancy and Presscart at my wagons. Felix was boy enough to return with us to Nugan

Ganway, but Hector was still an infant. I was uneasy about imposing him on Phoebe, not that I doubted her openness of heart, and I hoped I might find some establishment in Goulburn to take him and complete, or get close to completing, his education.

Phoebe was again waiting for me at Mandelson's and before we left town I must collect the convict woman Sarah Bernard from wherever the magistrate had located her. Upon inquiry at hulking Police Magistrate Purler's office I was surprised to find she had been placed with the Irish nuns, whom I had not met before, despite my regard for the lamented Catherine.

I rode in the four-wheeler the few streets to that place and was admitted to a parlour by a maid who muttered that she would fetch someone named Iggy. This Iggy proved to be a powerful little woman, Mother Ignatius, with full black garb and tucked-up sleeves, who entered the room in a flurry. She reached for my right hand with both of hers and laid her forehead against my wrists. 'You are the fellow now who took the right vengeance for our sainted Catherine. God bless and keep you!'

I told the woman that Phoebe and I were still most distressed at the mischief which had befallen Catherine.

'Mischief,' said Ignatius. 'That of course is a good way to put it.'

She called for tea and we sat talking in a worldly manner. 'Oh your wife is to have a child, is it?' she asked. 'Grand, grand! And thus you more than need a housekeeper. I think Bernard is the right one, you know. She's close, close . . .' Ignatius patted the side of her nose as if in imitation of some livestock trader she may have seen at market as a girl. 'But able to write very well, says she got it from her father, an old Jew. She's a Christian Jewess. A compelling mixture, wouldn't you say now? Why, having become a Christian in a sort of way at the age of fourteen, she needs to remind all that she is Jewish too, I cannot say. But she seems to be strong on the matter. She is a reliable girl and the police magistrate joins me in thinking her so.'

'You have a startling relationship with the police magistrate,' I remarked.

She did not choose to comment on this. 'Sit still there, Mr Bettany, and I will fetch her and see if she would be of any use to your wife and yourself.'

But I felt I must not deceive this remarkable woman, so I held up my hand to detain her a second longer. 'I should tell you that there are many lonely men due for ticket-of-leave on my station.' I thought of Long, who had always been the champion of this woman I had not seen. 'It's likely she will end as a wife to one of them.'

'Well,' said the remarkable Ignatius, 'that is nature's way, is it not? But on my observation, given that she is likely to be the wife of anyone, it is better that it should not be one rendered brutish by the lash. But such considerations, I think, we can leave to Miss Bernard herself, since she is a woman of quite a little character.'

She went, leaving me secretly to speculate upon this convict woman and lonely Long, with his convict theory that the passage of seven years with no news from his home, of failed or renounced communication with his marital cottage in Ireland, justified him in marrying in New South Wales. I realised that the idea did not shock me, as it might have had I first heard of it over tea cups in say a Manchester parlour. Moralists said that remote life in the bush weakened the strict ethic sense, and perhaps it was so. The Eve-less vacancy of the earth called for a European female presence on nearly any decent grounds.

I was in the midst of these speculations, innocent as events would prove them to be, when Ignatius brought the convict Sarah Bernard into the room.

I noticed at once that she was taller than most women, perhaps five feet nine inches. She had a lean and very pleasant face with a seeking quality to it, and was much closer to me in age than Phoebe. At that first meeting I did not place her as more than surprisingly pleasant and appropriately reserved, and yet I was aware there was a presence in this woman which placed her above the usual colonial categories. In her well-ordered features was that same vigilance which characterised many intelligent felons and ticket-holders, and so thoroughly characterised Long, the subject of my recent thoughts, as well.

I did my best, however, to see her purely as a potential servant. I was relieved to see that her wide-set brown eyes were studying me with perhaps greater attention and a more fervent hope than I her. And why not? If I made a mistake, I had merely chosen an unsatisfactory servant who could be shipped back to Goulburn with next month's mail. If she made the wrong move, the course of her life would thereby become skewed.

Yet for some unknown reason, as early as this I thought I needed some sort of defence against the scale of her being and, pretending I did this with all my servants, I found myself asking what she had been transported for, what her crime might be? She said she had stolen table napkins and other fabric wares from a haberdasher in York Street, Manchester. I did not tell her then that I could remember very dimly York Street, and my mother hurrying along it in fog with Simon and myself held by the hand. Either the poverty of being a law clerk's wife, or the poverty of being a convicted felon's wife, drove this young woman, my mother, on her blind way, ignoring the fabrics in the shops along this road in which porters seemed to do their best to collide with us and lights shone in early afternoon like dead stars. Manchester. She had the accent.

'They must have been expensive napkins.'

She looked me full in the face, as if making a declaration of Christian faith before a Roman procurator.

'They were, sir. Though I would not say that was the point of the crime.'

I saw Ignatius, behind the convict woman, smile and shake her head.

'Well what was?' I asked.

'One moment of great need,' said Sarah Bernard.

'You should have no such need in Nugan Ganway,' I said. 'It is at least far removed from the temptations of table napkins.'

I was disappointed that she smiled only with the greatest caution. But she said, 'Then it is the right country for me.'

I spanned the conversation out, asking where she had worked at housekeeping and kitchen skills, and she told me it was a good house, the Tib Street house of a Manchester merchant named Duncannon, in which she had worked. 'And did he have children?' I asked.

'Three,' she told me. 'Of various ages, one as young as seven. A girl of eighteen years.'

'I trust you may have children to tend to on Nugan Ganway,' I said, and heard the all-at-once empty echo of the words in my own head. 'My wife is due to give birth later in the year.'

Ignatius was growing restless. 'Sarah should fetch her linen bag now,' she suggested.

Bernard turned and as she did I saw in her something foreign, some darker features – her Orientalism, her Russian-ness perhaps, for I had heard of Russian Jews in Manchester. Bernard had through no fault of her own released in the room a riskiness I wanted to disperse.

'One thing,' I said hurriedly. She turned again, brown eyes on me. I thought of something to say which could as easily have been said later. 'My wife takes seriously her role as manager of all things non-pastoral at Nugan Ganway. What I am telling you is that you must wait for her instructions and obey them with alacrity. But if there is anything you have doubts about doing, refer to her first.'

'Yes,' said Bernard simply, and so went.

In Bernard's absence I was pleased to have another matter to raise with Ignatius. I had placed a half-cast foundling, and later a young full-blood foundling with Mr Loosely, I told her, and it had all seemed to work well for a time. She must have heard about the decline of Mr Loosely's Academy, I surmised aloud, and she clucked and shook her head in a way which confessed she had. Now I was for lack of other choices taking the grown half-caste child with me to Nugan Ganway, but the full-blood was still a child, and I did not wish to impose him upon my wife at such a time.

I offered a yearly fee of two guineas if Ignatius would take Hector in.

'What would happen if, without any persuasion from us, he decided to turn Roman? Would you be at the gate accusing us of swaying him?'

'Not unless swaying him had become the chief objective of you and your sisters.'

'We don't believe in ambush,' she said darkly, but like an ambusher. 'But there is no reason it should happen. We shall send him to the Anglicans each week.'

So I decided to go, while the convict woman Bernard gathered her things, and fetch him from the wagon camp, little wiry Hector. He entered the house of the Popish Nuns with a marked tranquillity and I thought that if such calmness was the price one paid for an inability to do long multiplication, I would willingly have sacrificed some of my own mathematical skills to possess it.

Thus Sarah Bernard was swapped for Hector, and my solid and placid life became feverish, and the world both narrowed like a trap and widened with an unplanned and limitless ecstasy. And all at the one time.

Letter No 15, SARAH BERNARD

Dearest Alice

A quick note before leaving this nuns house to say I am on my way to see my friend Long. I am to travel with Mr Bettany and his wife to Nugan Ganway. Bettany looks a man of reason but very serious not least when trying to be funny. It sounds that his wife might be hard to please. He asked me what my crime might be. Might be – I would say that is an important question.

I think though it is dangerous to surmise that I might have fallen amongst the just. Mrs Bettany must be a notable style of woman to choose such a far off marriage as that to Mr Bettany.

I am on my path and so are you – it is the same thing my friend. More news will come.

Your lasting friend
Sarah

OUR SON IS BORN

From their first meeting, Bernard turned into the perfect companion for Phoebe, and throughout the winter, the confidante of her pregnancy. The returning Felix also took to Bernard. Soon after their arrival I would see them sitting together in the vacated phaeton at dusk reading to each other from Felix's works on grammar. Felix liked particularly to translate, for Bernard's enjoyment, from Caesar's *Gallic Wars* and Bernard would say to me, 'Mr Bettany, this native boy is cleverer than all of us.' Later, during the winter, in mid-afternoons, Felix, who lived in the Irishman O'Dallow's hut, would come to see Bernard, where she lived in a little bark annex to the kitchen, and they could be found, at a small table, reading, passing books to each other, some of them borrowed from me. Each time I saw one of my books in her hand, I hoped with the silly hope of male vanity that she thought my possession of such a work (the history of the Punic Wars, for example) meant that I was a cultivated man.

As spring neared and I prepared for the shearing, I saw them almost daily, climbing the ridge behind the homestead in their boots, taller Bernard stalking ahead carrying Phoebe's easel and paintbox. On busy days the admirable Felix stuck with me, building new pens for my yet abounding flocks, impeccable with a hammer. When there was no work for him, he went and read to the women as Phoebe painted. If there were native women about in the foothills, where despite our former misunderstanding, conflicts and mutual murders, they still came in the spring by ancestral habit, they might also join the party. They mistrusted us men except as a source of flour and tea and chewing tobacco. But Phoebe would have Felix fetch from the house a chart she had bought in Goulburn. She would unroll it, hang it from a tree and conduct an alphabet class. Then with the greatest of ease, she would ask them to take up a brush. Sometimes they would, laughing, but make nonsense lines in her art book.

'But they do well, I know, for they hold the brush very exactly,' Phoebe would tell me. 'I mean, they know how to hold a brush, something a child needs to be taught.'

I had indeed once blundered upon a Ngarigo dance, or what they called *corroboree*, a dance by firelight, and the men had used the clays of Nugan Ganway – the plentiful brown, the rarer ochre, red and yellow, and the white from a particular white clay cliff cut by the stream of the Murrumbidgee some way west of Nugan Ganway, to enhance their bodies and faces quite graphically. But I hoped Phoebe did not look for too much improvement to derive from her intermittent outdoor classes. The last one who had put faith in the universal talents of the natives had been Mr Loosely.

Phoebe and Bernard had got to the stage of exchanging affectionate and sisterly embraces, and I was pleased that should Phoebe's confinement come on early, she would have the solace of that company. The familiarity of tone between them showed a democratic impulse in Phoebe which must have come from her mother.

I noticed all this, but what I most noticed was Bernard. It was as if I were a theatre-struck youth who could not see enough of the features and movements of a given actress. I was not aware of affection – that belonged to Phoebe. But a new need to *see* seemed to have arisen in me – at least, so I explained it to myself. I dimly remember as a mere fragment of speech the words Bernard uttered. The content was not significant. The gentle nature of her Yorkshire accent was the essential issue.

I might even walk out of my way to encounter my servant. But why? Who could match what pretty Phoebe had done – finding me in the bush, abandoning her home, embracing joyously the barbarous Nugan Ganway life? The valiant way she had behaved, the scope of her love, compelled a lifelong love from me. The sad truth was that a mindless oaf who occupied my flesh and passed himself off as Jonathan Bettany wanted for himself that familiarity of tone, that careful affection, those embraces, which he saw passed by Bernard to Phoebe. He could not be otherwise persuaded by intermittent common sense, this buffoon. To him, Bernard was a marvel.

The young loom-breaker Presscart drove Phoebe and Bernard into Cooma a week before Phoebe's predicted date – finer than I would have liked, but Phoebe was in this as in all things a girl of her own mind. I rode in three days later, and in the middle of a summer's night Phoebe went into labour. Alladair and the midwife were called, Bernard and Mrs Paltinglass were attendant, and at three in the morning our son was born. This emergency compelled my attention and respect – there were hours at a time during the delivery, with Phoebe robustly defying her own pain, when I thought the careless, covetous clown who had possessed me was gone. Phoebe's bravery compelled me! The sight of my son, fresh from Phoebe, raising a small robust fist before being wrapped in a blanket by Bernard, was a scene in which – blessedly – the squalling boy, my son, was the chief element, and, after comforting and caressing Phoebe, who made light of her labour, I fell asleep towards dawn, convinced that the birth of a son had saved me from all that was asinine in myself.

I wanted to call our son George, in honour of Phoebe's brother. When I had mentioned it earlier as a potential boy's name, Phoebe had made a mouth but not dissented. I was delighted. These family pieties were important to me, whatever her father might think. I was gratified to make any gesture to bring Phoebe and her parents closer together.

Later in that day, while I sat on the Paltinglass's verandah reading, in what I had assured myself was my old calm, the newly born *Cooma Courier*, a carriage driven by a male convict wearing a splendid blue jacket arrived at the gate of the vicarage. In a blue dress and large straw hat, Phoebe's mother descended. She accorded exactly with my memory of her, the slightly bruised and beautiful cautiousness which seemed to be the mark of the woman was still in place.

Making noises of welcome, I rushed down to meet her. 'You have a grandson,' I said, 'And his name will be George.'

I did not look to flatter the Finlays in any way, but my own filial instincts cried out for it.

She grasped my wrist. 'Well,' she said, 'it was managed then.' Despite a little discomfort at her frankness I looked at her to see if there was any form of accusation in this. But she said, 'No, no. *I* know, Bettany, you are a good fellow.'

'And you make me very happy by being here,' I told her, very nearly believing in the happiness I felt at all aspects of the day. What I knew more profoundly was that events had caused me to mimic the joy I should have felt. How, after Phoebe's suffering and the emergence of little George, could I say, even secretly to myself, that what I cherished and retrieved from that day was the sight of Sarah Bernard emerging from the Paltinglass kitchen with a cup of tea or a glass of tonic for my wife, leaving behind her the rude discourse of other kitchen servants. And my perceiving that here was a goddess amongst swineherds. Even while my mother-in-law's kindly hand was on my wrist, that is what I most knew and most celebrated.

But I said, 'How is Mr Finlay?'

'Mr Finlay will play the grandfather in his time, I hope. He takes great time to grow into the fullness of his position, which does not please me. But he will make a doting elder sooner or later. I tell you now, I am possessed by a fear that unless he and Phoebe desist from their stubbornness, our son will not come home soon, for who wants to travel all that distance to listen to orations and rants?'

In coming days on that same verandah from which I had rushed to welcome Mrs Finlay, I held my son, swaddled and moving his head with that infant quickness. I sniffed the Australian air like a man with all life's questions settled and for minutes on end escaped the ridiculous groove in which my head ran. My continual fear was that someone would notice a hollowness in my fatherly exuberance. And I *was* exuberant, and already loved my son. Bernard was something, however, which I feared would be visible to my friends, and sat in me not so much like the definite paternal joy I felt in George, but like a wound, or the swellings of a fever.

Phoebe and Bernard had not long returned to Nugan Ganway with little George, its heir, when an unlikely traveller arrived at the homestead by way of our now distinct track to Cooma. Even from a distance, he looked ecclesiastical in an old-fashioned way, with his large black hat and his leg gaiters, of a kind many colonial clergy found inconvenient. Closer up, he had the same pale and clouded eyes as new-born mice, and his skin was so pale that the summer had not turned it brown but brought out sore-looking patches of pink. His dray was loaded with sacks of flour, tea and sugar, and with boxes which proved to contain a supply of tracts.

He stopped on the north side of the homestead, where I stood by the home yard to meet him. He dismounted, sniffed the air, and said, 'Sir, you have not been forced to boil down!'

'No,' I said, 'I have been lucky in that regard, Reverend Mr ...'

'Oh,' he said. 'I am the Reverend Inigo Howie, Protector of Aborigines for this region.'

So this was the man Treloar had raged against. I felt an unease myself.

Had I behaved well towards the Moth people? This man might not think
so.

But his round, reddish-complexioned face seemed mild and even
hapless. 'Please,' he said, 'I would regard it as the greatest charity if one
of your men could turn my poor horse out, and yard it.'

I told him that was easily done, and called on Felix, who was at the
time seated on the verandah with Bernard, reading. Phoebe and George,
who had had a restive night, were both sleeping. I asked the man inside.
I had some port and gave him a hefty glass. He had the appearance of
a man who needed it.

Phoebe arose and hungrily questioned this inoffensive fellow. She told
him of her efforts to teach the alphabet to native women. Though she
had persuaded three of them to look into the house, they had not stayed
more than a hour or so, polite and timorous at one moment, and the
next loud and likely to pick up objects – tea cups, books, samplers – and
walk off perhaps innocently, calling on their fellows on the verandah to
admire what they clearly intended to take for their own use.

The Reverend Howie drifted away in the midst of Phoebe's account of
the natives, and even on the matter of his own family. Reverend Howie,
Phoebe and I told each other with a glance, was perhaps fifty years, and
too aged for the task he had been given.

'When I saw this post advertised in the *Church Times*,' he told us,
'I imagined something utterly different, something like the missions to
the Cherokee in the Americas. Maize gardens and a church built of
rudimentary yet charming materials, having about it much of the
natural aspect of the country, and a manse ditto. I did not, for example,
realise how truly wandering a race the natives are. Therefore how
wandering I must be. On arrival in Sydney, I was given a dray and
told to come to this quarter of the country without my wife or my
older daughter.'

During the evening, he frequently uttered sentences such as, 'It is so
hard to get a living in England, or even to get a curacy without influence.'
And so here was pallid, blinking Howie, newly appointed by the
improving Governor Gipps, who wished to be ensured that all random
slaughter of the sable brethren be proscribed and punished. Again, by
the way his mind drifted and his hand trembled, he seemed to me an
inappropriate person to be a missionary–policeman, a regulator of
malice.

Yet, particularly after Phoebe had retired, he had a few wily questions.

He remarked, 'I heard there had been a Ngarigo woman shot here some time ago.' I coloured despite myself.

'May I ask how you know?'

'One of Treloar's men told me.'

'It was not possible to report it at the time, especially as it seemed in any case to be an accident. I chose to take the woman's child and have him educated, and that process is still under way.'

'With the Roman nuns in Goulburn,' he murmured, with a somnolent vagueness which made me dream, despite his dusty black cloth, of hitting him.

'You are splendidly informed, sir,' I told him.

'It is my only strength. Inquiry. I realise that you have no ill will towards the poor nomads. I heard you did your best to raise the half-caste child who unhitched my horse.'

'Felix,' I said. 'I am very proud of Felix. He has the attainments of a good scholar and of a good stockman. I have mentioned to him the possibility, should my finances hold, of an English education.'

'You would consider sending this child, not your own, to Oxford or Cambridge?'

'He is a remarkable boy,' I said. 'I had intended, and still intend, to use him as a mediator with the natives. But we have not lately met any large numbers, nor have we had any quarrels with them. The worst was when they slaughtered some hundreds of stock. The pasture looked like a battlefield of fallen.'

'So you notice that the people are fewer in number, Mr Bettany? And have you seen how poxed some of the women are?'

'The women who present themselves to my wife don't appear poxed.'

'That is right, I suppose,' said the Reverend Howie with a sigh. 'The worst cases die on their pilgrimages from place to place, or are found on the edge of Goulburn, in a brawling, drunken camp-of-all-tribes. Would you object, Mr Bettany, if I had a conversation with your overseer?'

'What could he tell you?'

'Sometimes,' said the Reverend Howie, 'men talk to the overseers with a frankness they do not display towards masters, however friendly and humane.'

Having begun the evening thinking Howie a pitiable ninny, I now saw that he was, in whatever state of bewilderment, doggedly pursuing the clear light. I told him to ask Long anything he chose, and said I had noticed some absences among the Ngarigo in an indefinite way, and despite my trouble in drawing pictographs and ordering a breastplate for him, I had not seen Durra for more than a year.

The Reverend Howie slept in the parlour by the fire and at breakfast made a fuss of young George. Then he and Long spent more than an hour in Long's rough, orderly hut, drinking black tea. Next I loaned Reverend Howie a horse and we rode out to visit our hut at Ten Mile. The hut-keeper was in attendance, but above, on a slope, a Ngarigo woman loitered chewing some plug tobacco, and I wondered if she had visited my men for a purpose predictable enough.

We entered the hut, and Howie questioned the men about the behaviour of the Moth people. They answered in the clichés of their bush trade: 'Them blacks don't have regard for property of others.' This, without any irony, from transported thieves. When we emerged from the squalid little hut, the woman was still there and Howie stood regarding her. I wished we had brought Felix with us. 'Hello,' called Howie in a jolly voice, waving, but of all men to retreat from, she retreated from him.

'I noticed your man had a carbine in the corner,' muttered Howie.

'You will notice it is gathering dust.'

'Oh yes, oh yes,' said Howie. He murmured, his mind following one track, 'You mentioned not having seen this king of theirs, Durra. I think the Ngarigo have been much misused. Has Felix said anything?'

'He hasn't said much at all. He has had many shocks in his life, and they have made him reticent.'

'The boy may be in mourning, Mr Bettany. The boy may have heard what your overseer has heard.'

'And what is that?' I asked. The idea that Long knew more than I did about this country always frightened me.

'That somewhere north-west of this spot, the Ngarigo have been much misused.'

'Please, please, Mr Howie. Clear words!'

And Mr Howie told me in explicit words.

It would at other times have been a grand excursion – Long, O'Dallow, the strange clergyman and myself, riding north-west along the Murrumbidgee and breaking off into the mountains, into the indefinite country where we had stalked the sainted Catherine's murderers. From here I would normally have enjoyed the sight of plains strewn with those natural dolmens and, from one jut of earth we paused on, of one of my shepherds and his tranquil flock. Lambs may safely graze ... But you could see in the clear air that the man was leaning casually on his firearm.

'He is armed too,' the Reverend Howie commented.

The minister did not dwell on that point, but I felt I must offer the normal defence. 'Of course he is armed, Reverend Howie. If not, there is some risk he would be studded with spears like a porcupine, and whether it is his own fallible nature which caused it would not be the question, for he would be equally dead as any virtuous man. Yet he has the strictest orders to fire over heads first – the men know very well I am particular on that point.'

I sounded to myself like a temporiser, an evader. The Reverend Howie said, 'But you told me that you gave Durra an illustration of a white man punished for shooting a black. Would that happen if your shepherd down there killed a black now?'

'Why of course.'

'But not if it were an accidental discharge, as in the case of the child Hector's mother.'

'In the absence of other authorities I must use my own judgement, which I hope is not morally deficient.'

'One wonders whether people such as Durra understood these subtleties from the treaty of pictures.'

I exchanged glances with Long, who seemed rather to favour this pale clergyman.

Long had heard a circumstantial story of a disaster, which he had not shared with me until now. Why? Perhaps he thought until the Protector appeared that there was no suitable, no useful ear to pour it into. He had abstained from writing to his family for seven years, since his family, like the Ngarigo impasse, could not be mended. But now, I wondered, having seen him take Bernard off on afternoon rides, whether he was hoping to mend himself with her, and at the same time mend the Ngarigo through the sudden apparition of Reverend Howie. Under both these lights, he had an aspect more that of a rival than of my pastoral intimate.

Progress in the steeper country was hard, and we had no native tracker with us – we would have needed to send as far as Michelago for one. Nonetheless it was as if Long knew infallibly where to take us. It was high up along a ridge marked by red gums, where some force – who could say in view of what we were about to see that it was God? – had placed a majestic thicket of huge standing boulders. We could see these stones from quite a way off, and scattered over them, for all the world like the petals of Sydney's frangipani trees, were fragments of white. Beyond the boulders the earth dropped away to the west to become a brown limitless plain, and innocently I thought, surely there is pasture over there, in that flatness!

None of this mattered now, since it had become apparent to me what the frangipani white meant, settled there like ridges and patches of snow. We rode closer but were in no hurry. Some of these white remains represented to us the places where amidst the great boulders people had in their terror sought sanctuary from some wild onset. Others were thrown wide. The wind keened around our ears, and took up a new pitch, in case we did not understand this was a vicious place. As we reached the first heap of bone, Reverend Howie slipped with a groan out of his saddle.

'Dear merciful God!' he said. He seemed robbed of all competence, but then he told us, 'Gentlemen, let us all count skulls. That will be easiest in the circumstances.'

The rest of us, pleased to have been given a task, jumped from our horses and began functionally wading into the shelter of the standing stones, counting skulls large and small, O'Dallow now and then crying to Long, 'What do you ever make it now? I think I make it twenty-seven.'

So we continued to step and count amongst the dead. Long cried, 'Mr Bettany, there is something here.'

I joined him, moving gingerly amongst the thigh bones and fibia, the occasional shattered ribcage where a ball had found a heart. There was a punctured skull holding loosely in its widened mouth a tarnished silver-plated plaque which read dimly 'Durra, King of the Ngarigu' (the engraver in Goulburn having mistaken my 'o' for a 'u'), 'Chief of Nugan Ganway'. It seemed they had shot him and then, mocking him and me at once, stuffed his insignia in his teeth.

I found Howie beside me, blinking down at the awful terror here, frozen – so to speak – in the bone. 'Long tells me there is a stockman named Morpeth who witnessed this. He is a time-served labourer in Goulburn now. He may swear an affidavit.'

'My God. How does Long know these things?'

'It is his gravitas,' sighed Howie. It appeared that Morpeth, who was then Treloar's man, told Long when they met by accident on the plain, looking for lost stock one day during the last winter. 'If I were a man like Morpeth, shamed and condemned and far from home, and if I saw this happen, I too would speak to a fellow like Long. He has the air of a confessor.'

I acknowledged the truth of this amongst the shards of bone.

'An affidavit will be very important. Morpeth may not want to betray his comrades when it comes down to it.'

The Reverend Howie moved on and pointed out an infant ribcage, ineffably delicate, fallen atop adult remnants – a female pelvis, said Howie. It seemed that with satanic pride someone had felled Madonna and child with the one shot. I thought at once of Phoebe. I was forced to think of Bernard too. Since servants knew what masters didn't, had Long confided to Bernard that this Golgotha stood here, high above Treloar's, the wind scattering the murderous dust in Nugan Ganway's direction?

Long had now paused in his search and, leaning against one of the largest boulders, had begun to smoke a clay pipe. I made my way with awkward delicacy, fearing to shatter some brittle remnant under my boot, towards him.

'I must say I would have liked to have been told of this.'

'Mr Bettany,' he said, 'I thought of it, but then Mrs Bettany was there ...'

'Well,' I told him, 'you showed too much fastidiousness. I mean, you must surely tell your master these things, for God's sake.'

'There was no one to do anything,' he said in a near-whisper. 'Not until yon parson came. Now there will be one of those Alfred-Davids from the man who saw it.'

'So you keep me in ignorance of huge ... of awful events ... some official turns up and suspects I am hiding something, and shames me with what I haven't heard!'

'That wasn't for a moment what I set out to do, Mr Bettany,' Long assured me, standing upright and taking his pipe from his mouth. This was for him an apology.

I demanded he tell me about this Morpeth, and everything he himself, Long, knew of this place.

He began. 'You wonder, sir, why Goldspink was moved away and beyond reach? Goldspink was moved beyond reach because of this. A stockman is easily replaced, but not a good overseer. The Protectors like that wee parson there were coming, and Goldspink did his best to assure there remained nothing to protect. The orders may have come from an altogether higher level of society than Goldspink. But I had a bone to pick with Goldspink and he was gone in a trice.'

'Are you telling me, Sean, that Treloar ordered or connived at this monstrous business?'

But Long's cautiousness entered. 'Oh, that's for surmising, Mr Bettany. But this fellow Morpeth hated what had happened amongst these boulders. He hated Goldspink, who had had a great deal of trouble with the Moth people as they crossed Mount Bulwa station. They subjected him to much aggravation because he subjected them to the same. He dreamed of a thunderclap, an end to the botheration. But the amusing bit is this, sir ... Morpeth says Goldspink wasn't here for it.'

Morpeth had told Long that at the end of the muster Goldspink had made a speech at the campfire about 'settling the blacks for good' now that they were coming north from Nugan Ganway at the end of the summer. He made sure there was rum aplenty available to his men.

As for the Ngarigo coming north, though they might descend to the plain to spear sheep at night or loan one of their syphilis-infected women to a hut-keeper for tea and baccy, on Mount Bulwa, because of past confrontations, they travelled high up the slopes, and out of sight. They would need to be hunted by Treloar's men. A solid party of shepherds, stockmen and wagon-drivers, including Morpeth, set off to go to war against the Moth people and found a party of them here, amongst these natural high stones. There had been much drinking on the way to the site, Morpeth said, and bets were taken on particular shots as the people were chased and surrounded.

Shaking my head, I approached Howie. 'I shall get some of my men up here to bury this.'

'If you don't mind,' murmured Reverend Howie, 'not until I have shown the police magistrate.'

I nodded, for the sight of the bones was his authority. He was the Protector.

I managed to tell Phoebe the tale of the massacre the day before we received a week-old copy of the *Goulburn Herald*, reporting it. Even with this horror weighing on it, my wayward mind was gravid with Bernard. My fascination with her was outbalanced by my disbelief that it should be so. She seemed – for no reason I could define – the most august of beings. Even though I asked myself what had Bernard done to match the deeds and gallantries of my wife, the convict woman sat undeservedly at the centre of my brain.

Thus, half-distracted, half-resentful of Bernard, I was contemplating taking out some men to perform a burial when the newspaper reported that six of Treloar's men had been arrested. Goldspink was not one of them. Before the coroner, Mr Treloar had been vocal in defending Goldspink's probity, had made an affidavit to that effect; and though there was a sense that the overseer had incited the men, he had not participated in the massacre of thirty men, women and children – all connected by kinship to Felix.

With a student demeanour which could not have been bettered anywhere on earth, and despite the news of the massacre, which must have reached him, Felix came to the house, sometimes to read with Bernard, but increasingly to read in silence from my library of books and English illustrated papers. I felt that I must let him know that I had seen the bones of his people and was outraged by what I saw. So I sat him on our sofa by the bookcase. As I spoke, his eyes strayed to the book, and I had the sense this was not utter selfishness, but an instinct that in those pages was redemption. Almost to reassure him, I asked, 'What is the capital city of Scotland?'

'Edinburgh,' he told me.

'Well done,' I said. 'But then what does the Latin noun *drapeta* mean? Eh? Do you know?'

'It means a runaway slave.'

'And so would you use such a term for the father of Horace the great poet?'

'Oh no,' he said, 'there is a world of difference. Horace's father had undergone *manumissio*, the legal process of freeing.'

We were safely back in Horace's world, his Sabine farm, the Roman pole to Nugan Ganway, and this conversation was a delight to me.

Not quite as delightful was a letter from Treloar, full of rage, saying amongst other things,

I urge you, Mr Bettany, to raise your objections at the treatment of my men with His supposed Excellency the Governor. Tell him that a war exists between us and all the Ngarigo, that their ideas and ours cannot live together and that they are the blight on our landscape. How many fine Englishmen or Scotsmen have had their lives taken by such as these – for whose eradication my men are now required to undergo the travesty of public trial? But oh no, His Excellency does not count their raids and injuries against us, only ours against them, as if they were his children.

Now do write, my good fellow, for my men did only what you yourself might have done. I cannot believe the effrontery of this blinking idiot Howie who has been so praised by some elements of this town, and now he has been rewarded in that the government has given him charge of a coastal region beyond the Tinderies where the vermin of the land can be attracted by flour, sugar and tobacco, with him as virtual bishop! Yes, in the region of Bombala, Howie will have his black parish and fiefdom! And I tell you that if ever any of my men are damaged by natives in the future, I shall bring in magistrates and border police and demand of them and of His futile Excellency that the sable miscreant be punished to the limit, to the full length of the rope, to the gate of hell! Do, do write. There can be sheep or there can be natives!

I replied to the effect that perhaps Mr Treloar, during our brief meetings, had misread my disposition. I was for humanity for the native and equal justice. Yes, the natives could be distressful but not to the point where I could condone their slaughter. I was very pleased Reverend Howie had been rewarded with a reservation to which he could attract the pitiable blacks. One of Treloar's men, I said, had argued that he was pleased to shoot these natives since many of the women were poxed, and one had given the disease to him. But I knew the pox began not with natives but with white men, and the men themselves were the ultimate polluters, yet had murdered native women and children as if they were the source of the disease. I told him I was willing to meet him in Nugan Ganway, Goulburn, Sydney, depending on the pastoral season, to discuss matters of shared interest as graziers, amongst which I was willing to place the issue of some shared and humane policy towards the sable brethren.

Since I knew Treloar would not send a party to bury the bones, and since whenever I looked to the north-west I saw that horrific thicket of boulders all over again with my inner eye, I took a party of my own men and dug a pit into which went Durra and his brethren.

I was amazed to read that at the trial of his men, Mr Treloar declared on oath that he did not know where Goldspink was! No one challenged the assertion. At the time of the executions, I happened to be in Goulburn with my bullock driver Clancy. This was the town to which the condemned men were returned, and the execution, to which the tribes of the County of Argyle were invited, occurred in front of a new stone courthouse. Perhaps as many as one hundred Aboriginal men and women were present to see justice done, though one felt they had been conscripted from around Goulburn. One did not feel that justice was exactly what was happening as the string of hapless condemned shepherds and hut-keepers were paraded before us that day, moving under the care of priests of two or three faiths, and in a mass, up to the long platform of the scaffold. When the trap was opened and that horrendous thud assaulted the air, the men fell mercifully from sight, but the natives wailed, as if it were their relatives who had fallen. There was a lot of Treloar-like muttering amongst the whites who had seen the event.

Clancy himself was very sullen about it. 'Not bloody right,' he managed to tell me eventually. 'Governor's a bloody madman, Mr Bettany.'

'No, no, that's not the message,' I told him. 'The message is: "Be warned."'

I discussed the feelings of the crowd with Phoebe, who somewhat abashed me by entering the men's huts during meals, the delightful George in her arms and accompanied by Sarah Bernard as by her chamberlain, and saying, in the light of the judgement, 'Mr Bettany and I do not see that these men were unlucky. They have deserved their sentence. Whatever happens here, Mr Bettany and I do not propose to make our fortunes by wiping away the sables.' I did not witness this, but I heard men talking about it, and when I asked her, I found Phoebe was not ashamed to admit it.

After the horrifying execution, at the time of lambing, Long said to me with casual frankness as we rode, 'Mr Treloar was easy with the truth, would you say?'

'Or he may have been misquoted by the press.'

'Seven men were hanged,' he told me. 'Awful for them and for onlookers. And they were obeying Goldspink, who eats damper beyond the mountains. Over there.'

He seemed to want me to do something to bring Goldspink to appropriate punishment, but what could I do? I was busy enough as it was, and though there had not been an exact equivalence of blood between that awful bone-strewn hill and the Goulburn hanging, surely it was all close enough in horror to satisfy the scales.

'I have much to talk about with that Goldspink,' Long further said. 'He seems to be a good man at getting others to do the dying for him. It has happened before.'

'What do you mean, *before*?'

'Oh but he's sly,' was all Long would tell me, and I was aware yet
again that Long knew more than I did.

His power was increased in my mind too by the question of what
manner of friend he was to Bernard, and that itched away in me even
more actively than the knowledge that Mr Treloar had lied under oath.

For two more years wool prices were low and Barley showed me how
deep his pockets were by continuing to buy and warehouse my wool on
the expectation of sweeter times. Later in the year of the hangings,
Phoebe and I attended a good dinner he held in his house at Darling
Point – the guests being an interesting combination of colonial land-
owners and city merchants, many of the latter being Whigs rather than
colonial Tories of the Mr Finlay stamp. All very jovial, all very brotherly.
When it was over, however, and he and I were alone, watching a south-
erly breeze create ripples on the harbour, Barley said, 'My dear friend,
if you trust me, and you say you do, then I have some counsel for you.'

I said that of course I trusted him.

'Well then, I have it on good report that Bank of Australia – yes, that
bank used by New South Wales's better people – is in vast trouble, with
many bad loans, a portion of them to your father-in-law, who has
borrowed excessively on inflated value of his land holdings. For one
thing, his view is that since his son is now his sole heir – I hope it is not
painful to mention this matter – he has set boy up like a lord at Oxford.
He thinks that is way for a young man to place himself at very centre of
British society. Of course, this is only one item in Mr Finlay's large
expenditure. All depends for him on wool reaching no less than 8 pence
per pound, and so he has been bleeding money for past three years. The
purchase of a large property at Yass at height of market is one of his
less advised ventures, and he, and other grandees like him, are too proud
to take a loss, and too fixed in proposition of wool and pasture to believe
what is presently befalling them. Bank of Australia has indulged them to
its own and their disadvantage.'

'And the Savings?'

'Savings's underwritten by sundry merchants, is brass-bottomed. Sometimes convicts and democrats are more worldly than Tories. My friends
at Bank of Australia privately tipped me nod that two or three major
depositors are very worried about ratio between loans and deposits, and
if they withdraw their money as threatened, this will create a rush on

.

those esteemed premises and – hard as it is to believe – demise.'

'Are you saying that I should place all my reserves with the Savings Bank?'

'I think it should be done unobtrusively, over a number of days. I can ensure that it is done for you, if you give me a power of attorney.'

I did authorise him, and raised the question of whether I should tell my estranged father-in-law anything.

'I wouldn't,' said Mr Barley. 'Let him live a little longer in fool's paradise. You see, he has little to withdraw from Bank of Australia except his debts.'

It was to Mr Barley then that I would owe my survival when, two months later, the Bank of Australia collapsed, having absorbed the fortunes of many of its depositors. The credit arrangements under which Mr Finlay had been operating were at an end, though the bank's liquidators would require him to repay at least some of his borrowings. He was thus not obliterated as thoroughly as those who had life savings, rather than debts, with the bank, but he would be forced to sell most of what he owned.

Without telling Phoebe, who seemed to have heard nothing of their plight from her parents and who probably thought her father's wealth immutable, I took some mixed feelings (including perhaps vanity) in writing to Mr Finlay offering any assistance, including a loan of £4000 pounds free of interest, until he had realised his assets, and until those which he chose to retain had achieved their former value. He did not answer. I realised that he could not.

I wrote to George Finlay in Oxford, who had some of his father's and Phoebe's capacity to see things in absolute terms. He accepted my offer of a money order for £250, said that he regretted he could not thank me man-to-man, but that the collapse of his father's affairs had been a lesson to him. Through the influence of the Master of his Oxford College, he would proceed with his studies under a sizarship, take holy orders and seek a curacy in the English countryside, in Canada or in the Australian colonies. He asked only that God's blessings should be poured out on my head, and that of his beloved sister and namesake nephew, like ointment.

THE AIRSTRIP IN LOKICHOKIO TO WHICH Connie Everdale, the baroness, the professor and Prim delivered their rescued children was an extensive region of cracked cement. The Americans had built it, said Connie, as a base of possible operations into Uganda at the time of Idi Amin.

The bush around the hangar and workshops was sparse, and the earth stony. Four aircraft of varying size and function, decorated in Connie's livery, stood about the apron of the strip. Others gleamed in the dimness of the hangar, where her mechanics worked. The one resemblance to their last landing place was a *rakubah* near Connie's hangar, where Turkana women dressed in brilliant fabrics – emeralds, scarlets, electric blues – sat offering bright bead necklaces and wood carvings for sale.

No sooner had they descended from the plane than three four-wheel drive trucks came racing across the tarmac. Halting, they disgorged an angular, elderly white couple, Caleb and Dorothy Wagon – whose hewn appearance fitted more Prim's idea of a Montana ranching couple than of missionaries – and two young men who might have been Dinkas, possessing the facial scarring for it. Prim and the professor were cursorily introduced to the Wagons, but the liberated children were loaded with such dispatch into the vehicles before being driven off that it seemed almost as if they had been recaptured. The airstrip was left in stillness, with only the thin howl of a metal grinder remotely burring inside the hangar, the murmur of the women in bright cloth, and the languid noise of insects to fill the vacated air.

'Alleluia,' the baroness said. 'Take us home, Constance.'

Connie's place, on the northern edge of the scattered market town of Lokichokio, proved to be not unlike the bungalows of remoter Australia. Here Connie, the baroness and Prim drank tumblers of iced fruit juice brought out by Connie's Masai cook. In the dusty garden, by a date palm, the professor spread his little prayer mat and knelt compactly on it, his back to a blood-red evening sky.

In the morning, the baroness took Prim to the Wagons' Jesus True Saviour Mission, a considerable compound made up of one-storey dormitories and classrooms and a large white steepled chapel.

'Sorry we rushed off last night,' said Mrs Wagon in an accent from the southern United States. 'We had dinner waiting for the boys!'

The Wagons were energetic, devoted, evangelical, all according to the robust American tradition from which they came. They had accommodated the liberated children in dormitories in which a number of other southern Sudanese, and some Ugandan and Kenyan orphans, also slept.

That first day, Dorothy Wagon and one of the Dinka men who had met them at the airport gave English alphabet classes to the boys while Caleb Wagon, the baroness and the other Dinka, working as a committee, interviewed each child and made a record of his testimony of enslavement. Prim sat in on much of this, and made notes.

Over hours, the stories of the young, with names like Deng, Alier, Bol, Lagu, Garang, Along and Harika, blended. Most of the tales began with a Rizeighat militia raid on a village. In some cases, the militia visited second, after the regular army had already confiscated the village live-stock. When that occurred parents would cry and protest that the army had taken all their cattle the previous winter! Sometimes, according to twelve accounts, the militia then felt justified in putting a gun to the parents' heads and firing. Sometimes they made the husband watch the rape of the wife, a practice favoured as a means of implanting faithful seed in the infidel flesh of a Dinka woman. Or if the family were lucky, the militia officer cheerfully said, 'Your lack of cattle is not our problem,' and then marched the children away, telling the parents, 'Come for them when you have a bull to give me.'

Some of these children had been servants to militiamen, others were sold to army officers in the garrison towns. A number had been sent to Koranic school, and these had been given new names – Abdullah, said a child whose family name was Joseph Odongi; Fayed, a boy named Manute Kassiano; Jafir, a boy named Ismael Yagoub.

If the interrogated child mentioned beatings, the baroness would make a gentle demand that he take off his newly issued True Saviour white shirt and tan shorts, and would ask about his scars, mapping them on a diagram of front, back, and side views of the body. Over this the baroness spent great amounts of time, for she did not want to count a scar more than was valid. Some of the boys displayed burn scars – Prim presumed these were where cigarette ends had been applied by masters rendered brutal, perhaps, by the war. Each marked boy looked into the middle distance as his body spoke for him, yielding up the map of his captivity. If Prim's Arabic proved inadequate for understanding a particular debriefing, or if the child was too raw in his own familiarity with that language, or was simply too dazed to respond adequately, the baroness would have the Dinka man question him in his own sonorous, tongue, and then translate his story to English.

The way the tales accorded with each other was depressing, since there was in the boys' eyes no apparent knowledge of the fact that their master's work would remain with them enduringly in life and death; would be encountered by lovers, doctors, undertakers; would speak for them even at the most unconscious hour of sleep or ecstasy.

'Did your master ask you to do anything that was wrong?' the baroness, chin raised, would ask each child, not in Arabic, always through the Dinka man. It was a question best addressed in a language so intimate to the child that nuances could be conveyed.

At lunch, over more stewed beef and plantain, the baroness was reflective when Prim mentioned this side of the questioning. 'Of course,' she said, 'in a sense bodily scars are more eloquent. They can't be minimised. Sexual brutalism isn't as easy to prove. So we never make an explicit matter of this in our reports. We don't – as it were – headline it.'

'As for physical scars,' asked Prim, 'why don't you videotape the interviews, and supply the videos to governments and agencies and news services?'

'I am an old stick in the mud. I admit we have thought of it, but dismissed it for now out of consideration for the privacy of the child. And even filmed material is subject to accusations of trickery and staging.'

In the late afternoon, returning to the mission part-stupefied from a rest at Connie's, Prim paused by a window of a vast classroom and beheld through it the platoon of young Dinkas, sitting on benches for a class taught by lanky, grey-haired Dorothy Wagon. Mrs Wagon was telling the boys in Arabic that their bodies had been brought out of slavery by Christians, and it was her duty to break to them the news that their souls had been paid for by Jesus Christ. They might have heard of Christ and the Crucifixion in their Coptic childhoods, but had they said yes to Jesus in their hearts?

As she spoke, Mrs Wagon approached an easel on which was hung an album of brightly coloured Gospel pictures, to which she referred one by one: the Nativity of Christ, the baptism in the Jordan, the preaching, miracle-working, sacrifice by crucifixion, the Resurrection. 'I go on ahead to prepare a place for you . . .'

Prim moved along the wall and entered the classroom, still full of the day's heat, by its rear door, and sat on a bench at the back. Her arrival was registered with a smile from Mrs Wagon, who did not suspect Prim's feelings, which were edging beyond discontent into a dizzy fury. These children had been raised in a peasant mix of animist magic and Coptic Christianity, and had then been forcibly and rigorously instructed in Islam. Koranic sheiks had taught them that redemption lay in the most fundamental and sweeping observance of the Law. And now, within a day of leaving the Sudan, they were undergoing introduction to the Resurrection as perceived by American evangelicals! Their brainpans already brimming with loss and exile were assaulted with this third version, with American religious melodrama whose Christ must seem a different deity from the Afro-Arab Coptic Christ.

That evening on Connie's verandah, Prim tentatively sought the professor's opinion 'I just wondered ... I mean, I'm drinking Connie's gin ... but are you worried that the boys are subjected to such a strong and sudden dosage of Christianity? Not the Christianity they're used to either.'

The professor frowned at her – it did look as if he considered her question to be bad form. Prim rushed to define her unease further. 'You see, when the boys are questioned by the baroness and Caleb about whether their masters sent them to Koranic schools, there's an implication that that was an extreme thing to have forced on them. Why then, are the Wagons not an extreme thing too?'

She had half expected the professor to confess his own concern, kept secret because of his old-fashioned politeness. Yet he sipped his wine and did not seem fussed. 'But they're so well-meaning,' he said, nodding towards the interior of the house – Connie and the baroness – and the outer night, in the general direction of the True Saviour Mission. 'A minor solecism.' His voice was very low; he wanted nothing hurtful to be heard. 'It grows from the same zeal which liberated the children.' He held up his glass to the west's last light. 'These are the only people who are willing to speak for the slaves. I am willing enough to go along with their less harmful idiosyncrasies.'

Prim felt a considerable disappointment.

'You want large solutions, don't you?' said the professor with a smile. 'I don't mean you personally. I mean your generation. Safi's the same way. I think it's the film industry which has done this. It gives everyone mass emotions, and poses glib solutions to mass anguish.'

Prim felt her irritation collapse before the practicality of a man who said his evening prayers like a fundamentalist but drank wine before dinner. She said, 'I'm willing to be their ally, but I have problems with their methods.'

'They would not be offended to be told so,' the professor murmured.

Prim thought of Safi, who tried so hard and with a little stridency to utter smart, adult opinions. The professor's loving condescension did that to the boy.

Yet at dinner, tiredness, induced by the splendid meal, overtook her before she could express her unease – if it was suitable to do so in the first place – in the midst of Connie's aviation stories, and the tales of the baroness's genteel but somewhat deprived childhood in Vienna under the Reich and post-war.

It was not until dinner time the next day that Prim had a chance to talk properly with the women. She admitted her misgivings but begged that any quarrels she might have should not prevent them sharing information with her. When she had finished, there was a comfortable silence. Was it the same middle-aged complacency the professor had shown? Connie said, 'If you ask me, hon, I think the Wagons do come on a bit hot and strong. But you see, they're here. They're the ones who give the kids a bed and plantain stew. The rule in Africa is you work with what's to hand.'

As for the baroness, it was as if she had not quite heard the speech Prim thought she had just made. She stood up and adopted a pose which Prim thought of as pontifical. 'Be sceptical,' she intoned in her high, aristocratic English, 'as long as you accept the basic proposition. Slavery exists, children are bought and sold.'

At mid-morning on the fourth day of the visit to Lokichokio, Connie took Prim, the professor and their baggage back to the airport to fly them to Nairobi in one of her light aircraft. They took a little over two hours, traversing the Rift Valley on a diagonal, crossing huge landscapes. Prim, in the back seat, wondered if Connie and the baroness believed, as did anthropologists, that this was the landscape of the first Eden, the home of the Adam and Eve with whom Yahweh made his ambiguous compacts.

Landed in Nairobi on the vaste concrete of Yomo Kenyatta airport, Connie found a trolley for their bags, and walked them to the main passenger terminal – 'Pretty big deal for an old Masai watering-place!' – and then excused herself. She must fly back to Lokichokio. The professor who, as ever, spoke English with a slightly archaic *politesse*, thanked Connie. 'Dear lady, you have borne the expense of hundreds of litres of aviation fuel to get us here in time for our plane. I am awed by your generosity of spirit.'

Prim became aware as soon as rowdy Connie withdrew that she and the professor made odd travelling companions, although neither of them said so. There were some hours to wait for their plane, and Prim suggested to the professor that they might hire a taxi and visit the city sights. 'Thank you,' he said. 'But I have some work to prepare. Do go yourself.'

Yet Prim did not make a good solitary tourist, and so took out a novel while the professor made notations on pages of Arabic script. As the afternoon wore on, the professor decided to call home. Prim sat in the departure lounge, watching him speak to Kenyan and perhaps Sudanese operators. At last he was through. She saw him sagely nodding, then speaking at length. Looking sober, he returned.

'Is everything well in your house?' Prim asked him in Arabic.

'Everything is well,' he said, but she could tell that it was not so.

She bought a newspaper for guidance. The Air Sudan strike was still on. A brigade-strength force of the Sudanese Army had been overrun by the SPLA at Torit. The Sudanese pound was falling yet again, and the National Islamic Front was crying for a movement of national salvation. Khartoum would be its jolly old self, still in decline!

Prim suggested a meal. They sat in a café before slabs of tough steak and piles of chips. 'It's funny,' the professor murmured, preoccupied, but politely making conversation. 'On the level of popular culture and cuisine, the British made a much greater impression here in Kenya than in the Sudan.'

Their aircraft was called at last, and they went though passport control and walked out across the tarmac in pleasant night air. In this anonymous area, between terminal and plane, the professor said, 'There *are* some problems awaiting me, Primrose. Safi, my son, has been involved with some of his classmates in an anti-war riot. And of course, not a coy one – right along the *Sharia el Nil* and then past the foreign embassies. He has been arrested, charged before a magistrate, and is in prison on remand. Not the big gaol, Kober, I don't think, God be praised! Khalda is desperate.'

Prim felt a pulse of fear for the professor, fear for what she might need to witness, the police and army taking her companion away on arrival in Khartoum. What was she to do if el Rahzi was arrested? She was an aid eunuch, responsible for the survival of her NGO, and so with a professional duty to avoid trouble.

The professor said, 'I told my wife to get straight onto our friend el Dhouma – you met him, I think, at our place. He is an influential lawyer, and we have a home number for him.'

They took their seats, and sat in silence. Tea was brought when the plane reached level air, and Prim was aware that she and the professor sipped it with the wistful meekness of those who have run foul of a system.

Their plane wheeled in at last over the scatter of Khartoum's lights and landed. They were two of a handful of passengers who rose to leave the plane – most of the others were bound for Cairo and Athens, and were requested to stay aboard. Prim and el Rahzi descended the stairs, looking for signs in the dry, clear night. Knots of police and soldiers conversed on the tarmac, but the customs and immigration hall proved to be quiet. The questions the immigration man asked were blessedly routine, and the professor was not delayed. Their bags collected, they simply walked out of the terminal, hoping for a taxi. They found that, though access to the front of the terminal had been blocked by armoured cars, Sherif was waving to them from behind a barrier of shrubs in the near-empty car park.

'There's a curfew,' he cried as they drew near. He reached for their bags. 'But I got a police pass to meet your plane. I left Mrs el Rahzi just forty minutes ago.'

'News of Safi?' asked the professor.

'Not really. El Dhouma called and said he'd check things. Safi and his friends certainly picked a day to have a peace rally! This afternoon the army began occupying government offices. It's a coup. There's a rumour the prime minister is about to clear out to Cairo. A brigadier-general named Omar Bashir is said to be the coup leader and thus the new man.' Sherif looked Prim in the eyes and said in a lowered voice as if he did not wish to encumber the professor with this particular reflection, 'These guys will be very hawkish towards the war.'

Even beneath the weight of this news, Prim was elated by the urgency of his voice. He opened the boot of his car for their bags and had time to touch her wrist. 'Oh my love,' he murmured in Arabic. '*Ya habibti.*' She wished this was a banal night of no arrests and no civic uncertainties. 'Where have you been, you evil woman?' he whispered.

'Nairobi, of course.'

'Oh yes,' he said with a mock sneer. 'How is the mad baroness?'

'Thank you for helping my wife,' cried the professor to Sherif. 'Who told you –?

'Your wife knew I had been to school with the all-powerful el Dhouma. I believe his power has just gone up a notch too. This brigadier – Bashir – the National Islamic Front is in bed with him, and el Dhouma is their prized adviser. It seemed,' said Sherif, 'that el Dhouma was already busy making it possible for a number of prominent Islamic Front exiles to come home to work with what the brigadier called the National Salvation Revolutionary Command Council.

Driving along unpeopled avenues into the city by way of the New Extension, the professor sat with Sherif in the front seat, maintaining the proprieties. For self-appointed men with canes had recently begun to appear about the streets, stopping vehicles, chastising and sometimes striking men and women who sat on the same seat together. Sherif parked the car outside the el Rahzis', and though there was no one to overhear them, spoke mutedly as he took out the professor's luggage. 'Look there,' said Sherif. Across the broad avenue beneath a tree a driver smoked a cigarette in a ministry-black, parked vehicle. From a small staff on its front superstructure the green flag of the republic drooped.

In through the gate from the street, they were greeted at the open door by Khalda, her face twisted with distress. The embrace between herself and her husband was brisk and almost ritual, for both of them seemed distracted with fear for their son.

'Dr el Dhouma is here,' Khalda told her husband.

'A good thing,' he said.

They followed her into the strange heat of the house, a warmth which seemed intensified by the politics of the day. El Dhouma, Sherif's school friend, sat at a table in the living room, drinking Sudanese tea from a glass. Though the hour was late, and her son was at police headquarters, Mrs el Rahzi had found a plate of pastry to put within reach of the esteemed lawyer.

El Dhouma stood and greeted the professor formally, as did the professor in return.

'It is a pity you were away,' the lawyer told el Rahzi. 'I have had a long day with hardly any food, and so I shall come to the point. Why ever did you go to Nairobi with this woman?' He nodded to Prim. 'You must have known that this march was on the cards.'

'My dear fellow,' said the professor, 'I did not know it was on the cards. I had not even heard it was intended.'

'This is serious business,' el Dhouma told him. 'Your son cannot play at being political the way he might in an American university. I don't know what he thinks he is doing ... it is perhaps a means to attract women?'

'What can you do for me in this case, my friend?'

'My clients and friends in the National Islamic Front have been asked to join with members of the junta in the work of national salvation. This arrangement is extremely recent. And though I could use my influence with my clients to help Safi in his predicament, may I say that this is not a well I can return to more than once. There are emergency regulations in place now. But even under the present *National Security Act* there are at least ten sections which your son has violated.'

'Yes, yes,' the professor assented with a trace of annoyance.

El Dhouma lifted his right index finger and looked at his old friend Sherif. 'A word to all the wise, I hope. I know my clients well. I know the national war will be waged hard now, and the cultural war.' Over some minutes he exhorted the el Rahzis to control their over-indulged son. Then he relented and suggested that he and the professor go to the police headquarters and if necessary the ministry.

'Have no doubt,' said el Dhouma. 'Not all your son's friends will come out of this so happily.'

'My dear heaven,' said the professor, losing his temper at last. 'A protest, that's all it was! They didn't murder anyone! Freedom of assembly is in the UN Charter.'

'Please, professor,' said el Dhouma, 'don't be naïve.'

Mrs el Rahzi stepped between the two men. 'We're very grateful. We're very grateful, isn't it so?'

Prim and Sherif sat with Mrs el Rahzi until 4 a.m. Khalda spoke about visiting Cambridge with her father, an army engineer officer who had become a leading figure of the Umma party, and meeting the young el Rahzi, who was already a gifted tutor in Middle Eastern and East African affairs.

'You might not think,' she said drowsily, 'that with all that has happened I could still be astounded at my country. You might think, "Oh, Africans are used to oppressive regimes." I assure you they are as much of a surprise to me as to anyone. I don't care. As long as he gets Safi out.'

They drank more tea. Khalda nodded, her chin dropped, and she fell asleep, breathing audibly. At last Prim and Sherif could look at each other as they would if alone, and Sherif's annoyance was clearer than it had been as they had loaded the car at the airport.

'Assure me you won't go slave-trading any more with that Austrian lunatic. It is unwise. Believe me. El Dhouma is correct about one thing. These are not laughing matters.'

She patted his head. 'All right,' she told him. 'No more flights.' She heard, by the air he expelled, that he had not been casually concerned for her.

Mrs el Rahzi stirred then, forcing a close to a debate which still had some distance to run. She stretched, covered a yawn, and spoke. 'It isn't pleasant to be beholden to el Dhouma. He's changed. Politics changes all of us. I was embarrassed for you, Primrose, and for my husband, at the imputation that the professor was on some improper enterprise in going to Nairobi.'

It was first light when a car was heard outside, and the gates of the garden opened. Prim could hear the professor's voice and Safi's in discussion. Mrs el Rahzi rushed into the hallway and Prim and Sherif did not think it right to follow. There was a soft wailing, and much conversation. Something of Safi's argument could be heard. 'The Islamic Guard are permitted to parade in the university. Why aren't we permitted to parade for a peace settlement?'

Prim heard the argument move down the hall from the front door, past the door of the living room and towards the back of the house. It was as if Safi were prowling for food or medicine. A long parents-and-son discourse, marked only by the mildest traces of anger, settled in the kitchen.

Without warning Sherif wrapped Prim in his arms. There was urgency. After they left here, roadblocks permitting, the strenuousness of sex could be let substitute more fruitfully for the strenuousness of an argument. They could hear the kitchen debate become sporadic. Soon Safi appeared in the living room, in a white shirt with a torn collar and stained fawn pants. He was barefooted, as if the police had kept his shoes and he had been willing to forget them. He said, 'My mother tells me you have been absolute pillars. It was very kind of you to stay with her through the night.'

'Are you well?' asked Sherif.

The young man smiled. 'I go unpunished, even here at home.'

'But no doubt your parents counsel you to be wise,' said Prim, before Sherif could say something similar.

'Oh, yes. I do feel sorry for anyone who falls into the hands of police and security in their present uncertainty of soul.'

His father came in, put a hand on his son's shoulder, and gently told him to go to bed. 'Goodnight, my good friends,' Safi called, departing. The professor said, 'He is carrying bruises. I will not tolerate it.' But there was also that in him which knew he would – for a time – need to.

⌐

A TIME OF ANGUISH

Over the years of grazing at Nugan Ganway, Charlie Batchelor's Merino flocks had remained in the care of my shepherds, and, year by year, I calculated the natural increase due to him. In return he left to me all matters such as the management of the flocks and the annual sale of wethers, easier now that there were closer towns where some could be disposed of. He did me the honour of accepting without complaint or quibble my reckoning of his share of natural increase, of trusting that I kept strict stock books, and he never disputed any cheque that I might send him. Nor had he shown any panic when wool prices fell.

I was shocked and surprised therefore to get a sudden curt letter from my old friend and boyhood intimate.

Sir,

I would be pleased if you could deliver to my property at Inchecor, Yass, the proportion of your flocks which has been kept in trust for me. As is the normal business arrangement, those lost in the transfer shall be to your account, and I shall expect to be compensated for their loss. You may delay delivery of my share of the cattle until your next muster of them, but I expect to be in receipt of either the beasts themselves, or of the money from their sale, according as I shall direct, soon thereafter.

After years of freedom and ease in our partnership, Charlie wanted the harshest letter and not the spirit of our fraternal arrangements to operate between us.

'I should be obliged,' the letter continued, 'if this could be attended to with dispatch, and if my beasts were at Inchecor before the end of the month.'

It was fortunately an easy time of year, after lambing, but I cursed having to make this journey. George was now sufficiently advanced, though only in months, not in years, to know when he had my attention and Phoebe's. He would sit up in his cradle by the warm hearth and make faces at us as he mouthed, say, a little sweet currant damper, whose disintegration in his hand as he chewed and sucked it would create a comic amusement in his face, while causing Phoebe and me to dissolve into laughter. He loved to cause laughter, and knew how to produce that effect.

His eyes were quick, and his hair was growing quite flaxen, and I could see him as a tall, forthright, amusing New South Welshman of a future decade. One could tell by looking at him that he would develop great social ease, as distinct from his father, who for sundry reasons of temperament and history was often uneasy in refined company.

I did not want to leave George and my laughter with Phoebe. And in deciding whether it should be myself or Long who led the drive to Inchecor, I pretended to consider only the joys of the hearth. But I was also monstrously aware that should I leave Long behind, the affection between him and Bernard might perhaps reach some deciding phase. Yet I must go myself anyhow – to find what had injected rancour into Charlie's summons of his flocks, and remake that lifelong brotherhood. After all, Charlie was to me an instrument of mercy. One of the ways in which I knew myself to be a gentleman was that the Batchelors had declared me to be one! Any permanent rejection by the Batchelors would throw a deep shadow over my own estimation of myself.

It took some days for Long, O'Dallow and other of my stockmen to cut out and assemble Charlie's portion of all the flocks in my yards around the homestead. Long's admirable sheepdogs – we now thought of these offspring of my original bitch, Bet, as Long's – brought them to fold and then sat about the homestead with pricked ears, sniffing at and hoping for the coming journey.

To deliver Charlie's sheep and to inquire into the meaning of his letter would take me at least ten days, and I would have also to leave Phoebe and my little son at the coldest season of the year. But I now, both hating and congratulating myself in equal measure, devised almost without trying, a means to leave Long in charge at Nugan Ganway, the obvious and wise provision, without allowing Bernard to spend much time with him.

I thus found myself heartily engaged in domestic arrangements and willing to discuss them. I said to Phoebe, 'You'll have Bernard here to get up to baby George. She could rest in the same room as Georgie, after all.'

My ears reddened, since I thought it was transparent to Phoebe and to all intelligent persons why I made such suggestions.

'But I like to get up myself to George,' said Phoebe. A true and splendid bush mother – avoiding the usual intermediaries between herself and her child. It was yet again shown how criminal it was of me not to love her without distraction. 'However,' she conceded, 'I'll enjoy Bernard's company while you're gone.'

At the moment of this conversation, Bernard was in the homestead
kitchen. I had until now escaped her dark scrutiny of my plan. Again, I
thought my enthusiasm was like a rash – the wise would notice it at once.
Nonetheless I went to speak to her. The cooking fire in her chimney corner
raged merrily, and the range smelled of succulent contents – beef, as it
happened, slaughtered by O'Dallow. She was attending to it and before
standing upright looked around at me with her profound eyes in which
all the wistfulness of exile seemed to pool. She could not have faced her
judge in Manchester with the terror with which I now faced her.

'Bernard, I must take sheep to Yass. You should sleep every night in
the next room to Mrs Bettany and rise to help with George if he is
restless. I am concerned Mrs Bettany might become exhausted.'

'Then that's what I'll do, and very happily, Mr Bettany,' she said,
nodding. A slightly strange order of words, I thought, like much she
uttered. Her own strange guarantee.

It was not a small thing which I was about. Charlie Batchelor's share
of my present flock had grown, in spite of drought, fire, scab, fluke and
the incursions of the Ngarigo people in summer, to a majestic 9000
beasts. Along the trail, such a flock might spread for miles. If Charlie
really took these back, and was not just involving me in an annoying
gesture, would I replace them from my own resources? I had a certain
unease about spending my cash reserves, or borrowing. There was
another consideration: under the influence of Sydney radicals, the British
government was considering an end to the transportation of prisoners to
New South Wales – no more Longs, O'Dallows, Presscarts. No more
Bernards either. If it happened, where would my labourers come from?

Yet there was in strict business terms a positive aspect to Charlie's
demand. It would mean a saving on any further employment of shepherds, a saving on expenditures (shearers, soap, tar, woolpacks, and so
on) and would enable me to get my flock sizes down much closer to the
approved number of about 800 sheep per flock.

These were the provident considerations I made, swallowing chagrin
at Charlie, as I got ready to return his stock to him. It was only in the
matter of the ticket-of-leave housekeeper that I wrote fantastical cheques
against that other precious resource, my supposedly unassailable
affections.

O'Dallow, Presscart, Clancy, the dignified Felix, delighted to be asked
to come, riding a large-shouldered black waler and tall as a boy of fourteen, made up the team which – with myself – drove Batchelor's flocks

through the long hollow west of the homestead. I turned around and looked back, and saw half in shade by our verandah Phoebe and our son in Bernard's dutiful arms, and then, closer to me and by his hut, Long, who seemed somehow connected to the two women in understanding, a seamless thought linking three minds. It was as if all three of them saw me clearly and, from a generous unearned love, indulged me. I did not look back again until I made the top of the first rise to the north of the homestead, from which they appeared as mere patches of colour.

We followed our Murrumbidgee stream for some way north-west, before it veered away from our path. We crossed the Limits of Location, and traversed the western side of the Limestone Plains, their pleasantly folded hills and fine pasture. Here grass had returned to the broad common grazing lands, and I rarely needed to ask local pastoralists if they could accommodate Charlie's flock for a day or so. Our path took us well to the west of Goulburn, so I was saved the trouble of writing appeasing notes to either of the Finlays.

In this country, New South Wales seemed almost restored to its old self. Farmers who had survived were rebuilding. The little towns of Bungendore and Collector, though quiet, had more than one inn, and all the offices of civilisation from schools to apothecaries to police magistrates.

On the Yass road, as I galloped ahead of the mob, I encountered by the roadside a convict constable, wearing his thick leather belt, and guarding a very fleshy-looking female convict. As I passed he gave his cap a leisurely tip. I saw light chains, worn loose, around the woman's wrists.

'What is this?' I called to him.

'Nothing of yours, sir,' the woman herself told me.

'You know what it is, sir,' said the constable to me. 'Her master's sending her back to the Factory for unruliness. Happens with all you gents, so you'd know the story, sir.'

'I do not know it,' I told him with a heat whose source was similarly a mystery, and kicked Hobbes's flanks to get past.

'Lucky fellow you, sir!' the constable called after me. And he and the woman laughed as my flocks, or Charlie's, milled past. She was a version of what Bernard might have been. Had this woman been sent me as housekeeper it would have saved all anguish, put me to the small trouble of returning her, and kept me in dull contentment.

In camp that night, sitting last at the fire, I was approached by

O'Dallow. 'Sir,' he said, as ever like a notice of motion at a meeting.

I threw a branch on the fire. 'I'm very pleased with the pace of this drive,' I told him, because it was the truth but also to loosen him. 'We are truly old experts in these matters now, O'Dallow.'

'Sir,' he said affirmatively.

'Is there something with which I could help you?'

'I was thinking to marry the little cook Tume if you permit, Mr Bettany.'

This pertained to something I forgot to mention earlier, that Phoebe had become so dependent upon Bernard's company, and had sufficient demands on her time, we had decided to employ a ticket-holding woman from the Factory to cook for the men. I had asked my father's old friend Dr Strope of Parramatta, still Visiting Surgeon at the Female Factory, to select the right woman. Weeks later she arrived on one of Finnerty's wagons, a wiry, dark-complexioned but pleasant-featured little woman named Maggie Tume. She had been with us perhaps a month, and was loudly authoritative with the men. Now O'Dallow wanted to marry her after their brief acquaintance, though it was a fairly long courtship by the standards of the convicts. A woman of promise, she shared the same language-of-the-hearth as him.

'Oh,' I said, 'she will keep you honest, O'Dallow.'

'Sir,' he assented. And then released an extraordinary quantity of news. 'She comes from the one county as me, sir.'

'You were not married in Ireland?' I asked.

'Oh,' he said, 'I have long since had the sad news. My wife is dead.'

He took from his pocket a letter and handed it to me. The envelope had a Listowel, County Kerry postmark. Its contents were from a man who called himself 'Tomas', and was O'Dallow's brother-in-law. The letter broke to O'Dallow the news that his wife Bride had perished of 'the choler' and died with the sacraments and in the bosom of Holy Mother Church. Tomas mentioned that O'Dallow's sons were now close to grown, were in good health and had borne the loss bravely, in certain expectation of the Resurrection. All in the village of Knocknaboulna asked after him, O'Dallow, and would never forget him, though they knew they would not see him in this life.

I had never read such a heartbreaking letter, not even the one I had read at our first Nugan Ganway Christmas to Long. I held it out towards O'Dallow. 'My dear fellow. You bore this with such fortitude.'

He looked away, the only gesture of overwhelming regret.

'So,' I said more cheerily, 'since you are still serving time, you need only the permission of the Colonial Secretary. And of God, of course.'

'That's right,' he told me.

Even in this discourse I suffered from an irksome suspicion that he – like all the men – saw through me. Now that Eros, the god of love, rather than Ceres the goddess of husbandry, seemed to have undertaken to rule Nugan Ganway, I felt that all flesh was transparent.

Beyond the little town of Yass, where I had let the men visit inns in two watches, we left the track and came down to the homestead at Inchecor, in a valley somewhat narrower than the great plain in which Nugan Ganway stood, but with plentiful kangaroo grass.

As our flock neared Charlie's home, a hessian-booted stockman, holding a carbine as if it were a crutch, strolled up from the stockyards to meet us. 'Thou be early, zur,' he told me in a gargling voice. A Devon man. A plump woman bearing a shotgun also emerged from under the shade of the Batchelor's verandah. I asked the man why everyone was armed.

'Well, it be some native trouble,' he told me. 'Mr Batchelor himself's off after them Myall blacks who caused us trouble.'

'Are there sufficient yards for these sheep of his?'

'When he gets back, Mr Batchelor and the men'll be 'recting 'em, I'd say.'

I broke the news to my men and told them there had been trouble, and we set up our camp quite contentedly on a slope. I gave directions that two of us would ride the edge of the flock at all times, and the dogs, watchful even in their sleep, could be depended on to stop heedless rushes and to marshal strays. That arranged, I rode down to Charlie's place. As I approached, the armed housekeeper, still waiting on the verandah and darkly regarding me, reached her carbine back indoors as if to some hidden recipient. I would have said that I knew everything there was to know about the sort of house Charlie might run, but the housekeeper's gesture made it seem a household of mysteries.

I dismounted and tied my horse at the yard rails and walked across to her. I asked her could she tell Mrs Batchelor I was here. She nodded and went to do it. She was a time about it, and at last I settled myself in a wooden chair placed outside, in the winter sun. I was drowsing off when the housekeeper came back with a tray, laden with a tea pot and cup and some cake, somewhere between old English fruit cake and damper with mixed fruit.

'Mrs Batchelor said for you to have tea.' She laid the tray down, poured a cup – there was even milk there, which I declined. 'Some of my bush duff then?' the housekeeper asked me, and I took a slice of the stuff, though without appetite. As an afterthought, she wrenched a piece of paper from the pocket of her apron and gave it to me. 'Dear Jonathan,' it said, 'I regret the indisposition of children prevents my welcoming you indoors. Best you camp out pending a conversation with Charles. Yours, Julia Batchelor.'

I believed from its tone I was fortunate that I got away with being called 'Dear Jonathan', instead of 'Mr Bettany'.

So I would camp with my men, and what was most vexing was that Clancy would secretly make jokes about it – 'Batchelor don't want the boss in the house while he's away.'

By the next afternoon, having had in our stock camp on the slope above the homestead no further approach from Julia Batchelor, I was considering losing patience with Charlie, leaving the sheep in the care of the West Country man, and returning to what was, after all, my own business. I set my men to work cutting brushwood hurdles, a skill asso- ciated with their servitude. We had erected the first yard and driven perhaps 1500 sheep into it when further down the valley I saw a party of horsemen. I could see Charlie amongst them, in his wide-awake hat.

'At last,' I intoned, and got on Hobbes, irritated, and rode down to greet him.

Closing on him, I called with apparent lightness, 'Mr Batchelor, my friend!'

He glanced up and saw me but made no answering greeting. Naturally enough I felt foolish, but wondered if it was a matter of hearing, eyesight, or even a sad experience on his chase of the natives. I rode a little past his group of seven men and wheeled and caught up to his side. He, and the entire party, still looked grim.

'Charlie,' I said. 'Trouble with the sables?'

'Speared one of my shepherds, killed one hundred and fifty sheep, all for nothing.'

'My God,' I said. 'Did you catch up with them?'

'Two,' he said. 'Old man and boy. Left their bodies as a warning to the blackguards.'

It was true the natives could reduce one to shameful practice. But there was also something directed at me in his bluntness. He said no more, but a man riding on his right in a large straw hat nodded down towards two small objects hanging from his saddle by twine. 'Drying them out, sir,' this man told me. A cultivated felon by the sound of him. 'It's excellent standing for a fellow to have a nigger baccy pouch.'

I understood the hanging objects were the scrotums – or would my father have it *scrota*? – of the men they had caught. Could Charlie let this thing be done and talked about without some comment? It seemed so. An altered Charlie!

He saw the hurdles my men had made on the hillside. 'There is no need to trouble your men further,' he said briskly. 'Perhaps you could go and tell them to break camp.'

I was by now thoroughly hurt, and said that if that was what he chose then ... But I could not finish the sentence, and so turned Hobbes away and rode back towards my men.

'Bettany,' he called. 'Be sure to inquire of your father.'

'My father?'

'Meet me by the yard in half an hour,' he shouted, and it was all he said by way of clarifying things. 'Before you leave.'

I told my men to abandon their work on the hurdles and to break the camp. 'Had trouble with natives,' I said, nodding to the homestead. 'Not a good time for frivolity.'

I felt Felix's handsome eyes on me. But what a good lad – he had ridden and stood watch like a man.

'Would have thought he'd be glad to have bloody people round,' said Presscart.

My men began to gather themselves. We would want to be well on the road beyond Yass by dark. I sat and drank black tea, peering at the homestead. In a while, I saw Charlie emerge, coatless, and pace by the yard, smoking a pipe. By now of course he had spoken to Julia and the housekeeper. He knew I had not been inside the house. Perhaps that was the crazed idea he had had in the first place. That I might offer some affront to Julia! If so, what did he think of my honour?

I had intended to take my good time, but could not sit watching him for more than two minutes, and so, with a 'Keep at it!' to my men, I mounted and rode down the incline to join him. When he saw me coming he began knocking out his pipe against a railing.

I dismounted near him.

'Well,' I said, 'didn't you think the tone of our last exchange a little cold?'

'If so, it will not much improve,' he told me. He considered me.

'I don't know what in God's name you mean, Charlie,' I said, softening towards him, because in his reserve I could see some acute pain.

'It is all over Van Diemen's Land and you do not know? Of course, everyone does Mother the honour of pretending not to believe it and never mentioning it. But the knowledge is universal, and Van Diemen's Land is a closed place to me now!'

'Is your mother ill?'

'No, but I wish so. I wish she were dead.'

'Dear Charlie!' I said.

'Never *dear*, and never *Charlie* again! Your mother is the wife of a scoundrel, though herself a victim of his easy charm. You're the spawn of a scoundrel. "It was a mistake of youth," my poor father said of his crime. What about this crime? This one?'

'These are very appalling things you say, Batchelor,' I told him. 'What crime?'

'Just that my father's house is disgraced. My mother is disgraced by your father, and it is the gossip of Van Diemen's Land. And you have not heard, you say! It is inherited in you – the air of hurt and blithe innocence!'

'You be careful!' I roared, pointing at him. It was the subject on which I had least composure.

'Drop that idiotic, stage-gentleman finger of yours, Bettany. While your father was teaching us the politer lines of Horace, he was applying the more tempestuous ones to my mother. "... *nunc et campus et areae lenesque sub noctem susurri composita repentantur hora,*" and so on. "Now in the fields is the appointed hour for night time whispers ..." It seems he knew too well what such sentiments meant.'

I uttered the normal outrage and denials, then said 'Dishonour your mother if you choose, but do not dishonour my father!'

'But you always thought him better than he was. You thought him a statesman because your mother pretended so. But he was always a plausible scamp. Go to your brother! The story is he has known of the indecency for some time and sought out a station on the mainland just to get away from the shamefulness of his father. Or else, more son-like, go to your poor dishonoured mother, who still has to ride into Ross in a cart and listen to the whispers, while your father stays safe in the degenerate port of Hobart.'

Hence I heard from Charlie that my family was in ruins, and it seemed at once that my unfaithful yearnings for Sarah Bernard had somehow infested the past and undermined my family's honour in reverse. Yet I could not picture my father in my situation, as the besotted adulterer. My brain ached with the task of imagination.

Charlie stopped leaning on the rail, put his pipe away, and prepared to go inside. 'I know you have a competence for grazing,' he told me. 'But you will never become more than a low-bred fellow. And you will never have any honour.'

This statement terrified more than offended me to the extent that I grabbed his shirt collar. But he looked at me with such a calm contempt that I let it go again. Nothing he had said could be amended by blows or even the infliction of wounds. Perhaps in punishing the Myall blacks, he had also been punishing the Bettanys.

'I wish to see all of you off my land before dark,' he said and went inside. I could not follow. I walked back to my men with a pretence of dignity. I was reminded of the night when, after two rums, my father had said, 'There is no charity which is not the Master and Servant Act.'

I had not known then what he meant. I knew now. The Batchelors had mimed fraternity. Had my father thus been encouraged to punish them?

Phoebe was the first to mention Alice Aldread to me.

Sarah had told her story to Phoebe, describing her as a woman who had more played at murdering a tyrannous and aged husband than killed him. The victim himself a man who believed in taking arsenic and mercury for his health.

'She's a sad case,' said Phoebe, with that beautiful obdurate light in her eye, reciting lines which I believed had come from Bernard. 'She was locked in amongst the mad at Tarban Point, before languishing in the Female Factory. She has also been much weakened by some consumptive illness. It would be wonderful if she could live out her time in this country, which would be very tonic for her. She might be useful for lighter duties too.'

'But does she have her ticket-of-leave?' I asked.

Phoebe was busy at needlework but reading at the same time. I so admired her simultaneous talents.

'It should be possible for you to get her one by writing,' said Phoebe. 'She has a champion in Sarah, and I think we should be her champion too.' We had, she pointed out, been more than fortunate in our convict servants, our record was good, and so a letter to the Colonial Secretary petitioning for this Aldread's release and assignment should be successful.

How cruel it was of me that I could listen apparently lightly, seemingly half-jokingly to my generous girl-wife as she asked me to pursue a kind impulse at the urging of Bernard. In fact, so far was I from being easy and indifferent in doing Sarah Bernard favours that, with dinner ended, after engaging in pleasantly deceptive conversation with Phoebe, I excused myself to smoke my pipe. Hidden like some morbidly observant and moonstruck farm boy beneath the overhang of my bark verandah, I watched the light from the mutton-fat lamp glint through the woolsack curtains of the kitchen. This was the same light by which Sarah Bernard worked. I looked for every subtlety of that dull, muted beam and – I am ashamed to use the word – *trembled* when her shadow, generated by a step forward, fell across it. Then the light was quenched. Envy the lamp, for it had shared her breath, Horace might have said.

Then, in a wind which sharpened itself against the great boulders of my pastoral country, she appeared by cold and partial moonlight and walked out towards Long's hut, the blast flattening her dress against her shins. Her gait was leisurely, but the wind and I urgent. By now my pipe was snubbed out with my thumb and resting cold in my pocket, and I was at the one time raw and glowing.

Through the small gaps in the slab timber of Long's hut, a more sullen light showed. It looked to me like the light fit for a man who had finished his labour and drowsily renounced the day. Trailed by me, Bernard rapped on the door and it was opened a little by Long, who said, with his same old dolefulness, 'Come in, Miss Bernard my love.' I would have traded my own and Charlie Batchelor's flocks and herds to acquire somehow the right to make such a welcoming noise.

Seeing this much, I was not quite crazed enough to take my spying further. I returned to my homestead and my noble young partner. But my task of observation and pursuit became a regular nightly exercise.

One night, in my half hour of tracking Bernard's short progress from the kitchen to my overseer's, as I stood behind a damp tree trunk whose moisture was fast turning to hoarfrost, I was rewarded by the noise of a quarrel.

'You should not think that you have some claim on me, Sean,' I was delighted to hear her tell him. 'If kindness is a claim, then what is its value?' On the one hand, I found it hard to believe that anyone could quarrel seriously with Long. On the other I knew an uncontained joy

that it seemed improbably to be happening. I heard him murmuring a
little in baleful apology, or even, if she had driven him that far, in self-
justification. A careless caress, I assumed, and if he were chastised for it,
that might mean it was a rare gesture.

The next day I went to the kitchen and quizzed her on Aldread. She
is a good woman, said Bernard, claiming to have known her since the
ship that transported them both and taken such care of her as was
possible. She was a woman removed from the Factory to work on light
duties at the Parramatta Gaol hospital after the scandalous case of the
Pallmires, the former matron and steward of the place. 'She is in trouble
only when she lives in disorderly places. She will be very good here.' As
I questioned her I saw the little curtained alcove of slab-timber and bark
where, unless she slept by George's cradle, she spent her nights. After of
course first visiting Sean Long.

On the off-chance that she would thereby be pleased, I wrote the
following:

27th June 1842
To: the Rt. Hon. The Colonial Secretary
Macquarie Street
Sydney

Dear Sir,
I have the honour to address you in the matter of one Alice Aldread, per
Whisper *who is serving a life sentence for the manslaughter of her report-*
edly tyrannous and aged husband. My information is that the behaviour
of said Aldread has been in the colonies unexceptionable, and that her
illness, and time spent in the Female Factory hospital, and the hospital
of the Parramatta prison, have between them effectually chastened her.
It is believed that this prisoner's health is not good, and I am thus
pleased to report that my wife and I have the honour to reside in one of
the colony's more tonic reaches, which would no doubt be beneficial to
the well-being of this misguided but repentant soul.
Etc, etc

In the same season I received a letter from my brother Simon beyond the
alps. He had lost some 1400 sheep from catarrh, and it was a very
daunting prospect for him and his young wife, Elizabeth. He proposed
that I might kindly consider bringing a flock, some of which he would

purchase over two years, some he would pasture according to the normal arrangement, and some to be sold in Melbourne, where the market had revived. This journey would need to be done before the shearing season, but after the worst of the mountain snows. It struck me abstractly as not unwise to have investments on either side of the mountains.

The letter also contained a sentiment, and offered a challenge, at which my heart sank: 'The other great benefit to you would be that you could see Father, who has joined me here for a time.'

So I had pressing duties, one financial, the other familial. Yet even when my motives were reputable, my feelings had become so duplicitous that all I planned seemed uncertain and dishonest to me. Should I take Long on what might be a challenging crossing of the Port Phillip Pass to the south-west? It would be unremarkable if I did so, I decided. O'Dallow could stay with his sweetheart and soon-to-be wife Tume and manage Nugan Ganway with utter competence. For it was an unspoken arrangement that O'Dallow would become the permanent overseer in the coming time when Long would receive his conditional pardon for time served, ask for his share of the stock, and disappear.

So Long and other stockmen, including the enthusiastic Felix, ever the student of bush horsemanship as well as of the Punic Wars, accompanied me through fine, clear September air. We rose up a long valley, accompanied to the west by mounded peaks with the snow streaks of the past winter's storms adhering only to their more shadowy contours. We contended with steep, wooded hills, but the weather held and the ascent to the Port Phillip Pass itself was gradual on this eastern side, and according to report the western slopes were gentler and well-grassed even in dry seasons. Felix proved yet again what an admirably reserved and hardy boy he was, and in every evening camp, while the quart pot was boiled by Presscart, he would fetch one of the Latin texts I had bought him from his saddlebag and read it to me and translate it by last light. He had begun to study a Greek primer too, since though I had but a minor grasp of Greek, he would need it for his ultimate education. He would honour his race at Oxford or Cambridge, and make a way for my son, George. They would become used to robust Australian intellects in these distant academies.

In these lessons as in all else, the journey was pleasantly predictable. We came down through the great native forests into the clearings of the Broken River, which we followed until we encountered, by seeking out the origin of some smoke we saw, my brother's first shepherd hut. Here a bare-footed hut-keeper sat nursing a carbine and looking with surmise at further smoke, that of a native fire on a rock outcrop above.

'Having trouble, young man?' I called.

'Not as much as them'ns, mate,' called back the convict, nodding towards the native fire. A grenadier guard protecting the person of a monarch could not have sounded as clearly dedicated to his martial task as this fellow did.

The journey had by now become more leisurely, the sheep slowing us down as they luxuriated in these new and richer pastures. It was some time before we met stockmen mustering cattle, and the head man told one of his native assistants to ride to the homestead and warn my brother of our coming. This rider was one of the native horsemen my brother had brought with him from the Port Phillip area, and although, like Felix and Hector, his tribe had never laid eyes on a horse until less than two decades ago, the man rode off with the grace of an ancestral rider – such as we read of amongst the Indian indigenes from the plains of the Americas.

My brother had barely come a mile from his homestead when we encountered him. Simon was a well-made young man, less tall than myself, brown-haired, with a manly, pleasant face.

'Brother,' he said, leaning out of his saddle and grasping my right hand with his, and my upper arm with his left hand.

But behind the boyish features lay the barely disguised lineaments of care. They were worried eyes which stared forth at me, with no glint in them to make authentic the smile on his lips. I wondered had my father's presence anything to do with his worn looks.

'I've brought you prime stock,' I told him, smiling.

'You have been splendidly kind,' he said. 'The appetite for mutton goes unabated in Port Phillip. They even have their own architects' office now.' We smiled at each other, but perhaps each brother could see in the other that the plain, pastoral matters were of solace only if the soul was aright.

Simon turned back with us, and pointed out new-made pens amongst scattered tall trees where my men could turn out our sheep to pasture. 'They should mount shifts though,' he counselled with a careworn frown. 'For the natives are still somewhat active.'

We were at last, *sans* men and livestock, riding side by side down the slope to his homestead near the Broken River, with its sundry outbuildings and stockyards.

'Does Father live in the house?' I asked.

'By his own choice he stayed only one night. Since then he occupies that old overseer's hut. It's better. Elizabeth is hard put upon by what she calls anaemia. She complains of lack of strength. As soon as our daughter is two years of age, I propose that they return for a visit to her aunt and uncle in England. I hear that these new ships are more like health spas than the horrors we had on our 400-ton floating Hades coming to join father.'

My memories of all that were confused – uncontainable nausea, dimness, violent movement, the sharp, penetrating stench of overflowing privies and of bile, and beneath it the symphonic and enduring malodour of bilges, the smell which penetrated skin and cloth and dreams.

'Is she upset to have Father here?'

'She is very dutiful. She has never uttered a word of complaint. After all, the man is charming company when he sits at our table, and little trouble otherwise.'

'How does he fill his days?'

'He reads, he writes and – I confess – drinks rum. He gets his exercise through long rides with a convict, Tyler. Father has what he always wanted. Enough to read, some stationery and a pen, a few books, and a pupil.'

'Have you asked him about Mother?'

'He is cheery about Mother. He says he is giving her a rest from his company.'

'One of us must go down there to Van Diemen's Land soon.'

'Oh certainly. I intend on my next visit to Port Phillip to take ship. We must show our love and affection for her ... she is the wronged party.'

'Have you heard from Charlie Batchelor?' I asked in a lowered voice.

'I got the rummest letter from him. Full of obscure references to our returning to type. I decided to put it away and neither seek his company for the time being nor judge him too harshly. This life in the bush is a hard affair, and brings out flaws in the character.'

I said nothing to that in case I gave away something of my own especial flaws.

It got cold early in this trans-alpine world. I sat with Simon and Elizabeth, who did not look well, drinking tea in their parlour, with an Irish woman keeping a watch on my utterly healthy infant niece. I had one eye out for the return of my father and his companion from their ride.

And when he arrived, what would I say? My father had still not appeared when Elizabeth excused herself to rest before dinner. It was hard to tell whether her departure was an attempt to avoid the coming, awkward reunion.

I had gone out to look for him when Father finally appeared from the blind side of the house, galloping hard, in contest with his companion. He looked a wiry figure in his jacket of kangaroo skin. I went over to meet him as he handed the reins to his companion. I had not seen him for eight years. His head was barer and what was left of his hair hung in grey ringlets about his ears, yet the old intelligence shone in his eyes.

'My handsome and successful son,' he said, holding his arms wide with a frankness which I thought was new to him. 'Greet your twice-betraying and twice-betrayed father!'

I did not know what to make of any of this, so I took one of his hands and shook it to prevent the embrace I think he sought. 'You look so well, Father,' I said. He was the man I remembered, older and with the light in his eye which I had once trusted and thought the light of talent, but which I could now see was unreliable, or had somehow run that way.

Simon had suggested that Father dine with all of us that night.

'Does this sit well with Elizabeth?' Father asked gently. And then, 'I believe my daughter-in-law fears I may be some plague on legs.'

I realised the time might come when I would need to say, 'You are, Father, you are.' But my old reverence for him as mentor and parent and seer kept me filial. Besides, whatever shame he had, I had mine.

Inside, by the fire, Simon and my father and I drank rum and water prior to dinner, and when it was served Elizabeth came in, and her small appetite and weary look, I hoped, had nothing to do with my father's supposed sins. She excused herself early, the table was cleared and we sat again by the fire, as beyond the wall the tall trees seemed to creak with cold.

'Have you heard from your mother?' Father asked me.

'She is only an intermittent writer,' I told him. 'Her most recent letter told me to maintain towards you my affection as a son.'

'A virtuous woman,' he said. 'Of all who have eaten of the tree of knowledge, I believe that we males were most over-toppled by the experience, even if we have conveniently made it seem that Eve should take the blame. Did she tell you she would not have me back?'

I went red at this frankness.

'Well,' he continued. 'I have betrayed her twice, once with politics and the other time with my affection. I cannot complain if she, who has no treachery in her, does not want to see it happen again!'

'This is of great grief to us, Father,' I said with feeling.

'The conventional advice when I was young,' said my father, 'was for a philosopher to have a wife of simple virtue. As an anchor, you see? A woman of unthinking loyalty. I certainly achieved that.'

I noticed that my father was, as the stockmen said, giving the rum a nudge. He drank heartily, his eyes were alight. 'The problem is that if my mind was too active, your mother's, I'm sure you'll see, was too docile. There was no benefit in her forgiving me, and loyally trooping with the infants to Van Diemen's Land. The uselessness of that proposition has now been proven.'

'But you should not be apart now,' I said, lamely. 'After so much. With old age coming on. With all mistakes acknowledged and set aside!'

'I shall tell you something, Jonathan,' he said. Both his eyes and his cheeks were aglow now, and there was a wildness of thought and gesture there which I had never seen. 'I very nearly convinced myself that my early heresy against the state was wrong. But all the time there was a cool cell in my mind in which the prisoner writes on the wall: "I am right, and I do not recant." Wealth *is* an evil, though in a vast country like this its blunter wrongs are not obvious! There is no sense at all in invoking Christ's name unless we adhere to the radical nature of His message: "Sell all you have and give to the poor . . ."; "It is easier for a camel to pass through the eye of a needle . . ." Oh, we must appease the law of Christ when it comes to desire and marriage, since that is a good thing for mortgages and inheritance. But when Christ urged community of property, well then, of course he was engaging in parables and hyperbole! He did not mean Mr Huge Coffers, who eyes and begets bastards on his convict maid, but cleaves to his stupid colonial wife and thus is permitted to be called virtuous by the parsons and the Van Diemen's Land Philistines.'

'Father, don't excite yourself like this.' Simon tried to stop his flow.

But Father was reaching for the rum bottle without invitation. 'I say nothing about your mother,' he yelled. 'I say nothing.'

My brother looked at me with bleak eyes, and I could see what he had been through, with a sick wife and a father whose lack of repentance emerged in liquor.

'I say nothing about your mother,' he repeated, sipping his dram without benefit of added water. 'Although I could say this. She is a woman of genuine virtue. That is, she is the type of woman of whom men make fools.'

'I'm going to put away the bottle,' said Simon, rising to do it.

'My friend Horace would disagree with you. "... *dissipat Euhius curas edaces* ... Bacchus drives out voracious cares." Horace, you must know by now, was not a straightforward man or a man of one pedestrian affection. His life too was a set of betrayals. He was redeemed by his poetry. I too, Jonathan, am engaged in redemption.'

'Father writes a great deal,' said Simon in a thin voice which said it was all beyond him.

'It's nearly nine,' said my father with sudden energetic compassion. 'It's time you were abed, Simon. You're the true labourer in the vineyard. Perhaps Jonathan would indulge me by taking a final sup in my hut?'

'I must take my saddlebags to my room,' I told the old man. On this night I thought of him as that, an old coot, gazing at me with a feral eye. 'You go first, Father, and I shall follow.'

'Very well,' he said, snatching up the bottle to depart.

It still contained enough for a few drams. '... *mihi parva rura et,*' he intoned, '*spiritum Graiae tenuem Camenae, Parca non mendax dedit et malignum spernere vulgus.*'

Then he exited elegantly translating. 'Destiny which is no liar has allotted me a little farm, a capacity to attend the classic Muses and a soul which spurns the envy of the mob ...'

'I had no idea that you have been suffering this,' I said to my brother.

Simon told me, 'Mother gave us the greatest gift: of being content with the usual, with the world as it comes. Without that we'd be like him.'

The image of Bernard rose to mock this homely proposition. If only I did have my mother's steadiness. There had been indications of it earlier on. But now I was my dangerous father's dangerous son.

'Simply thank God,' suggested Simon, 'that your remoteness prevented him from deciding to visit you and Phoebe. Elizabeth will soon be gone back to visit her mother's English relatives, and when that is so, he will make fewer inroads on my happiness.'

'And when she returns?'

'We shall deal with that. My prayer is that by then he will be back in Van Diemen's Land, a mild invalid, taken out of action by *Anno Domini*, under Mother's management. Under that regime I believe she could bear being pointed at in that small society as the unfortunate wife of a traducer.'

We said goodnight and I went to join my father. His lamp shone robustly in his window, with a pedagogic intensity. When I knocked on his door, he bade me in joyously. He was already pouring two glasses of rum. By what moral authority could I say, 'No, Father!' I was too vividly conscious that we both drank from the one malign cup.

My father was living in this overseer's hut in one large, not unpleasant room. There was his old sea-chest, which the carpenter had let him make during his time on deck on that unmentionable, unfathomable first sea voyage of his. He had a good cedar table and a comfortable but narrow bed, and a long-legged cupboard on top of which his shirts and pants and smalls rested, for within its open doors sat books and journals, including Cruden's *Concordance*, the *Biblium Vulgatum*, the King James Bible, Byron's poetry, Horace, Cicero and Macaulay's *Essays*, which seemed to be everywhere in the bush and which I would have guessed he secretly dissented from.

He brought out from this cupboard some of the ill-assorted collection of books in which he had been writing – a ledger, a cash book, a commercial diary, all of various page sizes. Even an old half-empty stud book had not escaped filling at his hands. He plonked them, opened at pages of tight scholarly writing, on the cedar table. He sat beside me and took a long pull at the rum. 'What would you say was the greatest Christian virtue?'

I laughed. 'After seven years of sheep farming, I don't quite know. St Paul said faith, hope and charity, and the greatest of these is charity.'

My father said, 'That in a sense is true.' He went rooting through the stud book and found a passage of his own writing. ' "Charity is but equability under another name," ' he quoted. ' "But the emphasis is significant. St Paul was attempting to find a specifically Christian face for a virtue which the old world had practised with considerable dedication. This virtue was *oikeiosis*, kinship, affection. *Oikeiosis* led to equanimity, the acceptance of one's state. Perhaps it would have been better to leave kinship as a chief virtue of civic men in a civil society, rather than try to dress it up in the divine and purple robes of charity." '

He closed the stud book with a thump. 'I wrote that,' he told me. 'That is the burden of my book. What did Epictetus say? "Do not seek to have events happen as you want them to, but instead want them to happen as they do happen, and your life will go well." The greatest crime of Christianity may well have been that it took suffering out of the sphere of human courage, Jonathan, and turned it into something else – turned it into expiation, into the imitation of Christ. We suffer for our sins, and to be made closer to our Redeemer – so every cheap village parson tells us! Until perhaps the fourth century, civilised man was willing to bear the slights of the gods for his *own* dignity. Thus he was validated by the Stoic tradition. He suffered to show that he could suffer and still sing. He suffered to show that we could be at the one time bound by fate, a web of initiating causes, and yet be free. We have the right, whatever happens to us, not to complain. Oh, but no! Christianity requires that we should snivel, for it has smothered the Stoic tradition. These days we suffer because God is displeased with us, and because we have sinned. "Forgive me! Forgive me!" is the continual infantile cry in every Christian church from Port Arthur to Ultima Thule. Not, "I am a man who can bear anything for the sake of my name." Not that. But grovelling.' He mimicked a narrow, parsonical tone. 'Forgive me! Forgive me!'

I dared not say anything.

'Remember! Something I told you in the classroom at Hydebrae, Van Diemen's Land. When the Emperor Constantine conquered his opponents at the Milvian Bridge, what is he said to have seen in the sky?'

'I do remember this –' But I was interrupted.

'Yes, I probably told you this tale as a time-serving convict. Now I tell you as a free but flawed man and for a different purpose. Constantine saw in the heavens a cross, and burning beneath it the words: "*In hoc signo vincis*", "In *this* sign you shall conquer." Primitive faith, you see, replaced the Stoicism of the obedient soldier. Could it be argued that it was the swamping of Stoicism by other sects, including the sect of the Nazarene, which fatally weakened the legions and the administrative capacity of Rome? I believe so. I make a case in my book.'

'That is a fascinating argument,' I said lamely. 'Though there are some who would be offended by it.'

'They deserve offending,' said my father. He waved his arm about. 'I ask you, Jonathan, what virtue did Horace take a sane pride in? What does he most treasure amongst the resources of his soul? Not chastity, for unlike the worthies of Van Diemen's Land, he made no false claims to chastity, and was thereby more chaste! Not expiation, for he looked upon the republican crimes of his youth with whimsy, and on those who forgave him with frank but unkneeling gratitude. His virtue was an ability to bear adversity in an obscure location! Horace blessed the flawed but unavoidable world he found himself in. "Though I am poor, the rich seek me out," he wrote in recognition of the irony of his destiny.

I hope too to be in that position. He on his Sabine farm, me in trans-alpine New South Wales or Van Diemen's Land. Men are robust creatures, not ninnies. Under Christianity they pretend to be ninnies once a week, but apart from that one hour, their real life, if they have courage, resembles that of Horace, Horace the rationally sensual, Horace the forebearing.'

Again what could I say? He was looking at me with a raised, rum-blurred but still cutting eye. Who was I to defend normal Christianity against such a persuasive voice?

'This you see returns us to the question of myself and Mrs Batchelor and your mother. How *does* it happen that certain passages of Scripture are given literal weight, and others are not? Let me tell you, Christ himself was a Spencean Philanthropist, Christ himself was a revolutionary, and he howled down property more often than he howled down poor lapses of flesh and affection! How many times must he say it? "If thou wilt be perfect, go and sell that thou hast, and give to the poor, and thou shalt have treasure in heaven ..." Ah, but *there* – it seems – He is being an exaggerator, *there* He is working in figures of speech. It is His funny little way of exaggeration! The Lord could not possibly have really expected virtuous people to do that! And the message comes again and again. In Luke: "Woe unto you that are rich, for ye have received your consolation." And on and on.'

'But I could in some lights be called wealthy,' I protested. 'Am I to be damned?'

'How could I say that of my son?' he asked. 'But it is a problem you have.' He began hand-waving again, racing on with his argument. 'The Stoics call for good behaviour because reason and fraternity are thereby glorified. Virtue is simply politeness and fellow feeling. Vice is inevitable but must be its own education. Not a matter for pietistic grovelling before some altar, but an issue of calm assessment. The Stoics urged dignity in the face of both passion or desolation. Their founder Zeno exhorted them to perform "acts of which a reasonable account can be given". That was not good enough for the Gospels as interpreted by parsons! Not only did a man have to behave well in the street and the home amongst other men and women, he had to deny his interior and unbidden thoughts. Christianity, by bearing Stoicism away, made true virtue, the virtue of the man who applies reason to his turbulent thoughts, impossible. Hypocrisy was guaranteed. If a man is to be condemned for one infidelity as well as for a hundred, thinks the sinner, why not the hundred? And this all the more so when the other supposed sinner is a woman of robust thought, rare in Van Diemen's Land, as you know.'

'Please,' I said, 'please, I do not want to hear this.'

'No,' insisted my father. 'No. This is my book, you see. Stoicism could deal with betrayals. It drove out morbid jealousy as it drove out morbid guilt. Horace could regret our flawed nature but accepted it as the real condition of his own pilgrimage. Prim schoolteachers liked him for his statement about hating the vulgar and profane crowd. They do not copy for their students the passages where he imagines a bracelet removed from a white arm prior to the mysteries of love. And like them, a reforming convict, I tried to make Horace a Christian for the sake of getting by in Van Diemen's land. But it is not so. And I shall now expiate my hypocrisy in this book.'

'My God,' I called out, full of terror. 'Never mind Horace! What of expiation for my mother, for the Batchelors?'

He took a huge swig of his rum.

'They too,' he said, 'will be reconciled by my book.'

Stumbling back oppressed to Simon's homestead in double dark, I comforted myself that no one would publish his cracked book, if indeed he did not succumb to rum before finishing it. There you are, I told myself. See him! That is what you will become if you are foolish.

Steely skies overtook us as we returned from visiting Simon and my father. In the Port Phillip Pass, it was not yet snowing, but the sky was taut with grey, aching clouds. I let Presscart and some of the other men gallop ahead of Clancy's wagon, for amongst these high, dark crags the squalid yet familiar comfort of their hearths called to them. I stayed with Clancy and Felix, taking the same pace as the wagon. Though longing to see not only Phoebe and George, but in a different sense, Bernard, I felt delayed by the paternal mess behind me and the familiar but precious torment ahead. I had calculated that my rival Long would receive his conditional pardon within a year, and thus be able to marry Bernard without reference to me, and move away somewhere, taking her and his share of the cattle with him.

We made Nugan Ganway at last light with the wind screaming around the boulders above the homestead. The poplars Phoebe had planted as wind break between the homestead and the Cooma track were infant in growth and thrashed about pitiably. Some of the men were out piling extra stones onto their bark roofs to stop them blowing away.

Going indoors at least from this turmoil of nature, I found that my beautiful Phoebe sat wrapped in a rug by our fire indoors. She was reading a story of a carthorse to my sturdy little George, now a little under a year old. Her theory was that one read to a child whether they caught the specifics of what was read or not. But her cheeks were reddish and her eyes, if anything, desperate.

'We must get you to bed,' I said, strangely delighted to be of simple service to Phoebe.

I would make an excellent hospital attendant. First I went and rang the bell outside our back door which summoned Bernard. I could hear Presscart and Clancy drinking tea with her in her cookhouse and teasing her. She was in her way easier in manner with these men than with Long. She amused them with her own careful humour. When I rang she came at once – no last words, no delay. She would make Long a successful wife. Like him she was driven by tasks, and embraced them for their power to ease memory.

'Bernard,' I said, 'I think my wife has a sudden fever. She might need broth and tea, and little George must be looked to.'

Bernard's long hands crushed the apron at her hips. In the parlour Phoebe saw her coming and trustingly raised her jaw. Bernard admirably asked, 'Do you have neck pain, Mrs Bettany?'

'No,' said Phoebe. 'I feel generally out of sorts, and my joints ache.'

Little George Bettany sat in his chair and watched as the servant examined his mother, and then with fathomless eyes turned to me, the unworthy husband.

'I have senna in the kitchen. I might make up a tincture of it for Mrs Bettany.'

'Yes,' I agreed, exercising the creaky authority of the would-be paterfamilias.

'Mama!' said George, four-square in his infant boots and pantaloons and vest.

'Mama is sick,' murmured Bernard.

'But not for long, my darling,' Phoebe told him.

I went out in the raging afternoon towards Tume's lively kitchen. She had an eight-year-old boy, a reliable fellow named Michael, who had been involuntarily transported with his mother and whom I thought of as one of my future stockmen. I asked if I could borrow Michael to entertain little George, who clearly much admired the older boy. This child Michael was barefooted, and wore dungarees and an old shirt which had once belonged to someone much larger than he. A woollen jerkin was his only protection against the deepening winter's day. Though he had apparently been born in Ireland, he was the characteristic bush urchin, and every Celtic intonation had been bleached from his tongue. Michael suggested then in his New South Wales drawl that he carry a suitably coated George into the woolshed to play for the hour or so of light which was left. It was far too cold and blustery outside, but inside the shed was a large room, the tops of the walls lined with wool sacks, where men ate during the shearing or at the end of long musters. Here Clancy had made a little enclosure with wooden toys inside it, horses, cattle and a camel, and the sight of them always excited and diverted George.

Michael came with me back to the house, where by now Bernard had my wife's pale, neat feet in a basin of hot water to which English mustard powder had been added.

'I've put a warming pan in her bed,' Bernard told me. Such implements were some of the refinements Phoebe had brought to us soon after our marriage.

'Look after George,' I said to Michael with confidence, as I buttoned my son into a kangaroo hide coat one of the men had run up for him. 'No playing outside, not today, do you understand?'

'That's jake, Mr Bett'ny,' said Michael.

George, who at this stage could barely walk but who insisted on tottering rather than being carried, was wriggling inside his jacket with the prospect of being pick-a-backed down to the woolshed by this older boy. But to be sure, I held his forehead for a long time before I let him go. I held his pulse, and pressed his collarbones and the base of his neck, and none of that seemed to cause him any pain.

'No, no,' he told me as I fussed. For he was ready to go. I kissed him for the man he would become.

So Phoebe was helped to her room by Bernard, and when she was in place, in nightdress and shawl, with the wind playing the timbers and rattling the darkening window pane, I went in and began reading to her a new book of Carlyle's, *Sartor Resartus*, a study of the amusing Professor Teufelsdröckh and his absurd remarks on fashion.

As I read I could tell that Pheoebe was less and less comfortable, and I asked her how she was. 'I have a sore throat,' she said, 'and feel very ill.' At that second, perciypiently, Bernard lifted a basin from a bedside table and placed it in front of my wife. Soured tea and a concoction of senna burst from Phoebe's mouth. The combination of Phoebe's pain and Bernard's competence, the sisterhood between the two women, the hale Bernard and racked Phoebe, was a torment. In confusion I moved in and held Phoebe's wrist as the violence of the thing passed. Bernard said, 'You'll be fine and on top of matters in a day or so, Mrs Bettany.' Her eyes turned to me, full of profound, liquid confidence. Then she swayed off to her work in the kitchen as I reread the opening sentences, and I had perhaps not read more than a page when Phoebe went into an uneasy sleep.

I placed great reliance in what Bernard had said: Phoebe would be soon on top of matters.

George returned on Michael's back, his cheeks red and his eyes alight. I let Michael stay and look through my bound volumes of illustrated papers, with George propped beside him in a chair. As Michael turned a page and uttered the name of what was illustrated on that page, George would repeat the word. 'Look, a ship,' Michael would say. 'Sip,' George would reverently echo.

Later, Bernard put George to bed in the second room, where she would also sleep overnight.

At some stage I woke at Phoebe's side while she was suffering another paroxysm, which I attended to. 'I am so ill,' she said, uncharacteristically.

'Bernard says you will be on top of matters in a day or so,' I said to comfort her and myself.

'Bernard doesn't know everything,' Phoebe told me.

Indeed, Phoebe's extreme pallor concerned me. She seemed almost luminous in the dark, and I heard the traducing wind hungry at our walls, gnawing the daub from every seam. I felt terror for Phoebe, and for the solidity of my world. In my flawed mind, I wondered if I had somehow whistled up my wife's illness.

'Tomorrow I shall ride to Cooma to fetch Dr Alladair,' I promised Phoebe.

She held my wrist. 'Send a man, and stay with me.'

The next morning, with Phoebe still pallid and weak, I visited Long's hut, as if on normal business. The air was blowing sleet and the mountains were lost in a turbulence of snow clouds. Long seemed faintly confused to be asked to ride on an errand any other of my convict hands could have undertaken. He too had a fear – that I had changed.

I decided that Tume's son Michael would again keep George company in the house. Felix, who had been exhausted by the ride across the alps and woke late, also joined the children, and showed them pictures and maps, with the gentle expository skill of a born teacher. Bernard would need to cook, to change and bath George when necessary, and above all to bring her air of certainty to Phoebe's bedside. The boys could entertain themselves with a ball of jute I gave them to throw to each other, as much stationery as they wanted to make lines on with pencils, and further access to my library. In between stoking the fire, which sucked down the angry air from outside and blazed merrily, I would occasionally cross to my son and feel his brow, for what that exercise was worth.

Phoebe herself was, I was happy to find, cool, even icy to the touch. The climate without and not the fever within had influenced her, and I thought it a good sign.

The big-boned Scotsman Alladair, who had attended George's birth, arrived in mid-afternoon. He added his air of competence to that of Bernard, so that one did not believe anything bad could be permitted to happen to his patient. 'You must compose yourself, dear fellow,' he told me. 'It is – whatever it is – not bubonic plague you know.' He felt the glands beneath Phoebe's jaw, and inspected her throat. Was she still nauseated? No, I was pleased to hear her say, but she felt very weak. He smiled at me across the room as he felt her pulse. 'Fortunately frailty itself is not a fatal sign,' he told Phoebe through me.

He suggested more senna mixture, and rest. Since he had ridden all the way from Cooma, I asked him to look at my son, whom he described as being in 'rude bush health'.

So Doctor Alladair cheerily drove off home again in a dusk hard as steel.

When I woke late that night and lit a lamp, I found my wife convulsing. First senna and then quantities of bile came up her throat. She lay back so exhausted that she could not speak of it. 'My love,' I said, kissing her hands. 'Rest and don't succumb.'

I cursed Dr Alladair for making too rosy a judgement. I would have to fetch him back. I comforted Phoebe and slept fitfully. Bernard nudged me awake at dawn. My son was convulsing as his mother had. I sent Presscart out to summons Alladair – I might have gone myself, to ease anxiety with action, but George was calling for me. I felt his pulse and it was very irregular. They had both developed a racking cough and mucus rose up their throats.

Through all that horrible forenoon, Bernard went from one to the other, placing hot cloths on their foreheads. This was not the normal pattern of fever – it was not a matter of the vital spark raging and consuming itself. It was a matter of it sinking down into dim iciness. Bernard and I moved the boy's bed into his mother's room, and Bernard filled the space with the warm and comforting smell of camphor and hot water. Alladair rode up at one o'clock in the afternoon. Good Presscart had got the man here, and on fast horseback rather than by carriage, in rather better time than I had hoped. Alladair briefly warmed his meaty hands at the fire before touching Phoebe and George, and then Bernard supported Phoebe to allow the doctor to looked down her throat. Gravely, he then moved to my whimpering son, and I supported George in my arms as Alladair performed the same examinations.

I was appalled by his sombre look as he leaned on the lump of hewn cedar which made our mantlepiece.

'Do you have any rum?' he asked.

I said we did. I went and fetched it and poured him a glass mixed with water. It was a day for it, and obviously, from his face, it was a day for worse things as well.

'Their heads should be shaven at once. Could your housekeeper manage it? That is important. It diminishes the spread of the fever. Yesterday there were no signs in your wife's throat. Now I can see the appearance of a membrane. It resembles white of egg.'

'And ... what is it?'

'Your wife and son have the infection named diphtheria. The membrane will attempt to cast itself over the soft palate, the uvula, the pharynx and larynx. Have you noticed both their eyes are squinting – that is a symptom. Some of what your son is regurgitating comes through his nose. That too is characteristic. They will both grow delirious, but we must hope for the best. In delirium, they should have cold compresses on their forehead. I believe the woman has been using hot ones. That should discontinue. We must depend on the youth and strength of your wife and of your son. They are in God's hands now.'

I felt a surge of anger. 'You mentioned "rude bush health".'

'Yes, I was guilty of rashness. It was true yesterday. It is not true today. There is no earthly force I could have applied to prevent the development of that coating on the throat.'

'You tell me ... you tell me, do you? ...we must wait to see if this growing membrane strangles my wife and son?'

'Don't dwell on that, dear fellow. We must rely on the inherent strength of the two sufferers, and on the mercy of God.'

'God was not mentioned yesterday, sir!' I said. 'It seems that He only achieves a mention when the surgeon is bewildered.'

'You're probably right about that,' said the tolerant doctor, draining his rum. 'I shall leave doses of calomel. This is a disease which takes days or even weeks to develop, so I shall be back here the morning after next. Stockmen and their families should not come to this house, and I must inspect yourself and the housekeeper.'

I remembered to tell him that Felix and Michael had been close to George. He declared that Bernard and I showed no signs, but that we should stay in isolation around the homestead until the fever had run its course and not have close contact with any other person on Nugan Ganway. I thought I heard then, high at the apex of the wind, the laughter of ironic gods who had given me my perverse desire, to be locked away with Bernard.

Thus began a dreadful fortnight. Somewhere beyond our walls, like life on another continent, my affairs were run by Long – pastures patrolled in search of frost-blasted sheep, a steer run down and slaughtered for meat, carpentry attended to by Presscart and Clancy, rations drawn by Long and cooked by Tume. On some days I could hear Tume's barefoot lad, Michael, out there, as he leapt, sang and freely breathed. Felix, whom I would have loved to greet, did not come to read his Latin texts or Greek primers.

And what Alladair called 'the characteristic membrane' grew apace in George's throat, a force so small that the idea it could not be thwarted and prevented brought me hourly closer and closer to madness. My son and dear Phoebe were often in a simultaneous delirium. Phoebe cried that she was drowning in glacial Lake Geneva, raving as, in her perception, she went down. No stockmen visited Bernard in the outer kitchen, she cooked solid food only for herself and me, and broths and light junkets to be routinely regurgitated by Phoebe and George. Bernard asked me, her large, limpid, darkling eyes possessed by an unfeigned concern, 'Do you think if we could find some arrowroot it might stay down?' Alladair was back, humble as a monk, concerned, and abandoning by this time references to the Divine Will.

George suffered choking anguish as he cried to me – all the ships and bridges and dukes and soldiers Michael had pointed out to him in the pages of the illustrated papers were crushing in on him. I wept and howled with him, and Bernard said, 'Sir, I must get you a dram.'

In the mornings, when Phoebe's head was generally clearer, she would ask, 'How is George?' I would tell her that he was well. But the boy was losing even his infant power to communicate. He lay in torpor, profoundly sunk in his bed. On his fourth visit, Alladair insisted on staying. I let him have the ottoman in the living room. By candlelight I watched the flecks of white foam in the corners of Phoebe's perfect mouth. Dr Alladair had given her perhaps too much calomel, and she was salivating, weakly working the lips, and I rose quickly to feed her teaspoonfuls of water and then went back to the chair, which I straddled backwards, my elbows on its straight back, above my son. On my awkward roost, I fell profoundly asleep. I dreamt of Bernard with her hair lasciviously undone bringing me scones to eat. For the moment of the dream I managed to feign indifference, but I said to myself, 'It will be harder to do in Nugan Ganway than in this dream.'

Alladair woke me to steely light in the sick room. I knew at once that this would be a merciless day, knew it before I heard a word from Alladair. But he quickly told me, his great face twisted. 'Mr Bettany, George's struggle is over.'

I got up and went to the little truckle bed. Bernard stood above it, weeping. My wafer of child was sunk in it, deep as an ingot, determined already in death's velocity to recede from us. 'His earlier suffering was terrible,' said Alladair, 'but over the past two hours he has been very peaceful.'

'For sweet Christ's sake, why didn't you wake me?'

'I had crept in here and I mistook the tranquillity of the end for the beginning of a recovery, and thought it best to let you rest.'

I inspected George's face. I could see beneath the infant features the ghost of the man who would never be.

'Your wife however, your wife seems more settled.'

'How would you know, sir?' I yelled at the poor doctor. He, I thought, could bear a sympathetic face but go home to his wife and children. 'Diphtheria is a disease of slums. It's a disease of Manchester, for dear God's sake. How could it come all this way, to the open bush, and take my son?'

'The worst of ill fortune, my dear fellow. That's how.'

I insisted on raising the feather-light body of my son and embracing him. I was demented, and this was, of all my life, the greatest agony. This, I thought, is what people mean when they call something insupportable. I could not support this grief. I felt my body melting beneath it. I looked to Bernard but in her eyes, blurred themselves by loss, there was nothing to aid me. I wanted my heart to stop, and my soul to find hell.

The doctor persuaded me to let go of George. My next impulse was to flee the house, to go raging amongst those boulders, to be impaled by those screaming winds, and to discover at last, beyond a ridge some-where, this very moment, this very room again, but with the scene altered, my inheritor, my boy, having woken from profound sleep and saying in joyful recognition, 'Papa'.

'Steady, Bettany,' said Alladair, taking firm hold of my arm. 'Be brave. Think of your wife.'

That morning Dr Alladair permitted me to emerge from the house – I had clearly outlasted some phase of quarantine he had in his head. I saw my men move around the outbuildings, and heard Maggie Tume yelling from the men's cookhouse. In this clear, sharp day, currawongs shouted from the tall eucalypts whose every branch stood out in the clear air, whose every leaf was a dun spear point. I called for Clancy. We had got beyond improvised coffins. There was a man in Cooma who made polished and decorated ones. Clancy was to go to town with my son's height – two feet five inches – written on a sheet of paper and bring back one, waiting should the man need to make one specially. While the coffin was being prepared, he was to let Mr Paltinglass know that we had lost our adored son, and place in the fledgling *Cooma Courier* a memorial notice I had written. I warned Clancy most grimly against stopping on the way or the return at the public house newly established just north of Mount Bulwa station.

For the moment, George lay in the same room as Phoebe, who had utterly lost the wit and the strength to ask about him. In the parlour Bernard fed Alladair and myself a meal of bacon and fried bread and tea. Taking back my plate barely quarter-eaten from me, she said, 'Let us pray for Mrs Bettany, sir. A man as young and strong as you will have other children.' Had anyone else – Alladair, for example – suggested that, I would have become engorged with rage. But since it came from Bernard I madly set myself almost to considering that halfway a prophecy, a divine chastisement, and a cause of minute hope.

I had Long get the phaeton ready – it was appropriate as overseer he should attend the funeral with me. When I had bought this vehicle it had been in expectation of Phoebe, myself and our children proceeding in it to town for special occasions, to cricket matches and picnic race meetings. Now it was my son's tiny body which, coffined, was to travel roped to the ledge behind the main seat.

Before I left I went to say goodbye to Phoebe, finding her in a state of maternal clarity. Her eyes glazed with intelligence. 'George is gone,' she told me, and her face became sodden with grief. I caressed her, I kissed her forehead. I gathered her thin body off the pillows, embraced it, repented of my delusions. I said the usual things: the little fellow was with God, had died without suffering, but that she must not deprive me of son *and* wife, that she must recover, for her sake, mine, for the sake of unborn children amongst whom we would keep George's name green.

'You are going,' she acknowledged. 'But you are coming back?'

'I shall be back before night.'

'If you are back by night, my love, I shall make sure I am here to greet you.'

Abased and weeping, I left her in Bernard's care and took myself out to the four-wheeler phaeton. Felix was there, wearing boots and a jacket, and with moist eyes. Since he seemed, by the standards of Nugan Ganway, dressed for the funeral, I asked him, 'Would you come with Long and George and me, Felix?'

'With you and the little bloke,' he said. I recognised the phrase. Presscart had always called George 'the little bloke'.

Felix climbed into the carriage, his back holding the little polished coffin in place. Long, helping me board, inspected me carefully, as if loss had turned me into yet another person.

'You're such a good fellow, Mr Bettany,' he said, 'that God should be kinder.'

I raised a hand to prevent any other honest and quaintly phrased condolences from him. He climbed into the driver's seat, shook the reins, and the bright-cried currawongs and magpies mocked us on our way.

George was amongst the first of the scatter of young to be placed in the new churchyard at Cooma, and to have the benefit of the earnest, East Anglian-accented prayers of the Reverend Paltinglass, whose ceremonial style was a comfort to me and both sharpened and soothed my grief. Paltinglass and the editor of the new Cooma newspaper had between them spread the news of the Bettany calamity, and my old friend Peske, the District Commissioner, was there, full of suppressed excitement since he had just been given a post in Madras. Cooma Creek's first police magistrate and his family also attended.

After we saw George into the earth, Long supported me back to the parlour of the very manse in which George had been born. Family by family the mourners left, men and women muttering their helpless condolence. As the wind mounted outside I began to dread the coming bereaved night. But at least I had a simple contract to fulfil – to return to Phoebe by nightfall.

With Paltinglass's priestly best wishes, Felix, Long and I rose to the cushioned seat of the phaeton. Climbing the hill a mile out of town, I stood in my seat to reach for a cap beneath it, and was bent over in a very insecure posture when the wheels hit a large stone. I felt Felix clutch at my coat tails, but he could not stop me pitching head first from the vehicle onto the track. The disturbance caused the horses to bolt, and Long passed the reins to Felix and jumped down to run beside them and try to catch hold of their heads. But he could not manage it. With Felix their hostage, the horses left the track and galloped uphill, reduced to their untamed instincts, and making for a wooded spur to the right.

Sitting up in the dust, shaking my head, I saw with some dread that Felix was rising to abandon the vehicle. I wanted him to remain amongst the upholstered cushions rather than take that risk. But with the cushions spewing forth around him, he jumped to the ground and landed with grace. The phaeton disappeared over the rise, and vanished towards its ruination.

My head was ringing from the fall. Long limped, but Felix ran to us. 'I undertook to be with Mrs Bettany by dark,' I told Long.

The phaeton, if still intact, might be miles off by the time we found it. But we were a mile from the new public house along the track, Long reminded me, and suggested the three of us walk there. In the tap room were a few of Treloar's stockmen, who grew reverently silent as we entered. So they had heard the news of George. I asked the innkeeper, by rumour a former London burglar, whether there might be someone there who could loan me a horse. 'Now you mention that,' he told me, 'we've Mr 'arrington from Yass.'

I remembered the name; the man was a station agent I had met once in Barley's company in Sydney. He was fetched from the parlour and offered me his black mare, asking only that one of my men return the horse the next day.

I was strangely more consoled by the kindnesses of these strangers, the stockmen, the innkeeper, Harrington, than I had been by the funeral rite from *The Book of Common Prayer*, and gained hope again for Phoebe.

I gave Felix and Long a sovereign to buy them dinner and, if necessary, accommodation, and told them I would send horses for them in the morning. They were to find the phaeton or its wreckage and retrieve or, if necessary, shoot the horses. Then I rode off. Four miles along the road, as I mounted the side of a stony hill, another sign of hope. I saw off to the right my carriage and its two horses, their reins caught in the front wheel and a broken trace conveniently preventing forward progress. The dashboard was shattered and sundry cushions could be seen strewn about the hillside, but Long would have little trouble finding and repairing it tomorrow.

There was still plenty of light as I splashed on the good mare across the ford of the Murrumbidgee. As I came into the front parlour, Bernard was feeding logs to the fire. She read me with dark eyes. 'God bless you, Mr Bettany,' she said outright, in that strange way of hers, blunt yet elegant. 'Your wife has been asking.'

I went in with renewed hope to Phoebe. But it seemed that only her eyes had any capacity for movement, and she was already, I hated to see, a wraith. A mocking God had preserved my phaeton but would not preserve my wife. All that had happened that afternoon had been a series of divine teases, not gracious omens of hope.

I held Phoebe's hand. 'George is at rest,' I said, and with a sudden surge of belief which would have done honour to Mr Paltinglass. 'He would greet you in paradise, but he wishes you should live and remember him.'

She tried to speak through that pernicious veil which was crimping all her powers of voice and breath. 'But he is lying in that cold place,' she whispered.

All belief fled. 'No,' I insisted. 'He has ascended.'

After preparing a meal for which I lacked appetite, Bernard intended to be Phoebe's night nurse again. The contrast between this noble office, and the more intimate one my base mind had previously devised for her, chastened me. I thought of my father and Stoicism. What had Father quoted to me before I rode off from Simon's? Some rubbish of Epictetus. 'Do not seek to have events happen as you want them to, but instead want them to happen as they do happen, and your life will go well.' Want the death of your son, and your life will go well! Want your wife to choke, and your life will go well!

That night I set myself wakefully, on top of the covers, wrapped in a rug, at Phoebe's side. I watched her by lamplight, how fine-featured she was even in this extremity of disease. I allowed myself to sleep for no longer than ten minutes at a time. Thus, I was awake at two o'clock in the morning when, by the stump of candle that was left, I saw her straining to sit. Her breathing was strangled. 'George has come back anyhow,' she told me.

I denied it, but her face was full of delirious certainty. 'I knew the Moth people would not keep him. They are too kindly.' She began to choke, and as I tried to restrain her, and make her rest against my shoulder, a convulsion set in, arching her body. Then all the tension of the disease left her in a second. I was stupid enough to think her better.

Bernard removed the shawls and nightdress from my wife's tiny shell. I saw with unspeakable regret and remorse the breasts which had fed George, the stomach which had borne him, that girlish abdomen, and the mound of hair marking her womanhood, her motherhood.

'I'll look after the washing and laying out, Mr Bettany,' said Bernard. 'You should go outside and take some brandy.'

Through tears I said, 'You have been very good to us, Bernard. You might have caught the disease yourself.'

'It is an honour to serve a noble woman.' Bernard told me. 'It is for the crimes of others she has been punished.'

I went to the parlour and obeyed Bernard by pouring some brandy. As I drank I was sharply aware that in the next room the body of my wife, whom I had vowed to cherish unto death, was receiving its last mercies from the woman I had wantonly desired.

I was not fit to travel after the Reverend Paltinglass had committed Phoebe's coffin, itself remarkably small, like a young girl's, to the same alluvial pit in the churchyard at Cooma Creek as George's. I wrote to Mrs Finlay with the grievous news, but there was hardly time for her to have received the letter. We had not taken the chance of any more phaeton accidents and lashed the coffin, with Phoebe's wraithlike, stiffened body within it, to the tray of the bullock wagon. Alladair, who bravely attended the funeral despite the risk that I might begin ranting, unjustly or otherwise, at him, took me back to the Paltinglass manse as if I were an elderly person. Good Paltinglass sent his young children to bed early, lest their fresh complexions cause me to rail like Job. Alladair, with the connivance of Mr and Mrs Paltinglass fed me whisky and a dose of some opiate which utterly felled me. I would not later remember who had helped me to the bedroom I occupied that night.

Riding back to Nugan Ganway the next afternoon with a sombre Felix, I became aware of the unfamiliarity of my own self. It was as if I had met a plausible stranger, someone I did not choose to know better. I was aware of a parallel strangeness in the landscape about me. I did not wish to occupy that landscape. I had become so estranged from the world I had once so coveted. It could no longer provide me with an outer skin. I shook out the reins impatiently.

In the house that evening, I was aware that Bernard, who had not attended the funeral, had packed away all traces of Phoebe and George in sundry chests. Their ghosts occupied the death room, if at all, in the faint smell of naphtha.

'You may return to your normal pursuits now,' I told Bernard.

I could look with the composure of an already disembodied soul at her going to visit Long. Let the living look to their busy, fevered courtships. Though I believe I could see in her a touching intention to keep a vigil here. But from my point of view, the angle of a man who had resolved to put an end to all his lust, grief and treachery, to cast himself down upon the mercy of the deity, her delicacy was meaningless.

With a strange energy and appetite, however, I ate the supper she prepared. I thought of my father, a man like myself far removed from life's normal tide. I pulled down my copy of the four books of Horace's odes. The best I could find – a classic Stoic credo – was in Book Three: 'Quanto quisque sibi plura negaverit ...' 'The more a man deprives himself of, the more the gods will give him: naked I flee from the wealthy to seek a place amongst the unselfish ...' The most unselfish were the dead. And since grief was everywhere, virtue beyond me, vice inevitable, I began to think how correct it might be to go to greet both George and Phoebe in the shades. Bernard might wash and settle my body, a service of sisterhood rather than the coarser yet sublimer contacts I had imagined. Honest Long would conduct it to a dismayed but forgiving Paltinglass.

And yet liquor and sleep ambushed me, and I was disgusted to wake to a further dawn, and stagger into the parlour to encounter a solicitous Bernard. I was sure I would not so betray myself the coming night. I went outside and made a good play-act of discussing the day's order of work with Long. I wanted Long to think: he's taking it bravely. Yet that evening again I took drink and sleep overcame me and made a fool of my intentions. I knew now that within me lay yet another oaf than the one who had desired Bernard even as Phoebe sickened. This oaf cared not for grief. He sought merely to breathe and go through his bland animal functions.

Another morning saw me in the yard, squinting and swallowing bile, and conferring again with respectful Long. I must not drink early in the day – so I told myself. Yet how could the time be tolerated without the blunting influence of rum? Again I was stupefied, and prostrated by noon, but at least I woke at dusk with a head so gravid that my neck felt inadequate to the task of raising it. Since the column of my bones could no longer sustain me, and all was ache, I was calmly set to act during the coming dark hours. I needed of course to eat a meal – I did not want Bernard running out to tell Long I had refused to eat. I did not want her large-eyed concern. And I took rum even then to stoke in me that sense of distance from the universe of normal feeling. There would not be enough time tonight for me to consume it in those quantities which might steal away my purpose.

The time came. Bernard was occupied in the kitchen. I went to the trouble of collecting a jacket before stepping out of the door. No nostalgic looks back at this or that surface. I wanted to be quit of all. I did not mind that I might be seen by some transcendent critic as a ridiculous figure in a bad play: I would not be here to bear the sneers of that. The ground was cold and wet beneath my feet. There would be a frost by the morning; it was palpable that the night ached for a conclusion – a gale of snow, a death. I would do my best to satisfy the requirements of the darkness.

Careless of damage to my fingers, I unknotted a near-frozen length of rope from the wool press, cursing its obduracy. Taking it inside the wool-shed, to the best-constructed part of Nugan Ganway, where wool which had clothed Europe had been shorn and sorted and pressed, I could barely see the red beefwood rafters. I fetched a bench from the annex where the men ate during shearing, hauled the rope over the dimly seen roof beam and knotted it, testing it for a moment with my weight by lifting my feet off the chair. Then, summoning up the image of George and weeping for him, I made a hefty knot and placed the rope about my neck. As I waited on the bench a while, delayed by the interesting nature of my last second, I evoked both George's face and Phoebe's. The dead were palpable in every corner and shadow. I would meet in Hades earthy, sage Horace. I would encounter Phoebe to whom, as with God, amends must be made. I would encounter too the phantom man my son never grew to be, and greet with least shame the mother of Felix, whose killers I had tried to punish. The murdered Catherine would bully, on my behalf, a capricious Deity, and the absconders would delight to see me brought to my extreme moment by the same hand which had helped finish them.

I enjoyed these few moments of assessment but despised delay and prevarication in the condemned. I stepped off the bench.

In darkness I engaged a final hope that the rope was adequate to send me to oblivion. And indeed, as the base fell out of the earth beneath my feet, I felt gravity and the noose connive to produce an enormous blow to the right side of my neck, below my ear, nearly adequate to sever the head from its shoulders.

And yet it was not adequate to bear my senses away, and all was consumed by the sensation of choking and of futilely seeking solidity, desiring it all at once as nothing had ever been desired, neither woman nor property nor wealth. I told myself that I had now taken adequate punishment, and already knew hell, and was entitled to draw back. For the blackness of the woolshed flashed with light and burned and burned in great gusts of airlessness. The earth was my hard spouse and would not return to me now that I had abandoned it. My father walked in from the sheep yards and added the pages of his book to the flames of my agony. And I saw, as a concrete figure stepping towards me, in a rush, howling, Death in dark weeds, scythe in hand, eager to close the transaction. The dullest, most gelid moonlight delineated the blade as it sliced at my head. I fell, and there was solid ground again, the ground, I supposed, of my interment. A hand worked at my hangman's knot, and lost air, as painful as lost limbs, ached into my body.

'Mr Bettany,' said the reaper in Bernard's voice, 'whatever are you at for sweet God's sake?'

The reason Death had Bernard's voice was that I had misidentified. The one figure there was simply Bernard, straddling me with her thighs, shaking the air back into me. I felt great strength in her long hands.

'Do you think it can be as easy as that, do you?' she asked me, and so drew her right fist back and smashed it against my jaw. The woolshed filled up with light again, but I thought in a powerful, instant, fuddled way, 'This woman may well teach me to accommodate myself in the world again.'

Reborn of her, I found myself engorged with love of the living, and dragged her towards me, a huge endeavour towards which she seemed to add her own strength. Soon I who had had no air was howling and aching into her. Though within days of my wife's burial, all this did not have the cast of betrayal. Rather, of triumph, and a necessary rite of resuscitation.

I let myself be led back to the homestead again. She opened the door for me and let me in. By the light of two lamps and of the low fire at the hearth she looked directly at me. 'Look what you have brought us to, you poor fellow!' She sat me down, then went away to get tea and make some embrocation with both of which she returned. With the bowl of embrocation she began to wash the rope burn on the side of my neck. When in plain, brute need I reached for her waist, she pulled herself clear. 'No,' she warned me. 'No.'

In the subsequent days, I spent most of my time on my own in my desolated homestead, but attended by a severe Bernard. Suspended exactly between the living and the dead, I was suffused by an aura of azure sensual delight, shot through with a yellow sulphur of doom. I waited in a soporific daze for her to return to me and give me ease. I knew it would happen. My grief for Phoebe and George had begun to take on the colours of consolation as I waited. I waited stoically. In the face of hell, I was ecstatically stoic, grief-stricken and agape with wonderment at the one time. I drank and stumbled out for brief conversations with Long, none of which I could remember, all of them more meaningless chat about out-stations and stock.

On the second night I appealed to Bernard as she brought me food I was too feverish to contemplate. I appealed to her, and she said, 'I would be most evil.'

'If it was not evil when you scythed me down, why is it evil now?' I said.

'Dear God, the warmth of your poor wife's body has not yet left the deathbed!'

But I persisted. 'If it will not be wrong in a year, why – viewed from the standpoint of eternity – is it wrong now?'

She yielded at last. I did not know, I did not care, as I subsisted on Bernard's ivory lineaments, whether she had told Long and the stockmen about my attempt to jump into the pit. I was not, however, without shame, but was prepared to let it cohabit the house with me, as one might in an extremity share a cave with a large dangerous beast. And everything was two-edged with her, was at the one time guilt and redemption. Yet by throwing an arm about her body and drawing her close I could in the unity of that embrace reduce the world to one sharp, tolerable edge, sustained from the opening kiss into other intimacies of touch, into a fury of feeling and reaching. Then, as I gasped, all fell back again to two-edgedness. And of course at that moment I did not know for whose sake I should feel more ashamed. For Phoebe's and George's? For Long's? For Bernard's? For the sake of the steadfast condemned man I had been a few nights before?

During these days, Nugan Ganway functioned well, horses being reshod, my remotest shepherds greeting visits by Long and maintaining my flocks. On the fourth day I felt a passion to go out for an extensive ride, but first, and after thought, I tested Bernard with a question.

'Will not Sean Long expect you to visit him?'

'Long knows that I am needed here,' she told me, standing back from feeding the fire at my hearth. 'Long and all the men know how badly I am needed in your house now.'

'Badly needed,' I confirmed, and reached a hand for her wrist.

But of course as days passed the most unlikely, or some might say improper, of arrangements rose to be normal. After a week I emerged and went down to Long's hut, and discussed a coming 'bang-tail' muster, that is, a muster of all our neglected hill cattle, which he had been urging upon me. There was no sign of altered knowledge or resentment from him. But then there would not be, since he – like many of his people – had learned to swallow resentment more profoundly than the marrow of his own bones.

Long told me he would need a dozen riders, and I promised that he would have them. Felix wanted to go, he told me, even though he was still mourning Mrs Bettany and George.

'Are you sure he is matured enough to muster cattle?' I asked. 'We have had sufficient tragedies on Nugan Ganway.'

'He dearly wishes to be with us, and is as robust as many boys of sixteen.'

'You may count me in too,' I told Long. It was mere justice to him for me to join in the risk.

His eyes were dark and deep-set and could hardly be read. But in some distant corner of his brain, Long must have hoped that I would fall – such things were possible – and the mad, unbranded, so-called 'Bushian' cattle would trample my head to pulp. For he suspected, surely, that in offering to go on a muster with him I was declaring myself restored, in so far as anyone could restore me. And he must have apprehended too that I would not surrender up to him the means of that restoration,

Bernard. I did hope this was tolerable to him, but if not he could – since he possessed his ticket-of-leave – take his share of cattle and work as overseer for someone else. He was still remote enough from his conditional pardon however, which well-behaved men such as he acquired after fifteen years of their sentence, that I had power over him. Yet I did not want to see him anything but well used. As long as he did not try to take Sarah Bernard, my daily rescuer, away.

Bernard and I lay at night in George's room, awaiting for the time of grieving to pass so that the relationship could be formalised as a marriage. And in this ambiguous period, the thought of my father was a perverse comfort. Whomsoever I seemed to shock, I knew my father at least. There was ultimately a letter, conveyed to me on a visit by the new police magistrate, in which the Reverend Paltinglass urged me to consider the unspeakable sufferings of the Saviour and be wary of new and sudden and false attachments which grew merely from my present desolation.

News of my attachment to, or, more correctly, my passion for Sarah Bernard, barely needed lips to whisper it. The information was borne on the vigorous winds of the Maneroo, travelling further than pollen or bees. I confidently imagined Charlie Batchelor hearing of it in Yass, and the Finlays in Goulburn, and feeling justified in their attitudes. There were frequent confessional letters, published by the editor of the *Herald* in Sydney, from priests and parsons of all denominations, which declared that the communities of New South Wales seemed so debased and reprehensible that they deserved to be denied all rite and sacrament. I imagined I must reconcile myself to living not only beyond the limits, but beyond the sacraments too.

Part Three

In the year after Prim's visit home, Dimp's unease about the annulment of Bren's previous marriage had not diminished at all. She felt no rancour against Bren. As she saw it, the annulment itself was something he could not go back and amend. But it was the toxic root of her marriage. So she was able less and less to argue with him about it. Arguing, and raised voices, would have been a comfort. But what use was a debate between parallel universes, exchanges travelling meaninglessly on tangents into infinite space.

And then, some six months after Sudan's civilian government fell, while Prim was still involved in trying to clear the way for a health survey of the Red Sea Hills camp named Alingaz, or Hessiantown, Dimp suffered what she saw as another crucial and revelatory experience in Sydney, and believed that, though an account of it would annoy Prim, Prim would need to be told by fax.

As always, she began with a plea for Prim's return.

Your friends get blown up, and that awful regime comes in with – according to an article I read – moral police prowling the streets with power to take a person to court! Come home and bring Sherif too. He's graduated from a British university hasn't he? They'll let him practise here.

If you were home I could tell you this better. But I have to tell you anyhow: I know the marriage is finished now. I have to stop moaning and act. I know you won't be surprised to hear it's Benedetto who brought it about – and no, it's not Benedetto in the obvious sense. He kind of said the determining word, that's all. What an admirable fellow he is! The Archangel Gabriel of my poor squalid little life.

I remember you used to warn me that I was wrong if I fancied that behind Bren's old-fashioned front, and his ideas, and the functional way he embraced them and applied them, lay an exotic wizard, a sort of sage in a cave. You thought the cave was empty. And you said that's okay as

*long as you know it's empty, but don't go into this marriage thinking
there's something there, that the cave is full of charming goblins. You'll
deny having said it, but you did, once – during the Auger business. I
thought it was your mess that made you talk like that. But it's the truth.
Most of Bren's opinions are predictable to the core. Well, whose aren't?
But again it's that cautiousness! A man who'd seek an annulment . . .
But we've had that conversation. And his boringness is now out of kilter
with my boringness.*

*The conversation at our last dinner got on to this character named
Eddie Mabo. Only people in mining and those of like interest know
about him – as yet, anyhow. He's a Torres Strait Islander. With the help
of a few lawyers from Melbourne he's claiming ownership of his vegetable patch on an island, Murray Island. At the moment the case is being
heard by the Supreme Court of Queensland. Doesn't sound of much
significance. Except all the industry newsletters Bren gets say that if
Mabo wins, it will mean that Australia did belong to the Islanders and
Aboriginals all along and the lot of it was filched illegally from them, in
violation of international law. That may also mean Aboriginals have a
right to block mining and drilling! The industry newsletters are full of
panic at this, and the judge intends to go to Murray Island and hold a
hearing right there. This is seen by Bren's friends as an indulgence! See
what I mean by predictable? If this Eddie Mabo wins, the result round
here will be full-throated fucking hysteria! Gut fury amongst some of
Bren's set. You know the stuff: how dare those damn pinko judges give
away our country! The Aborigines had this country for fifty thousand
years and what did they do with it? Didn't build a single 747 or put up
one Sheraton. And now some Islander wants to turn the law of possession upside down just in time to bugger up the economic recovery! Etc.,
etc.*

*I think of Bren's associate, Peter Ignacy and his wife, Thea. Did you
meet them at our party? Peter was born in Hungary. Thea's a Scot whose
parents came from Glasgow. Tough little reddish beauty. Last year the
Ignacys spent three whole weeks with Bren and I in a chalet in Aspen
owned by an American bank. They've done well out of the Australian
earth and the bounty thereof. I find it hard to believe that a native land
claim could put a dent in the Ignacys' happiness. They've got a huge
Lloyd Rees in their dining room – it's like a great blob of liquid light
and it seems to gleam with love. Thea runs a second-hand shop for your
crowd, Austfam. So she's no primitive bigot and, unlike me, she's not a*

frivolous woman. But the rhetoric I mentioned above comes from Thea too. She has a sort of primal anger against this Mabo, just in case he succeeds. I get defeated by this sort of thing. I don't know how to utter my dissent, you know. This whole business strips the air out of the room at the moment. Or the air cries out for things to be said, the air's thirsty. And I find myself silent, and I wish I wasn't. Big Bren is spraying the bloody earth with opinions, of course. Incautiously. That's the whole thing – the sod is rampantly incautious when he should be wary. And cautious when he should be free! See the history of my life, under A for Annulment.

But again Bren, like the Ignacys, is a decent fellow according to his lights, and what else do any of us have to sail by? He has enthusiasms too. He bought a big Colin Lanceley for one of the lobby's walls recently and was so pleased with himself. He'd seen one in a bank and thought it was great and wanted one similar. Bren said he bought it because it looked like a map of childhood seen from above – rivers and painted boughs and the whole caboodle. So he did that for love, and that should cover a multitude of banalities!

Now I introduce the difficult bit, the bit designed to test your patience. Benedetto. I hear your smirk, if hearing a smirk is possible. It's not what I think of him though that's the issue. It's what he does. He's at dinner at our place the other night, the night the Ignacys are there, and he's brought along some sexy, glasses-wearing girl barrister from his chambers. And everyone's talking like the clappers about this Mabo case and Thea Ignacy says one of the expected things. 'My ancestors were Highlanders,' she says, 'and a person can't help asking if the descendants of Aboriginals are allowed to try land claims, why aren't the descendants of eighteenth-century Highlanders?'

And she's a bit more proud of the originality of this argument than she should be. But I must confess I've never known the answer to that one – I've known there must an answer, but have been too lazy to pursue it. And yet whenever that idea is uttered, generally by someone more bombastic than Thea, I develop an absolute itch to find the answer, an enormously intense itch while it lasts, but easily forgotten. I have this intense desire to correct them. I feel there's a place, and they ought to be put in it. But more, I feel if I knew the answer I would somehow understand being that curious thing: a woman of European (and as we now know, Semitic) descent living on this outlandish bloody continent.

Now Benedetto's got a lot of credit with Bren and Ignacy. He took and won some case over diamond drilling for them. So there he is, his broad face, close-cropped but thickly growing hair, his standard issue Italian brown eyes. He sits all through this talk about how the Mabo case is full of potential recklessness, and sits through Thea's lines about Highlanders and how she had better put in a claim for Banffshire. And he's able to say nothing. Dispassion is a great gift.

And after Thea's non-original point, instead of spraying their own annotations on Mabo about the room, the men ask Benedetto for his ideas. And Benedetto grins without malice and begins to talk. I do not think, Thea, he says, smiling, that you could successfully pursue a claim to your ancestral land before British courts. It would be an enormously difficult case to research. The point is that rightly or wrongly the Scots were seen as having forfeited their land by rebellion. Parliament enacted laws to that effect, and those laws have not been challenged, so that the common law is against you on this. But the Aboriginals and the natives of the Torres Strait never committed any act to enable forfeiture of their land, and they did not forfeit it voluntarily through treaties. In Australia, says Benedetto, country was taken away not because it was forfeit for some act of sedition but because it was considered terra nullius. *Land belonging to no one.*

God, says Thea, I'm sick of people rabbiting on about this terra nullius!

Yes, says Benedetto, but it means that either Australia was terra nullius, *or else the native peoples had title to it. No middle possibility. If Australia was* terra nullius *when we occupied it, this man who wants to claim his ancestral yam and banana patch will lose. But otherwise he'll win.*

Bren soberly asked him what he thought would happen.

Oh, said Benedetto, I believe terra nullius *is contrary to international law, and Mabo will win in the end.*

All of this said lazily, and with a casual grin.

This was the moment, Prim. I felt an exhilaration out of proportion to the substance of the information. I actually felt I had been all at once set free by a Torres Strait man I'll never meet and who wants secure title to his vegetable garden, and by Benedetto's clear exposition. It was as if he had made rain in a dry town. I had betrayed myself into marrying wrongly. I'd mistaken the annulment for something enchanting. But it had made me invalid, and I lacked the power to walk until Benedetto had turned up and freed me with his few words. I found myself clapping, and Ignacy turned to me and said, 'But you've always been a pinko!'

That's it. The whole incident. It's happened in a thousand places in the nation – the same opinions and elucidations. But at the end of this explanation the contract between Bren and me did lie shattered. It's a strange feeling. I feel that I must retrieve myself. It's a pressing obligation, even though you'll think it's self-indulgence, and I can't prove otherwise.

I'm trying to be more than serious. I've started looking for small houses for rent back in Redfern. I'll keep you posted.

And just because I eat well and have lived in a palazzo, don't be remiss with me. Accept this as an event of some moment in the life of

Your pilgrim sister,

Dimp

In Prim, panic revived. Dimp might say anything, and be socially rowdy. But Dimp's job in Prim's universe was to be, behind all the passion, steady, secure in her life and her marriage. If Dimp fell apart the world might too, in some radical way no one had thought of.

ould not help writing to her in fright and with even more of the usual and futile severity, of the kind which might itself serve as a provocation. She saw with some alarm that she could not refuse to believe in the idea of a word which once uttered changed the known world. She had had that same experience when she heard the word 'slave'.

When I read your faxes I don't want to read any more of the transcript. It seems Benedetto didn't do you much of a favour, giving you that stuff. I see that as having set up too big a sense of debt in you, as if now you have to take everything he says as some sort of prophetic statement.

As for the idea of scales falling from your eyes as Benedetto spoke, I just don't believe it happened. You sound like someone who's likely to be converted to a sect just because some swami comes up with the right, plausible line. Just because you fancy Benedetto – well, I don't have to complete the sentence. I could see the signs at your party.

You're lucky to find me still here. I was supposed to be off with Sherif to Hessiantown. But Sherif's finding it a bit slow getting Ministry of Health approval – they say they want to supply one of their own officials to work with us. I don't know what their problem is – they might be sick of negative reports getting out.

I'll let you know before I go, so your anguish isn't sitting unread in the fax tray for four or so weeks. I hope I don't come back and find you've done something extreme.

Your stern and loving sister.

She had not sent it an hour when Sherif appeared at her office door with a letter from the Ministry of Health. They were permitted to make their journey. A government health official would meet them at Alingaz when they arrived.

Prim knew she would take her sister's malaise with her on the journey, and had a superstitious fear it might poison things.

To take the road from Khartoum to Port Sudan, all informed travellers – and there are few of the uninformed variety in the Sudan – leave Khartoum at night and hope to reach the Red Sea Hills late the next morning. Thus Erwit, Sherif and Prim left the city after an early dinner. In two days the two nurses who had worked on Sherif's earlier health surveys would come on by bus, which also made maximum use of darkness, slipping away east into flat country to the north of the irrigated fields of the Gezira.

The rains were late again this year. Indeed, Prim by now took their irregularity as the norm. The night Sherif, Erwit and she left was breathless. The upholstery of the Toyota exuded that peculiar hot-weather chemical breath which had always made Prim sick when her parents had strapped young Dimp and younger Prim, still sticky from the surf, in the back seat and told them not to fight.

As they left Khartoum, all their papers were in order. It was thus almost welcome to Prim to be stopped at the checkpoint on the edge of the city, to have to get up off the vinyl and explain to the officials that she was not carrying sacrilegious books, whisky or rifles. At each of the recurrent checkpoints they encountered through the furnace night, there was a petrol pump, and an awning beneath which sweet tea and flat bread were served.

'Are you married to this gentleman?' men, sometimes in khaki, sometimes in civilian shirts and pants, politely asked at each road block. Prim told them no, that the man there was a doctor, the other a mechanic and driver. They saw Erwit was Eritrean which caused them to frown, but slightly. 'So you are not the woman of that man there?' they would ask Prim again.

'I am nobody's woman,' she would say.

Sherif was simultaneously denying Prim in Arabic to the two or three young men inspecting his papers. 'No, I am not her man.' Two denials by both parties. One more, thought Prim, and she and Sherif would match St Peter, who denied Christ thrice.

No, all three of them assured the men, we do not work for the infidel rebels from the South. We are going to Alingaz, to look after people's health.

Further out there were not any towns, but a desert of clay. At one in the morning, however, they came to a checkpoint as they entered Kassala province. Thirsty, they noted the border tea-house with lanterns attached to its poles. Again they had to show their sheaf of permits. Overhearing their conversation, some nomads, who had been camped opportunistically near the tea-house, came up to the truck, tall men in grey-white clothing. Even Prim could tell they spoke Arabic roughly – it was not their native tongue. They were Shukriyah nomads, semi-settled around waterholes drilled in the years of hope, the 70s and 80s. There had been government clinics all along this road once, which had since been closed because the Sudan was tyrannised by debt, could not earn enough foreign currency, and had the continuing folly of the Southern war to pay for. The nomads were powerless people and yet they moved with a dignified gravity, wearing huge crusader swords belted at their waists, and daggers thonged to their ankles.

'One of them has a sick daughter,' Sherif briskly told Prim and Erwit. A man went off with swaying gait and carried back into the light a bare-headed child, a girl of perhaps seven or eight. Her eyes were closed, there was a look of subtle pain on her face and her breathing could be heard. Sherif felt the child's forehead, fetched his medical kit and, putting on his stethoscope, slipped its head under the girl's *galabia* and gravely listened. 'Ai-ai-ai,' he said to nobody. 'Pneumonia. Nothing to be done!' Nonetheless he gestured that everyone was to follow him into the tea-house.

The proprietor looked a little uneasy as the half-dozen nomads crowded in, but was partially reassured when the urbane Sherif ordered *chai* for all the company. The child looked very ill by the lights of the tea-house. Prim sat and drank sweet black tea, convinced that in spite of its heavy quotient of sugar, it was the right drink for the climate, bringing out an astringent sweat which was the best response to the heat.

Sherif frowned and brought out of his kit a card of broad-spectrum antibiotics. 'Give your daughter two of these now, with tea, and then one in the morning, and one at evening. They will help your fakir's good magic.' For even in the cities the ill went to fakirs for help. 'Go on, open them.' The man obeyed him, releasing two pills from the foil, and forcing them into the child's mouth. The child sucked hungrily at the tea. 'She should have a drip in,' Sherif told Prim and Erwit.

Then, with bows and *shokrans* from the entire tea-house company, Sherif, Prim and Erwit went back out to the truck and the warm vinyl of the seats, Erwit and Sherif taking, according to the protocol most likely to appease checkpoint officials, the front.

Again on the road, Erwit – jovially swinging the wheel – began to imitate in Arabic the nomads' accents. For the first time on the journey, Sherif laughed. 'The Shukriyah speak Arabic the way the Cockneys speak English,' he said. 'The Kababish sound like the Irish. The ones up around the Red Sea Hills, the Beja – they sound like Glaswegians.'

'Which of them sound like Australians?' Prim asked.

'No one around here,' said Sherif. 'You have to go far out to the west, to Darfur, to the furthest Shendi village, to hear anything so outrageous.'

'Go to hell,' said Prim, and there was a salutary burst of laughter in the truck.

Now their lights penetrated apparent nullity, and it reduced Prim to sleep. She woke with an arm numbed from the pressure of the flanges of the door-frame against her shoulder. Sherif was driving and Erwit was napping in the front seat. She saw Sherif's set shoulders. He was utterly watchful as the sky to the east shed bluish light across this country of desert rubble. So, while she slept, they had passed through Kassala and its rocky nobs of mountains she had wanted to see, since she knew from pictures they resembled mountains in Central Australia. They had now turned north-east into a further wasteland. She watched her lover's back and head as the earth became very quickly golden. She peeled her lower right arm away from the seat and sat upright, reaching out to put a hand lightly on the nape of Sherif's neck.

'Who is that?' he asked, not taking his eyes off the single lane of tar which bisected this absolute landscape. 'Is that a mouse, or is it a grasshopper?'

'When they asked whether I was your woman, I didn't like to say no.'

'Oh well,' said Sherif, 'this is the republic of double talk.'

'When will we be citizens of the republic of single talk?' she asked. Before Sherif could reply they saw through the beautiful, unhazed light of the first of the day that a truck had run off the strip of tarmac and lay unevenly on the stony earth. Across the strip of tar itself, the limbs of fallen camels were indolently and hugely strewn. This was indeed a phantasm of the dawn. Sherif slowed the vehicle, and Erwit stirred as the Toyota made its way amongst the camels' legs and huge necks. There were two females and a young, smaller male felled there.

From behind the flung-open door of the truck appeared a thin Sudanese man. He began to draw his hands together with what looked to Prim an exaggerated motion, from far wide of his body to a joined-together gesture of pleading in front of his face. There seemed to be tears on his cheeks.

Sherif said, 'He has killed all three of them, silly bugger, speeding at dawn.' The man rushed in front of the Toyota, making his gestures of prayer. Sherif needed to stop or swerve. He chose to swerve.

'Take him on board,' Prim said, and could not keep reproof out of her voice. 'He probably just wants to go to Port Sudan.'

'There's nothing you can do,' said Sherif. The man wailed and beat at the side of the truck.

Erwit said, as if it were Newton's Law, 'He must pay for the camels or be punished. We cannot save him from it.'

'You can't mean this,' Prim told Sherif. She could see the camel-killing truck driver, receding yet still pleading in their wake.

'If we help him escape we would be liable,' Sherif explained. 'The owners would meet us on the road back. They have large swords. You saw that.'

His tone caused Prim to remember her otherness and she felt lost in a foreign nation. Sometimes, lying together with Sherif she forgot she was not an African woman. She suffered only occasionally revelations of who she really was, and it was always, as now, a painful and sharp experience.

'The girl with pneumonia might die too, and her father could wait to ask you why your medicine failed.'

'But he would accept that,' said Sherif accelerating, the truck-driver fast becoming a dot.

'How much does a bloody camel cost?' Prim asked.

'Up to £3000 Sudanese,' Erwit told Prim.

'He wouldn't get a thousand pounds a year for driving his rotten little truck,' said Sherif like a stranger. 'Our friends will cut his arm off.'

'Oh Christ, is that what you want?' said Prim.

'No. But he could escape. He could go to the South.'

The poor creature was left kneeling behind them, on the edge of the great mound of camel meat.

'This bloody truck belongs to Austfam,' Prim told Sherif. 'You go back and let him in!' But no matter what her commands or pleadings, she could not bring Sherif to turn around.

'How dare you treat me like this!' she cried.

Sherif said, 'So is it your authority or the truck-driver you're concerned about? Every fool knows you slow down at dawn. Camels are always on the way to wells in the mornings. Would Austfam pay for those camels?'

'It doesn't have a mandate to,' Prim told him.

'Exactly.'

He seemed at that instant a stranger to her, a petulant man on the edge of disappointed middle age. It was as if, conveyed by fax from Dimp, a virus of distancing had entered the air between them.

Prim had been correct in guessing that Dimp's confessional faxes were landing in the tray of Austfam's fax machine back in Khartoum, and pooling, like a rich centre of infection.

TO: Prim Bettany, Austfam, Khartoum
AT: 249-11-46951
FROM: Dimp Bettany
AT: 61-2-9550 3763 (NOTE NEW NUMBER!)
DATE: March 5 1990

Darling Prim,
I've signed a six-month lease on a minute cottage in Poldene Street in Redfern. The number above is for phone as well. Not that I've been here much as yet. I've been to Los Angeles for a week, and am just back this morning from that soul-sapping overnight flight. I called into Bren's to collect mail – no, he wasn't there at the time – and found your chastising note waiting for me.

All the way back home I had a window seat beside two nice Los Angelino gays on their way to the Mardi Gras. Unlike me they had a great calm, sitting very upright and very relaxed. Secure in each other's love, but maybe that's just my reading. I felt a kind of envy, as I always do now when I see the real article. But then I've made my bed, as you'll no doubt tell me.

So now I'm off on my own, as I predicted I would be. It's necessary, but I know you don't believe that. Just in case you wondered, I have not called Benedetto! I don't mind you wondering.

I do, however, mind you calling my dear friend and ancestor Jonathan a fool. Sure, he's a human, and thus he's your average fool and automatic liar. What do you want of our lying species? I am enchanted by the tenor of my ancestor's journal, simple as that, and I'm not going to apologise for the fact. It's not a matter of his or my morality. It's more a matter of the intimacy of it, and the attempts at honour! I began by thinking he was relating an idyll, a pastorale. But then there was this extraordinary frankness about the threat from the evil at the edges, at the edges of the landscape and the edges of his own soul. The touching way – I think it's touching anyhow – he finds it hard to do pure business in an impure world! And he doesn't name things bluntly and directly, but in his earnest style he seems to want to tell the truth. On the one hand a modern person might suspect him of telling less than the truth about 'the Moth people', to use his own term. On the other, as his tale progresses, he does not save himself from blame or self-reproach. In this he is a halfway reliable narrator, surely.

If you kept a journal, I bet you'd be subtly self-justifying, yea even the moral Amazon, Prim! You'd be sneaky about it, too. You're not a screaming sinner like me and Jonathan. But I have to ask, doesn't it touch you at all to find this pilgrim, Jonathan, so tormented amongst the gum trees and boulders? Don't you want to go back and offer him comfort, as our Jewish great-granny did? Aren't you glad he found her, to give him a little solace?

Anyhow, at the end of it and within those limits, I trust this voice, and you should trust it too. Of course you're not up with me yet. I've read the lot, and so am far behind in transcribing – I've spent my time doing a treatment, a rough screenplay and provisional budget.

What was I doing in Los Angeles you ask. Well, I need a lot of money for this film – or a lot by Australian standards. The preliminary budget I did tells me I won't get out of this with much change left from $15 000 000 Australian. And the rule of the universe is that those with the real money, development and production, are least likely to go for this story.

For one thing I'm getting an expensive writer: Hugo Ventriss, the

Aussie Peter Weir used to write Dos *and* Taboos. *It won all sorts of prizes, got five Academy Award nominations. Hugo won the Golden Globe for the script, and the film got the Palme d'Or at Cannes. Not bloody bad. This Hugo – a tall, solid fellow, built a little like Benedetto – is very successful, a phenomenon. He's a playwright really, sees himself in those terms. I met him at a party at the Australian Film and Television School, where he had come to make a graduation speech. Anyway, I approached him with the good old Dimple sashay and gave him my phone number scrawled on a scrap of paper. He studied it with a sort of gracious care. And he looked up excited. After we'd been through the normal ritual dance over Enzo and its abiding influence on him and everyone else, he asked me did I want to go out for dinner. He didn't mean with various student film makers in a Chinese restaurant. He meant* dinner. *I told him I was married, though every time I said it I'd remember that berserk annulment. Oh yeah, he said in a resonant voice. I read about it. Aren't you married to that rich guy – D'Arcy?*

I admitted it. Oh bugger, he said like an old-fashioned boy at a dance.

I told him that, like everyone in the room, I had some material. But unlike the rest of them, I'd let him write it only if he begged me. On top of that, I was prepared to pay him what the Americans would.

He laughed like an honest journeyman. He was still willing to listen, but in that frank, boyish way. Priapis, the god of the donger, had as much to do with his tolerance as did the Muses! But too many students and others wanted to talk to him, so I did end up in town eating a plate of pasta with him. I narrated my little arse off, and I could tell I had engaged his imagination – writers are easily enthused if you tell them a tale, and here was wool and convicts and the Moth people and betrayal. I haven't transcribed everything for you yet, so you don't know half the betrayals! And I built up the role of Durra too, the Ngarigo 'king', and the Felix experiment.

I told him that if he gave me his agent's number, I'd approach him, pass on my treatment and the transcripts I have. If he had any enthusiasm for the material – and I wanted him only if he felt driven to write it – we would proceed to contract, and I'd pay him 5 per cent of budget.

He used a cricketing metaphor. Five per cent would knock some of your rake-off to leg, he said. It's one of those, eh? Burning a hole in the old creative duodenum. Are you really called Dimple?

I told him I was, and he said, Shit. Fair dinkum eh? He told me then he preferred to write plays. Plays got produced, whereas the studios paid him to write screenplays that never got made. He said, I write the first draft and then I go off jet-lagged across the Pacific to some meeting in Burbank or Universal City and some idiot holds up the script in his hand and tells me that he doesn't see what's at stake between the bloke and the girl. And why don't we give the hero this pet bloody parrot? Everything goes to hell from that point, he said, and he satisfies no one, least of all himself, and the film isn't made. He said, I don't know why I'm complaining. Faulkner and Fitzgerald warned the whole world of writers what would happen if they took the Devil's candy.

I said, This will get produced. I tried to blaze with zeal, though I didn't even have the development money. I said, If I don't get development cash on that scale, I won't trouble you further. And he said, Okay. But 4 per cent of budget will be fine. I don't want to feel too beholden to you. Then he laughed in a way that gave me hope.

I got a call the next day from his agent, a Londoner, now domiciled in Sydney, named Max.

Hugo got $700 000 US for his last American screenplay, he told me, expecting me to faint.

I think I could run to that, I told him joyously. It is wonderful to surprise these people.

Look, he said, no offence, but it's a long time since you produced anything. I presume your husband's underwriting this one?

I told him to presume again. That made him really nervous. He wants me, when the time comes to contract Hugo, to present a bank statement. He doesn't want to start Hugo off on what looks like a generous payment, and find there's nothing left in kitty when he's done the real work.

This is what I promised: $200 000 on contract, $150 000 on delivery of first draft, with a bonus of $50 000 if it was delivered in three months, a term which balances creativity with urgency. The rest of the money is to be spread over subsequent re-writes and polishes.

My, you are keen, said bloody Max.

Then I bought an economy ticket to Los Angeles, even though I knew Bren wouldn't have blinked if I'd used one of the corporate credit cards and gone in comfort. I believed I would talk them round in LA the way I talked Hugo round.

But I'm afraid it's proved a pretty dismal trip. I've got to find Hugo's $700 000 somewhere, and a few thousand for me to live off while I'm putting the thing together. If I can get provisional commitments of *production money from a studio that would be the key – the rest of it could be raised in Australia, by way of the usual tax dentist investors, or else through the Film Finance Corporation.*

In Los Angeles, in the 'business' – that's the first mistake, that they call it a business, as if it's like making tractor transmission boxes or computer hard-drives – there are loads of people willing to buy me break-fast, drinks or dinner, and to say, No, I'll pay. Your treat when we make a movie in Australia. I met with production executives from Miramax, the crowd I really want to back me. I tried Savoy, and people whose cards I have from Fox, Universal, Sony. In the abstract they all want to put money into a picture produced by me in Australia. They've told me this in the past. But it always turns out to be any picture except what I'm proposing at the moment. But they all loved Enzo Kangaroo! Jesus, yes. They were just talking to Martin Scorcese or Sidney Lumet or Miloš Forman or Sydney Pollack, and it's his or their favourite film of all time. You Australians have a lot to teach us! Blah, blah.

One of the problems I have is that the word has reached across the Pacific from Sydney to California, and it's become one of those apho-risms these people 'in the business' like to fall back on, Aussie frock dramas are officially passé. American audiences don't get 'em. They're even going off the British frock dramas as well. And settlers and Abos? No one really gets that stuff!

So now I'm back home in my little house which I love and enjoy greatly. But no one's given me any development money. I'm looking out at brazen Sydney light, at the tangled roofs of Redfern terraces. The alternative is repentance, and then back to the art gallery-cum-dormitory which dear old Bren considers home. How can I turn back to a man who spent more time buying his mobile phone than he spent condoning my purchases of Australian glories, of Blackman and Boyd, of Whiteley and the great Fred Williams? Fred Williams saw the continent as I wish the film to see it, with its glories and its secrets seemingly there, behind the veils of trees, waterfall, boulders.

Anyhow, I have in my mouth something it will take a lot of the teas of China, and maybe later a bit of gin, to wash out – the taste of having been taken to the mountain top and told precisely why I can't inherit the cities of the plain! Well, that's the normal aftermath of a trip to that acidic place.

I have one more trip in mind. Remember Sir Malik Bettany? Dad talked about him once or twice. A part-Aboriginal part-Tamil descendant of the very Felix in nearly-Sir-Jonathan's journal. He turns out to be a very rich Tamil in Singapore. Owns import–export, hotels, and a bank! Knighted by Betty Windsor. Not related to us at all of course, unless Phoebe Bettany's first suspicion is somehow correct and Felix is Jonathan Bettany's kid. But as Bettany says, the dates are against it. In any case, this story is Sir Malik's story too. So I might go up there and see if he'd like to divert a few million into a film.

So I'm not moaning, or maybe I am, but if I don't moan to you, then to whom?

Dimp told her sister to be careful on her journeys and reiterated her plea that Prim return to Sydney. She could, she urged, share the rent of the Redfern house.

Then: 'As for me, stop worrying. I am where I must be.'

⌒

SARAH BERNARD AS HER OWN WOMAN

Sarah Bernard was, I felt, now established in Nugan Ganway as the staple of my life. She had not merely saved me from the noose but brought me Lethean forgetfulness. It was in her presence that I could survive the particular, horrifying idea that flesh of my flesh lay under the earth of newly consecrated Cooma, that mother and child lay in an unspeakable union of dust.

As she understood my sensibility, Bernard rarely uttered Long's name. Her demeanour towards her former possible husband did not seem at times nearly as guilty as mine towards the memory of Phoebe. It appeared to me in a way to be based on a hard-headed view of the world. May God look after my friend, Long, and heal all wounds, because I can do nothing more. This meant that her friendship with Long was conditional, and her love for my welfare was absolute. How could I not rejoice in such an outcome?

I had never known such transports as those with which Bernard's company rewarded me. Her skin to me tasted much more of salt than I think mine did to her, as if she had eaten enough bad Transport Board food to make of her an ocean. I had lost the blue opacity of Phoebe and inherited the deep green, salt turbulence of an honest thief. Her generosity of soul was so heedless, her unquestioning and unamazed discoveries of the limits of my body and spirit so wonderful that even the concept that she, like Long and like my father, had once fallen foul of judges, was one of the enchantments of her presence. Someone had presumed to judge this most noble woman!

In a lover's desire to know the beloved utterly, I did once idly, the savour of her skin on my lips, raise the question of her crime. She put the five fingers of her hand to my mouth. 'No,' she said. 'I shall say I was falsely convicted, as does every thief in New South Wales, and you will disbelieve me.'

'No,' I insisted. 'You know I cannot afford disbelief in you.'

But she could not be persuaded. Perhaps she feared that I might in some future and inevitable anger hold it over her. But I felt I could not know enough and would never know half. I might also have been possessed by the knowledge that in my father's case, we all pretended he had never been condemned and never seen a chain, so that the undischarged friction between his having been a prisoner and his seemingly solid, oblivious life in Van Diemen's Land went on chaffing and rankling unseen, bearing away in the end the peace of two families, ours and the Batchelors'.

But whatever my intentions, instantly thereafter I felt in her a strange reluctance towards my uncomprehending caresses. She pulled away from me and suggested we drink tea. The season was still full of occasional coldness, as this evening, and I thought of firing my black tea with rum, for which I had an increasing appetite, while she drank hers reflectively and penitentially, black and without sugar.

'The thing I did not want to be trapped into saying was that I am not a thief,' she told me then. 'But you would ask and ask, and so I am forced to say it.'

'I am certain you are not a thief,' I told her with too much callow enthusiasm. 'I would not so readily admit that you are not a nurse and an offerer of comfort, for these you are in abundance.'

'No, you are for some reason enchanted,' she told me, her dark and suspicious eyes on me. It was typical of this period, and of her problem, that she had found no name to call me except 'you'. She could not call a suicidal fool cut down from the shearing shed rafters 'sir'. She could not with a straight face call such a desperately joky figure 'Mr Bettany'. And she could not – across the gulf we had suddenly traversed – call me 'Jonathan'. 'You' it would need to be for some time yet.

'The only convenient thing in New South Wales,' she told me, 'is to have committed the crime they accuse you of. Then you are fitted to the place. But the innocent are the misfitted! Nothing they say is believed, and so they are reduced to silence.'

'But, Bernard,' I said, for I too was a hostage to names. She had been 'Bernard' when preparing Phoebe for the grave, 'Bernard' when she scythed me down, and remained still 'Bernard'. When she became known more profoundly she might become 'Sarah'. The Master and Servant Act would be borne away, the solemn ordinances of the Colonial Secretary's Department would die of irrelevance, and the pure and Biblical name would assert itself. 'But Bernard,' I said, awed by her hints of uncomfortable innocence, 'assert whatever you like with me. You will never have a more loving audience.'

'Is it love?' she asked. 'A child may love whoever feeds it. But that does not make the feeder its mother.'

'You know everything about me,' I told her. 'I know nothing about you except that your generous soul and splendid body are the source of my new life. Assert any tale you like and I will devour it like a meal, like manna in the desert!'

She shook her head. 'Would you really believe that the daughter of a Manchester merchant could become so bored, so full of infant envy, that she could find the swearing of false oaths a recreation, relief from a dull life?'

'I could believe it. The mysteries of human nature . . .'

She was impatient with my platitude and shook her wonderfully sombre head.

'I was a married woman,' she told me.

'It says so on your papers. But I believe,' – indeed I had heard it from Phoebe – 'that your husband is dead.'

'I had the task of a resident housekeeper for a silver merchant named Mr Duncannon. But though I had perforce to live there in Tib Street, my husband Corporal McWhirter, who was a Scot, was permitted to call at Mr Duncannon's, to visit me.'

Corporal McWhirter, dead of fever in Jamaica, marched for a second through the room with his ghost of a claim on her.

'We met mainly in the kitchen,' continued Bernard. But was there a small room beneath the eaves to which this freckled corporal took his dark-eyed, impeccable wife? 'Mr Duncannon's fourteen-year-old daughter used to find means to come to the kitchen while McWhirter was there. He was a jovial and even loud sort of man, full of teasing. He could make a cup or a fork disappear up his sleeve, and all watching him would swear these objects had utterly vanished. Young girls liked him. I had liked him. He was the opposite to me. "Long Face" he called me. "Even Long Face is laughing at this one," he would say. I don't know why I tell you all this.'

'No, go on,' I urged. I was desperate for this story.

She shook her head again. She wondered what was so compelling in what she recounted, and why I had urgency to hear it. 'Now Mr and Mrs Duncannon belonged to a strict Chapel and their life did not abound in joy or forks which disappeared before your eyes. And it seemed that their daughter, Miss Duncannon, took particular delight in the liveliness of Corporal McWhirter. And he had plenty of stories, tales I had myself already been told but which were renewed for me by Miss Lucy Duncannon's enjoyment. They concerned such things as what he had heard from other soldiers of the customs of the West Indies, where the dead were believed to rise and speak and steal the ability of movement from the living. They concerned the alligators and burial pyres of India, where McWhirter had served, and the houses and manners of the Dutch in the Cape Colony he had once visited as part of the guard on a ship. This was more colour than was ever admitted into the parlours of the Duncannons, who were decent but believed that all images in books and illustrated papers were a vanity and snare. But McWhirter had been everywhere, even to Nova Scotia.'

I was again for a moment envious of the much-travelled corporal.

'One day Miss Duncannon entered the kitchen while Corporal McWhirter and I were engaged in the quite normal endearments of married people, an innocent embrace. Since I lived with the Duncannons six days a week, and Corporal McWhirter was not permitted to remain there overnight, Miss Duncannon should not have been surprised to see an exchange of caresses. But I saw that Miss Duncannon was unused to seeing such displays. There was certainly none between her parents, and to the preachers of her Chapel this would have been seen as a flippant embrace or even an evil one.'

How I cherished and feared her bluntness, but also her occasional elegant phrasing. Like Phoebe she had caught the desire to talk like novels and not like felons. Speaking in the tongue of angels must have brought her some abuse from hard Londoners on her ship.

'So she was jealous, this merchant's child?' I asked.

'In her innocence, she thought the kiss was a betrayal. She had believed McWhirter's teasing of her, and his compliments, had been love. And she could not imagine a more intense connection than a kiss. So it seemed to her an insult to her feelings for the corporal.'

This assessment of Miss Duncannon was redolent of what my mother-in-law had once said of Phoebe.

Bernard continued. 'I knew there would be trouble. It was as if she was the wife and I the seductress, and I thought, "What will she tell her father?"'

'Did she have such power over her austere parent?' I asked.

'Perhaps she did not, since it wasn't to him she took her anger. But she did acquire all the cleverness of a rejected and jealous soul.'

'Oh,' I uttered, delighted that she again delivered the sort of sentence you got from novels as published in newspapers. *My* seductress educated by her own strong will and vigorous memory.

'Do you know I am Jewish?' she asked me then.

'The little nun in Goulburn told me,' I said. Indeed the fact had added to the sense that I had been engaged in a desperate Old Testament struggle, and was following a pillar of light to guide me out of desert places.

'My father was a tailor to the poor,' she continued. 'But he was learned and read to me and sent me to Christian churches. He wanted me to behold what the English believed. I could make my way if I knew that. "Do not be afraid of Christ, because he was Jewish yet these millions of Gentiles honour him!" he said. Now he went to the synagogue in Bootle Street, but he made sure I went to St Ann's and the Cross Street Chapel which the Duncannons themselves attended. He did not want me to be a Christian but to become learned in their ways so that I did not have the hard life he had even from other Jews. There was a German Jew clothing dealer by the name of Reichman who helped my father have a hard life. My parents had known him since they came to Manchester. My mother had collapsed in his warehouse before she died. I was a seamstress in his repairing shop from the time I was five. All the poor Jews from Poland and Russia bought their clothes from him, or sold them to him, and as they did it he would mock them, crying, "So here they come, I smell them, the Russians and the Poles, the Tsar's outcasts who know not soap." Statements of that nature amused him. Even when I was a child this Reichman was as good as blind, but he would feel fabric with his fingers and say, "That is a good one, that is good worsted." He could tell good cloth even if he could not swear as to who presented it to him.

'My little Miss Duncannon gathered up some of her best church clothing and delivered it to him, and he approved wonderfully of it and gave her a price of perhaps a third of its value, and she signed his receipt with my name, and answered to my name in a voice which, it must be admitted, was not a long way removed from mine, the voice of ordinary Manchester, which Mr Duncannon had brought with him from his childhood on his way to riches. She placed the money in a hole under a commode in my room, and then cried that her clothing was gone. Mr and Mrs Duncannon, who believed in their daughter's innocence and redemption above their own, called the constables, who were delighted with their cleverness at discovering money and the receipt in my damp room beside the coal hole. It was the sort of room of which a policeman might easily think: the person who lived here must have a grievance.'

'And this chapel girl,' I asked with a childlike awe, 'who believes vigorously in hell, would perjure herself?'

'She would also be believed in preference to a daughter of Russian Jews. In any case, girls don't believe in hell as strongly as they do in revenge,' said Bernard, and then, 'You don't believe this. I can tell you do not believe this as more than a thief's version. However, I don't require your belief.'

I did my utmost to reassure her. She smiled distantly, into a shadowy corner, and said, 'Women not equipped as I, and shipped as I was shipped on the transport *Whisper*, died of sorrow and the bloody flux long before they landed.'

'Equipped as you?' I asked.

'Equipped with that in my blood which makes me expect torment.'

'Do you expect torment from me?'

Again the smile, as if to an invisible audience, with more history to them than me. 'No, for in my blood I expect joy in the end.' I kissed her, but then recklessly set a test, one which she was entitled to resent.

'Your friend Alice Aldread however? She did kill her husband?'

'Oh, yes,' she said. 'Mind you, he had been poisoning himself with arsenic for years. But yes, she speeded the end. She filled his tea with poison.'

For some reason she began to laugh, and I joined in, and all at once we could not cease.

To me, as very distant thunder, came from Mrs Finlay a letter, sent from England, with the news that Mr Finlay, distressed at having neglected to become reconciled to his forthright daughter, and burdened with debts which, while not murderous, forced him to an agonising reappraisal of his place in the world, had perished in his sleep. A month after Phoebe's death, Finlay himself went into the bitter ground. Mrs Finlay was selling the pastoral station they had owned at Yass, had retained the house where I had first met the child Phoebe, but had closed it down while she visited her son George and other relatives in England. Her tone was anguished and consolatory. I was pleased she would have left Goulburn before news of my supposed disgraceful betrayal of Phoebe was likely to have reached her.

I did not grieve for Finlay, except for my mother-in-law's sake – though I foresaw that she would make a very successful widow and perhaps be happier in that state than she had been married to her acidic and self-important husband.

Phoebe had been some six weeks gone when I saw a spring cart crossing the ford of the Murrumbidgee down the long slope from our stockyards. I recognised as the driver of the cart the new Cooma Creek magistrate, Bilson, who had attended George's funeral. He was with a woman. His wife perhaps? The cart was attended by two border policemen, and a native tracker, his feet bare in the stirrups. It was possible the magistrate had been sent to chastise me on behalf of the colonial gentry, and the possibility gave me a strange, angry interest in his arrival. But as he swung the cart into the yard before the house, he had a grin on his face.

The woman beside him, whose nose bone and cheek points seemed at first to dominate her face, had eyes which burned with a notable fury of interest. Was this Bernard's friend, the murderess? I asked myself. It seemed to be. She wore the sort of cap and apron which came from the Female Factory. I signalled Felix, who was combing a horse in the yard, to come and help the woman down.

Landed on Nugan Ganway, Alice Aldread leaned fully and breathlessly on young Felix's forearm. The ghost of what had once been a splendid smile rose to her lips.

'You're a lovely boy for that,' she said, and her voice, though not refined, was melodic. Her praise for Felix had no archness but was authentic, and the boy blushed for that reason.

I presented myself and told her that I was Mr Bettany. And yet I felt a little like an impostor. It was an earlier and redeemable Bettany who had applied for her. The one who claimed her now was a different fellow.

'So,' she said, 'if I had the physical strength to kneel at your feet and rise again, I would do that. Since I was first in this colony, you are the only one to have treated me to the credit of being sane and able to be decent employed.'

I told her that bendings of the knee were not necessary on Nugan Ganway, and that her friend Sarah was here. 'And your wife?' she asked. I told her Phoebe was dead of diphtheria. She coughed and could merely shake her head in condolence. I instructed Felix to lead her inside.

Later, when I went indoors myself, I heard Sarah and her laughing from the cookhouse, and thought it a splendid sound. They might go, I thought, into my wife's room and convince her unreconciled ghost with their gaiety. Then I heard Sarah say, in a way I knew at once she would not say to any man, 'So I've brought you out of Egypt, Alice, as I promised.'

Bernard, the universal saviour. For she had brought me out of Egypt too, even though she was a rescuer held at a distance from me by layers of statute, of Home and colonial ordinance, and of universal pretensions of respectability. But it was, above all, with someone who had shared the stink, peril and bafflement of the convict deck that she could plainly say, 'I've saved you!'

I soon found that Aldread, though consumptive, had none of the earnestness of Bernard. She was what would be called a jolly woman, with a greying fairness to her hair and complexion, the flaming red of her disease in her cheeks, and its frenzy in her eyes. She was eager to help in the kitchen with Bernard, but her occasional coughing fits became so intense that Bernard and I devised a way to keep her busy with needle and coloured cottons, and she worked on my clothes, on Bernard's, ultimately even on Long's, Maggie Tume's and O'Dallow's, with the speed and delicacy of a true craftswoman.

Tume being quickly with child by her new husband O'Dallow, and breathing hard over her work, Aldread ran up nightdresses for her laying-in, and a christening robe for the unborn child. In the yard a few days later, I saw these items blowing in the wind from a rope, for Tume had wisely chosen to boil all traces of Aldread's breath out of them.

Despite her condition, Aldread was partial to rum in the evenings, sitting by the fire with Bernard and me. Perhaps it might hasten her disease, but it eased her breathing. From these conversations, I learned amusing facts such as, for example, that during their transportation, other women called them 'the miseries' because of their superior height. I heard a great deal darkly narrated of the Pallmires, the Steward and

Matron of the Female Factory. Bernard clearly did not wish to tell as many stories, nor make as many jovial asides, as Aldread. Her eyes reflected the fire flatly.

The Pallmires, according to Aldread, took women on drinking expeditions into Parramatta. Even in the early stages of her illness, Aldread had been required to travel in Mr Pallmire's wagon for such an event, though, unlike the women from amongst whom Bernard had been assigned to me, Aldread was meant, as a life prisoner, to occupy the factory's cells.

'The fellow liked to be utterly fenced with women,' said Aldread, 'and his wife, unlike a normal wife, liked to see him so fenced. They were a most rum pair, and thank God they were taken off through you, Sarah.'

'Through you?' I asked Bernard.

'Why Sarah watched them, all their dodges, and made a record.'

I knew that Bernard had been taken on such degrading excursions, for she said nothing, and said nothing in a particular way, a knowledge-is-dangerous sort of way. It was clear to me that to talk of the Pallmires was for Bernard an acute pain. She had suffered, I could tell, in other ways she did not want to detail, and with her immutable air of privacy, I understood with a pang that I might never hear of them. Even the outspoken Aldread could tell Bernard was ill at ease and retreated from the subject, letting her anecdotes die in a series of discreet coughs.

As at some periods in the past, after four in the afternoon, Felix began to come regularly to the door and, if it was convenient, was admitted to the corner of the parlour where my library was. He was the most advanced scholar of Nugan Ganway, and combined learning with skillful riding. His studies had, of course, been interrupted by our recent tragedies and by my reluctance to open the door to him, in case I read something in his eye. But now that he returned he brought back with him a book on surveying which I had bought to equip myself against potential disputes over boundaries. He had, on his own initiative, fashioned a device like a quadrant, involving two lengths of stick screwed together, with a peg glued to either end of the stick. By using this he could measure distances between landmarks.

He liked to sit and study in the presence of women. In a quiet way he even enjoyed an applauding audience. Alice Aldread regularly rose from her sewing table to make a fuss of him.

'My heaven, but you're a clever fellow. I guess you could even teach a fool like me some of that.'

'Trigonometry is difficult,' said Felix, politely closing his book. 'But I could teach you Euclid.'

She pulled her chair closer to his and, while searching for the page in Euclid, he motioned her to come even closer.

'No, I would cough all over you,' said Alread. 'You can show me from a distance.'

He held up the appropriate page. It was Pythagoras's Theorem. He pointed to the crucial elements. 'See this? This is your right angle. Straight up, straight down, no deviation. This one here is your hypotenuse.'

'Why is it called such a silly name?' asked Aldread.

'Oh, Aldread,' he told her, laughing. 'It is not a silly name. It's just from the Greek – 'to be opposite to' – you see, it is opposite.'

I thought that Pythagoras couldn't have put it better himself.

For six weeks or so, Aldread slept in the kitchen, from which, in Bernard's arms in the room built to honour George's unachieved boyhood, I heard her occasional paroxysms. One night they were so regular that Bernard and I lay awake waiting for the next.

On a mad impulse I said, 'It's draughty out there. We should put her in the other room . . .'

I felt her breath on my neck. 'It is . . .,' she said, '. . . it is your wife's room.'

I had wanted that very response, to be argued out of the proposal. And yet I myself argued for it all the more. 'If there were justice on earth, it would be Phoebe's room. Since there is none, Aldread might as well have it.'

The enormity of what I proposed hung in the dark above us.

'You must think seriously on this, Mr Bettany,' Bernard counselled me.

A new bed was found and Aldread moved, hacking and laughing, into the room where Phoebe and George perished. There was in me a distinct impulse to have her there, this colourful, generous yet vulgar being. By her hilarity she might change the aspect of this room and this house.

And yet sometimes when Bernard went to sit with her there, during crises of her breathing – when she nonetheless chatted busily on, the genial opposite of what one would think a spouse-murderer – I would leave the house, driven by some sense, akin to jealousy, of my not having been preferred. One thing I did definitely envy, and perhaps so did Bernard, was Aldread's lack of grief. She had killed a husband and it lay lightly on her. I wished sometimes for that same lightness, I who was tormented by the belief that I had whistled up my wife's death, and in doing so caught by accident my son in the malice of that intent.

Some nights, driven by the implications of Aldread's and dear Bernard's sisterly amusement, I might simply walk away, eight miles to a shepherd's hut, and surprise the shepherds at the fire.

'Oh sir,' the shepherds would say, from their little fireplace as the wind sluiced musically through every gap in the timbers of the place, 'What are you doing abroad on such a night without a horse?' And after we were settled and they shyly brought out moonshine, I might say, 'What was it you did again? What landed you here?' My awareness that we all had crimes ran very high on those nights.

If they were embarrassed to tell me the first time, I would again ask, 'What brought you here?' They were sometimes edgy at this moment, and I did not blame them. They thought I wanted news of their miserable and desperate acts, committed in England or Wales or Ireland as prelude to their Australian baptism, so that although living like them in slab timber, I could feel that I lay a distance above them in the human scale. They thought I wanted the assurance that, though they were criminals, I was an honest freeman. They did not understand that I wanted the company of their warm, anonymous ranks, their undistinguished crimes. Conscious of my leprosy, I wanted to lose myself amongst the lepers. I wished them to tell me about the lead they had stolen from the roofs of halls and churches, the locks they had forced, the livestock they had led away into darkness, so that I could measure, for the sake of my mind, the scale of my own guilt. I would walk back cold and consoled, and see by lamplight Bernard darkly, sombrely, studiously asleep.

Sometimes when I visited the hut there would be a native woman there, dressed in rags of burlap and skins and fabric clogged by mutton fat, some tribal outcast who had stayed on after the Moth people left in autumn. Where else was she to be? I had given up trying to win that moral argument, since I could not even win one with myself.

The Ngarigo woman might look at me with eyes even more unreadable than Bernard's and hug to herself her skirt of flour bag. Her husband was perhaps amongst the bones the Reverend Howie and Long and I had found. Or had he been informally shot, in spite of my best instructions and warnings, and the reminder that Mr Howie would return, by one of my shepherds for spearing a sheep? This was something one could not always prevent either! The war, oh the war. Its skirmishes went unrecorded and its thunders were borne away on south-westerly winds. Such was my life at its highest and lowest moments.

Maggie Tume, the men's cook, was a merry little woman and thought her taciturn O'Dallow such a wonderful fellow that she wanted to hold a woolshed celebration of their recent marriage, but was inhibited by the thought that I might be hurt to see happiness. Nevertheless, she asked Bernard to see if I would allow it, and Bernard, my chatelaine, did so, half-smiling at the enthusiasm of Maggie. Tume meant – if permitted – to reproduce a Celtic *ceilidh*, a rustic dance-party, deep in the Maneroo.

This request to licence merriment cheered me greatly. No sooner did I give assent than Tume had Presscart and O'Dallow cutting eucalyptus boughs to decorate the rafters and uprights of the woolshed. Clancy was heard practising the fiddle he had learned to play at sea in his youth and claimed to have played in bars in New York and Liverpool. Dear and dreaded Long rode a cart to Cooma Creek to buy kegs and bottles of porter.

On the night, Tume dressed with all the solemnity of a bride – she had found a good straw hat to substitute for a veil. Watching the celebration taking form from a chair by my window, I saw as O'Dallow and Tume went to the woolshed in late dusk that Tume had made O'Dallow wear a brown suit and a cravat. Her son, Michael, was also in a jacket, and wore shoes. Clearly, Tume was a coloniser, an improver!

To the woolshed in the next hour came seven stockmen; eight shepherds from nearby out-stations, their sheep safely in fold by this hour, and some of them with stoneware jugs of moonshine; a Ngarigo woman in a dress; Felix; beloved Bernard; and the consumptive Aldread. I had promised I might call in later, and after a fortifying glass of rum, I did so.

It was the first time I had entered the woolshed since my attempt at self-obliteration weeks before. I found it startlingly lit by all the station's lights, gathered together from the huts by Tume. Flagons of liquor and bottles of stout were placed at one end of a long table, and slabs of damper and warm, sliced mutton at the other. Here, many of the population of Nugan Ganway were presently feeding themselves for the energetic night ahead.

In the middle of the far wall Bernard stood chatting to Long as he took a hand at tuning Clancy's fiddle. From the sight of them a stranger would not have known that, in some lights, she might have been seen to have betrayed him. In Long's world the loss of a woman to the big house and the big name might not have been uncommon, and though my house and name were nothing to speak of, he had learned the limits of protest. He combined this profound knowledge with a furious pride, and his silence, his unaltered demeanour, was part of that pride too.

In full sight, dressed with boughs, was the rafter from which I had tried to break my neck, from which Bernard had scythed me down – her harvest. By considering it now, I concluded that every scene, every object – all which had once had a singleness of purpose – had become double, a sign of its own contradiction.

Clancy had by now assumed his duty as fiddler, producing a more than passable jig. The Ngarigo woman responded to it very lithely but when, at Felix's invitation, Aldread bravely tried, she was overtaken with convulsions. Michael Tume, dancing a Gaelic reel by himself, breath thundering in and out of his throat, frowned over the steps in a country where the children of fallen souls were blessed. I sat by the door, and a shepherd fraternally brought me some raw liquor. 'It's the cream of the mountains, sir,' he told me, recommending it.

Soon, Bernard had to help the poor gasping Aldread out of the shed and back to the homestead. Bernard's dark eyes communicated with me. 'I am going now, and so might you.'

So, between dances, I gave my final congratulations to the blessed couple and followed.

But even though Bernard was at home, I felt an undischarged embarrassment at the event. People had treated me as an elder and an invalid. I knew I was lucky to get out of the woolshed under that kind description. Yet how could I remain in that indefinite state and at the same time hold Nugan Ganway? Approaching the door to my homestead, I could hear Aldread laughing within, and, turning away in a kind of servant shyness, I wandered back in the direction of the woolshed, and far beyond it. Standing alone in the night I remembered the time I had lain naked under this exact sky and in innocence let its light wash my body. I dallied between woolshed and homestead, leaning to smoke a pipe by the stockyard, taking more note of stars than I needed to. In this state of uncertainty, belonging neither in the woolshed or the homestead, I understood how Phoebe had set out and succeeded in tethering me to the reality of things, of pastoral expanse and parlour intimacy. Now, it seemed that servants owned my woolshed, and servants – even the divine Bernard, and certainly the raucous Aldread – owned my hearth.

Thus, confused and shy, I swung away from the bright core of Nugan Ganway and strolled amongst the boulders a little way down the slope towards the river, then half a mile uphill towards the wooded ridge to the west. I took comfort from my ragged, punished breath the higher I got. At last I could look down in stillness at the bright lights shining through the gaps in the woolshed walls, and the smaller light of the homestead where Bernard and Aldread honoured their long-established sisterhood. The night was still and, in lieu of wind, there were the small, tinny judderings of Clancy's violin, and a drumming accompaniment as if one of the men had found an empty cracker or tar tin and was beating it. The central vale of Nugan Ganway lay before me as incomprehensible as the court of a Khan might have been to Marco Polo. This was how the Ngarigo had seen my occupation, from this height, an ulcer of light and fire at the centre of their world. Homeless as them now, I descended the hill merely because there was nothing else left for me to do.

It took me a great time to descend that slope. Clancy's violin ground itself through every extreme of feeling: of wistful despair and exuberant joy and heedless whimsy. I heard voices join in to bolster the fiddle music, sometimes with massed success, sometimes a mere raggedy chorus, sometimes the penetrating solitary voice of one man. I still paused often to confer with the neutral and upright trees. So much time passed that the closer I got down towards the homestead, and thus the woolshed, the greater I sensed a note of discord in the voices. The human race, as represented by my people on Nugan Ganway, was turning itself from two favourite activities – music and the consumption of liquor – to a third, conflict. The sort of shouting which goes with shaken fists drew me in close to the timbers of the woolshed.

I put my eye to a gap in the planking, through which I could feel the heat of the crowd within, the pulse of their intense hope and anger. The first figure I saw was Felix's. He looked stunned, big lips parted in the pained grimace which on his baby face I had mistaken for a smile. I then spied briskly on the faces of my servants, for once seeing them as they were when I was not there to represent the force of the larger world and the pastoral demands of the place. And so I lighted upon O'Dallow and Long at the party's centre. O'Dallow, who rarely spoke above a growl, flushed as one would expect the host of the celebration to be, was yelling at Long in Irish. But, legs spread wide and face glowing, he was soon forced to the English language by a desire to win allies to his denunciation of Long.

'So I'm the only honest bastard of a man here. You, you mongrel dog, what can you claim of honesty?'

O'Dallow's new wife held his forearm, trying to restrain him physically, trying to temper his voice as well. 'You blew the head off that poor bloody absconder,' cried O'Dallow. 'He didn't kill the nun. T'was bloody Goldspink who paid them to take the woman's cart away, and then put you and old Bettany on their traps. Says poor bloody Rowan, I did not kill the nun! With his dying breath he said it! With his own blood on his lips. As I go to God, says Rowan, I did not touch the nun. And you heard him say it and put a bullet in his brain.'

Long stood up on the far side of the pool of light, and I saw his hand extend like a lance. 'Were you there? Tell me, were you there?'

'No. But you confided in me.'

'Exactly. I confided ... It was the very stroke of mercy I gave the poor fellow. I couldn't take back the lead the magistrate had put in him, and he would not have been believed in any case.'

'Oh Jesus, that's a splendid mercy you've got there. You'd give it to me too, if I lay down to let you! But I won't lie down for you, you bloody dog! Such a man are you, such a bloody slave! You let old Bettany take your woman. I would die, I would go to Norfolk Island, I would be flogged raw before I let a man take mine! "God bless you, Mr Bettany," say you. "And you're welcome to her. And would Your Worship want me to hold her still while you take her?"'

I hurt my fist against the wall, though no one heard. There was too much hubbub inside, and to the credit of my servants, some aghast looks. I hoped Long would hit him now. In moonshine one had not only the truth, but it was viciously told as well.

Long said in a quiet voice, 'Don't say a word of Bernard. You are an ape beside her! She is no man's woman, and never will be.'

'Right you are,' yelled O'Dallow. 'For isn't she another woman's woman now?'

Tume, weeping, tried to gag her husband. 'She's the woman of that coughing Venus from the Factory who poisons husbands and spits blood,' said Dallow. 'So maybe you'll have your way in the end, Sean, you poor sawney bastard! Maybe she'll put sheep drench in old Bettany's tea!'

Why did Long not deliver the blow? Surely he did not believe there was any value in O'Dallow's drunken version of our lives? It was, in the end, merciful Clancy who laid down his fiddle, knowing it would not soon be needed, that the music was for now at its close, and picked up from the side of a stove used to boil tar in shearing-time a lump of wood. Crossing to the civil war, he brought it down behind O'Dallow's ear. The bridegroom's eyes rolled, his legs gave way slowly, but he did not fully collapse, for his dutiful wife held him up while calling Clancy a bloody pig and a foul bugger. Long cried, the most authoritative utterance he had made in the whole dispute, 'The wedding party is over now. God bless all souls here. All you have heard is talking drink.'

Full of more terror than fury I ran to the homestead before my emerging servants could manage to sight me. Entering my house, I heard Aldread's sharp cough in her bedroom. A murderous felon occupied Phoebe's room and poisoned that air. How could I have permitted that? But by a turned-down lamp light, how beautiful Bernard slept at the hearth, in front of a dwindling fire. A homely shawl sat on her shoulders. It would have suited my evil mood better had they been both together in there, had I heard Aldread's vulgar laughter, a woman whose girlish levity and well-ordered features were very likely what had saved her from the fall from the scaffold.

I made for the decanter of brandy. Let her sleep a moment longer, while I considered the other question O'Dallow had raised. Dying, and in Gaelic, the absconder had pleaded innocence. Well, a cynic might say, you would expect him to. Long had said both, 'It was the very stroke of mercy,' and, 'She is no man's woman, and never will be.' He had made these claims with the equal force of a man for whom there's no profit in admitting half the truth and shading out the rest. I took my brandy to the fire and sat down facing the embers. She did not stir. 'What a pair we are,' I murmured. And then, in thorough misery, I fell asleep.

When I woke, she was leaning above me. I gave her a weary caress. What else was to be done when we had defied heaven? I told her to go to bed and I would follow. She obeyed, and as she entered George's room, I heard a wide-awake cough from Aldread. I rid myself of the cup of brandy which had been sitting slack in my hand, and went to the door of the room now part-way converted from Phoebe's to Aldread's. Instincts of proprietorship, doubt and grief urged me to open the door and enter.

I found Aldread propped up by pillows, wide-eyed as if expecting me. By the light of her stub of candle, her brow looked unearthly pale beneath her fair hair and mob cap, and her cheeks as red as if rouged.

'I heard a riot out there, Mr Bettany,' she told me. 'I hope no one was hurt.'

I could not help a kind of sharp laughter.

'Isn't that a peculiar concern from a woman who murdered her husband?'

She looked briefly but without confusion towards the dark ceiling. In summer, brown snakes would sometimes penetrate the roofing and fall on the occupants, and perhaps she was invoking snakes now.

'It was a peculiar concern which caused me to take his life, Mr Bettany, as I told the jury. It was not simply myself who suffered his bruises and his outrages, but other women, though I do not expect you to believe that ...'

Indeed, I pretended to be a sceptic.

'So you are at one with the judges,' she told me.

'If I were a better judge, you would perhaps not be here.'

'I must say then that I bless you for not being so good a judge,' she said, with a smile some might have thought disarming.

'There is a story that I am so bad a judge that you are more than a friend to Bernard.'

I waited while Aldread's breath rasped away in my departed wife's room.

'I have been a sister,' she said at last. 'Do you expect less when women who have never committed any crime but one are hurled together into the floating pit? But what have you got to fear, Mr Bettany? I am dying, and dear Sarah loves you for your honest soul.'

I looked at her by the dim light, not knowing whether to damn or thank her. For even now there was a chuckle in her.

'Is nothing ever serious to you, Aldread?' I asked.

She got out of her bed and stood by it. I could see her two luminous feet on the earth floor.

'By God, Mr Bettany, everything is so serious that I have to laugh. But don't misjudge that – it is merely the hindquarters of wailing and tears.' She spat into the palm of her hand, and I saw that it was largely blood. 'I swear by this that you have nothing to fear from me. Sarah loves your decent soul and that is that. I am about to drop into eternity, so if you envy me as some rival, God help you. If you look at me as someone crooked and perverse, I ask you what is more perverse than marrying a young woman when you are an old man, as my husband was, and wanting not her alone but her sister of fourteen as well! Prussic acid was in my hand a minister of a just God. I shall not cease to love Sarah while there is breath. But I who will go to God with a mouthful of blood tell you again, if you fear me you are a pitiable creature, and if you mistrust Sarah you have a mean spirit. Now send me to the magistrate, and get me flogged!'

And she began to compose herself, as if to take to her bed again.

'Oh God,' I said, and leaned against a wall.

The merciless Aldread, though hard put for breath, had not finished haranguing me. 'If I have been too forceful in my utterance. I beg your pardon, Mr Bettany.'

Of course she did not sound as if she begged anyone's pardon, and why should she, for she did seem, as she justly claimed, close to an end.

And yet I felt that it was utterly true what Long had said, and that it would hang over my life like a banner. 'She is no man's woman, and never will be.'

I was aware of Aldread's eyes on me. The consumptive woman seemed to know everything, the doubled over and twisted and complicated history of my own clan not least. Or if she did not know it, she assumed it, and refused to accept my right to make complaints or fuss.

I was left lamely to say, 'I hope you're telling me the truth, Aldread, for I tell you I've had enough grief for one lifetime.'

She took a damp cloth and washed the blood off her hand and lips. I realised that it was time to go.

⌒

AT MID-MORNING, PRIM SIGHTED THE refugee camps of Alingaz 1, 2, and 3. They ascended the slopes of three distinct wadis on the flanks of a red-grey mountain named *Jabal Erbab*. At the point from which the camp could be seen, Erwit negotiated with caution the steep oil-slicked highway, past a blighted area where oil trucks dumped the dregs of their cargoes before descending to Port Sudan to reload. The rubbled earth, unsoftened by any vegetation, fell away awesomely to one side. Prim, maintaining her composure by concentrating on the high ground, thought the camps were, in their way, a tribute to military intent: people had been relocated here, eight hundred miles from their home ground, so that the Sudanese army could enjoy a clear field of operations at Nuba Hills.

They had been joined also and voluntarily by families of Beja nomads, who had a thousand years history here in the Red Sea Hills, but who had been driven in by the same factors which kept close to the road the Shukriyah they met the night before: uncertain seasons, the failure of ancestral wells, the increasing aridity of already dry hills, an acquired dependence on pumped water, and on Western, as well as traditional, medicine.

Even people from as far away as Darfur were said to be have come here, moved on from camps near Khartoum. They too were camped in their separate community, in a gully on gritty south-facing slopes, not far from the abandoned Port Sudan railway line. In its swathes of hessian, the entire refugee settlement might in a happier republic have passed for a post-modernist artistic gesture – desert hills say, in the Mojave Desert, or to the west of Alice Springs, wrapped as a statement by Cristo.

The Hessiantown clinic, a series of connected tents supplied by a number of NGOs, was located at the mouth of a valley in Alingaz 1. Around and above it, the shanties of the first 16 000 or so relocated Nuba rose. This part of the camp had been created so quickly, around a few old wells, that the normal blue UN plastic or well-ventilated tents of refugee camps were not in evidence. Adi Hamit, the Austfam-supported camp in Darfur, was a sophisticated city compared to this.

The clinic was run by a robust Red Crescent-supplied Egyptian nurse named Nuara, who had already expressed by letter her willingness to help administer Sherif's health survey. She was hopeful, she told Sherif, that a survey from such an eminent source might lead to more assistance – further nurses, midwives or Trained Birth Assistants, as the Ministry of Health called them. The team which would scour Alingaz 1 and delineate its sadnesses, its exiled skills, its crying needs would consist of Sherif as boss, Prim representing Austfam, the reliable Erwit, Nuara, two nurses Sherif had used for other surveys and a man who was being sent from the Ministry of Health, who might prove helpful or obstructive.

It had been arranged that Prim and the two nurses would stay at the clinic tent. After spending some time talking with Nuara, Prim and Sherif walked a little way up the valley to the only permanent structure in Hessiantown, the house of Hanif el Suq, the official of the Sudanese Commission of Refugees. Erwit had already parked the Austfam truck outside a vast, wire-fenced food depot within which the house stood. Inside the enormous compound, the rations of thousands lay beneath canvas tarpaulins.

Hanif el Suq's correspondence with Prim had been clipped: 'Please, Miss Bettany, ensure that you let me know in good time the date of your visit, since my work is extremely mapped out for me here, and seven days weekly.' But the man Sherif and Prim met, sitting in the dwindling shade on the north side of his two-room residence, was a pleasant-featured, stout, vivacious fellow in neat, sweat-stained khaki. Prim could see a well-made bed against the east of his house, where it would get afternoon shade.

Hanif stood up from the little anodised folding table at which he had been drinking tea. Simultaneously, by an open fire some yards to his right, a beautiful Nuba servant woman looked up darkly from beneath a white shawl, and then went back to stirring the pasta which was to be his midday meal. A large and unopened can of tuna sat on a red stone near the fire. Prim thought, where there is food, a woman can be bought with it. Hanif might be a man of honour. But the presence of food in a hungry landscape was a great corruptor.

Hanif called to have chairs brought from the house, and a slight Nuba boy with shaven head – probably the woman's son – appeared with two chairs. Soon Prim and Sherif were sitting and drinking more sweet *chai*, in one of the hottest noons of the year.

'So you are here to make a survey of our Alingaz?' Hanif asked, happy to show off his English.

'That's right.'

'It was built from nothing, you know. One day hills, a few camels, a goat. The next – phew! Hundreds of trucks and thousands of the Nuba.'

'Yes,' said Sherif. 'We understand. There are special problems.'

'These,' confided Hanif, leaning forward, 'these are very backward people. They are like children.'

'We might all be like children,' said Sherif, with an edge Prim heard and Hanif perceived, 'if we were ripped out of our villages on an hour's notice to be taken a thousand miles away.'

That concluded, the genial Hanif saw, one topic of conversation. 'Do you like rap music?' he asked, his eyes glittering. He shouted a command towards the house and soon the high-octane thud of a rap band could be heard, and the emphatic voice of a rapper.

> *I went to the store*
> *   and the man said pay,*
> *and I said I'll pay*
> *another day*
> *'Cause you poison the black man*
> *with all you sell,*
> *you send the babies*

to additive hell,
and you charge top dollar
to fry our brain
and you grab our dollars
*   for the same again.*
*   Well, listen, I'm here*
to collect my dues,
put in a little lead
to alter your views
and you'll see your body
on the evening news!'

Hanif's smile broadened, delighted at this plaint for black justice. He was sure it would win Sherif back. Sherif raised his eyebrows at Prim, but his innate Sudanese courtesy restrained him from saying anything.

When the track ended, Hanif hooted, raised his boots off the ground and slapped both knees. 'You must join me for lunch, sir and madam,' he said. The Nuba woman set enamel plates on the little folding table, and brought a mixture of spaghetti and tuna.

During the meal Sherif gave Hanif an Arabic copy of the questionnaire and explained that the process would be based on random cluster sampling, told the best method given that the residences of this hessian city were not numbered. It involved, he told the not entirely interested Hanif, the survey team walking to the middle of the camp with one of the camp leaders, to any spot he might nominate, and from there, facing east, selecting a house, then going to the next, and the next, and continuing thus for thirty or so interviews. Then the team would move to a new location, face east, and began again. The aim was to achieve a ten per cent survey of all houses in Alingaz 1, and produce some 322 family interviews out of a camp population of 3220 households.

Shovelling in his spaghetti, Hanif gave sceptical little snorts. 'And I can just hear them all,' he said. ' "The evil Hanif el Suq doesn't feed us enough!" They are lucky, lucky people, but like all to whom something is given, they are still hungry, hungry.'

'The matter of food rationing is not amongst the fifty-two questions we shall ask,' said Sherif, though with a glint of professional annoyance in his eye. In his peevishness, he might well have said, 'We don't need to ask questions about officials of the Commission of Refugees. We know enough about them already.'

'You know,' Hanif told Prim, anxious now about Sherif's coldness, and whether it was a threat to him, 'these Nuba people, they are rebels. Both the Christians and the Muslims, just as much as each other. So they must be moved here, far from home. But here the sanitation is not good and the water is not good, and sometimes it has stopped running and needs to be brought in by truck until the new well is dug.'

Sherif said, 'You must tell the man from the Ministry of Health.'

And there was the point, Prim thought. Sherif expected obstruction. He expected more obstruction because he was Sudanese, and perhaps because he had published. The uncomfortable testiness, which had been brought to the surface by the camel massacre on the Port Sudan highway, revived in him very easily. There might have been journeys once when a man like Hanif would have amused him. But this was not one of them.

Hanif blinked, and to clear the air, Prim asked him where he was from. He immediately sat up and beamed. 'I am a Kassala boy,' he boasted. 'A little to the south of Kassala. Is that right ... to the south?' He was asking for linguistic not geographic reassurance. He came from grass scrub country then, not far from the Eritrean border. 'It is beautiful,' he said. 'It is green, and it has the mountains, better mountains than these. Like fingers in the air.' His eyes were full of nostalgia, and perhaps the hope of a better posting.

In the early afternoon, the heat was murderous, though the day was still and empty of the threat of blowing grit. It was simple justice, Prim thought as Sherif walked her down to Nuara's clinic, that if the timing of the rains were dislocated, so too should be the timing of sandstorms.

On this stroll, there was time, before a stupefied afternoon retreat from the sun, for Prim to chat with Sherif, but he proved uncommunicative.

'What is it?' Prim asked. With each syllable she felt a weight of hot air on her tongue.

'Oh, it's that Hanif fool,' he said. 'He thinks he's such a rocket scientist. And we don't know what this joker from the ministry will seek.'

'We'll get on top of him,' she promised.

'Maybe I'm getting old. But I think: what is the point of understanding the processes of health in a refugee camp, if the refugee camps go on multiplying? If in number they outrun the very strategies?'

'It will not seem futile once we start,' she assured him. 'Once we meet with the camp committee and see their faces. You'll be all right once you're not working in a vacuum.'

That evening, Prim manoeuvred Nuara to invite Sherif for a meal of
rice and flat bread, so that he did not have to eat with Hanif. But the
meal was brief, and Sherif soon went back to his billet at Hanif's depot.
Black cloth pulled over her head, Nuara went forth on some visit, striding
out confidently in sandals. Alone, Prim lit her so-called blizzard candle
and picked up her current novel. It was a book Dimp had sent her,
promising it would explain something about Dimp's own situation. It
had won prizes. It was skilful. Prim could see why Dimp should be captivated by a tale which reproduced the anguish and desperation of divorce.
Yet the novel, which concerned the break-up of a marriage between a
painter and a television producer who lived in London, annoyed and
fascinated Prim in exactly the same way Dimp annoyed and fascinated
her. Relieved of the imminence of physical death, sure of their daily
bread, people turned to the death of love and friendship and endowed
them with the weight of mortality, and equated the omens of such failures
with a portentousness which in the Sudan applied to failures of rains,
crops, and the deaths of children. Both the chief characters were so
clamant in their expectation of happiness that they made a grating
contrast with the stoic politeness of the Nuba women Prim had seen
earlier in the evening, cooking by open fires. To the clients of Austfam,
happiness began when water flowed, when the pannikin filled with
sorghum, or when fever released its hand on a child. The griefs of the
Hampstead couple in the novel were far too pastel and decorative for
the absolute, ravenous latitude Prim occupied.

Impatience eventually put her to sleep. On the edge of unconsciousness,
she wondered if Sherif might break the dormitory rules and visit her
during the night. But Nuara was a formidable housemistress, and a reluctance seemed to have set in Sherif. She felt that his hostility for Hanif
was, in part, a hostility for her silliness over the camels and the truck
driver. In a marriage of souls, one partner could never predict what
would weigh most with the other.

Could it be possible that the camel business was the equivalent for
Sherif of what Benedetto's speech had been for Dimp? Surely it was too
minor a quarrel to have such weight.

The second day in Hessiantown was spent searching out the leaders
of the apparently twenty-seven distinct villages or clans in Alingaz 1.
The people derived from different parts of the Nuba Hills – Limon,

Doleibaya, Tabuli, Talodi, Talabi, Moro, Anderri in the north, Dimo-
dong in the south. Though to the government in Khartoum they were all
one in being a nuisance, the refugees themselves cherished, and might
kill for, the distinctiveness of their own group. As there was no end to
the minute particularity of atomic particles, there was none to the particularity of a given Nuba.

The morning passed pleasantly, and Sherif's spirits rose. Then at the
close of a stupefying afternoon, the committee of leaders met with Nuara,
Erwit, Prim and Sherif in a canvas-topped lean-to. In the sudden clarity
of late afternoon, the camp committee of Alingaz 1 sat on the ground in
a semi-circle. They wore a variety of faded *galabias*, shirts and cummer-
bunds, and thigh-length swathes of fabric.

Sherif spread a rug, and he and the rest of the team sat at the mouth
of the semi-circle of elders. Prim could sense at once that these venerable
men placed a reliance on this meeting, an emphasis of hope, which could
probably not be immediately justified. She had a sense that the same
thought had occurred to Sherif.

Above all, they seemed to think that Sherif and Austfam had come to
adjust their permanently unsatisfactory relationship with Hanif: the food
distributor, the man from the Commission of Refugees.

One elder rose and said, 'That man is no good. He sells ration cards
to the Beja round about and to shopkeepers in Erkowit and Sinkat.'

Acknowledging this, Sherif told the leaders that he had no authority
over the Commission of Refugees. His wish to question a significant
number of families was based on a desire to find out what capacities they
held within themselves, and how they could best relate to their situation
in Alingaz 1. This was a survey, said Sherif, which would be shared with
them and with their community.

The men became excited. One elderly spokesman with cataracts in his
eyes stood up and declared, 'We are ready to co-operate. We have been
sitting in our houses waiting for someone like you to come. Better that
we find people who can help us to be independent of such scoundrels as
Hanif el Suq rather than to wait for their gifts.'

Nothing Sherif said would persuade them to hope less.

Another thin, tall man rose and declared that the people of Alingaz 1
had lost their hills because of their ignorance. They did not understand
politics except in the most basic way, said the man. And now they had
lost their country, so different from these hills. In the Nuba Hills the
breeze was like sandalwood. Here it grated against the flesh. The trees

of the richly watered Nuba Hills gave shade and fruit. One day they would all go back there, said the man, and it was to be desired that they would go back better informed, and with wider skills, than when the army moved them away.

Many of the other elders applauded the man's speech, and Sherif looked helplessly at Prim. He began to explain that health problems would also be looked at. And those results too would be presented to this very council, so that it could decide whether it could do anything about them. Particularly, Sherif said, he and his colleagues wanted to inquire into the deaths of infants under five years. Leathery Nuba elders with greying, frizzled hair stared at Sherif with piercing eyes. Of course they had heard this argument before – Sherif was aware of that. Be numbered for your own good! Let your tears be numbered! They hoped and they suspected. They wondered had this man the power to take from them the authority of their children's deaths, to reduce the infant features, the intimately remembered screams or restiveness to numbers. Sherif began pedalling hard, to keep their enthusiasm for this project in place. 'No names will be put down on paper,' he assured them. 'And I *do* speak of the possibility of gardens – watermelons, tomatoes and cardamom for sauces. I talk about chickens, donkeys and camels. I talk about co-operatives buying a grinding mill, and renting it to others. I talk of modest but hopeful things. I cannot offer you more.'

Another lean Nuba rose, grey in his wiry hair, and said, 'We thank you, sir, for thinking of us.'

The meeting was breaking up when in the space between the food dump and the tarpaulin community centre, a white four-wheel drive vehicle drew up. On its sides was painted the green flag of the Sudan. Prim, watching from the shelter, saw a youngish man in fatigues get out, look about him, and head towards the *rakubah*. There was something familiar about him. Sherif obviously thought so too, for he rose and stepped out into the light, inquiring of the newly arrived government official, 'Siddiq?' The two men embraced. For this was Dr Osman Siddiq, a protégé of Sherif's whom Prim had first met at the el Rahzis.

'Come,' said Sherif, 'we are just finishing a meeting with the community.'

'That's wonderful,' said Siddiq in English, smiling at Prim.

'But I thought you were with the Ministry of Defence?' asked Sherif.

'I've been seconded here,' said Siddiq, still the smooth-faced, youthful man Prim remembered. 'When I read that you were one of the team,' he said to Sherif, 'I could barely believe it. Although, of course, I have read your earlier publications.'

'Oh, yes,' said Sherif, mockingly, 'you can recite them by heart. But how wonderful that you are here. You were being sent to Atbara, I seem to remember.'

'And was promoted to Port Sudan. You never know, my friend, one day I might make my way back to the capital and live a civilised life.'

Prim looked at Siddiq with gratitude. His friendly presence might turn the balance and bring Sherif fully back to the process.

'And are you a big wheel,' asked Sherif, 'in Defence, or Health or wherever you are? Are you worth cultivating?'

'Oh, yes. I think I am exactly the fellow a young chap like you must cultivate.' And Siddiq and Sherif burst into fraternal laughter.

Prim had been invited to join Sherif, Siddiq and Erwit for dinner in the yard by Hanif's residence. Sherif set up a meal of canned tomatoes, flat bread and pasta on a collapsible table, and Prim walked towards it, through the evening camp, the endless intricacy of hessian shelters, un-reinforced by brush, since there was none to be had. By evening fires, Nuba women dressed each other's wiry hair in strands which looked to Prim like maps of harvest. Women of the great Nuba evacuation! They looked up from beneath their eyebrows at her as she walked by.

The dinner guests served themselves from the common bowl, and Siddiq spoke to her across the table. 'And you had a good time with the camp committee?' he asked, making a slight mouth, as if he knew that a camp committee of Nubas could be difficult.

'It went well,' Sherif told him. 'Promising to show them the results – that goes well.'

'You always were such a democrat, my friend,' said Siddiq. 'I have some suggestions for additional questions, though perhaps we should keep the answers to ourselves.'

'Additional questions?' asked Sherif. 'I'm very happy to consider them. But with my present fifty-two questions I thought I had just about covered the field.'

Siddiq smiled at Prim, as if to imply that Sherif had now achieved a middle-aged retentiveness, a resistance to the new.

They ate their meal sitting on a circle of stones. It was as prodigiously hot as the night before, and Prim's flesh itched. Like all the best scorpions, the sun had bitten her through her clothing. She felt too a section of fried flesh in the V of her shirt, which she had failed to cover with her bandanna.

Erwit was, as ever, quiet. He was, Prim well knew, a very intelligent fellow, but he did not consider it his place to intrude in the purely Sudanese debate in progress between Sherif and Siddiq.

They were discussing whether it was a good or bad thing that a public health official could rarely expect to be permitted to interview a woman alone. Her husband was always present, sometimes a mother-in-law. When you asked a woman, for example, how many animals her family had grazed in the Nuba Hills, would she exaggerate the number out of regard for her husband? If you asked a woman was she willing to attend classes at the clinic, would she be inhibited by her husband's presence from saying yes?

Prim could tell that Sherif was anxious about the additional questions Siddiq had mentioned, of whether they would prove to be marginal or so intrusive that they would alter what he was trying to do. And so this secondary debate, instead of genuinely interesting Sherif, seemed to reduce him to the disequilibrium of earlier in the day.

He nodded towards Hanif's cot. On its far side, an oblivious Hanif sat in a chair, listening to a battery radio broadcasting music from Port Sudan, and drinking tea. 'They all complain about that guy, by the way.'

'Well, that's standard,' said Siddiq.

'Tell me what you want to do here,' said Sherif, sick of letting the main issue dangle in the air.

'Well,' said Siddiq, "the Ministry of Health is not paranoid, Sherif. As much as your rhetoric might be to do with breaking the dependence cycle, you still want to find the Crude Birth Rate, which you believe will be low – thus undermining the wisdom of the government's clearing of the Nuba Hills. And you'll come up with a figure for Infant Mortality that will be embarrassingly high. And we will live with that, if the verb "live" is not too callous.'

'No,' said Sherif. 'Let's not be particular. You mentioned added questions.'

'Well, these people are a security risk,' said Siddiq. 'There are supporters of pro-Southern groups here. I'm sure this news is of no surprise to you. Not only that, but there are operative cells supporting the Southern People's Liberation Army within Alingaz, tyrannising ordinary people and – you will not believe it, but it is so – raising anti-government funds.'

Sherif said nothing, and Siddiq sighed.

'I want to add some questions about the operations of these cells in Alingaz. I want to hear information from the people concerning pro-SPLA extortion here. You and I can devise the questions between us.'

'No, we can't,' said Sherif. 'I have undertaken to share the results of the questionnaire with the camp committee.'

'We don't need to let them know about these questions. We don't need to give them these results. I assure you I have the interests of the ordinary refugees in mind. They don't enjoy being under the thumb of the rebel machine.'

'I don't consider these people refugees,' said Sherif.

'You know what I mean,' said Siddiq.

'Now I understand why you were seconded from the Ministry of Defence! Are you a doctor? Or are you in intelligence and security?'

'Please don't insult me,' said Siddiq. 'You know I am a doctor.'

'Then let us not ask political questions!'

Hanif, Prim saw, was closely watching this painful argument between the toffs from Khartoum.

Siddiq said, 'Don't be naïve, Sherif. All health and all aid are political.'

'All I know is that I have guaranteed my results to the camp committee. If you are willing to do the same with the results of these few questions of yours, I might consider it.'

'You know I can't do that,' said Siddiq.

Prim intervened, 'I think you miss the point too, Dr Siddiq, that this survey is financed by Austfam, which is not a servant of Sudanese government intelligence.'

'God forbid,' said Siddiq, though she could not be sure it wasn't an ironic reply. He held his hands up in surrender. 'Look, let's discuss this again.'

'Let's not,' said Sherif.

Siddiq winked at Prim. 'Very well, I accept your position, maestro. Let's not.'

Sherif looked, frowning, at Prim, but still spoke to Siddiq. 'I hope you're being straight,' he said.

'What a thing to say to a maternal relative of the great Osman Digma, hero of our nation! "I hope you are being straight!" '

'I am sorry,' said Sherif, nearly inaudibly. He looked at Prim. He meant it for her too. 'Let us simply do good work.'

Sherif's nurses had at last arrived by the bus, which Erwit had met with the Austfam vehicle on the steep main road. Now Sherif arranged a dusk training session to the east of Nuara's clinic for the entire group, including Siddiq. Before beginning the questionnaire with a particular man or woman, it was important that the interviewers explain the reasons for the survey, stress the need for frankness, assure the subjects that the interviewers were working with the camp committee, and that the result, without names attached, would be made known to the committee, and would be published independently of the government. People far away, in Australia, had provided the money for these questions to be asked, and indeed, for the arm measurements of the camp's children to be randomly taken by the nurses.

When the three interviewing teams went to a household, it was the head of the household who was to be the person interviewed, whether man or woman. If both man and wife were present, both might answer, although a man could be expected to insist on answering the questions on his wife's behalf. If there were no adults present in a given hessian habitation, the interviewer was to go to the next one.

The reliability of data, said Sherif, might be affected by the reluctance of people to talk about births and deaths of young children for fear that such deaths had resulted from the evil eye or sorcery, and to speak of such things was to invite them to occur again. But the interviewers must be gently persistent. The figures – birth and death – would represent trends, and could be compared with figures for other camps and the general population, and the comparison would be significant for suggesting the sort of action which should be taken in Alingaz. For instance, a low crude birth rate, said Sherif, was infallibly associated with a lower fertility rate because of malnutrition.

'Ah,' said Dr Siddiq, smiling. 'At last we get to our friend Hanif.'

'Not necessarily,' said the terse and unfamiliar Sherif. 'They may have come here malnourished.'

Erwit, Dr Siddiq, Prim and the two nurses from Khartoum watched Sherif administer the questionnaire to Nuara, who tried to reproduce the answers her experience taught her to be normal amongst the Nuba. Ages and sex of family members, tribe, place of origin? Had any family members received any education? It was a matter on which, said both Sherif and Nuara, the Nuba were likely to be frank. They were not like European autodidacts who made up fictional university degrees for themselves. Then, occupation in the Nuba Hills – pastoralist? farmer? other?

Other skills? I have no other skills, said Nuara, in her role as a Nuba paterfamilias. I had cattle and they are gone. I grew millet and it is gone. Here, Sherif told the team, you must probe. There are always other skills, if not in the man then in his wife, who may not think of a capacity to produce handicrafts as a skill. But handicrafts from the far-off Nuba Hills would have great novelty value in the *souk* at Erkowit or Sinkat or Port Sudan.

So they got to question 32, a controversial one for Muslims. Would you be interested in introducing other subjects – maths, Arabic, health care, gardening – to the Koranic school, if there is one in Alingaz? Was anyone in the camp talking of starting a conventional non-Koranic school? If one was started, would you let your sons and daughters attend?

Would you return to the Nuba Hills if the war ended? Sherif asked Nuara in her role as a Nuba. Siddiq had a little indulgent chuckle at this, as if the answer were obvious.

And so the teams were drawn up – Erwit and Nuara; Prim and Nawal, one of the nurses; Siddiq and the second nurse. Sherif would oversee the process, but join Prim's group whenever he could to add male gravitas to the questioning. Interviews would take place chiefly in the mornings, from six o'clock onwards, but if necessary two of the teams could work at dusk. In the mid-to-late afternoons Prim and Sherif would collate the results as they came in, and keep a running score on death and birth rates.

On Prim's fifth day in Alingaz, the questioning began. Prim and Nawal, a sturdy, self-certain person rather in the mould of Nuara, entered houses in which the light through the hessian gave the air a tannin cast. The house furnishings consisted of bowls, and an enamel or plastic pitcher, a few glasses for tea, lengths of floral cloth which sometimes were the only beds, and sometimes a palliasse of straw. Prim and Nawal were at some predictable disadvantage interviewing young, earnest fathers of families, though Nawal's air of authority moderated that.

Over a number of days, and in retrospect, the answers of all these randomly chosen interviewees started to blur. The person whom Prim would remember best was a woman who had lost a leg and was raising

three young children alone in her dingy tent of hessian. Despite her muti-
lation, which had occurred as a result of some sort of cattle raid, perhaps
by the Beggarah militia, perhaps by rebels – the details were hard to
elucidate – she moved agilely about her house, sometimes using a crutch,
in which case she moved at lightning speed to the fireplace at which she
cooked outside her door. Her name was Wariba. She wore the ring of
her lost marriage in her right nostril, her hair was tightly dressed in the
Nuba manner, the rims of her ears were marked by yellow and red beads,
and a three-year-old son was asleep at her breast. The points of her
cheeks were marked with a triangle of scars, forked at the end. Her lost
leg disqualified her, she knew, as a future desirable bride.

When Prim worked at her laptop in the late afternoons, the morning's
uncollated harvest of questionnaires by her under one of Alingaz's
numerous red stones, it was Wariba she thought of, and it was in her
name that the majority of responses seemed to resonate.

There were not enough wells, Wariba had forthrightly told Prim and
the nurse, Nawal. She had no choice but to send her children to fetch
water in a plastic container, attached to a strap which they carried across
their foreheads. There was a salty well at a *khor*, a watercourse, to the
south. There was an old well at a place called Girgir, but it was difficult
to climb into. Prim had seen such wells, holes in the ground, with the
water running below. A slim person might lower herself and stand on a
subterranean stone from which a plastic container might be filled and
passed up to others on the surface. An occasional water truck came from
Port Sudan and sold water.

In the meantime Wariba was all for a school, but there was no money
to pay teachers. If we go to the villages like Erkowit or Barimeiya, she
said, and try to trade a little of our rations for others things – medicines
or clothes or sugar or kindling – the storekeepers take too much of our
rations for too little of what we seek. So we need a store too, owned by
all, and fair.

Wariba was also one of the small number of women who said they
might be willing to take training from the Ministry of Health as traditional birth attendants. But her parents were dead, and so she would
have to find a friend to mind her children while she took her training.

Now that the survey had begun and was going well, the two nurses
from Khartoum spent their dusks visiting the homes of those already
interviewed to measure the arm circumferences of the children. The sandstorms having held off, Sherif was more composed. His playfulness

returned, and one evening he suggested an assignation with Prim at a
secluded rock shelf behind the food depot. He took a rug with him, and
when Prim arrived fell on her with a welcome hunger.

'I have been a bastard,' he told her. 'But I have been so anxious. I
thought Siddiq would get in the way. But I tell you – I would not say it
to him – this needs to be *specially* written up. This camp should not
exist. Saving people from themselves by dragging them to a harsh sector
and dumping them? I've read of it. This is the first time I've seen it.'

On a second evening visit to the rock platform, Prim and Sherif found
the area being used by young Nubas. The two of them lay very still at
each other's side, beneath the sharp points of innumerable stars, listening
to suppressed laughter from perhaps as close as twenty paces away. Prim
imagined the young couples who had also chosen the place as lovers
brought together by the great dislocation of their lives, embracing each
other perhaps across prohibited lines of family and clan. She had assured
herself in a kind of spiritual or emotional vanity that the attraction
between her and Sherif was somehow separate from the herdish need of
the majority. She had reacted badly when Dimp used such phrases as
'your African boyfriend'. But such a sense of exclusivity could not be
sustained on the rock platform above Hanif's compound.

The interviews had been running smoothly for ten days, with only the
intrusion of one mild but irksome sandstorm, when Prim, at the collapsible desk with the mass of that day's interviews held in place with a
red rock, found in one questionnaire a strange, unrelated sheet of paper.
Even with her green Arabic, she could recognise two of the typed
passages.

She passed it to Sherif, wondering if it was the right thing to do, if
his new equability could stand it.

'What is this?' she asked.

He read with a frown and then stared at her. 'I think you know what
this is,' he said. 'Tell me what you think it is.'

'It looks like the questions Siddiq wanted answered. I think he's asking
them.' She translated creakily from the Arabic. ' "Is it to your . . .?" No,
let me start again. "Do you know . . . of any members of illegal groups,
opposed to the government of Sudan, operating in Alingaz? Is it to you
that they come for money or help? Is it from you that they demand oaths
against the legal government of Sudan? Do you . . . do you know the

names of any members of these groups in alliance with the SPLA against the legal government of Sudan? Do you realise that I now ask politely, for I do not want you to suffer from ... harsher questions later?" '

She handed the page back to Sherif who tore it up.

'I must not go off half-cocked,' said Sherif, struggling with an impulse to go straight to Siddiq and have it out, only to find on reflection that he had gone to battle incapacitated and invalidated by anger. 'I must sleep on this. But I have to eat with, and smile at the bugger!'

'I have to also,' Prim told him. 'He's invited me for dinner tomorrow night.'

She had not normally eaten at Hanif's – she made a point of eating with Nuara and the two Sudanese nurses at the clinic. But Siddiq himself had insisted that she come and visit them at the food depot for conversation's sake – as he put it – the next night. She was now more than willing to go with Sherif; it might help take the edge off his just anger.

There was still the question of how Sherif would contain his fury for the moment. But he seemed to get through dinner in an exemplary manner, meeting her as planned at nine above the food depot, after credibly enough feigning tiredness.

At the end of the next morning's work, Sherif intercepted the nurse who made up a team with Siddiq as she returned towards the clinic with that day's sheaf of questionnaires. He asked might he look at the documents. He proved right in suspecting that a man of such background as Siddiq would depend upon the nurse to separate his intelligence questionnaire from Sherif's survey, and deliver them to him later. She had not yet done so, and Sherif found, amongst the completed questionnaires the woman was carrying, eight of Siddiq's sets of questions on rebel activities in Alingaz.

In late afternoon Sherif showed these pages to Prim as she began work on the collation of responses. He seemed preternaturally calm. 'These questions poison all the others,' he said as if it were a weather report. 'These eight families, and God knows how many others, are now telling everyone not to answer us, or if they do, to hedge and mislead. The man has completely destroyed the process!'

Prim touched his wrist, despite the risk of Nuara observing this intimacy. She was unable to say anything adequate, since he had worked so energetically to get here. Siddiq was guilty of the grossest violation.

'Remember,' she said when she could speak, 'you decided yesterday to wait until you were calm. You'll have to do the same today. I'm coming up to the depot for dinner. We'll just pretend the others aren't there.'

It was, of course, the wrong thing to say. 'Pretend?' he asked her, devoting some of his fury against Siddiq to her. 'It's easy for you and Austfam to write off an expensive survey. To say, bad luck, old fellow. Too much static. We'll go somewhere else next time. Let me tell you, this place could become the worst of all. Have you seen the latrines? Have you heard of cholera? How will Nuara cope against an epidemic, with her popgun arsenal of nice little pharmaceuticals? And our data is worthless. The world knows nothing of Alingaz, and will continue in ignorance because of bloody Siddiq and his funny bloody questions!' He nodded and stood by her little desk. His head sunk. 'He has made me an arm of government.'

Prim said lamely, 'It is a dreadful betrayal.'

'But I shall not be angry,' Sherif declared. 'I shall not give him the satisfaction. Tomorrow morning, we'll simply pull our personnel out. I'm sorry, Prim. I did not choose to waste Austfam's resources. But I am sure you agree we can't continue.'

'It would be an obscenity to go on,' she told him. 'I'll complain to the Ministry of Health. So will Austfam. This mixing of health surveys and intelligence should not have happened.'

Sherif looked weary and had closed his eyes. 'Let him turn up tomorrow morning, with his bright face, ready to set out on further deceit. And I'll tell him then. I am going, you are going, Erwit is going, and the two nurses. We are turning away in protest. I hope it will have some negative impact on his career, though I doubt it.'

He managed a grievous smile, which Prim returned.

'It will be hard at dinner,' he admitted. 'But I will do my best to behave.'

The hour came. The women emerged from their hessian shelters, talked and dressed each other's hair, and the children ran and chirruped as if occupiers of their own ground, their ancestral gardens. Prim switched off the laptop, packed away the questionnaires in a box kept in the clinic, and walked up the floor of the valley with Sherif to dinner in Hanif's compound.

At the table shared with Erwit, Sherif and Siddiq, Prim guided the conversation to safe and fatuous subjects. She spoke of Sydney and of coming to the Sudan, and of finally being made Austfam administrator.

Siddiq said, 'It seems strange to the Sudanese eye that they would leave a woman on her own in a difficult post.'

'Well, they're all difficult posts, aren't they?'

'What would you say the average person in your country knows about Africa?' asked Siddiq, quite pleasantly, wanting to be informed.

'Very little,' said Prim. 'Australia is a country on both the Pacific and Indian Oceans. But the only ocean it has any consciousness of is the Pacific. If you asked most Australians whether they shared an ocean with Africa, they would say no.'

'Amazing!' said Siddiq.

'I do not say they are not good people. They are very good people. They are paying for this enterprise, after all.'

She stopped there, fearful Sherif may be provoked in some way by her comment.

'But,' said Siddiq, laughing indulgently, 'They do not make your black natives very happy, I believe. A state is like a great family, too crowded to work properly. And yet it is also like a great underground serpent. It burrows its way towards the light.'

Sherif swallowed the tinned fish and pasta which was the standard fare of Hanif's establishment, and said nothing.

Siddiq fell back to talking about the English-style grammar school he and Sherif had attended in Almoradah, a fashionable part of Khartoum.

Sherif spoke only once. 'It is no use talking about *that* Sudan, my friend. That Sudan is gone. So many urbane people have been driven out.'

'But they will come back,' said Siddiq. 'They will come back once the foreign press stops maligning us, once we win in the South, and when the economy is on an even keel.'

Sherif laughed, perhaps a little too loudly. For all the years she had known him, Prim had never had to worry about this, that he might turn volatile at dinner parties. Yet there was something to laugh at in Dr Siddiq, who was fascinated rather than challenged by the contrast in his own life – of being trained as a little Englander, yet being a thorough, modern Sudanese, a Sudanese who could live under the regime of Omar Bashir and his *éminence grise*, el Turabi, head of the National Islamic Front. Siddiq was narrating some faintly derogatory school story about Sherif, when Sherif's mouth took on a severely vulpine look, a prelude, Prim assumed, to unmanaged fury. An instant later, hawking sounds arose from his mouth, and suddenly she, Siddiq and Erwit realised that he was choking. Erwit took the most immediate and effective action, dragging Sherif upright and applying a fair Eritrean imitation of the Heimlich manoeuvre. Sherif's breath drew in with a long and agonised gasp, as some pernicious clod of food was released from his mouth into the night.

But you have been so humiliated in front of Siddiq! Prim thought, feeling for him. Choking, the most demeaning of human experiences. Painfully, Sherif got his breath back. He stumbled to Hanif, who, not one of the dinner party, had risen in alarm from the place beyond the table where he sat listening to his short-wave radio.

'Where do you get red salmon, you bastard?' asked Sherif. 'Where do you get red salmon, you prick from Kassala?'

For it had been Hanif's red salmon, sold at a reasonable price to Siddiq, which they had been eating with their pasta.

Siddiq moved in closely to prevent Sherif from violence. 'He buys it with his wages, of course. Let him go!'

In fact, Sherif did let go of Hanif's shirt. 'Do you know what I suspect?' he asked Siddiq. 'I suspect that this fellow keeps two sets of books. He keeps a set of books in which the population of this camp is inaccurately represented! And then he keeps his real books in which it is accurately shown, the savings made are recorded, and similarly listed are the names of all those in nearby towns to whom he has sold ration cards.' Sherif turned on Hanif again. 'Where is your second set of books, you prick?'

Siddiq tried to restrain Sherif by the shoulders, and his efforts worked in a way, for Sherif now turned to him.

'And you, you son of a bitch! I said no supplementary questions! But you are using us as camouflage under which to grill the locals. Or are they locals? After all, they've been dragged from the Nuba Hills! What are they doing here? What is a man who boasts about the grammar school he went to doing twisting things here? How do you put the two sides of your soul together, you bastard?'

He delivered an open-handed slap to Dr Siddiq's cheek. The act seemed to create a silence which encompassed nature and the camp. But then Prim realised it did not exclude the noise of Hanif's short-wave radio.

'You,' said Sherif to Siddiq, 'have violated my trust. You have used me as a front. When I tell the people who really matter in Khartoum about you, do you know what you'll be seen as? You'll be seen, in the language of our grammar school, as a cad and a rotter! I'm withdrawing my team in the morning. You can face the people of Alingaz alone, asking your poisonous little questions. *Old bloody chap.*'

Siddiq sat down and considered Sherif.

'You won't have to withdraw your team,' he said. 'I've tolerated you to this point. But in view of this assault and your refusal to be co-operative, I'm withdrawing the support of the Ministry of Health. I have the power to do it. The power to cancel you. I haven't disgraced your inquiry. You have made mine trivial. Are you Sudanese? And is this not a time of extraordinary peril to us? These people have been moved here by necessities of state. That means nothing to you beside getting your results published in some elegant British or American journal. To hell with you, Sherif. You always were a poseur. I withdraw *your* permission. You cannot withdraw mine. You can go tomorrow at any hour of your choosing.'

In a very small voice, Sherif, who had by now realised that his choking fury had deprived him of any advantage, said, 'You are totally ... *totally* ... despicable!'

Siddiq laughed, stirred the remnants of his dinner, and murmured, 'Who sounds like a grammar school house master now?'

⤳

A MURDER OCCURS

Even in the midst of condolences, my brother Simon had not ceased writing to me inviting me to bring more stock across the alps for ultimate sale in Melbourne. But I clung to Bernard, convinced of her salutary nature both by what Aldread had told me and by the daily pabulum of her kindness and sensibility. I delayed in answering Simon's assurance, supported by some newspaper reports he sent me, that the Melbourne market had re-entered a period of boom and bubble, using the coming shearing season as my pretext. But when the shearing was complete, I chose not to take the wool to Sydney myself, leaving that task to Long and sending a letter to Barley which said, 'Give me at least 10 pence per pound and let it go at that!' I could not, for one thing, easily face the excessively sympathetic Barley, who called me 'dear fellow'.

Barley met my price, exceeded it by a ha'penny, and wrote to urge me to put hope in work and time, the two great reconcilers! He said he understood that my usual reluctance to taste the pleasures of Sydney had been fortified by events.

I trusted Long to bank my return on the wool and carry a bank draft back to Goulburn to buy more ewes. For whatever reason, he did all that impeccably, remarkably so given his limited capacity to read. Exact copies of every document were brought back to me. I hoped it was not that he did not despise me too much to stoop to steal from me. I hoped in fact he had forgiven me.

When Long presented these records to me, I said on impulse that now he had returned it was time to drove over the alps the 4000 sheep Simon had been calling for. We would take them to Simon, and he and his men would take them on to Melbourne with a lesser number of his own flock, which he was still building up. So Long and I selected stockmen and assessed the low chance of mountain storms, all as if nothing at all had befallen our brotherhood. I was not chiefly concerned about mere friendship anyhow. I was concerned as to whether I could find my breath away from Bernard.

The expedition was gathered. Felix, who had not been permitted to take the wool to Sydney in case the men encouraged him in bad habits, wanted to come, and was one of my stockmen. His full-blooded cousin Hector, of whom much had been expected, was still living with the nuns in Goulburn, and was believed at eleven years of age to be content to stay on there as a familiar of Mother Ignatius and hewer of all the kindling she and her sisters required. In that, as in the mind, Felix was the more daring.

I barely slept the night before we left. I felt unbalanced, and doubted I would be much use aboard my dear old Hobbes. I murmured, 'I would not drag you through that country, but if only you could come.'

'No,' Bernard told me. 'It is time you found your bravery again without me, and it will return to you once you make your own tracks.'

All night, penned close in to the homestead, we could hear the flocks protesting, as if they were aware that a hard journey would be required of them. Next morning, departing, I felt dismal and ill. It was no normal start-off, and in the saddle my breath proved so impaired I doubted I would reach the hills to the south-west. I engaged in last looks back at the homestead, which would be under the general protection of O'Dallow, whose outburst in the woolshed had been, I believed, immaterial to his general sobriety and reliable temper. I saw that O'Dallow's step-urchin Michael, the boy who had provided George with the opportunity for his last dear games on earth, ran barefoot and grandly free of all disease at the tail of the flock we were taking to Simon.

Her face bisected by light, Bernard had come onto the verandah late, not wanting to encourage that dependence which made me feel I might at any second crumple and fall from Hobbes's back. There was no sign from her, her mouth was closed. Near her, on a chair, sat Aldread, and from a great distance her lifted shoulders gave her a brittle look. There was a way that Long, departing, put a thumb to the rim of his hat, a signal of some extravagant gallantry in him. Oddly, sullenness would have been more welcome.

The further we went, the more confident I felt. This, our first day out, was most clement, and the natural exuberance of my surroundings, the valleys of boulders and forested ridges, eased me along.

We awoke in our blankets the next dawn to the annoyance of drizzle and low cloud. 'It will burn off,' Long promised me. Yet the sky remained low and vile all day, and the sheep moved amongst ghostly gums in vaporous air. We depended on our dogs to sniff out those who would lose themselves from the flanks and vanish from the flock. The afternoon turned freezing and snow was aching to fall on the steep hills over which we took the sheep. In that air we found an abandoned hut of patchy construction – Long surmised it might have been a place used sometimes by the absconders. I had a sense that he had all the time known where it was. We crowded in, more or less cosily, except for those who had the first shift with the flock. By a mutton-fat light Felix got out his trigonometry text and began studying, and I felt a sting of tears on my lashes. I had introduced him to Horace and geometry as if they were unmitigated goods, instead of traps for the young voyager. We stayed there that night, and as wind howled, we drew our possum-skin rugs close. I moved my blanket to a halfway point of the hut, so that I might be Felix's rampart. As I settled, I was aware of Long, close to me.

'They reckon Goldspink is over where we are pointed. In the region named Treloar's Suggan Buggan station. There that rascal sits!'

I could feel the urgency in Long. Maybe it was urgency for land, rather than grievance at Goldspink's deceits. Here was Long, with his soberness of character, that commixture of skill and sense, and his awareness that the land though immense was not infinite, and might be all taken up soon.

'I hope we would not need Goldspink's hospitality on the other side of the peaks,' I said.

He would not say though whether he wished the same or not.

We moved the sheep along in calm first light, south through a gradual but wooded and fairly gloomy pass. At nine o'clock, at the top of the pass, with a narrow high valley ahead of us, the snow came on as I had never seen it before. Even though from Nugan Ganway I could distantly see snow upon these mountains, I had considered it more decorative than dangerous. I was now astounded to see it blown into drifts amongst these trees. By noon my sheep waded to their chests, and the light turned the colour of a dirty pearl, and all was lost in it except the black dart of an occasional alarmed dog and the sight of Felix riding at my side. I could not give the order to return to the hut – it was likely my flock would perish there from cold. Our better hope was to keep them moving to the far side, where the wind should slacken and the snow ease.

But in the afternoon the snow increased and blinded us. All we could do was find each other in the stinging dimness of a failing day. Unsure where any of our stock were and with the dogs reduced to whimpering, we made a miserable little tent by draping our blankets artfully around some snow-choked scrub. Within this bivouac we lit a little fire. I now saw by its dim light that Felix was too thinly clothed. Long and I took turns loaning him our heavy coats, and an awful, scaldingly cold and profound darkness came on. I knew that tomorrow I would need to ride ahead of the flocks and get Felix to Goldspink's. I had looked on such an arrival as contemptible. Now I longed to see Treloar's despised overseer.

In the morning, in unabated blizzard, we managed to light a fire somehow. Felix said little but shivered and muttered incoherently. We fed him tea and cold damper, and then I set him on the saddle before me, encircling him with my arms.

'Are you still well?' I asked above the wind.

'Yes, Mr Bettany. You are too kind.'

I asked Long to accompany me, and left Clancy, Presscart and the other men to find any protection they could. I presumed my sheep would perish, but I was prepared to yield up this portion of my stock to such a hungry storm if Felix could be saved. Following Long, who after all knew this country no more competently than I but who had assumed command, I had to dismount and drag my Hobbes and Felix's horse Whitey along, with Felix tottering in the saddle. It struck me that perhaps Long was leading us eastwards, and from my own guilt, I could not remove from my mind a suspicion that he was not acting in good faith.

'Are we not travelling too easterly?' I shouted at him.

'Yes, yes,' he called back. 'That is the way of it. The way to the rivers down here.'

Felix slipped into an uneasy, prattling sleep. At last, as the light icily cleared, Long indicated the way downhill, through fallen trees near buried in snow. Ahead lay stockyards and a little hut by a snow-choked river.

We hammered on the door, and there suddenly was a somewhat aged Goldspink, who nonetheless behaved as if he had been expecting us. He told us where to put the horses. Seeing my arm around Felix, and Long behind me, he grinned. 'Old friends,' he said, and Long said, above the wind, 'Yes. If that's what you want. Old friends.'

We moved Felix, who only said, 'Don't push me too far since I'll break,' into the hut, where the fire raged. Goldspink was on his own, and seemed drunk or in a fever himself. 'You hold the boy tenderly,' he said as Long and I carried Felix towards the fire. 'People always thought he was your boy, you know, Bettany. He has the manners.'

'Don't be an insulting bastard!' Long told him, and conversation waned.

We had no strength for a dispute with Goldspink anyhow, and his few square feet were the only place for Felix, and indeed us, to be. So I wrapped Felix up in whatever rugs we could find and fed him tea, and I heard him whisper, 'So kind, so kind.' We ourselves ate mutton and damper ravenously, and made halting conversation with Goldspink. Then we wrapped ourselves in our rugs and were happy to sleep, though as the wind raged we wondered about those we had left behind in their small tabernacle of blankets by Clancy's wagon.

With Goldspink still sitting up drinking rum, Long murmured to me as we settled, 'It's a matter of wonder he doesn't ask us to pay for our meal now, in the event we perish by night.'

I felt desolate, eroded to a shiver of dry wood by the storm. I wanted, with the simplest and most utter hunger, to be with Bernard. The fire raged and the hut had sometimes a fevered, sometimes an icy atmosphere. In the morning I bought a little of Goldspink's store of rum, flour, sugar and beef, and packed my bags to take all this as relief to my men who might in their snowy isolation use some of these comforts. I would need to find them myself – not, I believed, a hard task but one which if I fulfilled it might help re-establish me as head of this droving enterprise and of where it had begun, Nugan Ganway. Thus, I fancied, I was beginning to think like a master, a boss, again.

I told Long, 'I am sure, Sean, you'd rather be friends with the gale than with present company.' This late-season blizzard had done wonders in making us companions.

'Yes, sir, but you must know I'll do my best to ignore the blackguard.'

And that was how, the snow not being too heavy on that side of the mountain, I set off back uphill on Hobbes, laden with the comfort of supplies, in snow still falling but under a sky which gave some promise of clearing from the west.

It is curious how quick is the way back from places arduously departed from in anxiety and under adverse winds. Nonetheless I found Clancy and the stockmen very worried, huddled together under their makeshift blanket tent and without a fire. The admirable Merino sheep, however, the majority of whom could have been expected to die, had everywhere struggled up out of the snow and were now trying to dig down into it with their hooves, searching for buried pasture.

Seeing me coming, Presscart yelled, 'We'll have you to pasture soon, darlings.'

We roused the living sheep from the drifts and shuffled them down the ridge in cold afternoon sunlight. My stockmen had been cheered by a pannikin of the rum I had brought with me, and Clancy began singing pleasantly in baritone. Some hundreds of my flock were left dead beneath the snow, but Presscart, who had an eye for estimating stock *en masse*, argued that as many as 3000 still hardily travelled with us. A clear night of no wind overtook us on a platform of patchy snow, where we slept comfortably beneath intense stars and by a huge fire.

When, next morning, we found Goldspink's place, we could perceive, from above and through the thicket of trees which surrounded the hut and stockyards, some not quite decipherable activity, a mixture of the mobile and the static. As we rode closer, the sheep gratefully descending into warmer air, it proved to be Long, digging a pit in the red and black soil of the yard. The earth moved easily, for a warm morning had softened it with melted snow.

A little closer and I was shocked that the work he was engaged in was the digging of a grave. Nearby, wrapped in wool sacks, a figure awaited interment. At the sight, the fragile security the journey had restored to me vanished utterly. I galloped downhill in a panic, and the sheep rushed behind me.

'Felix?' I cried, hauling myself off Hobbes's back.

'No sir, it's Goldspink, gone to hell.'

I released a breath and covered my face with my hands. 'How?' I asked. 'How gone to hell?'

'He has been hit about the head, again and again, I think. A whole number of times.'

Indeed I could see a bloody mess on the burlap which covered the head. Clancy arrived with the wagon, went to the shrouded mess, lifted the woolsacks and looked underneath at the corpse. 'Jesus. It's Goldspink transformed. He looks better.'

'Is Felix recovered?' I asked further.

Long stopped digging and looked uncomfortable. 'I fear he's gone, sir. With proper clothing this time – the big sheepskin coat he found here. I think you might find him at one of Goldspink's outer huts. I'm sure he's well. But frightened.'

Naturally, since he had a stunned but intimate association with what had happened, I brought him out of his dazed labour of grave-digging by insisting he tell me events in order.

As first light came on that morning, said Long, having been wakeful all night, he fell profoundly asleep. When he woke the hut was empty. He came outside and found Felix's horse, the mare Whitey, gone. Gold-spink, the night before, had mentioned that he needed to visit some of his out-station shepherds, to see how the hard weather had affected their flocks. Could it be believed that he and Felix had ridden off on the one horse to make this excursion? For Goldspink's big mare was still in the stockyard.

Long unhobbled and saddled his own horse and followed the tracks of Felix's horse where they led with fairly hectic directness north-east over a ground of grassland and rock in which no shrubs grew to confuse the issue. But he had not ridden more than two hundred yards when he found Goldspink lying dead at the base of a trunk, with his head beaten front and back repeatedly. A thick coachwood branch on the ground nearby seemed to have much blood on it, and it accounted for the injuries to the brow. But then the back of the head seemed, by the signs on the tree, to have been thudded repeatedly against the base of the trunk.

Covering the broken head with his possum-skin jacket, Long had spent some hours following Felix's tracks – there was no mistaking Long's avuncular concern for what might have befallen his protégé in terms of horsemanship, mine in terms of Horace. Losing the tracks at a stream full of snow-melt, he reassured himself that the boy, however appalled and stampeded at what he might have witnessed that morning, possessed the skills to reach shelter somewhere. He thus returned to bury Gold-spink's body, a task at which he was willing.

Long had been working at a pace, and during his recitation of this tale his face glistened with his cold sweat. He wanted to be off again, looking for Felix in a more considered way. I got Clancy and Presscart to take over the digging and took Long aside.

'Sean,' I told him, 'you must be calm.' Though he could have said, 'Nice talk from you!' he merely nodded.

'Are you telling me Felix witnessed this? Or that he *did* this?'

'God knows he is strong enough, sir. Or else Goldspink was at last jumped on by a tyrannised shepherd. It cannot have been natives, though they like the hardwood club. But it is not their season.'

'And ... forgive me ... you did not do it?'

'Oh,' he agreed softly, 'better me than Felix, that's certain. I *had* proposed to myself having a few deadly things out with him this morning. But you see, I did not get around to it.'

'But why would Felix do such a thing?'

'I couldn't start to surmise,' Long told me.

'And why did you drag Goldspink back here?'

'I put him on my horse. It wasn't the right thing to bury even such as him under a tree with the blood of his murder on it.'

'Look, Sean,' I said. 'there is no magistrate here. This is cisalpine New South Wales, and the only law is you and me and the other lads with us. In fairness to Treloar, the shepherds will need to be told. Treloar himself can be told. But it is all very confused. One of Treloar's stockmen may have stalked him and done it. Who, in Goulburn say, or in Sydney, can tell? Let's be calm, and find Felix.'

We inspected Goldspink again, and verified he was certainly dead. This man who had shown me Nugan Ganway, this ambiguous messenger of the gods, as I had once thought of him. He deserved the recitation of a psalm, for in guiding me to my country he had awarded me both a great earthly asset and a great earthly burden. I perversely gave him Psalm 10, which seemed to relate as much to the situation of the living as of the dead. 'Lord, thou hast heard the desire of the humble: thou wilt prepare their heart, thou wilt cause thine ear to hear: to judge the fatherless and the oppressed, that the man of the earth may no longer oppress.' No one seemed to find my choice curious.

After the burial I left the flock on Goldspink's (and thus Treloar's) home pasture in the care of two of my men, and the rest of us rode off behind Long, following the line he had taken that morning. From the far side, in country with great verticals of timber, we formed a long, sweeping line and called for Felix. But Felix did not answer, and Long was sure Felix was not there. He would surely have answered to my voice, Long fancied, and the bark of the dogs he loved.

We spent a further day searching for him, some of my men even scouring caves in escarpments to the east. Had anything bad befallen him, we believed, our dogs would surely run to the scent of his familiar blood. We found some high pasture huts of the kind generally occupied only in summer, but Felix was not sheltering in them. In the afternoon of the second day we gave it up and rode back as fast as we could to the flock at the Suggan Buggan River, Goldspink's place.

Long seemed to have his hopes restored by the very absence of Felix in the country we had scoured. 'He is fled home,' Long told me, 'and there we'll find him, drinking tea with Bernard.'

Returning to Goldspink's house we found it full of his shepherds – nine of them, drinking rum, using the death of their overseer as a pretext. They were not mourning. They were telling tales of Goldspink's favourite weapon of discipline, a knout of rope enclosing a shard of flint. One of them had a facial scar from it, and said merrily that Goldspink had nearly taken out his eye. Then there was the short-rationing, they told me. Goldspink liked to store up tea, flour, sugar and tobacco, so that he might have plenty to buy native women with in the summer.

I remembered Felix's mother. The absconders' misused woman? Or Goldspink's?

Now the question arose of what was to be done. I sent one of my stockmen, a reliable Scot from the Border country, the sort of rustic with a lifetime behind him of lonely rides in harsh climates, riding home alone, to give the news, see if Felix were there, and if not, search for him. Should he find the Port Phillip Pass blocked by snow and was concerned for his safety, he was to camp and wait for conditions to improve or for the rest of us to arrive.

I had no choice but to take my flock westwards towards my brother's, and we started out. I dreamed at night, in the camps in the middle of our flocks, that Felix presented himself with a small wound in his hand, which he presented to me for inspection, and rejoined an expedition in which snow and precipices were the only peril. Even in dreams I did not fear for him as one would fear for someone who abandoned a scene of violence in Van Diemen's Land or say, Nottingham. A killing so far beyond the Limits of Location was a killing beyond the purview of authority, even if it could be shown to be Felix's work. We would find him somewhere soon, and all he would need to be rescued from was the weight of maligned Goldspink's blood.

At my brother's Broken River station we did not even pause a night. The place looked comfortless, for Elizabeth had departed on her journey to England, taking my little niece with her. I had time for a quick meeting with my father, who though he looked balder and more crooked in the legs, retained a young man's briskness. 'You would not believe how the book prospers, Jonathan,' he assured me, then lowered his voice. 'Simon is a generous son, but too long a contact with one's father may become tiresome. I may visit you.' His eyes flashed. 'Simon has heard a rumour you console your solitary state with the companionship of a handsome felon. Eh, is it true?'

I stammered, and left him while he was still laughing.

We were all dismayed to find Felix had not returned to Nugan Ganway. That fact diminished the joy of my reunion with Bernard. How much freer, however, could affection be now that I had shown myself I could continue to exist outside her salutary presence. Since Long was particularly full of self-reproach, I needed to take the unusual role of comforter. He is not dead in the mountains, I assured Long. He may be in some town, sheltering with a clergyman.

Within the next day, my less-than-confident guess proved itself correct. A note arrived in the forenoon from the Reverend Paltinglass at Cooma Creek, brought by the sixteen-year-old son of the surveyor there. The note said simply, 'Bettany, Please come at your earliest chance. There is someone harbouring here who much wishes to see you.'

I knew at once who it was that was 'harbouring' there, and after telling Long I might have good news for him soon, I drove the phaeton out, waving broadly and like a man almost jubilant to Bernard.

The Cooma manse looked inviting in last light, and I suddenly found myself asking why I chose still to live in rough-hewn timber and beneath bark roofing. At some cost and with now and then a broken axle, things could be altered. We settlers in these outer regions kept to our slabs and our bark roofs in part as a protest – no one would say, from Westminster to Sydney, whether we had an absolute right to our habitation and the ground beneath it. We paid licences, but our title had not been finally confirmed. It was as if we chose to live in bush squalor in defiance of all those administrations, imperial and colonial, which would not once and for all say, 'This land is yours.' But what was lost by taking a chance of something more solid, and four-square, within which I might pursue with Bernard a new order of life? And if we lost it, by some shift of law – well, government would have a fight on their hands! I would not live any longer in a rawness which had outgrown its charms! It was in part the expectation of seeing Felix which made me dream of such things.

I knocked at the door, unflustered at the idea that Reverend Paltinglass might greet me ambiguously. There had been no 'Dear Bettany' in the note, only the curt 'Bettany'. Paltinglass came to the door himself, in his shirt sleeves.

'Come in, Bettany,' he told me.

'You have Felix?'

'He is a remarkable boy indeed,' was all Paltinglass would tell me, as if sinfulness had diminished my need of information. He took me straight away into a small front room. Here sat wide-eyed, fresh-cheeked Felix in a clean shirt provided for him by Paltinglass, and thumbing a bound volume of an illustrated paper with such an intense interest that he did not at first notice me come in. I had to say his name. When he heard me, his hands trembled.

'Felix, it is good to see you well,' I told him warmly. But still he said nothing. 'I didn't understand why you had to ride away and leave us. We would not have done you any harm at all.'

He stared into the darker corner of the room.

'I was not frightened as much of you, Mr Bettany,' he said. 'I was frightened of other things.'

Paltinglass said, 'The lad claims to have had a most extraordinary ride. Isn't that so, Felix?'

'Yes, sir.'

'Tell Mr Bettany.'

Felix seemed to feel no pride in the narration. 'I crossed a range to Bombala. And then again to Cooma Creek.'

'Perhaps you could tell me what it all means, Bettany,' the minister suggested. 'The boy said, when I asked him why he came to me: "Sanctuary".'

'Sanctuary?'

'Yes. In the mediaeval sense. But he would not tell me why he needed it.' Paltinglass seemed almost amused by that.

'Confession is not a rite of the Church of England, Mr Paltinglass,' I told the minister as amiably as I could. 'Would you mind if I spoke to Felix alone, sir?'

The priest nodded. I have this to say for him: he engaged in no play-acting about whether it was theologically or morally safe to leave Felix in the same room as me. I wanted him gone, however, not least because the loss of Goldspink had not and need not be advertised.

Paltinglass excused himself, and I was left with Felix, with that edginess, uncertainty and embarrassment in the air which I realised was always part of our conversation. From the day I had found him we had been friends, yet had never been easy with each other or comprehended each other's mind in any but the most superficial way. He had been a potential son to me, but I had kept him at a distance.

'You said you were frightened of other things. What things?'

Felix lowered his head. 'Why blood, sir, and the spirit I had let out into the air.'

I put a hand on his shoulder. 'Tell me, Felix. You don't need to be fearful. Did Goldspink try to attack you?'

'No,' he said, 'No.' His answer had an air about it as if he were saying, 'Do your best to ask a question which means something!'

'Did you strike him? Did you strike Goldspink? None would blame you. But surely, that's why you fled.'

'The policeman here in Cooma Creek took me in charge for stealing my horse. That's because I was black.'

'You didn't steal your horse. It was a horse I gave you.'

'Yes, but Mr Paltinglass set them right,' he said with a small smile. 'And once the policeman went, I cried sanctuary!'

'A man, and a boy, is entitled to protect himself,' I said. 'His blood and his gods tell him. You did not need to escape. You needed solely to present yourself to me and say what had happened. In any case, I don't think you have much to fear now. If Goldspink attacked you . . .'

He looked at me frankly. 'Sir, you say "attacked". You have said it over and over.'

'I know. I have reasons for that.'

'I was escaping Mr Long.'

That set me back. Then, 'Why try to escape dear old Long?'

'He was in an awful fury. I had never seen such a fury.'

'*Long?*'

'He was throwing huge stones in all directions. Whitey saw it and galloped off, whether I wanted or no.'

'But you must tell me,' I insisted. 'If I am to help, you must tell me. Who hurt Goldspink?'

'I hurt him,' said Felix, beginning to weep. 'I found the right branch and beat in his head.' He wept more, as I held his shoulder. At last, he gathered himself together and delivered a clear line of unaffected narration. 'I woke early, you see, Mr Bettany, and went out to talk to Whitey, since I felt much happier in her company. Goldspink came from the house, walking softly and said to me that he must talk to me and tell me a secret. He drew me away, and after we walked a little way, I said, "What is the secret, Mr Goldspink? I think we are out of Mr Long's earshot." And he said, "By heaven, you speak like the very scholar, son. That Bettany fellow takes the credit for you and, I believe, will show you off occasionally. People even think he is your father. But I shall tell you who is your father. I am your father, sonny. I am your father. I knew your mother. You come from me."'

The horror of that moment brought a pause, but by swallowing, Felix bravely did his best to shorten it.

'I remembered some things from my babyhood. I remembered it might be true. I beheld like an infant a blow he directed at my mother. Oh I remember my mother and our first meeting, Mr Bettany. I shall never forget those times.' He spoke like the veteran of wars, rather than a fourteen-year-old scholar. 'But I could not bear for him to say he was my father. I felt my heart trying to get out of my chest and my brain ... my brain ... I could not bear it. And I chose the right piece of fallen timber and struck him. I struck him many times, since I wanted to drive those words back into the earth.'

He howled now, and added as if to a roster of anguish, 'And why did you curse Mrs Bettany and your son? Why did you sing their deaths?'

This was the most awful question and I grasped his hands. 'I did not curse Mrs Bettany,' I assured him, though I could not assure myself.

He was full of sobs now, and it took a time to comfort him, holding him close. He should not have to occupy such a doomed world, a world of curses and anger. 'Please, Felix, I did not curse Mrs Bettany or George. George was my son.' By now, I was adding my tears to his.

'You punished Goldspink for what he had said?'

'I did.'

'With many blows?'

'With many.'

'You said Long was angry. Did he add blows?'

'No,' said Felix and coughed. He had got beyond his worst fit of woe now. He explained he had gone back to the hut in terror, chased by

Goldspink's howling spirit, and had saddled Whitey, for he knew he must be hanged . . .

'No, not you,' I assured him, but he brushed that away.

He was mounted on Whitey when Long came running out, grabbed his bridle, and started asking questions. 'I told him to let me go,' said Felix, 'and that I would be hanged.' That was when Long began throwing stones, not at Felix, but at things, and at the air, and cursing, saying, 'It was *my* task to punish that Goldspink. It was *my* task!'

The hullabaloo and stone-throwing disturbed Whitey, who darted away. 'When I had her back in control, I kept on the way, back up the mountain.'

'Why though?'

'Away from the mess! Away from it all! From Long's crankiness too. I wanted to be gone, sir! From that blood!' And now, though his lips kept moving, no further explanations came. Yet he had a level stare.

Long had lied even to me for the boy's sake. Long's story had been designed to create greater doubt about Goldspink's death than Felix had allowed me. To open up the chance of hands other than Felix's! Even in Long's lies there was a flinty honour.

I set in seriously to reassure Felix. I repeated that if ever it were necessary to swear to Goldspink's malice, many of us would do it. Long would do it as fast as I would. And no one knew anyhow. Some shepherd would bring the tale to Treloar, but Treloar would write it all off to some brawl in the trans-alpine bush, where men might be expected to perish unexpectedly. Sanctuary was a fine idea, but he did not need it. Etc., etc.

'You can come back with me,' I told him, 'and you and Long and I will not speak of this any more.'

'You have been very kind to me,' said Felix, looking away again. 'Everyone tells me so. Mrs Loosely, Mr Paltinglass . . .'

'You are a credit to your people,' I told him.

'But I wish to go elsewhere.'

I asked whatever for. Of course he was fourteen years. Fourteen-year-old wanderers were not utterly unknown in the towns, in the bush, or at sea. 'What will you do?'

'I would like to trade,' he said.

'That's very well, but in what? And you will need capital.'

'I shall get capital,' he said, 'from working on a ship.'

I asked as expected, what ship? Where would he trade?

'The outside world,' he said. He picked up the illustrated paper he had been reading and brought it to me. He pointed to a picture of a tropic harbour. The picture was entitled 'The Commercial Settlement of Singapore'. There was a further picture of the *temenggong*, the Sultan Tunku Hussein. 'You see there,' said Felix. 'A black man.'

'And here,' I said, so that he would not have too idyllic a view of the place, 'here is the British Resident and the officials of the East India Company having tea.'

'I might achieve a concession from the East India Company.'

'No,' I said. 'Sleep on the matter? Do you think you can sleep?'

He nodded. 'I feel happier.'

I told him I was happy at that.

He said, 'You stand between what I have done and me.' But that reflection brought on tears again.

'We shall sleep in the same room,' I promised.

We shared the same room, provided, in spite of my moral unsatisfactoriness, by kindly Paltinglass, and Felix seemed to be comfortable, and slept profoundly. In the morning I left him to his illustrated papers and his further studies of Singapore and other places and went for a walk throughout the town, its three longitudinal streets, its four latitudinal. In the early air, the plain timbers of the *Cooma Creek Courier* building still smelled of sap. The question I was dealing with was whether indeed Felix should return to Nugan Ganway. Surely no one would want to prosecute him over this, but he was so open in explaining his guilt that if any inquiries were made, it was clear he would do little to protect himself. I could return him to my hearth and his books and Bernard that very day, but was it as safe to do so as I had been telling him?

Returned to the manse, I found Long looking hollow-eyed and waiting by the gate. He must have risen at three o'clock to be here now, and he had just heard from young Mrs Paltinglass that I was out but expected back very soon.

'You must have some tea,' I said, greeting him. He said he had been offered it. Treloar, he went on urgently, was at Nugan Ganway, had arrived the previous evening and been very disappointed to find I was not there. One of the shepherds who had sat in Goldspink's rejoicing at the man's demise had ridden behind us and reported the death to Treloar. Treloar was determined that action must be taken. He had come to my place with a notary from Goulburn and two servants, and he intended to take affidavits from all his men at the Suggan Buggan River. He spoke to Long and half-suspected him. He said significantly, 'If my men might be hanged for removing the sable nuisances from the country, someone should certainly pay for the death of such a good servant.'

Bernard had made up the room for Treloar and the notary, said Long. And Long had left at an early hour to prevent Treloar, who was resting in preparation to ride forth into the mountains that day, from seeing his departure. Treloar's intention to see punishment had impelled dear Long across frosty hills.

'You must get him away, sir,' Long told me. 'Treloar has very firm ideas. If his concepts come to nothing, we can fetch the lad back.'

'Away? What is "away"?'

'If perhaps you had friends in England.'

'But the priest here, Paltinglass, has seen him. If we got him away, Paltinglass would know that.'

Long stood frowning and we took thought.

'Then,' Long told me in a harsh whisper, 'it must seem that he has fled us too. He did so down at Goldspink's, didn't he?'

I found a ten-shilling bank note in my pocket and gave it to him, telling him it was best he not come in now, but take refreshments at the Royal Hotel, a long brick and plaster public house in the town. He turned back to his horse. 'Tell the boy,' he said over his shoulder, 'that Sean Long says he'll be a great man.'

'Yes, indeed,' I said. 'If he can be saved now.'

'If he had only waited an hour or so,' said Long, 'I might have found the means to do it myself! Finish that murderous Goldspink is what I mean.'

'Oh Sean, you would know as well as I that these things are always the matter of an hour. It is the hours which determine how we travel through the years.'

He got into his saddle and said, 'That's exact right,' and rode away.

Paltinglass, at his breakfast table in the parlour, was nourishing himself to ride out to visit the sickbed of the wife of Treloar's new overseer at Mount Bulwa. This English convict woman had cried out, according to a message he had received, that the sins of her London girlhood sat on her heart and oppressed her breathing. That being so, he wondered if it would be necessary for Felix and myself to enjoy his 'sanctuary' – again he made it a pleasant joke – during the day.

He clearly did not want to ask me explicitly to leave, yet he would be embarrassed for his parishioners if the scandalous Bettany stayed in the house alone with his wife! The truth was that I did not want his parishioners to know I had even been there. He offered me food, his faith strong enough to accommodate the presence of a sinner. But his near-departure was very handy for my purposes. I found Felix in the kitchen drinking tea with Paltinglass's old servant, a woman named Amy. I dragged him away, with Amy crying in outrage, 'But the boy has not even eaten his breakfast, sir!'

I took him anyhow and had him gather his few things. When he came back from the room we had occupied, carrying only the greasy and stained coat he had inherited from Goldspink's hut, I told him to wait in the corridor at the back of the manse, then went to the stables and told the parson's convict groom to saddle Whitey and put my team in the shafts of the phaeton, and after that go inside, since Mr Paltinglass wanted to see him. When the man had shambled inside, frowning his way past Felix to answer his master's apparent inquiry, I rushed the boy outside to his horse. I told him to ride fast out of town. He was to speak to no one and wait for me where Cooma Creek met Middle Flat Creek, some fifteen miles north. If he saw people, he was to conceal himself and Whitey.

Felix mounted and went off on his own at a discreet canter which became a near-gallop as he passed the gate. He was still cautious though. He did not wish to attract any inquiries from constables. Going to the front of the manse where I had once celebrated George's birth, I was delighted to see him, across some fenced paddocks, safely veering north past the police magistrate's and Land Commissioner's offices, and disappearing at pace over the hill beyond the north of the little town.

Happily, and as I had half-hoped, the pleasant Paltinglass had forgotten he had not summoned his groom and indeed engaged him in conversation for at least ten minutes. Towards the end, I knocked, strolled into the parlour, and said casually, 'Excuse me, Mr Paltinglass. I must go. For some reason Felix has ridden off.'

'Your way?' asked Paltinglass. 'Or towards Goulburn?'

'The latter, I think. But I shall track him. I must thank you for your Christian kindness and tolerance, sir, and hope you will pass on my regards and appreciation to your splendid wife.'

'Yes, yes,' he said, standing, and ordering the groom, 'Stay there, stay there!' he followed me into the hall.

'Please don't trouble yourself. I shall go straight to my vehicle,' I told him.

'No,' he said, shaking his head. 'I wished to say –– my Heaven, I must be a failure as an Evangelical minister, since I still have great regard for you, Bettany.'

I thanked him, though the compliment was very mixed.

'I ask you as your pastor. Do you hope to marry this Bernard woman?'

'Yes,' I said.

He touched my sleeve in a kind of relief. 'I am no social arbiter, and I leave you to pay the social price. It is the moral price which is my concern.'

'Yes,' I said, 'I understand.' I wanted to be gone. I must meet with Felix and then trail him by a mile or two all the way to that paradisiacal stew of a town, Sydney, a supposed chase and a weary one, which would take me away from what I needed, Bernard and Nugan Ganway. As Barley would say, away from my rudder.

At our meeting place at the confluence of Cooma and Middle Flat Creeks, I was careful to instruct Felix that if stopped by constables, as might happen to a half-caste boy, he should speak quietly and reasonably to them, and should mention my name. If that failed, he should show them a letter I had written on paper I had begged from Mr Paltinglass. It advised whomsoever that he was carrying a message from me to Mr Barley. I did not like to embarrass Barley by invoking his name as a ploy, but in any case he would need to be asked to help me even more concretely than that.

On another sheet I wrote a note to Bernard, and sealed it, and as I set off after Felix, gave it to Long, who had just finished breakfast at the Royal. I had utter confidence in all parties to the arrangement – in Long, in Bernard, even in my flawed self. A half-embarrassed tone had until now, I saw, marked my discourse with Bernard. Bernard herself had that reserve as well. So I was suddenly determined to alter things with a very heated letter, which the time I had now spent away from Nugan Ganway and her gave me the authority to write.

My most remarkable and beloved Bernard,

I must go to Sydney for reasons to be explained, but regret each mile that stands between and intend to be back with you in an unprecedented time. Hard riding is justifiable for the sake of the company of so incomparable a companion. Until then, retain a fond memory of me, since your humble supplicant and lover lives for the kindness of your eyes.

I have asked good Sean to deliver this.

Your loving servant,
John Bettany

Felix had his bed-roll and would sleep at night on the edge of bullock-wagon camp sites along the Sydney road. There were, of course, risks in that – brawls, assaults, shouted insults from ticket-of-leave wagoners and drivers who, from within the standpoint of their own flawed blood, were often willing to find fault with the blood of others. These taunts would be hard for Felix to bear, now that it seemed that the improbable truth was that his blood was half Goldspink's, that half his cleverness flowed from the same tainted well. But I had to depend on Felix's wisdom and physique to protect him, and also on the rough fairness of the sort of convict represented by Long and O'Dallow, the kind of men who would inevitably cry, 'Leave the poor bloody boy alone!'

I stayed in inns, occasionally talking to the publicans about how hard I had travelled, and wondering had they seen a young, half-caste go by on a bold grey mare.

I had to change my team of horses at the town of Mittagong, renting new ones and leaving mine in stables there. A few of the grooms had sighted Felix and Whitey. In the warming air of early November, Felix rode in shirt sleeves, according to their fleeting memories, and 'looked a handsome nigger'.

'Did he steal from you, sir?' they asked.

Felix and I were at one stage so close that I believe I sighted him from the crest of a long, low hill beyond the Black Huts and outside Liverpool. I had by then been chasing and not-chasing him for a week. It was the last I saw of him for the moment. I had told him to take a room at the Seaman's Mission in George Street, to tell the good people who administered it that he intended to find a berth on a ship, and that he would like a bed in the coloured dormitory. There he would find himself surrounded by Malay, Kanaka and West Indian mariners and whalers, yet again I had no choice than to be confident in his reserve and aplomb.

Arrived in Sydney, I visited the Colonial Secretary's Office in urbane Macquarie Street, where some very handsome residences of three floors had been built to look down, over the government's broad botanical gardens, at Government House, the harbour, and the Sydney Heads. I consulted a number of Imperial Gazetteers, from which I discovered the names of the Senior British Resident in Singapore, Sir Baldric Thorsen; the Bishop of Singapore, the Most Reverend Edgar Hamer; and the Chief Agent of the East India Company, Cecil Plumley. At my hotel I wrote letters, as one Briton soliciting the services of another, recommending

Felix Bettany, my ward, to all these worthy gentlemen and (in case malaria had been unkind to them) their successors. I then asked a few people randomly had they seen a young man like Felix around the seamen's boarding houses of Woolloomooloo, and in the dusk drove out along the South Head Road, seeing the early lanterns of convict night-watchmen at a sandstone quarry and by a timber yard.

At Barley's splendid hearth, the nature of my recent loss was made bitingly apparent to me. The man stood by his mantelpiece, his wife sewing, and his ten-year-old daughter reading to both of them from Boswell's *An Account of Corsica*. By the door, a Scottish maid was listening, holding in her arms the utterly sleep-limp Barley son and heir. It had come to a pass where I reminded myself for consolation's sake he and his wife had lost a daughter in infancy. So he was no stranger to the breath of that great furnace.

'Do you have someone with you, Mr Bettany?' he asked me. 'Someone to take to kitchen.'

'No, I am on my own,' I assured him.

'Ah,' said Mrs Barley softly, 'have the Sydney radicals succeeded to the point of punishing such a pastoralist as you that you have not a servant left to yourself?'

'No, Mrs Barley, not yet. Mine are all scattered about the Maneroo, growing wealth for the Barleys.'

I said this with some urgency to lighten the tone, for I could see it forming in their throats to commiserate with me at my loss. I did not want them to, not least since they did not know that I had now been both lost and found. But Mr Barley came forward and laid a hand on my sheepskin coat.

'We prayed that you might have fortitude, my friend.'

'That is so,' Mrs Barley confirmed.

The girl child observed me sombrely with Boswell's book in her hands.

'Thank you,' I told the little family.

'Oh please, my friend take up a seat,' Barley urged me.

'I would like greatly to sit at the heart of your family,' I told him. 'But there are some matters ...'

'Of course,' he said, standing again at once. 'You didn't come up here out of your normal time, dear chap, just to see how well young Clara here is reading. No, of course, not even for such a wondrous performance!'

Mrs Barley and Clara laughed – there was a genuine amusement in both – and I thought what a fortunate man Barley was to be so admired by both a wife and a daughter.

Soon we were in his study. 'So, do you for once have time to visit my new Darling Harbour wool stores? I am out of dark woods, dear old Bettany, and into birdsong, absolute birdsong.'

'I would be more than happy to have a friend in absolute birdsong,' I told him, 'though by the appearance of tranquillity I just saw in your parlour, you are already there. In any case, I have come for a great favour I have no right to ask, dear Barley.'

'We are friends and partners.'

'But you may now hear things of me ... Not that the gossip of Nugan Ganway would be of much interest to Sydney-siders.'

'Sir,' said Barley, 'only gossip I will countenance concerning yourself is gossip from your own mouth. I feel, however, there is something I might do for you.'

I told him how I had met the brilliant Felix a decade past, and that I wished for sundry reasons to send him out of the colony. 'Thus,' I asked, 'do you have any of your ships in harbour at the moment?'

'I have charter contracts with two ships in port at the moment,' he said with a casual shrug, used to the habit of proprietorship. '*Hindustan* with wool for Britain, non-stop, in search of a Sydney to London record in fact, and a partial charter with *Goulburn*, which is for Liverpool by way of Singapore and the Cape.'

'If you were to authorise the captain of the *Goulburn* to be of service to me, I would be very grateful.'

'I could take you aboard *Goulburn* in the morning.'

'Better for your sake not to, Mr Barley. But an enthusiastic letter of reference and a request that I be offered any reasonable service would do as well.'

He said certainly, and wrote me an excellent introduction to a Captain Robert Parfitt. By then Barley's womenfolk had gone to bed and so I said goodbye to my friend and drove back to town. I sent a message to Felix Bettany, Seaman Apprentice, care of the Seaman's Mission, George Street, telling him to meet me at the Dockyard steps at six o'clock the next morning. I thought that surely the messenger boys of the Australia Hotel would not be sought out and questioned by a vengeful Treloar.

That night was consumed with longing and sadness. I had lost my son by blood and was about to lose my son by wardship. The pillow beneath my head seemed full of the threat of subsidence, of fragility, and not having slept at all in my room at the elegant Australia Hotel, I rose at four and read a *Sydney Herald* in the cold smoking room to pass the hour to dawn. I was at the Dockyard in my phaeton before five, went to the hut where the boatmen congregated, and reserved as mine an old man with one glaucous eye and a second which did not seem much better. At half-past five I saw Felix walking beneath quenched lamp posts from the direction of George Street. At the meeting place outside Cooma, I had given him money to buy some sea kit, and I was pleased to see he carried a canvas bag, wore boots and the sort of droopy hat favoured by fishermen.

I intercepted him when he was close, put my finger to my lips, and fetched my boatman, whom I hoped had enough eyesight to take us to the *Goulburn*, but not much more. We were away at once, as the sun came up in the mouth of the harbour. The *Goulburn* was moored off Milson's Point, and looked a well-made four-master of, I guessed, some 700 tons, larger than the old *Fortitude* on which Mother, Simon and myself came to join Father in Van Diemen's Land. Felix and I were soon ascending the ship's stairs. Captain Parfitt, a little mahogany-complexioned man in a straight-fronted naval coat which reached nearly to his knees, was on his quarter-deck, and watched Felix and myself climb aboard. A sailor in the well-deck greeted us and I begged to be allowed to present Captain Parfitt with Barley's letter. The seaman indicated a companionway.

'Wait here,' I told Felix, and climbed towards the captain, who watched me through bright, narrowed eyes.

I told the captain that I carried a letter from Mr Barley. Parfitt's entire demeanour altered and he now dropped at once the air of treating Felix and myself as intruders. He accepted the letter, and when he had read it, took off his cap and smoothed his streaked hair, still cocked from having recently risen.

'Mr Bettany, sir,' he said in a Lowland Scots accent not unlike that of Dr Alladair of Cooma, 'how may I serve you?'

'I have a very promising native boy, Felix, in my care. He wishes to go to Singapore, and perhaps later return. He is both a splendid scholar and a skilled horseman, and he wishes to add a maritime education to his admirable battery of skills. I would be grateful if you took him on as an apprentice steward or clerk.'

'Mr Bettany,' said the captain, 'you must understand I am due to sail

on this evening's tide and happen to have already signed a manservant-
cum-steward all the way through to London. Which doesn't mean of
course that he is more reliable than your – is it Felix? – than Felix there.
Could not your boy travel as a steerage passenger, and I and the mates
will happily teach him the names of shrouds, the setting of sails, the use
of the sextant and other mysteries, as well as setting him educative tasks?'

It was very cunning of the captain, I thought, to get me to pay for a
passage and at the same time acquire a servant for no cost. I wished that
Felix should be well-used and not left to idleness, chiefly because the
boy, haunted and lonely as he might be, would need the bodily and
intellectual distraction of a maritime life. I doubted the occasional attention the captain and his officers extended to a passenger, however
charming they might find him, would fill his day with benign activity.

A middle-aged woman of average height and wearing a black dress
appeared, drawing breath, at the railing amidships. She stared out across
the harbour water at the town, or as Sydney-siders liked to say, city,
where already the crisp sound of a good axeman at work could be heard,
and the sizzle of cross-saws rose from the maws of saw-pits. I saw her
notice Felix, and come up to him and begin speaking. She had the smile
which, it seemed to me, everyone brought to meetings with this boy. I
was cheered that Parfitt too would see that a warm conversation had
begun between Felix and the woman I presumed to be his wife.

'I would not want him to travel steerage, sir,' I said in a lowered voice,
like a man who wanted to reach an understanding with another worldly
fellow. 'Given that to travel steerage is to experience everything a sailor
does, but to learn nothing. It is apposite to my needs that he take up the
life of a mariner or find business ashore somewhere. It is *very* apposite.'

So of course I saw in his eyes that he took it that the boy was my son
by a native woman, and that my motive for finding him a career on the
broad sea was that he might not embarrass my white children.

I said, 'I would be willing to pay his wages as far as Singapore, where
he says he wishes to land.'

The middle-aged woman in the black dress was now leading Felix up
the companionway to join us. Parfitt turned his head and watched her.
But clearly, she did not need the permission others did to invade this
deck sacred to males.

In a very jolly Scots accent she sang, 'Captain Parfitt, have you met
this splendid boy? Of a very fetching hue, but he talks like a Lord Chan-
cellor, and when I asked him what he was doing here, why he says,

"Madam, I wish to learn a little of the sea"! Do tell me, is he going to sea with us?'

I knew that this woman was a kindly visitation and Parfitt glanced at me in a way which said, 'Our secret, old man! Women would not understand.' In the circumstances I was happy to remain under the suspicion of being Felix's begetter.

'Very well, Mr Bettany,' murmured the little captain, 'I will put him to task as an apprentice mariner if you will meet his upkeep. My wife takes delight in teaching reading to many young members of the crew.'

'She will not be put to the trouble, captain. This boy is a prodigy. He reads not only English, but Latin and Greek as well.' He half-smiled, disbelieving, and looked away into the top masts. 'Then, maybe, Sir, he can read to the good wife.' He called to his wife, who was already pointing out to Felix a vegetable garden on Blue's Point. 'He is joining us, my dear, as apprentice mariner.'

The woman beamed so maternally that I thought Felix stood the risk of being coddled.

'What shall I call him for now on the ship's books?' the captain asked me in a lowered voice. ' "Felix, an Australian Native?" '

It would be convenient for him to be so listed. Then authorities in Sydney could never be sure, if they inquired, who Felix the Native was.

Yet I could not see him so plainly entitled. 'I would like him called Felix Bettany, Captain.'

'You are fond of the lad,' observed Parfitt.

I was invited below, and the captain gave me tea in his little dining room, quite separate from the officers' mess. Prints were bolted to the walls, and tartan curtains framed the ports. After he had extracted £25 from me for Felix's tuition and upkeep, we discussed where Felix might bunk, and the captain said it should be in a little cuddy forward, with the ship's carpenter, a reliable man and a strong Presbyterian. Now we were joined by Mrs Parfitt and Felix. Mrs Parfitt, having conducted Felix throughout the ship, drank her tea thirstily. 'Oh, Felix is no deckhand,' she told us. 'He will read to us in the evenings!' He would also be the target of blows and resentment from other members of the crew, if she were not careful.

'Perhaps,' the captain agreed. 'But he must be put to toils as well. Mr Bettany wishes it so.'

I had a sense now of my time aboard aching to a close, and found it painful to behold in Felix's eyes both the fear I had encountered there ten years past, but along with it the intelligent willingness to attempt anything which did not seem fatal to other humans. I asked might I say goodbye to the boy on deck? I shook his hand in a corner under the quarter-deck.

'You have the money I gave you?' I asked him.

He said he did.

'The captain will keep it safe for you. He has a locked box for these purposes.'

He nodded politely, for he had heard me say all this two or three times before, at the pier, in the boat on the way.

Then he began spontaneously to weep. 'Is Goldspink my father?' he asked. 'Do I have that curse on me?'

His eyes had no childhood left in them, and it was apparent he feared himself a patricide.

With other deceits behind me, I was now accomplished at lies. 'Goldspink was not your father. Your father was Rowan, the absconder, who was shot some years back.' Better he should think his father had once tried to drown him than that he had broken his father's skull. 'In the most real sense of the term, I am your father. But now, I liberate you.' I put my hand on his head, as the Romans did, freeing a slave. Manumission. But it struck me he could never come back to this haunted land, or at least, not back to Nugan Ganway. I said, 'Here on this ship, and in Singapore, you will be free of evil dreams, Felix. You will be God's favoured child.'

He began clearing away his tears. I looked at his arms, made muscular on stock rides at Nugan Ganway.

Mrs Parfitt now emerged from the cabin, and came towards us, putting a hand on Felix's shoulder. 'The tears of setting sail,' she said. 'In my day I've wept a lake of them myself, laddie.' In that reliably banal way, she smoothed out the strange angles of our farewell and turned it into a normal departure. Soon I was back in my boat waving a farewell to Felix who stood at the midships rail. I was weeping myself, knowing I would never see a boy like this one again.

Yet I too had been somewhat freed by my endeavours in Felix's regard. I was able to feel an unclouded joy, rather than a plaintive hunger, in returning to Bernard.

WHILE PRIM WAS IN HESSIANTOWN, DIMP went to Singapore seeking funds.

What she called 'a report from the front' joined an earlier of her faxes in Prim's in-tray in the closed office in Khartoum.

I stayed at Raffles, more or less to honour Great-uncle Ernest who'd gone to dances there when he was an Australian army officer, before Singapore fell. Do you remember how Dad had a box of his postcards from Singapore.

Raffles was the showpiece in those days. Now it's full of Aussies in shirts and sandals, all screaming for a beer, and it's surrounded by glass towers in which a person is told to stay if she wants less quaint and more predictable service.

Remember that time we went through here as kids on the way to England, and we stayed in the flashest hotel – the Marco Polo was it? I forget.

Anyway I'd already called Sir Malik Bettany from Sydney, talked to his secretary, claimed our common ancestor, at least in the spiritual or patronage sense, and he called back and said he would be delighted to have a meeting with me. He had only a very faint Malay accent. I was conscious that I sounded a lot more like the average rough Aussie than he did a Tamil. He seemed so curious too, so anxious to see an Australian Bettany, that I thought he would be very sympathetic to the cause. I confessed on the phone I had a proposition for him. He would certainly be interested, I was sure, in his esteemed ancestor's history. He nominated his office, May 1, 4pm.

The great tower where Bettany's Bank and financial services is located is near the junction of Orchard and Tanglin Streets, which is apparently a pretty serious commercial address in Singapore. The building sits on columns, which the Singapore guidebook says is meant to imitate the stilts of a Malay village. The guidebook also says Tamils are modest people who aren't much involved in big wealth. But Sir Malik is the exception. The reception area has great blocks of marble, and makes pretty extensive reference to Singapore's races. There're Tang dynasty horses in an illuminated case, a golden Buddha ditto, teak panelling from the mainland, and behind the reception desk, a mural incorporating Sikhs, Muslims, British, Malays, Chinese, all doing industrious stuff.

I began to think that somehow I might have made a mistake coming. It looked so formal, it took itself so seriously, it lacked levity and it certainly lacked ambiguity. When I was taken into the man's office, my panic got worse! Sir Malik is a slight, ageless-looking man, with a sculptured, bony head and handsome feminine wrists and hands. He has a cherubic smile and looks like a fellow who thinks positive thoughts. A descendent of one Moth person and many Malays! I believed I could just about smell the spices on his delicate hands. Apparently his father, Felix's grandson, was shot dead in a frightful massacre of community leaders by the Japanese. This man would have been merely a child at the time. After the war Sir Malik's mother ran the business until the man I saw before me graduated from Oxford.

His desk was clear, and there was a solidity to everything. He was beautifully dressed, in a blue, pin-striped western suit. Behind him was a huge photograph of the archipelagos of the Singapore Straits. His front yard. He bowed and did not shake my hand. 'You are only the second Australian holder of the family name whom I have sighted. I remember, when I was a very small boy, about 1940, an Australian officer visited my father.'

That would have been Great-uncle Ernest.

Sir Malik said it had not been forgotten in his family, and did not go unmentioned by his great-grandfather, that Sir Felix Bettany's fortune derived from a generous £50 given in time of hardship and ignominy by our ancestor. Nor did the family try to gloss over the fact that a part of them was in the truest sense Australian. 'What sort of fellow would I be,' he asked me, 'if I did not affirm and celebrate Sir Felix and his startling gifts?'

This was a promising start. I told him about the film, describing it as an attempt to bring the tale of Sir Felix Bettany's youth, of his escape from imprisonment, of the justness of my Bettany ancestor and Sir Malik's, to the screen! The difficulty of raising funding at home, since people had a prejudice against nomads and the telling of tales of the obliteration of nomads! People did not want to be discomforted by that story, but I did not want to discomfort them. I told him I wanted to celebrate both worlds – the pastoral and the nomadic.

Sir Malik listened to all this earnestly, with his beautiful brown-blue hands on the desk before him, resting from his normal work and available for the new, the unimagined. By the time I finished talking, hope was thumping in my ears. It was not to be left thumping for long.

He told me with a frank little smile that the development sum I had mentioned was not large by the standard of his company's operations. But there were other considerations. He had certain misgivings. He said the impact of Western films upon the youth of Singapore and Malaysia was less than edifying. We have strict standards, he told me, and they are routinely violated by films from the West. He said that through travelling a great deal he was aware of what the fashionable call 'moral relativity'. But he believed that there were areas of the family tale better not depicted on film.

I wouldn't mention Sir Felix's first, Indian, wife, I assured him. Felix had had one, who died in childbirth, and the mention of her caused Sir Malik to flinch. I told him that the film, except for an endnote, would be made entirely in Australia.

But your great-grandfather, said Sir Malik Bettany, cohabited with a Jewish woman prisoner – so Sir Malik's father had been told by Great-Uncle Ernest, who must have known the family secret. Are we to see that? he asked.

Straight away, I knew he wasn't going to help me. He explained he'd just underwritten the manufacture of a new car engine for his Tamil brothers in Malaysia. He wasn't sure they would understand his investment in a film which portrayed scenes of nakedness. Both as a businessman and an individual servant of God he could not contemplate investing in such a thing unless he had the last word on all scenes in the film, and even then ...

It was hopeless. We made the politest small talk and I left. A secretary took me to the lift, and was amazed when I launched a surreptitious kick at the pompous marble panelling, while the lifts whispered their way up and down the height of this great marble pile, sighing like Sir Malik. The old bugger would not give me my £50 and hadn't looked after me the way Jonathan Bettany looked after Felix!

So I'll have to fall back on less conventional options. I have the problem of money, and the problem that Bren thinks my living alone is a stage, and will pass. I might be able to wrap up the two into one resolution. Anyhow, further details to come.

ALL THE WAY BACK TO KHARTOUM, on that tedious, hard road south to Kassala, Sherif seemed depressed and chastened. A clod of food lodged in a windpipe had taken his dignity away, betrayed him in front of

Siddiq. So Siddiq had been able to sack Sherif, instead of the reverse.

Arriving in the city he asked to be dropped at his house, and it was apparent he wanted to be alone. As he left the truck, he placed a hand on Prim's wrist. 'I do hope none of this rebounds on Austfam or you, my dear friend Prim.'

'It doesn't matter,' said Prim. 'Austfam will believe me.'

'One betrays oneself,' Sherif said dolorously, 'not in hours but in seconds. And in front of someone like Siddiq!'

She accompanied him into the garden in which she had first waited for a consultation with him. She kissed him goodbye inside his gate. 'Do you think,' she risked asking him, 'you might just give it all up and emigrate to England or the US?'

He said, 'I would like to, but I have a girl here, you know. And in any case, I doubt I would be given permission to board a plane.'

'You got angry with a pair of crooked officials, that's all,' said Prim. 'That's not a hanging offence. Certainly not with me.'

A ray of torchlight from the street struck the garden gate. It was the block's so-called 'Popular Police officer' – a retired policeman armed with a torch and cane. These patrollers the new regime had installed were all over the city now, policing behaviour and morality. They were admirers and supporters of el Turabi.

'I will see you back to the truck,' Sherif insisted.

Prim said no, since she wondered if he still had a predisposition to make scenes. But he would not be dissuaded and, speaking in a normal voice, led Prim out to the truck, opened the back door for her, let her climb aboard. The old volunteer policeman watched intently from the pavement, frowning at Sherif's suspect association with a bare-faced infidel woman. As Prim entered the back seat, Sherif went and stood on the pavement by the old man, taking up a mock filial posture. 'Good night Erwit, good night Primrose,' he called, in English. Together, he and the morals officer watched the truck pull away.

Prim slept soundly, though the dreams she remembered were scarcely peaceful. She dreamt she told Sherif a number of times, 'I am willing to become a citizen too.' But then she was full of fear for what might befall the children she might have by Sherif: a boy conscript in the Sudanese army in the South. An infibulated girl embarrassed by her white mother.

She woke just before office hours, refreshed but in a depressed state. She tried to call Sherif but there was no answer. Irregularities of telephone service were not unknown. She would call him at mid-morning.

She called throughout the day, and in late afternoon had Erwit drive her around to Sherif's. She had a key for the gate and for the house, which was locked up, and there was no answer to her ringing of the bell. She called the Omdurman Women's Hospital and the hospital in North Khartoum, and asked for him. Both matrons said he had not been in.

Next, she called Helene Codderby. Had Helene heard anything? Helene went, at Prim's request, to the magistrates' court to look at the list of people presently on charges. Had Sherif got disconsolately drunk, and been arrested, and did he now face flogging?

Helene called back. There was a shudder in her voice, but there often had been since Stoner's death. She had seen three women protesters from a mothers anti-war group sentenced to flogging for prostitution, and the birching occurred right there in court, with only the lean, brown backs exposed under the rotating electric ceiling fans. 'It's reached a pretty bloody pass,' said Helene, disappointed Sudanese patriot that she was, 'when the only terms on which a woman can show her back in public is to be flogged.'

But there was no Dr Sherif Taha on the court list. Helene had also called the el Rahzis to see if the professor could check the police stations. He had done it, said Helene, even checked the morgue. But he had no news either.

Throughout the following night, Prim rang Sherif's number at all hours, and went again to his home at breakfast time. It was still locked. She let herself in. All looked normal, though with that wistful look of abandoned objects. The horrifying off-chance that his body might be there, that there might have been some sudden aneurism, was dispensed with. So was the chance that he might have been held by the police for some misdemeanour and then allowed back home.

Later, Helene called her again.

'Remember Sherif's school friend, el Dhouma? He's senior counsel to el Turabi now, and likes to think of himself as the acceptable face of Islamic radicalism. But he's not a bad guy. You could maybe ask him to see if Sherif's . . . well, in the system somewhere.'

Helene gave her the number. Prim called and haltingly asked the secretary could she speak to Dr el Dhouma. She cursed herself that her Arabic was least viable when she most needed it. Dr el Dhouma would be free in an hour, the secretary said. She waited an hour and called again, and then again, and at last, in late afternoon, when the ministry was cranking itself up for business after the torrid hours, she was surprised to have a call directly from el Dhouma himself.

'Miss Bettany,' he said in a courtly and apparently delighted voice. 'There has been some remarkable water passed under remarkable bridges since I last saw you.'

'Yes,' said Prim, less capable of urbanity because she was frightened for Sherif. 'I called you because your clients are now so crucially placed. The security system is in their hands.'

'And very competent hands they are, despite some recent slanders in the international press.'

If it had been a cocktail party, she might have mentioned the female protesters Helene had seen in the magistrates' court.

'I wondered if you knew anything of your school friend, Dr Sherif Taha? I was working with him in the Red Sea Hills on a health survey, and I haven't been able to find him since we returned two nights ago. I've had a friend check the magistrates' lists and another check the police stations.'

'Ah yes, I suppose that would have been el Rahzi, generous fellow that he is. His friends always have him ringing around the police stations these days.'

'I thought that you might be able to find out if anything has happened to Dr Taha? If, for example, he is somewhere in the legal process . . .'

'Do you suspect he is?'

'No. There's no reason he should be.' But she thought then a little information might help el Dhouma. 'He was part of a health survey team funded by Austfam which was ordered away from the refugee camp named Alingaz by an official of the ministry. But he had done nothing illegal.'

'Who ordered him away?'

'Another old friend. Dr Siddiq.'

'But Siddiq's with the Ministry of War.'

'The events were confused,' Prim admitted.

'You realise I am simply a counsellor, don't you? I would be delighted to find out what I can. But he may simply have gone somewhere for a rest.'

'Austfam and Dr Sherif work together. He would have told me. I would be very grateful if you could let me know anything, anything at all. He may, for example, need a lawyer.'

There was another stricken night, during which she had leisure to torment herself with the idea that had Sherif not known her, he might now be safe. She had ample time to talk on the phone to Helene, and inform Peter Whitloaf that Sherif was missing, and urge him as head of Austfam to begin making his own inquiries with the Sudanese Ministry of Justice.

When he called Prim at mid-morning, El Dhouma was not nearly so chummy as he had been the previous afternoon.

'Your friend has indeed been taken into custody by the security forces.'

'On what charge?'

'Under emergency regulations of the *National Security Act* and on summary charges of placing the government of the Sudan in contempt.'

There came instantly to Prim an image of the el Kober gaol, with its vast walls of ochre adobe and its high watchtowers. Whenever she had driven past it, it seemed to exude a malign promise of torrid confinement.

'Does he have a lawyer?' she asked. 'I must get him one.'

'A lawyer can't help him very much,' said el Dhouma. 'He's not standing trial, not yet anyhow. He is being detained, that's all. So there's no need for you to go running about the city.'

'But where is he?'

'I'm not certain. In some detention house or other.'

'You mean, a ghost house?' It was a term which had come to be used for unofficial and unregistered houses of detention, where the security people could do their work far from supervision. It was said the army men of the Revolutionary Command Council and el Turabi's security officials had got the idea from Pinochet of Chile.

' "Ghost house" is a ridiculous piece of Amnesty International jargon,' said el Dhouma, though he did not seem particularly annoyed.

'I won't argue with you,' said Prim. 'But can I see him?'

'The people I spoke to didn't seem to think he was in Khartoum. There was some story of his being detained in Port Sudan, or Kassala.'

She thought, Siddiq is in all this. Hence Port Sudan.

But there was nothing to grasp on. They had taken away her power to react with their inexact news – unspecified violations; unspecified detention centres; unspecified cities.

'Please,' she said, 'I have no trouble begging you. Should you hear anything more, call me. Any hour, day or night.'

'I would like to help you, Miss Bettany,' el Dhouma said. 'But you must understand you have not exactly been a pleasant guest of the republic. Could you be depended upon to behave within the spirit of any latitude the government might extend?'

'Of course,' she said, 'of course.' For there was no other source of help. If Sherif had taken the trouble while in Louisiana to become a US citizen – hundreds of thousands of other Africans had done so – she could appeal to the American Embassy. They went in to bat for US citizens. As it stood, she had nothing to hold over el Dhouma. 'If Sherif could be freed,' she said, 'you people can depend on my good manners.'

She set off before curfew to visit the el Rahzis, who seemed to her two rocks in a torrent of events. Led into the house by one of their Southern maids, she was alarmed to find the el Rahzis themselves in distress. The professor and Khalda had been comforting themselves with the standard medicine of sweet black tea.

Mrs el Rahzi rose with tear-stained eyes and embraced Prim. She asked, 'Sherif is still missing? Who could have grounds to arrest him? Even in this regime one has to think it's a mistake.'

'But you are not weeping for Sherif,' surmised Prim.

'No, it's Safi, our boy,' Khalda told her, sitting her down and pouring some tea. 'They came for him – the conscription people – a truckload of troops to conscript one boy. He violated his exemption when he was arrested. They've put him in the infantry, of course. He is in a special combat training camp near Wad Medani. No doubt they are telling him, as they tell farmers' sons, that all the loyally Islamic snakes of the South will fall from trees upon their enemies. No doubt they are intoning, "*Jihad!*", and promising him paradise should he tread on a mine.' And Mrs el Rahzi turned her head and began to weep quietly, regarded by her doleful husband.

'Did you speak to el Dhouma?' the professor asked Prim.

Prim said she had.

'Did he tell you where Sherif is?'

'No. He said it wasn't el Kober here in Khartoum. He said it might be Kassala or Port Sudan. Then he said a detention centre. I don't know where to look, or how to start.'

'I shall again talk to my tame policeman.' The professor had a former student who was a police captain. 'Wait with my wife, would you?' said the professor, and went out for his car keys. In the midst of his own anguish, he was going off to talk about Sherif. Perhaps it was a welcome distraction.

'Does your husband have any vices at all?' Prim asked Mrs el Rahzi after the professor left.

'Stubbornness,' said Mrs el Rahzi, 'but that means he is stubbornly faithful too. We could all make do with a little less of his determination.

Oh to be one of those families who know how to keep a low profile! That's the gift we should try to give all our children!'

'Safi won't be easily tyrannised by NCOs.'

Mrs el Rahzi's eyes filled with tears again. 'As long as that does not annoy them,' she said.

The professor was gone two hours, a period of time Prim and Mrs el Rahzi filled up by reiterating their chief concerns for their menfolk. At last the professor was back home, frowning.

'All I could find out is that he's in a house of detention. I'm sure my friend the captain doesn't know where. The way that system is run, it's hard to know. But I'd guess he's here in Khartoum. Why would they take him further? You take a criminal back to stand trial in the place the crime was committed. But this is not a crime. This is arrest on the basis of emergency powers. He has no charges to answer, except the charge of being himself.'

'El Dhouma put me in my place for using the term "ghost house",' said Prim, and began to cry in her powerlessness.

'Don't distress yourself, dear Prim,' said the professor. 'Why would they need to lay a hand on him?'

As well as her confusion, Prim was engorged with a fury which, for Sherif's sake, she must, by the second, minute and hour, swallow.

'Do you happen to know where any of these houses of detention are located?' Prim asked. She did not herself want to use the term "ghost house" any more. It was a description which hung heavy not only on the oppressors but on the victims too.

The professor looked at his wife. 'It doesn't serve any purpose knowing that.'

'But do you know?'

'There appears to be one in the old Khartoum City Bank building.'

'Right in the middle of town, near St James Circuit?'

It was barely a mile south-east of where they sat.

'Yes. The bank was bought by someone bigger and it moved out and ... You notice the windows have been whitewashed, the ones facing the street. The back windows have been wired over. It's unlikely he's there. But that's the point. No one knows. A fellow can't be extricated from any one ghost house by due process.'

'Jesus Christ,' said Prim. 'What a system!'

'You're quite right,' said Khalda. 'The totalitarian imagination is so fertile in absurdity.'

'Any other places?' Prim asked the professor.

'There's a boarded-up restaurant in North Khartoum,' said the professor. 'I forget its name though. And that's just a rumour.'

'Where's Connie Everdale when we need her?' Prim asked. 'If we could get her to fly up here and put Safi and Sherif aboard, she'd have them in Kenya in three hours.'

She saw the el Rahzis exchange glances, as if she had blundered upon a stratagem they had also thought of for Safi. An impulse of caution made her step back from pursuing that idea. But if it could be arranged, and if Sherif could be found, what a dazzling moment for them to ascend to neutral heavens under the care of Connie.

'I'll report Sherif's name to Amnesty International,' said Prim.

'A reasonable thing to do,' said the professor. 'Though you should perhaps wait a couple of days yet. Amnesty are not enthusiastic about people who have just recently vanished, and might be let go tomorrow. And ... their lists of missing are so crowded. I don't want to dampen your hopes, Primrose, but they will present his name to the government, and the government will say they don't know where he is, he is not on the records. That's what ghost houses are designed for. Deniability.'

The concept that Sherif's location and existence might be indefinitely denied panicked Prim. She rose. 'Look, forgive me, but I must go. I have to talk to Helene Codderby.'

'You are understandably enraged with us because we are Sudanese,' said Mrs el Rahzi, a tear breaking on the lower lid of one of her eyes.

'I will never be angry with you,' said Prim. 'You are two of the most noble souls I have ever met.'

She knew she should stay and comfort Khalda, but there was no time if she was to get to Helene's before the curfew.

Since Stoner's death, Helene Codderby had got, if anything, thinner. She had taken on a stoop too, and her old air of citizen-of-the-Sudan had vanished. She had almost become tentative, though her reports for the BBC African news still read well.

It happened there were four ghost houses she knew of in Khartoum alone. One was in the old Khartoum City Bank building – the professor had been right about that. Another was located in the Fashoda Restaurant in North Khartoum. There a number of amplifiers projected music into the street, so that the place seemed like a dance club. There was another house on the way to the airport in the New Extension, and a fourth on the northern edge of Omdurman. 'Not counting el Kober prison, which has its own interrogation centre.'

'Can we find out which one a particular person is held in?'

'No. They even move them around. It's a system to confuse any well-meaning inquiries.'

'I can't even contact Amnesty tonight,' said Prim. 'They'll be closed, won't they?'

Helene said, 'Well, there are such a multitude of prisoners the world over, held in violation of their rights, that I read somewhere the London office has to be staffed twenty-four hours. Simply to deal with concerned parties, such as yourself. Would you like to use my telephone? I know the press man there. I have his number.'

Prim took the number and raced home before the curfew. As she drove, she began to curse herself for not accepting Helene's offer of her telephone. Blows might be landed on Sherif as she used up time on the road. She rushed into her office and called the London number directly. Only a year past she would have had to go through the exchange, where the government would have been able to employ people to listen to sensitive calls. Possibly, even in the awful condition of the Sudan, they could still afford it, though she suspected with direct dialling it might be more technologically difficult.

She got on to the duty press officer at Amnesty. It was a woman with a well-bred voice who was still new enough to treat incoming calls without boredom. Prim explained how her friend had evaporated, had not appeared on any police or court records. It had been informally confirmed that he had been arrested.

Prim must keep in contact, said the sympathetic woman. If by the end of the weekend Dr Sherif Taha had not reappeared, they would make an inquiry of the Sudanese government about his whereabouts. 'I'm sorry we have to wait so long,' said the woman. 'But they love making fools of us by releasing those we inquire about prematurely.'

'Give them the name prematurely! Get him released!'

'I can understand how you'd feel like that. But we have to think about what works for the mass of prisoners. So maintain contact, and we'll act in a few days time.'

Prim wanted to ask, 'How many times will he be beaten or shocked with electrodes by then?' But in a world full of nations in which so-called state security preyed on the citizenry, it was too banal a question which

even a woman as newly oppointed as this would have already answered
a number of times. Besides, a scheme had descended out of the air and
upon Prim, taking her up for once into tolerable air. It was a plan
contrary to her own welfare, contrary to the welfare or the standing of
Austfam, but she was certain it was good for Sherif.

'Just confirm one thing,' she asked the press officer. 'Your research
shows that it's better for the prisoner if you draw attention to the fact
he's being imprisoned. Isn't it so? Treatment then generally improves?
Because they, the captors I mean, know that we know?'

'That's right. That's why we get ordinary people to write letters to
governments, demanding the release or fair trial of this or that prisoner.'

The world must be full of such letters, thought Prim. They must be
thicker than snow.

'Then would it help my friend if I brought public attention to what's
happened to him? I mean, he'd be better treated.'

'There's . . . gosh, I couldn't swear to it. There's no absolute guarantee.
Just the same, it's what we've found.'

'Thank you. You've been very helpful.'

'But you will keep in touch?' asked the press officer. 'You won't take
any action likely to endanger yourself?'

'Of course not,' Prim said and hung up.

An impetus had grown in Prim as she had spoken to the press officer in
London. Her intentions solid within her, and with the comfort of coming
action, Prim did not mind as much the next crazy fax from Dimp. Instead
of being oppressed by news of her sister's extreme acts, she could read
about them now almost as if they were gossip. They had already wrought
any damage they could. Under the impact of Sherif's detention, they
possessed that degree of remoteness.

Bren, said Dimp, was gone for the moment, was off to his Chicago
office, and in his absence she had decided how the seeding money could
be got, decided that she was going to get it, and decided she was bloody
well entitled to it.

Did Prim remember one Binky Enright? Dimp asked. He had a gallery,
but he was also once very keen on Dimp. He had no objections when
she asked if she could use his number 2 van. 'Because, you see, I still
have the receipts for all the paintings I bought for Bren, and all of these
documents, including guarantees of authenticity, carry the measurements

of each painting, each Blackman and Williams, the Arthur Boyds, the two Sali Hermans, the huge light-filled Lloyd Rees, the five Sidney Nolans, the two Olsens.' Already she had a joinery at Woolloomooloo run up packing cases for her, which she collected and stored indoors overnight. The third step in her plan was the most audacious.

Dimp confessed that like Bettany she was somehow pleased when nature reflected her moral tonality. Thus she was gratified when, driving to Double Bay the next day, she saw a steely sky settle over the city. The harbour might all at once have been a dour loch in Scotland. The stealthy colour of the day was an aid to a stealthy wife. That's what she fancied anyhow. She knew by instinct Bren had not changed the alarm code at Woolarang, that he didn't have that particular degree of narrowness; a fellow of limits, but not as paranoid as some. He believed too she might one morning wake, get in her car, come back, punch in the code, make a cup of coffee in the kitchen and wait – reading the *Herald* and cured of all discontent – for him to get home.

Not living there any more showed Dimp as soon as she entered that Woolarang was a memorable house. And silent too. For it was the day off for the maid.

She wrote:

You remember, you come in through the loggia into a dining room, a bit overpowered by one painting from the Burke and Wills series, and another of the Ern Malley sequence, which Bren – God forgive me! – particularly likes. As a visitor now, I asked myself why I'd done it this way. Why the walls of a room built for egregious pleasure, for epicureanism, should be covered with the anguish of Australia's explorers and its equally lost venturers: poets? On most days of course the corners of the startled eyes of Burke and Wills – lost and dying in the merciless centre of Australia, poor bastards – weren't immune from the sparkle of the harbour. But they were today. They looked as if they knew they were about to be purloined and put in a crate. And the figures in the Arthur Boyds – the Aboriginals, brides, World War I diggers – had the fugitive look of children about to be sent to a boarding school from which they doubted Bren would have the will and affection to retrieve them. I spent a busy hour easing the first half-dozen into their crates.

By lunchtime she had got to the warehouse of another old friend, Tim Huxpeth, whom she'd had had a crush on when he played rugby for

Knox. He was now a famed broker of paintings. Dimp told Tim that her husband had business problems and wanted the paintings quickly capitalised. Tim and his staff started removing the first shipment from the back of the van, for he was used to the tale Dimp told him. If someone was going broke and wanted to liquidate paintings without letting the world know, or if a couple were splitting but didn't want to advertise the fact or have it turn up in the papers, he'd pay cash for paintings and retrieve the outlay and a percentage more through sale to his network of private clients. He liked to deal, but he was also willing to take a bit of a risk. Due to Bren's delusions about Dimp's possible return, there had been nothing in the press about the split-up of the D'Arcys. But it might not have stopped Tim if there had been.

On her second trip to Woolarang, Dimp fetched the insurance documents from the safe – all in her name.

She made three trips in under four hours, and left Bren all she thought he needed – a Grace Cossington Smith, a Margaret Preston he liked, and one Nolan, the Colin Lanceley – and a note for the maid saying that she had taken the other paintings for reframing. Tim had the works valued within a day. Before Bren returned to find his paintings gone, Dimp had received by express delivery a cheque somewhere in excess of $1 600 000.

Before you unleash judgement on your poor sister's head, let me say that this is all I want from the marriage, ever, and I solemnly assure you I'm willing to sign a settlement to that effect. Woolarang itself is worth $8 000 000. So he's getting off very, very cheaply. I've called the lean screenwriter, Hugo Ventriss, and put him on notice to start work for big bickies! All is movement. I know you won't approve, but necessity is necessity, and Bren will be better for this, not to mention

Your adoring sister,

Dimp.

I refuse to satisfy you with a starchy letter, Prim thought, too preoccupied in any case. Play with legalities if you wish! My love is in a real prison.

Seeing her sister's fax on her desk the morning after she had received it, she was ashamed of having read it, and tore it up.

I VISIT LONG, AND AM MYSELF VISITED

I drove gratefully and innocently past Cooma Creek without knowing that I was passing Sean Long by. My thoughts were now upon manifesting myself to Bernard as more than a dependent child. In late afternoon I splashed across the Murrumbidgee with the last light on my shoulder, a man whose sorrows had been amended to scale, whose anxieties could be appeased by hope, and whose promise had been retrieved. I saw that Michael O'Dallow, riding a waler bareback and without boots, was playing at annoying some sheep in the pasture below the notched hill which was once more for me the centre of things, the hill both of skulls and of resurrections. He spotted me and raced away to tell Bernard and his father. He would willingly unharness, rub down and stable my team, and I could walk straight into my homestead and repossess its spaces.

Alerted by Michael, Bernard stood before the house, her hands wrapped up in an apron. O'Dallow and Maggie were also out in the open to welcome me. I got down from the phaeton, grasped Bernard's arm briefly, and shook hands with O'Dallow. Bernard's welcome surprised me by being muted even by the standards of her reserved nature. She assessed my face, my rare willingness to be jolly and make happy plans, with a little dispassion.

'You have not heard about Sean?' she asked.

'Sean?' I asked. 'Sean Long?'

'He was arrested here by the police magistrate, Mr Bilson. Eight or so days back. Did you not read the papers, Mr Bettany?'

I had in a way been too blithe about returning, too wistful about Felix, to read much, though I now remembered that the innkeeper at Bredbo had looked at me a little strangely, as if gauging what I knew. He must have read something of the arrest in the *Goulburn Herald*.

'What did Bilson say the charges were?'

'Why it was murder,' said Bernard, distress in her eyes. 'The killing of Treloar's overseer. He had given me help, but I could not save him.'

'Sean is in the cells at Cooma Creek,' O'Dallow called. 'He awaits trial before a circuit judge. He would admire to see you, Mr Bettany. He would like to know whether you found that young fellow, Felix.'

I turned and told him earnestly I had not. I had barely found a soul who saw Felix pass. He nodded in a way which was either acceptance or belief, and said in his leaden, reliable voice, 'You should look Long over, sir. He might have an idea to hang and be done. He is of a peculiar mind, Mr Bettany.'

It was more than apparent they looked at me to save Long – Bernard, O'Dallow and Tume were all equally awaiting my word. I was aware of harbouring my first secret from Bernard.

'He shall have the best counsel,' I told them all. It would have to serve.

Bernard had few questions for me that night. Her attentions to me were if anything more tender, augmented by her concern for Long. Do you notice I am a new man? I wanted to ask her. But was I a new man, now that I was myself in a bewilderment over Long?

Late the next morning, Police Magistrate Bilson, a wiry little fellow, greeted me in his office in Cooma, in a manner to which I was getting used: sympathy combined with an air of inquiry which bordered on full-blown suspicion.

'The native boy who fled the manse?' he asked. 'Did you find him?'

When I said no, Bilson blinked and said, 'That is indeed a pity, since he may have witnessed the killing.'

'He was always sensitive to ghosts. The child, seeing a body, may have been put to flight in terror. He may also have had an irrational fear of punishment.'

'Well, he need not have feared that, since your overseer swears the boy did not commit the crime, as convenient as it would be for him to swear the boy did.'

'And what then does Long tell you?'

'He says he was not at the killing. He raises the idea that one of Treloar's stockmen did it. But there is no evidence of that. There is much evidence, however, of Long's abomination for Goldspink, and evidence of past threats. Treloar is frantic to convict him, and the Crown Prosecutor, Mr Cladder, is anxious for Long's head, to show the colonial Tories that a white overseer is worth as much as a native. The circuit judge, Justice Flense, however, is a native of Ulster and, though a Presbyterian elder, has shown himself lenient towards Pats like Long.'

Long, I soon found, occupied a quite spacious cell, one of three, in a free-standing stone building behind Bilson's courthouse. He was let out under the guard of a constable with a carbine, so that I could talk to him in the police office which made the fourth room of this cell block. Not for the first time in his life, Long wore bracelets attached by a chain to anklets. The constable led him companionably into the office, and sat him down at a broad table, bare except for a lantern, where Bilson had already asked me to take a seat. Sean managed to seat himself by landing sideways on the chair and then heaving his chained ankles under the table. The constable had a brand from the fire ready for him to relight his pipe. 'Thank you, Mr Hewitt,' Long told the man.

'Let Mr Bettany talk with Long,' Bilson told the constable, and waved him away through the door into the corridor by the cells, and himself walked out of the door to the yard and back to his office.

Sean Long craned his neck to look into the corridor and see if the constable was listening, was satisfied he was not, and then stubbed the light within the bulb of his pipe out with a great leathery wad of thumb.

'Mr Bettany,' he said softly.

'Oh my God, Sean, what are we to do?' I replied, slumping as if I were the prisoner. 'Is it safe to talk?'

'In careful tones, sir. Is the boy away?'

'I found it impossible to catch him,' I lied, knowing that I would never exceed or even recover my honour from this deceit.

'Then he is well out of it.'

'Sean,' I said, 'let us be honest men. You cannot be happy that Bernard turned her affections to me.'

'Well then,' he murmured, 'it would not be right to think she had ever turned them to me. What was I to do? Rant? Fight a duel? Life has taught me to be calm, since I suffered greatly for what was done in fury. She is your woman, sir. It's she who decided it.'

I was humbled by this dispassion. 'I mean to get you an excellent defence, Sean.' I lowered my voice further, and continued, 'You must, if necessary, throw suspicion on Felix. He is, after all, the perpetrator.'

'But the boy's life will be poisoned,' said Long. 'I shall swear that I was not the murderer, and Felix was not. I shall tell of all the murderous things said to me by Treloar's stockmen.'

'You must play it safe, Sean. To swear falsely on a Bible, and before a court – that could complicate your chances.'

'Oh, but I have the jump there, sir, since it has never been my Bible, nor has it ever been my court.'

'We must think hard about this. To save you, I would confess to what I had done in all this.'

'Oh that would be something of a folly, sir, after your trouble. Have you had enough of life? I have. I have had enough. I am composed, sir, I am reconciled, and trust my Saviour.'

I said he must not think like that, that his friends needed him, that I was his friend who needed him. I remembered I had brought him a gift, and I pulled from my pocket two quids of negro-head tobacco –

something to return him to a sense of the world of pleasures. 'Some extra supplies,' I said. Then I passed him too a flask of good rum. 'Enjoy them in expectation of your release from this place.'

He said, 'I am the man who lies in the sights of the musket. I fill the bill, you see. You may try to save me by destroying your life. But what's the purpose? I am already aboard my boat.'

I put my forehead in my hands. 'I shall return soon,' I promised, 'and see how you might be saved.'

He merely looked at me, and suddenly the constable was back.

To add to the already abounding disorder of my mind, there was a strange roan horse by the stockyards as I drove in on the afternoon of my meeting with Long, and a barefooted Aboriginal stockman in a kangaroo skin coat seated on the verandah with a pannikin of tea. I fancied I had seen this stockman at my brother Simon's, and now I thought, 'Oh God forbid it is Father.' Whoever had come it was a welcome stranger, since I could hear Aldread's lyrical yet strident laughter inside. Entering the house, I found my father and Aldread drinking tea by the fire, while Bernard occupied herself at the table trying to read Goldsmith's *The Vicar of Wakefield*. By keeping pace with Felix, she had become a reader, but I could tell by her eyes that she was concerned for my reaction to this arrival, and to the way my father and Aldread conducted themselves.

There was in the way my father now rose from his seat the over-eagerness of a man who is burning with some cracked-headed views of universal brotherhood, the same fevered enthusiasm I'd seen in him at Simon's place beyond the Port Phillip Gap.

'Ah,' he said, 'my son, my student, my friend. The women of this household have made me very welcome, while, I believe, your overseer is accused of murder. What an event!' He held up his rum pannikin. He had not been like this in Van Diemen's Land when I was a child, or if he was, I had never seen it.

'Would you have a spare stockman's hut for your old scribbler of a father? Somewhere I can lay my head and place my manuscript?'

'But you must stay in the house,' I said, yet feeling lost, for if he did he would know everything, and knowing everything, might take it as a licence to continue on his present drift.

To my ineffable relief, he said, 'No. It is not a good policy. I lasted only as long as I did at Simon's through my insistence on my own quarters.'

'Surely Simon has not ejected you, Father?'

'I am not liked by the lady of the house,' he told me, 'who – being Australian-born – found the climate of England oppressive and wanted her station back. The result is neither her fault nor mine. I must say in pure honesty that one cannot win over a woman if she is set against it.'

And he actually winked at Aldread, who was overcome by coughs of amusement.

'You would have always been welcome here, Father,' I said with too much enthusiasm.

'And there is the tragedy that your own dear wife is gone. Poor, poor child she was, by Bernard's account.'

'There was no justice in her death,' I found myself saying. But dear Phoebe deserved to be more thoroughly bewailed than I could manage in front of my father in his new, rabid state.

'There is never justice,' said my father. 'Hence, Stoicism! Join me perhaps,' he suggested, tapping his pannikin.

Through all this Aldread smiled broadly, a handkerchief not far from her thin lips.

'You could have my overseer's hut for the present,' I said. 'When he is acquitted, some other arrangement might be made.'

My father found this hilarious. 'If half humanity had their way, I should soon follow him,' he said. 'I would imagine a hanged man makes a jolly ghost.'

Bernard was crossing the room to bring rum to me. She did not drink herself, saying she hated it and had no head for it, as well as that it reminded her of people of less than solid character she had known. And so I found myself, sinner-with-sinner, invoking Bacchus with my father.

That evening, Father moved, as he had promised and without qualm, into Sean Long's hut. Young Michael O'Dallow was, over the coming days, attracted to his company by the blazing fire of eucalyptus boughs he kept roaring. I called on O'Dallow. 'Order Michael to stay away from my father's company,' I told him. 'I do not choose that he should succumb to spirits.'

O'Dallow nodded. He had become a safe man to talk to, and as sturdy and reliable as Long had been.

As summer came on, Father settled in. He would write his book each day from dawn until eleven o'clock. Then he would ride out for two hours, meeting my shepherds and conversing expansively with them. He ate a large meal prepared by Tume, slept, drank the dusk away, and frequently wrote again. Whenever I visited Long's hut I hated to see my father's pages of exact manuscript and their heretic ideas. If his prose were as disordered as his life, however, it must surely fail publication. His family would be delighted, but I wondered what next erratic level literary failure might drive him to.

It was in his favour that he liked to drink companionably rather than alone, and sometimes came to my homestead to be jolly in the late afternoon and to eat, according to his preference, a plain evening meal of soup, bread and cold mutton.

One evening I came in from a conference with O'Dallow to find my father and Aldread sitting by the fire with their hands linked. I looked to Bernard, who had a hunched and guilty appearance, as if she had not done enough to prevent this obscenity. My beaming father spoke.

'Since I am without companionship,' he told me, 'young Miss Aldread here has done me the honour of agreeing to be my companion, for bush purposes.'

Aldread, to give her credit, told me with an embarrassed smile, 'You must know that I am soon enough to die.'

'And I reply,' said my father, 'that she is not on her own in that.'

'Sarah, dear Sarah,' Aldread continued, 'knows that she is my truest and firmest friend, and has treated me with such kindness, as have you Mr Bettany. I would be pleased to stay in your house, a friend to both. But in this country a woman who lacks a man lacks all protection. Both Sarah and I have seen this, during our separate imprisonments.' Aldread kept her eyes on Sarah, wanting her permission.

Though I was not party to the licences which were being exchanged, I believe Bernard did not yield. 'You must make your own decision, Alice,' she said, 'in a lifetime in which the decisions have not always been fit ones. But you seem ever to need the company of a man.'

My father chuckled again. 'I am content to qualify under that simple heading. A man.'

'And so, it seems, I qualify too,' I said, as if obscurely challenging him.

Bernard now performed what I considered one of the most gracious of gestures. She held out her hand towards me, to reassure me. I had a value for her beyond simple headings. I was so temporarily delighted by this that I felt my world was restored to me despite all.

'You wish me then,' I asserted to my lunatic father, 'to condone a cohabitation of my father and an assigned convict woman while my very mother is still alive?'

'Your mother will always be your mother,' said my stoic, Horatian father. 'But I have divorced her in all valid senses except the civil, and the latter is the least important of all, a mere description, as Horace's republicanism was, for a time, a mere description. And if I have not divorced her, she has divorced me. And after all, I see my son has no aversion to an assigned convict.'

I could have strangled him.

'But my wife, I'm afraid, is dead. Yours – who faithfully followed you to a remote and barbarous port – lives, and in the civil and sacramental sense is still your wife. I cannot countenance this association you propose because of the hurt it would do her. You may have learned cleverness, Father, but she has always been somewhat warmer and wiser. She has possessed purity and fidelity.'

'I will not disabuse you on the question of purity, my boy,' he said in a reasonable tone. 'As for fidelity, it would be more highly prized if it was not so often the bedfellow of stupidity.'

'Epigrams don't save this situation. I intend to marry Bernard. You cannot marry Aldread.'

Bernard shifted in her seat.

'Does the young woman herself know this?' asked Father. 'Do you Bernard?'

'It has not been formally broached,' I told him. 'And it is not possible in the mourning period.'

'Yes,' he said. 'I see how you weep.' And he dared grin at Bernard.

I surprised myself by being almost numb to this insult.

'If word of your living with Aldread gets back to Van Diemen's Land, my mother will feel betrayed – not by you, for that has already happened – but by me. Her son.'

'It will get back quicker to her if young Miss Aldread and I were to find a little house in Cooma, I should think. I shall write to your mother and inform her of this new shift of fortune, and I shall tell her how you ably and eloquently protested for her sake. But the point now is, she has expelled me, and an outcome such as the one I propose should not astonish her. Consider this! If you cast your father out, where do I go, and how do I live? At heart, your mother would accept the force of such questions. She is a Philistine and a Pharisee, but she is not a fool.'

And to clinch his arguments he began to recite his Horace, part to me, part, no doubt, to impress Aldread.

> *Sin visum Veneri, cui placet imparis*
> *formas atque animos sub iuga aenea*
> *saevo mittere cum ioco.*

He was delighted with himself. 'Thus Venus's plan – she is pleased to put to her brass yoke pairs of bodies which make a good joke.'

I saw that Charlie Batchelor was right about the pernicious influence of the old Roman poet. But as if I could win this argument, I was quick to respond with another quotation, from the very next stanza of Ode 33. '*Cum peteret Venus* ... "When Venus sought me out with someone I remained with my freed woman, happily tethered, stormier though she may be than the waves of the Mediterranean battering the Calabrian coast."'

'Ah yes,' he said, applauding me. 'But you see, that's the problem. *Libertina*. Freed woman. I am a *libertinus*, a freed man. Your mother, on the other hand, is a *mulier libera*, a *free* woman. The line between free and bond ran through our marriage, and your mother, may I tell you, was not always as merciful as the Convict Department or the Governor of Van Diemen's Land.'

'You malign her!' I said. 'You malign her here at my fire!'

'No, I am merely making my case,' my father protested.

Bernard and Aldread looked amazed, as if they had stumbled into lines of battle in an unpredicted war.

But for Bernard's sake I would not sustain hostilities, and sank into weariness. 'You must make your choices, sir,' I told him. 'You are not a captive here.'

'And nor are you, my son,' said my father, his face bland, leached of all irony.

There was at this stage, Dimp could see from the documents Benedetto had given her, a final exchange of letters between Sarah Bernard and Alice Aldread, Sarah being too enraged to trust herself to converse with Alice.

Letter No 16, SARAH BERNARD

Thursday
Dearest Alice

I cannot pretend you have not made me look somewhat poor in Mr Jonathan Bettany's eyes. This is all the more so at a time when he is distressed about the vanished boy Felix and the arrest of Sean Long. In silent moments too I am aware I have kept the memory of Mrs Bettany very poorly. Sometimes it seemed to me I was saving the living Mr Bettany and saving myself too. But at other moments I see clearly and in pain how I have disgraced my friend Mrs Bettany. So do not think I wag my finger at you from on high. I wag my finger in the same pit in which we all live.

But in the same way as Long spoke for me I had spoken to the late good Mrs Bettany about you. When I did so I could not foresee or would not have prophesied that you would move so quickly towards living in the same hut as the older Mr Bettany. If you did it only for the sake of having a protector then you should have stayed in the house with me. I could be your protector enough.

It is not worth pretending otherwise but that your lack of thought in this makes an uneasy household and an uneasy station. In spite of all your grief in Parramatta I might not have opened my mouth for you had I known. And I am not sure you have grabbed happiness by grabbing old Mr Bettany.

I speak as your friend

Sarah

Friday
Sar

Well! What a sour old thing you have become since Mr Bettany looked kindly at you! But remember you are not yet Lady Muck of the New South Wales bush. In your letter to your friend Alice you seem to be girding yourself for that! I wonder will you next give sewing classes to us poorer reckless creatures?

We both know how things work in New South Wales and how women are used. I come here to find that you have taken to Mr Bettany not long after his wife was laid in the earth! You and I have been taught at length that a woman cannot find a place on earth and more so on this earth of New South Wales unless it is by grace of that poor creature known as

*A MAN. You bowed to that truth first Sar. I bowed to it only second.
Is the young Bettany a fine choice and the old Bettany an evil one? My
very illness disposes me for more tenderness and caress than I had in
your parlour over there in the bark palace. And does it not make good
sense that the older man suits me since a young man would outlive me
by too many years?*

*I am pleased to be here, Sar. I say it is your doing. But do not expect
me to say it on and on and on and to live solitary like a sick saint. That
is not my way. You play Miss Scowl and pretend it is your way but you
behave different. It is the old quarrel. We have – the two of us – each a
different manner for making our journey. But we end at the same point.
No more sermons sister Sar. And no more tracts. I have ever done what
fate and my blood asked of me. And so have you. But you make a solemn
play out of it.*

*Enough! I hope Long is not hanged. I hope Bettany marries you – old
Bettany will not marry me. But I am not your fallen woman to be snarled
at.*

And I am still by the way your friend and

Your Alice

THE DEFENCE LAWYER FOR LONG, MR HANDLER, arrived in Cooma
Creek at the end of what was for him an unprecedented and wearying
journey, some four days prior to the trial before Mr Justice Flense. When
I came to town to meet him on the eve of the trial, I found a man barely
older than myself. He had the same sort of dark handsomeness as Sarah
Bernard, but a glowing, forgiving amusement shone in his eyes. We sat
in a quiet parlour-cum-reading room, surrounded by racks of papers
from all over the British Empire, many of them months out of date.

I knew at once he suspected some sort of collusion between Long and
myself, but he was hard put to decide quite what it was.

He told me that since neither Long nor the native lad had battered
Goldspink to death, it must have been one of Treloar's stockmen. Did I
believe that?

'I was not present,' I said, looking away. 'But ... yes.'

'Now,' he said, his eyes glittering in that alien, incisive way, 'you
pursued the native boy Felix all the way to Sydney. Did you think he
was guilty?'

'I think he was frightened he might be thought so. I think he was in a panic over the malign spirit of Goldspink too.'

'When you searched for the boy, did you try to discover if he had stayed at any seamen's inns or dormitories?'

'I . . .' It was the trouble with lawyers. They were cunning always, and we poor pilgrims only sometimes; we were dabblers at archness. 'I had no need to.'

'Well, I had my clerk inquire, and we discovered that a young Australian native boy who gave his name as Felix stayed at the Seaman's Mission in George Street for three nights. One of the dormitory wardens told my clerk the boy was going to sea. There has been no other trace, and thus one presumes it is true.'

'I hope he survives the adventure,' I murmured.

'But, sir, the point is that if people such as yourself and Long are concerned with protecting him, your concern should be diminished by knowing that he appears to be safe away. So there would be little need for Long to sacrifice himself, if that is what he is doing.'

I said nothing, and he leaned forward and murmured, 'Think about it, Mr Bettany.'

I said, if Felix was at sea, I hoped he was well. But did he believe a boy of fourteen could have done such a murder? I said. 'If Long says he did not do it, and Treloar's stockmen say they did not do it, can it be proven either way?'

'Perhaps not,' Handler conceded. 'Yet I do not know how strong a case of circumstance Mr Cladder, the Crown Prosecutor, might make.'

I was in anguish, but instead of twitching, I called for some tea and, while waiting for it, shook my head as if genuinely amused. I asked flatly but with a thin smile, 'Am I to confess to this killing myself? Or that I know Felix to have done this, and to have helped him somehow to have escaped onto the ocean? Is that what is being suggested?'

I was hoping that cunning Handler would say, 'No, no. No one would claim that!' But he said nothing. His dark eyes lay on me, and his ear was cocked, as if he was open to just such a story as I had uttered.

At last he murmured, 'Long is a deep fellow.'

Thus I was deftly persuaded to ask another question, 'Could it be by any means suggested I had aided a witness, or perhaps a perpetrator, to escape?' The man, after all, was counsel, for whom I was paying.

Handler said, 'I am sure we could cast that story, if by any chance it happened to be true, in a way which stressed your honest motivation and innocence of the facts.'

'There will be no need,' I said.

It was the sole interview I had with Mr Handler before the hefty yet delicate-featured Justice Flense of the New South Wales Supreme Court opened the trial in the diminutive stone courthouse at Cooma Creek. I had left Bernard's protection before dawn to climb into my phaeton and get to the court when I saw my father emerge in flannel shirt and pants and boots, all inexactly put on, from Long's hut.

He stood by the side of the four-wheeler.

'I have been speaking with your man O'Dallow,' he said. 'It seems your friend Long is determined to be hanged. So O'Dallow says.'

'I fear it may be the case,' I confessed.

'I would like to observe this fellow, should he be hanged. It seems he is a true Stoic by nature, experience and conviction. Stoicism is, in the end, a religion of but one sacrament. Suicide!'

I was so disgusted I left without a word, and made that by now habitual journey to the town not sure with whom to be most angry – my cranky father, myself or Long. By nine o'clock in the courthouse, there was barely room for the spectators, who milled outside in the sun, most of whom had to wait with the witnesses waiting to be called. The bench, the jury (made up of townsmen and settlers from Braidwood, Michelago, Bredbo, as well as Cooma Creek), the counsel, and Long in the dock, took up two-thirds of the available space. Treloar, with his determined, grim demeanour, seemed to take up at least a tenth of the courtroom – he was not an abnormally large man, but he had an abnormally large fixity of purpose. I nodded to him like a man with nothing to be afraid of, as we stood for the entry to court of the judge. Treloar frowned intractably and bobbed his head curtly at me.

When Long was brought in, chained as on the day I spoke to him, and placed in the wooden dock, I could not for a time catch his eye. He stood while the murder charge was read, and to those who believed in his guilt he displayed a commanding indifference, supporting his right chained wrist with his left hand. Some seconds passed before he saw me. He nodded very economically, raised his hand a little and then extended his fingers and thumb, like a man calming someone else's outburst. But then of course I understood: though he did not know how cravenly I would cling to silence, it could only be inferred that he was absolving me from confessions and gestures.

I was nonetheless in predictable torment. To save him despite his wishes – that was what a true man should do. He pleaded 'Not guilty', which meant that the law would descend on him all the more severely if he were found guilty.

I was the first witness called by Mr Cladder, the small, flinty Crown Prosecutor. I took the oath on the Old Testament, but no sooner was it uttered than it seemed to fly away out of the courtroom's opened window, like a bird too elegant and flimsy to bear the hot breath of equivocators like me.

There is time for truth, I assured myself. I might confess to subterfuge in the midst of testimony, to save myself from perjury, an evil crime in man's eye, a worse in God's. I began by explaining the circumstances of the snow storm, and of how I returned to Goldspink's hut to find Long in the process of burying Goldspink. Cladder asked me did I believe the remains were being rushed underground, and I told him not at all, that Long was doing the right thing in view of the fact that we needed to move on *instanter* to my brother Simon's station. As it happened, Felix had fled the scene, and there were many of my stockmen who could tell the court what a desperate search we had for him.

Mr Cladder asked me whether Long at Goldspink's hut or Felix at the Reverend Paltinglass's manse had said they had killed Goldspink. Neither of them, I said.

He said, 'But wouldn't it be the first thing you asked the boy?'

'No,' I said, in faked outrage. 'The first thing I asked the boy was an inquiry after his health. Any other and he would have instantly fled.'

'And,' said Cladder, 'he is what? Fourteen. You could not stop a fourteen-year-old boy from fleeing?'

'I did not know he intended to flee,' I said. 'Having found him at last, I did not wish to do anything to make him take flight again.'

'When you first met Long . . . did he suggest who might be responsible for the murder?'

I inhaled for a moment and pushed on into my perjury. The world was the same unsatisfactory place on the far side of my lie. The air did not alter. There was no immediate vengeance, as I told Mr Cladder that Long thought it was definitely some attack by one of Goldspink's stockmen with a grievance.

'You did not,' said Cladder, 'report the matter of the killing when you returned to your station here, Nugan Ganway? Why was this?'

'I did not have time to report it either to the magistrate, Mr Bilson, or

Mr Treloar. I intended to inform both in due course.'

'In due course? How long is due course?'

I told him I had had long experience of reporting crimes to magistrates and being told that no action was possible. As it turned out, I had not been put to that trouble, since Treloar had been told by one of his stockmen who galloped through from Treloar's trans-alpine station, and Treloar had himself undertaken to pursue whomever was responsible.

Cladder now quizzed me on my chase of Felix, but I was inured, and survived that. Mr Justice Flense, humane-looking and of a scholarly beefiness, took serious notes of my prevarications, and continued to do so as Cladder sat and Mr Handler questioned me.

Handler asked me to affirm that I had intended to let the world know of Goldspink's death.

I so affirmed.

Then I was asked to relate the escape of Felix from Mr Paltinglass, and what I told Handler and the Creator was a necessary and total misrepresentation. Handler reiterated that a native youth named Felix had stayed at the Seaman's Mission in Sydney on certain nights. Could I swear to the court that I had not abetted him in this, or any other fugitive act? I assured the court I could, and did.

Next, Handler asked me for a summary of my relationship with Long. I praised his honesty, indeed his sense of honour, his competence and his loyalty. Then he asked me of my experience of Goldspink. I painted a less than complimentary picture of the man. But Cladder returned at the end of this process and asked me whether it was true that Goldspink had pointed out my run to me, my beloved station, and I had to admit he had.

Long nodded to me marginally as I left. If he still wanted my virtual silence, I had done nothing to thwart him. Yet he must have despised me in at least an abstract way for my evasions, for in saving Felix I was also saving myself. I left the stand a perjurer, but still hopeful that Long would be saved. I assured myself I would consider confessing to my perjury if by some obscene juridical shift he were found guilty.

I did not count on the number of witnesses Cladder had marshalled against Long. An interminable succession of Treloar's Mount Bulwa stockmen came forward to testify that Long had frequently uttered threats against Goldspink's life. They said he told them why, too. The absconder Rowan, before dying, had told Long in the Irish tongue that Goldspink was responsible for the death of Sister Catherine. As for Long's capacity for inhuman rage, a border police sergeant was called who testified that he had seen Long point-blank shoot the wounded absconder, Rowan, as he lay dying.

Mr Treloar was called after the noon recess. He had gone to the trouble of having his servants exhume Goldspink's body for transportation in a coffin to Cooma Creek, where Dr Alladair had inspected the skull. Cladder therefore called Dr Alladair, and asked him whether he thought the grievous damage inflicted on Goldspink could have been the work of a boy of no more than fourteen years. Alladair said that it was unlikely that Goldspink could have been overpowered by such a child. One blow could have been surreptitiously delivered, but Alladair believed it would not have brought instant unconsciousness and that against a boy, Goldspink would have made a successful riposte.

At the end of the day, I met Mr Handler and asked him what his assessment was. He thought the Crown case was even stronger than he had expected, but that it was largely an argument of circumstance and that he might be able to circumvent it.

'By the way,' he asked me, 'have you seen Mr Barley?'

My heart clenched. 'No,' I said. 'Mr Barley of Sydney?'

'Cladder has brought him in by subpoena. He is at the Royal.'

I walked back to the hotel with Handler, my legs quaking and threatening to give way. What could I do, plead with him to back up my perjury? I had always imagined Barley's visit as a scene of collegial joy, of his exclamations about the splendour of the country, not the squalor of its occupant.

Entering the Royal, I found Barley sitting in the lounge. 'My dear old friend,' he said. 'Who is this scoundrel Cladder? But at least it gave me a pretext, eh? What is happening? Is my good fellow Long standing trial?'

It was a splendid act. I ate dinner with him, and the act continued. Or was it innocence? I could barely remember precisely what I had asked and told him that night in Sydney.

We slept, and I rose ready for judgement to descend on me. At ten o'clock, Cladder swore Barley in, and I sat and flinched.

'Did Mr Bettany tell you why he travelled to Sydney almost immediately after returning to Nugan Ganway from the far side of the alps?'

'He was distressed, looking for a runaway half-caste boy for whose education he paid as a Christian,' said Barley, so brightly, so confident of being believed. 'But since he was in Sydney he took the opportunity to visit me and discuss my new wool stores at Darling Harbour, and other matters.'

Cladder asked him what the other matters may have been.

'Well, he seemed to think his ward might have hidden on one of ships in harbour. He asked me to write to a captain I knew, Parfitt, captain of *Goulburn*, asking him had he seen this lad.'

Was this a possible interpretation of my request for a letter to Captain Parfitt? It probably was, if one had an innocent belief in one's friend, as Barley seemed to have.

I sat in a dream as Cladder asked his questions, but when he finished and Handler rose I realised that the greater peril would arise from him.

He asked whether Barley had received the impression that I wanted to be introduced to Parfitt to remove a potentially guilty ward from the scene.

'Of course not,' said Barley. 'You have a very poor estimation of sort of man my friend Bettany is.'

And Barley was thanked, and left the stand, and I was left to wonder at how thoroughly lies could be reinforced out of the mouth of innocence.

That evening I promised Barley that he would make his first tour of Nugan Ganway the following day. When Handler was out of the room, he said, 'I know that you reside with a convict woman. I raise the matter merely in case of your discomfort.'

'That is not the least. My world has gone to hell, dear Barley. My mad father resides with me as well.'

We laughed together.

'My eye,' he said, 'my eye will be for landscape.'

I thought that God should ensure that every scoundrel and liar had a friend like Barley.

Barley admired Nugan Ganway, took my arrangement with Bernard as a given, and admired that splendid woman too. My father's confident assertion during the evening that Long was, besides himself, Nugan Ganway's only Stoic, brought frowns of bewilderment to Barley's brow.

Bernard set him up a comfortable bed on the ottoman, and when I came out early the following morning, he sat by the fire he had revived himself, with a blanket over his shoulders.

'Did you sleep well?' I asked him.

'I was conscious of being far from home,' he said. 'And even in another age – with this talk of noble suicide by Long. What will happen to your father's ideas if poor old Long is acquitted?'

I wanted to plead with him to bear with my chaotic household. But I realised that the day before he had told the Crown Prosecutor the truth as he knew it. He had simply begun from the innocent premise that in any dealings with him, I operated in terms of honour. His belief in me had coloured his testimony. Perhaps after a day at Nugan Ganway, he had begun to ask whether it should have.

So, as Long's trial entered a third day, Barley and I rode from out-station to out-station, looked at flocks and boulders, climbed ridges to enable him to exclaim on the splendour of the country. But sometimes he would look at his watch. He meant to be well on his way back to Cooma Creek and Sydney. He did not choose to be baffled into insomnia again by my father, nor to have his faith in what he had thought of me, and in what he had said in court, undermined by another night under my roof.

While Barley and I rode, O'Dallow had kept post at the court, and as Barley went north by carriage, O'Dallow passed him, coming home on horseback to Maggie Tume. O'Dallow reported, 'I don't believe they can in any way find the poor fellow guilty, even with Treloar roaring and cheering in the Cladder's ears.'

But I knew that O'Dallow's one trial, years ago in some Irish County Assizes, had not necessarily equipped him to be an expert on justice in New South Wales.

The next day, not wanting to betray grief or relief I sent Presscart to town to wait out the verdict. He came back after dark. It had taken till mid-afternoon, but the jury had found Sean Long guilty, and Justice Flense condemned him to hang subject to an appeal to His Excellency the Governor of New South Wales.

PRIM HAD THE FAX NUMBERS OF HELENE and various other journalists and stringers of the Western press around Khartoum. Overnight she contacted them, notifying them of a demonstration she intended to make, telling them to assemble as if informally at ten o'clock that morning one block north of the Hotel Rimini. The fax suited her in Helene's case, because she did not want to have to argue her intentions on the telephone.

In her mood of fiercely adhered-to purpose, she was equipped still to read and hear almost recreationally of Dimp's ruin or redemption in

Sydney. Dimp had recently given her a rare call. 'So you *are* back from that Hessian place,' she'd said. She had told Prim that in a few days Bren would return to Sydney from the United States. She had checked with his office. She was in a state of 'a little tension', knowing that Bren would walk into a house from which the hoarded art had been stripped. While he stood there shocked, she would have to call him and tell him flatly what she had done, and why.

Prim had wished her a slightly derisive good luck, and Dimp asked if anything was wrong. But Prim had not been able to bring herself to share the news of Sherif's disappearance. She had been able to share it with Amnesty. Why not her own sister?

In a fax sent the next day, Dimp had confessed herself consoled that Hugo Ventriss was at work on the screenplay – or if he wasn't, he bloody well should have been, after the advance he'd received. And then she passed on what she considered more solemn news. Drinking a glass of wine and in a fraught state, she had answered a knock on the door and, answering it, found Frank Benedetto. Dimp announced this as if it would greatly surprise Prim, which it did not.

It was the person I most wanted to see, all the more disarming for being in a suit slightly too small for him. I was delighted to see him looking as I've never seen him before. Harried. He had been sweating over something, and I got the musk of that, which I liked pretty much. I wanted him to come in and fill my little hutch with it. Always been one for the sweaty fellas! No, I shouldn't say that. It's flippancy, brought on by nervousness. I'm more scared of your judgements than of anyone else's on earth.

No, Prim had mentally promised her sister. No judgements today.

Benedetto had told Dimp he had taken delivery from Tim Huxpeth of an Arthur Boyd painting which he suspected used to be Dimp's. She was flattered he had used that form of words – 'used to be yours'. He'd tried to reach her at home, and one day the maid was in and said she was gone. Then he'd thought of Max, Hugo Ventriss's agent. She'd told Benedetto earlier that she wanted to use Ventriss as a writer, and Benedetto knew Max was Ventriss's agent. She'd told Max she'd rented the cottage as an office.

In the doorway of the cottage, Dimp and Benedetto discussed the painting. It was one of those Dimp had sold. She congratulated him on acquiring a lovely work. God, said Benedetto, I've behaved so crassly. He asked could he come in and have some of Dimp's wine.

So, dazed with the glory and shame of what he'd just purchased from Huxpeth, he came into her little living room, and Dimp sat him down at the side of her desk, because he seemed in a mood to be told where to sit. He asked her what was happening – had something gone wrong?

Dimp told him, 'I've left Bren. That's the sum of it. For good.'

'And Bren gave you the paintings?' Benedetto asked.

'The paintings were actually mine from the start. You don't have to worry about any *caveat emptor* stuff. Your title's secure.'

But he looked pretty agonised still, and on more than legal grounds. He said, 'It doesn't feel like a triumph, having the Boyd. It feels like theft. It feels like the meanest thing I've ever done. I felt I had to come around here straight away and apologise.'

Dimp told him that that was irrational. But she saw that buying the painting had certainly made him look less certain than he was the night he had helped – with clarity of argument – to put an end to her marriage. She told him to enjoy the painting in peace, and mentioned the crucial dinner.

With a flushed face he told her he hadn't been the same person since that night. 'It's hard to ask this question without seeming a vainglorious bastard. But here we go. I'd had a fair bit to drink that night, and I just wondered if I had ... if something I said ... somehow caused trouble between you and Bren?' Even as he asked it, he shrugged and shook his head and laughed at himself. When he'd awoken the next morning he'd had this feeling that he'd trespassed in some sizeable way. He had the impulse to call Dimp and ask her. But he didn't. A man would need to be either very drunk or very desperate to ask such a question, he said.

And then Tim Huxpeth had told him a lovely Boyd was available, and he'd gone and seen it and suspected it was the D'Arcys', but didn't specifically ask. He'd thought, they're splitting up, and you, Benedetto, you smart alec, you bloody did it! He said his offer to take the painting off Huxpeth, was a sort of defensive, panicky gesture. He'd believed it would put him back on the rails, give him a centre. Well ... it hadn't. He'd really felt like scum then. What a futile, vain, stupid purchase. And the question went hammering on all the harder ... that's why he'd had the temerity to come and see her.

'What happened that night, Dimp?' he wanted to know.

She told him about the accidental impact of his speech that night, the oblique power of his exposition of the Mabo case. She began unevenly but was sure she covered all the points of law, at least well enough for someone like her, someone inexpert but willing. As she spoke, he occasionally shook his head and began to lift a hand, as if he might want her to stop speaking. But he never completed the gesture.

He was totally out of balance and Dimp said she felt she could reach forward and with one finger adjust him to the equilibrium he wanted. She told him to drink his wine and not to worry. 'You were right all along,' she said. 'You took the curse off me, and you've had to carry it around yourself!'

He laughed and said that was a Calabrian way of looking at things. Then he reached out and stroked her wrist.

Prim was woken at 7 a.m. by a concerned Helene Codderby.

'What does this press release you've sent mean, Prim? You're not going to do anything stupid, are you?'

'I am going to do something very sensible.'

'Look, you're in a special position. You're on an NGO passport. You are not a tourist. Tell me, what do you have in mind?'

But she did not yet want to expose her sustaining plan to the banal light of day. 'I might treasure you as a friend, Helene, but you'll just have to find out at the same time as the others.'

'For God's sake,' Helene said, her voice thin in that new way, as it had been only since the grenades of operatives of the Muslim Brotherhood had torn apart the Rimini dining room and Fergal and Claudia Stoner, 'between now and ten o'clock, do re-examine the wisdom of anything you have in mind!'

'If I'm mute, will they show their gratitude by letting him go? You and Amnesty are the first to tell me it's not the way they operate.'

'Are you doing this for him, or only because you need to do something for your own sanity?'

It was true that the need to act was nearly superior to all other needs. 'It's a good question, Helene. But again, you name prisoners, even in your reports. And Amnesty. I asked the woman – she said they're likely to be more careful in their treatment once they know the world knows.'

'Don't pin your hopes on what some faceless woman told you late at night from an office in London.'

'I pin my hopes on my instincts for what will work.'

'Please reconsider. You aren't a human rights advocate, you aren't a journalist.'

But the conversation sputtered out into barely more than monosyllabic expressions of concern from Helene.

At half-past nine, Prim had Erwit drive her into central Khartoum, to the Rimini with its blackened upper floor. They sat in the truck outside until, at a few minutes to ten, she emerged holding a sheet of rolled poster cardboard in her hand, and walked down the street to the Khartoum City Bank building. At her appearance there, a number of white and brown-skinned journalists emerged quickly from vehicles parked either side of the road. Some of them were fiddling with cameras. They knew they might not have long to do their work.

In front of the closed iron doors of the bank building, Prim stood still, and the folded cardboard she held in her hands was unfurled. It said in Arabic and English: 'Dr Sherif Taha of Khartoum is a prisoner in a ghost house like this one. He is illegally detained. Please protest at the unrecorded imprisonment of Dr Taha and many like him.'

Stringers for *The Times* and the *Guardian* were there, and the man who sometimes got stuff published in the *Washington Post*, the US paper which was best on Africa. Helene was there with a microphone and asked Prim in her shaky voice what she hoped to accomplish. Under the blanket of the *National Security Act*, said Prim, men and women from all over the Sudan were summarily arrested and held in unacknowledged detention centres. One of them was her friend, Dr Sherif Taha. It was time to call on the detainers and the interrogators to cease, she said.

Others threw in questions: What was Dr Sherif Taha to her? the man from the *Washington Post* asked. A respected friend and colleague, she told him. An eminent public health expert who had tried to keep health records separate from security records. Before she could explain, she saw a white police vehicle double-park in front of the bank building. Two immaculately uniformed police lieutenants descended. One of them asked Prim in English to accompany him and his friend. There was no reason she should not go with them. The stringer from the *Guardian* was closest to her as she stepped off the pavement to enter the police vehicle. 'Get it published,' she told him, 'for God's sake. You see, I'm being detained for a mere placard.' The lieutenants put her in the back seat, from which she saw Helene's strangely wan face amongst the ruck of journalists. God bless them all. She had called them, they had come.

The two lieutenants drove her to the police headquarters opposite the river-front parkland of the Blue Nile. They had nothing to say to her on the way. One of them led her indoors, the other followed with her placard. No one in the downstairs office looked at them as they waited by the lift, and on the second floor Prim was put in an unused office with a bare table and barred high windows. There she was left to wait more than two hours.

In the first hour she had the exultant sense of having made exactly the correct gesture to rescue Sherif. But in the second hour the sort of questions Helene had raised began to intrude. There were no utter guarantees, as the woman at Amnesty in London had told her, that in a specific case the tried strategies would work. Amnesty had in its care prisoners from Chile to Siberia. Its brief was very reasonably what worked best for the majority of that sad army. But the minority must be numerous! Prim told herself: don't doubt. This is not the hour nor the room for it.

Sometime in the third hour the door was unlocked and Dr Siddiq entered.

'Hello, Miss Bettany,' he said pleasantly. Prim remembered the time she had first seen him, at the el Rahzi's, where he had looked something of an outsider. Now he had, even more than at Alingaz, the relaxed gestures of an insider.

'So here we see the connection between the Ministry of Health and the security system,' Prim told him in defiance.

'I am a doctor, and an army officer,' Siddiq told her. 'So why not? They asked me to call in because I know you. They're puzzled as to why you'd do such a reckless thing.'

'That's a naïve question, Siddiq.'

'Of course. You did it because Dr Taha is your lover. You miss his caress.'

'I don't need you to belittle my motives. You must know better than me what's being done to him while we spar here.'

Siddiq spread his hands. 'Damn it all, Prim. He is being questioned, he is being held. That's what I know. But you are a guest in the Sudan, and so is the NGO you represent. Why would you choose to make such a crass intervention in our legal process?'

'Because it isn't a legal process, and you know it.'

'I'm told this isn't the first time you've acted beyond your brief. You have made an unauthorised journey to the South and helped to remove Sudanese nationals into a foreign country. You have collected subversive and libellous information in interviews with Southerners, and denounced our government to sundry world bodies to whom you sent copies of those interviews. Your superiors can't be too happy with you. You show an astonishing hubris. You can't be amazed that the government is not enchanted by your activities.'

Prim was not even particularly astonished that the government knew about her anti-slavery activities. Perhaps there was someone, some friend of the Sudan, in the organisations to whom she had sent her reports.

'So I'm the sinner,' said Prim. 'Why is Sherif paying the price?'

Siddiq opened the palms of his hands to her. 'How do you know he's paying a price? You can't be sure of any such thing. He might have a wife and children in Shendi. He might be visiting them. I wouldn't put it past him. It's difficult for him having a turbulent woman such as yourself for a close friend.'

'You know he's detained somewhere. He's detained for getting angry about your damn questions.'

'I see.'

'He's suffering for wanting to blow the whistle on camps like Alingaz.'

'Do you think so?' asked Siddiq. 'No doubt you wonder why we attempt to instil and enforce Islamic values, when we could instead be splendid hypocrites like Westerners! Do you really love these people, Primrose? Do you love the Nuba, do you love the Southerners? Is that why you are part of an aid alliance whose chief job is to service refugee camps here in the Sudan, refugee camps which put our administration under such great stress? But where are the helpful immigration officials from the West? They are outraged by Alingaz. But will they take the Nuba? No. It doesn't suit their domestic policy. Oh dear! But let's do the right thing. Let's feed them where they are, as a means of keeping these people out of America, out of Europe, out of Canada, out of Australia! Keep them alive in the Sudan, oh yes! But for God's sake don't bring them over. And when some inevitable glitch occurs, why then we can blame Sudanese barbarity! Do you and your dear friend Sherif really believe that in the wonderful West your Dinka and your Nuba and your Northern Darfur peasant would be safe from all harm, all violation? Well, it's something you won't be putting to the test anyhow. Feed them around Khartoum! Feed them in the Red Sea Hills! But for God's sake don't let them settle in Clapham, or rent a room in Brooklyn. Or in . . . in Sydney! In white Australia! For God's sake don't let them go there!'

Prim resisted an impulse to weep in bewilderment, for he was very nearly outdoing her in genuine rage.

'For God's sake,' she murmured, 'what you say is fair grounds for despising the almighty West. But that's not the point. The point is, why these ghost houses? Are they the fault of Sydney or Clapham? Just let Sherif go!'

Siddiq grew thoughtful. 'You know I don't have that sort of power. Nor do I have utter control over every angry turnkey and interrogating police NCO.'

Prim said, 'If you people tell me what I have to do, I will do it.'

'Oh yes. And then you would take him, if you got him back, to Australia. Shouting, "Come and see a real political prisoner! Risen from the awful Sudan prison! Alleluia!"'

'I just want to see him safe.'

'Well then, you do not go scouting for ghost houses. And you do not stand in front of any building with a placard. These are times of emergency. There are emergency laws.'

'If I agree to behave myself, will you move him into el Kober, put him on the books, let him have a lawyer?'

'I've just said I can't control every twitch of the penal system! But you may, in the coming weeks get a call from the Foreign Office. You must be patient. That's the way the government works, you know. One more stunt, though, and all bets are off. Talk to Amnesty if you want. They mean little to the people who hold Sherif. That's all I can give you.'

LONG AND OTHER TORTURED QUESTIONS

I went to see Long three days after the sentence and two weeks before he was meant to hang, subject to the appeal Mr Handler had made to the Governor. He had put on some weight under Mr Bilson's care and without the regular exercise of Nugan Ganway, and when I saw him come in, merely in wrist chains this time, as if he had earned the concession by good behaviour, I thought that he might have through eating well repented of all his talk of world-weariness, and his desire for a better place. The two constables handled him almost affectionately, having got to know him.

As they withdrew we uttered the banal pleasantries.

'Are you well, Long?'

'Yes, thank you, Mr Bettany.'

We stood at a table, the same table in the barred office where we had last talked at length, and he sat down at my invitation, and by then we were alone, and I could think of nothing to say. So I passed over some more tobacco.

'Thank you,' he said. 'I consider you've been very square with me.'

'No, I have perjured myself,' I said.

'Not in my book. Treloar and Cladder got me, as I knew they would.'

It was intolerable to be there with him and to be burdened with my knowledge. 'I am determined to come forward. To hell with any charges of perjury. As for Felix, he can live secure and distant. I am determined. I must speak if I am to tolerate myself.'

It was so apparent I rose to call for constables and for Bilson.

'For dear Christ's sake, sir, sit still. Come, sit. Please.'

I obeyed him rather slowly. Disgrace could be delayed an hour.

'Good, sir. Now, have no doubt you have given me what I seek, and all other actions are ruinous to the three of us – yes, to Felix, yourself, but above all me.'

'This mad concept I should help you destroy yourself!'

'And you should help not to destroy two others. For sweet Christ's sake, don't be a torment to yourself and to me. I mean it.'

I shook my head weakly. 'I have written to the Governor, by the way, Sean,' I lamely told him.

'Then I hope your best efforts of rescue do not count, since I do not want to be sent to Norfolk Island for life. But you know my increase of cattle? You have banked money for me?'

'Yes.'

'I would like it sent with news of my death to Bride O'Lúing, care of the parish priest, Glock-na-ballagh, Sligo. It is on this sheet of paper. Now, let us not be gloomy, Mr Bettany. Let us say that we had adventures . . . sometimes I wish I could go back to one of the old hearths at home, just to unburden the stories I hold.'

'Would they believe you?' I asked.

'Oh,' he said, 'that's not likely now. Justice Flense didn't, and I had a better kind of jury than they have at home.'

And now, we knew, somewhere on the road, from Bathurst or Goulburn or Sydney, a man was preparing to travel with a noose in his bag, while the Governor would soon be reading Mr Handler's appeal.

'Mr Bilson,' Long said, holding his pipe clamped in his teeth, asked me what I thought had happened to Felix. I said, "Oh, he will never be seen again until he takes on a man's face. He's gone far down the

Murrumbidgee to live with the Myall blacks. He'll take a lubra for wife. He was a clever boy, that one, but never happy unless amongst his own." '

'But he liked his Latin and Greek,' I said by way of gentle contradiction.

'Oh,' said Long, 'but there's no need for Mr Bilson to be so informed.'

'I have advertised for him,' I said. To prove my lack of complicity, I had done so. People had mentioned seeing the advertisements in the *Goulburn Herald*, and the *West Maitland Gazette*. They had been very particular advertisements in regard to Felix's age and features and character.

'Our Mr Handler tells me not to hope,' said Long, puffing away at his now-lit pipe, held in a cuffed hand, with the tranquillity of despair. 'Handler tells me that His Excellency is under a shadow for tolerating and, as they say, favouring Irish lads. He thinks we tend to be given to breaking down doors and houghing cattle, but not to thievery – that's the explanation for his liking, and he is a Whig that way. Last February, six Irish were charged with absconding and firing on their master, and His Excellency saved the lives of five of them. Now people all say to His Excellency, show us your firmness or you'll find us writing letters. I am that firmness, sir. I am the sign that no white man, however far out, can be harmed without punishment. This is what Mr Handler warns me, anyhow.'

'I have told His Excellency of your admirable record and qualities, and expressed the severest doubt about your guilt.'

'Yes,' said Long with a terrible plainness of tone, and as if he were distracted by something more important. 'In regard to all that, there is one service, Mr Bettany, you could do.'

I nodded.

'We Ribbonmen of Ireland, who swore to punish landlords, if you'll forgive the fancy, are not given to the idea of quick lime. The same can be said for unconsecrated ground. I spoke of the money you banked. I would have you ask His Excellency to give you my body. If I cannot be buried in open or priest-blessed ground then Nugan Ganway would serve – west of the homestead say, where I could be trodden on by little lords like Michael O'Dallow. And I would care for a little headstone of the local granite and on it a cross and the name of my ship, *Fairley*, so that any later comers will not mistake me for another Long, or another Long for me. It can say I was hanged, if that is what is needed, it can say that I murdered, if that is what is decreed. But it must say that I was Long of *Fairley*.'

I told him I would write a letter at once to the Colonial Secretary, that if the awful thing happened I would be there with a wagon, and his friend Clancy would carry him back. I also urged him to send for me in time if he were to change his cast of mind. I was willing to make the sacrifice for him, I assured him again.

But he said nothing and we seemed to have covered all his concerns. As for my concerns, after I left him I went straight to the Royal Hotel and drank three rums to quench for a second my rankling sense of my own fall, even though I would prefer to be fallen with Bernard than risen with any other. I took it too for the limitless treacheries I was still growing my way into.

On the principle that a man who consigns another to the gallows should be willing to look him in the eye, I was bound to drive in from Nugan Ganway to Cooma to witness Long's public execution, having merely as armour the Governor's permission, which the press would ultimately think an eccentric decree, to accept the remains. By my side was my father, eager to observe Long's death for the purposes of his writing. What a philosophical dog's breakfast he would make of it, coming to it as he did with such fixed ideas. He might well be the ultimate indignity for poor Long.

Sarah Bernard had lain sleepless by my side, but loyally expatiating on the idea that Long had somehow been fortunate to have me for a master. She was my courage and my one solidity in a world of vapours. She had become the wifely consoler, and I rebutted but welcomed all her plain soothing utterances.

She said, for example, 'Sean Long is a great believer. That's the thing surely. That to believe you're going to go to paradise is as good as going.' And I reached my hand and stroked her thigh, to honour her pithiness, her kind cynicism.

'You have done all you could have done,' she told me more simply.

'But how do you know?' I asked.

'Sean Long told me. He wrote me a letter.'

There was a pause.

'May I see it?' I asked.

'No,' she said definitely. 'It's simply mine.'

I laughed. It was as if she had been expecting another response, and she asked, 'Why are you laughing?'

'It's the possibility of secrets between lovers. All fallen creatures need their secrets.'

'Yes,' she said. 'All fallen creatures.'

We lay at a sort of peace with our separate and sometimes unutterable sorrows about us.

I was pleased to rise half an hour before a glorious dawn, rosy as a morning in a print of the Resurrection. I put the horses in the traces some twenty minutes before Clancy emerged to rig up a dray to bring Long back. I wished I could have ridden on horseback – I wanted the good, distracting jolt of a ride. But in Long's hut my father was already rising, and gathering notebooks and pencils.

I had known in my blood, from the day the trial began, that this was how it would end. With me silent and compliant. And now I expected, at the end of a two-and-a half-hour journey during which my father gave a repetitious commentary on the parallels between Socrates and as much of Long's history as he had gathered from O'Dallow, to roll into the town to see Treloar and a vulgar mob. Their cries would scour and flay my soul, as it deserved to be scoured and flayed.

But the truth was that the crowd which gathered before the courthouse seemed valedictory and almost shy, as if come more to ease Long upon his way than to hoot and mock. An hour before the time, a number of Mother Ignatius's nuns arrived, having come all the way from Goulburn. They knelt in a line before the gallows and began reciting their beads aloud. Sundry Irish ticket-of-leave men and servant women arrived from throughout the area, formed lines behind and on either side of the nuns, some of them producing their own beads and murmurously following the good women. Irish housekeepers huddled up to the back of them, introducing their resonance into the prayers. I wished that I could have been joined into their utterances, barbarous – according to some commentators – as they might be. I wanted that exalted company of virgins and that rough company of felons to stand between me and the painful light.

The day became hot, and bright enough to make one squint. 'Heaven and hell are opening with equal vigour to our friend Long,' my father told me, blinking under the sun as we walked from the Royal after drinking early morning spirits.

At seven minutes to the hour, Mr Treloar's carriage drew in behind me. Treloar tipped his hat, but did not dismount, sitting there sourly instead, a pastoralist waiting for a bill to be paid. He was the only one there for the victim, Goldspink. He made a miserable retinue.

I attributed it to the merciful nature of Mr Bilson that when the seconds had ached away to eleven o'clock, Long was brought out promptly and hustled up the scaffold. There Bilson, a priest from Goulburn, and the executioner awaited him. Long responded to a prod from Bilson as he stood like a reluctant groom, and stepped forward.

Men and women in the crowd began to cry, 'God save ye, Sean! Go to it Sean! For God and the old land, Sean!' There seemed to be a communal desire that he behave well. I heard Treloar behind me make a noise in disgust and say to his driver, 'They're a dramatic set of rogues.'

Long's face seemed that of a man at ease. He said, so that the crowd could hear, could perhaps later relate for the consolation of his lost family: 'Into your hands do I commend my spirit.' Indeed he did not look heavenward. He looked to what I supposed could be called the people of his communion of saints, Ireland's penal family as reconstituted on the high plains of Maneroo. He said, 'I did not kill the man ...'

There were shouts from the crowd. 'No! That you didn't, Sean.'

A woman cried, 'You are not the first martyr of our race, Sean boy.' So they had injected politics into this horror, they blamed it on powers and principalities, and I stood on the edge, unblamed and unpunished. 'I had hoped to run sheep and cattle of my own, but this rope ends that hope. Did the immortal Christ say, "It is expedient that one should die for the multitude?"'

'Yes. He did, Sean.'

'I know He did and I go without malice.' He did not look at me at any stage of this handsome, scalding little speech. Mr Treloar sucked his teeth and tossed his head, for I could hear his movements behind me. Long's legs were strapped, the noose put around his neck and his head covered a last time, all very suddenly and as if it were a normal function of society. Over the heads of the nuns, the sound of whose *Aves* had increased, I saw Doctor Alladair and a convict constable go to the underside of the scaffold and trapdoor. When it was sprung with a sound I shall indeed remember to my dying second, since it reverberated in my own spine, I heard above the prayers and sobs Dr Alladair quietly directing the constable to drag on Sean Long's legs, which he did. The faint trace of Long's dying urine reached me. But there were no sounds from him, and after a second Alladair told the man to desist, listened to

Long's heart and, as far as I could see, was satisfied. Everyone waited for two minutes, only the convicts praying, and at last Alladair instructed the constable to slit the rope. Inanimate Long fell to the ground. Clancy was to receive him later, from the back door of the cells, after Alladair had again examined him.

My father shook his head. I could see that he was genuinely touched, and there were a few scatters of tears on his cheeks. 'That was a case of a herdsman showing how to die, Jonathan. That was noble and, thank God, quick. But it is wearing. I shall meet you at the Royal.'

He wanted to drink, for in his philosophic approach to Long's execution, he had forgotten what a jolt to the human system it is to see a man mechanically destroyed. I saw him walk away, chatting to the town's new apothecary, his head nodding at points of emphasis.

Magistrate Bilson and his men now hustled everyone from the scaffold as if they were unwelcome guests. The crowd, some still reciting their Hail Marys drifted away. Some men looked at Treloar as they passed, and spoke gutturally but indistinctly. Treloar himself, convinced that further waiting was not likely to produce more vengeance, turned to me and said, 'I can understand you would want to hold on to a good man, Bettany!'

It was his version of reconciliation.

'I would want to hold on to an innocent man,' I told him.

'Yes. But the court and the jury didn't agree with you.'

He turned to his driver and told him to turn home. But I waited by that scaffold vacated even by the corpse, and emerging at last from the courthouse, Doctor Alladair came over to me.

'You'll be pleased to know, Bettany, I'm sure, that the fellow did die instantly.'

I was pathetically hopeful at the news, even as it plunged me deeper into the flames.

'I am grateful, doctor, for your delicacy. But perhaps you will not judge me harshly if I ask you how you know?'

'The break between the first and second cervical is palpable with the fingers and could only have happened at the drop. There was also no priapism, as would have happened had he lived ten seconds.'

'Thank you, sir,' I said. In departing, noble Long had avoided a last wave in the direction of Priapus, god of male fertility. Almost at once young Magistrate Bilson was at my side, his black cap tucked under his right arm.

'The prisoner left you this,' he said. 'He thought very highly of you.'

What could one say to that? I took the letter. Bilson, whom I had recently heard had been an ensign in the cavalry in India, saluted and left.

The paper said, on its first line, in Long's deliberate, raw hand: 'Sir, In case you are distressed I say to you I know all and take all as it comes and forgive all.'

And on the next, 'God save the boy.'

A last line said, 'Pass my affection to Miss Sarah Bernard.'

I saw then that he had owed me hatred, but condemned me to his forgiveness.

As he had hoped, Long was brought back to Nugan Ganway and buried the better part of a mile west of the homestead, far enough out to be remembered, not so far as ever to be forgotten by any of us who had known him. The burial was attended by a muscular young priest newly come from Ireland to Cooma. In time Long's presence and his tragedy could nearly be forgotten.

Meanwhile, Bernard and I did not lack for other distractions. To my horror, towards Christmas in that first year of his cohabitation with Aldread, my father borrowed my phaeton and rode into Cooma Creek with Aldread at his side. So the shame of his arrangement was not limited to Nugan Ganway. I heard later that he had called in at the Reverend Mr Paltinglass's brick manse and argued the point with him over the Church of England's doctrine on divorce. If divorce could be countenanced doctrinally by Judaism and Islam, why not by the Established Church? Why was it not within a man's – or a woman's, for he was democratic on this point – means to divorce within the context of his religion, if the one God was the same God permitting divorce under certain conditions as the Yahweh of the Jews and the Allah of the Muslims?

As Paltinglass was later kindly enough to tell me, he had himself indicated that more was required of Christians because of the mercifulness of their dispensation.

Bernard began to spend some time by my father's hearth, talking to Aldread. It was a friendship in which I presumed I should not interfere. Bernard also had food taken to my father and Aldread from the homestead by Maggie Tume, O'Dallow's wife. Bernard explained to me, 'She coughs up all her heart's blood, and cannot cook for herself.' And so, even as I rode to the out-stations, I retained in my mind an image of my rubicund father sitting by a blazing hearth with brittle Aldread on the nights when the wind turned south-east and grew unexpectedly chill. Aldread was, even in my view, fading a grain at a time, her cheeks blazing, her breath, as anyone could tell, so short that her pretty little mouth was always slightly agape.

'My little blazing girl,' my father would say.

In the late summer, before the first snows could bring down any peril or criminality on the scene, I made with O'Dallow and other of my men one more droving journey to Simon's place. We took some 400 head of cattle with us. I was aware of being trailed on the far side of the mountains by anthracite natives, whom Simon would later tell me belonged to a tribe named Jaitmatchang. They had greater power to frighten my men than the Moth people – they moved quickly and silently ahead of us, and it needed four armed men on horseback to guard the flock at night, and large bonfires to persuade them we would not be taken by surprise.

Apart from that, the descent on the far side, which I had once thought breakneck, and could be if taken at speed, seemed a mere amble now. It was as if the gods had decided, after all, that I should never be surprised again. Neither by virtue nor by glory, neither by malice nor by storms.

Riding down to Simon's homestead on the Broken River, I found him restored to his wife. Elizabeth sat at the fire with us, and chatted in a lively manner. She had won back her house from my father. And I knew by now, with whatever surcharges of guilt, how delightful that must be.

When Elizabeth went to bed, retreating from her husband's gloomy predictions of the livestock prices to be had in Port Phillip, I told Simon about Aldread and my father. I told him about myself and Bernard. He took it in a very worldly manner. He said, however, with filial hopefulness, 'Perhaps he feels towards this Aldread exactly as you feel towards Bernard.'

'Perhaps,' I painfully admitted. 'But is he of a mind to make a sane choice?'

Simon laughed harshly. 'Are any of us? But no, I see what you mean. Poor you. Have you told Mother?'

'I wrote her one plain letter,' I admitted. 'But how do you say it? I began by telling her that Father's behaviour on my station – were she to hear of it through rumours – was not condoned by me. And then it struck me that not to specify what the offending behaviour was would leave the poor woman in torment. And so I specified what it was, and told her to forget him forever. I also promised that within two years I would leave the property in the care of an overseer and go and visit her.'

Simon frowned. I asked him why.

'You will need to confess your own situation, Jonathan. That would hurt her too if she were to know.'

'My God, Simon,' I argued. 'The woman saved me from all manner of crazed options after Phoebe died. I intend to marry this woman, Bernard. She is a woman of strong qualities, and my mother herself chose to marry a felon.'

'Ah, but he was not a felon at the time of the wedding.'

'Well, at least,' I said, driving the stakes of irony as high as I could, 'at least she is not a Papist. Her mother and father were Jewish!'

'Oh my dear Lord,' said Simon, with such boyish forlornness that I could not, with the best intentions to do so, drive my anger higher.

'Do not judge me, Simon,' I said, gently. 'I am living the only life I can, and by the time I see Mother, I shall be a married man.'

'Do you think there is something wrong with our family?' asked Simon. His face was so fretted that again I could not dismiss the silliness of this question. 'Is it in the blood, in the heart, the brain?'

'Charlie Batchelor thinks so. But damn him. May I remind you that the first adulterer was not a convict.'

'Who was the first adulterer?'

'I don't know. But it can't have been long after Adam.'

'That is the moral cynicism which pervades all the colonial regions. I have sworn to live my life not as you and Father, but to take my grief without madness, like a simple man. If you should ask my ambition, then it is to live my life in such a way that whatever happens to me, I shall not react with mad displays. I shall not write books, nor dance with convict women. Whatever small sins will be left to my record, they will be so average as to vanish into it.'

I found myself shivering and understood it was anger. 'You speak of small sins,' I said, 'yet you arm your shepherds with carbines.'

'And so do you.'

'Yes, and how closely after a time do we inquire into the murders?'

'I have no guilt about deaths on my property,' said Simon. 'Am I to let my shepherds and my livestock be impaled and clubbed? By a race so sunk in cunning and aimlessness that one might think them the first creation of the Fall? I shall not be inhumane to them, but equally I shall not weep when they are gone. They are in this region impertinent and aggressive.'

'It is a sign of advancing age,' I said with a relenting smile, 'to use the word "impertinent".'

'Then so be it. If I have the wisdom of age before my time, I shall not complain.'

And he had at least achieved this – in his desire to fit the norm of goodness, he had achieved the normal concept of the native people.

'If Father gives you his crazy book to send to London or Edinburgh,' Simon continued, 'drop it in a deep passage of the Murrumbidgee, so that we can live free from shame.'

'Don't worry,' I said. 'He is becoming more and more exorbitant. His book will not be published.'

HELENE SAID, DESPITE EVERYTHING, Prim had got off easy from her demonstration, and that it had even seemed to bear fruit. Her picture with the placard had appeared in the international press – the lean, fair-featured woman in long-sleeved shirt and floral skirt holding her plea aloft must have appealed to picture editors. She was the Page 3 girl of the oppressed, said Helene.

Dimp faxed. She said she was on her way, making airline bookings to stand by her sister in Khartoum. She would bring Benedetto, who knew his international law. Prim called and dissuaded her.

She was tortured by the thought that her trip to free slaves in Loki-chokio might have contributed to whatever isolation and pain Sherif was now suffering. Nothing happened to ease that concern. Yet in the punishing weeks in which she waited for a call about Sherif, she took guilty comfort from the account of Jonathan Bettany, which had accumulated during her absence in Alingaz, and from tales of Dimp and her problems which seemed like the dilemmas of someone fantastical, of a character in a soap opera which, like all good soap operas, dealt only in lives of privilege. But Prim had a particular hope for how it would end. Surely scales would fall from Dimp's eyes and she would return to Bren and they would adopt a child.

Dimp had told her how when Bren returned from America, he was justifiably offended to find his paintings gone, and had instituted civil proceedings to recover them. To disabuse him, Dimp had a set of divorce documents drawn up and delivered, in which she offered in return for the withdrawal of his writ concerning the paintings – which both he and she knew to be only of nuisance value – to relinquish all further claim on him.

Though she distantly disapproved, and in the darkest of all dark hours suspected a connection between Dimp's Sydney chaos and the disorder of the republic which was toying with and devouring its child, Sherif, Prim thus felt subtly cheated when a definitive instalment, dated July 2 1990, arrived.

Dearest Prim
I've been talking to that miserable lean character Whitloaf, who says he's watching Khartoum and has a replacement or an aide ready to send. I just hope you're okay, and that Sherif's okay too. I called the Department of Foreign Affairs, but we don't have an embassy in Khartoum. They told me they've instructed the Brits and the Americans to represent you if anything bad happens. I really am very worried, and ready to leave the moment you tell me you need me.

Everything's settled here anyway. The terms of the settlement are engraved in legal jargon. My lawyer, Pynsent, a family law whizz, went to see Bren by appointment at his office a few weeks back, and said, 'Look, it doesn't make sense. My client is willing to waive all claim on you if you drop all charges and give her indemnity from any possible prosecution.' And the worst thing is, Bren stood up by his big picture window, with the whole reach of the harbour behind him, and began to weep, in front of Pynsent. Then he said what a bloody silly thing that was to do, in front of a lawyer, and started sobbing again. When Pynsent told me this I thought, What have you done, Dimp, you flippant bitch? Pynsent himself was embarrassed for these tears, and it must have been awful for Bren. You see, he is complex – he's willing to sacrifice his dignity. I have to remember that that's as far as it goes. He's not willing to sacrifice his soul. But when Pynsent told me ... I was weeping too, at the idea of Bren being so stricken. And he told me Bren said, like a man who couldn't be bothered to hide anything anyhow, 'If I drop the charges I'll lose contact with her.'

It sounds so plaintive. I did consider turning back for his sake and growing old unhappily with him. I'd be the forgiven spouse. I think Bren would go for it. A small matter of course: I'd lose Benedetto, and the universe would be a cold place. But love's more than a gesture. Though this was quite a gesture. He was suing me above all to keep contact. He was willing to be mocked in the press and whispered about amongst his peers just to keep a claim on me. And that's a very cunning instinct in its own right: they talk about suing for someone's hand – at least that's an old-fashioned phrase. Well, he was suing for mine, if he can be believed. I feel guilty for the way I must have mystified the poor sod.

And he's suing for heaven too, at the same time. I asked him once in an argument what redemption would be like, what pictures of it he carried in his head. It's ineffable, he says. It can't be talked about or defined. But I say, if it can't be discussed, why be so driven by it? There are enough things on earth which can be discussed, I told him, which can be defined by us poor suffering bastards. Including the price of molybdenum and the death of love. So let's stick with them. But then, you wouldn't believe it, he broke down. It was all a huge stress to him. This venture conquistador! He rarely shed a tear, but as with Pynsent, he wept then, trying to imagine heaven or deal with my agnostic mockery. And at that stage I was still simple-minded enough to think that sobbing – particularly in men – is love. But I've never seen anyone crying at the prospect of hell, have you? Bawling for salvation?

All this added up – willingness to weep before a lawyer, willingness to be thought foolish – instead of causing me to feel regret, caused me to feel even more relief, even more conviction. I did the right thing. I had the right instincts. How can I regret my removal – theft it is not! – of pictures, when that was the finest way to get my earnestness across to Bren?

Anyhow, Bren told Pynsent that he needed time to think about the proposal, and he was going to San Francisco to speak to commodity dealers at some big seminar, and he hoped that would clear his head, and he would talk when he got back.

Well, he came back yesterday, and this morning he called Pynsent and told him that yes, he would drop the case, but he insisted on making a proper settlement with me, minus half the cost of the paintings. What a generous, miserable thing! Half the cost! Though he didn't express the idea, he doesn't want people saying he was too mean or vengeful to give me anything. So he comes up, no doubt on lawyers' advice, with this 50 per cent forgiveness. For me, that was the finish! I told Pynsent, No. Not a chance! No maintenance, no cash. Remind him that the paintings were all in my name. And so to save Bren's self-esteem a clause had to be put into the agreement saying that the arrangement was confidential and no one would reveal the details under threat of legal sanction. Bren's lawyers made Pynsent and me turn up at their offices, and we all signed. To his credit, Bren signed without any reproach. I was sheathed in cloth covered in rainbow lorikeets, and he said to me with a lenient smile, 'You're still dressing in the old style,' and I forgave him for sicking Cara Motley onto me once to try to teach me haute couture. He was dry-eyed when it was his turn to sign.

And, with a hush and a nod and the scrape of a ballpoint against paper, my sole marriage as good as reaches its end – not quite yet in the technical sense. There's still the automatic and uncontested process to go through, but I think this agreement document is the real separator.

But then I found that there was a reason Bren might have been dry-eyed at the signing. Benedetto and I saw him at some Sydney Theatre Company bash at Walsh Bay and he had an American with him, a stylish woman who clearly understood how to dress and was enviably made-up. She looked an utter Venus, although slightly sharp-featured in a way which won't become marked for decades yet. She looked credible beside him. I was almost proud of him! I laughed all the way home – not in mockery at all, but in utter delight. Benedetto tells me she was saying at the party that she was arranging a tour of duty in Bren's office here and praising his chutzpah in running an international headquarters from Sydney. His tears have been wiped away by her admiration!

I don't blame him at all for finding a companion in what is for him fairly fast time, or perhaps even of beating the gun a little – after all he was in her city and within her ambience while I stole his paintings. After an inappropriate bitch like me, why shouldn't he comfort himself with a woman who knows the skills of womanhood as it is practised in his circles. Maybe he'll be man enough to marry her, and if he does, I'll be cheering from the sidelines. Laughing in the face of hell.

So, nothing to keep me from my sister's side! Even the writer, Hugo, is steaming away. He shows me stuff. It's beautiful. He has the tone and tempo of the speeches between Bettany and Phoebe, Bettany and Bernard. It's so rare this happens in a screenwriter, that he reacts so well so early in the process, but it means I can come to support you at a second's notice. You assure me there's no chance you'll be arrested. I hope that's the case!

Ready to roll at any moment on your behalf, I am

Your sister Dimp

⌒

MY FATHER'S BOOK

Bernard and Tume, a Jewish woman and an Irish, ensured we celebrated a hearty Christmas, energetically bearing us through all the rituals of the bush Yule. My father, O'Dallow and I drank and talked enough to keep away all the ghosts and other absences at our tables.

One or two days later, my father asked me to go walking with him one hot morning around the stockyards. I was intrigued by the one tassel of smoke on the hill above. Some of the Moth people came back still, a scatter, though most of them had been drawn away into the Reverend Howie's mission near Bombala, where he sustained and kept them in place with rations of flour, tea, sugar and tobacco. It was as if, when they first ate flour, or took tobacco into their mouths, they were doomed to lose connection with their earth.

'I've been to see Mr Cantyman, the solicitor in town,' my father told me. 'I want you to listen calmly to what my intentions are as regards my estate, which is not insubstantial, as it happens. My law practice in Hobart still functions under the management of a somewhat better lawyer than Mr Cantyman, a young man named Fletcher.' I remembered Fletcher as a fresh-faced junior clerk when I was a child. 'The practice was somewhat devalued when my sins were made public. Had I misused clients' funds, I might have been treated with slightly more lenity. The colonial Pharisees, who had come to me at Mr Batchelor's kind urging, vacated the practice. But more recently, the population of Hobart has chosen not to punish Fletcher for my sins, and he is a man of such innate integrity that all goes well in that direction. The law office is not without its inherent value.'

I told him I was pleased to hear it.

'Then there is the house at Sandy Point, which must go to your mother. Then there are cash and certain bonds, to be divided between you, your mother and Simon.'

I said the normal things about being confident we would not soon receive these benefits.

'And then,' he continued, 'the 250-acre farm at Ross, and its livestock. Small enough by the standards of New South Wales, pitiable by the standards of Nugan Ganway. But a splendid little place not without value in Van Diemen's Land terms. With this property I must seek your indulgence, Jonathan. I intend to leave it to be held in trust by my dear friend

Aldread, to pass to yourself and Simon at her decease. In this regard, all your pious wishes about her survival will probably go unanswered. She will not last long, I fear. And I did it for the poor little thing without her asking or even suggesting. But on the way back from town in the cart, when I told her, she was as happy as a bird. She had never been thought of as a recipient of the usufruct of a property, and it seemed to me that her heart was elevated by the very idea that I had seen her in those terms, and signified as much in a legal document.'

'But Mother will hear this will read,' I protested, 'should anything happen to you.'

'You presume that Aldread will live longer than me,' he said with a genuine dolour in his voice. 'I wish it were so. You even presume that your mother will live longer than me, which is somewhat a better wager, since she does not have my vice of soaking oneself with rum. My God, you should see yourself, you are so priggish, Jonathan. Where is your obedience to the Biblical injunction, "... a bruised reed he shall not break ..." Is not poor Alice a bruised reed? But of course, that verse is not a matter of the sensual temper of humanity and so it is not taken seriously by good Christians! By and large, good Christians bruise all they can!'

'It's not that,' I said. 'Your first duty is to your wife, to whom your vows were eternal.'

'Oh Johnny, do you think you are in a position to enlighten me? The one difference between you and myself is that a fortuitous disease struck your spouse and delivered you of your so-called "eternal" vows.'

And he stood braced on his bowed legs, waiting and – I believed – hoping to be struck. I confess that I was angry enough to consider a patricidal blow, all the angrier of course for the truth of what he had said.

'I shall write to Mother and tell her that I have no part in your decisions,' I told him.

He brought his legs together, no longer seeking aggression, and took both my wrists in his hands. 'Jonathan, I must be permitted – the law says so – to make my own testamentary arrangements. Your mother will not want. She may even be a literary widow, my son. Great days, great days! I believe I am no more than two weeks removed from the close of my manuscript! You must come to my fire and drink with me when it is all done.'

I said, 'Of course.' But I sounded like a churlish boy, and he laughed.

And why not? He had ensured that both his life and his death were calamitous to my mother.

It was more than two weeks though before my father finished and copied his grand essay. It was late summer at Nugan Ganway when he finally came to the homestead with the manuscript under his arm and hammered deliriously on the opened door. The evening was dry, far removed from the arts and the muses. A furnace wind was gusting and swirling, south-west one second, north-west another, all from a blazing interior. Ruby lines of fire swayed along the ridges, their confused smoke blowing all ways. From the distant peaks was blown ash which lay extinguished and sullen over the homestead yard, and on the bark roofs like dirty snow.

Yet our door was nonetheless opened in expectation of kinder breezes – even though they may not reach us for days. And there, as I worked on my accounts and stock books, my father appeared, wearing a hat and a good shirt and polished boots, with Aldread, smiling beneath her mob cap. 'I am here,' he called, 'with the last scintilla, the last full stop!' Aldread's breath could be heard, grating away, part excitement, part disease. Her cheeks had sunken, and the rounded cheekbones seemed close to the surface of her skin – there was a collapse occurring within the planes of her face. I had come to fear both their smiles, though in many ways one could not have found a more pleasant-looking couple, both frayed by life, appearing genially at a door in the remoter Maneroo. The manuscript, tied in a cord of jute, looked like a work of true industry.

'So it is done, it is done, my boy,' he told me, bustling in and pushing the leaf-light Aldread before him. They hastened to their customary spots by the empty hearth. Bernard was at that moment visiting Maggie Tume's sick son, Michael, who had chicken pox and was, according to Tume, uncontrollable by anyone but Sarah. Had she been present, neither my father nor Aldread would have entered quite so glibly. For in sundry ways Bernard was becoming particular about the homestead. She had lined the walls of our room with yards of blue cloth instead of the old device of pages from newspapers. She was a studious polisher, wiper and duster of most objects, expending particular care on the condition of the books in our growing library. She approached the volumes with her lovely long hands, tentative from reverence. Her manner was not quite that of a proprietor, yet she had become possessive enough to make her a little resistant to my loud, intrusive father.

In any case my father and his book and paramour having entered, I fetched rum and water. While I was doing it, Bernard returned. She greeted both visitors, but then went to make herself tea, returning with it in a cup and saucer to sit at the far end of the table, a little distant from the rum-bibbing, enthused pair by the hearth. How readily she had absorbed my unease, and her frown was a guarantee to me she would not let them go too far. But she also applied her frown to Aldread who, against the normal wisdom of consumptives, insisted on fuelling her illness with heavy draughts of spirits, clearly for the sake of maintaining pace and companionship with my father.

After savouring a mouthful of rum, Father rose, passed across to my desk and undid the string around his manuscript. He poked the paper with his finger. He whispered, 'I expect without any vanity but simply on the basis that a man knows the value of what he has written, to be within a year of this date in some editorial offices splitting differences with Carlyle, and J.S. Mill, and perhaps especially with Benthamites.'

Though I did not know exactly what differences these gentlemen represented, it seemed an exorbitant ambition.

'Carlyle,' he continued, 'is a good open fellow, and so is Mill, and neither of them likely to summon up the unquestioning prejudices of the British Philistine against me. As for all the Pharisees,' – it seemed to have become his favourite term of denunciation – 'of the Established Church, I shall bathe in their hatred!'

His eyes gleamed, and behind him Aldread, who had merely witnessed this quiet conversation and thought my father a sage, blazed and beamed. He turned to Bernard, 'Excuse me, madam, a second, while I point something out to my son.'

He went raking through the manuscript and found towards its close the pages he sought. He gave them to me, his eyes alight in expectancy of my praise.

Obediently, I began to read. The text embodied all that Father had told me in his discourses, both at Simon's station and here on Nugan Ganway.

'Farewell to the Stoic, for he has been long banished. The first of the heretics, he was punished long before the Arians, and centuries before the Cathars and Albigensians of Southern France whom the Crusaders put to the sword. For the Stoic practised the talents which struck the

Christian dispensation of St Paul at its base, which undermined all the Christian temples, as humbly as they began, as exorbitantly as they have spread upon the earth and clawed at the sky, steeple upon steeple! The Stoic needed to be crushed since he knew both how to take pleasure and to bear pain, gave an equal value to both, took equal authority from both, and needed no nod towards the suffering Christ crucified to give specious value to that what he either bore or relished.'

'You see, you see?' asked my father.

I saw it was an attack on Christianity itself. He would become another destroyed Stoic, and the rest of his family would inherit that destruction.

But I read on. 'Nor did the Stoic's wry self-knowledge, and his impulse to be wise, depend upon the standard Christian belief in the utter unworthiness of humankind and of oneself. Instead, he took to his judgements of humanity a wiser sense of the fallibility of all men, including high priests, than is found amongst the eunuchs of the Established Church. The Stoic adopted, in the face of humankind's universal frailty and foolishness, the spirit of forgiveness and – what is closest to forgiveness – of amusement. He knew the weight to give love, and perhaps above all, the weight to give death, and in dying, relied on the strength of his own resources of wisdom, rather than on the false pieties of a whimpering Christianity. He could thus never be permitted any peace by the villainous castrati of Christianity . . .'

All I could think to say was, 'This is strong material, Father.' This assessment seemed to delight him. But privately I thought that no one would publish this. Would not decent people stand outside the editorial offices of any publisher who dared to print such blasphemies and bay their rage against author and printer alike? Yet that was what he wanted. He wanted the Pharisees to bay!

'Your approbation means everything to me, my son,' Father said, his eyes threatening to fill with tears. 'You have yourself the makings of a Stoic – it is the way you have lived here, in this hard country. In the end, like me, you evaded the observances of hypocrisy.'

At this unwanted compliment, I looked at Bernard in astonishment. Her dark eyes understood already my discomfort. She knew too that I had been insufficiently stoic to wish to hang myself, for she had cut me down. Her eyes seemed to me to suggest ploys we could find.

I said, 'You misunderstand me, Father. I have not proceeded by some plan of wisdom. I have stumbled along in blindness. Sometimes in increasing dark. Do not misinterpret me.'

Indeed, I hoped that I was not some case in point amongst his wad of pages.

'Madame Bernard,' said my father, sitting back and smiling after I had returned him his extraordinary pages. 'I wonder would you sit with dear Aldread, your old friend, when I ride to town in two days to commit these pages to the English mail? Would be you so good? They say a package can now make its way from Cooma Creek to a London address in a little less than three months, dependent on shipping.'

'Mr Bettany,' said Bernard, moving her limpid eyes to meet his, 'I must go to Cooma Creek with your son within the next few days. If you will trust us, we will commit your pages to the English mail, and you yourself might then continue to keep Alice happy company.'

Though I knew nothing of this proposed journey, a saving instinct prevented me from denying it was planned.

My father seemed delighted. 'It will be properly packed, and I shall give you two guineas to cover postage.'

'And I shall bring you change then,' said Bernard.

My father turned to me. 'I am pleased, my boy, that you have the courage to profess your attachment to Bernard so publicly. As indeed you should.'

If this excursion took place, it would be the first time Bernard and I appeared in that tiny settlement in the same carriage, creating a buzz which would certainly reach the Reverend Mr Paltinglass, one of my father's Pauline eunuchs. My friend the police magistrate would be similarly thoughtful. I found myself for a second thinking like my father – it is mere hypocrisy which makes them think that way. Would they rather me abuse Bernard in secret or acknowledge her as a soul worthy of my honour? The truth was that they would all probably prefer private vice over frankly declared frailty. It was blatancy that the people my father called 'colonial Pharisees' most objected to. But was there not at least raw truth in blatancy? If it revelled in sin, at least it did not pretend otherwise.

Bernard was still waiting for me to confirm her offer. I was all at once very pleased that she regarded herself well enough to require of me a public avowal, the avowal of moving in the same phaeton in Spring Street, Cooma Creek. And I could read her plan, a reasonable one: to benefit herself, to benefit me.

'Yes, Father,' I said. 'Allow me to commit your work to the mails.'

So an evening later, my father brought the manuscript to me, packaged in oilcloth, bound with that same strong jute we used to bind the wool bales. And two guineas. I protested that I could afford the postage myself. He forced the money upon me. Bernard and I would leave a little before dawn, I told him, so he should not expect to see us before we went. I did not wish to be waved away by him.

It had rained during the night, damping the fires in the mountains, quenching the ashes in the stockyard. Bernard and I emerged from the homestead carrying *The Death of the Stoic* into a splendid late summer dawn, the early sun marking each of the great glacial boulders which littered our high plain. Thus Bernard and I, side by side in the phaeton, made our public way towards the outer world, in so far at least as it was represented by Cooma Creek. We reached and crossed the Murrumbidgee, which flowed well for the time of year and the hot season we had just passed through, and would soon, I hoped, be replenished by autumn rain. We drove on some miles until we encountered one of its bends.

'Stop here, Mr Bettany,' Bernard told me. Unobserved by anyone but myself, she reached into the second seat of the phaeton, extracted *The Death of the Stoic*, and unbound the oilskin with its inked London address prominent on it, took out the wad of white pages covered with my father's frantic hieroglyphics, and walked alone along the stream, to some rocks which in the best times of the year were sometimes near-rapids. She-oaks on the banks protected the place from too close an inspection by passing travellers. Resting her left knee on the pages, she extracted some from the wad and began tearing them into small segments and launching them on the river, which flowed away, however languidly, some hundreds of miles to the west. It bore *The Death of the Stoic* into the interior of New South Wales, into an Australian oblivion rather than towards the world of argument, heresy and renown. In this weather and in the Murrumbidgee's muddy stream the fragments, edging along on a sluggish tide, would very quickly lose the appearance of something laboured on by my father and take on the aspect of mute fragments of bark or sere leaf. Bernard barely looked at me through this process, but she worked with frank determination. The clause-less contract had been forged between us. She was willing to be ruthless for me.

She returned to me with the jute and the oilskin with its London address: Evans & Pauley, Publishers, St Martin's Lane, London. Holding these, her eyes alight with intent, she grimly kissed my cheek. There was

no air of triumph nor of malice, but rather the sort of sad wisdom my
father professed to admire in Stoics.

'If he had been of right mind,' she said, 'he would have done the same
thing himself.'

In awe I helped her back into the phaeton. But as we passed the inn
where, in the wake of George's death, I had once borrowed a horse to
ride back to dying Phoebe, I saw a convict groom saddling a horse, and
with the sight the practical issues arising from Bernard's sacrilege began
to intrude.

'We must send a package of some kind,' I argued. 'He is likely at some
time to go to Cooma Creek and speak to the postmaster.'

Bernard seemed already to have considered this. 'These publishing
gentlemen,' she told me, 'may be surprised to receive a great wad of
copies of the *Cooma Creek Courier*.'

'They might write though in return and thank the sender.'

'We ought erase the sender's address,' she said simply. The corners of
her rich mouth turned up in the most subtle irony. 'The gentlemen in
London will have to think that the gift from Cooma Creek is the work
of an unknown and generous soul.'

Even in this treachery against the book, the great display of paternal
energy the manuscript represented, I was confident Bernard had an answer
to every problem cast up by her drastic action. I said, in what might have
been a panic had Bernard not been there, 'He will want a letter in return.
He will need a good and authentic letter telling him it has been received.
Since he is no fool, I doubt I can counterfeit such a letter.'

'Don't fret,' Bernard told me. 'That is easy.'

'How is it easy?'

'Mr Pigrim – the owner of the *Cooma Creek Courier* was once the
forger of share certificates and bank bonds.'

'You can't tell me that seriously.'

'Sir,' she said. 'This is New South Wales! He also has a printer, a little
fellow who works on the heavy press. He can forge any postmark:
London, Dublin, Edinburgh. He's done it for a number of people I have
known.'

Again I had a sense that anyone who had been through the convict
institutions had an alternative map to the society of New South Wales
than the one I carried in my head.

'Why would people want forged postmarks?'

'They might want well-forged letters and postmarks to show a minister of God that a husband or wife in one of Britain's kingdoms – someone they will never again lay eyes on – is dead. And thus they are free to take a spouse here.'

'Are you talking of O'Dallow and Tume?' I remembered O'Dallow's affecting letter, supposedly from Ireland, telling of his wife's death. Was this the work of literate Mr Pigrim of the *Cooma Creek Courier* and of his printer?

'I would not speak one way or another of Maggie Tume, Mr Bettany. You must judge her on her merits, which seem to be notable. But you might think of Mr Pigrim for your needs. If you would like me to, I could undertake the business with Pigrim, so that if by some awful outcome your father discovered the plan and became enraged, his rage could be against me.'

I laughed. It seemed the era's final weight had been lifted from me. I did not feel that this was any dreadful onus to carry either. Bernard had saved my father from himself, I was certain, as well as saving Mother, Simon and myself from him as well. It was an admirable morning's work.

'I'm pleased to see you prefer me over the world of philosophy,' I told her, smiling and speeding my team along past the inn with a shake of the reins.

She said, 'You are the one I wish to keep in the breathing world.'

THE CALL CAME ON A DAY WHEN A little rain had fallen on the grateful capital and people confidently expected more. A secretary from el Dhouma's office told Prim to expect to be collected at 8p.m. that evening.

She was ready by 7.30, had gone to the extent of carrying a head shawl, and though in need of a gin and tonic, thought she had probably broken sufficient of the republic's laws and did not want whatever official was coming for her to sniff the liquor's acrid juniper berries on her breath.

A white police vehicle like the one she had been loaded into outside the City Bank building arrived in the street at 7.45. She heard it draw up and from the window she saw a lean and wiry police officer, with epaulettes on his shoulders and wearing a white uniform shirt and trousers, emerge and lean on the bonnet, smoking and savouring the kind air which followed rain. Prim put the shawl over her head, and picked up her NGO passport and a few Sudanese pounds. She went to the window again to see if the policeman had moved, but he had not, and was still looking idly up the broad street.

She turned back indoors and took the stairs, emerging by way of her small front garden through the gate, and went right up to him.

'Hello,' she said. 'Good evening.' '*Masaaha l-khayr.*' The greetings she had learned six years past in Arabic class. 'You were sent for me, professor?' Out of respect, ordinary Sudanese often addressed strangers as *ustaz*, professor.

He turned his clean-shaven, neatly made features to her. His uniform was spotless, though he must have been hours on duty.

'You are not Miss Bettany,' he accused her.

'I am,' said Prim, though fascinated by the chance that she wasn't.

She produced her passport. He looked at it for some time.

'You have darkened your hair then,' he said.

She denied it.

'They said at the ministry you were blonde,' he said.

'You are here in connection with Dr Sherif Taha,' Prim reminded him.

'I have a Swedish penfriend,' continued the captain. 'He sent me a picture of Britt Ekland, signed in her own hand. She is a wonderful actress. But I think she is old now.'

So at the ministry this was how they had persuaded him to do this job – 'She looks just like Britt Ekland, captain.' Prim had found an Arab–English dictionary in a store in Khartoum once, and there was within its covers a whole chapter entitled 'Swedish blondes'. Did it come from the attraction of opposites? Britt Ekland would herself probably not be averse to this trim, enthusiastic captain.

'Come to the truck then,' he told Prim, reconciled to her merely light-brown hair.

'Are we going far?' Prim asked.

'Across the river,' he said. 'Omdurman.'

He held open the back passenger door for her, and when it shut it locked instantly. A metal grill separated Prim from the driver's seat, which he now entered. She found herself shivering, and believed it fever, though then decided she did not like any form of detention. When she was small Dimp had for a joke once locked her in a pint-sized luggage-lift in a small hotel somewhere – Brisbane or the Gold Coast. She had beaten in terror at the grey walls, while Dimp laughed outside in the breathable air.

They turned left into the main road out of the New Extension, and rolled smoothly over the railway line, through the city, across to North Khartoum. There was a slightly greasy moonlight on the White Nile as they crossed to Omdurman. They passed the wall of the el Murradah stadium, and the shanty town and old cemetery of stately but decayed tombs through which Sherif had taken her once to see the dervishes reel in fervour towards unity. She remembered the appropriate Sura of the Koran on God's closeness to man: 'We are closer to him than he is to his own jugular.'

'Lovely,' she heard the captain say. 'Lovely night. There will be more rain.'

The Omdurman military hospital, like many official buildings in the Khartoum region, in less menacing days had reminded Prim of Kipling. Despite the fact that it lay beyond a high wire fence, its long shaded verandahs and large windows seemed to her to evoke cheeky Cockney redcoats recovering from Dervish lances, Mahdist muskets, or fever.

A solitary sentry waved the captain's truck and the captive Prim through the gate. A sentry was also sitting with the curious listlessness of a museum guard beyond a counter in the chief office inside the door. There were a number of desks with medical files open on them, of which this man had care, and on the counter lay a log book. 'Write your name and address and sign it,' said the captain. 'English will do.'

'What is my friend Sherif Taha doing in a military hospital?' she asked, pausing before signing, trying to make the signature worth something.

'Because we care for him. Sign your name.'

He led her past one ward full of men lying behind mosquito nets in dim blue light. By a bed from which the mosquito net had been taken lay a corpse beneath a sheet, the nose sharply delineated. It was of credible length to be Sherif's. Had the captain brought her to sign for the body? Had that been the nature of the log book? Then she discerned, crowded into the far corner of the bed by a chest of drawers, two slim figures in white, weeping, the woman with her grief covered by a veil.

'That is a young martyr,' said the captain. 'Your man is not a young martyr.'

Prim thought of saying, 'And a bloody good thing!' but was prevented by the fact that she did not know either Sherif's condition nor the nature of the contract inherent in her being permitted to come here.

'In there, two beds beyond the young man there,' the captain told her then. Strangely as she trod into that lethal blue light, she wanted his company. After the second bed, in which lay a thin, sleeping boy, profusely sweating and twitching with cerebral malaria, – the 'young man' indicated by the captain – her control of numbers fled. She was helped by the fact that the next bed contained a man whose face, under heavy ointment, had had its pigment altered to blood-red as if by some explosion. He was chewing *khat*, not a habit of Sherif's.

But the next man said, more or less, 'Primrose.'

She would have in any case recognised him, for he was pathetically present behind the ballooning head, the engorged lips, the scarred ears. There was so much damage that her name could barely be forced out. 'Im-ro,' he had said.

His upper body was bandaged, not tightly as if for broken ribs, but loosely enough for tufts of cotton wool, a rare commodity, to emerge from the edges of some of the swathing. His hands were in delicate cotton gloves. She took a seat and leaned forward, refraining from the easy affection of touching or kissing. He looked like a man to whom even the weight of lips would be painful. And even so padded, he was thinner, had had half his substance taken from him.

'I will get you out, Sherif. Yes, darling, you don't need to go back. I will get you out.'

'That'd be nice,' murmured Sherif with a little stutter of laughter.

'Where were you?' she whispered. She looked around to see if anyone was listening. No. The captain was outside by the counter, talking to the guards.

'Don' know,' said Sherif, struggling with the words. 'They said Kassala but I think I was here all the time. Moved me once. But only a short way.' He got a fit of stuttering laughter again. 'They don't give you any exact address.'

Prim stood and took firm but gentle hold of either side of the hem of the sheet which covered his lower body. She lifted it deftly, in a manner meant to cause no pain. No one was there to tell her to desist. His penis and scrotum were swaddled more or less in the manner of his ribs. From Amnesty reports she knew that torturers, from Chile to Northern Europe, infallibly settled on the genitals, male and female, converting love to loathing, fertility to ashes. Beloved Sherif had the mark on him of the twentieth century – the bite-marks of electro-genital torture. Prim swallowed tears, said nothing, lowered the sheet.

A nurse, frowning behind an elegant white mask, emerged from the deeper, bluer corners of the room and wagged a finger. The nurse remained, supervising, for about twenty seconds during which Sherif turned his eye slits satirically to Prim. His pervasive attitude seemed to be one of manic amusement, more odd than welcome.

'Forgive me,' Prim whispered to him. 'You had a beautiful body and they've ruined it.'

'A few dents,' said Sherif, overtaken by painful hilarity. 'No permanent harm.'

Behind her Prim was aware that orderlies were moving out the shrouded body, and the two white-clothed parents moved by in its wake, guttural grief in their throats.

But the spirit, thought Prim, weeping for Sherif.

He muttered, 'Don't let them make you do anything ...'

'I'd do anything,' she said. 'I'll sign anything. I'll take you back to Australia ...'

'Waltzing Matilda,' he said. 'Awt-zing Matiya,' it came out. And was he trying to wink with one of his swollen eyelids? 'Don't do everything they ask.' Then he grinned painfully and seemed to say, though she couldn't have sworn, 'I'm at home in the cupboard of screams.'

She wanted to ask, 'Cupboard of screams?' Yet it was cruelty to make him reiterate.

'Don't feel you have to talk,' she said. She sat close by him so that he could hear her breath. She thought for some reason that might be a comfort. It may have been, for soon she could tell by his breathing that he was all at once asleep. She got up and walked to the door. The captain was not visibly there, though she could hear him still talking to someone in the office. The parents of the dead boy occupied a bench, the woman mourning softly, the tall husband leaning across her and holding her with a hand on each shoulder. Their posture, a little short of intimacy and all the more poignant for that, jolted her. She had not had time to recognise them earlier, but she recognised them now. The man looked up when he felt the weight of Prim's inspection. It was Professor el Rahzi.

'Primrose,' he said, 'Did you hear?'

He thought she had come to console them in something. But the boy in the corner? The captain had called him a young martyr. He must have presumed that. A hero of the Southern war.

'You were in there?' asked Khalda el Rahzi.

'I was visiting Sherif.'

The el Rahzis stood and Khalda's lovely eyes rose to her but they were blurred and unknowing – loss had driven all reason from them.

'Sherif?' asked the professor.

'He's safe,' Prim said. 'They are letting him go.'

'Oh,' said the professor. 'Thank God.'

'See,' insisted Khalda el Rahzi, 'how we are placed, Primrose? Our son Safi . . .'

Her mouth cracked apart in a low, twisted plaint.

'That was Safi?' she asked.

The professor helped his wife sit again on the bench. He said, 'We are waiting for the undertakers.' He too was overcome a second. 'The funeral is to take place in the morning. We will bury him here in Omdurman, for he has ancestors buried here. You cannot join the funeral procession, of course. You must be with Sherif. But would you, if you have time, join us for *hidad* tomorrow evening? Or the next day?'

'Of course I would. What . . .?'

'They tell us a truck hit a mine. But it is not a mine injury. It's all contusions and fractures. A mine is different. We think he was beaten and thrown from a truck.'

'Oh dear God!'

'We wonder which indiscretion we have been blighted for. Our only child and only son. Too late for Connie Everdale now. Too late to send him to England or America for graduate work. We might bear an accident. But we cannot bear the conviction that it was capital punishment.'

He reached his hand down to Khalda's shoulder but did not himself sit. 'Is it for one of those articles I wrote about the university crisis? Our people deserting a dozen at a time and going away. The entire economics department. Teaching cost-accounting in America. And here in proud Khartoum, no one but senior students teaching the undergraduates! My silent colleagues seek safe refuge in Nebraska and California and the University of East Anglia. And their children breathe.' He looked away a second, not wanting Prim to see his dolorous eyes. 'Or was it the slave thing? Was it that? Or was it Safi's own activism? He was such an opinionated young fellow. But that's what being young is for! We are a reckless family but do we deserve the death penalty?'

Prim sat by Khalda and held her, felt the woman's convulsed and juddering frame within her arms.

The professor said, 'But they have let Sherif go, so not everything is destroyed.'

Khalda began to murmur to herself in rapid Arabic, but her voice rose, so that el Rahzi also sat down to console her. At that second the captain appeared in the office doorway.

'Well, Miss Bettany?' he asked.

Prim turned from the el Rahzis. What could be done for them anyhow, in the absoluteness of Safi's loss, and the absoluteness of Sherif's redemption?

'I shall drive you to the ministry,' he said.

'Tonight?'

The policeman nodded.

'I will say goodbye,' she said.

'He is asleep,' said the captain, squinting into the ward.

'But I shall say goodbye.'

'Be quick.'

She went and woke Sherif. She did not want him to find her gone and wonder was her visit a delusion.

He smiled creakily through his engorged lips.

'I'll be back,' she said.

In her weeks of waiting for the reappearance of Sherif, Prim had received many faxes of counsel from the director of Austfam, Peter Whitloaf. The picture of Prim and her placard had appeared in most Australian newspapers, it seemed. The board of Austfam felt a responsibility for Sherif, who had worked under contract to them, and had written letters of protest to the Sudanese Command Council, the Sudanese Foreign Ministry and the Ministry of the Interior. They were negotiating with the Australian Department of Foreign Affairs in the hope that a formal Australian government protest might be mounted, though Peter Whitloaf said the gorvernment was loath to act without due investigation, given that Sherif was not an Australian national, and the true nature of his crimes could not be ascertained.

Whitloaf had apologised to Prim for leaving her on her own without colleagues to turn to. Austfam was sending a man named Mike Lunzer from the Melbourne office. Mike had the benefit of being a lawyer as well as having headed a large Austfam team in Cambodia. He was due in a week – there had been delays getting an appropriate visa, not least because of her public protest in Central Khartoum, and Whitloaf, on the very morning of the day she saw Sherif in the Military Hospital in Omdurman, advised her to go on holding her fire until Mike arrived. She should hold off any further demonstrations, and not enter any negotiations with the Sudanese government, if that was what she was thinking of.

But on the drive back to Khartoum that night, all this advice was distant static to Prim. She neither objected to nor felt afraid at being locked in the back of the vehicle on this journey. What she had seen in the blue-lit ward made all caution seem fatuous. Trailing behind the captain along verandahs and through corridors at the ministry, she was distracted by fear and hope, but also seemed to be walking into distance, like someone walking down one of those long chutes which, at modern airports, funnelled passengers into planes. The misery in which the professor and his wife Khalda were sunk seemed already part of the landscape of an abandoned country.

Through outer offices, past abandoned desks, the captain took her straight to a double door. Here, he reached for her elbow, as if to position her correctly, and then knocked.

'*Idxulu*,' she heard uttered softly from within.

The lighting of the office into which she was ushered was low, but a computer glowed splendidly at the large desk behind which sat a youngish man, slim and handsome, in a cream suit. His tie was a ribbon of plain green silk. He had the features of an unviolated Sherif. Dr Hamadain, Sherif's cousin. He had been out of the country, part of some delegation, when Prim in desperation had tried to contact him to help Sherif. The captain led her to a seat opposite this stylish bureaucrat, said 'Good night' twice in English, and left.

'I shall send you home with my driver, Miss Bettany,' said Dr Hamadain, one eye on the glowing machine, one hand entering or altering data.

'There is no need,' she said. 'I could catch a bus. Khartoum has been my home city for six or seven years now.'

'Ah,' he said, still distracted by the screen, 'but I don't think it was quite your home, was it?' He concluded his work and hit the enter button. 'For example, I'm not sure that you ever quite understood the Sudanese way.'

'I regret it if I haven't. But if the Sudanese way has anything to do with what happened to your cousin, I don't mind not understanding that bit.'

'Fair enough,' he said. 'I am sure Sherif was beaten. Of course, this would never happen with Western justice systems.'

'Sherif seems to have been through genital torture.'

'That didn't happen,' said Dr Hamadain. He was very sure on the point. 'Blood is thicker than water. If there were so-called "ghost houses" and electric shocks, would I not be concerned?'

'Visit him! Look at him!'

'We are trying to create a particular state here in the Sudan. An Islamic revolutionary state, secure, prosperous and fraternal. In the process – well, every penal system has its sadists. The world over, Miss Bettany, revolutionary, reactionary. The French police? Well, I don't have to say more! If Sherif were an Algerian, how do you think he would fare if he refused to help with the processes of French state security?'

Prim asked, 'That's why Sherif was tortured? For refusing to help the – what is it? – "processes of state security"?'

'I'm told something like that. But don't quote me. It's not my area. This is the Foreign Ministry, and you are more an issue for me than Sherif is.'

It was true. The only question was what she must do to make Sherif safe. Dr Hamadain returned to his computer, brought up a file, and as he pressed keys, his printer began to hum. A page rolled from it. He picked it up and handed it to Prim.

'This is the statement you must make. Once you do so, the security people are willing to clean the slate on Dr Sherif Taha. The police and the Justice Department are willing to take into account the time he has served and do not intend to proceed to charges. So read it, Miss Bettany. Amendments are possible. But in the end you can sit in the Sydney Opera House and tell everybody how benighted we are. Is that a fair contract?'

She scanned the page. It said,

My name is Primrose Bettany, and I am an aid worker representing the Australian NGO Austfam in the Sudan. In my time in the Sudan I have been guilty of a number of unauthorised acts, including espionage. Contrary to the permitted and agreed limits of my task, I interviewed enemies of the Sudan and broadcast their unfounded opinions of the Sudanese revolutionary government as fact throughout the world and to sundry international organisations. I was guilty of being involved in unauthorised landings in southern Sudan and of participating in the removal of a number of Sudanese nationals without authorisation to a foreign country. When a friend of mine was detained under emergency laws, instead of working through appropriate government channels, I orchestrated a prejudicial and vainglorious event for the international media. I regret these activities, and acknowledge that the Sudanese revolutionary government has no choice but to expel me. I ask its pardon, and the pardon of the Sudanese people whom I have wronged.

Prim looked up at Dr Hamadain. The words 'prejudicial and vain-glorious' coloured her mind and threatened to undermine her. 'Which Sudanese people have I wronged? I haven't wronged Dinkas, or Nuer, or Nuba.'

He sighed. 'Do you care to quibble, or do you want to get Sherif out?'

'I want to get Sherif out. Will he be given an exit visa?'

'I can't give an absolute guarantee, but I shall bring my influence to bear on that. I mean, I'll seek to ensure it happens. You have my word.'

'And will you expel Austfam itself?'

'That's still being considered. It's very likely. But after your poor behaviour, I can't make any deal on that!'

'But you solemnly pledge Sherif's visa.'

'I do, to my utmost goodwill and ability, yes. Let him go away and complain about us to the kangaroos!'

'When will I see him again?'

'When he's released from hospital. I believe that will be in a few days.'

She knew she must sign the statement. 'I would like to add Austfam to the list of those I apologise to.'

'I'm sure the government has no problem with that,' he said, looking at the screen. He keyed in a sentence, and the printer whirred again, producing three pages, one of which he passed her.

She read it and nodded. 'Do I sign it?'

'You sign all three pages of the statement. Then you will read it. We have a television and audio studio here in the ministry.'

'When will I read it?'

'Tonight. As soon as you're ready.'

'My God,' she said, and began to tremble.

'You'll be fine, Miss Bettany,' Dr Hamadain told her as if she were a nervous actress.

'But if it will be on television, I must see the Arabic translation.'

Hamadain shook his head in amused disbelief. 'We don't have the time to argue over an Arabic draft. I tell you it will be fair. You are making a very thorough confession anyhow. It will not be softened by Arabic. On the other hand I assure you we won't call you Satan incarnate or such. We want you to go home safely.'

He was solicitous as he guided her from the office and, trailed by some sort of bodyguard in a white *galabia*, accompanied her into the small strobe-lit room where two men – a camera operator and a sort of floor manager – were covering with white cloth the wall-sized view of

Khartoum in front of which members of the Command Council generally made their pronouncements to the people. She was unworthy to be identified with Khartoum, unworthy of the Elephant's Trunk, the confluence of both Niles.

It was Hamadain himself who became her director: after the first read-to-camera, he said, 'Maybe once more to be safe.' Both times she read without emphasis but without playing tricks, without twitches, winks, or avoidance of the camera with her eyes. What was the point of ambiguous gesture when the confession was so comprehensive? And in so far as there was life in the confession, she wished to convince herself that it was the sort of life which would signal to those she loved – the el Rahzis, Helene, Dimp – her fundamental unrepentance.

'Thank you, Miss Bettany,' Hamedain said.

The cameraman stood back from the one fixed-angle camera. He looked very bored for a man who had just heard the utterances of an enemy of his people. Accompanied at a distance of perhaps four metres by the bodyguard in white, Sherif's cousin escorted her out of the front door of the ministry. Any idea that she could find her own transport now was a little fanciful. All her efforts went to combat the numbness in her neck and shoulders, and the grotesque urge to lean against a wall and vomit. A Mercedes stood below the stairs, and a driver, smoking, was propped against the passenger-side door.

In a lowered voice, Dr Hamadain said, 'I'm glad we could finalise this. There will be policemen in cars placed either end of your street to prevent harm to the Austfam offices and to you. They may follow you when you drive too, so don't be alarmed. You won't hear from me again. But if you get anxious because Sherif seems a little time in hospital, call me at this number.' He gave her a card. 'Don't worry. We are not playing ducks and drakes. You are too ruthless. What you did in Central Khartoum, that was ruthless.'

'There are societies,' she said, swallowing, 'where it would be a routine little gesture.'

'And a futile one,' said Dr Hamadain. 'Peace be with you. I believe your Sydney is a golden city, and perhaps in happier times I shall see you there.'

'Then you should look in the telephone book under Sherif's name.'

'Sherif's name? Very well.'

Pulling her head shawl tight so that the driver could not see her tears, her facial tremors, the agony of her nausea, she stumbled to the car.

There was a sibilant expulsion of breath through his teeth as he extinguished his cigarette and prepared to drive.

I CONSTRUCT A LETTER

Before an answer was even possible from Messrs Evans and Pauley of London, I noticed with some alarm that my father was fretting in expectation. His appetite had certainly waned, yet he drank even more. Scales of dead flesh appeared on his cheeks and around the rim of his beard, which he let grow wildly. I had hoped that the book was a fad and would now be half-forgotten. In fact it was the dominating issue of his life, more significant than his sins or the matter of what my mother might be doing, and how faring, in Van Diemen's Land.

Each evening he would hobble bow-leggedly to my hearth to talk feverishly about his hope for his manuscript, and each day seemed to undermine the bright-eyed confidence with which he had sent it off.

'I expected them to read it at a gulp,' he would say, 'and put it down at last excited and determined to use every means to get an answer to me quickly, lest I take it from them and give it to another publisher.'

'You cannot yet know they are not doing just that,' I – his treacherous son – told him. 'That they are not employing as we speak every most urgent means.'

As the autumn drew on into winter, and my men and I attended to lambing amidst occasional early winter blasts of wind from the southwest, I argued he could not expect anything before late June, if then. He would shake his balding scholar's head, as if that span of time was beyond tolerating.

Bernard too, reading in her seat by the table – she never held a book one-handedly, but laid it open on a table, and reverently avoided any unnecessary contact with it – became aware that a mania about time was growing in my father, and that no short, formal notice of rejection would satisfy him.

'Will you take me to Pigrim and his forger?' I asked her eventually. For I felt that the betrayal was filial, and the son, myself, should attend to it with what was left of honour.

Bernard and I thus found cause to visit the town again as partners in life, an action which had an air of normality about it since we had done it the first time. We entered the premises of the *Courier*, and Pigrim, a solid, bald man, greeted us pleasantly at the counter. He was very much in character with his paper, which while attracting the advertising of all the community, being yet the only town newspaper, pursued like the *Goulburn Herald* a democratic, progressive line of a kind which gave people like Bernard, my father and himself an equal claim on the benefits of colonial society as someone like Treloar.

The time I had dared read what it had said about the trial and execution of Long, it had been fair and compassionate. The fact that I had a convict beloved – or 'paramour' as some people would no doubt put it – whom I was willing to bring to town seemed to have increased rather than diminished my standing with Pigrim, not that his was a sector of society from which I could receive benefit.

I could receive the benefit of his printing press however, and of his elegant red ink, and I asked if I could speak to him privately. He invited Bernard and myself to his office, which was not properly an office but a mere chest-high wooden enclosure.

I told him the problem frankly. My father waited on word from some business in England. The lack of it was undermining his health, and I was concerned. Could he produce a few good pages with this particular London company's address on it, and then I would compose a reassuring letter? I had no idea of the look of this company's stationery, but I was sure anything official-looking would be adequate.

'Oh,' he said, 'I could certainly do it. I have an inordinate love of such japes. After all, they got me to this country. But my English crimes were based on need, not on criminality, and not, I think I can say, on greed. My father's tin mine was burned by some Chartists. I forged share certificates to help him raise the money to re-equip it. He himself was innocent of their falsity, as your father will be of this. I know of your father. I have seen him ride through the town with the consumptive woman. One day he called to visit me to discuss similarities between Sean Long the convicted murderer and Socrates. I believe he too was transported, and his view was that for a fallen society, one needed a fallen Socrates – Long.' Pigrim shook his head. 'I can see that he might need soothing, and reassurance, even reassurance kindly counterfeited. And I might or might not have provided some services to my fallen but not inglorious brethren. But I am here above all to make my way as an editor.'

'This conversation will never be referred to again,' I assured him. 'I shall not admit it even to my dreams.'

He smiled and said, 'That is a bold assurance, and I trust it. But Mr Bettany, if you are to send such an encouraging letter to a fellow of your father's cleverness, you will need a good replica of a postmark on it.'

'Yes, I shall,' I confessed. I did not tell him that Bernard, who had sat quietly and let me attend to the business, as if I were my own prime mover and all my instinct of joy and survival did not arise from her, had already told me he could provide postmarks.

He nodded to a man wearing a cap of paper and quietly setting print on a machine in a dim corner. He dropped his voice, 'That gentleman there, Joseph, is a skilled Londoner and can make postmarks. He is one of the Hebraic tribe, and yet has done postmarks chiefly for the convenience of Australian men and women who hope to marry in the Christian way here, since there is no hope of reunion of spouses. Your father is right in that, Mr Bettany. This is the Hades of the earth, and while in heaven we are not married nor given in marriages, as both St Mark and St Luke's Gospels say, in Hades we must be. Now my little Cockney can make you a London postmark, and charge very little more than his time.'

I looked at the thin, industrious, beak-nosed features of the compositor. This was indeed a world of mysteries.

'So,' said Pilgrim, 'you choose the date for the postmark, Mr Bettany.'

He passed me a calendar and, as I looked at it, he spent his time on galleys of copy for the next Tuesday's edition.

I chose a date. May 5. Had the manuscript been received in April, and promptly read and after much discussion rejected, the letter would be drafted in early May, and posted about that date.

'Very well,' said Pilgrim, looking up and approving my choice. 'Could I please have the London address you would like the letter to come from?'

I handed the address to him, and he sighed and shook his head, no doubt at the words 'Booksellers and Publishers'. 'You may pick up your pages whenever you wish. Write your letter at your leisure, since it would not be arriving for some months yet. But – I stress this – burn any residual pages. And one other small thing, do not put a date on the letter that is later than the postmark date you just now chose. Then bring it me in its envelope, with three penny stamps on it, and my friend Joseph will do the postmark.'

I shook his hand. He was a minister of mercy, and I thought how more useful he was to this disordered society of New South Wales than the Reverend Paltinglass with his pallid charity and Dr Alladair, who had

promised so much yet in my experience had chiefly proclaimed the death
of people I loved.

Bernard and I walked out, me seeming to support her, but the reverse
being the truth, and while passing in front of the haberdasher's and
dentist's, encountered my father emerging from Lattimore's apothecary
shop. He had been to the post office and held a modest sheaf of mail in
his hand, which he passed entirely to me. 'Nothing for me,' he intoned.
'Still, nothing for me.'

One of my letters was from Treloar, proposing a bang-tail muster, a
muster of all his and my cattle, for the following September. Another
had Mother's handwriting on it, and I did not open it. I packed Treloar's
letter back into its envelope.

'I was going feverish at Nugan Ganway,' Father told me. 'So I rode in
on horseback. And here we are in the streets of the same town on the
same day, pillars of the community. Shall I buy you both a drink, or
shall you buy me? The Royal Hotel is nice, but back behind that copse,
beyond the manse, lies Carolan's shebeen, and the company is good and
rowdy there.'

I could think of nothing worse than a shebeen, and I looked at Bernard
and saw that she too could think of nothing worse. But I followed him
into the teeth of the wind, over the fallen deadwood of the gum trees,
blowing up against my ankles beyond the manse. Inside the shebeen's
dark slab timbers, a fire was raging in the hearth. There was a pallid
fiddler at the bar, some unsatisfactory ticket-of-leave man. Approaching
the counter my father clapped his hands in time to the music. He asked
Bernard what she would like and she said tea, and he glimmered and
said he doubted they had tea here.

'Don't these Carolan people drink it?' she asked.

'Not, I think, at this hour,' he told her.

'Then I shall have porter, thank you Mr Bettany.'

As for himself and me, he ordered two drams of the best firewater,
and a little dumpy woman with eyes like marbles set in suet poured them
for him, and he brought them to us, and said the woman would bring
the porter.

I drank my rum quickly, hoping we would leave, but my father
matched my pace and signalled for another dram.

'Whoa!' my father told me, intending to prevent me slipping away.
'Your lady has barely touched her porter yet. And as for me, I don't
dislike the profane crowd as much as I pretended in my Van Diemen's

Land days. As I found in my youth, they have a great deal to recommend them. Many of their faults are the faults of innocence and naïve courage and generosity, of a kind into which gentlemen never let themselves be betrayed. God, I think, must love even the brutish frankness of their decent impulses.'

A red-haired, thin man with crazed eyes approached us and asked, 'Have you seen my Mary?'

My father softly denied that he had.

'Should you see her,' said the red-haired man, who reminded me a little of the dead absconder Rowan, 'you warn her! You understand? Warn her!'

'And well she should be warned,' said my father.

'Well indeed,' said the man, and went on to ask somebody else the same question. My father put his glass down and I saw his face suddenly wet with tears.

'Aldread is certainly dying,' he told us. 'I spoke of her when I spoke of decent impulses.' He turned to Bernard. 'Be indulgent to her,' he urged.

Bernard looked away, over the head of her undrunk porter. She had been indulgent long before he had been.

'And I suppose my mother lacks decent impulses?' I asked him. 'What of her courage and generosity?'

'Ah, she has it, but it is all strangled by her terror.'

I thought then that he deserved whatever might happen to him. He had the compassion to find delight in the mixed virtues of felons, but not in his own wife. I relished now my cunning deceit. I wondered what moral story he could make out of my forger, who was engaged with me in deluding him. Would he extend his universal fraternity to Pigrim?

'I must be back to Nugan Ganway,' I told him.

'Let us have one more dram, and I shall put my horse to the tail of your cart and return with you.'

That was what happened, and happily he slept nearly the whole way home, as I hurried my neat team back to the true centre of my earth, Nugan Ganway.

Lambing over, and in secrecy even from Bernard, I composed on the handsome pages run up by Pigrim at two o'clock one morning, the Evans and Pauley letter for which my father had been waiting. Pigrim had manufactured sufficient pages to allow for practice attempts.

May 4th 1844
Dear Mr Bettany,
I must thank you for having shown us your highly original tract, The
Death of the Stoic. *My editors and I found much in it that was intriguing
and provocative. In a perfect world, where readers might not be so
readily outraged as they are at this time and in this century, your work
might be able to be published. But given the high sense of orthodoxy
which marks this era, in which the slightest exuberance of ceremony or
church decoration brings cries of outrage from the mass of the members
of the Established Church, I cannot see how we can with safety publish
your admittedly admirable tract. Perhaps it must await a wiser time, and
I hope that in that thought resides your comfort as an author in this
rejection.*

> *Yours sincerely*
> *Thos. Pauley, Esq., Publisher*

This done, on my next journey to town, I ensured that I travelled alone.
At the counter of the *Cooma Creek Courier*, Mr Pigrim was engaged in
discussing some printing contract with the young lawyer named
Cantyman, the one who had executed a new will for my father, and who
happened to wish to advertise a Queen's Birthday Gala Ball. I left the
office and circuited the block, passing some boys playing cricket in a
street of soft ochre clay, before returning with the envelope in my hand.

Pigrim seemed to understand why I was there and invited me inside.
In the dark interior of his printing shop, he called the Cockney forger
away from his semi-mechanical press, which, due to his pulling of
handles and turning of wheels, had been producing dodgers with a
massive, thumping-and-swallowing noise. We all entered Pigrim's little
waist-high office, half opened to the shop, where amidst the clutter of
copy and proofs, I withdrew the envelope. The starved-looking forger
glanced at me.

'Does sir want to keep the stamp device?' It came out, very nearly, as
'dewize'. He held the wooden dye he had cut to reproduce a London
postmark. It was inked with red.

'No. I appreciate the craft, sir. But with your permission I shall put it
in the fire.'

The little man stamped my envelope, dropped it to the floor, scuffed
it with his hand. 'You should do this a few more times before delivery,
sir.'

I agreed to. So I put the wooden dye, beautiful in itself, into the fire in the bricked inglenook of Pigrim's office. I watched it consumed, and then took the letter and, too proud to threaten them towards secrecy, gazed as meaningfully as I could at both their faces, which suddenly looked like the faces of fallible men, before picking up my hat and leaving.

I was certain, returning to Nugan Ganway, that my father watched me approach the stockyard and homestead from the doorway of his hut, Long's old hut, thinking, 'Mail perhaps?' For I carried the letter in my saddlebag. I did not visit him however. I rehearsed in my mind how to be blithe and offhand, and how to just manage to remember that the letter, with whose contents I was so dismally familiar, had come.

I went into the homestead, finding its very air warm and tranquil, a gift to me from Bernard. I could hear her talking to Tume in our cook-house, both their voices brightly raised. I crossed the brief few yards of open soil from the back of the house to join them. As I arrived, Tume stepped out to leave.

'Your father has been here once already,' Bernard told me.

'I have it here,' I said. 'I shall take it to him.'

'Let us pray he'll be satisfied.'

But as I re-entered the homestead to retrieve the letter artfully placed in a wad of my own mail, as if indiscriminately shuffled in by some postal clerk, my father arrived at the door and began hammering.

'Madam Aldread could not accompany me,' he told me when I opened up. He bobbed his parrot head and blinked at me with his bird-like eyes set in a face as willing to hear only the best of news as a child's might be.

'I believe there is a letter here for you,' I said.

'Ah,' he said, forgetting he had been waiting months. 'Prompt enough. A good sign.'

I said, as if amused, 'You thought it overdue when I spoke to you last.'

'Well,' he explained, 'there we have the impatience of an old man with a strong sense of the limits on his time.'

I had at least a just sense that I must bear the moment with him. 'Would you care to open it here, over a glass?'

'That is gracious, my boy. But I must be back to Madam Aldread. She is really not well today.' And he made a gesture of the hand and a further bob of the head which indicated his sad doubts about Aldread's survival. Did he foresee, I wondered, a first-class ocean voyage, a return to

England, triumphant for him, therapeutic for Aldread? Did he see her smiling that wild smile of hers beneath a blazing sun, in the Indian Ocean?

I went and fetched the letter from my desk, trying to bear it forth with the casual equability which attaches to a document capable of being a lucky one.

'Let me know if it's good news,' I asked him.

He held the letter up. 'Oh yes,' he said, waving it at the air, certain that it was his return ticket to a world he so obviously cherished.

In the instant before he turned to go he seemed to me brave and admirable, an undefeated cock sparrow of a man. My flawed father. I wanted the letter back to pack it with further regretful prose, to imply that a more orthodox text, if he had one in him, might succeed with Evans and Pauley.

'You shall know,' he reassured me over his shoulder, 'whether your father is a fool or a literary man. Or perhaps both at the one time.'

He threaded his way, as I watched him from the window, an old man with a young man's step and a fatuous hope, down the slope with the shadow of boulders reaching out for him. In Van Diemen's Land, where she lived purely out of fidelity to a betraying spouse, my mother walked in uncertainty too. It was for her sake I was engaged in this deception, I assured myself. Or did I still wish to stand well, to appear non-heretical and unsullied to the Finlays and the Batchelors of the earth? I sat down by the hearth and drank the rum I had offered my father.

Bernard appeared with dishes. 'Is your papa reconciled?' she asked me softly.

'I wish I knew. He has taken the letter off unopened.'

I heard nothing that night, though I waited up. But one does not go at two o'clock in the morning, in the bush of New South Wales, to inquire of one's father what he makes of a letter supposedly from an English publisher. I went to sleep and woke at dawn. Outside, I heard curlews cry and Maggie Tume's chirruping, as if trying on the new day's clothes. I looked in the direction of Long's hut. Distantly, on a knoll, and discernible only if you knew of its presence, was the little molar of Long's grave, obscured by grass.

But there was no sign from my father's direction, from the direction of that extreme and whimsical ambition. So Bernard and I ate our breakfast without any visit or message from the old man. I had no urgent duties that day, for O'Dallow managed Nugan Ganway as if it were his own station, not with the wakefulness of the eager, but with a sort of enduring, watchful, relentless energy. I hoped vaguely that the watchfulness did not derive from Long's example, that to be my overseer could be a perilous thing. So I sat at my desk reading a biography of Pitt the Younger, knowing O'Dallow would call on me if he needed me.

He came about eight. He said he was surprised to see lamplight from my father's hut and, going to the window, could see my father nodding, it seemed, by the fire, with Aldread, her head back, on the far side of the hearth. She seemed to have been overcome by a profound weariness. Had they sat there all night? Had they drunk too much? I thanked O'Dallow and went hastily to the door of my father's hut. My father watched me enter with wide-open unblinking eyes but failed to perceive me. His tongue was fallen into the corner of his mouth behind teeth more crooked and stained than I remembered them. His skin was blue and the features swollen. He had perished in some paroxysm.

I turned to sleeping Aldread to accuse her, the practised poisoner, of having produced this alteration, as I then thought of it, in him, but of course she was gone too, the same way. There were spilled mugs of tea beside both of them. They had died parallel deaths.

Unable to breathe, and shaking and gasping, I hastened back to breath's sole provider, Sarah Bernard. I found her in the outer kitchen with Maggie Tume again, but she saw my face and came straight out to me.

'What is it?' she asked me, while I felt a childlike gratitude for the instant recognition of shock and yet more grief at this place once so Arcadian and now swept by curses.

'My father and Aldread,' I said.

'Ah,' she said, holding me by the wrist. She looked very pale herself, nearly as blue as Aldread. She led me back to my father's cottage, and inspected both their faces, murmuring, 'So she was willing to die with him.'

'She poisoned him,' I said, thereby railing against the opposite proposition.

'No. If she had, she would still be here. Look at the spilled tea. It was a mutual self-murder. They died together.' So though she had a farm in Van Diemen's Land to inherit, she inherited it for, at most, seconds.

With her deft housekeeper's hand, Bernard closed Aldread's eyes, and then my father's. The death of the Stoic. 'He was the only man she had regard for,' she said. 'I was unkind in my thoughts.'

Her tears came on and reached a pitch where I thought selfishly, if she cannot be comforted, who will be left to comfort me? I held her. For it was insupportable to think he might have gone into the shades, had taken the Stoic sacrament, to wait in Hades for his tract to be recognised, honoured and celebrated. A tract which Bernard herself had committed to the Murrumbidgee River.

'Had I known it was a killing matter, that silly manuscript ...' I started.

Bernard said, 'Oh, but hush, how were you to know? Had I known ... It was not a matter for taking poison. That silly book.'

But I was my father's defender. 'It was not utterly silly. It was well-reasoned. It was not however ... decent and appropriate.'

'Poor Alice,' she murmured. Helping me outside, onto a bench on the verandah, she said, 'I will get Maggie to lay them out.' I sat there shuddering as the sun came up over the eastern range, turning the earth and the pasturage a rich, wet brown.

Soon Maggie returned with Bernard, and the two women, passing me, Maggie exclaiming but mercifully restraining her feelings, looked altered by the hour's solemn demands. Bernard's hand trailed over my shoulder, and I felt its living blood.

'Sit still, love,' she whispered. 'Sit still.'

When the women had finished, I sent Presscart to town for Dr Alladair. Appearing in his role of coroner, he should at least be able to name the poison they had taken.

Nugan Ganway, August 23rd 1844
My dearest Mother,
You will perhaps by now have heard news of my father's, your late husband's, death by an apparently accidental poisoning. Such was the verdict brought down by the Cooma Creek coroner. I find it hard to believe that a just God would keep him stringently answerable for actions which in the past year have proved extremely volatile, and I hope you might, as the capping nobility of your life, forgive him for the hectic dance he led us. He was buried in Cooma with the rites of the Established Church. I did not call on a Wesleyan minister to fulfil the task since the excesses of Wesleyanism had tainted his youth.

I can guarantee you a few things: his book, of which Simon may have told you, will not be published, which is a blessing both to the family and to the world, and he is not buried with his paramour. And since the coroner, a friend of mine, steered clear of any verdict to do with suicide, preferring to accord to Father's convict associate all the suspicion of possible homicide or suicide, the entirety of his estate will pass to you.

I am thinking of remarrying, after a suitable period, and I must warn you that my intended bride, though a woman of the greatest honesty, devotion and probity, is a former convict. I know that you would have questions about this, but I do ask you as an indulgent mother to approve my choice. I am resolved to give happy children, who are not acquainted with the sins and follies of the fathers, to this world. Despite the history of my father, I refuse to believe there is anything irreparably tainted about transported felons. I believe that crime is in the blood of us all, and that Father's crime, to which we owe all that we are at present, good and bad, did not of itself condemn him to the follies of his later life, which were follies not unfamiliar to free men of no proven criminality.

My wife-to-be convinces me of these realities through her own goodness and generosity. Indeed, I believe I could not have sustained the loss of Father, or the circumstances of that loss, without her aid. One day I hope to present to you your innocent grandchildren.

> Your ever-devoted son,
> Jonathan

The apothecary Lattimore had the temerity to present himself by my father's grave as, on Paltinglass's lips, *Paternoster* gave way to the final words of repose. I felt a rage at this impudence mount in me. I had seen my father walking with the apothecary after Long's hanging. In my sleepless desperation I lost sight of all other culpability, including my own. This man seemed to me, above all others, responsible for my father's stupidity, and somehow its encourager. This man was the one who had handed the poison over the counter to my father. This man had encouraged and catered to my father's heresy that Stoicism was a religion whose one mystery, dogma and sacrament was self-destruction. I could barely find patience to hurl the clod of resignation in on top of my father's coffin before I cornered Lattimore, who was beating a fast retreat as if he had read my fury. So anxious was I to confront the apothecary that I postponed the saying of the normal grateful sentiments to the Reverend Paltinglass.

'Sir, I believe that the chemical substance which contributed to my father's death was purchased across your counter. What possessed you to give it to such an unstable old man?'

I had an image of my father's bandy gait and plausible smile; he was almost physically in our conversation.

'It was a dyeing substance, Mr Bettany. He said that his companion wanted calico dyed. Blue was her colour. Indeed, every time I saw her in town she wore a blue apron. I sold him a few grains of cyanic sulphide in the best of professional faith. I can understand your sense of loss, sir, but not your accusation.'

And he squared his shoulders, this oafish little man with an East Anglian whine in his accent, as if he dared to fight me.

'That substance should not be sold,' I told him, 'in quantities sufficient to cause death.'

'Then you would put, Mr Bettany, such an inhibition on industry and commerce, indeed on the beautification of the world, such as could not be borne.'

I began to raise my arm to strike him – had I started I would not easily have been restrained. But Reverend Paltinglass was by my elbow, and across a few rude memorials to Cooma Creek's recent dead, my eye caught Bernard's. She was waiting for me in the phaeton and had not wanted to join the few men at the grave side.

'You've done everything a son could, Jonathan,' the priest told me.

I began to laugh. 'Indeed I have.'

'You are distressed. There has been too much loss. But delivered of this burden, which like a good son you did not seek to shirk, you are free now to remake your life. If you accept the sacraments of the Church, notably the sacraments of Matrimony and of the Lord's supper, I look forward to rewelcoming you fully and joyfully to the Communion of Saints.'

'The Communion of Saints,' I said, not without mockery. Lattimore had turned and gone. 'Where is this Communion?' I asked. 'Where have I seen it?'

To give Paltinglass credit, he did not attempt to lecture me. 'I have spoken too frankly for a season of loss, Jonathan, forgive me.' He too nodded and moved away.

'But I have your stipend, sir,' I called after him. I took a small purse from my pocket with three sovereigns in it. Two for my father, and one for Aldread who would be buried later in the day, also in consecrated ground. Alladair had suggested that the clear self-destructive colour of their final act had obviously derived from Aldread, but he did not pursue the subject for fear of making my father into a suicide.

The awkward exchange of cash took place. I walked away to rejoin Bernard and await the burial of Aldread.

It was now nearly spring again. As Bernard and I approached Nugan Ganway at the close of that awful day, a blue line of snow punctuated with the dark dun of eucalypts showed to the south-west on the furthest mountains. It was a crystalline afternoon, and as we splashed across the first loop of the Murrumbidgee, flowing strongly with snow-melt and winter rain, I identified the place where Bernard had destroyed *The Death of the Stoic* so energetically. I had never thought that any blame attached to me, nor did I now see it as attaching to poor Lattimore. I brought the phaeton to a stop, all its four wheels on the stones and silt of the bumpy ford below the homestead. The water flowed north-west, and was silvered with late sun. I do not say that in that second happiness returned, but a plan of life certainly arose. This tortuous river was the Jacob's Ladder which would lead me out of tainted Nugan Ganway.

'My dear,' said Bernard softly, 'are you well?'

'I am reflecting,' I said, looking into the dazzle of bright water. 'This river has been followed by sundry gentlemen hundreds of miles to the due west.' The word 'hundreds' itself was a comfort. 'It has been assumed because rainfall is not as ample over there that that country will not serve a pastoral purpose. And yet it is said to be covered with native saltbush. It is not as if our sheep here have proven delicate, or are unfamiliar with drought.'

I wanted to investigate these propositions. I would be a less fanciful occupier of that country than I had been of Nugan Ganway. In expecting too marked a paradise I had made it a tainted garden. But out there, beyond the ranges and due west, the rain would be sparse enough to remind me that I should not expect the Elysian fields. I would travel from an overwrought landscape into hard and honest earth.

Perhaps.

'Before shearing,' I told Bernard, 'I would like to ride off with O'Dallow and inspect that country.'

'I can ride,' she announced. 'I shall discover it with you.'

PRIM'S ADMISSIONS HAD BEEN PUBLISHED in the Australian press and made much of. Whitloaf said the statement Prim had signed came as a surprise to Austfam but was obviously extracted from her under duress. He said he had spoken by phone to Ms Bettany and she was fine. He praised her work for the Sudan. But his letter to her was – if not lacking in compassion – more hard-headed.

While the Austfam board acknowledges it has been negligent in giving you support in your post, it is a matter of some disappointment that, prior to the arrival of Mike Lunzer, you unilaterally chose to make your statement, virtually ensuring the closure of our office in Khartoum and Austfam's expulsion from the Sudan. Mike Lunzer will attend to those matters, of course, so you don't need to be too stressed in the days before your departure. You have on a number of occasions brought us considerable kudos, Prim. But I trust you understand that whatever coercion you may have been subjected to in this matter, your confession creates a problem both for the Australian government and – a very different thing – for Austfam. This is another excuse, if it were needed, for NGOs to retract aid operations to the Pacific Basin and south-east Asia, and to withdraw from Africa. I'm sure you understand that it also confirms the accusations of some more conservative members of the Australian parliament who believe that Austfam is far too politically motivated, and is in part, as I have heard a minister say, 'a civil rights monitor'. So, subject to your ultimate explanation for your actions, I would be less than frank if I did not tell you that we feel bemused, and as if ground has been lost.

Waiting in nervous uncertainty for Sherif to be discharged from hospital, Prim received daily phone calls from Dimp.

'Did they torture you? Tell me. Is this call being listened to? Are you free to speak?'

Prim reassured her. 'I expect to be expelled within a week,' she told Dimp, who was cheered by such an immediate time frame.

Trailed by a police car, Prim attended *hidad*, the three days of mourning, at the el Rahzis.

Helene, who had declared she would attend the el Rahzis every day, was there when Prim visited. 'Congratulations, Primrose,' she said unaffectedly. 'I wish I could get out by declaring myself an enemy of the regime, which I am. You'll be a heroine in the West, but I suppose you'll be totally incapable of exploiting that, God bless you.'

Primrose blushed stupidly. 'The only way I could be a hero is for the worst reason. An Islamic government says a person is a criminal, and the West believes the opposite out of pure prejudice.'

'But sometimes out of wisdom too,' said Helene, kissing her cheek. 'Try to see me before they send you out!'

The mourners at the el Rahzi's were chiefly fellow-students of Safi, some in army conscripts uniform, who looked at Prim in what she knew an impartial observer might call awe. Either the more senior mourners – the professor's remaining colleagues at the University of Khartoum, for example – had already paid their respects or had stayed away, motivated by the damnable caution of the mature.

Prim did not dare ask Khalda whether el Dhouma had come, or even Siddiq. When she rose to go, and went to the twin chairs in which the professor and his wife received and farewelled mourners, Khalda held her close.

'You were not harmed?' she whispered.

'I was not,' said Prim.

'The day will come,' said Khalda, 'when the world will say there is slavery in the Sudan.'

Prim wept and joined her tears with Khalda's. It was Khalda's nobility of soul which enabled her to speak of slavery when her son had been murdered by the state.

Prim spent her time otherwise in briefing a young woman at the Oxfam office on Austfam's development projects – midwives-under-training, proposed health surveys. At dusk one evening, at the hour of muezzins' call, her phone rang. It was the police captain, Britt Ekland's admirer.

'You can collect your friend the doctor from the front of the hospital in an hour. You are to take him to his house, and to leave again before curfew.'

Prim ran down to her truck. She barely had wit to turn the key in the ignition and wondered if she would need to call Erwit. But she did not want anyone with her. By concentrating she was able to move the four-wheel drive out into the broad streets of the New Extension. With its stunted palms and neem trees it had both the air of an artificial city, which Khartoum was in a sense, and that peculiar intensity which the familiar takes on when it is about to be left. She and Sherif were about to depart! Every line of rooftop had an extra edge to it.

When she was routinely halted by a white-uniformed Sudanese traffic cop near the White Nile, her hands trembled on the steering wheel. When he waved her on she had to let a shiver pass through her body before she could put her foot on the accelerator. She crossed the river, brassy with the last of the light. Beyond the cemetery she missed her turning, and uttering the usual antipodean curses – 'Bugger it, bloody hell!' – made a perilous U-turn in the face of an oil truck and a string of donkey carts.

She saw him waiting by the gate, he and a sentry standing together, but with their shoulders turned from each other. He wore a light suit, very stained, as if he had worn it in the ghost house. A battered straw hat sat on his head – perhaps a gift from the hospital. She waited for him to see her coming, but he persistently looked the wrong way. Even when she parked, his eyes were averted, and she had to run to him, and touch his elbow. Turning, he seemed startled, as if he had been told that someone else would fetch him.

'I'm taking you home,' she said with a smile.

The sentry watched, wondering would he see a rare sight, a kiss or caress between a Sudanese and a white woman.

'Ah yes,' murmured Sherif. 'Home it is! Are you well?'

'Come on,' she said. 'We're going to your place.'

'Home, James!' he cried.

Sherif had always walked with what Prim thought of as a slow dignity, but more so now. Climbing into the passenger seat as she held the door, he said, 'Would you do the seat belt? My neck is a little stiff still. My back – you see – it's a problem.'

She reached over his waist, spilling tears. 'Don't cry,' he told her brightly. 'It won't make the Nile any higher.'

It was a Sudanese proverb, and his loyalty to his own idiom moved her to increased tears.

'Do you have any coffee?' he asked.

'I'll stop at the corner and buy some.' She slotted herself behind the steering wheel and slammed the door in the face of the sentry.

'Are you in pain, darling?' she asked, pulling away. 'Do you have pills for it?'

He unleashed his strange new laugh. 'They gave me ten aspirin,' he said, and anyone else would have thought he was hugely tickled by that, the gesture, the precise number.

'And sleeping pills?'

'I've got them at home.'

'They won't let me stay with you the night.'

He said nothing, neither in fear nor disappointment. She wondered if she needed to mother him perhaps more than he needed to be mothered. Wherever they lived in the future, she would take courses in how to live with the victims of torture, and behave with greater certainty than she knew how tonight. How many questions did one ask? Was a person meant to inquire, 'What did they do to you?' Or was it the right thing to ignore the fact that the beloved had spent some time in the pit?

'It's cooler,' he said.

'Yes,' she agreed.

He began to laugh again. 'That was Safi, you know. Safi el Rahzi. Under the sheet.'

'Yes,' she said, 'I saw the el Rahzis in the hospital corridor.'

'I fared better than him,' said Sherif frankly, turning his face however, looking out the window at the near-curfew streets. 'Remember that meal at the el Rahzis', when el Dhouma talked about that mad theologian and the Big Bang, and time running backwards? All the evil deeds taking place and then feeding themselves back to their beginnings. All our good deeds connected by a golden thread – he said that, a 'golden thread' – to their founding impulses. I haven't seen too many golden threads in recent times.'

And he kept laughing in that same odd way. Prim dreaded that laugh since it put him back in a cell of his own. She felt less than a secure hold on events as she parked outside the corner store, in which a dim yellow light still shone, and bought some coffee. As she emerged, she came close to collision with a tall, Southern man. He wore a cloth around his lower body, but on his upper body a shirt and vest and tie. His head was bare. 'Would madam like Scotch whisky?' he murmured.

Prim could think at that moment of few things more necessary to the hour. But of course, she understood, the man was an *agent provocateur*, put there to drag her and Sherif back into official torments. It then graciously came to her that such a minor instigation would be unworthy of the system. The fellow was merely a black marketeer. She found the requested £60 Sudanese in her pocket. From within a slot inside his waistcoat, the man extruded a full bottle of whisky sheathed in corrugated cardboard. He dropped it into the large paper bag which held the coffee. He too was making his way in the Sudan.

As Sherif and Prim entered the withered garden of his medical practice, Sherif moving with upright wariness. 'Is your back hurting?' asked Prim, walking behind with the coffee and whisky.

'A little,' he said. 'One of the vertebrae.'

'You may need an x-ray.'

'Oh, they x-rayed me for free at the hospital. The doctor said it would give me some discomfort all my life.'

'Some discomfort?' asked Prim, and then, tentatively, 'Did he know how you got it?'

'I told him it was a fall I had, getting down from a truck.'

And the laughter again. Should she ask how it happened? Did she have licence to ask? There would be time to do it, in safer latitudes.

They went in past the surgery. 'Perhaps I should get the rubbing alcohol,' chuckled Sherif.

'Oh, I didn't tell you, I got some Scotch from a man outside the store.'

'Good girl!' he said. 'Very good girl! Nothing like a party!'

At the head of the stairs Prim unlocked the living room door with her key, and, somehow amazed that throughout Sherif's time in torture the filament of this living room light had remained intact. She had feared the punitive darkness, yet was now able to consult her watch. 'We have an hour and a half before I must go,' she said. She wanted him, her maimed man, but it was unlikely he could yet consider such things. She opened windows and the door onto the balcony, but near-closed the jalousies.

'I believe there's some pasta and a few cans of tuna,' he said. 'We can spice it up with Worcestershire sauce. The mainstay of my student years.' And again he laughed. Almost anything he found hilarious, yet he could not look away from her quickly enough.

'First, you sit down,' Prim said, helping him to a seat. She went to his kitchen, poured them each a glass of Scotch and filled it up with bottled water from the refrigerator. She raised her glass in a toast. She had intended to say, 'To us, Sherif and Primrose,' but an uncertainty overtook her. He was looking sideways in any case.

'Happy days,' she decided on.

'And smiling dawns,' he said, but again avoiding her eye. She took a sip of acrid liquor, standing above him as he left his untasted. Then she put the glass down and drew him gently sideways to her, so that his shoulder lay against her hip.

'Sherif, my love, I will go anywhere with you. England, Germany.'

'Oh, I think I'll stay here,' he said in a dazed, muffled voice. 'Home base.'

'You can't mean that,' she said. But there was no point in arguing with him when he was barely home from an unimaginable planet, from events so obscure that they occurred in places called 'ghost houses'.

'I want to stay here. And have my patients back.'

'Yes,' she said. 'But what if you took Australian citizenship as a precaution?'

He drank. 'How could I achieve such a precious jewel?'

'Well, I don't want to be forward, but by marriage. That's a good way.'

'That's a very good way,' he said. 'And the Scotch is wonderful. I want to stay here.'

She chose to laugh now, when he was not laughing at all. 'It's such a short ride from here to the airport, dearest Sherif. Your cousin says he'll get you an exit visa. You can go to Riyadh or London or Rome. Or Sydney. Marry me, for God's sake, Sherif. There, I'm doing the proposing. I can make you an Australian.'

'And live in Australia?' he asked.

'Why not?'

She sat and pulled him closer, but again with regard for his scars, his tender points. His head lay still between her breasts. It was utterly unmoving, and she began to wonder if she was hurting him. She relaxed her hold.

'Will everyone pity me for being a Sudanese? I wouldn't want to be pitied for that.'

'No one will pity you. You will have respect. You can practise medicine.'

'Yes. But they'll want to talk about the wardrobe!'

'The wardrobe?'

'The little space they lock you in. It's called a wardrobe. They would want me to say my people are uniquely cruel. Well, they are not!'

'They ... no, look, you wouldn't need to talk about anything. You could just ... practise medicine. You'd walk straight into an Australian job.'

'But they would want to know. They would ask.'

'Ask what?'

'The wardrobe,' said Sherif again. And then he spoke with abnormal rapidity. 'And you see they wet the bedstead to increase conductivity and put clips on nipples and balls and there's a little hand generator on the table, and he turns the handle and zippo! it's all fried and shouting alleluia.' His voice took on the tranquillity of a craft which had just shot the rapids. 'They'll want to know about that but they won't be equipped to understand it.'

'Please. Relax. You don't have to decide anything. And you don't have to explain.'

'Well,' he said, 'that's pig's arse, Primrose. That's supreme pig's arse. Until I explain myself, no one can understand me.'

'Tonight,' she said, holding his shoulders gently, 'none of that applies.'

'No,' he said, 'some of it does. Why is your Arabic so pedestrian, Primrose? Why did you resist it?'

'I didn't resist it. But I've found it difficult.'

'If you did not consider us contemptible, would you have learned at a greater pace? Would you have had the same difficulties with French or German?'

She stepped back. She wondered whether, as well as burning and bruising him, they had indoctrinated him?

'Arabic is a reach for me, Sherif. We share common words with French and German.'

'You don't even see the point,' he said, and he took his glass of whisky and drank it very quickly, all but draining it. 'Ah, that is very nice. Forbidden, fermented grain. John Barleycorn, as they say. You say you are my beloved, but you resist my language.'

'No,' said Prim. 'That's untrue.'

'And if I leave the Sudan, I cannot tell anyone anything. For they do not have the ears to hear. They don't know the language. They see themselves as bringers of something to me, and me as a bringer of human rights gossip to them. My tale, if I could tell it, would give them a *frisson* but change nothing. If I wish to speak, I must stay in my country. It's here that the meaning of anything I say will be understood at once. No one would say, "Those contemptible Muslims! Those contemptible Sudanese!" Only here, in this city, in this bloody, bloody desert, do I have anything to say. Elsewhere, I would be rendered dumb.'

It was a statement of too much weight to argue with. She disengaged herself.

'Let me make dinner.'

'Yes,' he said.

'Do you want more whisky?'

'It causes insomnia,' he told her, and there was the turned head and the laughter again.

So she found the dry spaghetti and began to boil water and salt, and she shed tears as she worked. She opened two cans of tuna and put them in a bowl. When she went into the living room to look at him, she saw that he had poured more whisky. She had already bought him a ticket, Khartoum–London–Sydney. She had thought he might report to Human Rights Watch in London. It had not occurred to her that although he believed passionately that he had been tortured, he did not believe in the capacity of outsiders to hear.

She was reduced to domesticity, to taking plates to the table.

'How are your anti-slavery people?' he asked suddenly.

'There's some hope the UN is listening.'

There was a mirthless snort from Sherif. 'Well,' he said, 'we can all rest easy now.'

She tried to make it a joke and told him he was a cynic, as if any other posture were appropriate for one who had seen what he had seen. She had an image she wished to dismiss, of Sherif spreadeagled against a wall, a crucified Muslim. Had he screamed to behold the electrodes?

She shook her head. 'You know,' she said, almost for something to say, her words sounding to her shrill with nervousness, 'there are still parts of your body healing . . . I know you are a private and proud man. I didn't come here with any expectations . . .' And yet her voice would not stop trembling with expectation. She wanted to consume his vulnerable flesh. He turned his head in acknowledgment or rebuff.

She went to test the spaghetti, which proved to be *al dente*. She poured it through a too-small strainer, so that ropes of it fell to the floor. I've done very badly, she thought. I have handled this meeting very poorly. As she stooped she saw by her watch that she had a little less than an hour to resolve all questions. There would be other meetings. But would his face always be turned? She put the tuna on top of the bowlful of spaghetti. It looked like a less than satisfactory meal for a man released from a ghost house. She bore it to Sherif anyhow.

'I saw your friend el Rahzi again,' she said on an impulse as she filled his plate, as if it might serve as some sort of shock tactic. 'I went to *hidad* at the house. Helene Codderby tells me they are planning peace meetings with the relatives of other dead soldiers. They intend to compile lists —'

'El Rahzi himself is safe enough,' said Sherif. 'Half the cabinet were taught by him.'

'I hope he is safe,' said Prim, but she was aware that her instinct, that this news would act as a catalyst, had been mistaken. He seemed more grafted in place, here in his rooms in Khartoum, than ever before. So she set herself to the task of heaping his plate, refilling his whisky glass and asking, 'Shall I pour some more sauce? Say when.'

Standing above him she saw his skull, dry beneath wiry hair. She bent and kissed it.

'I'm sorry, my love,' he said, putting his arm around her. 'I cannot become a foreigner again. When I was a foreigner before, I was still young.'

'That's all right,' she said. And yet in a kind of desperation, 'We can live anywhere you choose. Egypt. That's not so foreign. Saudi.'

Above his untasted food, he had a sip of his whisky.

'I'm a broken man,' he said.

'And I'll mend you. Somewhere.'

He turned his head and did the laugh. 'But I'm Sudanese.'

'I was aware of that.'

'I'm Sudanese,' he said again.

Then he began to eat, forking up the spaghetti and tuna quite hungrily for a man with scars. He resembled someone eating a solitary, not a shared meal.

She had no option but to sit opposite him and eat some spaghetti and tuna herself, hoping that she would turn him back into her betrothed by demonstration. Look, I eat from the same bowl as you! She was to leave within days. She presumed but could not be certain that she would see him again. But she could not hold through a night and persuade him.

He took another swig of the whisky.

'Prim,' he said, 'there was never any need for you to buy into this curse. It was a kind of wilfulness. Misdirected. Nothing could come of it. Of course, I didn't know this at first. I'm culpable in my desire.'

Prim pushed her plate aside and wept as quietly as she could.

'Don't be upset, baby,' said Sherif. 'Baby' was not a normal endearment for him. It had the sound of threat. And she desisted, since she did not want to cause him any more pain. The regime had done that: the courses open to normal lovers – devices, stratagems, pleadings – had been stolen.

'I won't be upset,' said Prim. 'Don't be upset yourself. Eat.'

But by the time she forced another forkful down her throat, it was nearly time to reach for the keys of her truck.

'You'll be okay to get to bed?'

'Not a problem,' he said. 'I'm looking forward to a good sleep.'

And as she gathered herself, he said, 'You are such a good friend.'

Arriving home before curfew, she saw that the two policemen in their car at the corner were observing an olive-skinned male waiting by her gate. His demeanour, even the nonchalant way he gathered himself as her vehicle pulled up, declared him Australian.

As she got out of the truck, he called, in those unmistakable vowels, 'Primrose?'

Enraged, she approached him.

'Lunzer,' she said, unlocking the gate. She was irrationally angry that they had chosen this night to give her company. If he had arrived earlier in the evening she might have assessed him and sent him to sit with Sherif.

She unlocked the gate. He said, 'I was supposed to be in at dusk, but we were late taking off from Frankfurt.'

In the office, she said, 'There's a folding cot out the back. You can sleep in here.'

'Okay,' he agreed brightly. 'Are you all right?'

'I'm fine. I don't want any smart-arse advice, do you understand? Until I go, you are a guest here.'

'Fair enough,' he said.

'I've already briefed Oxfam on our projects. All you have to do is deal with the government.'

He smiled almost disarmingly. 'That's all I have to do.'

She began trembling. 'I've got a booking on tomorrow night's plane to London. I don't know if they'll make me go at once. Two things: I've written a reference for Erwit the driver–mechanic. He's a good man. Can you find him work with another NGO? I haven't had time, but he really is a pearl.'

'I should be able to fix that,' said Lunzer. He had that air of lazy efficacy which some Australians had. Her anger subsided.

'And Sherif. The one I did all this for.'

'I know,' he said.

She covered her eyes and shuddered with grief. 'He says he isn't coming,' she said, her voice muffled by her hands. 'It'll take him days if not weeks to make the decision. I'll leave you his ticket, and I'll wait for him in London as long as I can. I don't know you, but stay with him, be a friend to him! You'll have back-up from others – the BBC woman Helene Codderby is what the Brits call a 'good stick'. He's got Sudanese friends too, but they have crises of their own.'

'I'll look after him as long as I'm here.'

'He's been ... well, worked over.'

'Hell,' said Lunzer, shaking his head. 'I understand.'

'Look, sleep in the living room if you like.'

'The office is fine for now,' he said.

In the morning there was a call from the Foreign Ministry. She was to leave that night; her NGO visa would be cancelled at noon the following day. She would be collected from Austfam and taken to the airport.

She took Lunzer to meet Sherif, and was relieved when they hit it off. Sherif started asking about Australian politics, and Lunzer's descriptions of sundry cabinet ministers – Sydney bovver boys, Melbourne ideologues, Western Australian primitives – amused him. A shiver of laughter passed across the surface of the morning.

She sent Lunzer away then; he knew she had to be obeyed without question.

'Come on,' she said to Sherif. 'I mean, come on wherever I am.'

He looked away. His looking away was deadly. 'I'll try,' he said.

She had read of people like him. People not equipped to be political exiles. Sometimes those, like Hamadain, who were the greatest champions of a regime one week were the next week's exile, and sometimes those who had seen the regime's worst visage and borne its convulsive electricity in their muscles were the ones least willing to catch a plane and inveigh against their government at NGO meetings and in church halls in Bavaria, Oregon or New Zealand.

'Let me see your body,' she said. 'I want to see what they did, and how you are.'

But he shook his head. 'You have to leave all that to me,' he said.

When Prim arrived in Sydney, she seemed, in Dimp's view, beneath her Sudanese suntan, to have a somewhat shrunken, stringy look, and to be much in need of building-up. Dimp Bettany, producer *redivivus*, had newly achieved her civil divorce from Bren and moved into Frank Benedetto's domicile, a splendid apartment on the north side of the harbour. Every Sunday, Benedetto's Calabrian parents drove in from their acreage in Bonnyrigg on Sydney's south-western margin, to sit with their son and his fiancée on the balcony. Since Prim had at first nowhere else to go, she lived there a confused month, bewildered by return.

She found her sister in a highly purposeful state. The Ventriss screenplay was attracting investment – Twentieth Century Fox had put up some $9 000 000 in the form of a distribution deal. Other money came from private investors and the New South Wales Film Commission. Dimp would go off location-spotting in the Monaro in a Beechcraft Baron not far above the treetops, looking for the right bouldered hillock above river flats on which to build something not unlike Jonathan Bettany's first hopeful, pastoral shanty. She had recruited a woman named Augusta McNiece, an Aussie screen queen married to an American hyper-star, to play Sara. Bettany would be played by that darkling hunk Patrick Merrimée, who – though a New Zealander – was generally claimed by Australians. Benedetto got a Singapore bank to underwrite the amount, and Australians who wanted to lessen their tax borrowed lots of $200 000 from that source as a tax break.

Dimp was the fortunate sister. Prim had undergone penance and been damned for it. Dimp had stolen paintings and wilfully left a husband – or so it seemed to the husband – and had grown plump with love and reward. 'Crime pays,' chirped Dimp. 'Nothing has ever been as free of grief as this! It must mean the film will be shitty.'

Prim had returned with a grim intent to embrace her sensual, prawn-eating, wine-crazy home town, so that she would have thoroughly relearned it by the time Sherif arrived. She still had rational grounds to believe he would, and did believe so under certain lights. She kept in touch with him by e-mail and fax sent via Helene Codderby's little office, or letters sent via Oxfam.

Within a month of her departure, Austfam had been closed down, and Lunzer had come home, bringing plenty of news of Sherif. He was getting along, said Lunzer, working under supervision in the clinic at the university. He had hopes of being posted soon to a government hospital in Shendi.

Prim had by then found a flat at Neutral Bay and a job in administration at the Coast Hospital. She made inquiries about possible openings for Sherif in public health or epidemiological research. There was also much demand for doctors in remoter towns, and she imagined herself and Sherif aging at the centre of some community of sheep, wheat, rice or cotton farmers.

Sherif contacted her then, in a practical, straightforward, affectionate e-mail, to let her know that, instead of sinking himself in obscurity in Shendi, he might take a public health or infectious diseases job in England. Besides, he said off-handedly, he suspected his back might need surgery, and Britain would be a good place to have it done. The ticket he needed, the one Prim had bought, was still deposited with Oxfam. With a more flexible neck and less of a crazy laugh, Prim was sure, he could travel on to join her.

He wrote to her after he got his exit visa and a few hours before he
flew to London.

*Prim, this ticket is, as is all your nature, extremely kind. But I must tell
you I intend to use it only to get me as far as London, where I shall cash
in the remainder and send you the amount, plus the cost for Khartoum–
London. It is not pride or a crass rejection of your friendship. But I think
that if I must go, I must also be in place for a quick return. I cannot
become one of your people, for my people did these things to me. I must
keep my eye on them until they are no longer permitted so to act. I have
nothing but the warmest feelings for you, and exhort you to live a long
and rich and pleasant life.*

This letter, written in the world of electronic mail and faxes, had been
deposited in post offices, had travelled conventionally in aircraft, and
had at last been left in her mailbox. It had a nineteenth-century character
of finality to it.

Partly to distract herself, Prim started to go out with an anaesthetist
from the hospital, the child of Polish Jews. She had warned him, she told
Dimp, to expect nothing. Nothing! He seemed willing to string along
with a sort of stubbornness, occasionally exclaiming over her grace and
beauty and being reprimanded for it. In the end the relationship would
bear more than Prim expected, and a little less than the anaesthetist
hoped. Her reserve, and the contrast between herself and her exuberant
sister, baffled him.

Prim would come home from the hospital, unless going out for a drink
and a quick Thai meal with her anaesthetist, and sit at her personal
computer, call up her internet server, and type into the search engine
terms such as 'Southern Sudan', 'Sudan Human Rights', 'Sudan Prisons',
'Sudan Ghost Houses'. She complained to Dimp that the word 'ghost'
was likely to cast up the web pages of a Virginian theme park, cheek-
by-jowl with sites in which victims told the tales of the violation of their
bodies and minds. One day, she hoped, Sherif would be ready to
contribute his story to such a site.

But it was from the confessions of other victims that she tried to put
together a credible pastiche of what Sherif might have suffered. A Sudanese trade unionist, escaped to New Jersey, told of sleep deprivation and
of permanent damage to his circulatory system by his being suspended
by ropes with his feet and calves in a bucket of ice for hours at a time.

A young southern Sudanese man from Malakal on the White Nile told of having a bag full of red pepper tied around his head, and of a slow, burning asphyxiation. A former Sudanese army officer now living in London reported having been suspended from what was known in the West as a Saint Andrew's Cross. Tales of beatings and electrical torment lay printed out around her living room. Dimp picked them up, glanced at them, said, 'Jesus! Poor bastards!' and put them down again.

Prim also printed out denials of such pitiable stories by Hassan el Turabi, now Sudanese Vice-President and perhaps a more powerful man than President Omar Bashir. Benedetto, visiting Prim with Dimp, picked up by accident, and became fascinated by, some of el Turabi's elegant rebuttals. But Benedetto, the Calabrians' child, was so firmly rooted in Australia that he had room only occasionally to inquire into the Sudan. It was Prim, fourth- or fifth-generation Australian, who was the exile. Benedetto spoke to her at length about Aboriginal health. But it was as if Prim felt distant from Australian affairs and politics because they lacked the Gothic scale of Sudanese wrong and folly.

Her anaesthetist, surrounded by hundreds of pages of print-out from the pro-government Sudan Foundation, from Human Rights Watch, the Southern People's Liberation Army, the Southern Sudan Association, Amnesty International, the United Nations, the *South African Mail and Guardian*, and Fielding's *Danger Finder*, felt he could barely compete for scale. He knew no one whose arteries had frozen in a bucket in a shuttered house in a torrid republic. His parents could tell such stories, but his childhood and youth had been unmarred. He knew he was with someone who was recovering from a profound shock.

He tried to understand her excitement when the UN appointed a special rapporteur to look into the question of Sudanese slavery.

The contents of the website *www.amendsuk.org* which, once accessed by Prim, changed everything, were modest, a mere four pages. Its opening tag had attracted her: 'Observer report, 13 July 1992, "Ghost House" Doctors working for National Health.' The body of the text read:

A Sudanese researcher in the Infectious Diseases Department of St Thomas's Hospital, London, has identified two other Sudanese male doctors employed in National Health Service hospitals as having worked

in a 'ghost house' or secret imprisonment and torture centre in which he
was detained as a prisoner.

Dr Sherif Adam Taha, an epidemiologist, was imprisoned for a month
in one of the infamous detention centres, run by the Sudanese government but not acknowledged by them, and named 'ghost houses'. Dr Taha
argues that many doctors who participated in human rights violations
were allowed by their government to come to Britain as a form of reward
or because they themselves had fallen foul of the regime. Dr Taha claims
that Dr Jafar Gadir Khalig, now a registrar at the Royal Free Hospital
at Hampstead, was brought by prison guards to visit him at the end of
a three-day period during which he was strapped hooded to a metal bed
frame and subjected to electric shock for as much as seven hours a day.
Dr Taha had also been heavily beaten, and a resultant broken vertebra
had brought on a partial paralysis. Dr Taha said that at the time he had
pleaded with Dr Khalig to give orders against further beatings, as the
danger of permanent paralysis and death existed. But, he alleges, Khalig
refused to examine his neck and spine, or to remove him to a hospital.
Two days later, after Taha had suffered a further blow to the back of
the neck and was semi-conscious, the government doctor was again
summoned. He was angry to have been brought from the military
hospital at Omdurman on such a busy afternoon and again refused to
conduct a physical examination of Dr Taha, instead kicking him in the
hip and telling the guards, 'Let the dead get on with the business of
dying.'

Dr Taha has also accused a virologist at the Royal Infirmary, Edinburgh, Dr Osman Hatim Siddiq, of having been in attendance at 'ghost
houses' in the Khartoum area and of having failed to give any medical
attention or conduct any examination of prisoners. Dr Taha says that
Siddiq declared him fit to be locked in the minute cells named 'ward-
robes'. An academic from Khartoum University, says Dr Taha, had
pleaded with Dr Siddiq for medication for a rare muscular disease, but
Siddiq had ignored him, and the man had died.

Dr Taha has brought his case against his two fellow Sudanese physi-
cians to Amends UK, a British organisation which counsels and gives aid
to the victims of torture. Other witnesses amongst Britain's community
of Sudanese exiles have identified Drs Khalig and Siddiq as having
worked in detention centres and given orders which exacerbated the
treatment of prisoners. Amends has brought the case of Dr Taha and
these other witnesses to the General Medical Council, which has agreed

to investigate. The existence of 'ghost houses' and the complicity of some doctors has been reported by the United Nations Special Rapporteur and by Amnesty International. Dr Taha said, 'I sometimes saw regret or reluctance in guards, but I never saw it in Doctors Khalig or Siddiq. In giving their professional approval to what happened, in being complicit, they were more guilty even than the torturers.' But Dr Khalig, of St Thomas's, under suspension by his own hospital board, says, 'These people are fanatics who hate the Sudanese people and government. They are saying what one would expect them to say.'

So Sherif was liberating himself, was shouting testimony on the internet. Delighted, Prim called the *Observer* in London and spoke to the journalists covering the General Medical Council's inquiry. She was anxious not only for justice, but for every piece of evidence of what Sherif had been through. Only then would she be reconciled. Anger kept her going by day, though depression hit her at night. She told the team of English journalists – there were three of them working on the story – that she had been party to the situation which led to Taha's imprisonment. She begged them not to let Sherif know she was talking to them. She did not choose to use them as messengers. She told them what he had looked like in the military hospital, his swollen head and face, and what she had seen of his body when she lifted the sheet.

Sherif did not contact her. His soul was obviously consumed, thought Prim, by what must have been a near-physical need for justice. And gradually he was satisfied. Khalig and Siddiq were disbarred by the General Medical Council. The Home Office began investigating their immigration status. Prim herself was soothed and appeased as the wheels of equity rolled on over the careers and hopes of Khalig and Siddiq.

She began to confess these events to the anaesthetist. She began too to comment to Dimp on the charms of Sydney. 'They have really good delicatessens in this city,' she told Dimp studiously one night. It was as if she were limping her way back towards average enthusiasms, as if she had only just noticed. She gave up her work at the hospital round about the time principal photography began on *Bettany's Book*. She began to do promotional work for some NGOs: Community Aid Aboard, Save the Children, Doctors Without Borders. Slowly, over the course of the year, and particularly after the two Sudanese doctors were expelled from Britain, she settled herself to become what Sarah Bernard had no choice in becoming: an Australian.

Epilogue

From the Jerilderie Advocate, *June 2nd, 1883*

The death of respected grazier, Mr Jonathan Bettany Esquire, former Member of the Legislative Assembly for Riverina, at his home, Eudowrie Station, via Jerilderie, was a shock to all the community and in particular to his generation of pastoralists. Jonathan Bettany was one of the founding graziers of the Jerilderie area, and therefore a person who above all proved the suitability of this country to the Merino sheep. He served the district in the Legislative Assembly between 1869 and 1873 and again between 1876 and the elections of last year. He held the portfolio of Minister for Lands in the Cowper government and of Colonial Secretary in the government of Sir Joshua Lyons. Legislation for which he was responsible included the Registration of Poisons Act, *the* Pastures Protection Act, *the* Stock Diseases Act *and the* Flood Mitigation Act.*

At eight o'clock last Sunday morning his oldest son, Simon, arrived in town on horseback to fetch Dr Mellor saying that his father had suffered a stroke or paroxysm. Dr Mellor, reaching Eudowrie, one of the most splendid houses in the district, found that Mr Bettany had expired in the arms of his wife, Mrs Sarah Bettany. Mrs Bettany and her children, Simon, Antonia, Jonathan and Andrew, are left to mourn the death, at seventy-four years, of an exemplary father and affectionate husband. The funeral is to depart St Jude's Church of England for interment at Eudowrie tomorrow morning at eleven o'clock, after a service at ten.

Babyroussa Ape Monkey

Malay Race

Cuscus

Nutmeg Simlar

Nutmeg Tree

Anak Green

Cocatoo
Aust. E.I. &c

Cocoa Nut Palm

C. Rose Hen.
(Aust.)

CHINA

110 · 120 · 130 · 140 · 150 · 160 · 170

Bonin I.
Peel I.
Volcano

NORTH

Bishops
Volcano
Mears

Tropic of Ca

Lunira   Deserta
Halcyon

Formosa   Eastern Dist. of the

P
Vela
Mariana or   Ladrone Is.
Supaira Sarigan

Marshall Is.

Canton
A
Guam

Radack Is.

Hongkong

C
Luzon
PHILIPPINE
F
Yap
Egoi I.
Sinavin

Manila
ISLES
I
Peleu I.
Enderby Mortlock I.
Lukor
Oualan

C a r o l i n e   Islands

Charlotte I.
Henderville
Gilbert Is. Nautil

Mindanao

C
O

Deysters I.

BORNEO
Moluccas
N. Ireland

L

N. Britain
Salomon I.
Admiralty I.

Banda Sea
PAPUA
or
New Guinea

New Hebrides

Macassar
Torres Str.

Esp. Santo
Mallicollo
Banks I.

Gulf of
Carpentaria
and W. Monsoons

Melville
Bathurst
Edgecumbe B.

Extent of the
Sandy C.
Spring Summer
& Autumn Rains

Norfolk I.

NORTH AUSTRALIA

Macquarie I.
L. Howe I.

Three Kings

N.W. Cape

**WESTERN
AUSTRALIA**
The Interior supposed to be
a vast Sandy Island

NEW S.W.

Pt. Jackson
Botany Bay

Anchland

Cook Str.

Sn. AUSTRALIA

Spencer's G.

South I.

Winter
Rains

Kangaroo I.
P. Philip
H.C. Wilson

Bass Str.
VAN DIEMEN'S
LAND
Rain in all
Seasons

Hobarton
Storm B.

Dusky B.
Favourite Str.
Stewart I.
Snares

Auckland I.

Campbell I.

Swan R.
C. Leeuwin
Albany

Macquarie I.

Babyroussa Hog (E.I. Isles &c)

Duck Billed Mole (Aust.a)

Brush Tail Opossum

N. Zeal.